1957

Baxter Sinclair was well known around Orchard Coils Country Club for his acumen with a driver, which he used to devastating effect on the course that played long and open and wasn't overly burdened with water hazards. This had earned him the nickname Screws, which he was quick to adopt, flattered by the moniker. To that point, no one in his foursome was particularly surprised when he cut his tee shot left to right, a draw by design, and landed the ball clean in the center of the fairway. He let out a polite whistle by way of satisfaction and returned to his group. Baxter's wife of almost three years, Ruth Sinclair, gave him a loving if slightly rote pat on the shoulder as if to remind him they were all aware, if not mildly sickened, by his prowess in the tee box. Ruth was seven months pregnant with their first child, the gender a secret they wanted revealed at birth. Ruth, mired in her third trimester, had been feeling cooped up of late, the pregnancy taking its toll on her active lifestyle, her busied sense of motion. Too round in the belly now to actually golf, she'd insisted to Baxter that she could at least join him and their best friends, Peter and Mary Sullivan, for a loop around the course—even if she couldn't play.

The Sullivans were all too happy to have Ruth out there, even if Baxter had his concerns about overexertion. That said, Ruth was going to get what she wanted—not only was she a determined woman, but she was also holding all the cards, albeit in the cradle of her body. So if she needed a few hours out of the house despite her swollen feet and achy back, it was going to happen—Baxter never stood a chance. Besides, that was what those newfangled golf carts were for. If Ruth couldn't walk far, she could just ride along with her usual foursome, taking in some club gossip, breathing in some fresh air under the banner of sky that reminded her of crushed oyster shells on the beach—a thought she kept to herself as the pregnancy had made her uncharacteristically greedy with random observations, as though a new sense of possession had flooded her body and mind, which it had.

As a result, she remained quiet and watched Peter "Corporal" Sullivan tee off a three wood, his driver banished to his basement until hard feelings passed, and his scorned heart mended. His tee shot landed thirty yards behind Baxter's, though equally playable. The two men, brothers in arms, joshed each other over the distance gap and commented on the fickle nature of the long ball, more than comfortable enough to rib each other over safety shots and excommunicating certain clubs that suddenly refused to obey their masters.

They'd had separate war experiences in the previous decade: Peter in France and Baxter in Italy. This had taught them how to treat a game as a game and not to confuse it with anything more.

The foursome advanced to the ladies' tee box, some fifty yards ahead, where Mary Sullivan, who technically had the purest swing of the group, toed her drive in a most inconvenient and unacceptable way per the standards she'd set for herself. Her disgust was apparent and vocalized through a quick burst of obscenity. An appropriate amount of empathy was offered for the mis-hit; a swing observation was offered by her husband, the only man who could get away with such an intrusion. Peter stifled his desire to remind his wife she'd promised to curb the vulgarity as it was frowned on at the club. But he knew when and how to pick his battles. And that wasn't one of them.

Mary recouped some of her grace quickly but inwardly fumed she wasn't hitting her second shot from where the two men had landed. There were principles involved, stakes around gender, bragging rights in the Sullivan household. She resolved to do better on her next shot—one of the nicer aspects of the game, there always being a next shot to redeem oneself with. She would rally and post an excellent round, or she would not.

Again, golf is a fickle game.

The two couples returned to their carts and slowly motored to their respective shots, oscillating talk from golfer to spouse and the shared territory that frayed the line. There were more than a few fairway sand traps to mind, boulevards of trees coming to life in the spring thaw. They were presently playing the fourth hole, a par five almost the distance of six football fields, by far the longest hole on the course—the kind of design that, when things were going sideways, took a certain measure of grit to soldier through. Otherwise, one was destined for crippling defeat, infinite sorrow, and a crooked scorecard.

Baxter drove the little cart easily enough, despite having only used one once before. He glanced over at his wife and noticed perspiration on her temple, pooling on the down of her cheek. It wasn't hot out. He squeezed her knee with one hand, the other hand reserved for the steering wheel. His eyebrow lifted in a way she was most accustomed to: a mild tell of his—concern over her.

"How are you feeling, cherry drop?" he asked. Cherry drop was his pet name for Ruth.

"Fine. Nice to be outside," she said in a clipped tone that suggested otherwise.

"You sure it's not too much? You look a little pale."

"How long did you want the pregnancy glow to last for?" she said, giving Baxter a look that he knew all too well, an indication he should back off, that silence was golden—or, at the very least, not to bring up the pallidness of her skin.

In truth, the home front had been a little shaky over the past month. With Ruth's pregnancy advancing toward her June due date, new forms of malaise had set upon her that she hadn't experienced during trimesters one and two. The biggest culprit was intense heartburn and digestive issues she was reluctant to discuss with anyone apart from her OB. Baxter needn't know every little detail of her daily struggles. This was on top of the Christmas hams she now called feet and the mood swings orchestrated by her topsy-turvy hormones. Then there was the psychological toll. She loved carrying her child but hated being pregnant, a contradiction she felt guilty over. If she were to be very honest with herself—and she was an honest woman by nature, if not blunt at times—she'd admit the pregnancy was harder than people had tried to warn her of, a message she'd tried to absorb once the joyous news broke. It was harder than her mother and mother-in-law had advised. Her friends and doctor. She felt unprepared for all of a sudden feeling ugly about herself, less desirable in a physical way. Again, more warnings from others, but she hadn't been able to fully receive the message, adopt the sage advice.

That may have been where some of her strongheadedness, the bluntness, was working against Ruth. For some reason, she thought she should be enjoying the pregnancy more, as though it were a communion with something deeper, more spiritual, maybe even a closeness to God. But she wouldn't have imagined that type of transcendence riddled with so many foot bunions and thigh chafing. No God was worth this amount of acid reflux. Yes, she was over the moon to be a mother soon, to see Baxter as a father—her only true care was that the baby be happy and healthy, ten fingers and ten toes without deviation. Though she longed for her figure back, for the bloating to be a thing of the past.

To eat a single slice of pizza without drastic repercussions.

Compounding all these concerns was Baxter, doting in his way, loving, but not always the best at reading the room, at deciphering when less was more. She knew he was terrified, often felt helpless, though he tried not to show it. Not because of some cowardice or flakiness— he was neither of those two things and very much looked forward to the big day—but because he couldn't take the burden away from Ruth. This was a common impotency of good men who could only stand by and leave it to their better halves to shoulder the heavy lifting. It could be dispiriting. And in doing so, managing *his* anxieties had become yet another facet of the pregnancy for Ruth to navigate. It hardly seemed fair to her; it would be a lot for any one person to handle. So it was no wonder she'd hardly been feeling her best recently, why her guts felt crimped and her skin sallow—despite the excursion outside, surrounded by her husband and friends—feeling unsettled had simply become her default setting of late.

After the Sullivans found their respective tee shots, both were striking three woods dead straight for their second swings. Baxter carted closer to his ball, noticing a favorable lie puffed up on some springy grass. He pulled out his own three wood, still aptly named for its makeup, despite the intrusion of more metal worming its way into the game's equipment shed. It seemed wholly unnecessary to him, perverse even. The club was meant to be fashioned out of mahogany or spruce; that was the ancient way, no more, no less. Besides, holding metal reminded him of his time in Italy, and those were associations he didn't want creeping into his leisure activities. Things he did not want to be reminded of. His hope was that the metal fad would fade away in due time, though he had his doubts.

Baxter stood before his ball and sized up the shot, sailing the little orb into the horizon, a clean whip of the wrists, hands turned over, and a fresh divot in its wake. He retrieved the beaver pelt of sod and placed it back in the hole, tamping it down with his foot. He was more than pleased with the shot and looked back to his wife for that attention, that approval he cherished, even when he knew he couldn't hit the ball any better. He looked over not to find her admiring gaze or even a pursed smile, but a grimace of stricken pain on her face. Frozen features. Tensed body. He dropped his club and sprinted over as she was still sitting in the cart, unmoving, though a thin stream of brownish-maroon was now puddling on the leather seat. A substance Baxter was all too familiar with, had seen too much of in his young life. His wife's blood freely flowing. Their eyes met and locked, and she snapped out of her fugue long enough to speak in a startling tiny voice, unlike her, laced with fear and confusion, words no expecting couple ever wants to utter, to hear.

"Something's wrong," she said—then the pain arrived.

* * *

Five years prior, back in 1952, Baxter Sinclair met Ruth Kent on a quiet beach, off season and mostly empty, though an alcove still had its loyal followers even in February, particularly on mild days. There were the dog walkers, beachcombers, shell seekers, metal detector enthusiasts and those who just enjoyed a good stroll to feel the bite of the winter wind, the smell of sea salt on their clothes. Not to mention those who fancied a good sunrise or sunset.

Baxter, in recent months, had taken to plopping himself down into the sand and just looking out over the rolling tides, ceaseless and amoral and guided by a higher celestial power. He'd come to appreciate the tide; it just did what it did and wasn't subject to judgments against it. He envied it in that respect. Lately, Baxter had been looking over his life, particularly his behavior over the past few years, and questioning the kind of man he'd become—or, at least, was becoming if he didn't change his ways. To put it bluntly, he'd become hedonistic, a womanizer, who was running wicked and loose and caring less and less about who he left in his wake. Or who got hurt in the process. And his justifications were wearing thin even to him, hanging like an albatross around his neck. He was buying into his own bullshit at a rapidly accelerating rate. The insurance job he'd taken in Hartford after his return from the war hooked him into a boom-or-bust crowd that was surprisingly fast company for an industry that had always struck him as dull, stodgy. Which perhaps it was. And that may have contributed to some of the hard-drinking culture, late sessions in the rain-slicked nightlife, sun-soaked happy hours to help forget about the monotony of the day. And how the same was in store for tomorrow. Baxter, like many of his contemporaries who had skipped college to fight, who were lucky enough to return from overseas in one piece, did indulge in a certain level of excess upon their return, not necessarily unwarranted as they tried to settle into the lives of peace-time men. They'd left the country as boys, grown up fast in a tableau of atrocity, then returned aged beyond their years and looked to collect a silent debt, one that promised more perfume and lace, less bloodshed and rationed crackers.

A debt they felt owed and would not hesitate to collect on, as one doesn't easily forget the years sleeping in a trench of mud, skirting barbwire.

For five years, Baxter lived a roaring life. And as those years fumbled on, as his friends and coworkers gradually laid down their armor, sheathed their swords, and settled down in the name of love, family, and community, Baxter increasingly found himself on the outside looking in, somehow feeling very old for only being in his mid-twenties, able bodied, though relatively vacuous inside. A sudden emptiness had jarred him, pronouncing to him just how little introspection he'd cultivated over half a decade. Even if there were a few random fellows in the office to knock around with or the new crop fresh out of college keen on chasing skirts, something had finally snuck up on him, chased him down, shamed him. A certain reflection had finally set in, casting an image he barely recognized and didn't approve of—twenty-seven years old, he found it unsettling how he now despaired himself.

So, by way of baby steps, he took to the beach and winnowed out the late-night excursions. He dried out. He got sleep. He reconsidered God. He allowed himself to think, really think in a way that, if he were being honest with himself—which, unlike his future wife, he wasn't always   he'd come to identify some of the rationalizations that had been governing his life. This was not an overnight change. The whole alone-on-a-beach-with-only-my-thoughts routine didn't suit him at first, but he stuck with it, perhaps not solving anything immediately but laying the groundwork for something more profound, where the real work would kick in. The more he sat in the sand, the more he thought, the less it felt like a chore—until he came to look forward to it. He'd take to the beach on the weekends or early evenings if the conditions were tolerable, if he could duck out of work early without reprisal. He thought it was doing him some good. He thought it was a start.

It was Ruth Kent's brashness that had led to their actual meeting, or maybe just her inquisitive nature. Either way, she was walking along the dunes of that same beach, where the sand abutted the battered boardwalk, choked with unruly sea grass and little else. It was a frigid day, and there were only a smattering of people out. She'd walked by Baxter, who was backside deep in the hard sand, his eyes glazed over from looking at the gray-blue water for too long. Ruth was about to walk past him, then tarried, her face pruning in a way to suggest confusion, maybe even a restrained annoyance. She took a step forward, then about-faced, scrunched her hands up into tiny balls, white knuckled. Then she positioned herself right there next to the seated Baxter, still standing but close enough to the man to catalyze something that had been on her mind, even if he seemed all but inanimate, lost in thought. It still took Baxter a few moments to fully register that there was a human being beside him, angling for attention—*his* attention, not some other aspect of the beach that interested her. He adjusted his weight, buried in on his haunches, and looked up to see this girl, this woman, clad for the weather—rain slicker, boots, bucket hat— staring down at him intently, as though he would be her last meal. He didn't know what was going on (the perils of daydreaming on a beach) and was relieved when she spoke first.

"What exactly is your problem?" she asked.

"Sorry?" said Baxter, apologizing by way of confusion.

"You've seen me on this beach for a few weeks now. I'm always alone, and you've never found a way to introduce yourself or even cast a quick smile in my direction."

Ruth spoke in a huff, and Baxter was quick enough to parry, mostly out of instinct.

"I've never noticed you before in my life," said Baxter, not trying to be cruel or dismissive, just a knee-jerk honesty that seemed to match Ruth's forthright offensive, as though setting the rules of engagement.

Both Baxter and Ruth would harken back to that day, that moment, for all their lives. Their first interaction. It was delicate in the sense that if one were to blurt out to a woman that he'd never noticed her before, it wouldn't be a stretch to imagine her storming off, leaving the chump to continue sulking in the sand. It could have played out that way. It almost did. Ruth would often talk about the swirl she'd felt that day, the knife-stick of those uncurated words, *I've never noticed you before in my life*. Hardly pleasant. Burned into her memory. The twitch it prompted in her body to move away, an almost animalistic impulse to distance herself from airborne toxins, to protect herself. But she didn't. She regrouped. She remembered why she'd said something in the first place to the forlorn-looking young man with the wind-swept hair. She wanted to know more about him. So she decided to carry on just a bit longer until she learned what he was doing there. What answers he thought the waves might carry. What were even the questions? Maybe he'd actually have something interesting to say.

Then she could storm off the beach in protest, putting that sad sack back in his place.

"Well, I've noticed *you*, and I've been haunting this beach way before you ever showed up," she said. "So what's your story? You waiting on some message in a bottle to run ashore?"

Baxter was starting to regain his senses, coming to the conclusion that this odd woman, perhaps touched, wasn't going to let up on him without some sparring—he'd somehow stumbled into a row, despite being seated in the cold, gritty sand for the past hour. Maybe he could have just told her he wanted to be alone, which in a sense he did. Maybe he could have been contrite about it. Or summoned anger. But now his interest had been piqued, a curiosity strummed toward a pleasing chord. *Who is this interloper? Why is she dressed like a fisherman? And what exactly does she want with me?*

"I'm sorry, but do we know each other?" said Baxter. "'Cause I'm just minding my own here."

"Jeez, what planet are you currently on?" said Ruth, flailing her fingers like little starbursts. "We've already established you don't know me. What I'm asking you is if you're OK? I've seen you dozens of times on this beach, always staring out, and now the Samaritan in me feels compelled to make sure you're not contemplating something . . . drastic."

Baxter blinked at an alarming rate; maybe sand blew in his eyes, maybe the chill, maybe still trying to catch up to all the words coming out of the mouth of this woman—who seemed lengths ahead of him in a race he hardly knew he was participating in.

"Sorry, but do you talk to all strangers like this?" he asked.

"Feel free to stop saying 'sorry.' And yes, mostly, but only the ones I think I can help," said Ruth, who then took it upon herself to plop down next to him. "So I'll repeat, are you OK? I'm Ruth Kent, by the way."

Ruth extended her hand toward Baxter, who eyed it with a fair amount of trepidation as though it were a giant tortoise, and his fingers were carrots. He came around eventually and took her hand in his, offering it a hearty, if not leery, pump.

"Baxter Sinclair. And I'm fine, thanks."

"Fine, eh? Well, that's a state of mind, I suppose," said Ruth. "Listen, Baxter Sinclair, you mind me asking what exactly it is you're doing here?"

Baxter did mind but now was too intrigued to call the whole thing off, vaguely mesmerized. Plus, they were already sitting, and there was no graceful way to get up and out of the deep sand.

"You first, since apparently, I don't haunt this beach nearly as much as you do," he said, one corner of his mouth fish-hooked into a smile, or a smirk, take your pick.

Ruth liked it. The man was finally showing some signs of sentient life, maybe even intelligence—not just a piece of driftwood washed into the dunes. The wind had picked up a tick, and the sand was noticeably cold on her legs, even through her trousers. She didn't mind, either used to it or something to be dismissed in the interest of her current jaunt, finally engaging with the sad-looking young man.

Overhead, seabirds refused to shut up their persistent begging for calories—nature's zero-sum game, where even the apex had to struggle and fight for nutrition.

"I like to study this place—nature, that is," she said. "You ever hear of the Audubon Society? I'm a member."

"Is that the bird-and-tree club for gals?"

"We're a lot more than just birds, and there are plenty of men who are members," said Ruth proudly. "We believe in appreciating the outdoors. And conservation. My mom has gotten me involved, and I adore it now."

"So you're like a defender of the beach," said Baxter lightly.

"You may be joking, but that's exactly how I'd like to see myself."

They turned silent for a moment, their attention back on the crashing waves, the sun that had started its slow descent. They looked at the beach which Ruth Kent had professed a protective mandate over. She was giving the strange man some space, allowing the moment its breath, wondering if he'd have anything else to say, if he would even bother to speak again. Baxter himself was wondering how his path was now crossed up with this odd woman who fancied birds. Was it coincidence? Was he spending too much time on the beach? Was it a sign of something more? He'd allocated months of his time to purging his misdeeds in the bosom of nature, slowly leaking away the poisons that had built up for five years. Was Ruth's arrival an indication of atonement, that he was ready to move on? He was hardly sure but acknowledged that he certainly wasn't bored by her company, and perhaps that was enough of a sign to take a small plunge.

"You asked what I'm doing here, so how about I tell you the abridged version?" said Baxter, sans emotion, as though reading the warranty on a new toaster. "I've been a callous and flimsy man with people, women if I'm being honest, for longer than I'd care to admit, and I don't particularly like what I've become."

"I see," said Ruth.

"I'm trying to do better, but you may want to know this about the stranger you've sat down next to," concluded Baxter, returning his gaze to the water, providing Ruth with the space to chew on what had just been revealed, to stand up and take her leave if that was her prerogative.

It was now Ruth's turn to be caught off guard. She'd approached the young man, long having noticed him on the beach, angling to maybe procure a simple date with the fellow. She'd found him handsome and vulnerable the first time she'd laid eyes on him, a sentiment that had grown over the weeks of her quietly clocking him while he'd seemed lost in his own world, unseen narratives playing out in his mind. She'd speculated that he'd recently had his heart broken. Suffered a death of someone close. Perhaps an unrequited love. But a playboy trying to reform his ways was not one of the pictures she'd painted in her mind about the lonesome figure. And it wasn't necessarily a project she was looking to take on. That said, the admission struck her as genuine, if not a bit stoic, ringing true in a way that wouldn't be faked. She wondered if she was the first person he'd admitted this aloud to. And if so, what relevance should be assigned to that? Ruth realized she'd been playing at this little game but was now getting swept into something that bore greater consequences. Was it her place to judge? To march off? To stay and soothe? Wouldn't retreat be tantamount to casting a stone she'd never intended to launch in the first place? She looked at his face: flecked with sand, hair tussled, eyes of dark molasses. She liked what she saw, undeniably. She wondered if she was the one meant to change him. Fix him. And how many of his women before her may have thought the same thing?

A classic pitfall she'd been adroit at avoiding with men, but—what if he was different?

Ruth knew the heart was a fickle thing; it wanted what it wanted—never ceasing to amaze her, the wild leaps it was willing to take—so maybe this Baxter fellow wasn't the poet or grieving spouse she'd imagined, but that didn't make him any less redeemable or desirable.

"What do you say you take me out to dinner some night?" she asked. Ventured.

"You want to have dinner with me?" said Baxter, somewhat flummoxed. "Even after what I just told you?"

She paused for effect, braided a clump of dried-out seaweed around her hand without breaking a single strand, clearly practiced in the art form.

"You said you're trying to be a better man, right? Well, that's great, but hiding on a beach won't get you there," said Ruth, casting her hands out to encapsulate the vastness of their surroundings, the seaweed taken by the wind. "Maybe you need to start practicing on real-life people."

Baxter couldn't help but cough up a dry chuckle at Ruth's frankness.

"And I should start with you?"

She took off her bucket hat and shook some loose sand out of her hair, some of which landed on her face, though she made no effort to brush it aside.

"Why not? I'm good company once you get used to me. Besides, I guess I want to get to know you better."

Baxter had heard all he needed to hear—at some point, his mind had been made up on an almost subconscious level.

"Would you like to have dinner with me tonight?" he asked.

She lightly punched him in the shoulder.

"Thought you'd never ask."

* * *

Baxter slid Ruth off the golf cart and now had her lying on the grass, crimson trickling down her legs. There was blood everywhere she was moved to. Her legs were bent at the knees, and she was moaning in pain, taking in shallow sips of air like a person desperate to retrieve their breath. Baxter, for all he could tell, thought Ruth was going into spontaneous labor, which seemed impossible given she had two more months to go—two more months of what had been a relatively safe and steady pregnancy. Clearly no more, the situation now spiraling and marred with danger. He yelled over to Peter and Mary Sullivan, who could be seen directing their golf cart toward their downed friends, accelerating as much as it would allow.

Baxter continued to ask Ruth what was wrong, what was going on. But between her grunts, her thin voice, she articulated little through gritted teeth. Her eyes told most of the story as she gripped Baxter's hand with much of her strength. He tried to assure her with words that fell flat, unspoken prayer cycling in the back of his mind. He was afraid but already knew that fear must be plowed through, that he must not allow it to debilitate his thinking or dull his senses. In a way, it was simple enough. His wife was in peril. So was the baby. She needed his help, and the seconds, literal seconds, could make all the difference.

It was life and death—he'd seen it before, been there before. He steadied himself, prepared, as Sullivan's cart arrived. They ran over.

"God, what's happened, Baxter?" asked a shocked Peter Sullivan, Mary by his side.

"Don't know. I need you to get back in the cart and make for the Restaurant and get any doctor or person with medical experience you can find. Get them here now. Then tell someone to check the pro shop too. Find Clark, in case there's someone out on the course who could help us."

"On it," said Peter, tearing off, not needing any more than his marching orders, not needing anything more than what Baxter's eyes were telling him, the tone of his friend's voice. He was a soldier once too; he knew the score. This left Mary Sullivan behind; she dropped to her knees near Ruth's head, stroking her hair, her temples, anything to calm through human touch, to find out what may be going on with her. She whispered in her friend's ear, tried to suss out the truth. The best Ruth could manage was *fire*, a single word—*fire*, softly spoken through violent coughs, writhing on the ground less a human and more a wounded animal.

Mary Sullivan crawled over toward Ruth's feet, told her she had to look, catching Baxter's eyes. He nodded in agreement. Ruth seemed to lack the energy or wherewithal to protest or argue, not that Mary would have been deterred anyway. She took some of Ruth's semi-long maternity skirt in her hands and positioned herself to get a better understanding, woman to woman. After some time, she laid the skirt back over Mary's legs and emerged looking ashen, her eyes sharp with something new and terrifying. She got to her feet and spoke softly to Baxter, harnessing her calm.

"She's soaked through," said Mary.

Baxter felt the giant hands of a clock ticking against them.

"Where's the fucking doctor?" he yelled, the heat of the moment kicking in.

Stragglers from around the course started making their way over to see what the holdup was, to investigate what those wails might be. Was that a human making those noises? Did a cart somehow hit an animal? The newcomers arrived on the scene to form a sort of perimeter, a protective barrier around Ruth, asking questions about what happened, not a doctor in their ranks. A smattering of equally confused people murmuring to each other, couples holding hands out of fear. Some ran off, presumably to find any help available. Others dipped their heads in silence, maybe prayer. Everyone was now fully aware they were witnessing something horrible.

Baxter and Mary repositioned themselves by Ruth's head. She was still plenty conscious, though the fear in her eyes was slowly replaced with something more lucid, less wavering. It looked more like resolve, survival—her mind catching up to the reality at hand. Her breathing had found a tentative truce. Her bellows were more strategic, though no less frightening. Baxter stared down at her, able to see the back of her teeth when she opened her mouth to vent the pain—a sick chorus that rang across the country club's fourth hole. They fell into a concise holding pattern, minutes that lasted lifetimes, until Peter Sullivan's cart came bombing back, cutting through the course, nearly crashing into a bunker. Peter was driving the cart with an older man beside him and another literally hanging onto the back where the golf bags would rest.

They skidded into place aside the cluster of onlookers, almost tipping over as the driver's side wheels maintained just enough purchase to level the cart upright. The three men exited.

"We got two doctors, Baxter," said Peter, hope in his voice. "And one's an OB."

The two docs now on site, including a specialist—the small miracle of MDs and their affinity for private golf courses. The older of the two took a hurried knee beside Ruth; the younger backed him up.

"Ruth, my name is Corey Smith. I'm in obstetrics my whole career," said Dr. Corey Smith calmly, looking Ruth right in the eyes. "With me is Dr. Harvey Lanier, cardiology. Can you tell me exactly how many months along you are?"

Ruth mashed her teeth, listening to the man she'd never met before, trying to focus on the question she'd been asked. She was able to choke out a response, "Seven months," then whimpered as though the words had cost her dearly.

"OK, Ruth, that's good. I'm going to examine you now, real quick," said Dr. Smith, still calm, though not without a sense of urgency, authority. "Just you and me. Harv, can you move these people back and away?"

Dr. Lanier corralled the gathering crowd to where Dr. Smith wanted them, efficiently and with zero resistance.

"I'm told the husband is here; is that you, sir?" asked Dr. Smith, looking at Baxter.

"Yes. Baxter Sinclair."

"Baxter, good now. I'm going to need you to hold your wife's hand, talk to her as best as you can while I take a look. Can you do that for me?" Baxter nodded in affirmation. "Good man, off you go."

Baxter attended to his duties, and Dr. Smith positioned himself around Ruth's southern hemisphere, where he was able to manipulate her legs a bit as though they were in stirrups. He called out to her to get any assistance from her she could muster. He called out to her to squinch up the best she could so he could remove her undergarments. She complied where she could, exhaustion coming on in waves between the agonies. Dr. Smith brought down her legs what was left of them, tossing them far out of sight like a doused rag. Then the doctor, literally on his hands and knees with Dr. Lanier assisting with the maternity skirt, conducted the most emergent, makeshift examination of a woman he could recall in his thirty-plus years of gynecological practice. No additional light to work by. No sterilization. Only his learned hands to guide the way. The old practice, stoic training, but in that moment, enough knowledge at his disposal to conduct an examination that didn't last long, that in a very real sense didn't have the luxury of time. Dr. Smith quickly understood the situation for what it was, determined Ruth didn't have a moment to spare. He pulled himself out from the canopy of her dress, blinked hard a few times, and gulped some fresh air. He still looked calm, gray-haired, and wizened, almost like a reverend before the pulpit, if not for the leisure wear he sported. A presence quickly crept into his calm manner, tugging at his chiseled-in laugh lines, furrowing his brow.

He called out, and tension belied his authoritative voice.

"Baxter, first child, first pregnancy, correct?" asked Dr. Smith.

"Yes."

"OK. Where's Sullivan?" asked Dr. Smith, looking about.

"I'm here," said Peter, standing beside Mary, edging toward the doctor.

"Peter, get up to a phone and you call Memorial. You tell them on Doc Smith's orders, code vulture; they shouldn't question you; they know what it means," said Dr. Smith, a rat-a-tat to his speech. "You tell them I'm about to perform a delivery on the fourth hole fairway at O Triple C, and they need to send an ambulance immediately. You got all that, Sullivan?" Peter nodded vigorously, and Dr. Smith continued.

"Tell them the ambulance is to drive straight onto the course to us, no parking lot, no gurneys," said Dr. Smith. "The ambulance drivers need to know the code, and I want their tires five feet away from us ten minutes from now."

Peter understood, anxious to take off.

"Ruth, what's your blood type, dear?" called out Dr. Smith to his patient.

"B positive," she whispered, repeated loudly by Baxter, stroking his wife's head.

"Good job, husband, keep her talking, keep her comfortable," said Dr. Smith, then back to Sullivan. "You tell them bring four pints of B positive." Then the doctor lowered his voice, spoke just to Sullivan. "You tell them to get ready for a critical patient, possibly two."

Sullivan's blood froze at the doc's last words. *Possibly two.*

"Off you go," commanded Dr. Smith.

And for the second time in twenty minutes, Peter Sullivan spirited away in that golf cart as fast as its little engine would take him, his heart pounding like it hadn't since he was stomping around the obliterated French countryside in 1944, uniformed and teenaged and afraid, his head on a persistent swivel.

Dr. Smith took a quick moment to compose himself, to wipe off as much blood as possible from his hands onto the back of his clothes. He didn't want his patient to see it. Or the husband if it could be avoided. He also needed his hands dry as they were currently the only instruments at his disposal. He tidied them up and took to his feet with a workman's grunt, fished a set of keys out of his pocket and handed them to Dr. Lanier.

"Harv, get to my car—the white Skylark—and bring me the medical bag from the trunk, would you?"

Lanier took the keys and sped off on foot without further questions. Dr. Smith then made his way to kneel beside Ruth, who was looking increasingly pale. Baxter was still by her side, reassuring her that everything would be OK, trying to convince himself of this too.

"OK, Ruth, you still with me?" asked Dr. Smith. Ruth nodded her head slightly, then rested it back on the ground.

"You two may have surmised, but those are uterine contractions causing all this pain you're going through. You're clearly dilating," said Dr. Smith. "So you and I are going to have to work together and deliver this little one right here, right now, OK?"

Tears streamed down Ruth's face for any number of reasons. She didn't respond to Smith.

"All the blood, doctor?" asked Baxter quietly.

"Can't say for sure at the moment, but given the amount, I'd say we're dealing with an abruption of the placenta," said Dr. Smith. "And it has forced our hand."

The doctor then got back up and addressed the dozen-plus people who had gathered around the scene.

"Folks, if any of you can get to the Restaurant, bring me any clean linen, any buckets of hot water that can be fetched." A few from the crowd took off at the doc's instructions, then he turned his attention back to the Sinclairs.

"OK, Ruth, let's do something about propping your head up now a bit, get you a bit more comfortable, a bit more ready for what's to come," said Dr. Smith, in a way that let Baxter know he should take a quick look around to see if anything could be used as a makeshift pillow. Once he'd gone, Smith continued on with Ruth. "I know this isn't what you bargained for, Ruth. Between the pain and the lightheadedness, you're thinking it's impossible right now. I've delivered babies like this before, but not without the mother fighting by my side. This is about to be the most important half hour of your life, and we're going to make parents out of you yet. But I need to know, are you with me?"

While Ruth could hardly categorize her thoughts in that moment, she did come to understand the gravity of the situation, the stakes that were being played. She thought of the child she'd carried for seven months and the distress it was in. She thought of Baxter and all he'd gone through in his young life and just how much he meant to her. She thought of his dark eyes and, despite his best subterfuge, the fear that had so plainly overtaken their surface in the past ten minutes. She thought of the crowd around her and the doctor barking his efficient little orders. What she didn't think about much was herself, the danger she was in, the toll being taken. What came to bear was this holy task, those who counted on her, those she was absolutely willing to die for. She would gladly sacrifice herself if it meant the child would live. She listened to the doctor's words and understood his notion that a mighty test had been laid before her, truly a test that was pass or fail with no in-between. Despite her cloudy mind, she understood it for what it was, and the slightest of calms settled over her, an eye-of-the-storm clarity. She resolved not to fail and, in doing so, matched Dr. Smith's concerned yet determined gaze and answered back without equivocation, "I'm with you."

Dr. Smith allowed a smile to pass over his face and took Ruth's wrists into his own hands, an act of compassion while also masking what he'd been fearful of: a weakening pulse under the skin. He looked right back at her, comrade in arms, reminiscent of his own service days a lifetime ago in what was once thought of as the great war to end all wars.

"Then let's get to it," he said.

* * *

They ate their first meal together at an Italian restaurant Baxter favored on the outskirts of Hartford: garlicky food, dim lighting, worn-down wooden floors. It was the kind of place where you could have a conversation with somebody without raising your voice: low, moody music and an unspoken understanding between the patrons that hushed tones were preferred. A senior waiter who was quick to inform customers when they were getting too loud, raucous. A bartender talented at ejecting the noncompliant in as civilized a way as possible. A head chef who had literally been in prison brawls and knew how to use a knife for other things than preparing veal.

The place was called Rochettos, and they weren't going to tolerate your bullshit.

Baxter had taken more than a few women to Rochettos over the years and was particularly keen on bringing Ruth, given the spell she'd cast on him earlier that day on the beach. He could hardly believe on his drive home he'd been so enchanted, maybe even duped into taking this strange woman out to dinner on a Saturday night. He hadn't been out on a Saturday night in months, lately preferring to stay home to get some light paperwork done, dipping into a bottle of whatever struck his fancy and listening to music on the radio. Now he found himself before this tallish firecracker of a woman with sharp features and loads of flowing hair when it wasn't tucked under her practical but not unflattering bucket hat.

She now looked a far cry from the intrepid birdwatcher of twelve hours earlier—he thought she cleaned up exceedingly well and confessed as much to her, parsing his words about her beach attire.

She was not immune to the compliment of the handsome man, even if she did note he was shorter than she'd realized when he stood up to greet her, to pull her chair out in a gentlemanly way. Ruth had insisted they meet at the restaurant, despite Baxter's protests that he was obliged to pick her up. She wasn't interested in such social mores. She was more than happy to drive herself the fifteen minutes. She was hardly afraid of street parking or the fringe neighborhoods of Hartford.

They were seated at a sturdy wooden table that would easily support the weight of their elbows, now face to face, separated by only a few feet of faded walnut. Some house red showed up to facilitate the loosening up, getting through the awkward beginning chatter, allowing them to laugh a bit about the weather conditions they'd met under, her preparedness for conditions that he dressed indifferently to. When she laughed, she instinctively knew to keep it reserved for a place like Rochettos. Or maybe she was just familiar with the joint. They drifted on to opening topics to further dispel their jitters, the inherent weirdness of first dates. He talked about his work at the Hartford, a premier insurance outfit in the county, where he specialized in account management, a focus on commercial property. By Baxter's own admission, it wasn't an exciting vocation, but it was stable work one could succeed in if they hustled and exhibited a certain amount of charm. It was also a job where a lack of college education wasn't frowned upon, held against you as some paper ceiling. Ruth asked him all sorts of questions about his day to day: good questions, informed and well-intentioned ones. He appreciated the effort, though she did come to agree that the work didn't sound particularly compelling, an opinion she kept to herself.

Baxter asked Ruth what she did, apart from shaking down young men on cold beach fronts for dinner invitations. She offered him a smile by way of touché. They'd already noticed some similarities in their humor; mordant, some self-deprecation, though used sparingly for greater effect. Ruth told Baxter she'd gone out West to attend a small university, Pepperdine, where she got a bachelor's in liberal arts. He asked her what that degree actually meant in the real world—not in a condescending way; he sincerely wanted to know. She took the question in stride. All she could really say was that it was a hodgepodge of curriculum to expand one's mind without necessarily making them useful in the real world. Again, humor. He nodded, finding her candor interesting, even if she was being cheeky with her explanation.

Their meals arrived, Rochettos also being known for fast service: chicken parm for Baxter and penne for Ruth, who proclaimed herself an aspiring vegetarian though she didn't handicap her chances of success, particularly high given her love of beef and fish.

Baxter's impression of the woman was that she came from money: not just how she carried herself or the West Coast education, but some of the more hopeful observations she'd made smacked of an easy upbringing. She didn't seem to have a steady job. Had her own car. Spent a great deal of her time at this Audubon Society thing. Plus the occasional quips she'd made at her own expense, alluding to privilege and comfort. It all rang to him as someone who'd never gone to bed hungry, never heard their parent's tense, whispered conversations late at night, deciding which bills to pay and which to default into late notices, collection calls. He didn't hold it against her or at least promised himself it wouldn't color the first impressions of the woman he was trying to connect with. He was not unskilled at reserving judgment.

They ate, and Ruth went on about her love for golf—another clue as Baxter had always thought of golf as a rich person's sport, though he'd had notions of picking it up, mostly for work-related reasons.

Some of Ruth's self-deprecation was in response to how she felt Baxter might perceive her. Now that she'd landed the man for a first date, she could tell his interest had grown—the chess game had begun, the two feeling each other out, seeing just how viable a potential match was. Her sense was that he was a bright fellow, but their backgrounds were obviously different. It would be in her best interests to take some potshots at herself, maybe not overdo the cushy life she'd come from. She joked of some failed clerical work, assistant positions. It became clear enough that Baxter hadn't attended college, her talk of Pepperdine punctuating the distinction in their educations. She frankly wasn't sure if he'd completed high school. But what had come up as she probed lightly into his formative years—the tack many women Ruth's age employed when courting a man they had certain suspicions about—was he'd gone off to war instead. Not always said aloud, not at first, sometimes it had to be teased out, like an errant thread that needed to be cut without damaging the whole. And it was precisely that topic the two of them would remember decades later, a critical moment in their courtship when matters of lesser consequence were tabled, and some important cards were laid before them.

Over the candle glow, the din of silverware, the flavorful food, Ruth saw her opening and took a shot at their first real conversation.

"You served, Baxter. I feel like maybe you did?" asked Ruth, plunging into the chop, unsure of the depth.

"I did. Tried to enlist when I was sixteen, but they figured it out," said Baxter. "They told me to come back in a year, which is exactly what I did. On my birthday."

"When was that?"

"Summer of '43."

"Then what?"

Baxter rotated his wine glass by the stem, noticing the liquid bob away, as though it had a mind of its own, as though it weren't being puppeted by a higher power—him—though of course, too much of the stuff, and the wine would become the puppeteer, manipulating *his* strings.

"Boot camp, few weeks of training, then by the end of the year, I was shipped off as part of the Italian campaign, by way of Sicily."

Ruth listened intently, truly wanting to know more but conscious enough to not push too hard. She'd had conversations with veterans before, similar stories; she understood the inherent weight. Their now-empty plates were cleared from the table with great efficiency, their drinks topped off to finish the bottle. Dessert menus were wordlessly placed before them. They both had a little wine glow going for them. Ruth decided to press on, her curiosity trumping certain reservations, decorum one might exercise with a young soldier newly met. It was hard to help herself—she wanted to know more.

"What was it like?" she asked warmly. "That is, if you're comfortable discussing it."

Baxter took a pull from his glass, felt the restaurant, the city narrowing in a way that, while he'd become accustomed to it, never sat well with him. Though the earnestness with which Ruth spoke did assuage his tunnel vision, kept the walls from inching in. No, it wasn't a topic he was fond of discussing. But he would that night. He puffed some air silently out his nose and dove in, relenting some trust to this woman who made him feel surprisingly safe, an openness he'd never felt before, let alone shared with another human. She had plucked him off the beach after all; he was in her care.

"No, I can tell you some, but you may not like all I have to say."

"Please, try me." Again, with warmth.

"OK, well, you know how they say war is hell," said Baxter. "That doesn't even come close to explaining it. Hell is something you could argue some people truly deserve. But to see it with your own eyes, it's hard to believe anyone deserves it, even your enemy."

Ruth nodded, sipped her own wine, unsure if they would order dessert but very much wanting Baxter to continue on his own time, to share more of what he'd experienced, which he now seemed amenable to.

"I got there in early '44 with tens of thousands of allied soldiers, so many different countries it was a miracle anything ever got decided. Too often, it didn't," said Baxter. "Anyway, we were tasked with breaking the spine of Italy—that's how the officers always put it."

"Couldn't have been easy."

"It was Churchill's pet project, thought it the weak underbelly of Europe," said Baxter. "Which in retrospect it was, but the cost to take it was far greater than anyone figured."

"The Italians fought back as hard as they could?"

"Kind of. The Italians actually folded pretty quickly. It was the entrenched Germans that would put up a long and bloody fight."

"It was must have been so . . . so terrible, Baxter," said Ruth, really hanging on his words.

"It sure wasn't good. I was over there six months trying to break this very specific front called the Gustav Line and some key areas in Monte Cassino. Taking those would be our linchpin into Rome."

"I've heard of Monte Cassino before, I think. But I can't seem to recall much of it."

"The slow victories there kind of got overshadowed by Normandy, but the kraut paratroopers dug themselves into every inch to defend Monte Cassino as though it were their actual homeland," said Baxter. "I think we had to lose twice as many men as they did to finally force their retreat."

"My God, Baxter, how did you survive?"

Their waiter circled by discreetly, and Baxter waved him off with matching discretion.

"I still ask myself that question to this day. The combat I saw, the soldiers and friends that didn't make it home, men infinitely smarter and stronger and braver than me. There's just no accounting for it, like some type of plan I'm not meant to understand."

"What happened to you after Monte Cassino?"

"Well, that's where I got really lucky. I caught enough shrapnel from a grenade blast to keep me in Italy, part of the occupying force that would secure Rome, where there really wasn't any combat anymore," said Baxter, a faint hitch in his voice, survivor's guilt. "A lot of people I fought besides carried on into the wolf's den. Plenty of them didn't make it back."

By that point, Ruth could barely contain her concern for the man in front of her, his harrowing tale, even nine years removed—she was gobsmacked in a way that surprised even her.

"You were hit by a grenade?" she asked, louder than she'd intended.

"Fragments from one, yeah, into my back and upper arm," said Baxter. "Probably saved my life by getting me stationed in Rome. They gave me a Purple Heart for it."

Ruth started to shake her head a bit, as if it were all too real.

"I just don't know what to say when I hear a thing like that."

"You don't have to say anything, Ruth," said Baxter. "I just hope I haven't ruined the rest of your appetite prattling along."

"No, not at all. Were you going to order something else?"

Baxter cracked his knuckles, stretched his fingers as though he were about to break into a safe.

"One thing my experience abroad taught me was to never skip a chance at dessert," said Baxter, a big smile on his face.

Ruth smiled back, and when the waiter made a fresh pass, Baxter flagged him down and ordered coffees and carrot cake. They fell into a comfortable lull. Baxter had revealed so much of what he'd been through overseas, even if he knew it was only the tip of the iceberg, the sanitized version. He certainly believed that war was hell and felt oddly at ease sharing that insight with Ruth, even if it did make for heady first-date material. In their silence, he reached his hands across the table, like a young married couple might on the precipice of great joy or sorrowful news. She took his hands, an unexpected yet tender gesture. It felt right enough. An honest moment. He liked her. She liked him. They had that in common. And when she held his hands, Baxter Sinclair resolved himself to treat her well. Maybe he could feel that new beginning ready to kick in, to finally return from a war he'd never fully left. To abandon the glitz of the city streets. To give up his solo post on that cold beach. He felt like he was going to be all right with this one, in a hopeful way that had been elusive during his young and frenetic life.

Time would prove him right. Both of them.

Dessert arrived. They indulged.

* * *

For ten minutes, Ruth screamed and panted and caught her breathe between waves of contractions that pulsed through her body, pain she'd never imagined, that she could barely fathom as natural. No nitrous oxide, no drugs to induce any sense of drowsiness. Ruth tried to leverage her breathing training from the Bradley method but to little avail. It was all happening way too fast. But also somehow slowly. She felt weaker and weaker by the minute. Dr. Smith was right there with her, encouraging her to push, to push with all her might, all her heart—a heart Ruth felt primed to burst. His satchel had been retrieved from his car by Lanier; he now had some fundamental tools at his disposal; latex gloves, forceps, cutting instruments, a small flashlight. It was a bare-bones collection, an emergency kit he'd never really needed to rely on, almost a prop. Until now. Despite its austerity, the tools were a godsend, enough for him in lieu of a well-provisioned hospital. For the time being. He'd cleaned off his instruments with the hot water and crisp linen fetched from the Restaurant, sterilizing them in his makeshift operating theater that, half an hour ago, had simply been the fourth-hole fairway. As dangerous as infection could be, it was only the fourth or fifth thing down the line that posed a mortal risk to Ruth. Or the baby. They were in a precarious and dangerous spot. He knew he needed to get the child delivered soon, even if he had to wrest it from the bounty of its mother, whose blood loss continued to sap her strength. He needed that ambulance with fresh supplies, ready to spirit them away the second it was safe to do so. He was positive the baby would be dangerously undersize, in need of incubation. If it were even viable. Dr. Smith tried not to think about it, tried not to get ahead of himself. As if even thinking the word *stillborn* could summon the outcome into existence. He coached his patient onward, mopping his own brow with his forearm, an active sentry under Ruth's maternity skirt. His patient writhed, moving too much, then moving too little for the doctor's liking, nothing pleasing him about the rhythm being achieved, this presumed abruption, if that were the case, complicating the delivery every which way.

While the doctor did his work, Baxter did all he could do to comfort his wife, encouraging her on. It felt too little to him, that he should be doing more, much more. But he stayed at it, kept vocal in her ear. Told her to clamp his hand—she had strong hands from golf, hardly a dainty grip. He tried to get her to reply to him. To the doctor's commands. He wanted her working, lucid, equally vocal. It ate him alive that she was in such horrible pain, a clear danger to her and the baby. *Feckless* didn't come close to explaining how he felt about himself in the moment. But he had a job to do, and he'd be damned if he was going to roll over and not follow through. He kissed his wife's fevered head, tasted the salt off her brow. He told her how great she was doing, that she was amazing. He promised her they'd be a family soon. He tried not to think about all the blood he'd seen, all the blood that kept materializing on Dr. Smith every time he needed to pop up and assess Ruth, ask her a question, relay an order. Baxter flashed on all the preposterous luck and randomness that had carried him through Italy, barely a young adult, barely cognizant what it would mean to survive such a hell. Now he found himself praying that all the providence hadn't been squandered on his measly life, that there was enough grace left in this world for his wife and child. The universe could strike him dead, pummel his brain, scorch his heart in whatever way the ledger demanded, just so long as the other two were spared. He thought it not an unreasonable barter, not an unfair trade.

The delivery carried on—Ruth, Dr. Smith, Baxter—while seconds moved liked epochs.

By that point, so many others had joined the scene. Members, guests, the skeleton crew running the Restaurant and pro shop, some maintenance staff, and the few teenagers out of the caddy shack. All of them clustered together, woven together behind Ruth, out of her eyeline, agonizing along with her in solidarity. Some of them knew the pregnant woman. Others didn't. Some had eyes wet with emotion. Others were wringing their hands like steel braid. No one would recall the first who actually took to their knees in reverence. Maybe it was Beverly Stomm, a devout practitioner, mother of two. Or John Eischenchance, one of the young kids who gathered practice balls from the range by hand after the machine had made it's pass, collecting the ones left behind. Or Hank Pillar, in his eighties, not a religious bone in his body, now compelled to offer up the meagerest of humility, taking a knee in the hopes it could do anything to usher this woman, who had always been pleasant to him, through this inexplicable trial. It really didn't matter who started it; soon enough, almost all the gallery was prone in some way, whether they realized it or not, whether they were worshippers, whether their lips conceded to prayer or pursed in silence—including Peter and Mary Sullivan, who clasped their hands together and begged for mercy from any higher power that deigned to listen, to hear them out, to tip the scales.

Then from the faint distance, over the grunts of labor, the blare of an ambulance could be heard, imbued with the hope of choir bells.

Dr. Smith continued to bellow his instructions, silently noting the makeshift congregation humbling themselves ten yards behind Ruth. He was a man of science, medicine, though not godless, taking any and all help he could get, recalling his own vows to do no harm and believing in the divine tenets of his own training, his experience and successes. He found himself in a greedy frame of mind. He would save these two human beings who dared challenge his earthly abilities, his limitations. This delivery would be his crowning achievement. He would make his move. The usefulness of his sparse instruments all but exhausted, only a small incision with his scalpel left to attempt. The baby positioned and readied to the best of his manipulation. There was no pain left to spare Ruth, nothing left to do but to incite more. Now or never. She was as ready as anyone could ever be. With his cutting device in hand, he flicked his wrist in a calculated, textbook motion, then dropped the tool and freed up his ten digits. He screamed at Ruth to push, that there was nothing left to hold back. "Push," he roared.

She complied, more animal instinct than logic, as the ambulance could be heard loudly now, spinning lights seen in the distance of the parking lot. But not for long as it hopped the curb and concrete barriers and sped across the golf course, the message of "code vulture" clearly received, tearing up the ground to arrive at the visible scrum of people.

Though he could sense the commotion stirring over his head, the loudening sirens, Dr. Smith was ready to make his final move. His hands and their tactile precision, his most valued instruments, reached in and pulled the baby from the vacuum of its mother. The wail of the approaching ambulance was almost deafening now, all but consuming. But under its oppression, a small child now appeared in the world, one who could faintly be heard crying its first breaths. A viable baby who fit so easily in the cup of Dr. Smith's large hands—a baby who cried, who carried life in its spongy new lungs.

The ambulance arrived and was right on the scene, cutting its sirens as its crew could be heard pouring out. Much quieter now, they were all left to hear the sounds of a newborn.

"Doctor?" asked Baxter. It was all he could say, still holding his wife, spent but breathing, lucid in a dreamy haze, hopeful in a way she'd never been before.

Dr. Smith retrieved his scalpel and applied it to the umbilical cord, wiped the detritus of birth from the child with fresh linen, and cradled the new soul in the crook of his arm, close to the blast furnace of his own chest, his heart pounding in a way that somehow surprised him. He moved slowly, deliberately, to position himself before mother and father, the tabernacle ten yards behind them looking on expectantly, as though news from beyond the mountaintop would be delivered. Even the paramedics had stopped with their gurney to behold Smith and what he had to say, what his edict might be.

"Ruth, Baxter," said the good doctor. "Welcome to this world your new son."

* * *

An excerpt from the *Orchard Coils Courier*, weekly print edition, April 24, 1957, page 2, column 2, paragraph 4.

Concerning to some that day was the Orchard Coils Country Club's lack of emergency planning around this potential disaster and what other predicable and unforeseen calamities the institution is ill prepared to handle. When asked to comment, the current head pro and clubhouse manager, Clark Nealy, responded, "We're a golf course, not a maternity ward, and I think we performed admirably given the circumstances."

Hardly everyone in the county agrees with Mr. Nealy's assessment, and strong accusations have been levied against the club for being negligent in the face of a medical emergency—and certainly not just a spontaneous delivery, but other such serious maladies as heart attacks, anaphylaxis, dehydration, and respiratory distress, just to name a few. If O Triple C, as the club is commonly referred to, is allowed to operate with such disregard for their members' own well-being, then what does it say about their ambivalent standing to the community they purport to serve?

It's this reporter's personal opinion that . . .

1966

Ruth Sinclair could feel the storm clouds accumulating in her mind—her second cup of spooky punch running its blitzkrieg, opening pathways less prone to charitable thinking, fast lanes toward petty thoughts, long-held resentments. If she were being honest with herself, she'd been having more of these thoughts lately—the alcohol, part of a blood-red Halloween concoction, was just an additional means to lower her inhibitions, to dwell on dark sentiments more than she should.

Somewhere on the other side of the Restaurant was Baxter, in the men-only section of the Orchard Coils County Club, undoubtedly guffawing with his buddies over tall tales of three-hundred-yard drives and bender stories from the functional drunks the club enabled and catered to.

For his own part, Baxter had all but given up the sauce fourteen years ago when he fell in love with Ruth, had since become a drink-counter, a steward for moderation, leaving behind the bingeful behavior of youth. This change was further reinforced when their second child was born, a daughter named Lynn, after Ruth's mother.

His temperance was well received by Ruth, though not always mirrored through her own actions.

It was October 27, 1966, at the O Triple C Halloween party, and Ruth had it in her mind to do the drinking for both herself and Baxter, consequences be damned.

Ruth stared daggers through the solid walls that separated her from her husband, hiding in his little guys-club sanctuary, the whole notion positively archaic and outdated to her—an estimation shared with plenty of the wives at the club, though not vocalized nearly enough. That there was an entire section not permitted to women was like a bad joke to Ruth, a poke in the eye. On the floor, huddled around her left leg, was little Lynn, wearing a bumblebee costume, fiddling with some Silly Putty that, while mesmerizing, was not to be nibbled on as she'd been repeatedly told. Somewhere outside the building, Leo—their little miracle born two months premature on the fourth hole—was being taken around with other club kids on the Halloween Trail by their college-age guides, a tradition at O Triple C for well over fifty years. This would mark Leo's first trip down the trail. Ruth would have preferred he go next year once he'd reached ten years old but was ultimately overruled by Leo's insistence and Baxter's ambivalence in a way she didn't have the energy to buck. With two kids and a husband, one had to judiciously pick their battles. But if Leo had nightmares that night or the following week, so help her, she would send Baxter to deal with their son's distressed calls in the middle of the night. It would be Baxter calming him back down and watching him fade into sleep, not Ruth—she'd made that much clear to her husband, who had rubber stamped Leo galivanting about that night.

Eventually, Ruth took her eyes off that dividing wall, glanced at Lynn to ensure she was sufficiently preoccupied, and scanned the decorated banquet room, teeming with men, women, and young children, some of whom she could recognize despite the costumes, others she hadn't the foggiest. A few of the guests were wearing masks that totally obscured their faces, though not many—too difficult to talk and eat and drink with, particularly the spooky punch, a club classic, which Ruth had on good authority was a rum mix from back in the day, when a Haitian chef ran the Restaurant and introduced them to the fruity drink of his homeland. Apparently, when the chef left, he passed along the recipe and touted that if it were followed to the letter, it would remain a hit at the club for years to come. He wasn't wrong. And it was literally something Ruth had looked forward to since her own younger days at the club, back when she was fresh out of college, and her years were a bit aimless—too many balloons and not enough anchors in her life.

Ruth continued to scan the scene, playing a little mental game of hers when she felt a touch antisocial, in which she could hide behind the illusion that she was attending to Lynn when, in truth, the Silly Putty was doing the lion's share of that work. Ruth inventoried the people around her: those she'd known since being a teenager at the club, those she'd come to know over her first decade of being an adult. As her thirtieth birthday fast approached, a thought filled her with a childish dread she couldn't quite place but knew she should disregard. She observed, sitting in the corner, Constance Marlough, a gal from her prep school days, who had not married despite being wholly suitable and not without a head full of wits and an hourglass worth of curves. Though maybe that first part was the problem. Or maybe there wasn't even a problem. She always seemed to enjoy the attention of suitors, then merrily dashed their hopes over a coast of jagged rocks. Constance had been like that since she was in knee socks, and even now, Ruth could see some fellow trying to chat her up, costumed as some type of sailor, unaware he should be steering his ship elsewhere—but that was Connie for you, not an easy nut to crack.

At the very same table sat a stodgy old couple Ruth had known her entire life, friends of her parents, though she suspected her parents didn't so much enjoy their company as tolerate it out of habit. They were Bernard and Eloise Wentworth—he'd made his fortune in textiles; she'd made her fortune through marriage. They looked the dour pair, as though they'd rather be elsewhere but for the life of them couldn't conjure a better idea between them. Across from that table sat three young men she'd met over the last year at the club. All of them were in their mid-twenties, a group of prideful bachelors who had dubbed themselves "the stooges," currently shoveling seafood cocktail down their gullets, chewing with their mouths open. There were others in this stooges clique: some type of counterculture statement, earnest or ironic; no one could tell. Ruth had given up tracking their names as these were somewhat interchangeable men, mostly consisting of inept skirt chasers or failed comedy writers who had resorted to being goofballs who fancied pranks they thought would change the world for the better. No one thought much of their outlook. Or their antics. And Ruth viewed the whole lot of them as imbeciles and vaguely remembered a previous iteration of the stooges fifteen years ago at the club, equally ineffectual and prone to tomfoolery—different decade, same sad, recycled nonsense, packaged in a different container.

Across the room, Ruth spied Gloria Allister, one of her contemporaries she actually had an affinity for, ladling spooky punch into her cup: a fellow mother and wife and golfer who could free a ball from the sand like no one's business. Her husband was undoubtedly on the other side of the building; her kids, too young for the Halloween Trail, were probably at home with a sitter. Ruth had been trying to convince Gloria to join the Audubon for the better part of a year now, though with little success. Maybe she'd give it another go tonight.

She spied Haldermann—his first name a mystery, an old-soul libertine, barely costumed and out on the prowl—the kind of guy who used the word *bed* as a verb.

At a more secluded table, sitting by himself was Ronald Reymore, the current club champion, two years running, having secured his second title a few weeks earlier, edging out Bart Moreland, who could be seen as far away from Ronald as possible, wearing some kind of wolf costume that fit snuggly over his Appalachian shoulders. Ruth guessed that under that hairy mask, old Bart was staring icicles at Reymore as it had been a contentious loss that, while short of an official dispute, did leave some uneasiness behind as to the circumstances of the repeat victory.

Golf was a funny sport like that—an encyclopedia of rules, though still subject to some interpretation for home-course nuances, human failings.

Ruth glanced back down at Lynn, still fully absorbed with stretching apart and reattaching the gray goo. Sometimes it boggled her mind that five cents worth of anything could so enthrall children.

When Ruth looked back up, she saw Percy Huntington had made his way over to Ronald Reymore, shaking his hand, perhaps congratulating him on the club championship. Ronald's eyes livened up. He enthusiastically pumped Percy's hand, and they proceeded to exchange what Ruth could only guess was mild chitchat between two men who didn't have enough in common to warrant a real conversation or enough animosity to skip a few meaningful words about the weather or even some light politics. Maybe speculate on how well the redesigned Mustang would sell come next spring.

Ruth sipped from her punch cup and tried to imagine how banal their conversation would be and the probability that certain types of grass seed would get brought up. She knew she was being petty, jealous even, but at least she'd kept it within the confines of her mind. The thing about Percy Huntington was that, in Ruth's estimation, he was one of the—if not the—most handsome man at O Triple C. This wasn't a slight against Baxter, who was plenty handsome in his own way, but Percy was classically good looking in an objective way that no one was willing to deny. The kind of good looks that literally changed the atmosphere of a room once he walked in. Consequently, everyone at the club wanted to be his friend. Ruth didn't even know if he was a particularly nice guy or a good golfer, but she did know he was unmarried and loved to play the field, parading around his four-star chin and heavy brow to the top pickup spots in Orchard Coils and surrounding towns.

Ruth found herself studying Percy's and Ronald's body language, imaging conversations, until her dear friend Mary Sullivan sidled up, wearing a tastefully provocative nurse costume, holding a bottle of Budweiser, and offering Ruth a little hip check, minding Lynn by their feet.

"Penny for your thoughts, doll," said Mary, the vowels running loose in her mouth.

"Hubba hubba, look at you," said Ruth, sizing up her friend. "You're not playing around this year, are you?"

"No, ma'am. You should have seen Peter's face when he first saw me," said Mary. "He wasn't sure whether to demand I change or carry me up to the bedroom."

"You'll cause a stir tonight."

"Good, this place could use one from time to time. Besides, it's smart to remind Peter just how good he's got it at home," said Mary, turning her attention to the floor. "And hello, Miss Lynn, how are we doing this evening?"

Lynn looked up from her Silly Putty and smiled her assortment of baby teeth, said the word *clearly*, then returned to her fun. Mary gave Ruth a quizzical look.

"I don't know. It's her new favorite word now; she just doesn't know how to use it yet."

"Well, it's adorable, and she's adorable in her little bee outfit."

Mary took a long pull from her Budweiser, lifting her head, exposing even more of her plunging neckline, the delicate skin under her throat. Some of the nearby partygoers were clearly gawking.

"And where is Chip tonight?" asked Ruth. "Let me guess. Peter volunteered to stay home with him to give you a free night out on the town?"

"Ha, that'll be the day. My mom's watching him," said Mary. "I'm sure Peter is already egging Baxter on to try some new holiday potion and wagering on the number of fruit flies hovering near the beer taps."

The mention of Baxter prompted Ruth to cast a fresh dirty look through the banquet hall wall, taking a sip of her spooky punch only to see that the cup had been drained. She tried to remember if it was her second or third drink. Had she actually had a third glass or only imagined what it would be like to cross the room and fill one for herself? Was she to become a drink-counter like Baxter; was that her lot in life? And in what book was it written she couldn't have a third glass? Or maybe it would be her fourth? At a party for adults, celebrating a child's holiday, what was the point of any . . .?

"Earth to Ruth, come in, Ruth," said Mary, waving her hand in front of Ruth's face. "You getting a little tipsy tonight? Keep drinking that punch, and eventually, you'll really see through that wall."

From across the way, some of the stooges were casting appreciative glances at Mary and her homage to the profession of nursing, not that she seemed to mind. It made Ruth wish she'd chosen a less frumpy costume—her gingerbread woman outfit left *everything* to the imagination and wasn't bound to turn any heads. She felt invisible to their moronic leers, typically a good thing, though that night, it hit in an unflattering way.

"Don't you think it's preposterous in this day and age that Baxter and Peter are over in their little clubhouse as if they desperately need a safe haven from us?" said Ruth, her tongue suddenly forked, coated in red. She was pretty sure she did imbibe that third drink.

"Boys will be boys," said Mary. "Even if we're the ones that rightly need a break from them."

"I tell you, I'd like to march over there and give every single one of them a piece of my mind."

"Now who's the one looking to cause a stir?" said Mary, flagging down a passing waiter. "Hey, my friend here needs a cup of spooky punch, extra spooky."

She handed the waiter Ruth's empty cup and sent him on his way.

"You've always been a bad influence on me," said Ruth, patting her friend on the back.

"It's Halloween. What better night to exorcise a few demons?"

"Clearly."

The waiter returned lickety-split with a full cup for Ruth and handed it over.

"You may have just saved a life tonight, doctor," said Ruth to the waiter, who treated himself to an extra-long look at the nurse in front of him before plunging back into the throng of guests.

The two women clinked their glasses. Unspoken pacts abounded—they'd have each other's back no matter what the night devolved into, no matter the commotion they might cause in their own disparate ways.

* * *

The Halloween Trail at the Orchard Coils Country Club was about a mile and a half long, maybe a little less if one were to cut some corners. It ran through the interior six holes of the course, known as the I-6, then across a seldom-used utility road, only to begin in earnest through some of the remaining holes across the way, known as the exterior twelve, or X-12 for short. On that night, the entire path was guided by plastic lanterns filled with small, burning candles—positioned by the maintenance staff who would hand lay them parallel to each other, hundreds in total, only to be stored for 364 days until the following year, when the process was repeated anew.

It was hardly the maintenance staff's favorite night of the year.

On that October evening, there were fourteen children embarking on the Halloween Trail for the first time, including Leo Sinclair. The youngest of these fledglings was seven, while the oldest was eleven. Accompanying these first timers were a few teenagers who had walked the trail before and wanted to do it again. This wasn't necessarily discouraged, but they were told, as were all who had walked the trail before, to not speak of their previous experience so as to not ruin the fun for the new batch of explorers. These kids and young teenagers were chaperoned by two seventeen-year-old girls—high school honor students, cool and level-headed, entrusted to mind the back of the line. The entire production was led by William Rost and his girlfriend, Brenda Hicks, both sophomores at the local college and club members under their parents' contracts. They'd met each other at the club a few years before and had walked the trail themselves a decade earlier. They shared an affinity for local lore and had volunteered to serve as tour guides as their predecessors had relinquished the roles, the same way new guides would be called upon once it was time for William and Brenda to spread their wings and move on to what life had in store for them.

Shadowing the entire process were the two grounds crew workers who remained hidden through the deep woods—usually the two who drew the proverbial short straws. Sometimes they'd shake tree trunks to create extra rustling effects. Occasionally, they'd clap two pieces of wood together to create a spooky echo effect. Blow a whistling tune out of an aged wood flute. Maybe bellow a turkey call or mimic some animal. All of it an attempt to build more ambiance for the kids, which was meant to be fun for them—adventuring sans parents, guided by candlelight—and even if most of the trail was just the cart paths, it still had the feel of a late-night excursion. All that theater was leading the group to a fenced section of the seventh-hole green, where they would all settle in, allowing William and Brenda to recite a story that had been passed down for generations.

It was the story of the Quarry Witch.

For his part, Leo had been looking forward to walking the trail, had had a serious meltdown when he was denied last year; his mom—a former trail walker herself—thought eight years old too young. Baxter had remained on the sidelines of that fight back then but swore to himself that Leo would not be coddled and would be allowed to participate next year if that was what he wanted. When Ruth had looked to Baxter for help putting Leo off until his tenth birthday, she found none and acquiesced to her son's insistence that he was old enough to go. Leo knew it was a big deal when club kids got to walk the Halloween Trail. He'd heard some of the adults use the term *rite of passage*, though he wasn't totally sure what it meant and hadn't wanted to ask his parents out of fear it would somehow change their minds. The whole idea of being away from his mom and dad, under the authority of some older kids, traipsing about in the dead of night—even if it was only seven p.m.—was very appealing, like a grown-up thing to do.

There was no way he was going to wait another entire year.

Leo walked side by side with his friend Denny Nurasco, also nine years old. And while Leo didn't consider Denny his best friend—that was reserved for his classmate Tony Maine—Denny was Leo's best good friend as far as it went out of the kids from O Triple C. The two were stationed in the middle of the pack, listening to occasional instructions from William and Brenda about the history of the land they were walking on, way before it had been developed into a golf course. It was really dark out, but the lanterns and leaking moonlight from the thinly clouded sky made it a little less creepy. There were so many trees around them, weird noises popping out from the branches, from the deep dark. Even the flagsticks on the greens, the rakes along the bunkers, found a way to look intimidating. The kids knew the walk would end with the telling of a ghost story, a really important one to the town, so that only enhanced the sense of unease they were all experiencing, trying to be brave or at least pretending to do so.

Leo's heart was beating noticeably faster the farther they got along the trail. He was thrilled and scared and curious and happy all at once—feeling bigger than his body, that he was up to this challenge that his mom hadn't thought him ready for yet. He pumped his little legs and arms in strong motion, knowing he was exactly where he wanted to be—where he belonged. He and Denny would look over to each other every time something seemed to skirt above the tree line, some bird of prey or maybe a squirrel jumping the canopy of branches. Everyone knew that bats were common to the area, their erratic flight easy to spot. There was even the occasional coyote howl, maybe a fisher cat—though often, that was just a random dog baying at the moon.

Between nature and the dark and the lanterns and the weird noises, there was an awful lot for the kids to process, particularly when they were all trying to muster their own brand of courage, no one wanting to look weak in front of the others.

The two boys continued to walk the pathway, Denny eventually breaking the silence after a weird volley of what sounded like stick smashing from the heavy woods off the fifth hole dogleg.

"You scared at all, Leo?" asked Denny.

"Not really," said Leo, old enough now to know when he was telling a lie.

"Come on."

"OK, a little, but so are you."

Murmurs from the teenage guides at the back on the line, more encouraging words from those leading the charge up front.

"What do you think's going to happen up there?" asked Denny.

"I don't know. But we'll have to watch out for each other, no matter what."

"Really?"

"Scouts honor," said Leo, patting his friend on the back, reassuring him they were in it together, would face down any danger as a team.

It felt interesting to Leo to make that sort of pledge to someone, to see it calm their nerves. He wasn't sure he'd ever done anything like that before. Maybe for his sister when she was acting fussy, but that didn't count. These two were marching toward the unknown—maybe mortal danger, monsters, who knew?—and there weren't any parents around to protect them or whisk them to safety. The fact that he'd promised his best good friend they'd take care of each other felt, again, like something an adult would do. It sat right with him, even if he wasn't a scout and just liked that saying of late. The whole thing got Leo to thinking exactly what it meant to be brave—really brave, not just horsing around or playing make-believe. And not just for himself but what it meant to be brave for others, to make other people feel at ease, protected. He wondered how much of it he had inside him. He wondered if he was yellow. Or if Denny was thinking the same thing. He wondered if people would be proud, like his mom and dad, if he proved how much of that courage resounded in him—especially since he was hardly the biggest kid in his class. If anything, he was clearly on the small side, which could make a big difference in the complicated hierarchy of elementary school. It was all kinds of heady stuff for a nine-year old to be thinking, but that was sort of the point of taking them out of their comfort zone and introducing them to a different experience, a small taste of independence. They didn't know exactly how each child might react. But to Leo's credit, as they got closer and closer to their destination, he resolved to give it his all, to be unafraid, not just for his benefit but for Denny's and anyone else's who might need him. He knew what the word *coward* meant and was going to avoid that label at all costs. Even if he had to fake it at first. He was going to be one of the strong ones in the pack. He would be brave.

* * *

Baxter was nursing a second bottle of Budweiser while Peter Sullivan was yammering on about some shady financial venture that Baxter was welcome to come into on the ground floor lest he miss out on the chance of a lifetime. As much as Baxter loved Peter, he was plenty comfortable missing out on his friend's can't-miss opportunities—not so much get-rich-quick schemes as get-rich-easy schemes, as Sullivan liked to put it. He was half in the bag, which only enhanced his tales of dragon's gold and pirates' booty. Not that they weren't entertaining yarns—Baxter had just heard many of them before. For his part, Baxter was happy with work and family and weekends at the club, and there just wasn't much more he needed past that. He'd survived one war, avoided Korea, had turned over a new leaf meeting Ruth, and eschewed his hound dog days, retiring his own personal roaring twenties. He'd found a way to get along with Ruth's parents and knew they had some financial backing and safety nets should ever the need arise. All was rosy in his book, and the last thing he needed was to throw money into a pit like Sullivan, even if the man did seem to have some talent at alchemy. Still, the juice wouldn't be worth the squeeze, as they were prone to say around Baxter's office.

In the men-only section of the Restaurant, there was always a sanctuary feel, despite Baxter knowing Ruth resented the ever-loving hell out of it. Sometimes guys just needed a place to be a little crude, maybe even vulnerable, without the fairer sex bearing witness. He hardly considered it a slight, and thought that women-only clubs were equally fair and just as needed. He scanned around to see the thirty or so men, most of them poorly costumed, laughing and hooting over bad jokes and bawdy stories. Fueled by way too much booze. Amplified with wagers, many of which would be forgotten or not honored. Plans for long February weekends in Naples or Miami mused over, more likely to be scrapped than actually crafted. It was a raucous party, and just about everyone in the room knew each other. And even if Baxter's heavier drinking days were long behind him, he still knew how to have a good time, to be social without overdoing it, an acquired talent—unlike Sullivan, for whom moderation proved elusive and who now clamped Baxter around the shoulders and started whispering sweet nothings about amortized commercial property in his ear, another of his many siren songs heralding capitalism. Baxter nodded along with his inebriated friend, allowing him to hold court, trying to suck others into a debate over high-rise versus riverfront condominium development. There wasn't much point trying to slow Peter Sullivan down once he got going, particularly when he was convinced he could make the entire room rich via arbitrage maneuvers. Best bet was just to let him spin down of his own accord, maybe confiscate his car keys if the opportunity presented itself.

Baxter finished his bottle and ordered a club soda from Tracy, one of the two female bartenders working that side of the Restaurant—both comely employees accustomed to manning the men-only section, an obvious contradiction, though forgiven as the overwhelming majority of the male members had insisted on this exception long ago, preferring to be served their drinks by girls decades younger than their lot. From a business point of view, it was a fair play. Tracy and her colleague had no complaints, knowing full well these country club types were big softies compared to the creeps and malcontents found at other bars and clubs in the area. Plus, these guys seemed to have the money to one-up each other, never sweating an additional round, a juicy tip. Even if the finances weren't going so well on the home front, there always seemed to be cash to spread around the Restaurant—a disconnect Tracy and her ilk were happy to benefit from, a gig worth holding on to, despite the occasional catcall.

Baxter took his drink and found some distance from Sullivan, who had absorbed some new barflies into his orbit. He took a moment to himself, enjoying the cold soda in the hot room, his monk costume not well designed for comfort or coolness, even with the heavy hood pulled behind his head. Baxter had never thought much of the holiday since he'd become an adult—people pretending to be afraid or evil and all that jazz. He'd spent enough time in Europe being afraid for real, witnessing true evil; it seemed silly to him to fake it, even for a single night. He took in some more of the room, noticing an influential cross-section of members gathered in the corner, their lips moving in a way to suggest a private conversation, discussing their high-Machiavellian strategies, cloaked by a cloud of cigarette smoke permeating the room's atmosphere. The conversation looked serious to Baxter, maybe a little too serious for a bunch of middle-aged men dressed in cheap and hastily thrown-together costumes. Among them, you had the head of the members' committee, Grant Cornwall; the head of the greens committee, Jack Barker; and the head of the tournament committee, Trent Rawski, all cloistered in the dark parlor, buffered ten feet on any given side, given a wide berth by the rest of the party who understood their unspoken message: stay away. Baxter knew them to be good enough men for what they were—though not a soldier among the three of them—but a powerful little cabal in their own right, the likes of which you wouldn't want to offend or run afoul of. O Triple C was no different from any social hierarchy, with its ladders and fiefdoms, infighting and rampant gossip—not dissimilar to Leo's elementary school or even an ant colony, with the exception of some occasional golf that got played on the more pleasant days.

At the bar, Tracy lined up a dozen drinks for a dozen men to down: an assembly line of shooters with plastic spiders floating in each and every glass. Through the sound system, weird werewolf noises seemed to be playing on a loop, though they were barely heard over the din of drunken men and their seventy-decibel bullshit.

So there was Baxter, feeling pretty good about life, surrounded by friends, his family on the property, Leo out on the Halloween Trail per both their wishes, riding a very slight buzz with a soft workday tomorrow, a foursome already lined up for Saturday morning provided a frost delay didn't jam them up. He felt very much content, present in the moment—not always his best skill, but he had to admit there wasn't much to complain about during those autumn days, the big holidays on the horizon. In short, life was good—and not by accident, he'd worked hard at it. It felt earned.

Then Ruth appeared in the doorway of the men-only section, looking unsteady in her posture, a rictus grin barely concealed under the subterfuge of a smile.

Baxter's spirits plummeted. Diplomacy would not be an option.

She barged into the room and beelined for her husband, whose mood quickly shifted. He cursed himself for ever taking a moment to believe that things could be perfect. He wondered if it was too late to throw on his monk's hood and hide in the storeroom where they kept the excess bottles and bartending supplies. Ruth had set upon him, and her eyes were somehow glassy yet sharp, which should be impossible, but she'd managed it all the same. He knew he was in for something. He'd actually had a sense of it for a long while now. Her will was too steely, her annoyance too pronounced as varying cultural shifts had expressed themselves more recently in the country as part of a growing effect. Let alone if she'd gotten into too much of the spooky punch, which she almost certainly had given how much she favored that old Haitian recipe.

He would have his hands full, that much he was assured of.

Ruth approached and put her hands on his chest, smoothing down his robes in a way that suggested that the fun was over. All eyes in the room had shifted to the two of them, most of them anticipating that Baxter would nip the situation in the bud, not all of them knowing exactly how headstrong Ruth could be once she opened a salvo. The room hadn't necessarily ground to a halt—it wasn't quite a record-scratch moment—but a pinch of surrealism had been leant to the mood, an air of curiosity. Tactics would need to be employed to avoid an all-out crisis. Damage control. Baxter was glad to be holding only a club soda, and that was when his borderline teetotaling worked to his advantage.

He got down to the task of de-escalation, the way a cabinet secretary might try to talk down an enraged sitting president.

"Hey ya, cherry drop, how's my favorite seasonal cookie doing?" he asked, in full-charm mode.

She hiccupped—another troubling sign.

"Here to make sure you're not having all the fun," she said, not slurring her words but getting close, maybe one drink away.

"Oh, I never have too much fun without you guys," said Baxter. "And how is our little Lynn doing?" A question of veiled reproach.

"She's showing Mary the time of her life with that goo," said Ruth. "More importantly, how do you think Leo is doing? You don't think he's terrified, do you?"

A sore subject, thought Baxter. *A minefield.*

"I bet he's doing great," said Baxter. "And I'm quite sure you'll be the one he wants to tell all about it to first."

That seemed to soften the starch out of Ruth momentarily.

"You really think so?"

"I know so."

Ruth rubbed her hands at the side of his face dreamily, mollified.

"Would you order me a chardonnay from the bar?" she asked.

"My love, I think you know this isn't the place for . . ." said Baxter, cautiously. "Why don't I join you and Lynn and Mary in the banquet hall, and we'll put some food in our stomachs?"

The starch immediately returned to Ruth's demeanor. No more face caressing, no doting tones.

"I haven't come here to retrieve you, Baxter; I'm here to join you," said Ruth, taking note of Peter Sullivan and calling over to him. "Hey, Peter, what's a girl got to do to get a drink in this place?"

Sullivan smiled brightly at Ruth, then ducked away as quickly as he could. He didn't want anything to do with the nonsense the Sinclairs were about to bring, was thankful that his Mary was just interested in turning some heads with a low-cut outfit, not restructuring the social norms of the club.

Tracy, from behind the bar, in some act of womanly solidarity, handed Ruth a drink, though she motioned to Baxter in her bartender sign language that it had been watered down. Among her many mandates, keeper of the peace was one Tracy took seriously. Though she wouldn't be the one to kick the gingerbread woman out; that was for the club members to enforce. To that end, Baxter felt the bore-drill of eyes upon him, including the three committee heads who had broken from their scrum and were now silently observing the rift at the bar.

Baxter felt an ominous clock ticking in his head—the click-click of his own downfall. Perhaps Halloween was meant to induce a real fear in him?

"OK, Ruth, you've gotten your drink in the forbidden section," said Baxter evenly. "May we go now?"

Click.

"How about a tour of the room first?"

Click.

"How's about we get some fresh air?"

Click.

Too late, time was up. Grant Cornwall, the quote-unquote highest-ranking member in attendance that night, broke away from his council and joined the Sinclairs, his reasons obvious to anyone with half a brain and working knowledge of club policy.

"Ruth, Baxter, nice to see you tonight," said Grant with his trademark smoothness. "Having a fun time?"

"We are, thanks, Grant," said Baxter warily. "Ruth's just a little nervous for our oldest who's out on the Halloween Trail. First timer."

"Oh, I'm sure he'll be just fine. Who can believe our little miracle from the fourth hole is already out and about on the trail. Where does the time go?" said Grant, laying it on a bit. "You know, I was reminding Jack the other day that I was the deciding vote to grant Leo his lifetime membership on the arm. Only been done one time prior, more than fifty years ago as I recall."

Ruth glowered over her drink at Grant, who never seemed to miss an opportunity to bring up that fact, even if the Sinclairs had never asked for that gift, even if it had always felt like a stunt to get good press, even if the whole deciding-vote business might have been utter bullshit. All those kinds of decisions were closed door anyway. Hard to separate the fact from fiction with Grant's fuzzy relationship with the truth muddying the waters.

"We're aware, Grant, and we do appreciate it," said Baxter calmly, with a mechanical smile.

"Of course, I had less clout then—a junior member of that committee going so far as to buck the direction of the sitting chair, Robert O'Halloran," said Cornwall, amusing himself. "Old Robby didn't see that one coming, God rest his soul."

Both Baxter and Ruth silently recalled that Robert O'Halloran had stroked out back in '61. Grant couldn't be bothered to hide the smile on his face, an effect that looked odd against his sad caterpillar eyes and bushy brows. *Trim those fuckers, would you?* thought Ruth, stifling a giggle.

"Well, it was good to see you, Grant," said Baxter, touching his wife on the elbow. "Ruth and I were about to step outside for some air."

"See that you do," said Grant, still smooth, as though it was his idea.

Baxter would have liked to snap his pencil neck in two, would have a decade ago in the mudholes of Italy, but instead forced a tight-mouthed grin and steered Ruth toward the exit, but not before she could offer her parting shot to that room of supposed movers and shakers.

"So this is your little boy's club," she said loudly to Grant, to anyone within earshot. "Well, let me tell you, it's not so fucking grand."

She hiccupped, somewhat neutering the point she was trying to leave on.

Then she bailed with Baxter in tow, he looking a might sheepish, she more than a bit satisfied. His passivity quickly pivoted once they were out of the room and back in the hallway as he led her toward the coat check. He gave the attendant a sawbuck and told him to go grab a smoke under some streetlamp or whatever. The kid complied. They entered the enclave, now confined among the jackets and furs and stoles, Baxter used the seclusion to address his costumed wife, who always seemed charmed when her pragmatic husband had a bone to pick with her, as though his ire was adorable.

"What's gotten into you tonight?" he asked.

"You know I hate that room, those rules; don't pretend to be so surprised."

"You embarrassed me in there. And it's not just that. You haven't been yourself lately."

"Blame the spooky punch," she said, suppressing another hiccup, still clutching that watered-down chardonnay.

"I think you know what I mean," said Baxter. "You haven't been yourself for quite a while."

"Who have I been then?"

"A malcontent. You know, Ruth, if you're going through something, why don't you just talk to me?" said Baxter. "We'll figure it out together, but stop treating me like a mind reader."

Ruth observed the coats around her, the recessed lighting; sipped her drink; and felt her stomach turn slightly. She sighed deeply, her breath both tropical and rotten from the punch.

"Sometimes I'm surprised I'm not happier with my life," she said. "Maybe I just needed something exciting to happen."

Baxter, not one for contrived drama, frowned.

"Like one of our kids getting hit by a car. Maybe a brain tumor," said Baxter angrily. "'Cause that's the type of tragedy one courts once they've grown complacent with peace and quiet."

Ruth looked back angrily at her husband, the kind of man who would conflate excitement with tragedy, as though nuance didn't exist—such was the binary he lived his life by.

"Don't be fatalistic," said Ruth. "And you know those are horrible things to say."

Baxter flinched, and with his schoolboy tendencies quickly taking the reins, hugged Ruth and kissed her cheek. He'd long been tenderhearted with her, a lovesick fool willing to tip his king over before she'd taken even one of his pawns. What could he do? He credited her for saving his life.

"I'm sorry for the brash point," said Baxter. "How can I lift your spirits? Do you want me to cancel golf on Saturday? We'll take the kids to that orchard you've been talking about. Or maybe that DDT rally you've had circled on the calendar."

"It's an anti-DDT rally," she corrected him.

"Whatever it is. You want me to go? I'll hold a placard and everything."

Ruth felt very tired suddenly, Baxter's zeal zapping the last of her energy.

"Let's just scoop Lynn up and wait for Leo outside," said Ruth. "Cut the night short."

He nodded, though for the first time her really looked around to realize he'd been having it out with his wife in the club's coat closet, a first for him, including greasing the attendant to take a hike. He saw Ruth running her hand along the racks, swaying the outerwear on their hangers, bobbing like pendulums. She scoffed.

"I've always hated fur," she said.

Baxter reached under his shroud of monk robes and retrieved an item from his pants pocket. A plastic egg. He opened it and procured some more of Lynn's silly putty. A spare, they had eggs and eggs of the stuff. He proceeded to wad it around his fingers and smear it into the collar of some finely crafted jacket lined with animal tuft—a mink or a lynx or a minx he supposed, didn't know and didn't care—and really mashed it into the hairs and fibers, deep and unextractable and probably not easy to spot at first glance, particularly at night.

He returned the egg to his pocket and smiled at Ruth. It was the little gestures that counted in this world.

"Then so do I," he said. "Let's scram."

* * *

Once the kids were gathered and sitting around the heavily lanterned and fenced arena of the seventh-hole green, William Rost and Brenda Hicks, with the additional effect of their flashlights, proceeded to take turns in their rehearsed recounting of the Quarry Witch story.

Around the late 1800s, the town of Orchard Coils was known for two things: apples and springs of precious stone, granite in particular. Both industries imported laborers to conduct the work. These laborers brought their families if they could. These families needed services: churches, schools, stores, utilities, and recreation. That was how certain towns in the Northeast flourished and others died by the wayside, only to be absorbed into other municipalities or cordoned off as unincorporated land. That was the patchwork for hundreds of years in America, resulting in towns, counties, and eventual states across the land, many of them founded through the grist of business, the lubricant of blood, and the fuel of coin.

The Orchard Coils Quarry, as it was more commonly known, was an open behemoth set in the shadow of a massive protrusion of rock—not the size of a mountain, though larger than a hill. The surrounding land was mostly agrarian; varying crops could be planted and rotated during different growing seasons. The noise from the quarry kept most residential housing away; there weren't any proper homes for a mile in any direction of the mining site. There were plenty of makeshift shacks and cooking stations for the men to use, though much like the workers themselves, these structures had a very temporary nature to them. Disposable. Left to erode. The harsh winters and frozen conditions made the quarry viable for about eight months out of the year, resulting in a mad dash to extract as much granite and limestone as possible before the snows rolled in and compelled even the heartiest of men to lay down their tools until the spring thaw.

The owner of this specific quarry was a cruel man, even by the standards of 1892, and the human loss it took to procure his precious building materials truly meant nothing to him. It was all replaceable labor—literal boatloads of willing participants, a flood of whom seemed endless at the time. The owner's name was Arnold Holm, and many men died on his watch, a fact he didn't shy away from and all but embraced. Holm was a shrewd businessman with little imagination; he couldn't fathom a world where there would be a comeuppance for his callousness, where he could be dragged down from his gilded tower and be held accountable for his flimsy appreciation of life.

He would be proven wrong.

Despite the Orchard Coils Quarry being bountiful, the slow pace of extracting her sought-after goods frustrated Arnold Holm to no end. It was bad enough he was forced to shut down operations for four months every year, but to see him depleting his little money mine so slowly brought a sense of dread to the man, as though conspirators were endlessly plotting to steal it from him somehow. Given Holm's standing in the business community, or any community for that matter, he might not have been paranoid on that count. His was a mining operation before the times of sophisticated enhancements: electrification, advanced steam, and motorization. This was also before dynamiting became a refined art. There may have been some rudimentary steam-powered cranes to assist with certain free-load slabs, but whether Holm actually sprang for one in any of his Northeast quarries was unknown. They did have sets of crude tracks to guide carts filled with materials; evidence of that could still be seen in the present day, the aged tracks vaguely visible through the ground. Not that there was any activity down in the old Orchard Coils Quarry anymore—it has been plastered with NO TRESPASSING signs, private property that local law enforcement tried to keep unmolested, as much as it was in their capacity to do so, which, honestly, wasn't much, given it was a small-town PD with limited resources.

Arnold Holm was so perturbed by the slow pace of hammer and wet chisel that, in his greed, he decided to occupy the mine site further by boring into the side of the mini mountain, confident he could find similar materials that could bring him profits on the open market. He was advised by more than one geological expert against this, the reason being that the structure might not be stable enough to endure his proposed gutting; cave-ins and loss of life were possibilities. These were the wrong arguments to make with a man like Holm, who placed little value on the lives of the Poles and Swedes and Spaniards who had crossed the Atlantic looking to make a better life for themselves and their families. In Holm's mind, Europe was an entire continent rife with fodder for his mining operations—who cared how many of them had to perish in order for him to succeed? He fired his geologists and so-called experts, replacing them with ones who would testify that drilling into the mountain, despite its proximity to the quarry, was perfectly safe. He would proceed to cut into the vertical rise that had long shaded the giant hole he'd gorged into the ground.

With Holm's effort now doubled on the same site, he envisioned double the revenue, if not more, a reward for his boldness and ingenuity.

By that point in the story, Denny had raised his hand and was acknowledged by William Rost.

"Wasn't this supposed to be a ghost story?" he asked.

"And what's a Swede?" added Leo.

William and Brenda exchanged tired looks, clearly having gone through this line of questioning before.

"Please just continue to sit still and listen," said William patiently. "All will be revealed."

"And let's hold our questions until the very end of the story," said Brenda.

Leo and Denny looked at each other sitting cross legged on the seventh-hole green, shrugged their shoulders, and returned their attention to the storytellers, who continued on.

To the surprise of few, early in the spring of 1893, Holm's newly mined cavern collapsed and killed six men, including a German-born emigrant named Paul Schrader, who'd only been in America for thirteen months.

Holm, as it were, would not be deterred by the tragedy, particularly as he barely viewed it as a tragedy. Act of God, worker negligence, futility of life—it was all the same to the captain of industry who thought himself better than his fellow man, especially immigrants. He certainly gave no thought to the families of the fallen men, those they'd left behind. Maybe they'd receive a pittance of insurance money, policies that probably favored Holm way more than those bereaved. Holm was a notorious policy holder and loved sparring with these agents and lawyers in court, grubbing for every ill-gotten penny he could.

It was practically sport to him, something to excel at.

In time, the rubble and debris of the collapse was cleared away from the mine, presumably by hand, and the corpses were recovered, smashed beyond bodily recognition. Clothing and boots were primarily used to identify the six departed souls.

That's what survives a collapse like that—clothing and boots, not bones and organs. Not people.

The remains were carted off for their respective families to perform whatever burial rituals and funeral processions were mandated by their cultures, what traditions they could afford, including Agnes Schrader, wife of Paul Schrader. They'd been married more than twenty years before his untimely death at Holm's quarry.

Once the mine shaft was fully cleared out, Holm set his mind to getting it up and running anew. Again, certain advisors, even the yes men, now cautioned against it. The actual quarry was producing well enough and would be more stable if he didn't bore farther into the vertical rock, which had been yielding minimal value, continually flirting with a vein of minerals that had yet to fully reveal itself or prove to be worth the effort. These same advisors were also quick to remind Holm that his many other ventures around the Northeast were turning profits, that his balance sheet was strong and there was no compelling reason to risk another cave-in with such an unnecessary endeavor. But Holm didn't see it that way, and the more his advisors protested, the more he dug his heels in, convinced there was something precious buried in that skyward rock. It became almost a matter of faith to the man, ironic as he was as godless as the day was long, substituting for divinity the pursuit of ripping up the planet in search of innate treasure, only to convert it back into man-made notions; fiat currency, paper money, black ink in a ledger—an endless cycle that mesmerized Holm, powered his existence.

By that time, the mining industry across the country was starting to receive more than its fair share of bad press, now in the form of exposes around unsafe working conditions, corporate greed, and the slow adoption of technologies that could make mining encampments more tolerable to the workers. That type of journalism—which would usher in the needed era of the muckraker—was slowly bringing to light the cruel conditions the miners were living in. It sparked a new electricity in the air, though slow moving, and in the interim, more people were needlessly dying through the avarice of men like Arnold Holm, who, during those middle months of 1893, was routinely lambasted in publications as large as the *Hartford Courant*—even among smaller ones in the state, including the fledgling *Orchard Coils Courier*—a bold editorial decision, given Holm's sway in the town as a key employer and greaser of wheels. As a result of this onslaught of scathing commentary against him, Holm took to traveling with a full-time bodyguard, a mustachioed and heavily cologned former ranger who seldom smiled and wielded a carbine rifle that never seemed absent from his hands.

If Holm had truly known what was coming for him, he would have hired more than one—or, better yet, hidden in his West Hartford mansion and lived like a curmudgeon until the prevailing winds changed and the coast cleared.

On the day his mine was set to properly reopen, Holm invited some press to commemorate the occasion, to show that he was employing some additional safety measures, which, in truth, were scant, more smoke and mirrors than anything. He'd hoped to gain back a little of the favor he'd lost in recent months, to apply some luster to his tarnished image. Maybe make some inroads with the press, see if he could line some pockets and divert their attention to other industries that were surely exploiting the working man as they so often accused him of. Holm did this mostly off the advice of others—he didn't give a damn what people thought of him, what they printed in their rags—but he could see that bringing down the temperature would better serve his business interests in the long run. And bribing people was far more amenable to the man than investing in the costly and frivolous demands of his miners and their precious safety.

So the site was busy the day of the reopening, with the comings and goings of many different types of people. As a result, it wouldn't have been odd to see a plainly dressed though presentable, small yet sturdy woman having a look about, exploratory in a nonthreatening way. Agnes Schrader wasn't much to look at, nearing fifty and showing noticeable signs of a roughshod life. Probably why no one had really bothered to question the demure woman and her presence at the encampment. Probably why people were prone to offer her a quick, polite smile and be on their way. Probably why Holm's bodyguard hadn't regarded her with scrutiny, there being others more worthy of his attention. And the whole time, Holm persisted on holding court, yammering on about the future of mining to anyone who would circle around and listen to him, pontificating on his new square-set timbering that would make his mine even safer, neglecting to mention he'd skimped and would be using a less sturdy wood than local oak to buttress the shaft.

There was no shortcut the man wasn't willing to employ.

It hadn't taken long for Agnes Schrader to clock Holm's whereabouts. She knew the mining baron from his picture in the papers, which she read as often as her time allowed, teaching herself English over the year before the accident removed Paul from their fledgling American life. She set her sights on Holm, the crowd thinning around him, growing tired of his industrial soliloquies. She was a patient woman, and if she felt fear, she concealed it well, closing some distance between her and her target, waiting for the right moment, an unobstructed view. When that time came, as the legend goes, she reached into the gunnysack she carried as though it were a modest purse and pulled out an old thumb buster and loaded, then cocked, then aimed, then fired her shot into Holm, dropping him limp like a bag of grain. The event, witnessed by many, including members of the press, would chronicle Schrader as totally unassuming; many of them couldn't even remember noticing her prior to the attack, as though she had walked through them all like a ghost. But she was skilled enough with a pistol to hit her mark with the shot allotted to her, calmly and with the satisfied look of someone who had already made their peace with Lord and Creator. Whom she promptly met seconds later, when Holm's bodyguard regained his wits and proceeded to remove Agnes's head from her body with two blasts of his rifle.

She'd anticipated as much, wouldn't have held it against the bodyguard for doing his job, protecting his charge.

Suffice it to say, the mining site was again shut down that morning before it even had a chance to open, a cadre of police arrived, and various stories were written up and set for publication in evening editions or the following morning.

By that point in the story, as was usually the case, William Rost and Brenda Hicks had the kids' rapt attention—they'd settled down, eager for more of the tale.

One particular note to the legend, though it would take a few weeks to come out after the events at the quarry, was that Agnes and Paul had two children back in Germany, neither of whom had survived into their teenage years, one passing from tuberculosis, the other of consumption. Then Paul was ruined by a shabby mine in America, where the tales of a better life had never fully materialized for the already-heartbroken couple. By that point, given the untenable weight of tragedy in her life, Agnes figured her earthly plans weren't going to match those of her dreams, not by a long shot, so she'd have to fashion a new reality. Her existence then brimming over with sorrow and anger—a dangerous mixture—she'd set her mind toward revenge, as worthy an endeavor for any widow who'd also buried her only two children.

As Agnes would ultimately land upon, murdering Holm in cold blood seemed a good use of her final days on the planet.

That told, Agnes did fail at first as Holm survived the single shot, which found its way past his heart and lodged in a more non-organed part of his chest. He would lose half his mobility and strength in his left arm, nerve damage that would never return full functionality to the appendage. One might have thought such an assault would alter the man's mind and prompt him to change course in life. Maybe keep the mine closed and allow for some reflection. But Holm, bedridden and incensed, barked orders for the opening to continue, that work should resume despite the land now being a crime scene, despite the fresh blood still visible in the dirt. He'd had enough of these setbacks and delays, even if he was now somehow a part of it, even with his surgeon yapping in his ear that he'd lose the arm outright if he didn't rest and allow some healing to occur. The people around Holm kept going on about bad omens. Whispers and rumor circulated freely in that West Hartford mansion. His medical attendants were giving him tonics for the bodily pain, enough to induce periods of loopiness, forced slumber. But during his more lucid moments, his orders were crystal clear and ultimately carried out—open that damn mine and get back to work!

Once the site resumed, it didn't take long for weird things to begin to occur. Provisions would spoil at a rate that defied logic. Potable water tasted of silt and salt. Freshly laid track broke. Rail ties snapped. Surrounding birds flew into the mini mountain and broke their little necks, writhing on the ground as though they'd never mastered the sky, as though they'd been compelled to give up their birthright in service of a higher portend. Scores of little birds seemingly suiciding themselves before the workers' eyes. Then came the turkey vultures, attracted to the carrion, known harbingers of death that no one wanted to see loitering around the manic territory. The men's work instruments became less effective against the quarry itself. The mine would have rock tumbles from seemingly sturdy areas, resulting in numerous close calls, not killing anyone but further terrifying the already-jumpy men. They started to see these things as signs, a worsening energy that went beyond dangerous labor, something more unnatural, otherworldly. These may have been men who desperately needed the pay, but when even the worms deserted the soil and the pooled, stagnant water hued black and the wind carried the faint perpetual stench of gun smoke and sulfur, they started to question the wisdom of money in the face of lands that, for lack of a better term, appeared to be blighted, maybe even cursed.

Then the actual sightings started to occur.

The first was by the foreman, his name undocumented or lost by history as Holm was always replacing his foremen on capricious whims. He was at the quarry one morning before the other workers arrived, where he was finishing up his business in the outhouse. He exited the little structure to see Agnes Schrader, headless, still holding that gunnysack, surveying the worksite as though it was her job. She proceeded to stare at the befuddled foreman—if you could call it that, considering she didn't have a head. She regarded the foreman, who was frozen in his tracks, and eventually went about her own business of inspecting the site before she disappeared into the now-open mine shaft, only to vanish completely.

The arriving workers would eventually find the foreman hiding in the aforementioned outhouse, half-catatonic. In time, they were able to coax him out and retrieve the story from him. This information would be relayed back to Holm, still convalescing in his sickbed. He quickly fired the foreman and forbade those lies from ever being repeated on any of his worksites. The sacked foreman put up no protest to his termination, preferring destitution to sharing the haunted grounds with that spectral being, a turn of events not lost on his fellow coworkers.

But it didn't stop there, The Orchard Coils Quarry had many more sightings.

It mostly started with one man at a time, the early bird responsible for getting things going at the site or the last man to leave, just when darkness was shutting things down for the day. Same thing happened every time—Agnes Schrader trolling the grounds, minding her own business, yet somehow aware of those around her, tilting her headless neck in their direction, then disappearing back into the mine. It got to be so all the workers were scared to be alone on site, particularly in the morning or at dusk. All who saw the apparition would inevitably claim a disorientation, a fuzziness not unlike what the first foreman attested to, though somewhat less as eventually, the workers anticipated they'd see Agnes at some point and thus prepared themselves as best they could. The miners started traveling in packs of two or three at all times, hesitant to be alone. Undeterred, Agnes continued to materialize, as though growing more comfortable on the site with the workers around her as they grew more fearful that her benevolence would cease, that she might lash out at some point. She was a ghost of some sort, after all. More and more men saw Agnes in her meandering glory, and they all complained of mild headaches, buzzing in their ears. And all of them, eventually, much like that very first foreman, quit the site the day they encountered her or soon after, quickly realizing when enough was enough.

In one month's time, Agnes Schrader had cleared out almost all the quarry's workforce, and many of the others who hadn't seen her yet decided not to stay around for it to happen. A few actually did hang around to see the specter, to become believers with their own eyes—which happened in many instances, also resulting in speedy resignations from Holm's employ. Word of this exodus could not be kept from Holm forever, as he slowly recovered and shuffled around on his feet, though still mostly confined to his garish mansion. He was learning how to navigate life with a half-crippled arm, constant pain in his chest, and an even larger chip on his shoulder.

When the positions the workers abandoned couldn't be filled fast enough, the output of the site dropped off noticeably—ironic, given that Holm had always taken for granted what he viewed as the endless stock of workers for his excavation projects. It appeared word of the newly dubbed Quarry Witch had spread around New England, and even the laborers fresh off the boat couldn't be recruited or tricked into working that site.

Agnes Schrader had effectively turned off Holm's spigot of abused and maltreated miners.

When Holm's advisors tried to visit the site to see this astral projection for themselves, Agnes never appeared. Whether she was only interested in scaring off the workers or those willing to disrupt the land was unknown, but after a while, it did seem there was a certain method to her madness, and it didn't involve manifesting in front of fancy-dressed men with waxed mustaches and no callouses on their hands. Once it became unavoidable, Holm was informed of the supposed haunting at his worksite. As the tale goes, he flew into a rage, tongue-lashed his messengers, and flailed his busted arm around counterproductively, like an equally busted propeller. He proceeded to put on his own fancy clothes and demanded his advisors ferry him to the quarry in Orchard Coils. There, he would see the skeleton crew that remained, barely working, not really enough of them to tend the site properly. He chastised them as cowards, despite their being the ones who hadn't left, promised them famine and death and that they'd never dig up so much as an earthworm east of the Mississippi if he had anything to say about it. The men, nonplussed, fearing things greater than Holm's wrath or being excommunicated from the mining community, took their final exit, leaving their former boss and his advisors on site, alone and unattended and at the mercy of forces they couldn't explain.

Holm proceeded to circle and stomp around the site almost comically, calling out for this alleged witch to reveal herself as the same Agnes Schrader who had put the .22 slug in his body. He dared her, taunted her, insulted her. And her husband, a fool who couldn't mine the rock properly, a man whose name Holm couldn't even remember, if he ever knew it at all. Such was Holm's frenzy, screaming that he would not be run off his own land, that the honey was deep inside and belonged only to him.

Now maybe Holm's rant had an effect on Agnes, drawing her out. Or maybe it was her plan all along, if such entities were even capable of crafting plans. But after a few minutes of raving, Holm stopped dead in his tracks and stared into the maw of the mine, as though something were there, as though he might actually enter himself—an action he'd never considered before, behavior he'd deemed beneath him. He called out to one of his advisors, asking if he was hearing what Holm was hearing. The advisor could hear nothing apart from Holm's blathering; none of them could. It was only Holm who could hear something and now pleaded to his advisors: "She speaks; she speaks." No one said anything to their bedeviled employer as he crept closer and closer to the open mine, entranced by a siren call only he seemed to acknowledge. The closer he got, the more his head nodded, as though in agreement with the phantom words. The onlookers watched on. Holm continued to agree with whatever it was he heard, engaged in a one-sided conversation. Until he stilled himself, let out a final agreement, as though an accord was settled. He turned back to his employees, clad in finery and pocket watches and, in a trancelike state, fired the lot of them. He ordered them to clear out and said the site would be closed until further notice. The message lacked his usual firebrand, delivered to the men dispassionately, almost like a question. He told them all to leave him alone with his land, with his stone and tools. Then he turned his back on them, posting his attention back to the cave that seemed to be instructing him as his new sole advisor.

The living souls who, until very recently, had been employed by Holm left the old codger to his own devices, with hardly a regret. They seemed pleased to be freed of the man, even if he had been their meal ticket. The worksite was soon deserted, and Holm dragged an empty pear crate with his good arm before the mine and took a seat. He then proceeded to have an hours-long conversation with the mouth of the mine, with the Quarry Witch herself, the sounds of which only resonated in Holm's addled mind.

This détente carried on for six consecutive days, Holm alone in front of the mine, engaged in what looked like a lively conversation that ranged the full spectrum of emotion from sullenness to rage to disbelief. No one intervened, no one particularly cared what the tycoon was on about, treating it like a respite from his harsh ways. Maybe he would regain his wits. Maybe he wouldn't. It wasn't like he had a wife or children. Or friends. He wasn't a beloved man by any stretch of the imagination. No one gave a damn that Arnold Holm had succumbed to something down in that pit, content to argue with things that weren't there, or had fallen prey to an elaborate trick designed by those who ran his mine, who probably had reason to hate Holm the most.

In any event, on the seventh day of his vigil, rather unceremoniously, he arrived to his empty crate carrying his own gilded pistol—the type of weapon that looked more ornamental than practical, though it still had its utility. After what some people believed was his final fruitless back and forth with the witch, unable to outflank her demonic logic, Holm cocked the hammer and blew his own brains clear out of his skull, his lifeless body and suicide weapon falling aside to the ground, now caked with his blood. His body was found two days later, picked over by animals and insects, by one of his junior clerks who desperately needed Holm to sign off on legal documents concerning mineral rights in Southern Massachusetts. The clerk was rumored to have ultimately forged the needed signature, pilfered a ring off the corpse, then left to notify the authorities as to the condition of his dead boss.

Arnold Holm was buried in a large cemetery in his own personal mausoleum near his West Hartford home. His ceremony was sparsely attended and uneventful, barely a sermon or a kind word to usher in whatever came next. In the years to come, his plot was never visited.

And while no one knew exactly what he and Agnes Schrader debated for those seven days, the speculation was that Agnes eventually convinced Holm that the world would be better off without him—not that Holm would particularly care if that were true. But despite all his protests and wild mood swings and calls to earthly logic, it was Agnes who prevailed after the week, a checkmate that cemented her victory from across the ephemeral plane. If Holm ever really stood a chance against the supernatural being, it would have been chalked up to the man's keen survival instinct—much like a rat's—but ultimately, he was outmatched, and Schrader's lust for revenge proved too much to overcome, even from beyond the grave.

After that, the quarry and mining operation in Orchard Coils were abandoned. Even if there were still granite and limestone and minerals to be unearthed, no one was willing to set foot and muck about on that haunted ground, to unsettle so much as a skipping stone from where it lay. The only thing left for that site to produce was legend, ghost stories—a headless Agnes Schrader, who used the mouth of the cave to extract her punishment on the man she blamed for her husband's death. Who was to say she wouldn't try her trick on others who crossed her? Or so the cautionary tale had grown; those who would trespass on territory she'd laid claim to did so at their own risk. The Quarry Witch story had been told and retold to the children of Orchard Coils for some time now, part of local lore, a Halloween tradition on a golf course built atop her stomping grounds, though in no violation of the territory she held sacred below. A tentative peace, a well-respected truce, between two town institutions.

William and Brenda finished the story for their audience, the children, who collectively exhaled, unaware just how much they'd been clenching their little lungs, holding their little breath—now indoctrinated to one of the older traditions of the club they belonged to, the town they lived in.

* * *

The group walked the lit path back toward the Restaurant, where their parents, if a bit tipsy, would be eager to hear how the kids' little adventure had gone. Did they have fun? Did they learn a little something? Many of these parents had walked the Halloween Trail in their youth as well, though certainly not all of them. Some had heard the story as adults, which was never quite the same.

Leo and Denny had drifted toward the back of the line, right in front of those two teenage girls tasked with making sure no one got left behind. The lanterns were still aglow, but somehow, the walk back felt even spookier, maybe even dangerous. The clouds were now covering the moon almost in full. There seemed to be more animals out. Darker, colder, louder. The energy among the children had changed. They were uneasy, in no small part from the story they'd just heard, the knowledge they now possessed.

Leo, for his part, felt pretty good about the whole night, still wished he'd been allowed to do it last year when he'd wanted. The story was fun. He was not sure how much of the Agnes Schrader bits he actually believed, but he certainly knew a cool ghost story when he heard one, especially when some serious stuff actually took place. It felt like an adult type of tale they'd all been let in on. Probably more decapitations than he would have figured for a campfire story. He would definitely have to remember not to mention any of this to Lynn, lest she have nightmares for weeks—plus she'd walk the trail in a few years, and he wouldn't want to ruin the fun for her. What surprised Leo the most was how fond of the first part of the story he was: all the stuff about the miners and the conditions they worked in and having a mean owner and just how valuable certain junk was that was buried in the ground they walked on. That all seemed very real and more plausible than a woman walking around with no head. Then, as a bonus, all that stuff actually took place in his very town, literally below the land they were currently walking on. It just seemed really interesting to him that these were actual things that took place a hundred years ago—that people were traveling by boat, crossing an ocean, trying to make money and raise families, kind of like what he and Mom and Dad did, with the exception of the sea travel stuff. When he thought of it in those terms, it seemed even more realistic, more so than a cave that could talk, even if the ghost stuff was the real intent of the Halloween Trail, the bits that were meant to creep people out the most.

Denny, on the other hand, wasn't faring as well as his counterpart. He was jumpy and kept swinging his head around at every little noise from the snap of a twig to the hoot of an owl. The two maintenance workers were still shadowing the group but had cooled it with their own theatrical flourishes. About halfway back to the Restaurant, it sounded to Leo like Denny was snuffling a bit, that he was rubbing his shoulders in a weird way, as though cold to the bone. Leo tried to ignore it at first, unsure what to do, not wanting to embarrass his friend. Denny was being restrained about it, or at least trying to. They'd been silent, though as they carried on, Denny seemed to be getting worse, and Leo could no longer pretend not to notice. He felt compelled to ask his friend, whom he'd made a pact only an hour ago to watch over, who he promised to protect no matter what occurred: "Denny, you OK?"

"Yeah," he replied, hardly sounding OK.

"Come on, you sure?"

"I guess I'm just a little afraid for real now."

"From the story?"

Denny silently nodded, stilling rubbing at his arms.

"I don't know how much of that stuff is actually true," said Leo, still keeping his voice down. "And it all happened a really, really long time ago."

"But what if the witch comes looking for us kids that came here tonight?"

"I don't think that's how it works," said Leo. "Kids do this trail every year, and nothing bad happens to them. My mom did this walk and heard the story when she was a kid, and nothing happened to her."

Hearing that bit seemed to settle Denny down some. He wiped at his eyes with his shirtsleeve, clearing away the moisture from his face.

"You think?"

"Sure. Plus it sounds like she'd only go after people that were trying to rip up her turf down there."

"But we play golf up here. Stuff gets ripped up all the time," said Denny. "Maybe she still thinks we're on her land."

Leo had to take a moment to consider that one, formulate his counterpoint.

"Naw, I think she likes golfers," said Leo, aware that he was now stretching the truth for the sake of calming down his friend. "Besides, the grounds crew makes everything as good as new each day."

"That's true."

"We're not the problem. Think of it this way: so long as you don't go down there and start stealing granite or that stone made of limes, you'll be OK."

"How can stone be made of limes?"

"I didn't understand that part either."

Denny stopped rubbing his shoulders, his wits coming about.

"Well, I'm never going down there, Leo, ever," said Denny, deathly serious for a nine-year-old. "What about you. Would you ever go down there?"

Leo didn't answer that right away, tried to imagine what it would be like to actually explore the old mining site, but could then see that much was riding on what his answer would be. The wrong response would only freak Denny out further. He figured the truth could be stretched some more.

"Nope, not for me. Maybe when I'm really, really old, like my parents," said Leo. "But for now, no, thank you."

"That's a good plan. So you think we're going to be OK tonight?"

"We'll be OK. The only scary part is that we still have school tomorrow."

"Bleh," said Denny loudly, making a pretty authentic retching noise, which drew a belly laugh from the boys, their spirits lifted, more pep in their step as they marched along.

Back at the clubhouse, Baxter and Ruth were waiting outside, along with Lynn, who was near the putting green, all of them waiting on Leo's return. They'd grabbed their coats from the closet and were pleased enough to be wearing them over their costumes as the temperatures dipped. There were other parents scattered around with the same thing in mind, waiting for their children to return from the Halloween Trail, anxious to see how they fared. Baxter had his arm around Ruth, who was coming down a bit from the spooky punch, contented, pleased with herself that she finally gave that boys club a piece of her mind, though also aware that a hangover of epic proportions might be coming for her tomorrow. She'd try some water and aspirin to lessen the blow before she went to bed, if she remembered. Lynn had now found her way onto the actual putting green and was rolling strays balls into the practice cups with another little girl around her age. She seemed to have finally grown bored of the Silly Putty.

After a few more minutes, the silhouettes of figures could be seen walking near the maintenance road, shuffling nearer to the clubhouse through the lantern light. The group got closer and closer until they could be discerned, with William and Brenda leading the pack, far taller than those in their assembly. Eventually, Baxter and Ruth could see Leo walking with his friend Denny, his arm around him, whispering about the things children find important: new revelations, treasured secrets. A few minutes more and they were all reunited, and just as Baxter had predicted, Leo went straight for his mother and gave her a great big hug, which she bent down to return, exactly what she needed that night. Denny hung around the Sinclairs as it didn't look like his parents had made it outside yet. Baxter playfully knocked the two boys' heads together and asked them how it all went.

"It was kind of scary," said Denny sheepishly, seemingly eager and pleased to admit this to an adult, any adult.

"Well, sure," said Baxter. Then addressing his son, "And what did you think of it, old man?"

"It was fun. More like a history lesson though."

To that, Ruth let out a bolt of laughter, catching the kids by surprise, even Baxter raising an eyebrow.

"No, he's right. I can remember thinking something like that too all those years ago," said Ruth, looking around to make sure Lynn was still preoccupied on the putting green. "Though that Quarry Witch stuff was a hoot back then. You boys make sure you don't go telling any of the younger kids about this. Don't want to ruin their chance to have fun once it's their turn on the trail."

The boys nodded in agreement, though Denny wasn't so sure he was ready to categorize the experience as fun.

"You really did the Halloween Trail when you were a kid, Mrs. Sinclair?" he asked.

"Sure did."

"And nothing bad ever happened to you because of it?"

"Of course not, dear, it's just a story."

Leo motioned to Denny as to reinforce the notion he had nothing to worry about; his mom was living proof. At that point, one of the young teenagers who had been minding the back of the line approached the group and introduced herself as Jane.

"Hi, I just wanted to let you know your son did a really sweet job taking care of his friend here," said Jane, cuffing both boys lightly around their necks. "You can tell they're really good buddies."

Baxter and Ruth looked at Jane with some confusion, unsure of what she was on about.

"Oh, I thought they might have been telling you. Denny took the story to heart a bit, but Leo helped calm him down," said Jane, doing her best to not embarrass Denny. "I was going to step in and help, but Leo had it all under control. Then they both cheered up and had a fun walk back."

"Is that right?" asked Baxter proudly.

Leo met his father's eyes, modestly nodding in confirmation.

"I don't see my parents anywhere," said Denny, a bit anxiously.

"They're probably inside," said Jane. "Come on, Denny; I'll help you find them."

Apropos of nothing, or maybe something very obvious, Denny gave Leo a hug and thanked him and said they'd see each other soon at the club or at least for the Thanksgiving feast. Then he took Jane's hand, and the two walked off toward the Restaurant in search of Denny's parents.

"So your friend had a hard go of it?" asked Ruth.

"Yeah, but he's better now."

"Because of you, it sounds like," said Baxter.

Leo just shrugged his shoulders, but the smile on his face gave away the pleasure he'd received from his father's admiration. He couldn't recall ever feeling that swell of pride before. It was very new to him, like another adult-type thing bestowed on him that night. Ruth called Lynn over from the putting green, and she joined the rest of her family, registering Leo's return.

"Was it scary, Leo?" she asked.

"More fun than scary," he said, minding his mother's instructions on not revealing too much.

That was about as much interest as Lynn had in her brother's exploits. She quickly returned to her friend on the green, still rolling those balls around.

"What do you think, my dear, shall we pack it in and head home," asked Baxter. "Or would you care to go back inside and get anything else off your chest?"

Baxter slipped his monk's hood out from under his coat and cloaked his head, pretending to pray on his wife's decision, hoping for one over the other, hoping to peacefully end the evening with as little bloodshed as possible.

"I think we can go home. Mary and Peter can tell us all about what we missed," said Ruth. "Of which there'll be plenty."

She headed over to scoop up her daughter, who would undoubtedly protest their departure from the practice green.

"You hungry at all, young man?" asked Baxter.

"Nope," said Leo, who was about to ask his dad something, then seemed to think better of it, then quickly changed his mind again and asked away. "Dad, how good of a thing is it to help people?"

"How do you mean, Leo?"

"Like, can people help people as their job? Can they make money doing it?"

"Sure they can."

"Really?"

"Scouts honor, buddy," said Baxter. "How's about I tell you all about those kinds of people this weekend. We'll make a big list of them for you to see with your own eyes."

Leo smiled in agreement, a new and influential idea now popping into his impressionable mind. *Helping people.* A concept that would hold sway for much of his life, first conceived on the trek of the Halloween Trail, put into motion on a night he would never forget.

Ruth joined her men holding Lynn in her arms, back to fiddling around with that Silly Putty egg. The Sinclairs made their way toward their car in the parking lot—a family eager to depart the cold for the warmth of hearth, the comfort of home.

* * *

An excerpt from the *Hartford Courant*, daily print edition, April 29, 1893, page 1, column 1, paragraph 3.

To speak of ghouls and spirits in these modern times is laughable, and to attribute Mr. Holm's untimely death as such, equally so. Irregardless of what some may have thought of the Quarrymaster and his work conditions, along with his treatment of labour, the very notion that he may have been somehow "coerced" from the afterlife to execute himself flies in the face of logic and moral certitude. A more probable explanation, as related to me through certain inquisitions of learned and medical scholars is that an unchecked fever or side effects of the "medicines" Holm was imbibing through his convalescence over an unrelated gunshot wound may have brought about a delirium and led to his tragic misstep.

To suggest otherwise is akin to an old-world heresy that must continue to be stamped out and eradicated until . . .

1974

Little Leo—though not as little as he used to be—the unofficial prince of the Orchard Coils Country Club, was feeling as far from royalty as one could be, his arms submerged in the slop sink, helping clean dishes and glasses and flatware for the Friday night dinner crowd at the Restaurant. The dishwasher was on the fritz again—equipment that wasn't even that old and might have still been under warranty if anyone had the wherewithal to track down the paperwork, though that seemed unlikely, given the current management and their haphazard filing system. The backup dishwasher, the human version, a kitchen aide named Olaf Johnson—no one believed that was his given name—had asked Leo to cover for him. Why? Because that afternoon was pleasant by Olaf's standards, and he felt summoned to sit under the shade of the remote walnut trees out by the fourteenth hole and smoke his pipe, a musky tobacco that smelled so much of figs most people figured Olaf cut his stash with shredded fruit.

By most accounts, Olaf was generally a solid worker, nearing fifty and well liked among the staff at O Triple C—his pipe indulgence and impromptu breaks to commune with nature were peccadilloes and inconveniences that everyone around him had silently agreed to forgo, to look the other way on. Besides, when the man worked, he was a horse, and he also had tons of stories from the old country, though where that country was or if it even existed was still up for debate—Olaf could spin a good yarn but was weak on details such as names and geography. But in the service industry, if you're only beholden to one vice and generally don't behave like a psychopath, your coworkers will cover for you, and your boss will look to accommodate a quirk or two, provided you don't ask for a pay raise and mostly show up on time. So the acting general manager at the Restaurant, Mike Connolly—currently occupying a job with a higher turnover rate than a hotel mattress—had tacitly blessed Olaf's sabbaticals, and the bottom-down staff knew when and why to protect their own. And Olaf was certainly one of their own. He wore a hat garnished with turkey feathers and sported a full beard that could best be described as *aromatic*. He fit right in. So while Connolly was on the horn trying to hunt down a dishwasher repair man who might be willing to work for a free round of golf or a few trays of sausages and peppers, Olaf was gazing off into the woods, back against a tree, pipe in one hand, rolling two walnuts together in the other.

In response to the Olaf situation, one of the club's little runners, a twelve-year old scrapper by the name of Jimmy Jay, booked it over to the caddy shack, where he sought anyone who wasn't working at the moment to cover some kitchen prep. None of the staff relished the sight of Jimmy Jay heading their way, less than a horseman of the apocalypse but certainly a harbinger of some shit assignment about to be forced on an unlucky soul. As it was, Leo was the odd man out, having mostly just arrived for his shift, early as usual, but no one was requiring his services to lug clubs around the bifurcated seven miles of course and solicit his advice on distance and corresponding wedge choices. The caddy shack itself had been seeing less and less action with the growing popularity of golf carts over the past fifteen years, the industrial revolution alive and well in the Hartford county golf scene, automating jobs out of the hands of slacker teens everywhere from Bristol to East Granby—an epidemic not limited to Connecticut but continually spreading across all the golfing communities in the nation, probably the world.

Jimmy Jay, having arrived at the caddy shack, assessed his prey, pointed one carrot-stick-thin finger at the floundering Leo Sinclair, and commanded one fully understood word: *Olaf.* The rest was history. Leo immediately knew his fate: a hike up to the Restaurant, kitchen detail, the bane of any teenager's existence, even the hard-nosed ones. There would be no protest; he knew the code around the club: the staff was in it together and was to cover each other's flanks, particularly around well-known blind spots. In reality, the staff at O Triple C was a patchwork of misfits and outcasts and broken toys and rumored ex-cons, ranging from prepubescent to Medicare eligible, cobbled together in a way that fostered a makeshift family spirit, albeit the type of brood that enjoyed viciously arguing during get-togethers. They'd become Leo's second family. So he slumped his shoulders and shuffled his feet behind Jimmy Jay's lead, not quite a man resigned to the firing squad but silently cursing Olaf and his affinity for leisurely respite.

Leo, who was only a few months past his seventeenth birthday, was trying to be better at not taking things personally, even when these slights felt epic and wholly reserved for an unlucky nature. His outlook had been improving, and, though annoyed in the moment, he held no ill will to Olaf, didn't begrudge him a siesta, even if he thought smoking in the August heat was a pretty disgusting pastime. Leo had been looking to transcend such childish pettiness and would scrub the hell out of whatever was put before him, giving tonight's patrons the cleanest cups and forks and soup spoons they'd ever dined with.

These were the mental gymnastics he plied himself with, the games one plays to soldier through the grunt work.

Once Leo was inside the kitchen, he asked for a pair of rubber gloves and was almost laughed out of the back room. Almost. He was then told by some senior staff person to mind the steak knives at the bottom of the industrial sink and to use water-proof Band-Aids if things took a turn for the worse. Then Leo was left alone to his work. So he settled in and got to it, dutiful and helpful as always, wishing his girlfriend was with him, just to have someone to talk to, to pass the monotony and critique his sponge work in her playful way. Her name was Samantha Morris, Sam for short, and she was a waitress at the Restaurant, who'd be working that Friday night, though her shift didn't start until four p.m., still hours away. Sam was one year older than Leo and attended a different school; some nuance in the four-plus code had her in the neighboring town's high school, so she claimed. Sam and Leo had met at the club earlier in the spring, though only working part-time hours when school was in session. Then their schedules opened up during the summer to take on additional hours and raise more pocket money. As their proximity increased in June, so did their ability to spend time together outside work, school no longer in their way. They didn't share the same circle of friends—their prime connection point was the club, where it had become common knowledge they were an item. Leo wasn't particularly interested in trying to juggle a second relationship and very much wanted to consider Sam his main squeeze, to put a stamp of exclusivity on the twosome. When the subject was broached, Sam would tell Leo she wasn't into labels and was more than happy to continue spending time with him, provided he knew how to be cool. Leo could read between those lines and figured she had a suitor or two at the high school she attended. Probably some hip guy with long hair who thought playing the guitar was the most important thing in the world, more than likely wore a coat adorned with tassels and beads, used the word *man* a lot. Leo didn't like to think about this other side of Sam, even if it might have been imaginary, but he also wasn't going to mess with a good thing just because it wasn't perfect. Leo had had some girlfriends in the past—little relationships that didn't amount to anything serious—but for the past four months with Sam, he'd been head over heels, an experience unlike anything he'd previously encountered. And even if he didn't seem to have much leverage, he knew they were having fun together, which was plenty reason for him not to muck it up. Hopefully, she'd stick around too, despite his inherent uncoolness.

That fun they were having also included what one might expect from teenagers of that age—and while they hadn't quite gone all the way yet, those days were feeling numbered, as though it were only a matter of time and convenience.

That was the stuff Leo daydreamed about while soaping down wine glasses and salad forks.

When Olaf finally returned from the grove he'd been taking his constitutional in, reeking of pipe smoke, he heartily thanked Leo and relieved him of dishwashing duty, sending him back to the caddy shack. When Leo returned there, the head pro was minding the space. The man, named Cobb Webb, had been the top dog for a couple of years now, a cherry gig, given that O Triple C was flourishing through increasing membership; strong profits; and, in general, a favorable economic landscape. Cobb, poached from a prominent club in West Texas, had mostly been brought in to help modernize the place a bit but not too much, given that the old Northeast clubs weren't all that interested in getting too far ahead of the curve. They were happier with the illusion of it as those types of places relished their traditions and all the mystique that went along with them.

Cobb regarded Leo's return with a friendly enough guffaw and went back to his *Golf Digest* magazine—research, he liked to call it, billing the club for his subscription. His assistant, Jerimiah Bell, was apparently minding the pro shop and undoubtedly wishing he was elsewhere—like a public pool or Siberia. That was August in Connecticut for you. It was getting to that point in the summer, an inflection point in the dog days when people weren't overly interested in going outside; the sun was too relentless—somehow always in your eyes, despite the direction   and the humidity too oppressive. There was a downpour predicted within the next forty-eight hours, though the accuracy of that forecast was spotty at best. No one was in need of Leo's services in the caddy shack. Perhaps in a few hours or so as the sun dipped, when the twilight golfers ventured out to exploit the cooling temperatures and reduced glare. But then again, even those guys were using the carts more often or just playing nine holes and forgoing a caddy. So he took it upon himself to ask Cobb if there was anything else he should be doing. To which Cobb replied, in his typical Cobb fashion, "You mean in life?" Ever the ballbuster. Leo was confused, and Cobb just told him to check on the runner minding the range, see if he needed any help shagging balls. Then Cobb went back to his magazine, reading an article about new moisture-wicking technology in outerwear.

Leo was fine with Cobb's suggestion. It sure beat more kitchen work or hanging around Cobb's unnerving energy, particularly when the Texan found himself in a fanciful, if not philosophical mood. Leo had already figured out that once a golfer—really, of any skill level—tried to compare the facets of the game and life for your benefit, you'd best politely remove yourself from that lesson. Leo simply wasn't ready for that type of wisdom yet. So he walked the short distance over to the range and found Bucky Taylor pitching off the mats, trying to stick a ball into the basket at the hundred-yard marker. No one was around; even the range rats were staying away because of the heat. Bucky was just lofting shots and listening to a baseball game on the transistor, a good one from the sounds of it. Leo picked up an errant ball, cracked cover, and threw it down the range just for kicks. Bucky was now aware of his presence. Leo had always thought Bucky's grip was too weak but wasn't moved to offer advice or debate the issue, even though he thought Bucky was an OK guy whose swing would improve with a better union of his hands. Sometimes it was just easier not to critique someone else's game.

"Anyone been around lately?" asked Leo, just for the sake of saying something, just to hear his voice over the radio.

"Just One-Session-Away Andy," said Bucky, still pitching those shots.

"Oh yeah? How'd he hit them?"

"He'll tell you great," said Bucky, smiling but not smiling. "He'll tell you he's only about one session away from figuring it out if you happen to run into him by the pitching green."

Code for: stay away from the pitching green.

"He told me last week that the toughest distance in golf is between your two ears," said Leo.

"He told me ten minutes ago that it's two steps forward, one-point-nine steps back if you're ever going to make any progress in this game," said Bucky.

Code for: move along; I'm doing fine here on my own.

Leo left the range, clearly understanding his services weren't needed there, and went on a walkabout, maybe to find some work, maybe to find some trouble, mostly killing time now until he got to see Sam again.

He crossed the maintenance road, ambling by the buildings that housed the machines used to keep the course healthy and pristine. The main building on that lot had been dubbed the Monastery, given its size and exclusivity—no one without express permission from Jocko Whalley Sr., the department head, was allowed to set foot in there. Those buildings also hosted the rotating ensemble of roughnecks and hard asses employed by the club, though, in fairness, the grounds crew had a far better retention rate than anything seen in the Restaurant staff. There'd always been a lot of stories about those guys, their exploits working the club, their understanding of what exactly took place on so many square miles of property. They had their secrets the same way the kitchen staff did, the same way the caddy shack and pro shop did, the same way Judy Miller—who crunched the financials in a little office hidden somewhere on site did. The trick was to get these different sects of workers to mostly get along, to abide each other's fiefdoms and privacy, which mostly did take place at the club, a reason for their success—with a dash of mutually assured destruction mixed in.

Leo, all of seventeen years old, certainly wasn't allowed anywhere near the Monastery or any of her sister buildings. Nor were any of his contemporaries at the club, who thought sneaking by an ajar window or propped-open door might yield some snippet of overheard gossip, some bawdy tale spoken loudly. Alas, no one was under the impression these guys were discussing Shakespeare in there. But what they did know, about the club and the members and the hookups and the land, was well-guarded and sought-after information held close to the vest, like a card sharp protecting their tradecraft, a magician unwilling to reveal their secrets. Information that one day may be leveraged, bartered with. Or vaulted up and never used. Some of their exquisite talent wasn't just the maintenance of the course—which was top notch—but actually blending themselves into the landscape, fixtures that somehow moved, necessary for a well-run operation. Some went so far as to consider them spies. Others thought they were con artists with green thumbs. Either way, it gave them a power that was understood by most and ignored by those too ignorant to realize that the property itself had eyes and ears, that it was a living thing.

In short, these were men not to be trifled with—and they had the rap sheets to prove it.

Their feared and fearless leader, Jocko Whalley Sr., was the king of the hard-asses, and God help you if you mistakenly called him Jack, let alone attempt it on purpose. When summoned to see Jocko, he was the kind of guy who was going to speak first and last, and if you ventured too many extra words, he'd berate you for spilling your life story. He was a giant dude through an all-but-defunct Viking line of genetics that refused to stop pumping out future giants, both boys and girls—simian, but in a healthy way. He was a hell of a superintendent, revered by his staff—at least by those who made the cut and learned to live under his management style. He'd been running the show at O Triple C for ten years now, unchallenged by newcomers or those in his ranks. At most, behind his back, some would joke that he was born and raised in a radish patch. It may have been true.

Leo did his best not to think about Jocko Whalley too much. Better to avoid the man, the Monastery, and the other buildings he held domain over.

Leo crossed the maintenance road and through some strands of oak to see if anyone was tooling around on the deep-cut holes farthest away from the clubhouse. There were three par fives spread out around the X-12, which gave the entire section a more expansive feel than the snugger interior six. Leo was really hoofing it and easily breaking a sweat when he heard what sounded like an argument, words heavy in the moisture-laden air. The dew point had a bad way of exacerbating certain dispositions. So did the game of golf in general. Tempers could flare. There'd certainly been something in the air that summer already, both at O Triple C and the country at large. Nixon's resignation had put some folks on edge, supporters and detractors alike, contributing to an uneasy climate, like tinder primed to ignite. The country club wasn't immune to such tensions, an enclave that skewed Republican, though in a state more aligned with Democratic sensibilities—a cranberry mixed in with the blueberries. That said, politics mostly expressed themselves in the Restaurant, less so on the actual course—there were already enough things to worry over while playing rather than weighing in on geopolitics. Truly, when you're contending with low-hanging branches, energy-sapping heat, and crooked numbers on a scorecard, it was probably best to keep Washington, DC, out of your mind. Plus, the Restaurant's policy on generous pours always added fuel to the debate—the Watergate stuff dominating the discourse for much of the summer, a noticeable spike in chatter since Nixon peaced out and flew the coop. So much so that the respective staffs of the club had been made extra aware of it, even had to intervene to break up some kerfuffles and hullabaloos in the Restaurant—nothing too serious, but there had been some spillover at the range and pro shop, where even Leo has had to interject himself between hotheads in pink polos arguing over the solidarity of Nixon's Southern base and his chances at a comeback. Leo, to his credit, performed admirably, rising above his pay grade, displaying a knack for diffusing outrage between larger men, usually two or three times his age though often wearing checkered shorts and woven belts.

Now Leo could hear a fresh volley of loud voices and wondered if he'd be forced into more diplomacy, talking these local fools off the ledge and reminding people there's not much to be done over the alleged audio missing from the Oval Office. To his relief, he happened upon two younger members of the club, not engaged in a battle of leftist-righty wits but deciphering whether a ball had technically landed on the green or the fringe. Clearly a dispute over a prop bet, probably a greenie, just good old-fashioned testiness over sawbucks, not party loyalty. Leo breathed easy, then was clocked by the two and called over to render an impartial ruling—which Leo obliged, determining the ball was more fringe than green, channeling his inner King Solomon, purity in truth. The decision left one man elated, the other crestfallen, though both abided the young caddy's decision.

Leo walked away having done his service for the people, uninterested in getting more embroiled in whatever foolish gambling those two were on about—though he did remind them to mind the ticks in the tall grass, that they wouldn't want a trip to the hospital with a nasty bullseye rash.

In the back of his thoughts, he was also kind of curious how those two fellows had avoided dying in some rice paddy a world away—there had also been a lot of Vietnam strife in the news over the past few years, plenty of which was also fiercely debated at O Triple C.

Leo walked away and thought on the politics stuff, which interested him in the sense that he didn't find these born-on-third-think-they-hit-a-triple-politicians to be all that spectacular. He understood they wielded great power. But the notion that these were public servants, not overlords, seemed preposterous to him. He'd had lots of discussions on the topic in his JROTC classes at the high school, where other like-minded kids—some who even preferred to wear their cadet outfits every day—would debate the varying forms of service to the country, the merits of a more political path as opposed to a militaristic one and vice versa. Leo thoroughly enjoyed those sessions at school, found them to be what he looked forward to the most. He didn't really get into math or science or English in a meaningful way—not that he thought them unimportant, they were just disciplines that didn't appeal to him. He enjoyed his history class, gym, and shop class—anything that allowed him to work with his hands. He was still trying to figure out the path he wanted to pursue, using a process of elimination method to winnow his life down to correct choices. He'd grown pragmatic during his formative years, some might argue to a fault. When it came to those debates about Vietnam and the communist threat in JROTC, he found himself deeply conflicted. As he also did when discussing it with his parents over the years, returning home in the evening to see the television scrolling through the lives lost, those names of a bright and unique future snuffed short. Lynn, who was then twelve years old, was too young to really notice or care. She'd taken to golf strongly over the past couple of years, was showing an aptitude for the game far surpassing Leo's, and she busied herself with improving at the sport, almost fanatically. Everything else—school, parents, boys, wars on foreign soil—was just a distraction to her.

In Leo's defense, he was in the minority of his peer group who really gave a damn about stuff that was happening around the world, who valued charity and service at a young age. It seemed to him that the draft had changed so much of the landscape, and it hardly felt that long ago. It had fostered strange times, and he'd just come of age before it's dissolution but maybe wasn't totally out of its crosshairs. The dust was still settling on that one. The JROTC felt like his most salient class because they actually broached what was going on in the real world, even when those things were horrific and destabilizing and thrived in the gray areas. There weren't a lot of his ilk at the high school, but they did take pride in how they were trying to make sense of the world. Plus, though Leo wouldn't admit it aloud, he liked the way he looked in his cadet's outfit, even if he didn't wear it too often. He thought it added some needed gravitas to his smaller stature, the softness of his face. He'd grown to just shy of five feet, nine inches before the mechanism shut off on him—the growth plates in his bones calling it quits—not quite average and a daily reminder of what being born two months premature meant as one became an adult, even if that was more correlation and not causation, Leo believed them to be linked; how could he not, when tall men ran in his family?

He once tried to show Sam a picture of him in his cadet's outfit, in which he felt seven feet tall, but she just smiled and stroked his jaw and said that aspect of his life wasn't for her. He got the message and didn't bring it up again.

Leo's mind was really straying as his feet took him anywhere and everywhere, eventually out toward the farthest reaches of the course, near the crook of the fourteenth hole's dogleg. There was hardly a soul out playing, and those who were probably staying close to the clubhouse and cruising the I-6. Leo thought about plopping down, laying his back against a white birch, but he really wasn't that tired and would be mortified to get caught slacking off too much, even if his current responsibilities were scant. He relieved himself in the woods more out of boredom than an urgency to go, minding the underground hornet nests prone to the area, dangerous if disturbed. He watched a woodpecker scrutinize the bark it was about to drill into. He watched some squirrels bounce around like little ocean waves, already foraging for acorns. He'd always enjoyed the wildlife around the club, thought it to be one of the more underappreciated elements of the experience, a bonus to enjoy while the game was driving you crazy.

With nothing left to do, Leo headed back to the pro shop, still at a snail's pace, to grab a soda pop, maybe clean some stored clubs just to pass the time. Who knew? Maybe someone would need a caddy by that point. On the way back, he replayed a recent evening with his father in his mind, from just the previous week, when he'd had the kind of family interaction that would somehow stay with him his entire life—though obviously, he didn't know it at the time. He tried not to dwell on it, but given the amount of free time he currently had, it was kind of hard not to. In fact, he'd been wanting to tell Sam about it but was still organizing his thoughts in a way that would allow him to properly convey the story, what it meant to him, what it meant to those in his circle. He'd been practicing and was nearly there and thought tonight would be the night he spoke to her on it. Not so much because it required an unburdening—it was nothing that severe—but he was curious about her take on it, how the weight of it might feel to another. Someone he trusted, who he wasn't related to, who he could conceivably be in love with—for the first time.

Leo very much hoped Sam was indeed that person—and that maybe she felt the same way about him.

* * *

"Where are we going?" asked Leo, not thrilled with his dad's cloak-and-dagger routine, rare as it was. After they finished dinner, Baxter had made a point that Leo would have an errand to run with him, though he hadn't disclosed to his son what that errand would be. They were alone in his father's car now, a Pontiac Catalina, overdue for a wash and wax.

"We're going to visit your grandparents," said Baxter.

"So why aren't Mom and Lynn coming?"

Leo wasn't one for petulant teenage tropes, but he was feeling a bit picked on and had other things he'd rather be doing with a night off from working at the club.

"We're mostly going to visit my dad," said Baxter. "And I want you to do me a favor and just try to listen tonight, even if we're talking about you. *Especially* when we're talking about you. Understand?"

"Not really."

"Just pay attention. You'll figure it out," said Baxter, putting the car in reverse and backing out of the driveway. "Tonight would be a good time for you to be both quiet and smart."

Leo didn't really know what to make of that. He thought his dad was acting odd, edgy, maybe even a bit aloof, which wasn't his disposition. He may not have been the type of father to coddle his son, but he wasn't withholding, adverse to praise or encouragement from some archaic mindset. So Leo, confused as he was, piped down, resigned, and just looked out the window at all the familiar houses on his street, Yellowjacket Drive, still bustling with activity on a pleasant-enough August evening. Leo knew it was a good place to grow up, had figured that out at a young age—a quiet neighborhood where you could hear the rain sizzle off the power lines, the hum of landscaping equipment like so much white noise. He'd always had friendly neighbors. Pretty houses, picket fences, shiny cars, aboveground pools. Even the pets were good and well behaved. There were always these great sunsets behind the property lines, the kind of stuff people purposefully waited around for, tarrying for an extra ten minutes before they'd go inside. Leo tried to pay attention to those sorts of niceties, aware enough that there were a lot of people in the world who never got so much as a whiff of the tranquility he experienced on a daily basis.

It also didn't hurt that his parents tried to drill these blessings into his mind, his heart, on an equally daily basis.

They continued to drive silently, Leo not pouting, Baxter seeming less anxious, as though the movement of the car had calmed him. They were listening to an FM station out of Hartford that played newer rock music that Leo was coming around to. Baxter didn't really get it, thought it sounded like screeching compared to what he was brought up on, though he acknowledged it might have a certain appeal to a younger generation. He knew he was getting older, not so many years away from the big four-oh, and maybe those advancing years now disqualified him from understanding modern rock. He wondered if he should try to spend some time listening to the stuff at home with Leo, maybe make a real effort to see what this Aerosmith was all about, 'cause according to the DJ, they were breaking down barriers one catchy earworm at a time. He could tell Leo was enjoying it, his head bobbing a bit to the music, absorbed in some preposterously long guitar solo that Baxter thought would never end.

At least Leo didn't demand they turn the volume up.

Baxter looked over to his son—really, it was more of a sneaking glance. He didn't want to make any more of a fuss in advance of what was to come. He loved the boy with all his heart, his daughter too. They were never far from his thoughts; they were the stars that guided his night sailing. So this little sojourn to visit his own father had hit him from a few different angles. They had their own complicated history, involving multiple fallouts and reconciliations, stemming from as far back as Baxter's teenage years. And it wasn't like Leo had been kept from his grandfather, far from it—he'd spent time with the man fishing the lake and watching the Friday night fights, plus all the birthdays and holidays and family get-togethers. All the type of stuff Baxter considered normal grandson-grandfather activities. But today, they'd need to seek the old man out for something different—not a visit where Leo would be viewed as an innocent kid, but instead a young man who was very seriously considering putting on the uniform and enlisting during a dangerous time, just as his own father, Baxter, had done before him. Just as his own grandfather, Roy Sinclair, had attempted to do but was denied enrollment because of a gimpy leg from polio, back when a vaccine was only an unanswered prayer on the lips of mothers and fathers alike.

Roy still carried a slight limp with him, along with the decades of pain and shame the affliction cost him—in turn, hardening his world perspective.

Now, almost halfway through the 1970s, the word itself, *polio*, seemed antiquated, almost barbaric, from a different era. But its stain, though fading, was still a noticeable mar on the planet. Roy Sinclair was a prime example: old, nerve damaged, and still bitter that Uncle Sam had turned him down, when all the man had wanted to do was die in a trench on some foreign land, maybe have a medal pinned to his corpse, be laid to rest in a national cemetery. He'd tried enlisting three times when he was a teenager, not unlike Baxter, though even younger. They'd both jockeyed to get to Europe—different wars, same enemy—only Baxter making it across the ocean and eventually tasting that kiss from a grenade. Roy never got out of rural Connecticut, had missed his birthright because the government thought him lame, thought him unworthy as cannon fodder. It was a bitter pill to swallow and colored his life ceaselessly, tinged his relationships, shaped his mind—all the while, never speaking of the dark fire that singed his leg daily, though it would slowly dull over time. He was the kind of man who would fight you if you said something about his leg. He would fight you if you even looked at it a hair too long. It took him decades and decades to develop the patience and workman's grace he now tried to display, a happenstance that didn't particularly help Baxter, growing up in that house thirty years ago. Or his mother. The thought of Leo having to deal with some of the situations that he dealt with sent a bucket of ice water down his spine. He knew he'd done better for his son and, in his more sullen moments, wondered how he'd escaped the matrix of his own childhood. Then he would recall the scar tissue that marked his back, his side, and recall the truth—*I fled*—leaving his mom behind, one of the greatest shames of his life, something he'd barely ever confessed to anyone apart from Ruth. When he thought back on it, there had been so many ways for it to go bad permanently. He marveled that it didn't. More grace he couldn't account for. The clearest notion he could attribute to their safe passage was that time was the great healer, a rote notion, but battle tested and pure and true. Time did heal, if you allowed it to. Of course, you had to have the luxury of time, or a stomach for it, or a fortitude against it—take your pick. And not everyone did. And those who did still needed reminding that time was undefeated. There were always so many different ways to lose hope, to throw your hands up at what seemed like a dead end, for the umpteenth time. To give up and lie down and roll over and die. Just the thought of it forced Baxter to shake his head to himself, silently driving that Pontiac, a physical reaction to how close he'd come to maybe never being able to take that drive with Leo, to have a real conversation with Roy Sinclair, still tucked away in a quiet corner of Connecticut, holding down the family house, Baxter's childhood home. So much that almost never came to be—perilous to think where some of those other roads may have led.

Trancelike behind the wheel, Baxter thought, *No one has ever taken a step in this world without it being on a knife's edge. They just don't realize it, even the ones who pretend they're in the know.*

Apropos of nothing, but also of everything, Baxter broke the silence to speak.

"Your grandfather can be a very hard man," he said. "Try not to show too much surprise if he says something crass to you."

Leo just nodded, still not totally sure what his father was on about but already heeding his advice about speaking less, listening more. It wasn't like he didn't know his granddad was a relic from a past era. It was hardly a family secret between all the branches in their tree. He tried not to think about it, focused his thoughts on something better, like Sam, which always cheered him up.

They arrived and trundled their way into the small cape house—old, though well maintained, not musty or mothballed in odor as one might think, but cleaner, like fresh linen. Baxter and Leo were greeted at the door by Esther Sinclair, Baxter's mom, Leo's grandmom. Hugs and kisses now abounded. Esther had always been an affectionate woman to those who would allow it, very much in the mode of doting on the men in her life, even if some of that mindset had become less en vogue over the past fifteen years. Esther had been married to Roy since 1923 and wasn't likely to change under the direction of shifting cultural winds. She was who she was and planned to die that way—such was her dignity. Her husband, who had not made an appearance yet though surely aware of their guests' arrival, remained upstairs, living and acting on his own time, as he preferred it.

Esther sat them down and for ten minutes pumped Leo for all the information he could offer up about how his summer was going, how his girlfriend was doing, what her name was again, what it was like caddying at the club. Are you getting along with Lynn? What's it like seeing your parents at your place of work? And so on. And so on. Esther could ask questions until you were dizzy and under her spell, peppering you with freshly baked morsels from the oven, a cold drink, only for you to realize two hours had passed, and you hadn't had a chance to ask her so much as a single question edgewise. Such was her magic. And prerogative. But that night, she knew in advance that it was going to be more of a Roy visit, that she might not have as much access to the two as she was accustomed to. So she maximized the time allotted and didn't ask any questions about what was to be discussed upstairs. She had her suspicions. She told them that Roy would be waiting for them but didn't quite let them go up yet. Just a few more questions, take your time with the answers—as if she hadn't just seen them a month ago for a long Independence Day celebration. She still had to ask about Ruth, Lynn. She still had to ask about Baxter working in the tall buildings of downtown Hartford. Still had to offer them something more from the kitchen; anything they could think of, she'd whip it up. She'd jump to Christmas planning, despite it only being August, always with such verve to bring family together. She adored seeing Ruth's parents. Adored hearing about Peter and Mary Sullivan, Leo's beloved godparents. And their son, Chip, getting closer to his own teen years. She asked how the weather was behaving where they lived, despite it being only an hour away. She might have been a small and unassuming woman, but when it came to the gift of gab, she was a juggernaut—coming alive when the opportunity arose, though Baxter could tell she was nervous, saw it in her bony shoulders, the cords in her neck. He started to sense she was stalling, as though afraid of how things might play out upstairs, as though all might not go well, which, in fairness, was a possibility. Baxter assured her they'd have a nice chat with the old man, that Leo was getting older and ready for some family advice. She smiled weakly. Esther might not have been formally educated, but she was cunning in her own way and easily understood how quickly a splinter can wedge, and a wedge can fracture, and that's how you break even the strongest of structures, the best and sturdiest of people. Sledgehammers were overrated; it was the chisel that did more damage.

She planted a big kiss on Leo's cheek—he was always a good sport about his grandma's affection. Having detained them long enough, she sent them on their way but not before reminding them of their Labor Day plans, a barbecue promised in Orchard Coils. Baxter agreed, and she released the two into the wilds—a thirteen-step staircase of hardwood leading to the second-story landing, then a single turn into Roy's study, which was actually the master bedroom that he'd reappropriated decades ago for his own use. He and Esther slept in a second, smaller bedroom, adjacent to a twenty-by-twenty bathroom with slightly outdated but exceptionally well-performing plumbing and amenities.

Baxter's old room, a refurbished attic crawl space, was seldom used by that point and mostly went unremarked on, as though it would conjure old thoughts no one wanted to relive.

Baxter knocked on the study's closed door and heard a booming "Come in" from the other side. Father and son entered to see Roy Sinclair seated behind his desk, wearing glasses he barely needed but liked the erudite look of as he aged into his sixties. He wore a flannel shirt with a cardigan over it, despite the summer heat and the house running warm. Roy still had his lion's mane of hair that any man from any century would be envious of, preposterously immune to thinning, flecked with silver. He put down the book he was reading and stood, then walked around the big, heavy desk to greet his son and grandson. Baxter extended his hand as was their custom over the years, but Roy just regarded the hand as though it were an alien object and opted to embrace his boy in a short, firm hug. He repeated the uncharacteristic gesture with Leo. Both father and son were caught somewhat off guard, their little session already off to a weird start.

Roy saw the looks on their faces and addressed their confusion head on.

"Don't bust my balls, all right? Your mother wants me to hug more, so there you have it," said Roy, the last he'd comment on it. "You kids have a seat."

Roy pointed at the two as though they were interviewing for a small business loan, maybe a mortgage, the warmth from the hug already long gone.

Baxter and Leo took seats in some wood and leather-bound chairs: solid, comfortable, nice looking despite probably not costing much—more than likely bought secondhand from an estate sale. The old man had a good eye for that sort of thing, could suss out a bargain when he needed to. Roy took his own chair behind the desk, another stately purchase, and eyed his kin with bemusement, maybe a bit of skepticism. He wasn't unhappy to see them; quite the contrary, he was very much looking forward to a spirited talk. He could be loquacious when he wanted to be. Maybe not as much as Esther, but with a little liquid courage, some piss and vinegar, he could dial it up and spar with anybody, especially his own family. But that night, he was in no rush—they'd come to him.

"How are they treating you at the club, Leo?" asked Roy. "First real job for you. What's your assessment after three whole months of work?"

A playful dig that Baxter recognized, though Leo didn't or maybe just chose to ignore.

"It's good. I like the people there."

"Making friends will help the hours pass," said Roy, studying his grandson. "So will doing the job right and without complaints. Are you a complainer at work?"

"I don't think I am."

"I wouldn't think so either, but it's something worth bearing in mind," said Roy, adjusting his glasses as though they were actually doing something to improve his vision. "You see your old man at the club a lot? I tell you, I never had time for golf when I was his age."

"I don't even play that much anymore, Dad," said Baxter, kind of a lie, subject to interpretation. "And a lot of the time, it's for business."

That was less a lie. Baxter wondered why he still felt compelled to justify his schedule to his father, as if he were still living under his roof, eating at his table.

"Fine, then, enough catching up. To what do I owe the pleasure of your visit tonight?" asked Roy, not one for excessive small talk when there was a real topic at hand. "Not that I ain't glad to have you here."

Baxter sighed, feeling as though they were about to cross a Rubicon that couldn't be avoided, that there was no turning back from.

"Well, Dad, Leo's heading into his senior year, and he's got some really big decisions on the horizon," said Baxter. "The kind of stuff I think you'd have some good opinions on."

Roy tried not to crack a smile at that, but there was enough surprise from Baxter's request to contort his poker face just a bit.

"You want my help weighing in on Leo's future?"

"I do. It's important. Plus I know you got a few thoughts on a man once he turns eighteen."

The room took a beat and fell silent, the sounds of something mechanical clicking away, probably some clock shelved among the books in the cases. Leo looked to his grandfather, then to his dad—at least now he had a better idea what this sit-down was all about, his future. He was glad someone was finally going to let him in on it. He had questions.

"What happens when someone turns eighteen, Grandpa?" asked Leo.

Roy had answers.

"What happens is he's truly beholden to no one but himself. Which puts you still one year away, but getting close," said Roy, getting up from his chair, still plenty of spring left in his legs for a man who worked on his feet for an entire career, a man who was still only semiretired. "I won't lie; I'm proud to be asked about Leo's future. So we'll have a drink and talk. I'm not going to tell you how to live your life, Leo, but I won't pull my punches either."

Roy walked across the room and pulled a bottle of rye off the neatly arranged bookcase, producing three ornate glasses from the drawer. He poured a collective six fingers, neat, to be sipped like gentleman in their private atmosphere. Beer or wine simply wouldn't do. Baxter and Leo knew not to protest, despite neither one of them really wanting such a prop. But they'd drink it all the same, slowly, in bird sips that burned smooth, not wholly unpleasant once one acclimated to the sensation. They clinked their glasses. Then Roy returned to his chair, feeling ever more like a wise man holding court, addressing the assemblage that had traveled a distance to gather before him, seeking his counsel.

"I can more than guess where some of this consternation is coming from," said Roy. "Maybe Leo has notions of running off to war, even though we may be out of the war business for a bit. You still doing the toy soldier routine at the school?"

"The JROTC, yes."

"And you like it?"

"I do."

"And *they* want you to enlist, correct?"

"Yes."

"Do they expect you will?"

"They don't say it outright, but yeah, I think so."

"But maybe you're not so sure yourself," said Roy. "That maybe it's not the best thing for you?"

Leo said nothing, his silence enough of an admission to what his grandfather had intuited, what he'd considered for his grandson over the years, observing it when the family was together, reflecting on it during his own quiet moments. He loved the boy and of course had given thought as to how he would pursue his future. Leo, continuing to heed his father's advice, remained mute. He'd be angrier at the tenor of the conversation if it wasn't so true—he was at a crossroads with important decisions fast approaching. And he was unsure of how to proceed. Roy put his attention back on Baxter.

"And what sage advice have you offered so far?" asked Roy of Baxter, who leveled a look of displeasure at his dad, now not being a time for intergenerational potshots.

"Hard to see what's been going on the past five years and not be influenced by it," said Baxter, swirling his drink a bit, like a nervous child playing with their food. "The draft has more than proved that."

Roy grumbled in what could best be interpreted as agreement.

"So you don't want Leo to serve, but you're—what? Afraid that would make you some kind of hypocrite or something?"

"It's not that I'm so utterly against it. A part of me still very much believes in it," said Baxter. "I just wonder if there's a better path out there for him."

"Sure. But it's his life, right?"

"I understand that."

"And what does Ruth think of all this?"

"She doesn't want it for him."

"No mother does."

Then, with a start, Roy belted out a big belly laugh, slapping his meaty palm on the desk, reaching for his rye to finish it off, then leaning back in his chair like there was no place else in the world he'd rather be, which was true a homebody at heart, just him and his boys comparing notes on the endless circles men scurry through, the walls they bang their heads against.

"Well, Baxter, my boy, you have to admit some of this should sound awfully similar to what your own mother was going through a few decades ago, the trick bag you stuffed us into," said Roy. "Can't say I'm not taking some enjoyment seeing you wrestle through it from the other side."

"Glad you're enjoying yourself, Dad," said Baxter coolly, not unaware of the irony his father was speaking of. "But let's remember we're here to give Leo the benefit of our experience, maybe even a little sound advice."

Leo looked on, starting to understand that while plenty of this was about him, plenty of it was also about shit between Baxter and Roy, old grudges and the unresolved nature of deep grievances.

"Yeah, sure, well, of course, Leo, you know your daddy ran off barely after he'd started shaving his face to become a bona fide Nazi killer," said Roy. "Maybe that makes it sound heroic or something, which it was, but also don't think it didn't come back with a whirlwind of shit that lasted for years and years."

Roy looked at his son, who just nodded softly in agreement, taking his first real pull of the rye, now a little grateful for its bite.

"Of course, I tried to pull the same shit, but those damn pencil necks didn't see me as whole," said Roy, fuming; the man could go from zero to sixty in the course of half a sentence. "I wouldn't wish that type of failure on you, Leo. I've carried that around with me my whole life, reminded of it every step I ever took. It's a bad fit on a man."

Roy's own personal fourteen stations of the cross—admissions he was loathe to make, reluctant to openly discuss.

"But if it didn't happen that way, Dad, then maybe none of us would be in this room today," said Baxter, cautiously.

Roy regarded his son's statement, the words he used, the words he didn't. It seemed to him the boy had a fair enough point, in a philosophical sort of way.

"I suppose life is screwy like that," said Roy, allowing his son's fanciful statement to pass.

Roy drained his drink, got up, and tumbled another finger into his glass, added to his companions' with a fresh splash, though they'd barely made it halfway through their first pour. Leo was warming up from the brash liquor he'd never had before, listening to his dad and grandad talk in a more candid way than he was accustomed to. He knew their relationship had been strained, back to Baxter's own childhood. And they'd had to repair it slowly over the decades, almost learning as they went how to organize and reconfigure pieces of a disassembled machine back into working order without the benefit of a master or schematics. He found it interesting to watch the two men navigate each other, around their blind spots and jealousies, toward the common interest of Leo's well-being. He felt cared for, loved. He also knew the rye might be dancing in his head a bit. Probably another good reason to keep his piehole shut, to mostly listen—seldom a bad approach. But that sort of silence wasn't going to work forever. His father and grandfather would jaw on some more until they put it back on him, where it belonged, the question he'd been unable to pin down an answer to, the million-dollar question, as they say—what was it that *he* wanted for himself, his own life?

All these roads that lead to the one true place—but still, how do you know which road to take?

* * *

There was less than an hour of daylight left, and the sky was taking on a streaked quality across the expanse. Ribbons of pink and yellow painted over the blue canvas, the background dimming. Leo kept looking up. It was hard to ignore those contrails of color, marbled clouds tinged with orange, the occasional glint of silver as planes headed back to Bradley. The humidity had finally dialed back a smidge. It would be a pleasant night, trilled with insects and the frog chorus. Beetles would flit. The fireflies would swoon. Leo absently thought about all that nature stuff while cleaning the golf clubs of members who had just come in from a late round and were now in the Restaurant, having dinner and kicking off their weekend. He didn't mind cleaning clubs, actually found it relaxing and certainly preferred it to the grime and sharp edges of kitchen work. Also, he liked clubs, liked being around them, liked handling them. He got a kick out of seeing what members were carrying—who was spending money trying to keep up with advancing technology and who was hanging in there with the antiques, trying to squeeze an extra season or two out of hardware long past its prime. Plus, unlike the kitchen work, he could actually do well on gratuities when people returned from dinner, maybe a bit tipsy, and dropped some money on him. It wasn't such a bad aspect of the job. Some had already tipped him out, trusting Leo with their keys and asking him to load up the clubs in their car—some of these were the people who tended to make a night of it at the Restaurant, particularly on the weekends, when the bar stayed open as late as needed to accommodate the night owls.

Leo was chipping some caked-on mud out of the fine grooves of Mr. Reymore's three wood, a club he'd seen the man use with devastating efficiency out of the tee box and onto the fairway—equal amounts accurate and ferocious, with a crack reminiscent of a loud bowling strike. Reymore could still dance out there, even if his club championship days were now behind him. Leo appreciated the man's acumen with the three wood, an underrated club and Leo's personal favorite in his own bag, in part because of its versatility but also because as one lost heart with the driver—which all players did at some point—the three wood awaited and was ready to serve during any given time of crisis, often to perform admirably, until the driver was called on anew. And while this could be an emasculating admission, swallowing one's pride in favor of the three wood was more often than not a prudent move—not so much a retreat, but a strategic recalculation, until the lay of the land changed, until an alliance with the driver could be reforged.

In between cleaning Mr. Reymore's varying clubs, Leo looked over to his coworker, a kid his age by the name of Garth Streng, who was also cleaning clubs, though with less reverence for the equipment, a scowl on his face. Their differing enthusiasm levels for club cleaning aside, Leo liked Garth well enough and knew he'd just come in from lugging a chimney stack of clubs for eighteen holes with one of the more surly players—a specific kind of member who tipped directly based on how well they shot, which was really junk logic on any level other than professional caddying, a notion certainly held by the shack workers.

Now between the carts and the August heat and the cheapskates, it was increasing tough to survive in that racquet, to squirrel some meaningful money away for the approaching school year.

Garth hadn't been saying much, so Leo presumed he'd busted his back for four hours, chased down tossed clubs, and listened to a host of woeful obscenities only to get skunked into a lousy tip. It was the kind of treatment that would pipe down any kid, so Leo allowed him to stew, but he also knew it wasn't a good idea to let Garth, or any caddy for that matter, tank in their head for too long over shekels before throwing them some sort of lifeline. He considered telling Garth a joke to cheer him up, but after rummaging around in his brain, he was dispirited to realize he didn't know any, just some dopey puns Lynn would drop on him from time to time. That struck him as a bad sign and something he'd have to remedy on his own. Then, apparently, without really realizing it, he'd already turned his body toward Garth, as though to address him, as though he'd already had a belly buster lined up, only to come up blank. Garth had taken notice and was waiting on Leo to say something, at first with mild interest, then confusion over the delay, then sheer annoyance. He was still holding a rag and using a wire brush against a four iron when he took it upon himself to speak first.

"Something on your mind, Sinclair?" he asked neutrally.

"Um, I was going to tell you a joke, but then I couldn't think of one."

"Well it's the thought that counts," said Garth, going back to cleaning the four iron, before adding. "Besides, narcs don't know any good jokes."

"What? No, don't say that about me; don't spread that."

"Relax, Leo, *that's* just a joke," said Garth, smiling now. "You know you can be kind of high strung sometimes."

"I've been told," said Leo, thinking it over, wondering if narcs actually would know a lot of good jokes to ingratiate themselves with the people they were trying to infiltrate—seemed feasible. "I was just trying to cheer you up is all."

"Well, mission accomplished. Sorry it was at your expense," said Garth, bagging the four iron, then leaving for the pro shop that was only a few feet away. He returned with two bottles of pop, a cola and a Mello Yello, which he offered as a choice to Leo, who opted for the cola. They tapped their bottles, and Leo thanked him.

"So, are you hanging out with Samantha, tonight?" asked Garth.

"Planning to."

"Good, that'll help you relax some," said Garth, trying to bait something out of Leo he wasn't interested in discussing. Garth pressed the point. "No offense, but she kind of seems out of your league."

"Meaning?"

Leo didn't take too much offense, mostly because he'd thought the same thing, though he didn't relish hearing it from an outsider's point of view.

"Nothing bad. I guess she just seems more . . . worldly than you. Again, no offense."

"I'm not offended. And it's only been a few months, mostly just the summer," said Leo, brushing dirt and dust off his shirt. "Maybe she'll grow tired of me by the time school picks back up."

"Seems likely. Good on you for recognizing that."

They both laughed at that one, Leo proving he could be a good sport and Garth snapping out of his funk. They continued talking and cleaning clubs.

"Is Jeremiah still minding the shop?" asked Leo.

"Yep, counting the minutes I'm sure," said Garth. "With the intensity of how many suns do you hate that dude?"

"He's not *that* bad."

"Better than Webb."

"Webb. Twenty bucks says that guy prefers to eat his chicken undercooked."

"Dude has the diet of a seagull," said Garth. "I've literally seen him eating out of trash cans."

The two laughed some more at the silly reference, starting to really loosen up, the earlier tension abating, the reality of a workday coming to its end in full view. The boys had a weekend upon them with some fresh cash in their pockets, sun on their skin, and full tanks of gas in their beater cars—all the freedom one needs at seventeen. Leo would spend his time with Sam, and Garth would do whatever it is he did, probably troll around Orchard Coils for girls who wouldn't be interested in him, having too few sharp angles in his face to ever be desired by the opposite sex the way he felt he should be, a realization he was too young to grasp, to come to terms with.

Jimmy Jay dashed by for no other reason than to call Leo and Garth dorks, then ran back to the maintenance buildings. The kid was like a deer, sprinting around the grounds for no real reason sometimes, just to prove how fast he could move. He was also the unofficial runt of the grounds crew, technically a runner for the pro shop, but the roughnecks loved him and were grooming him to take over a mower job once his feet could reach the pedals. The idea of Jimmy Jay, latchkey kid extraordinaire, under the tutelage of Jocko Whalley scared the bejeebers out of everybody at the club, though it had all the makings of a fait accompli, an apprenticeship that would not be denied.

"We work at a weird place I think sometimes," said Leo, ragging down a putter, packing up the bag into the storage room.

"It has its upsides," said Garth. "Speaking of which, didn't see Lynn here today. What's she up to?"

"Not sure. She may have had a lesson with Jeremiah this morning. Maybe did some range work."

Garth eyed Leo from the side, tacking closer to something on his mind.

"And she's going to be at our high school next month?"

"Yep, first year. Why?"

"You worried about that at all?"

"What's to worry about?" asked Leo as Garth clammed up a bit, maybe getting a bit over his skis or just getting to the crux of what he was on about—perhaps a little of both. Leo used the whites of his eyes to reinforce the question he'd asked, to compel Garth to spit out what crude or delicate point he was dancing around. Nuance be damned; they were teens, not diplomats.

"Well, she's kind of turning into a stone cold fox."

"Dude, she's thirteen."

"Fourteen."

"Barely, just turned."

"Still. She's a high school freshman now, Leo. You've been in that building for three years; you know how it goes," said Garth, holding up like an expert witness under cross examination, staying true to his story.

That gave Leo pause in a way he hadn't considered before: the implication Garth was not so subtly trying to suggest to him. Though to hear it aloud kind of made sense. He'd been so wrapped up the past year with his own life he hadn't really thought of Lynn as an overly influential cog in his machine. Between his first real job, his first real girlfriend, Vietnam, JROTC, and trying to map out his future, his kid sister hadn't seemed more than a distant moon in his orbit, the two not having much impact on one another. But now, Garth, in his creepy way, was making it sound like it should very much be on Leo's radar. Lynn was about to enter the big school the two middle schools dumped into, an ocean much bigger than anything she'd encountered before. Lots of minnows. Lots of fish. Lots of sharks—many of them wearing letterman's jackets, driving slick cars. Leo could remember what those first few months were like, how scary they could be, confusing at best. It took real time to settle in, to get used to brushing shoulders with kids four years older, basically adults who were allowed to drink and vote and die fighting communism in far-off lands.

Though he didn't want to dwell on it, let alone agree with Garth on his assessment in any way, Leo was mildly aware that Lynn was shaping up to be the looker in their brood. Less from his own observations, because that would be unsettling, and more from the greetings and reactions of family and friends and acquaintances and strangers and vice principals and you name it who always seemed to comment on Lynn's comely appearance while the most Leo could garner was a polite comment around something banal, like his posture or straight, yet un-orthodontured teeth.

These musings over Lynn had accelerated over the past year or so, really since she became a teenager, as though that somehow gave the world the green light to open a floodgate of vaguely sexualized comments—or so Leo had noticed and done his best to ignore. Now Lynn was showered with praise for doing nothing, basically just being alive and growing into her predetermined genetic code, like everyone else doing without the excessive fanfare. That said, almost inexplicably, she wasn't one to preen around, didn't stop before every mirror or reflective surface, didn't tidy her hair using the glass of every car window she passed. In fact, she was hardly what anyone would call boy crazy—Leo couldn't remember her having any sort of little middle school boyfriend or even a crush for that matter. She'd never had a boy at the house.

Never went to a dance. And he'd certainly never been called upon to intervene in some brotherly way against a hostile or jaded dirtbag who couldn't take no for an answer. Nothing even close to that. All Lynn ever seemed to care about was golf. She had natural talent for the game; anyone who knew anything about the sport could recognize that in her. They'd tell her so. And she believed it. She believed it in herself. And that stirred something protective in her, a fear of squandering such a gift, to the point that becoming exceptional at the sport had been her primary interest for as long as Leo could remember, probably the better part of a decade now. And that *was* something he admired in his sister, not her accelerated journey into womanhood but the hard calluses on her hands and the hamper of sweaty ankle socks and the gallons of mint-scented joint cream she used freely just to get back out there and practice another day, despite the aches and pains, despite the boys who were apparently clamoring for her attention, evidently of an increasingly wide age range. That, in his estimation, was something worth feeling pride over, particularly in a family member, in someone he loved, though he wouldn't be quick to admit it aloud.

Nevertheless, Garth's scenario rang true and was begrudgingly a valid one that Leo would have to put much more thought into, maybe even act upon over the next year while they shared the same building, passed in the same hallways.

The Sinclair siblings, caged under one roof. He could steel himself for it. He would start immediately—with Garth.

"Just make sure you stay the fuck away from my sister, Garth," said Leo, not joking.

"Hey, man, I'm just the messenger," said Garth, then thought it over. "Why, does she ever ask about me? You know, I'm not so bad either."

"You're plenty bad in the creepiest of ways," said Leo, taking his leave of Garth, chucking the remaining half of the cola in the trash. He'd had enough of the kid and was eager for the sun to set and to find Sam in the dark.

* * *

Roy, Baxter, and Leo sat around the study for another hour, drinking rye—mostly Leo and his grandfather—while Baxter sipped along, given the long drive home still ahead of him. Baxter wasn't of the habit of letting his underage son drink around the house, aside from the occasional beer at a barbecue or while watching the Red Sox. But some of the point of the evening was to allow Leo to bond with Roy on a more adult level, and sharing a bottle had the ability to fast-track such an endeavor. Plus, it was one of Roy's preferred pastimes. It also felt reasonable, given the heady topics they were discussing—provided neither of them got too sloppy, which they'd avoided so far. Baxter could tolerate the rye loosening them all up a bit, sharing a few laughs as Roy's spirits were soaring now, pontificating on Leo's path, listening to the boy discuss what he liked, what he didn't, and how to translate that into a future that suited him.

Roy started to move around the study like a jungle cat, abandoning his chair and desk for the sake of getting some blood flowing, building up a lather listening to the younger men. He beseeched his own son's opinion, to weigh in on the probability that any seventeen-year-old out there would really have a clue what they wanted to do with their lives. And even if they did have a notion, how often it might be misguided or foolhardy, altruistic for the wrong reasons. He reinforced to his grandson that his choices need not reflect his life or his father's, that what had been laid before him were different circumstances, that he shouldn't have reservations about striking out on his own, not following in footsteps already marked in the sand. The elder men agreed on that point, agreed on most of them actually, something Baxter was particularly appreciative of, even a bit surprised by. They understood Leo's concerns and his indecision when faced with daunting decisions, what it would mean to choose poorly.

Even if Roy was a little all over the place toward the end, the rye having some effect, it really was a corker of a conversation among the three, though perhaps a bit too ambitious on Baxter's part to think anything would be fully solved in one night. Or that there wouldn't be some snapback or repercussions from bringing Roy Sinclair into the loop, which had been mostly avoided, but not totally.

As their conversation was winding down, Roy took it upon himself to share a story he'd never thought he'd speak aloud, let alone to his high school grandson, with Baxter, their common denominator, present. The old man might have been high on comradery. Patriarchy. And the rye. All that talk of the future, the airing of the past. Surely a combination of factors that led to revelation, an openness one might have thought no longer existed. But when that quiet moment developed, Roy took the opportunity to try and help his grandson out the best he could, even if it meant consequences against him. And Baxter. The whole lot of them.

"Leo, did your dad ever tell you what happened between us once he returned from his post in Rome?" asked Roy, standing before the seated men. "How he came to move out and stake his claim in the city?"

Leo looked blankly at his grandfather, shook his head—then at his father, who straightened up in his chair, almost as though he was about to launch out of it.

"Dad, you don't need to get into—" said Baxter, though he was cut off by Roy's upraised hand, a reminder of whose house they were in, whose counsel they sought.

"Let him hear what I have to say. It might be the thing that helps in the long run," said Roy. Baxter reluctantly conceded the point and allowed his father to continue.

"Look, Leo, I'm going to give you a bit of the condensed milk version here, but what you need to know is that I wasn't always such a good man to your dad or grandma as I should've been. It pains me to admit such a thing, especially to you, but there was a time in my youth when I could raise a hand in anger, and it shames me to no end. Do you understand what I'm telling you?"

Leo nodded slowly at his grandfather, feeling quickly sobered—family squabbles and rifts aside, this was news to him, something his mother and father had never divulged.

"Good. Well, it took me plenty of time to see how it was me that helped drive away your father overseas, that he'd rather take his chances against the axis than be in my house one minute longer. Of course, Esther knew it all along, tried to warn me, not that I could listen back then," said Roy, who then paused and took a belt of the brown liquor, his eyes cast into its slosh, clearly not reveling in the current disclosure, not like he had been previously in the evening. Some of the lightheartedness was gone—much of it, actually—his pacing reduced to a tight circle, almost a shuffle, as though he had transformed into a pigeon. He continued with the understanding that his grandson might come to hate and resent him before the night was over.

He continued all the same.

"Baxter was gone for two years, and all we can think of is that we'll never see him again, never get another chance at being a family, to be better at it. Then, by God's grace, he returned to us. I'd never seen my wife happier in all her life as when she got to hug him again, when she knew it was real."

Baxter remained stoic, remembering that moment, that embrace, seared into his head in a way that he knew not even Alzheimer's at its most rampant would be able to erase from his memory. It forced him to gnash his back molars together at the thought of never seeing her again, of her worrying that she'd never see her only boy again, the countless nights of sleep lost, years, really. How he'd circumvented the only aspect of death that would have been worse than his own—leaving his mother in the lurch, alone, with Roy, for the rest of her days.

"You and I shook hands on my return," said Baxter to Roy.

"We did. Shows you the pathology I was up against back then. My boy returns from war, and I didn't have it in me to hold him," said Roy, shaking his head. "Hell, I don't know, maybe that's just how I figured a returning soldier would want to be welcomed back. The point being he made it back, even if not all of him wanted to."

The room went quiet; even the mysterious ticking noise seemed to have ceased. Roy and Baxter seemed lost in thought, transported through a time warp, reorganizing their memories, telepathically comparing how the story tracked, where they agreed, where they differed. Leo was the one most at a loss. He didn't understand why the two seemed drawn into an abrupt stalemate, but knew he was ready to hear how it played out, what had clearly gone sideways and maybe, over the course of time, how it had been righted.

"So, go on, Grandpa. How did things go after that, once Dad was back for good?" asked Leo.

Roy set his jaw as evenly as he could, quietly hoping the men before him couldn't see how brittle the façade was, the delicate infrastructure of a man trying to put on a brave face, to sell the room on it.

"Not long after your father's return, he's back in that tiny bedroom of his that hardly fits anyone, and he's up there alone trying to figure out what to do with the rest of his life," said Roy. "Then one day, he hears a commotion and comes down to see me giving his mother a push onto the couch. Not the most terrible, nothing he hadn't seen before." Roy paused a moment to look Leo straight in the eyes, then resumed. "Your dad proceeds to crack me in the chin, twice, until I hit the floor. I can still remember that string, almost still feel it when I want to."

Baxter averted his eyes downward, as though fascinated with the grain in the hardwood floor.

"Then your dad told me if I ever laid another bad-intentioned finger on his mother again, he'd bash my brains in with a garden stone," said Roy, now looking at his son. "That he'd done it abroad and wouldn't think twice about doing it here. Those were his exact words, more or less."

No one said much of anything after that for more than a few moments. Leo looked to his dad, someone he'd always viewed as a friendly and affable man, almost to fault, what some might view as a bit of a pushover. Sure, he knew that Baxter had seen combat, but he seldom spoke of those years, and it was a topic reluctantly mentioned in the Sinclair household. Plus, it also seemed like it had happened a lifetime ago. Baxter was always quick and pleased to tell his children that his life really began, really took shape, after he'd met their mother on a winter beach, He'd often recount their first date at the Italian restaurant, a family-favorite story, particularly when the kids were younger and willing to hear anything to delay bedtime for an additional twenty minutes.

Now, Leo was learning from a different Sinclair man, the elder, a glimpse of the gauntlet Baxter struggled through when he really wasn't much older than Leo currently was. He felt very confused, childlike in that moment, about his grandfather, about a version of his father he'd had a vague notion of but never had such a fine point put on it—a murderous, vengeful point. Leo had more questions, but as if on cue, Esther called up from downstairs asking if they needed anything. Roy shouted out to her, as pleasantly as he could through the closed study door, that they were all fine. He called her "dear."

"Why are you telling me this story now?" asked Leo.

"Because I want you to know that what your dad did was right. He was right," said Roy. "That if things hadn't gone that way twenty years ago, it would have been far worse for all of us. I'm positive of that."

Leo shifted in his chair to address his father, to size up the man in a new light.

"Why'd you do it?" asked Leo.

"What would you want to do if you ever saw me hit your mother, Leo?"

"I suppose I'd threaten to kill you."

"Then you already know the answer. The real question you should be asking me is why did I wait so long?"

"Why did you?"

"Because I was afraid. That's usually the answer, fear," said Baxter plainly. "Then through life, you become unafraid, and you finally do the thing, and it actually becomes kind of easy, like you can hardly believe you waited so long."

"Like knocking out your dad," said Leo, trying to follow Baxter's logic. "Would you really have killed him if he didn't change his ways?"

"I thank God every day that I never had to find out," said Baxter. "That by some miracle, me and your grandfather made it through."

"That's not really answering my question," said Leo, pressing. "Would you have done it?"

Baxter paused, but not for long. He knew the answer, and it wasn't the right night to be disingenuous.

"I knew exactly where in the backyard I'd have buried him."

That was enough to further silence the study for a bit—there'd been plenty of that going around until Roy spoke up.

"It's a strange thing to be humbled by your own child, Leo," said Roy. "But your dad and your grandma were the two that kept this family together. Don't hold that against him."

Leo felt heavy in the room or that the room had become heavy around him or that the house was sinking into its foundation. Either way. He put his glass of rye down on the floor. He'd had enough. He didn't know how any of this was supposed to help him. His confusion hadn't improved.

"Listen to me, Leo. Life is going to be full of miracles for you, big and small," said Baxter, more optimistically. "I think what your grandpa and I are trying to impress upon you tonight is that your decisions are going to start counting soon. And maybe we'll be able to give you some advice along the way, but it's about to become *your* life, which means you'll own the decisions, as any man should."

Leo looked around the study, trying to make sense of what the older generations of Sinclairs were telling him. He recalled asking his father once years ago why his granddad had such a big study in the first place, in a house that really wasn't all that big. After all, the man was a lifelong plumber—what did Roy Sinclair actually need to study? Baxter's answer had been candid, more candid than Leo had expected, and now made more sense, given when he'd learned that night. Baxter told Leo that for forty-plus years, Roy had been humping around on state jobs, always on his feet or his back or prone under some godforsaken sink. That all the manual labor somehow made it important for him to feel like a learned man, to be regarded that way, even if he didn't have the opportunity to attend college and barely finished high school. Even if he had a career that was very much seen as a trade, as blue collar. So building up his study had taken on the form of a hobby—part of a quest, part of his path toward redemption with his wife and son, where he learned to quiet his mind and control his base impulses and educate himself on a world he was unlikely to travel.

That pastime took the span of decades and slowly changed his temperament as he'd become proud of his station in life: a tradesman, a grandfather twice over, a volunteer in the community. Roy's study had helped him balance out some math in a ledger that wasn't crunching in his favor, that had been liened against since his birth in 1903, in a small hospital that also tended to animals on the other side of the building. Esther let him take the room, seeing he was trying to grow into a kinder, more attentive human—a peaceful, hardworking provider. She'd loved the man, always had; it was hardly a sacrifice to move into a smaller bedroom where the radiators actually functioned better. The study wasn't the only thing that had helped slowly leach the poison out of Roy Sinclair, but it was one of the things—a goal, a symbol. And twenty years later, he could now host his son and grandson and talk openly about the past, in hopes of guiding their youngest generation into a decision that was best for him.

A study, when a room was more than just a room. Leo looked on it with fresh eyes as he now did his dad and granddad—funny how things can change in the course of two hours, funny to consider all the things you don't know, whether they've been withheld from you or you've been willingly ignorant.

"I guess it's all about to come for me real fast, isn't it?" asked Leo, less a question, more a statement of fact.

"You'll be ready," said Roy.

"And you'll be lucky for it," added Baxter.

"Why lucky?"

"'Cause lots of folks never get their shot," said Baxter, thinking back to the day Leo was born out under the open sky, so small in Doc Smith's hands one could hardly imagine the child would pull through.

"Well . . . fuck," said Leo, for lack of anything else worth saying at that point, though it was enough to get another belly laugh from Roy, a sly smile from Baxter.

"Leo, you got that glass still by your foot. Pick it up and finish it off; don't go wasting my good hootch," said Roy jovially. "We ain't quite done yet, and I'm going to have a drop more before I ask about the most important topic of them all."

Roy took a splash more rye, hardly any, more out of ceremony, and he knew not to top off Baxter and Leo. The three clinked glasses, and Roy took his seat back behind the desk among his dog-eared books on the industrial revolution and the poppy trade in Afghanistan—Roy Sinclair, among his letters and baubles, a reformed man, a master plumber and aspiring intellectual. He now had a big old smile on his face as though he couldn't wait to get on with it and leaned forward in his chair, a wily king still holding court, all he'd ever wanted in the autumn of his life.

"Now, why don't you tell me and your dad about how things are going with this little girlfriend of yours?"

* * *

It was well past the dinner rush, to the point where even the bar flies had buzzed off for the night. Leo was back in the kitchen, doing dishes again, only this time of his own accord. He'd been off the clock but still needed to hang around until the head bartender that night, a prematurely balding goon named Gordon something-or-other gave Sam the greenlight to take off. Gordon was just filling in because of some scheduling snafu created by Mike Connolly, who was loathe to admit the skeleton crew was his fault, not penitent enough a man to stay past his own shift and lend a helping hand. Even if Connolly did have a young wife and baby on the way and was understandably more interested in being home, Leo thought it was a weak move, as did the Restaurant staff working that night. He'd also struck out finding a dishwasher repair man, only compounding everyone's frustration for the day. So Leo dried while his old buddy and smoking aficionado Olaf Johnson washed with his old-world vigor as though an ensign assigned to scrub the deck of an important gunship, too green to realize it was a shit assignment. Truly, you never saw someone so determined to scrub the crud off the desert forks, putting Leo's earlier effort to shame by his own reckoning.

By that point, Leo wasn't really in the mood to overcompensate by doing a great job with a drying cloth, so at best, he was sopping up the soapy liquid and mildly preventing water stains from setting in, little more. Olaf just shook his head at Leo's effort and harrumphed in foreign sounds, possibly forgetting that Leo had covered for him earlier in the day, that he was helping out now for lack of anything else worth doing.

They worked like doubles tennis teammates who weren't on speaking terms, and Leo silently wondered if there was anything more "spiritual" that Olaf might have cut into his tobacco apart from fruit.

By the time eleven p.m. rolled around, even Olaf had had enough of Leo's youthful assistance and kicked him out of the kitchen, telling him to find a dark corner in the bar and ask Gordon to pour him a draft of the cheapest beer they currently had on tap. Leo wasn't overly keen on drinking and driving, considering he hadn't been doing either one independently for that long, considering it was illegal, but figured one cold one wouldn't hurt. The prospect flashed him back to the night last week at his grandfather's, drinking whiskey and getting a front-row seat to a father-son dynamic he'd never witnessed before. Threats of violence. Talk of death. Razor-thin reconciliations. The ties that bind. It wasn't something he would soon forget, nor was the hangover he'd suffered the following day. He'd tried to eat some dry toast before going to work, hiding his nauseousness as much as possible. Baxter took pity on him, offered him a reprieve from the club that day if he needed one. But Leo went, determined to white-knuckle through the early shift, which he did, though he had to dry heave a few times in the men's locker room. He eventually finished up work and got home and crashed in bed, a lesson learned. He could hardly believe people did that to themselves on purpose on more than one occasion.

Leo ponied up to the bar, staying away from the smattering of members still in the Restaurant, which was mostly just one table in the back, equally shadowed. They seemed mired in some less than jovial conversation, and Leo shrank himself out of their eyeline as he wasn't technically supposed to be there for a number of reasons. He did come to realize that his godfather, Peter Sullivan, was among them, his back to where Leo was sitting. Gordon approached, and Leo ordered a beer, mentioning Olaf's blessing, which seemed to hold sway with the fill-in bartender. He served him a foamy draft in a mug, and Leo wondered if it was one of the mugs he'd cleaned by hand earlier in the day. Once the suds settled, there was only about eight ounces of actual liquid, and Gordon seemed unconcerned with the lackluster pour, probably not thrilled to indulge the seventeen-year-old kid with a full head of hair and pretty young girlfriend anxious to call it quits for the night so they could elope or do whatever they had in mind. Leo wouldn't hold that against Gordon—maybe the bartender even knew his reputation as being somewhat charmed around the club, the free lifelong membership—so Leo just sipped his pilsner with a workman's satisfaction and enjoyed the air-conditioning blowing on the back of his neck. It wasn't such a bad thing to wait on Sam, particularly when everyone left in attendance knew the score. Not that Leo minded. He was proud of the fact, felt almost envied.

He continued to sip his beer, rationing his precious ounces, and watched Sam deliver a fresh round to the lone table, chatting them up a bit, maybe flirting, probably saying she'd be knocking off soon for the night, that Gordon would close up with them. She'd undoubtedly been putting up with their antics all night, mild as they usually were, though the alcohol could hit people in unexpected ways, forcing out-of-character behavior, strange calculus. But their quorum just waved her off, lost in their muted conversation, though Leo could make out the occasional rise in Sullivan's voice, almost in protest of something, his godfather tending to be the loudest one at any given table.

None of this was any skin off Sam's nose. She returned to the bar and whispered something into Gordon's ear, then joined Leo beside him on a stool. She took a pull of his draft, leaving him a few ounces left over. She licked her lips, and Leo found it sexy as hell. Her perfume had mostly faded under the duress of her shift but lingered just enough to be detected. Also sexy. Gordon busied himself elsewhere, either opting to give the young lovebirds some privacy or simply not wanting to be around for the canoodling. Either way, Leo and Sam were inches apart, their connection palpable and charged from their day apart.

"Long day?" asked Leo, pleased to be looking at her lovely face.

"Remind me to call out sick next time this place offers lobster thermidor as the special," said Sam. "People were high on themselves all night."

"Lobster is overrated sea bugs that the poor used to pull from the rivers to avoid starvation," said Leo. "No one else wanted them, especially the rich."

"Is that true?"

"According to my grandfather it is."

"Well, times have certainly changed," said Sam. "Wait till you see what the special is next Friday night."

"What is it?"

"Blueberry-fed bear filets with roasted tubers and leeks."

"Really?"

"No, it's just spaghetti and meatballs," said Sam, grinning. "How was your day?"

"I almost took a nap under a tree."

"Sure you did."

"I said almost."

"Sure you almost did," said Sam, somehow inching her stool closer to Leo. You could hardly fit a leaf of paper between the two now, get-a-room kind of energy in full effect.

"I did have a weird conversation with Garth, though. How worried do you think I should be with Lynn going to the high school next month?"

"You're just getting around to this?" asked Sam, as though it were the most obvious concern in the world, to which Leo could just meekly nod. "She's going to be a stick of dynamite."

"She hasn't really shown much interest in boys before."

"Wait till she finds one that does interest her."

"Then what?"

"Kaboom," said Sam, pantomiming a large explosion with her hands, a hushed explosion from her mouth.

"Shit, I'm not prepared for this," said Leo, rummaging his mind for a game plan. "Maybe this is something you can talk to her about?"

"Me? What did you have in mind?"

"I don't know. That she should be leery of upperclassmen, I guess," said Leo. "And lowerclassmen. Really, all men. That you dealt with plenty of creeps when you got into high school, and she'll need to watch out for herself. You know, impart some wisdom on her if you can."

Sam took a prolonged look into Leo's eyes, watching him flounder for a solution to a problem he barely knew existed. It was sweet, if a bit clueless. She liked him, truly did. He had a real heart and wanted to be certain that Lynn was watched over or, at minimum, well informed. Sam rubbed at the skin right below her scalp: some latent dryness, a splotch of sunburn peeling over, slow to heal. It gave her the expression of one either deep in thought or battling severe frustration, of which neither applied. She was content and appreciated Leo's blinders when it came to his sister, cute in an illusionary way, innocent to the point of obtuseness. Though it did appear the veneer had deteriorated, and Leo was now scrambling to catch up, to gain ground. Not that she minded the request. Sam had gotten along well with Lynn during their limited interactions at the club. She found Leo's sister to be an aloof girl, though not with pernicious intent. She was lithe and pretty and apparently had hand-eye coordination of great renown. Leo wasn't wrong to worry about her, even if he was late to the game, and he wasn't out of line soliciting advice from Sam, someone who had gone through the wringer of high school, who occasionally had to deal with the quips and whistles of the usually well-behaved denizens of O Triple C.

She was the right woman for the job, and she knew it would sate Leo's anxiety if she intervened.

"OK, I'll talk with her," said Sam. "Next time I see her, we'll have a little girl chat."

"Thank you, Sam," said Leo, giving her a quick kiss, which elicited a few hoots and hollers from the occupied table in back, apparently jettisoning their conversation in favor of spying on the two from afar. Leo noted that Peter Sullivan was no longer among their ranks, having slipped away, perhaps to the bathroom, maybe even home by now. The cacophony was probably the last straw for Gordon, who materialized from the storeroom and shouted over from across the way.

"OK, Sam, you're good to punch out," said Gordon, not that there was a punch clock. "I'll take it from here."

Sam gave Gordon a mock salute and hopped off the stool. Leo finished the dregs of his beer and followed her into the back where she grabbed her purse and said good night to Olaf, who bid them fare thee well and a bountiful night, whatever that meant. They made their way out of the building and into the parking lot, their bodies brushing up against each other in that labor-worn way, rife with expectancy, swaying until their hands met and clasped, young skin, tinged with electricity.

Universes were born this way, even if they couldn't be seen by the naked eye.

Leo walked Sam to her car. They still hadn't decided what they wanted to do. It was late; they'd worked all day but were still hoping there'd be something out there for them. He looked up and paid mind that the moon was nowhere in sight, obscured by clouds, maybe that storm front that was supposedly on its way arriving early, finally the promise of a break in the heat wave. Before Leo could mention its absence, suggest going to a diner or something, Sam took the reins as she was prone to.

"Can we take a walk, Leo?" she asked.

"Really? You've been on your feet all night, and you want to take a walk?"

"Yes, walk me to the snack shed near the tenth hole. We'll sit in the gazebo and talk," said Sam. "I want to hear more about this nap you almost took."

"OK. There's actually something kind of interesting I've been wanting to tell you that happened last week with my dad and grandpa, kind of a long conversation actually," said Leo. "I wanted to see what you think."

Sam took Leo's hand again.

"I'm all ears. Lead the way."

Before they headed off, Leo noticed someone stretched out against a car, mostly obscured from their vision but just recognizable in a way that prompted Leo to call out, "Uncle Pete?" The figure came to life, moved with a start, then seemed to pry himself heavily off the car against which he was leaning. Maybe it was propping him up; maybe he'd even nodded off. It was indeed Peter Sullivan who was now approaching Leo and Sam, unsteady on his feet, though none too concerned about it. He seemed surprised that the parking lot would allow others, as though it was his own personal domain.

"Leo, Samantha," said Sullivan, a slur infecting his voice box. "Some evening out."

"Yeah, we saw you inside. Whose car is that?" Leo knew it wasn't Sullivan's. "You heading home for the night?" Leo also knew that Sullivan should not get behind the wheel.

"No, no," said Sullivan, either biding his time or losing his train of thought. "Just getting some fresh air before heading back to the firing squad."

An uncomfortable moment passed. Leo and Sam exchanged looks. Sullivan was worrying over a piece of gum stuck to his shoe, lacking the balance and motor skills to properly remove it.

"Uncle Pete, is everything OK? You want me to call my dad?" asked Leo.

"I'm fine, my boy, though I do cherish your concern," said Sullivan, taking a woozy step backward to better take in the two before him. "Look at you both, so full of hope and life. Don't ever lose that."

"Mr. Sullivan, we can wait around to see you off with someone if that would help," offered Sam, but Sullivan just put his hand up gallantly.

"Kind of you, Samantha, but I'll manage. Leo, tell your parents I said hello," he said. "Or better yet, perhaps don't mention me."

He left it at that, making his way back to the Restaurant in no particular hurry, almost a saunter, his coordination clearly compromised, never looking back once at the teenagers and the conversation he wouldn't remember the following day.

"How do you know him again?" asked Sam. "Family friend?"

Leo couldn't say why, but his blood immediately felt cold—reptilian, if he hadn't known better.

"He's my godfather," said Leo. "He was there the day I was born, called for the ambulance that saved my life."

They watched Sullivan turn the corner and disappear from sight. They stood in silence for a few moments until Sam rubbed Leo's back and gave him an encouraging nod. It was time to go.

So they walked and, after holding on to the story for ten days without telling anyone, Leo recounted the highlights of his conversation with Baxter and Roy for Sam. He didn't skip over too much of note, wanting Sam to have the benefit of the full context. He wanted her take on what his family was trying to do for him, but maybe, more accurately, he wanted to know where she stood when it came to his future, their relationship, and how it might all fit together. They'd only known each other for five months, and Leo was well aware of the sway she held over his thinking, how important her opinion had become to him in such a short time. What she thought about that conversation from last week counted very much in Leo's mind, so much that he was holding his breath at intervals, observing Sam take in the story, asking small questions, listening intently.

They spoke and walked across the maintenance road, not a soul around given the late hour. They traveled quickly without walking particularly fast, wrapped up in Leo's tale, Sam patiently attuned, allowing Leo to get the weight off his chest. By the time they'd reached the closed snack shed, Leo had completed all he'd wanted to share, omitting very little. They found the gazebo tucked against the turn, adjacent to the tenth-hole tee box. They sat beside each other on the bench, her arm now over his shoulder, his face in the crook of her neck, taking in her scent, her collarbone pressing against his jaw in exquisite fashion. He waited for her to deliver a verdict of sorts. But she just looked him over. Silently. It was all so silent around them, apart from the earth's soothing noise. Peaceful. He wanted her to speak, desperately so. Instead, she kissed him, passionately and with an expressed meaning. And even Leo, with his half-baked naivety, knew they were done talking; there would be no repartee. They pawed at each other until they slid off the bench, laid their bodies out on the planks of the gazebo, hardly comfortable, hardly a concern for the young.

The Restaurant stood two miles away, out of sight, Gordon something-or-other undoubtedly trying to shoo the remaining patrons out into the moonless night.

Peter Sullivan, facing the music, taking his medicine for some minor transgression, a dressing-down levied on him by the constituents of that clandestine table he'd meekly returned to.

The Quarry Witch, if the stories were to be believed, was lurking hundreds of feet below where Leo and Sam lay, haunting her cavern, protecting the territory she'd tricked Arnold Holm out of.

In their charged moment, the older girl and the would-be lover struck their accord through hands and body and tongue and wordless admissions of "I'm sure." Leo had been waiting for that moment for a while. Their clothing cinched down, though not fully off. Some guidance was proffered. The gazebo responded to their bodies, made its own creaky noise in the dead of night, an altar for a commitment deepened between the two, roiling in heat, gratitude. The act didn't last remotely long, but it was satisfying for the two, though in different ways. They did not rush to redress themselves; they were neither ashamed nor embarrassed. There was no rush to explain themselves to one another. They just scrunched their bodies up against the bench, Sam collapsing into Leo, where they got as comfortable as possible, held each other, and peered into the black landscape their eyes weren't fully equipped to discern.

Sam rested her head on Leo's chest, lulled by his respiration, heightened, then slowly coming down. A beating and brimming heart underneath. Organs and systems peacefully at work. They listened to the world around them, and it was a good one, filled with beauty and grace, and Leo couldn't help but think a better world or better setting couldn't possibly exist for him to become a man. He was so tempted to speak, to say anything to Sam: a silly joke, an epic proclamation. But he recalled his father's advice from just last week, to be quiet, to just listen. So he did, sewing his mouth shut in his mind, allowing the trance to remain whole, a distant train whistle their sole reminder that there were others out in the world, that they hadn't conquered the planet, even if it felt they had. Of course, he had so much to say, to ask of her. But he just let it be and allowed Sam the same dignity, and together they found felicity and weren't wrong to claim it—together, they were justified.

* * *

An excerpt from the *Orchard Coils Courier*, weekly print edition, February 21, 1975, page 7, column 2, paragraph 1.

Vietnam Casualties

Washington, DC—The Defense Department has announced the following casualties in connection with the conflict in Vietnam.

Killed in Action—Army

Sgt. Robert W. James, Modesto, CA
SP4 Antonin R. Squintilli, Medford, NY

Killed in Action—Marine Corps

Col. William "Billy" Huffington, Lexington, KY

Died of Wounds—Army

PFC Daniel "Denny" Nurasco, Orchard Coils, CT

Died of Wounds—Air Force

A1C Benjamin Gilpin, Vinton, LA

1983

Selected excerpts from the personal journal of Officer Leo Sinclair, Orchard Coils Police Department, dated September 1982, regarding case number H724-01: Open date April 17, 1978, no close date. Incident type: Death under Questionable Circumstances—Victim: Peter Sullivan of 1131 Howling Wind Road, Orchard Coils, CT 07215. Survived by Mary Sullivan (wife), Chip Sullivan (son).

(I won't stop writing this out. It's helping; it's going to make a difference.) On Saturday, March 31, 1978, Mary Sullivan, living at the same address as the victim, called local law enforcement to report her husband missing. She confirmed it had been more than forty-eight hours since she last saw him. Mrs. Sullivan was asked to come down to the headquarters to speak with an officer and determine if an official report should be filed. She agreed. An hour later, Mary arrived on site and was brought into conference room B, where Officer Tim Leary would conduct the intake interview. Mrs. Sullivan would recount for Officer Leary that it had been more than two days since she'd seen her husband, the last evening being Thursday, March 29, 1978. Mary would volunteer that she and Peter had quarreled after he returned home from work, and he had stormed out (her exact words per the case reporting, "stormed out") with no further explanation or elaboration as to where he might be heading. When asked about the nature of the dispute, Mary called it a private matter, would offer little more, but made mention of it being an ongoing issue. At no point did the confrontation become physical per her recounting of it. (Leary noted no obvious signs of abuse on Mrs. Sullivan's person e.g., black eye, bruising, split lip, etc.)

Officer Leary proceeded to ask Mary why she'd waited two full days before notifying authorities of her husband's absence, inquiring as to her level of concern when Peter didn't return home that first night, the 29th. Mary indicated that it was not uncommon for Peter to stay away from home after a fight, and if anything, it had become more commonplace over the past two years. (I wish I had known this at the time. So do Mom and Dad.) She felt it would be premature to involve law enforcement when in all likelihood he was sleeping it off somewhere on a buddy's couch or his office in Hartford (which apparently had a large couch) or had simply found a hotel to crash in. When asked about Peter's increasing disappearances, Mary indicated that her husband's fuse had trimmed with age, and his vocational stress had done little to help his disposition at home. When asked what Mr. Sullivan did for work, Mary relayed that he was an executive VP at Travelers, a prominent insurance carrier well known to the area. When asked to expound on her husband's exact work at Travelers, she admitted she couldn't quite detail it, though she understood it to heavily involve numbers and risk assessment.

Officer Leary confirmed that despite Peter's behavior in the past, per Mary, his absence for more than two days with no communication of any kind was very much out of character. Mary had taken it upon herself to finally reach out on the morning of the 31st to call some key friends that may have an idea where Peter was hiding (again, her exact word, "hiding"). No one she contacted could recall seeing him in the past two days or speaking to him. The Sullivans had one child, Chip, seventeen years old then and studying abroad in Paris at the time as part of an exchange program (though, oddly, the Sullivans didn't take in some French student; it was the Crosbys from across town that hosted the swap for some ill-explained reason). Mary had not reached out to Chip about his father's absence or for any information he might have, which, in her opinion, was extremely unlikely. Ultimately, she did not want to worry her son over what might be nothing, at least not yet. Officer Leary explained to Mary after hearing her story that she was well within her rights to file an official missing person's report if that were her decision, and, if so, she would need to supply a recent photograph of Peter. When asked directly if she'd like to file such a report, she agreed and worked with Leary on its construction, returning to the station later in the day with a recent polaroid of her husband (a Christmas picture from a few months back).

Over the course of the next three weeks, Mary Sullivan reached out to anyone and everyone who knew Peter: friends, family, business associates, all the club guys, O Triple C staff, even all Peter's favorite watering holes from Orchard Coils to Hartford and back. No one claimed to know anything about his disappearance. The police networked the identity of the missing man through their channels but had so far come up blank. Sullivan's disappearance was not nearly as common as a child that might have gone missing or been taken by someone they knew (which was usually the case), let alone when it was a teenage runaway scenario. Also, when an adult goes missing, there are the usual concerns of gambling, prostitution, street living, mental retardation, and hosts of other contributing factors that might lead to an adult willingly fleeing their current situation. The success rate on actually finding adults that end up having missing reports filed on them is low and would not inspire much faith in those trying to find the wayward soul. (I've seen the statistics. They're abysmal.) Now compound that with a person that seems mostly sound of mind, lucid, healthy, of means, intelligent—chances are, if they don't want to be found, that's how it will play out (even with the understanding that Sullivan had a family that loved him). But people are unpredictable and willing to walk away from even good scenarios. (Some of the older guys on the force have more than apprised me of this.) Many times, these absences resolve themselves within the first forty-eight hours. But after three weeks of searching for Uncle Pete, there were those very much convinced that he didn't want to be found (though his banking records didn't indicate any major withdrawals prior to his disappearance).

Of course, there were also those who thought it not impossible for Sullivan to have some caches not accounted for. His car had never been found during those three weeks, further evidence (albeit circumstantial) that he lit out of his own free will. By the end of that third week, some of the resources that were looking into Sullivan had to be shifted back toward more traditional town matters. (I've been told some of the officers were not upset with that development as they'd truly come to believe the man had left of his own accord.) Some thought he simply started a new life elsewhere, across the country, maybe in a bungalow overlooking the Pacific. Perhaps he had company, a lover unbeknownst to anyone. Though there were officers on the other side of that coin, also those that knew Peter best, that would have insisted that even if he'd snapped, he'd at least phone Mary and Chip, even just once, to let them know he was alive. (This was certainly my parents' belief—mine too as this was all taking place during my UConn years, and I was a bit removed from the town.)

That said, and while it's possible he escaped of his own volition, that didn't seem to be the overwhelming sentiment of those at the Orchard Coil's PD. The town was both big and small in a way, and Sullivan was well known to a few of the investigators as an attentive father, so it was hard for them to imagine him putting his boy through such terrible uncertainty on some capricious whim or tidy plan to start life anew elsewhere. And even if a wedge had formed between Peter and Mary, it was still hard to imagine he'd willingly put her through such turmoil.

Mary had been forced to call Chip on the fourth day of Peter's disappearance, no longer able to protect her son from the circumstances. He immediately returned home from Paris despite his mother's mild protests about interfering with his school year. (We all know she was relieved to have him home during that awful time.) Unfortunately, despite Chip viewing himself as the dutiful son, there was little he was able to provide that lent to the investigation (I've read all his transcripts, multiple times), and he mostly served as comfort to his mother, who seemed to be holding it together like someone convinced it was all a bad dream, the missing person would reappear, and she'd do her best to keep the situation from getting messier than it needed to be as it was sure to resolve itself favorably any day now. When Chip Sullivan was asked about the state of his parents' marriage, he had little to offer. When the police continued to press Mary during those three weeks as to the state of her union with Peter, she'd reiterated they were going through a rocky stretch but wasn't interested in any more elaboration. (Again, her thinking why air their dirty laundry when Peter would return soon enough.) Apparently, this wasn't uncommon in certain domestic cases, not even necessarily missing persons, just anytime the police may need to involve themselves between family members. Of course, people withholding information when they're not really qualified to do so doesn't help the police resolve the issue at hand, but it's proven to be an intellectual hazard that comes with the job, as I've learned over my first few years on the force. (In short, they're called secrets, and there's a reason people are reluctant to part with them.)

The search carried on until the Saturday afternoon of April 17, 1978, when Peter Sullivan's body was discovered by two teenagers in the abandoned quarry below the O Triple C property. He'd been missing eighteen days per the official report, twenty-one since the last time he was physically seen. This entire duration, his body had presumably been less than two miles away (as the crow flies) from the Restaurant, what many would say was his favorite place on earth, also the last place he was seen alive. The call had come in on a Saturday from Hal Jenkins and Luke Ferrier, two local teens not known to law enforcement as troublemakers or bad seeds. Calling from Hal's house, with his parents present and on the other line, Hal informed the police officer he'd been connected to, Officer Patty Rese, that he and a friend had made their way down the old quarry where they discovered a slumped figure on the ground. As they approached, it became clear that it was human and very much deceased. Hal and Luke took off back for home and told Hal's parents, who immediately contacted the PD. Technically, Hal and Luke had been trespassing in an area well known to the community as off limits and where violations were heavily enforced (theoretically) to deter the exact behavior Hal and Luke had engaged in. The boys were aware of this but also knew it would be chickenshit (their word) not to report what they'd discovered. Even an anonymous tip felt wrong to them. Hal's parents, and Luke's once they learned of the situation, would insist no repercussions be taken against their kids for the trespassing infraction, which the police easily agreed to. (They had bigger fish to fry, a corpse on their hands now.)

Once Officer Rese took that phone call, it did not require a lot of brainpower to link the possible discovery to the Sullivan case. Little progress had been made over the three weeks, and what Hal Jenkins was detailing over the phone was by far the most promising lead they'd had, if it was to be believed. Two officers were dispatched, Joe O'Malley and Tim Leary (same officer that conducted the initial interview with Mary Sullivan), and they drove their cruiser down to the O Triple C maintenance road, through some little-used roadwork that was underfunded and mostly dilapidated. Eventually, the two officers got as close as they could before they had to get out of their car and hoof the two-plus miles down the old path, littered with rocks and overgrowth and other natural barriers that in part helped the area from being trespassed upon, including the numerous signs (though, from a law enforcement standpoint, the truth is, if people wanted to trespass, no matter the obstacle, they'd find a way).

The two men treaded carefully down the slope, dark in areas from canopy, slippery in areas from cold and organic rot. Both men would later agree it was a creepy descent, especially thinking about what it was they were searching for. After an hour of slow and tedious walking, maintaining sporadic radio contact with HQ, the two officers reached the expansive opening that cleared out into the abandoned mining operation, well below the surface level they'd set out from. With improved visibility to the area, it did not take them long to discover what the two teenagers had stumbled upon hours before. They approached cautiously and all but confirmed that the face-down and battered corpse was, in fact, Peter Sullivan, based on height, hair color, gender, and general build. Even the clothes seemed a match to what he was last seen wearing in the Restaurant on the night of the 29th by various members and staff, which included Samantha Morris (Sam!), who'd been working that night.

The officers hovered over the body, and O'Malley, being the higher rank, took the lead to crouch down and try to get a better look at the face, which was planted firmly down into the earth. Cognizant not to disturb the scene as much as possible, but also needing more information, O'Malley manipulated what was left of the head in an effort to make a more conclusive identification. (They'd all reviewed the photos of Sullivan a million times.) And while he couldn't be 100% sure, given the state of remains, O'Malley felt 99.9% (his number) sure that they'd just found their missing man. He radioed it in and requested the full resources of their department to be dispatched to initiate a formal identification and determine if they were, in fact, standing on a crime scene. (All this would have taken place whether it was Sullivan or not.)

Neither O'Malley nor Leary had any real experience with a dead body in such a capacity: out in the wild, picked over by animals, bugs, decomposition, rigor, cold damaged, weather strewn, and bloating. They would agree it was a horrible thing to bear witness to, even if it was part of the job. And while neither man could say how long the body had been out there or what the exact cause of death may have been, one glaring thing they independently agreed on (after the fact) was that the broken and mangled nature of the corpse suggested a certainty around Peter Sullivan's death—he was either thrown or jumped from the cliff above (the seventh hole, where the Halloween Trail and the safety fencing end, where those quarry stories begin). O'Malley and Leary waited for two hours for their colleagues to arrive in full force, almost sitting a vigil (Leary's words). They lightly canvassed the area, minding their footwork, though the ground was too cold to leave footprints. They would say they didn't even see fresh ones left by the teenagers only a couple of hours ago. They would say when they piped down, it was very, very quiet there, canyon-like, spooky, and desolate.

(I'm back, had to take a break. This can be tougher than I realize sometimes.) The remainder of that Saturday was dedicated to elements of the OCPD getting their select vehicles and resources down as far as the path would allow, not unlike O'Malley and Leary before them, not unlike the two teenagers before them. Then they needed personnel to walk the remaining distance, where the body was extensively photographed. An on-ground examination of the body took place as best as possible where it lay, then it was eventually bagged and tagged to be carried via a collapsible stretcher by two of the more junior yet sure-footed members of the department that were on scene. They used an ambulance to haul the body away once topside. (Dental records would ultimately be used to confirm what everyone figured to be true, the coroner noting that despite the catastrophic condition of the jaw and remaining teeth, there was enough to make a verification through that time-tested method.) There were others on the force that knew Uncle Pete and assisted with this process, sparing Mary and Chip from viewing the distorted body, having to put them through a cruel and redundant process. They would be told that his remains had been discovered and would request permission to conduct an autopsy, which Mary would agree to with little hesitation or cajoling. (Apparently, not everyone thought a blood relative shouldn't be a part of the identification process, but these were uncommon things in a small town unaccustomed to such incidents, so every letter in the book may not have been followed, though at the end of the day, it made no difference.)

As I've reviewed all the materials I can get my hands on, the word "drained" comes up often when describing Mary Sullivan's reaction to learning her husband was officially deceased and recovered. (I personally remember coming home from UConn that Sunday once the word had gotten out, not that there was much help I could offer at the time, but I spent the day with Mom, Dad, and Lynn, all of us upset, eating a meatloaf dinner quietly until I had to drive back to my dorm very early Monday morning.)

The autopsy ended up proving more with what it eliminated than what it could clearly establish. The deterioration of the body was consistent with a three-week period (tissue samples, *insect burrowing), which would have put the rough time of death exactly when Peter Sullivan went missing. There were no glaring puncture wounds to be found, nothing deep or serrated in nature like a sharp instrument or cutting tool. There were no bullet wounds of any kind. No real bruising or ligature markings around the neck, though the body was badly broken, lacerated, including significant damage to the skull. Ultimately, no one could say with perfect authority that Sullivan hadn't been manhandled or clubbed over his head in some way. There was more than enough trauma to keep that theory in play. The medical examination's conclusion really wasn't so dissimilar to what O'Malley and Leary had initially guessed, that Sullivan had been crushed to death from a fall from an extraordinary height.*

The toxicology that could be performed at the time did not return anything useful, though it was well known that Sullivan had been imbibing alcohol heavily. (Some less than friendly accounts and descriptions surfaced during the investigation that I won't repeat in this journal.) At the end of the day, the examination couldn't conclude whether Sullivan was forcibly ejected from that precipice or he willingly threw himself to his own demise. (The default position of the OCPD was homicide, given the absence of a suicide note, his missing car, and other factors, the correct view in my opinion.) Mary Sullivan would later confirm that Peter owned a legal handgun and that it was still neatly tucked away in an old cigar box in the back of the closet shelf, oiled and provisioned with ammo kept on the shelf below. The obvious question was, if Sullivan owned a working gun and was intent on taking his own life, why would he jump to his death on a golf course? (I can't believe he would. He wouldn't.)

The spot where Sullivan likely fell to his demise was combed over easily enough with the help of officials at the country club. The season had technically started, though there weren't many golfers out yet, given how hard the ground still was. That said, they closed the area down for a few days to conduct their work. Officers were shown the fenced-off area near the seventh hole, how if you were to climb up and look down, you could sort of make out the quarry below. (In a general sense, it wasn't all that clear. Using binoculars certainly helped.) It wasn't such breaking news to the PD that the spot was well known to the club members and even the town to a certain extent, that the area was associated with that Halloween tradition and the kids walking by lantern light, the ghost stories, and the Quarry Witch hoopla. The investigating officers didn't seem to put much stock into that, coincidence or not. They had more practical matters to address than chasing around country club fables. The fencing was more than adequate for safety purposes, but if the intent was there, they could see how someone could hoist themselves up and jump into the abyss below (particularly a youngish and healthy man). The grounds were continually searched in those days, but nothing of note was detected. (It had been three weeks, after all, with enough foot traffic to render the site all but useless for the investigation, through a forensics lens.) That would be the end of their physical evidence trail, with nothing new resurfacing even as I'm writing this out, now years later. It had been long hoped that his car would resurface, be discovered, though it hasn't been to date (another indicator that suicide

* * *

Ruth Sinclair had been looking forward to the Easter weekend since the slow turn of the season. While she'd always had an appreciation of the holidays, they'd taken on a more acute meaning over the past few years as her children had spread their proverbial wings and left the nest. Not that she would begrudge them their freedom, but it was still a new reality to acclimate to, particularly when so much of her time and identity had been pinned to rearing them, bringing them up. But now she had two college graduates on her hands—well, hopefully two, provided Lynn eked out some magic over her last two months at Tulane. It had been harder than ever to get her to focus on academics; everything with her down there was golf, golf, golf. If she graduated on time with her degree in communications or if she needed an extra year—what the kids call a victory lap—it would certainly be absent any scholarly honors or Latin-sounding distinctions. That wasn't to say Lynn was dumb; she was anything but. Ruth and the rest of the family were well aware of her sharp wit and crafty mind. Lynn was just an individual who, at a young age, knew what she wanted to be and actually had that tools and determination to pursue that goal while letting the less important things slide—which was just about everything.

The truth was, she never would have even bothered with college if Ruth hadn't insisted on it, which required much research on her part. She had informed her daughter that the most promising springboard to the LPGA was the collegiate track, preferably a warm-weather school with an existing program of repute that functioned twelve months a year. And while it pained Ruth to encourage Lynn's travels far from the freezing corridor of the Northeast, she knew it was the only pragmatic way to get a degree of higher learning into her daughter's callused hands. Such was the nature of realism and compromise. That was almost four years back, and since then, Lynn's trips home had become fewer and farther between, her team commitments keeping her stationed in Louisiana or traveling across the country for various competitions.

They'd last seen her Christmas week of 1982, about four months before, but she'd had to depart just prior to New Years, returning to a clinic she was helping run with the head coach of the university's women's golf team, a young man by the name of Sachin Moore.

As for Leo, Ruth worried about her son in an entirely different way. The good news was that he'd been settled in Orchard Coils for some time now, after his four-year stint at UConn. He'd landed in a one-bedroom apartment, an eight-hundred-square-foot fortress one would cherish in their twenties, that he kept clean and orderly, though he hosted guests infrequently because of its size and spartan nature. He'd also never really gotten into the whole party-throwing scene. It wasn't the type of place Leo took excessive pride in, and he thought of it more as a spot to crash or to bring home the occasional date that had gone well—apart from that, he thought his hours were better spent elsewhere.

Given his proximity in town, he was able to see his parents quite often, whether at the club or at their house, also close by. The bad news, as Ruth saw it, was the dangerous profession her do-gooding son had chosen, becoming a police officer after graduating from the state academy after his matriculation at UConn, where he majored in history, a line of study that greatly pleased his grandfather, Roy Sinclair, who was still up in that study reading his books, now fully retired. Roy was pleased by Leo's zeal to join the force. The women in Leo's life were less thrilled about it, though were hardly surprised by his decision. Ruth, leery as she was over such a vocation, did concede it was better than some of the other options Leo had been considering his senior year of high school. All the Vietnam and armed forces discussions back in the day had boiled her blood and chilled her body temperature at the same time. It was during those years that Ruth had very much subscribed to the school of thought of "not my son" and wasn't always so tempered when delivering that message to her boy or her husband or really anyone who would listen.

Millions of mothers had felt that way, justifiably so.

Ruth had always had that fire to her, and it was hardly extinguished during those years when Leo was weighing his future; if anything, it glowed white hot. She'd cringe at those photos of him in the JROTC cadet's uniform, as handsome as he might have been, adorned and looking serious. Those photos reminded her of a path he could have chosen—almost did—though she was grateful he'd opted for a safer existence in Storrs. That said, the allure of some type of uniform was bound to ensnare the kid, basically by his own admission; it just ended up being dark blue, more local. And while his career decision may have assuaged some of Ruth's concerns over the more militaristic options, it did not expunge the fact that Leo had chosen a dangerous profession that required a sidearm at all times. To link oneself to that thin blue line was to put oneself in harm's way every waking hour, on or off duty. Any traffic stop. Any domestic disturbance. Any time sitting in a parked squad car, running a plate or minding a speed trap. Any jaywalker you felt compelled to offer a warning to. Any of these moments could go sideways and spell the end for those sworn to protect and serve. And they knew it. They knew the deal. So, poignantly, did their loved ones—all too much. They lived it. They feared it. It kept them up at night. It was a package deal. The fact that Leo was assigned to Orchard Coils did bring Ruth a modicum of solace. It wasn't quite a sleepy town, but it was hardly a big city or a hotbed of criminality. There also hadn't been a police casualty in the line of duty for twenty-seven years—she'd gone to the library and looked that one up, then found herself praying that another twenty-seven years would pass along the same trajectory, a similar statistical outcome that would protect her boy.

Those were the burdens Ruth Sinclair carried with her—two small birds nested in her heart—though she had less power than ever before to watch over them, which tormented her to no end.

So it was hardly a surprise to her that once she was seated in the Orchard Coils Country Club banquet hall, tastefully decorated for the Easter holiday, with Baxter to her left, her two adult children to her right, and her own parents, still very much alive and kicking barreling into their seventies, seated directly across from her, that Ruth found herself so overcome with joy and gratitude that she could barely hide it. She wasn't about to cry in the crowded room—she'd never been a public crier to begin with—but she wore her happiness on her sleeve, in the radiance of her face, still lovely and relatively unlined, which she'd attributed to her frequent nature walks and hats designed to block the sun. Baxter gave her hand a squeeze under the table as if to reinforce her good cheer, to further prove that she wasn't imagining it; the day was real. Her parents gave her approving grins. Even her kids, grown up as they were, accustomed to their mother's doting, beamed smiles upon her, letting her know it was good to all be together. Easter was a blessed holiday like that, a mom's holiday, and everyone knew it, and the day was only enhanced by the sun streaming through the Restaurant's oversize windows, bathing the collective families in magnificent light, uplifting in a way that was hard not to notice, not to feel a little cleansed by.

"What a day for all of us to be together," said Ruth, once they were all seated, fortifying her composure, kicking off their ceremony. "So beautiful and warm out already."

"An early spring graces us," said Archibald "Archie" Kent, Ruth's father and recent retiree, selling off the last of his ownership stake in a successful demolition business that had been passed down to him by his own father some thirty years before. "A needed respite from the winter we've just endured."

Connecticut had seen near-record snowfalls as 1982 gave way to '83, the last big storm a late-March surprise that had taken the wind out of everyone's sails, relegating them back to their homes with the heat still cranked, musing over notions of living in Florida full time, humidity and alligators be damned—at least the taxes were cheap, and their department of transportation didn't need to budget for snowplows and rock salt.

"I do believe that winter gets a bad rap," said Lynn Kent, Archie's wife of forty-six years and Lynn Sinclair's namesake.

"How so, Grandma?" asked Leo, wearing his Sunday best street clothes, opting to keep his service revolver in the car, his usual prerogative when off duty despite his affinity for certain weaponry and the art of pistol marksmanship, a skill he'd developed during his academy days, taken a natural shine to, and now practiced religiously at the shooting range.

"It offers us a chance to rest and reset," said Lynn Kent. "Both humans and nature."

"Plenty of chances for rest now, right, Arch?" said Baxter, who got along swimmingly with his father-in-law, always had. "How's retirement treating you so far?"

"Lousy. I went from a world of well-controlled blasts to saving the whales with these two in a manner of months," said Archie, playfully pointing over to his wife and daughter, having now been conscripted into the Audubon world, a new and somewhat reluctant foot solider on their behalf.

"Don't listen to him, Baxter. He loves keeping busy, and it does him a world of good to get back outdoors," said Lynn.

"I do enjoy seeing Ruthie more, even if it means I got to shake my tin cup in a way that's going to save the koalas or whatever."

"The organization really has become very strong, with a reach the likes of which it's never had before," said Ruth proudly. "We're even looking to get into TV this year or next. Maybe some educational videos that can be shown to school students."

"That's right. Indoctrinate them while they're young," said Archie.

"Young people should know what we're doing to the creatures of this planet," continued Ruth, steadfast.

"Perhaps they should," said Archie, relenting to his daughter, raising his water glass in salute, taking a sip. "Besides, everyone at this table knows I only went after the dilapidated buildings and razed land. I left Mother Nature alone, mostly."

There might be some debate about Archie Kent's role in the natural landscape over the past forty years, let alone the checkered history of Kent Demolitions dating back to his grandfather founding the company in 1919. Archie could hardly identify himself as a naturalist, but he did like to think he left the world a little better through the cleansing efforts of his family trade, removing man-made blight and paving the way for something better, if not more profitable. Even if much of that effort revolved around sodium nitrate and wrapped wood pulp. But on the Easter holiday, the Kents and Sinclairs were all inclined to indulge the man's outlook—or delusions—and not dispel his reality one way or the other.

Their waiter approached, a man by the name of Raul whom most of the family had known over the years. Warm wishes and the like were exchanged for the holiday, and Raul jotted down a few specific drink orders from the Kent side of the clan. Praise was offered to Raul for the decorations, the beauty of the banquet hall, which he graciously accepted on the Restaurant's behalf. The meal was a buffet-style affair, so the table was free to serve themselves at their leisure, though Raul impressed upon them that if they required anything additional, they need only to ask. Thanks abounded as Raul took his leave, and the family joined the buffet line to load up their plates with carved meats, vegetables, starches, salads, and other tasty options.

They all returned to their seats, after some dawdling with other members and guests, wishing all a happy holiday, commentary on what they hoped to be a fast-approaching spring. There was a friendly murmur in the room, comforting, well calibrated. Many of its inhabitants were wearing what looked to be church clothes, kids dressed in their finest, looking appropriately itchy and uncomfortable yet hopped up on Easter bunny candy since sunup. The Sinclair-Kent table dug in, falling back into their conversation while sipping a fresh round of mimosas that Raul had delivered while the table was empty. Of all their plates, it was that of the youngest, Lynn Sinclair, that towered the highest with sliced turkey and ham, sides of roasted asparagus, and a dollop of rice pilaf to boot. She ate as though it were her mission in life, which didn't go unnoticed by the table in an amusing sort of way—they at least half understood what she was on about but weren't about to let it go uncommented on.

"They feeding you down there at college, Lynnie?" asked Archie, never one to miss a chance to rib one of his grandkids. "Or do you just miss our Yankee food that much?"

Lynn swallowed a mouthful of turkey, took a long sip of water, then cleaned her mouth off with a napkin and placing it back down on her lap—if golf had taught her anything over the years, it was to operate at a tempo she could control—then she answered her grandfather on her time.

"Coach thinks I need to gain five to ten more pounds—muscle, obviously," said Lynn, tending to a new forkful of protein. "Past few weeks has about getting more calories in me, the right kind."

Lynn ate the ham, never touched the mimosa.

"Such an odd thing to hear a man wanting a young woman to put weight on," said Lynn Kent, clearly amused by the notion.

"Indeed. And do you happen to agree with Coach Moore on the matter?" asked Ruth of her daughter. Lynn just nonchalantly shrugged her shoulders and worked her plate down to the porcelain.

"Aww, come on now, who doesn't like a gal with a healthy appetite?" said Archie. "Especially when she's a star athlete."

What Archie didn't know and what Ruth had come to suspect over the past year was that her daughter's golf mentor, Sachin Moore, was having undue influence over Lynn that might be crossing the boundaries of coaching a sport and more consistent with trying to lord over another's life. When Ruth previously pressed the issue, Lynn would always defend Coach Moore as a real savant of the game, conditioning, and nutrition who had incredible powers of both focus and motor control, the likes of which she'd never seen before. Lynn had truly come to believe that under his tutelage at Tulane over the past four years, her game had significantly reduced its trouble spots. And while a coach's direct connection to such improvements could be tough to quantify, no one would argue the consistent strokes shaved off Lynn's game during her time in bayou country. That said, the enigmatic Coach Moore was a bit of a mystery to the family. While they saw Lynn infrequently, the coach had free rein to guide all aspects of her life, including schedules, travel, academics, tournament play, and now, apparently, dietary choices. It had sort of a grooming feel to Ruth, but she never quite had the words to express her concerns to her myopic daughter, who seemed convinced that Sachin Moore was her ticket, in part, to the LPGA. It was unsteady ground at best for Ruth, not wanting a blowout confrontation with her daughter, especially since she was the one who had nudged her onto the college track. So the best she could do was imbue subtle messages to Lynn of her own sovereignty: that it was her life, her talent that would get her where she wanted to be, not her demanding coach. Lynn wasn't so sure. And these messages, like so many others delivered to a younger generation who'd lived on the planet a whopping twenty years and already knew more than their parents and grandparents combined, tended to be met with exasperation or worse, the dreaded eye roll and shoulder shrug, when their retort didn't even meet the criteria for speech, warrant any sound.

Nevertheless, Ruth wouldn't be giving up probing the exact relationship between her stunning daughter and this supposed golf guru some ten years her senior anytime soon. She'd just have to pick and choose her angles of approach until she found one that revealed the truth, whether it be wholesome, torrid, or, God willing and more probable, somewhere in between.

* * *

Selected excerpts from the personal journal of Officer Leo Sinclair, Orchard Coils Police Department, dated October 1982, regarding case number H724-01: Open date of April 17, 1978, no close date. Incident type: Death under Questionable Circumstances—Victim: Peter Sullivan of 1131 Howling Wind Road, Orchard Coils, CT 07215—Survived by Mary Sullivan (wife), Chip Sullivan (son).

I'd arranged to meet Mary Sullivan in her home, still on Howling Wind Road after all these years, never having departed Orchard Coils after Peter's death or taking up a new residence. (She didn't even revert to her maiden name.) I'd had to screw up some courage to reach out to Mary for a number of reasons, the first being her somewhat fragile state. It had been known over the years since the incident that while Mary was still a member of our community, in many ways, she no longer acted as one. She'd withdrawn so much from her previous social life, had quit O Triple C, and was hesitant to even entertain one visitor at a time (quite a reversal—the Sullivan parties used to be things of legend around town). She no longer liked dining out, taking in a movie, browsing a bookstore, or even walking in a park (all things she used to love). Sadly, an aspect of paranoia had taken hold and kept her frozen in a certain way, which was odd in a sense, given the community outpouring of support she'd received when the news of Peter's death was made public. She was well liked, and folks wanted to care for her. One may have imagined a colder reaction from people as though fearful Mary's misfortunes might be contagious, might taint their own well-being. (This is New England, after all, and everyone loves their superstitions.) But by all accounts, the town did their best to rally around Mary, to make sure she didn't feel like a pariah, shunned from the larger group. I have to admit that I got plenty of this intel from Baxter and Ruth Sinclair, my own parents, who detailed Mary's slow regression, a pulling back from society over the years. They were very much adamant that despite their continued best efforts, years of them, they hadn't been able to coax Mary Sullivan back to a semblance of her former everyday life, that she had mostly chosen isolation. (Maybe in the circumstances she's been forced to face down, coming back just isn't an option. I truly don't know.)

So for me to secure this interview of sorts with Mrs. Sullivan was a bit of a flyer. She had long given up believing that law enforcement would have a breakthrough in the case (or maybe barely believed they still cared). Even as a cop myself now, I had to recognize that the real reason she agreed to sit with me was because I was her godson, little more. I doubt she thought I'd be able to shed new light on the case, considering I'd only been on the force for a couple of years, considering she probably still regarded me as that child that used to run around her property with Chip years back. Nevertheless, when I called to ask for some of her time, nervous as I was, she mildly accepted the offer for me to come over.

Another sticking point for me asking to meet Mary was that I technically wasn't assigned to the Sullivan case, which had basically gone ice cold over the five years and hadn't garnered much activity from what I could tell during my short tenure in the police building (zero progress to be exact, at best some outlandish process-of-elimination work). From what I've seen, the

Sullivan case moves like a literal ghost through the walls of the stationhouse, occasionally mentioned and then quick to vanish. It's a sore spot in the department for sure: a potential murder on their watch that can't be accounted for. Apart from the body, there'd been no further evidence recovered. No suspects. No motives. No car to be found. It truly felt like the planet might have called out to the man and sucked him down as though a sacrifice to what lay deep below. (Unfortunately, this hasn't helped the Quarry Witch stuff, only emboldened it, so much so I've recently learned that people are now calling the fenced area on the seventh green, where Peter presumably went over, the Devil's Altar, which is truly the last thing this town needs.)

When I tried to ask some of my fellow officers about the case, I'd run into a spectrum from utter indifference to wild conspiracy. There hadn't been a suspicious death in Orchard Coils since Peter Sullivan, yet the inability to generate viable leads or headway on the case seemed to have neutered interest in the small-town PD that one would have thought would be constantly obsessing over. (This part has been a real education for me, also a case study in the numbing impact of time.) A few years in and I can more than confirm that the trail is so cold no one even feigns interest anymore, despite it feeling like a blemish on them, a failure. This has obviously been a disappointment to me and, as a result, prompted me to photocopy any and every scrap of paper I could regarding the case (mostly nights when I'm manning the front desk, on the shit shifts, taking my lumps used to indoctrinate rookies, which I was always fine with—I got it). But over the course of all those nights, on the sly, I recreated the full version of the case just for myself, which was certainly against protocol. (Everyone thinks I'm such a little rule follower, but guess what? Not always!) Though it was hardly the biggest infraction in the world, and frankly, I don't think anyone would have even missed the original case file or told me I couldn't hold on to it for as long as I liked, but I still wasn't about to draw attention to my efforts. After all, if everyone else had stopped trying, and I was relatively new to the force but now had my feet under me a bit, maybe it was my turn to take a stab at the thing. Fresh eyes— maybe there was something still to unearth.

Which led me, logically, to Mary Sullivan's doorstep, armed with the knowledge from reading the entire case file over numerous times, much of it committed to memory.

It was surreal being back in the Sullivan household after so many years absent. But there I was, sitting on a couch, with Mary serving me coffee and butter cookies. It almost felt normal, like when I used to visit her with my mother. I'd play with Chip if he was around, some type of bank robber game, or we'd just run ourselves ragged in their spacious backyard. I actually spent a fair amount of time there in my youth. I have nothing but fond memories of it, so close were my parents and the Sullivans back when things were good, like an extended family. Now Mary sat before me, and I was quickly reminded how everything had changed for the worse. She looked much older, rapidly so. (She wasn't even fifty yet but honestly could have passed for sixty, maybe older.) I had to imagine the torrent that was roiling under her calm demeanor. Now that I actually had proper training for this sort of thing, stuff I'd learned in the academy, stuff I'd watched through one-way mirrors, even participated in, I had to remind myself this wasn't a purely social call, that I hadn't even pitched it that way to Mary when I phoned her. It was true that I wasn't there on official business. But I was trying to straddle some ill-defined line, an in-between. The question I'd had prior was how much of it would she allow, tolerate? How much would she respond to? I knew that recording our conversation would be a nonstarter, so for the sake of this journal, the files I keep, I endeavored to recreate some of the conversation from memory, erring on the side of caution but committed to steering clear of embellishment or too much emotion. (This is meant to assist me as a person, as a would-be detective, not to rewrite history in some pleasing way or sugarcoat the facts.) Here it goes.

LS: How is Chip doing in school? (Always prudent to start off with a topic you know they'll like, children especially.)
MS: Very well. He's enjoying the city. I wasn't so sure he would. (She spoke softly. The city was Boston.)
LS: Third year, right? What's he studying again?
MS: Yes, architecture. In the city.
LS: What a field. Please let him know I was asking about him, glad he's doing well.

(I knew I'd have to circle back to Chip at some point. I remember there being an awkward beat as I needed to pivot past the opening formalities. I looked around the room and found it mostly unchanged from how I remembered it. Then I tried to recall the last time I was actually in that house, which was probably for Peter's wake, though that barely seemed possible to me. I'd had plenty of contact with Mary and Chip over the years, but it must have fallen short of actually stepping foot inside their home. Weird. But again, in retrospect, much of this was by her design, her solitude. I wanted Mary to speak again, to get talkative, so I purposefully piped down, made a small show of looking around the room, the little tricks they teach you to entice a conversation out of others, which oftentimes, if one is patient enough, if one refuses to be embarrassed by silence, can work in their favor.)

MS: How are your parents doing?
LS: Very well, thanks. They miss you terribly you know. They wish they could see you more often.
MS: Do they know you're here today?
LS: No one knows I'm here today. Not my parents. Not the police.
MS: You're the police, Leo. (A not-so-subtle barb.)
LS: Yes, but more importantly, I'm your godson, Uncle Pete's godson. (A gambit, I admit, to evoke his name so early in the process, though warranted, or maybe I panicked a bit, but it did unsettle her briefly, that much I could see in her frame.)
MS: Do you think there's more to what I know? That I would hold out on the police but not you because of that bond? (She was being direct, quickly so.)

At that point, I tried to remember if anywhere in my photocopied case file there was anything mentioning whether Mary definitively thought her husband had been murdered or if he could have ended his own life voluntarily. While homicide had always been our operating theory, suicide or even a bizarre accident could never be fully ruled out. But had Mary ever come out and explicitly said what she thought happened? I wasn't so sure there was a long explanation in there, perhaps something brief. In any event, it was more than worth me asking the question to hear her answer with my own ears.

LS: What do you think happened to Peter that night? (She took a long time to respond.)
MS: My husband was many things, but a suicide case was not one of them. (She spoke with dignity and chose her words specifically. My training had taught me to look for that, particularly from the more intelligent people I came across doing the job. But I was also cognizant that people who are careful and deliberate with their language make mistakes, can overcurate their speech in a way that reveals more than they'd intended, which has a way of inadvertently opening doors to information they'd rather not have seen the light of day.)

LS: Can you tell me some of the many things your husband was? (She nibbled on a cookie and wouldn't answer, made me persist.) Mary, please, tell me about my Uncle Pete. I've read all the interviews that were conducted those years back. Staff and members at the club, his bosses, coworkers. Yours. Chip. Even statements from my own parents. They paint a picture of a man growing erratic, struggling against something in some slow, drawn-out fashion. He was a high-functioning guy, a decorated veteran, but it sounded like his personality was shifting into something . . . different. (I had to stop myself from sounding too desperate, pleading, showing inexperience.)

Mary continued to chew that butter cookie for a bit—one of those that had a dollop of raspberry jam on top—maybe not trying to be disrespectful (I think) but more out of varying considerations, trying to make sense of why I'd think she might know more than she was letting on. (Which I did, but plenty of other people thought that as well. It's only natural with a surviving spouse.) I remember asking her basically the same question again, looking for any slightly different vector of approach, probing codas. I wanted to impress upon her that I was determined to get to the bottom of what happened. And that she'd have to trust me, to allow this pursuit even if she felt the police had failed her, even if maybe she was unsure she wanted the pursuit to continue. And the really weird thing was, on top of all of that, this was the woman that was there the day I was born, who comforted my mom when she thought she and her baby might die out there on the lousy golf course. A woman who watched me grow up from my first breath, and now I had to intrude in her house, basically her last sanctuary, and dredge up all this unpleasantness and still expect her to be civil and accommodating about it. (Christ, Leo, she's even still feeding you—you were stress-eating those cookies.)

MS: You're sort of not a cop, in a sense, to me.
LS: I get that.
MS: Peter would have been so proud of what you've become, what you still want to be.
LS: I miss him every day.

Then she talked because, in the end, they all want to talk in some capacity, often when they don't think they have anything to hide—it's just a matter of figuring out which button to push. (Again, my training, plenty exhaustive for those that take it seriously.) I'll do some paraphrasing for the sake of this journal as the conversation started to get blended, washed between the two of us. And the up-front fact is, all Mary had to share with me were some thoughts and feelings, vibes almost. There was nothing of concrete value for her to offer. She told me she didn't know what had been bothering Peter over the past year or so, only that it wasn't imagined, but at the same time, he wouldn't comment on it, disclose anything. For a long while, she chalked it up to midlife, the crisis, recognizing one's own mortality, a fear of irrelevance and the fleeting nature of life, those old chestnuts. She did find it odd that none of the materialism that seemed to accompany those pitfalls landed on Peter, who still mostly eschewed anything too flashy. He liked his personality to garner the attention. He'd also seemed less interested in his work, which was also an oddity, as he was one who assigned much of his value and status to the operations he carried out in those Hartford sky-rises, to the financial security he brought back to the home front. He still performed his duties in a way that satisfied those around him (per his colleagues, boss), but there was a certain ambivalence now present, a noticeable lack of verve, which really wasn't so uncommon in that industry. People burned out, went into down cycles, grew bored or complacent, sometimes to pull themselves out of their funk, other times not.

I was then reminded of my parents' own statements about Peter Sullivan. My mom was utterly distraught over the man's death, this vivacious and charming soul that had meant so much to our family. The changes she'd observed in him were always unsettling to her. Mary was unwilling or unable to fully confide in her best friend (Mom) as to what Peter might be going through. Ruth saw the dark clouds gathering. (She always had a good perception for things like that.) They were plain as day to her, even when others wrote them off as harmless malaise (including my father). While some saw a passing overcast, Ruth could see the true maelstrom behind it, and when she tried to press both Peter and Mary on it, she was rebuffed, not always with courtesy, which I know without directly asking her wounded her terribly. (She was only trying to help.)

My dad, a man's man through and through (apart from the lack of hard drinking), crestfallen as he was to lose his best friend, placed much of the blame on himself for not doing more, for not believing more strongly that there was a legitimate problem at hand. He wasn't as overt with his concern as his wife, didn't want to embarrass Peter or sully his pride. If anything, he'd tethered himself closer to the man, tried to keep a better eye on him, as though proxy was his only solution. (I know my dad. That's exactly how he'd go about it—be available, allow Sullivan to come to him.) Obviously, I can imagine my parents discussed the Sullivans at great length during their private moments. They'd have their theories, their concerns. My father would be mindful of the agency Peter held over his life, his family, his freewheeling days at the club. They all agreed he drank too much. Comments were made in the file about his deteriorating golf scores. (More of a tell then the layman might think. I know for a fact he was proud to shoot under 80 somewhat consistently, from the tips.) I imagine my parents thought Peter was chasing something that people wouldn't understand, that he didn't want to divulge. And not something banal like infidelity. I don't think that was Sullivan's style. (But still, who knows?) I know my parents shoulder much of the blame (far too much in my view), thinking they could have saved their dear friend. It's taken a real emotional toll on them—that much I've seen up close and personal, along with their failed attempts to bring Mary Sullivan back into their orbit. It's been tough for me to watch, and I don't fully know how I'll explain to them at some point that I'm investigating the case. I don't suspect that conversation will go particularly well. (Sorry, I'm digressing, but I am stalling on telling them.) I recall asking Mary two very specific questions.

LS: What do you think he was chasing? Why would he be out on the seventh green so late at night? (The presumption was that whatever happened, happened well after operating hours, even after the Restaurant closed for the night on the 29th.)

(More paraphrasing from me—too much verbal churn to write specifics.) Mary didn't know, but she didn't think her husband would be after anything conventional. He wasn't a gambler or a womanizer. He wasn't even much of a thrill seeker. As for the drinking, she thought of it as almost a prop, an affectation he used to highlight his tolerance, to bolster his personality. (I think she has some blinders on around this point.) It was almost as though he couldn't think of anything else to do, that he wasn't using the booze to numb the pain or bury the past, and that's why he'd always been able to keep his vice in check (debatable). If anything, she'd thought he'd grown bored with much of what he loved, but never to the point where he'd leave it all. He loved her, loved Chip, and would not willfully abandon them (her words). She thought maybe at some point he'd bring up God, religion to her, but he never did or chickened out of the conversation. She didn't know. And she certainly didn't know why he'd be out walking the course at night, except that he loved the place so much, and nothing would surprise her about his affinity toward it, how it would hardly be the first time he had walked the course after hours. (A statement I knew to be true as I'd had a few walks with my godfather around some of those holes after the sun had set.) I could tell she was growing a little resentful of me, her inquisitor, the mood shifting, and I tried to conjure a way to press her on Peter's relationship with Chip, but I didn't have it in me—neither the guts nor the skill to tease that thread without pushing my tenuous connection with her over an irreversible edge, my failing as a cop, as a seeker of truth. I punted. I bailed.

LS: Did Peter ever seek out any professional help we might not be aware of?
MS: No. (The face she gave me contorted to borderline disdain, and I knew the ice was thinning)

We had reached our impasse for the day. I'd learned as much about my Uncle Pete's mindset, if not more, than the fair amount chronicled in that report. Mary had delivered on some additional context, though still nothing absolute, no brass tacks, no motives, no enemies. If anything, Sullivan might have been his own worst enemy, which would speak to an accident or *suicide, though it doesn't necessarily rule out homicide. Even if none of us wanted to believe he'd do that to himself, one had to leave room for the notion that he'd had enough and did something rash (but the missing car, no note). I tend to believe Mary doesn't know the truth either. She has her suspicions and holds on to them for dear life, though the life she has left seems to grow paler each day. (Thank God she has Chip, though I wish she got to see him more often. Maybe on that I could find a way to discreetly intervene.)*

I got up from my chair, believing I'd maxed out my welcome (an unimaginable notion only two years ago) and began to take my leave. I told her I wouldn't be giving up on Uncle Pete anytime soon. That I would always be there for her if she needed something—anything, big or small. These weren't useless platitudes, though I didn't expect her to take me up on much of it anyway. She saw me as something different now, ill defined. My guess is she struggled with it. (I know she loved me like a son, but the relationship had become complex.) Before I could exit her house, she seemed to offer up one final thing for me, for the benefit of my gumshoe investigation, maybe my own personal safety.

MS: Are you still a member at the club? Do you still go there?
LS: I am. I don't get there as much as I'd like, what with working full time now, but it's still a part of my life. Why do you ask?
MS: You asked me what I thought Peter was chasing. And I told you I didn't know exactly. But whether he found it or not, I'm quite sure O Triple C has something to do with it. (I wasn't remotely sure what to make of this. It sounded accusatory. I actually retook my seat and asked her to elaborate.)
MS: You haven't really been there a long time, not as an adult. I'm sorry, but you haven't even really been an adult for a long time yet either. What I'm telling you is there's a dark undercurrent there.
LS: I don't know what that means. Is there a name you can give me, something I can pursue?
MS: If I had a name, I'd have given it to the police years ago. It's an intuition, Leo. I think it's a fine thing you became a police officer. I actually think you'll do some good out there. And in a way, it's good you're also embedded at the club. (I thought she was finished, but she had more to say.) But you'll need to watch your back there. Some of them will never see you as a real member. You'll always be a cop. Many of them won't trust you.
LS: Mary, where is this coming from? You're making the club sound sinister. My parents and grandparents have been members for decades. (I'd grown a bit defensive, lost some objectivity.) Is that why you left the club? Do you think someone there killed Peter? (It took her a while to respond, clearly assessing how much she'd divulged to me, how much more was worth saying.)
MS: Just keep an open mind, Leo. (Her exact words, though more ominous than hopeful.)

I left after that, feeling almost chased off, like I'd lost, eager to get home and write some of this down while it was still fresh in my head. I'm not sure if these notes will ever see the light of day, but I do think they'll assist me with discovering the truth about what happened to my godfather. But I don't know. I guess the only thing I know is that I'm glad I'm doing it, proud of it. I owe that much to Peter's memory. I owe him plenty . . .

* * *

"And how is our resident crime fighter doing these days?" asked Archie Kent, his tongue and inhibitions loosened through some bourbon and a hot fudge sundae. *Not an unimpressive combination*, Leo thought, also noting, as he had in the past, that both his grandfathers enjoyed their libations while that particular preference hadn't rubbed off on either Baxter or Leo, though it might explain why Archie Kent and Roy Sinclair got on so well, famously so, whenever their paths crossed at family get-togethers.

Leo had been pleased to keep away from the sauce, and becoming a police officer only reinforced that decision, given the amount of drunken buffoonery he'd come across, the number of closet alcoholics who were now on his radar. Leo liked his grandfather Kent, loved him, and therefore tolerated his antics as the man was now toasting him and his presence on the streets of Orchard Coils, keeping everyone safe and sound, earnest in his jocular way. Leo raised his coffee cup in salute to the man, accepting the compliment, allowing the old-timer his fun. He was newly retired after all; he had to find his kicks somewhere.

"Ignore him, Leo. He's letting all this newfound free time go straight to his head," said Lynn Kent, tossing her husband a look thick with unspoken marital code. "In all seriousness, how is your work going?"

"It's going well. Very different from the academy, but everyone warns you of that," said Leo. "I'm happy enough so far and glad to have gotten assigned to Orchard Coils."

"Have you pulled your father over yet for speeding?" asked Archie, which actually did draw a round of laughter from the table as it was known that Baxter had the opposite of a lead foot.

"I'd probably catch Mom on that sort of infraction. But I suppose I'd let her off with a warning," said Leo. More laughter from the table, Ruth throwing her hands up in mock surrender.

"Just keep staking out the rotary. Plenty of crazy drivers in that part of town," said Baxter, who was still adjusting to hearing his boy talk about his position of authority, of actually having to enforce the law.

"Have you had to arrest anyone yet?" asked Leo's sister, who, after putting away two full plates of buffet food, was noticeably skipping the full desert bar. Maybe she was full, or more likely, maybe concentrated sugars and caramel drizzle didn't fall into Coach Moore's dietary regimen, the wrong kind of calories.

"Sure, I actually had to arrest someone my first month on the job."

"What for?"

"Domestic battery."

That quieted the table. And Leo quickly realized he should have parsed his words. He was still learning how to navigate that aspect of the job, particularly around family and friends.

How to blend it in with other aspects of his life. Or completely firewall it, which was probably impossible and somewhat unhealthy. People were going to be curious, inquisitive. They were going to treat you differently. Be leery. Jockey for favors. All the thin blue line stuff they try to teach you in advance, but most of it you have to learn through experience—no fast tracks or shortcuts to speed that along. It was new territory for Leo, and he marveled at his older colleagues who'd pulled it off, juggling spouses and children and coaching softball teams as though they led normal lives. It seemed impossible to him. Being a cop did not seem conducive to leading a normal life. But those around the station advised him to give it time. Plenty of the old guard were willing to guide Leo as he was the kind of young man amenable to receiving good advice, had a strong enough filter to block out the bad, even if the difference wasn't always obvious at first.

That said, Leo knew it must be somewhat jarring for his family to hear of domestic battery in their town, handcuffs going on someone for such a terrible offense. But given Orchard Coils had surpassed twenty thousand residents in the last census three years ago, it was far from inconceivable that the town would have its share of heinous actions—even if Leo's family would rather not consider it, even if they could hardly believe it was their sweet boy's job to bring such a person into custody.

For his part, what Leo had learned about his town and its citizens in only a couple of years had been a radical education to a truth he'd been blind to his whole life. A variety of abuses lined the seamy underbelly of what he thought was a bucolic little berg—that illusion had been thoroughly dashed the first time he saw someone's face split open with a frying pan, his second month on the job, about five miles from his apartment.

"What's some of the other stuff you've done these first two years?" continued Lynn, showing more interest than usual in her brother's vocation. He supposed if she couldn't be out doing golf stuff, she'd practice at being a willing participant in the family.

"Oh, nothing fancy. Plenty of patrolling, speed traps, lots of hours checking in on people," said Leo. "Plenty of shifts the radio barely cracks. Those are kind of the boring ones, to be honest."

"Good," said Ruth, a bit suddenly, though with emphasis. "I want you to have as many boring shifts as possible in this job."

Everyone understood what Ruth, Leo's mom, was getting at, including Leo.

"Thanks, Mom. I promise I'm being careful out there," said Leo. "It's really not so bad. I honestly feel the most vulnerable when I'm trying to direct traffic on foot—you know, like at the scene of an accident or some construction work getting done to the roads. People always drive in such a hurry, even when they have no place to be."

"So you do feel safe out there?" asked Lynn Kent.

"I do. Obviously, you always have to prepare for the unexpected, but let's face it, Orchard Coils is hardly New York City. It's not even Bridgeport."

"Not a lot of serial killers roaming our fair streets, right, Leo?" joked Archie.

"Nope, no murders since five years back, and we're not even sure about that one."

Another showstopper, as everyone at the table knew the last death Leo was referring to. Discussion of Peter Sullivan among the family wasn't necessarily taboo; enough time had passed, and it could be broached, debated openly, but always with a measure of caution. There was a time when the emotion was so raw, the nerves too exposed, when it was far wiser not to bring the subject up in front of Baxter and Ruth. There was more room to maneuver with the topic now, though in hushed tones. Whispers. Solemn respect. It was doubly dubious to discuss Sullivan at O Triple C, his home away from home, the literal place of his demise—as though his ghost might haunt the topside, take umbrage with being gossiped over. That said, people still talked of him; it was hard not to, and it's what people do.

"I mostly knew Sullivan through your parents, some random club events over the years," said Archie, modulating his voice down from the bourbon bravado. "Always struck me as a damn good fellow."

"He was that indeed," said Baxter.

"It really was such a terrible thing that happened," said Lynn Kent.

"Maybe we don't even need to talk about it," said Lynn, looking directly at her mother, who'd always shared a kinship on the topic and its macabre nature. "Especially on Easter."

The table looked to Ruth, knowing full well she was best suited to arbitrate, to set the tone—they would abide by her ruling, and they didn't have to wait long.

"No, it's OK. Obviously, we loved Peter, and what happened to him was such a blow to us, to the club, even the town," said Ruth, composed, soulful. "I think it can be nice on a day like this to remember him, what he meant to us. We don't ever want to forget that. We want his memory to carry on."

Murmurs of approval from around the table, relieved smiles.

"Well said, cherry drop," said Baxter, giving his wife's shoulder a squeeze.

Then Leo decided to contribute to the conversation, instead of maybe just piping down and letting a soft moment be.

"I met with Mary Sullivan a few months ago to discuss it," he said quickly, basically a blurt.

He hadn't been sure if he was going to tell his family about the meeting. It had been five months, and he hadn't mentioned it. He and Mary hadn't spoken since. She hadn't reached back out to Leo. And he, wanting to be respectful of her boundaries, had done the same. He knew he wasn't going to talk to people at work about it, apart from fishing for information where he could. And it wasn't something he wanted to discuss with his buddies or college chums or a girl he might be dating at the time. It was going to be his family, the people who actually knew Peter Sullivan, who knew Mary and Chip and the club who he would ultimately confide in, if he chose to do so.

That said, they could also be unpredictable, too close to him, to the situation. It would be a gamble either way. There were good enough reasons to keep his mouth shut; he'd done so easily enough for five months. But the truth was he didn't like the way it sat with him, like a secret that needn't be, like he was engaged in something unseemly. Maybe it hadn't been as easy as he liked to pretend. He wasn't sure, but he thought it was time to lift the burden, to spill, as he thought of it, in that impulsive moment, what his training had taught him, his early experiences, that people wanted to talk. It was far more common than not, and even he wasn't immune.

"You met with Mary? Why? Why would you do that?" asked Ruth, genuinely surprised.

Before Leo could answer, Raul did a lap around the table to see if anyone needed anything, in the great tradition of even competent waiters arriving at inopportune times. He was politely waved off as the focus returned to Leo.

"I wanted to know more about what she thinks happened to Peter."

"Have they assigned the case to you, son?" asked Baxter.

"No, I'm just poking around on my own," said Leo delicately. "Truth is there doesn't seem to be much of an investigation to speak of."

"How was Mrs. Sullivan when you saw her?" asked Lynn. "Did she seem OK?"

"I don't know, kind of, maybe not really. She's happy for Chip. I told her we all miss her."

"Did she give you any new information to go on, Leo?" asked Archie. "Anything that might get the wheels in motion again?"

"Not as much as I'd hoped, no real specifics," said Leo, deliberating in his mind whether he should mention the next part. Then he did because, if he couldn't trust the people at that table, then what was the point of anything anyway? "She did make mention of no longer being a big fan of this place anymore."

That detail floated out there, and Leo wondered how it would land.

"Why would she feel that way?" asked Lynn.

"Because she thinks the club factored into his death," said Leo, choosing his words purposefully. "She just doesn't know how exactly."

"And you believe her?" continued Lynn, to which Leo offered a noncommittal shrug.

More silence, though Leo noticed a lack of protest around the notion that the club could be involved in some way, as though it had occurred to some of them before, a theory they'd only admit to themselves in dark hours, cloistered thoughts.

"I remember the police being here so much during that time," said Baxter, thinking back. "Felt like they interviewed everyone knew Peter, those who were working here."

"They did. They actually did a pretty exhaustive job when it came to that."

"So you've read through all the old reports?" asked Baxter.

"I have. I've also started to approach some of the people I used to know, informally, trying to learn anything that may have not made it into the official statements," said Leo. "I even met Samantha Morris for a cup of coffee last month. Do you guys remember her?"

They all remembered Samantha—Sam—Leo's first real girlfriend, his first *time*, his first real heartbreak.

"Wow, Sam, how's she doing?" asked Lynn.

"Good, I think. Married with her first kid on the way. Lives out by Stamford."

"Was she happy to see you?" asked Ruth, who'd been noticeably quiet since Leo brought up investigating the Sullivan case.

"I think so, kind of. We ended on weird terms all those years ago, even if there wasn't that much animosity," said Leo. "But then I turn up out of the blue, a cop now, asking her questions about Uncle Pete from the Restaurant days. She humored me, but I don't think she was that interested in a trip down memory lane."

"Not everyone is," said Ruth.

"If she's pregnant, it would make sense that other things were on her mind," said Lynn. "I always liked her. Sorry, Leo."

Leo shrugged it off, understanding Lynn's point and not taking offense, even if Sam had rather abruptly broken things off with him his senior year without much in the way of explanation, which made for some awkward encounters at the club until they found a new stasis, until Leo went off to college. Then it became less of an issue; people move on, especially the young.

"Did she have anything to volunteer about Sullivan?" asked Archie.

"Not really. She remembered that he was my godfather and understood why I'd be so interested," said Leo. "She always thought of him as a chatty barfly, eager to talk with anyone and everyone. She said his death came as a total shock to her."

"I suppose some people might imagine that about Peter, particularly in those last years . . ." said Baxter, trailing off. Leo nodded along with his father in agreement. He'd read the statements, spoken with Mary, knew his Uncle Pete was spiraling toward something that some couldn't predict, that others were fearful of.

"So Leo Sinclair is officially on the case," said Archie. "Have at it my boy. I hope you nail the bastard."

"Not officially, so please don't mention this to anyone," said Leo to the whole table. "And besides, we don't even know if there's someone to nail."

"There is," said Baxter, leaving it at that. His thoughts were well known: Sullivan never would have shimmied himself over a fence and thrown himself off a cliff with no explanation, no matter how odd his behavior had become; he wasn't nearly that erratic or despondent.

One could tell Archie wanted to continue lauding Leo, his grandson potentially tracking down a killer, but his wife rested a hand on his arm, wordlessly indicating for him to hush up. Lynn's Kent had cast her eyes on her daughter and knew the floor was about to be taken. A mother knows.

"I don't like this one bit," said Ruth strongly. "This all sounds too dangerous, and I don't care for Leo being around it if he needn't be."

Everyone at the table adjusted in their seats, mostly backward. It was only Leo who straightened, then pitched forward a few degrees.

"Mom, it's my job," said Leo, trying to not sound like a petulant child butting heads with their caretaker.

"Actually, it's not. The case hasn't been assigned to you," said Ruth. "And you haven't even been in the department two full years yet."

"Everyone says the best way to learn is to dive in."

Ruth was unconvinced by Leo's point, wore her disapproval visibly on her face.

"Look, Mom, I promise to be careful. I'm just checking into it on the side," said Leo, holding Ruth's gaze. "In all probability, I won't find anything anyway."

"Everyone says they'll be careful, even the ones where something bad happens to them."

"Please don't make me regret telling you all," said Leo to the table, but mostly to his mother. "I wanted you all to know that someone in this building, at the PD, still had Peter's back."

A somewhat impassioned plea, at least by Leo's standards.

"It really means something to you to pursue this?" asked Baxter, to which, Leo nodded his head. All eyes volleyed between the boy's parents now—Baxter grinning with admiration, Ruth looking mildly defeated.

"I obviously can't stop you, Leo. I just hope you know what you're doing," said Ruth, as close to an approval as her son would ever get on the issue.

"I know how to go about this cautiously, I promise," said Leo. "Sorry I had to bring it up on a day like this."

"We're glad you told us, Leo," said Baxter. "We're all proud. It's just going to take some time."

And that was just enough to get everyone over that little hump in Leo's plan, a further glimpse into what it would be like to have a loved one in law enforcement: their daily activities, their personal side quests—there would be nothing easy about it.

The remainder of the Easter holiday played out well enough. They would all go back to Archie and Lynn's house to play some cards, watch some golf on TV, sip from a little-known small batch that tasted more like degreaser from one of Kent Demolition's heavy machines, despite Archie proclaiming it was so pure you wouldn't feel a speck of it in the morning. It ended up being an enjoyable, loose Sunday evening, some of the turmoil from earlier put behind them, at least on the surface, though it would certainly leave an indelible mark on the clan, particularly Leo's parents—the kind of new information you can't unlearn.

Once it was time to leave, Leo spent a few private moments with his mother, hugging her extra tight, her doing the same, probably more so. He knew she worried about him, and he had now compounded that burden. It was her job, and she took it seriously. But she also had to know that despite the peril and heartache of the world, her kids needed a chance to venture out and make their own mistakes, cultivate their own regrets they'd have to learn to overcome, to live through and grow stronger from. Yes, there were flags to plant, but what parent doesn't know the truth, a difficult one to pass on and express through words: that as much as they wanted to protect their babies long past childhood, the fact was no one was going to get out of their lives unscathed. With the benefit of that wisdom, experience, it was a terrible thing to see coming down the road for those you held most precious. But, in a nutshell, that was what it meant to attempt a brave life. So what real choice did Ruth Sinclair have for her son and daughter? None, really. Not that she wouldn't stop worrying about them or trying to offer guidance where she could. Not that she wouldn't say a prayer for their safety or summon a guardian angel to watch over them during an hour of need when she couldn't be there. When they didn't want her there. These weren't small things to do, even if they seemed so—on the contrary, when one poured their heart into those whispered words, those intimate pleas, it was a covenant you couldn't fully understand but would nevertheless pledge your fealty to it if the request was honored, if your loved ones were delivered out of harm's way. These would not be hollow words, something Ruth eschewed—language offered in defense of her children was a wartime oath, a religious decree, a pact she'd honor until her body returned to the rightful cycle of life and death, the circle completed.

* * *

An excerpt from the *Orchard Coils Courier*, weekly print edition, May 1, 1978, page 15, column 1, paragraph 1.

Obituaries

Corporal Peter J. Sullivan was laid to rest in State Veterans Cemetery on April 28 with full military honors.

The heavily attended service celebrated the life of Mr. Sullivan and his unwavering dedication to his country, having earned a Bronze Star for his heroics in France in 1944.

Those closest to Mr. Sullivan have described him as a man "larger than life" and a force in this world that will surely be missed.

He is survived by his wife of 24 years, Mary Sullivan, and their beloved son, Chip.

Mr. Sullivan's family has expressed gratitude toward the community that knew and honored this tragic loss and has humbly requested patience and privacy during these mournful times.

1994

Lynn Sinclair-Moore tapped in a twelve-footer with a kind of flowing effervescence that made her feel five pounds lighter in her Reeboks, like she couldn't miss even if she tried. She almost lamented wasting that type of flow on a non-tour event, as though the magic would be better reserved for when some real money came into play. But when that incredible focus appeared, elusive like pixie dust and just as likely to dissipate without warning, one had to capitalize on it—even when it was just a charity tournament.

Lynn had seen this phenomenon firsthand out on the circuit—equally talented people divined on certain days, cast away on others. A force that builds on itself, feeds, and powers in a loop. You might wake up feeling that way. It might manifest early in the round, maybe even on the first tee shot. Or show up at some critical juncture, help create a turning point that carried the day. It was the kind of sorcery that doesn't answer to anyone, but in a packed field of competitors, all will court its grace to give them just one lucky bounce, one friendly roll—anything to find that groove. That was what it took most often, on any given day, to separate the winners from the losers.

Books had been written on the subject. Trainers preached and offered paths to tap into it. Even some hucksters and gurus promised to sprinkle this magic on your Wheaties if you hired them as your swing coach or short-game consultant. To Lynn's credit, she'd never really bought into that type of serendipity being bottled and delivered to your front door. She knew the only way to tap into that state of mind was through a murky accord with oneself: fleeting, mercurial, different for everybody and not just something you can will into existence. In fact, the more you beseeched it, the less likely it would manifest. So you had to work around its absence, polish those rough edges, create situations in which it might appear, lure it, and when it didn't arrive, not begrudge it—another surefire way never to experience nirvana out on the course.

That was how Lynn came to think of the zone, and though it would be nice to enjoy such privilege more often, particularly during a televised tournament, she knew it was reckless not to appreciate the muse when it arrived, shaving strokes off her score like a deli slicer while she played a game she truly loved—especially knowing the juju would fade sooner than later, as was its nature.

Lynn bent down and retrieved the ball from the cup, birdying O Triple C's par-four twelfth hole, a layout she'd played hundreds, if not a thousand times in her life, thousands of times in her mind. Her mom, Ruth, performed a cheeky golf clap in the direction of her daughter, knowing full well Lynn was dialed in and having an outstanding round. She'd seen Lynn on TV more than a few times playing strong golf, was good at noticing the signs apart from the leaderboard: certain body language, certain types of shots made to look effortless. She'd also seen Lynn play not so well at times, amplified on TV, not the easiest thing for a parent to watch, particularly when the broadcast is intent on highlighting your child's presence for reasons other than stroke play. That said, Ruth very much enjoyed watching Lynn play in the flesh, up close and personal like the old days of their roaming the club, some of their former gestures and mannerisms still very much alive between the two of them, as though time hadn't passed, as though not all her former self had been weeded away and pruned by Sachin Moore and other various coaches who had taken the reins on Lynn's training over the past decade. Ruth could still see the slight shadow of the girl in the woman before her, some of the foundations she'd taught her as a child—maybe in the slight hitch of her waist or how she approached the settled ball from a certain angle. The traces were there and always would be to her mother, for only her to see, where even the ghosts couldn't hide from her.

And it was Ruth's smile that corrected Lynn's awkward thinking, reminding her there was nothing inconsequential, inferior about the day's event, just because it wouldn't count toward the league standings or cumulative earnings purse. In fact, when all was said and done, these might be the days she remembered most for the year. It wasn't a small thing to return to Orchard Coils, to the course you cut your teeth on, and play in your own inaugural charity tournament: a women-only event with all the proceeds going to breast cancer research. To serve as host and key benefactor at a place you cherished, partaking in a game that had become your livelihood, surrounded by people you loved. To think of it as anything less than special or worthy of your top game was silly, foolhardy when Lynn really considered it. If anything, now was a great time to show these wonderful women exactly what she was made of, the prodigal child returning home. Besides, Lynn wanted to lay some groundwork that day. She had big ideas for the event in future years, and making a splash would only help her cause, more so if she broke her own personal course record. There were so many ways to broaden the scope of its fund-raising arm; she just needed this first year to go off well and then plan accordingly, strike while the iron was hot—a well-honed talent of hers.

Lynn had just turned thirty-one. The past few years of her life had been a blur and wash—she could hardly believe how fast the time had gone and had recently become aware that she was past due to start giving back, that she'd slipped behind the curve. The inception of that charity tournament was the first step in that plan.

She joined Ruth, waiting for her in the golf cart, and readied for the thirteenth hole.

"You trying to show up all us old ladies with that enchanted putter of yours?" asked Ruth, teasing her daughter.

"It's funny how I still remember so much about these greens," said Lynn, cracking open a bottle of water from a local distributor, an event sponsor. "It's all bringing back a lot of fond memories. Maybe that's why I'm playing well."

"You also play some of the toughest courses around the world now," said Ruth. "Play and win, I might add. So I think it would make sense that your little home course would become pedestrian to your talents."

The thought had occurred to Lynn, but it felt like a betrayal to dwell on it.

"I don't really win that often, Mom—only four times in the last seven years," said Lynn while Ruth whipped them around the cart path. Lynn took in all the familiar sights, waving to those who might seek her attention—something you'd think she'd be exceedingly used to by that point, though it did take on a different patina nestled back in Connecticut, playing in the deep X-12, no cameras or media hounds. She felt insulated, protected from the lesser aspects of her public life. Though she knew there would be some publicity to deal with later in the day, to help boost the signal of the cause and her own standing in the LPGA, where aligning oneself with charitable events was practically page-one advice from their unofficial handbook, their guidance on crafting a marketable image, a branding strategy.

"Don't be overly modest, Lynn. Besides, too many trophies can be garish," said Ruth, still teasing her daughter, having a lark over it. "How many top-ten finishes have you gotten this year?"

"You know that answer."

"But I love hearing you say it."

"Ten."

"Ten, exactly. You know how amazing that is, don't you?"

"Most days, I just feel like a grinder out there," said Lynn. "Been kind of the trademark of my career."

"Until now. You're still coming into your own; 1995 is going to be your year."

"That's what Sachin keeps telling me."

"And what do you think?"

"I like where my game's at. But it's up to me to execute over the next year or so to bring my CV to the next level," said Lynn. "Before the window starts to close on me."

"What window?" asked Ruth, but before Lynn could elaborate, they'd arrived at the thirteenth hole, a nifty par three that forced the player to shoot over a fountain of water anchored into a small body of water directly in front of the rolling green—not quite an island hole, but with some of those characteristics.

Ruth and Lynn got out of the cart and joined the two women they'd been paired up with. One was the current female club champion, Sally Wright, early twenties, who, like Lynn, had been a member of O Triple C her whole life. Sally was a gangly girl, all limbs and angles, though possessed a savage golf IQ, which she used very much to her advantage. The second was Elizabeth Cornwall, wife of influential club member Grant Cornwall, who surely pulled a string or two to obtain the coveted spot in the foursome with the tournament's star attraction and local celebrity. Lynn knew Elizabeth mostly by reputation. Ruth knew her well enough from her years at the club. They weren't enemies by any stretch, but "friends" might have been pushing it. Ruth had always found Elizabeth more than a bit stuffy, the kind of woman whose highest life ambition was to own the anchor house on a cul-de-sac, to befriend families whose lineage could be traced back to the Mayflower. Elizabeth, for her part, could hardly understand why Ruth cared so much about cataloguing birds, thought she was too prone to emotional outbursts, sometimes alcohol related. Basically, two women cut from different cloth. Ruth had wondered how Sally would get along with Elizabeth in a golf cart all day. It might not help that Sally was less than half Elizabeth's age and already a far superior golfer. Or maybe the two had a preexisting relationship Ruth wasn't even aware of. When in doubt, there was always the option of silence, never a terrible fallback and a tactic Elizabeth Cornwall could unleash with devastating efficacy.

The four of them congregated in the tee box, admiring the fountain in all its glory, watching the mist plume around the water, refracting light into broken rainbows.

"I almost holed this pin when I won the club championship last month," said Sally, throwing a few tufts of grass in the air to gauge the wind, hoping what she said didn't come across as bragging. "Missed by two feet. Still chasing my first hole in one."

"How many strokes did you win by?" asked Lynn.

"Just one."

"Nail biter."

"I was so nervous on eighteen trying to close it out. I thought everybody could see right through me, like they were wondering who this imposter was," said Sally, who hit her nine iron off the tee and found the backside of the green—the ladies chitchatting, playing ready golf, not hung up on the proper sequence, rightly so for a charity event. "Do you ever still get nervous out there, Lynn?"

"Sure do. I'd be nervous if I ever stopped getting nervous out there," said Lynn, a friendly detail, an encouraging smile for Sally.

They hushed up for Elizabeth, who hit her eight iron, which cleared the fountain but found a dastardly placed bunker to the right of the green, crowned up tight, not so far away from the pin, what would create an awkward shot—Elizabeth looked less than pleased though would not dare vocalize it.

"Unlucky," said Ruth to her contemporary, who nodded modestly in return.

"Why would you be nervous about that?" asked Sally, returning to her earlier thread with Lynn.

"Being a little nervous lets me know I still care after all these years," said Lynn, dropping a ball, forgoing a tee, then striking a blooper with a very lofted wedge, easily clearing the water and landing the ball ten feet from the hole as though it were nothing—she might have had her eyes closed for all they knew. "The trick is not to let that little bit of nervousness adversely affect your play, to get in the way of the goal at hand."

The three women looked to Lynn's ball on the green, which actually caught a phantom dip and rolled an extra three feet closer to the hole—the rich getting richer—which Lynn would tap in for an easy birdie, a fait accompli.

"Now you're just showing off, young lady," said Ruth, hitting her own ball into the light rough to the left of the green, mumbling an obscenity just out of the group's earshot.

"Well, I suppose we all did avoid the water," said Elizabeth, trying to find the bright side of the game after some unfortunate breaks for the elder players.

"Come on, Mrs. Cornwall, show me how it's done, getting that little fellow out of the sand," said Lynn, hell-bent on and fully committed to schmoozing everyone in her crosshairs that day, including and maybe especially the wives of the board members.

Not that Elizabeth minded or was opaque to being buttered up a bit. In fact, she was enjoying the attention from their guest of honor. And why shouldn't she? Aside from being a professional golfer, as many people at the club knew Lynn had strived to become since her early days struggling at the range, her formative years at Tulane, she had also matured into a truly beautiful woman, radiant from a career spent outdoors applying reasonable amounts of sunblock. It was a powerful one-two punch that Lynn Sinclair was working with. And as her career began to pick up steam over the past few years, so did the attention from sponsors that were always on the prowl for the next fresh face that might launch some new campaign or endorse a flagship product.

Lynn's magnetism was quickly noted and impossible to miss on the tour, as early as her rookie season. She garnered a little extra TV time despite not being able to break away from the pack on most Saturdays and Sundays. And that was presuming she'd made the cut, which often didn't happen as she was coming up, when there was zero TV time allotted to the woman's tour prior to the weekend. It wasn't until her first tournament win that the golfing industry took a much more serious look at Lynn Sinclair-Moore. The first call came from Srixon, not the most well-regarded name in the field, but solid enough when they were offering you a one-year deal for some print ads to advocate their brand, to wear a small patch on your sleeve while on tour. Lynn, excited at the prospects of her first endorsement, discussed it with her former collegiate coach and now husband, Sachin Moore, who also served as her business manager and closest confidant. Neither of them bristled at Srixon's offer, even if the terms were short and the money far from earth shattering—it was still a way to get Lynn in the door, to mug for some glossies that might appear in prominent sports magazines. And if she continued to win more tournaments and sell more Srixon balls while flashing her pearly whites and stretching her lithe body for the camera, more offers were bound to roll in. Better ones, more lucrative. So she took the deal with Srixon and prepared herself for the bigger and better things that were right around the corner.

Lynn proceeded not to win a single tournament over the next two years. Srixon had re-upped her for a second year, but once it looked like her lone championship in South Carolina had been a fluke, they parted ways with her at the contract's expiration. She was now twenty-seven years old, making a living on the tour through volume, traveling almost nonstop, grinding out every stroke for a bit more prize money—the difference between eighteenth place and seventeenth place could mean a few thousand extra in the coffers, crucial to keeping the show on the road, the dream alive. Sachin had quit his job at Tulane years ago to travel with Lynn full time, and though he wasn't bringing in revenue, the two considered themselves a team. But some of that momentum from Lynn's midtwenties had dissipated and felt long ago as she was steadily closing in on the big three-oh. Everyone knew an athlete had a certain shelf life, and in that regard, Father Time remained un-bested. And while they didn't speak about it aloud, it certainly put a strain on every joint and pillar in their marriage—a union that was not devoid of scrutiny and scandal, given their age gap and previous coach-student dynamic, prodded from both outsiders and their families within.

But Lynn continued to believe in her abilities, despite her lack of results; her game was actually improving, becoming nimbler, sharper in areas not easily seen by the untrained eye. Her mind had grown strong, reinforcing itself with disappointment, then against disappointment, opening new doors that might lead to future success. Sachin agreed with his wife. Whether because he truly believed it or because it was just the prudent thing to do, he was savvy enough to avoid undermining her confidence or casting doubts on her talent—a cardinal sin when dealing with high-performing athletes. He knew no one would be her greatest advocate apart from herself; he'd have to be OK settling for second best. He wasn't wrong—it was the smart play. So they carried on together, through thick and thin. Mostly thin. They took cheap flights. Stayed in modest motel rooms. Did their own laundry. Didn't dine out much. Or buy stuff. They had a small one-bedroom apartment back near Tulane with a beater car parked in the lot. They were seldom there, and Sachin had a buddy check in on the place from time to time, take the old Nissan out for a spin to keep the battery alive. Their goal was low overhead and steady, if not slow revenue, meant to increase over time. The decade was about to turn over, and while frugal living hadn't been celebrated in the eighties, perhaps the nineties would be different, more austere. Lynn and Sachin hoped to hunker down for winter, come back strong and survive another year on the circuit—if they could.

Then, in the spring of 1990, the very first tournament of the year, Lynn went out and won the thing outright, convincingly so, by a margin of four strokes. She looked different out there: a determination in her body language and some of her sanguine nature now shucked away, replaced with a little anger, some resentment, maybe desperation. They'd white-knuckled through the winter, and there were a few weeks they were unsure if they could hack it for another year. The pundits and announcers speculated throughout the weekend, some wondering if Lynn had grown up a bit, an odd calculation given she'd never been a frivolous or callous person but perhaps lacked the heart of an assassin, the pedigree of a killer. That was what maturing meant to some people, leaving a trail of bodies in your dust, holding a crystal trophy over your head for all your detractors to see. They may not have been wrong. Whatever the change was technically, she proved to be a different competitor those four seminal days in April, and it was the exact thing she needed to happen—*they* needed to happen.

She finished in second place just two weeks later, barely missing back-to-back tournament wins to a grizzled veteran of the tour, a fan favorite who'd played out of her shoes to beat Lynn—a swan-song victory that would be her last, being forced to retire a year later with back and hip injuries. That veteran would openly admit to herself and to the press that it was a small miracle she'd held Lynn off that Sunday. Lynn remained graceful in defeat and offered homage to her victor, though she silently stewed over the loss that night, brooding in her dumpy hotel with its leaky faucets and unpredictable climate controls, barely sleeping. Sachin had never seen her so angry over a loss and considered it a good thing. Despite that loss, the money they made from that April alone would fuel them comfortably for the year, even if they didn't earn another nickel in 1990, which would hardly be the case. A few days after Lynn's second place, Sachin received a call from Adidas, and by the end of May, she was signed to a three-year deal with the sports apparel juggernaut for an aggregate $2 million, not including bonus and incentive clauses.

Their ship had finally come in.

Since then, over the past four years, there had been three more championships and many more endorsement deals to boot. In fact, the impressive career earnings Lynn had amassed during the first half of the nineties paled in comparison to what she would make from Adidas, TaylorMade, Titleist, and other staples of the industry. There had even been some non-golf work for Delta and Radisson that brought in a pretty penny. But the big opportunity Lynn currently had her eye on, the one she really wanted and was waiting to hear back on, was the Gap. The clothing retailer had brought her in for some test shoots, a mock-up of her modeling chops for their upcoming spring line of 1995. She knew that if she could land that gig to represent that kind of cultural and fashion touchstone, it would cement her crossover appeal and fully introduce her to the non-golf world, where it might never matter if she ever sunk another improbable putt again. In other words, she'd become undeniable; her future opportunities outside the sport would increase exponentially. In her mind, a partnership with the Gap would be a perfect fit. She just needed those corporate kingmakers to land on the same conclusion. She was supposed to hear back from them by the end of the week, which had come and gone with no word. Now she was forced to patiently wait, not wanting to appear too eager—in that sense, hosting the charity tournament at O Triple C had come at a good time, a worthy distraction as she did her best to place the prospective Gap contract in the recesses of her busied mind.

* * *

Pair of aces checked and the whole table opted for a free card, taking a round off from betting into the anemic pot, currently worth about twenty bucks. Fifth street was dealt, and Sachin deferred his aces again, despite their still being the best hand showing. The table wasn't quite sure if Sachin had figured out how to set a trap or just didn't realize that now would be a good time to lead out with those bullets and take it down. Regardless, the other active players—three of them—were willing to defer in hopes of catching up. Leo, who folded after the first round of betting, had been giving Sachin some on-the-fly tutorials and advice throughout the night, as Sachin had never played seven card in his life. In fact, Sachin only had a cursory understanding of what beat what and was still confused as to why trips beat two pair—wouldn't four cards be better than three? Leo had been sitting to Sachin's immediate right, and the table tolerated him getting the novice up to speed. But two-plus hours into the game and many drinks later, the other five players were ready to stand Sachin on his own two feet and send Leo's assistance back to the peanut gallery. Leo wasn't in total disagreement with this notion and had curbed his involvement in the current hand, though he was telepathically trying to convince his brother-in-law to bet those damn aces to high heaven. But Sachin wasn't receiving the message or wasn't open to such alternative methods of communication. Hence, all the checking. Sixth street got dealt, and Sachin was inexplicably gifted a third ace, to the communal groans of the table. Either realizing he had a monster or heeding the table's guttural cues, Sachin finally threw in, under-betting the pot with a paltry five dollars—though you'd never seen three men fold so fast. Even a small bet by mathematical standards wasn't going to solicit an additional wooden nickel with trip aces exposed. He raked in the small pot, pleased with the win unassisted by Leo, and smiled earnestly at his fellow card sharks, who smiled back at him, all thinking roughly the same thing—*dead money*. They just needed to give it some time.

Poker was funny like that. Novices were welcomed, if not encouraged, though mostly in the hopes of fleecing them by the end of the night.

It was the Saturday night of Lynn's inaugural charity tournament at the club. The golf had ended many hours ago, as had the raffle and giveaways and pig roast and all the other little events that had contributed to the day's success. The small smattering of media was long gone, and the club, which had been humming since sunup, getting prepared for the festivities, was winding down as midnight approached, with only a few people still left on property, mostly congregated in the Restaurant. The bulk of these stragglers were playing poker, seven players to be exact. The star of the table was Sachin, who'd been working for months to help Lynn craft and pull off the day. The tournament's success had very much weighed on him, and its favorable outcome had been a massive weight lifted off his shoulders. Not surprisingly, some of the more influential members and staff wanted to show him a good time, pick his brain a little about golf, about traveling the world. There was also some curiosity about the man in general, not least of all how he'd been able to snatch up Lynn Sinclair in both love and life, let alone sport.

Sachin had always had an air of intrigue about him, almost mysterious if you didn't know him well. He was certainly a handsome man: very dark hair, expressive eyes, rich skin color, bone structure that stood for something. His Indian ancestry only added to the effect, as though it made him wise beyond his years, a rarity despite the fact he'd been born in Poughkeepsie and spoke without much of an accent. For all those reasons and more, women adored him, thought he was swarthy, cultured, when really, he considered himself more of a glorified jock. He hated museums, reading, loved golf, hobnobbing, winning. But if Sachin was anything, it was shrewd, that trait probably coming directly from his parents, who were born in New Delhi and immigrated to the States, newly married, both to take jobs at IBM. He knew how to play up his charms and was also good at letting people believe what they wanted to believe—particularly when it worked to his advantage. So when he was invited to throw a few cards around for an impromptu game, normally something that wouldn't appeal to him, his initial impulse was to pass, to claim exhaustion from the long day, which would have been understandable. But the fact was he wasn't tired. On the contrary, he was still amped up. The day had been a rousing success, thanks in part to his efforts, and while being the husband of Lynn Sinclair was a tremendous thing, it was also nice when people wanted to treat him like the center of attention, when he didn't have to share the spotlight with his better half. Lynn, who wouldn't have been caught dead gambling at a card table with a bunch of dudes, her brother included, was undoubtedly tucked back in at her parent's house, gossiping with her mom and dad, letting the adrenaline of the day dissipate, eventually lulling her into a near comatose sleep—though not before replaying missed shots in her mind, how she could have approached them differently, chastising herself even after superb play in an exhibition event. The pursuit of greatness and its price—a gear not easy to downshift.

So Sachin was a free man for the night. He took a small hit from an eyedropper of THC on his tongue, a mix he'd picked up overseas, and planned to sip some tequila and let these Connecticut stuffed shirts fawn over him a bit, maybe make some inroads or just see how much of an edge he could take off for the night. The microdose would help. And besides, Leo had shown up at the tail end of the tournament, his shift finally over at the station, and was sure to join the card game, whether some of these guys actually wanted him there or not. Sachin had some ideas of Leo's standing at O Triple C but made it clear Leo should be reserved a seat at the table. No one openly objected. Leo was family to Sachin, after all, even if Sachin had always thought his brother-in-law was a square. But he would keep an eye out for Sachin in the unfamiliar clubhouse with these unfamiliar men playing an unfamiliar game. Leo was good like that; Sachin would readily admit as much. The truth was he liked the guy, always had, even if they seemed to view the world through very different lenses.

So around nine p.m., Sachin was wrangled in by some committee head, Grant Cornwall, the longtime big swinging dick at the club who was looking to entertain their honorary guest into the late night. Sachin knew that Cornwall's wife had wormed her way into the foursome with Lynn and Ruth, knew they were big-fish-in-a-small-pond kind of people. Which was fine— plenty of that in the world. He allowed himself to be treated hospitably, open to flattery. It wasn't so terrible to have his ego stroked. Who knew if this Cornwall guy had some ulterior motives or was just genuinely trying to be a good host, a steward for the O Triple C experience? In Sachin's opinion, it was probably the former. But it didn't really matter; he'd roll with it all the same. Casually, Sachin and Grant, with Leo now in tow, made it inside the Restaurant and sat at a table in the corner farthest away from the bar. There were already a few other men dealing out chips and fiddling with two decks of cards, drinks before them. It was hardly late yet—still plenty of time to let your fuel of choice do its worse, which was likely once the testosterone and bravado took over. Plus the money. No one wanted to look soft in front of the other, so there was bound to be some jockeying, even in a friendly game—welcome to a card table of men. If one were searching for nuance and civility, feel free to look elsewhere.

Sachin had mentioned to Grant that he didn't really know how to play poker well. Grant just slapped him on the back and told him they'd walk him through the bullet points, that Leo could get him caught up while playing. That was the first time Grant seemed to acknowledge Leo's existence, that he would indeed be joining them at the table for the evening. They exchanged terse smiles, Leo giving Grant a brief glimpse of his cop stare, which he'd been perfecting over the past decade, enough to make Grant flinch, to look away first. There'd always been a little uneasy blood between the Cornwalls and the Sinclairs, and it hadn't lessened through the younger generations, even if they'd mostly been polite about it—something about New England manners and quietly holding those old grudges close to the vest.

Sachin, Grant, and Leo joined the other four men at the table and put in a drink order with an overly attentive waitress Leo had never seen before. He recognized three of the four players immediately. Across from him was Cobb Webb, the head pro for the past twenty years—the Texan transplant who had found his footing in Hartford County, of all places, though Cobb would swear fealty to his lone star roots to anyone who would listen. This was the same Cobb Leo had worked for in his youth, during those heady high school and college years—a guy Leo never fully understood, given Cobb didn't seem to have the strongest work ethic but did just enough to maybe not get shitcanned. Not an easy trick to pull off for twenty years, so Leo figured Cobb must have some sleight of hand he wasn't privy to. He was a personable dude, Leo would grant him that, particularly with those who counted the most at the club, which made Leo think Cobb had stronger political instincts than he let on, a skill set Leo sorely lacked but knew he'd have to develop if he wanted to get anywhere in the PD. Funny thing about Cobb was he couldn't golf worth a damn. No one in their right mind would take a lesson from him; those services were best procured from the assistant pros, a revolving duo who didn't hang around too long, given the lack of upward mobility. In Cobb's defense, though, the man did know how to run an efficient and tidy pro shop—good wares and fair prices—a portion of the proceeds of which he'd pocket as per his contract.

Leo and Cobb had always gotten along well enough, dating back to when Leo was a kid and Cobb entering his thirties, still wondering if he'd regret leaving the big sky expanse of Borden County for a shot at something bigger and better, albeit it in drive-through Connecticut, with its whopping four highways. Now they were both adults and continued to get on well enough, seeing as their respective interests seldom clashed. Fact was Cobb liked to take a little credit for helping Leo come up. Fact was membership at the club had done extremely well under Cobb's tenure, so rightly or wrongly, some accolades were bound to stick to the man, who was adroit at leveraging a favorable outcome without talking about it until blue in the face. He had some of the hallmarks of a blowhard, but it would be a mistake to label Cobb as such; truth was he was anything but. His was a more internal hubris, a hidden cunningness.

Leo and Cobb nodded heads at one another, that was all it took in ways of recognition, and a formal introduction was made to Sachin, though he'd met Cobb briefly earlier in the day, right before the tournament had kicked off. Grant Cornwall had taken it upon himself to deal the first hand to the table, two hole cards down and one face up, while another man shuffled the spare deck behind the dealer to keep the game moving. They were using a decent set of composite chips, not plastic, with an almost clay-like feel that would be tricky to manipulate with your fingers if you hadn't practiced on them before. The blinds, antes, betting amounts, and pot maxes had been preordained without much controversy. Ultimately, it was designed to be a friendly and relatively low-stakes affair—the knives out wouldn't injure anyone's wallet so much, but other targets—heart, mind, balls—were open season at any card table.

The eager waitress—her name was Judy—returned with pure agave sipping tequila for Sachin, a pint of Coors Light for Leo, and a club soda for Grant, which went uncommented on, despite teetotaling being good fodder for ribbing as it was known Grant had been sober for the past two years after some adverse medical news—rumors that seemed true enough—which allowed the man to drink soft and not have a federal case made out of it by the degenerates at O Triple C: namely, his best friends.

The high card showing per the first hand, after the initial deal, was a king to the player sitting directly to Cobb's left—a kid in his late twenties named Wes Baker, who'd become, over the past five years, the sort of de facto leader of the newest incantation of the stooges, that weird sect of formerly merry pranksters, counterculture advocates, the club had never been able to fully rid themselves of for close to a century. A fifth column as they were, though perhaps their history and antics were more tolerated than people liked to rail against and, therefore, were allowed to persist. The stooges had almost faded into obscurity in the eighties when club membership downticked, and the world seemed ferociously hung up on the acquisition of wealth—more so than usual. And not just those in the usual power structures, but everyday folk who suddenly pinned their entire self-worth on squeezing out a few extra digits to the left of the decimal, only to flash it around in a slightly bigger house, a somewhat shinier and noisier car. During that time, it had never been less en vogue to act a fool at a country club, the vice culture having sucked the joyful folly out of everyday life, forcing a single-minded materialism into the zeitgeist and rendering the stooges into a quiet period where more than a few people at O Triple C felt they permanently belonged. But, with the passing of time and an uptick in Clintonian-era peace and globalism, the stooges ended up just having to abide a soft reset. They had, indeed, returned.

It was Wes Baker who seemed to bring about the resurgence in this subgroup, invigorating the contrarian sect at the club, which now, in the mid-nineties, took on the form of technology: more specifically, home computing. Apparently, Wes had a high-paying job at United Technologies that revolved around the tower, monitor, and mouse. Most people hadn't really developed a need or even a desire to use a personal computer; they saw it as an alien concept, something to be leery of. But if you allowed him, Wes would talk your ear off about weird stuff you'd never heard of before in what sounded like made-up terms, like *modems* and *motherboards* and *graphic cards*. At the club, through many of his diatribes, Wes discovered a few more computer enthusiasts and subsequently banded them together and took on the stooges' moniker, replacing antiquated pranks with a different kind of dark magic, one that conjured its energy in microprocessors, in a symphony of ones and zeros. Suffice it to say not everyone was thrilled with this resurgence—mostly the old-timers—and viewed Wes and his cohort as stitched-together heretics, openly discussing sorcery that ran afoul of the pencil and pad, that eschewed the great outdoors. Of course, there were others who just viewed them as an amalgam of nerds, hardly stooges, and they were fair game around the club, subject to derision, much like a middle school locker room, though with a little less towel snapping and more open criticism about wasting one's precious hours in front of a lifeless screen, probably absorbing levels of cancer-causing radiation that would express themselves in the brain or bowels ten years hence.

You know, pleasant comments like that, among *friends*.

All that said, Leo still found the young man exceedingly intelligent and polite and socially well adjusted, despite the quote-unquote nerd label that had been slapped on him. He also showed a very clear reverence for the game of golf, even if he was prone to talking jargon on the course when truly, that kind of tech speak was better reserved for when they returned to the pro shop, maybe the Restaurant, There, Wes could bore them all he wanted, so long as he was buying. Leo hoped Wes would mind his audience at the card table and not hijack the banter with one of his Computer Science 101 lectures. In fact, Leo was rather curious how Wes had even landed a seat at the table in the first place. Were they short a player? Was it dumb luck and timing or some other motive that got him into the fray? It could be nothing, random, but the cop in Leo always let his mind run out those kinds of threads, figuring it would keep him sharp, lest he abuse it, forget to turn it off, and drive himself paranoid. He wouldn't be the first cop to go down that road.

Leo was sure of one thing—if Wes dove into that internet thing he was always blathering about, someone was going to pop him one in the nose and send him packing. And it might very well be Leo.

With the first action still to Wes, his king high, he threw in the first bet of the night, a red chip to build the pot, worth ten dollars in the exchange.

To Wes's left was Ronnie Kemper, who had also taken the time to introduce himself to Sachin, offered his hand to him and Leo. Ronnie and Leo already knew each other well enough from around the club. Plus Ronnie worked in the town's treasury office, which technically made the two beholden to the same employer, the town of Orchard Coils. But how Leo knew Ronnie best was from recently pulling him out of a wayward car that had semi-crashed into a gnarled patch of back roads, clipping a guardrail and spinning a couple of times into excavated land, formerly a Macoun orchard. There was an awful lot of cosmetic damage to the car: one side caved in a bit, smashed mirrors, blown-out tires. Ronnie got his bell rung something good, the blood thundering in his inner ears, though it wasn't easy to separate the concussion from the inebriation, both with similar traits, both playing their part. Leo had been working a rare late shift; his seniority in the department now kept him out of the graveyard and more in the light of day. It was past two a.m. when Leo stumbled on the car in the desolate area, taillights still blazing away. He actually preferred trolling the back roads during those types of shifts, always had. He figured if something bad was going to go down, better chance it would take place off the beaten path.

Leo was able to get Ronnie out of the car. He miraculously didn't seem to have any bad injuries, not even a busted nose from the deployed airbag. In Leo's ten years on the force, he'd become accustomed to the weirdness of automobile accidents: how some people can walk away from horrific wrecks with nary a scratch while some bump their heads the wrong way in a fender bender and wind up in critical care with some hematoma blossoming in their gray matter. It was an odd body of evidence to accumulate over the decade, but one Leo had grown a good antenna for and leveraged like a triage nurse. He propped Ronnie up on his squad car and started to ask him a bunch of questions, shone a penlight into his eyes to see how his pupils would react. The man reeked of alcohol but was coming around and sobering up enough to slowly grasp his predicament. His drunkenness. The late hour. The accident. And now he was talking with Leo Sinclair from the club, only this version was wearing dark blue, and it was Officer Sinclair, in full uniform, and the awfulness of the situation had finally dawned on him. He would be arrested and probably lose his job in the town office. He would lose his wife. Then he remembered why he was out so late to begin with, drunk as a skunk, which further compounded his despondency with a swiftness that his addled mind could no longer contain. He broke down and sobbed, slumping out of Leo's hands and onto the ground, his back up against the car tires, his head wobbling under the crook of his arm. Ronnie wanted to die right then and there. And Leo was left to observe, then consider what was most often his primary thought: *How am I going to repair this situation?*

Leo got Ronnie back up from the ground and dusted him off, got him to sit in the passenger seat of his squad car, very deliberately not putting him in the back seat. He then told Ronnie to compose himself and explain exactly what the hell was going on. Leo was pretty sure he already knew the answer, or at least the core of it. Guys like Ronnie tended to fly off the rails for one reason alone—big trouble with the wife. And that was basically what Ronnie confirmed. A pressure cooker at home had been building around money and fidelity and regrets. Leo allowed the man to pour it out, as patiently as he could, hoping his patrolling services weren't needed elsewhere. It was a sob story for sure, but Ronnie's to purge, to get the toxins out. Leo ran Ronnie's license through the car's onboard, just to ensure he didn't have any extracurriculars out there that Leo needed to know about. He didn't; the man's record was squeaky clean. That counted for something when trying to figure out if someone was a threat to society or just made a bonehead decision. Leo was now dealing with a decent-enough guy who may be having the absolute worst night of his life, and it was up to him whether to make it exponentially worse or to staunch the bleeding, both of which were in his power. It was the type of conundrum they didn't teach in the academy, that couldn't be broached in a classroom or a printed manual. It could only be learned through experience, through hushed conversations with veteran officers in the taxpayer hallways, grabbing a beer after a session at the firing range. *What kind an officer of the peace do you want to be? How do you mete out justice? What rules can be bent, broken? What will it mean to you saving a life? Ruining one?* Leo had wrestled with his understanding of this variety of questions for years, still did, which led him to believe he had a lot to offer the world with respects to his type of policing but also that he still had plenty more to learn. That one could truly never learn enough. He would have been fully justified slapping a pair of bracelets on Ronnie's wrists and bringing him up on more than a few charges. By the letter of the law, it shouldn't have even been a debate. But Leo wasn't willing to work that binary, at least not ten years in—to view the world as only black and white and pretend nuance didn't exist, that no room need be made for the gray.

Ronnie had made an incredibly reckless decision, 100 percent, but at the end of the day, he didn't have a pattern of such behavior, and no one was injured. No one was even around to witness it. He'd blasted through his crying jag and cathartic spiel and now sat docile, spent—no longer possessing the energy to beg Leo for his life. He looked out the darkened window, seemingly beaten or resigned to relegate his fate to Officer Sinclair, a man he kind of knew from the club, friendly enough, average golfer at best. It wasn't a slam-dunk decision for Leo, but he pretty much knew what he was going to do, which was to let Ronnie sleep it off on his couch.

He'd write the crash up to a deer strike, common on those back roads, and doubted anyone would raise an eyebrow. He'd call Ronnie's wife and further the lie, sure to wake her up, though who knew? Maybe she'd been up all night worrying about Ronnie. The somewhat tricky thing was to keep Ronnie awake for a while, just to ensure he didn't have some type of real head damage, that his breathing wouldn't falter in his sleep. A small risk, but Leo wanted to avoid the hospital if he could, where they would surely pick up on Ronnie's inebriated state, poke holes in the notion the man had any business behind the wheel of a car, deer or no deer. That wouldn't be good for anybody, including Leo. Basically, it all amounted to a great deal of aggravation for Leo over the next five hours or so—hours needed to clear Ronnie of his immediate troubles with the law and mild concussion. Then Ronnie would have to attend to the pressing issues he was facing back on the home front, where the trouble all began.

It played out well enough for Leo. No one at the station batted an eye as to his whereabouts that night while supposedly patrolling the town; his walkie had stayed on without so much as a crackle. Ronnie was kept awake for a bit, then allowed to snooze on the couch, Leo keeping a watchful eye on him, paying note to the man's snoring, a reasonable enough indicator that he was alive and breathing. By seven a.m., it was time to rouse Ronnie and give him a lift home. Ronnie, groggy, though more alert than he'd been eight hours before, thanked Leo for saving his bacon, professed the massive debt he would owe Leo for the rest of his life, relieved he still had a life. Leo didn't argue, but neither did he feel compelled to further spell it out for Ronnie. He was tired and wired, and his compassion for the man had reached its summit—even if he was just a smart-enough dude who had done a very dumb thing.

Leo still had to return the cruiser to the station and hope no one picked up on him shirking his responsibilities for those few hours, let alone allowing a drunk driver off the hook. He gave Ronnie the name and number of a discreet wrecker to call and get his car towed back home or to his mechanic. He reminded Ronnie that it was a deer strike, to leave it at that, to say little else. Then he told Ronnie that if he ever caught him drinking and driving in Orchard Coils, or any town in the county for that matter, that Leo would personally see that the charges got bumped up to the point where Ronnie would be using taxi services for the rest of his natural life. Ronnie understood and thanked Leo profusely, despite the less-than-subtle threat. Leo drove the man home to see his wife waiting in the doorway of their split level: a well-manicured lawn, an honest-to-goodness white picket fence border. Leo hung around long enough to see them embrace on the front steps. The complexity of marriage: he'd seen it plenty of times in these civilians. They were all a shade of the same color. Just the way cops are all kind of the same. Human frailty, contradiction—it was a recipe for disaster. Leo knew his thoughts were going dark; he'd played favorites and didn't feel overly good or bad about it, but still, it was a dicey habit to indulge, to grow comfortable with. He needed a few hours of shut-eye to reset. That would help put the ugliness of the night to bed.

That was only four months back, and the two men hadn't spoken much about it—and "not much" meant not at all—which suited them both just fine.

Ronnie folded to Wes Baker's bet, and the next time Judy came around, he made a point of ordering a water, which would be the only thing he drank for the remainder of the night, ridicules aside—more than remembering his promise to Leo, more than noticing the sly stare the cop fixed on the man when the waitress asked if he'd wanted another whiskey.

"No, water's fine. Thanks."

Ronnie's fold forced the action to the only person at the table Leo didn't know; somehow, introductions had been skipped. The mystery man was seated directly to Leo's right, and he promptly raised Wes's bet to an even twenty dollars. Leo regarded the bet, then the man. He then took it upon himself, despite the hand in progress, though Wes clearly deliberating a slow decision, to make the man's acquaintance on his own.

"We haven't formally met. I'm Leo Sinclair, and this is my brother-in-law, Sachin Moore," said Leo, extending one hand, pointing toward Sachin with the other.

The stranger now regarded Leo warmly, seemingly unconcerned that he was in the middle of a hand, still the first hand of the night and one he'd just raised.

"Pleasure to meet you both. I'm Kirby Keener."

The name didn't mean squat to Sachin, but Leo immediately realized who he was seated next to.

"The same Kirby Keener who owns the *Hartford Courant*?" asked Leo.

"My family does, yes."

"Which you're the head of, the patriarch, right?"

"If you like. We own others as well, including your very own *Orchard Coils Courier*."

Leo was somewhat taken aback to find himself in a card game, sitting right beside this newspaper magnate and the owner of the local paper that, for as long as Leo could remember, had relished taking potshots and all but maligned O Triple C every chance it got, as though the club were some scourge on the town.

Which then raised the question, what would bring Kirby Keener to the lion's den?

"So what do you say there, Officer Sinclair?" said Kirby, clearly well informed about his surroundings, Leo having said nothing about being a cop. "You going to call my bet?"

Leo shook off the surprise, practically forgetting he was still in the hand he'd mentally folded two minutes before. He checked his hole cards for the theater of it, then mucked to Kirby's raise, as did Wes Baker. The table looked to the dapper man, silver haired and scented with mint aftershave, as he raked in the first pot of the night, casually, as if it had always been his, and everyone else was just catching up to his reality.

Kirby fucking Keener in the house—*Welcome, welcome*, thought Leo, who drank half his pint in one gulp, signaled for Judy to bring him another one.

* * *

Lynn, Ruth, Elizabeth, and Sally's round was heading into the final stretch. They were teeing off on seventeen, back in the I-6, not so far away from the smaller maintenance buildings that Lynn thought could stand a fresh coat of paint, which she bet was on Jocko Whalley's to-do list. The

Monastery loomed behind them, immaculate as always. There was a cooler by the tee box, and the ladies grabbed various drinks, including Ruth, who plucked a light beer from the icy dregs. Their round had been going surprisingly well, and spirits were high. Ruth was so pleased to spend the day golfing with her jet-setting daughter. Sally had sufficiently picked Lynn's mind without being overbearing about it. Even Elizabeth Cornwall had been on the warmer side of her behavior, keeping the sniping to a minimum while cozying up to Lynn and discussing future altruistic projects. Some of that grace was attributed to information Elizabeth revealed on the eleventh hole, when she asked Lynn how she'd chosen breast cancer as her charity. Lynn told Elizabeth she really wanted something specific to women; her time in competitive athletics had revealed to her just how far back a woman's starting place was in the annals of history. Truly, it still blew Lynn's mind that women had only gained the right to vote about seventy years before, in a country twenty years past its bicentennial. She wasn't trying to be a feminist about it; in fact, she found looking through a prism of identify first and foremost to be self-defeating and, frankly, banal. That said, women helping women without resorting to grievance peddling made an awful lot of sense to her.

So breast cancer research became an obvious choice to her.

Elizabeth, not one to wear her emotions on her sleeve, told the three women that her older sister had passed away from such a cancer a decade earlier—a woman who'd barley reached forty years old. This wasn't a secret, but it also wasn't commonly known information. Elizabeth didn't advertise and rarely opened up to the other women at the club over matters she viewed as personal, if not morbid. Death happened and shouldn't be dwelled on, brought up excessively around polite society. That said, Elizabeth spoke to the three women of the reverence she felt toward her older sister, a woman she adored and emulated, professing that a day didn't go by that she wasn't saddened by her absence, would give anything just to have one more long conversation with her big sis. It was about as humanizing an admission as Ruth had ever heard from the woman. Elizabeth's sister had left behind a husband and two children. They should have had decades as a family. But then some terrible miscoding kicked in, turning her own cells against her, and even an early diagnosis wasn't enough to curtail it. The treatments wouldn't take; the scalpel could do no more. Then the rest became a tragic history. So, as it turned out, the cause Lynn had picked was deeply personal to Elizabeth, and it buoyed her heart that O Triple C could play a role in the event to raise awareness and help stamp out a terrible affliction. All three of the women were moved by Elizabeth's candor, and Lynn assured her it was only the beginning. She had high hopes for it to become a reoccurring tournament, only to grow bigger and raise more money to combat cancer.

Elizabeth put her hands on Lynn's shoulders and gave them a pump, an act of solidarity, decorum fit for the golf course. It had a unifying effect on the women. They knew what the enemy truly was.

The foursome played the seventeenth and eighteenth hole is a breezy, lighthearted way, comfortably praising good shots and ribbing bad ones. Lynn birdied the final hole and figured she'd just shot her best score at O Triple C ever, or at least very close. The zone she'd found earlier had stayed with her the entire day and was very much reflected on her scorecard. They closed their putts out on the green, removed their hats and visors, and shook hands in a way that underscored success, satisfaction. Ruth hugged her daughter mightily and professed her pride. Lynn, not one for dramatics, had to choke back a little of the swell, but she knew an emotional day when she lived it. And there was still plenty more to go. They made their way back to the carts and went to the clubhouse to report their scores, which would be tabulated with and without handicaps, net and gross. There was no prize money, just items donated, so the standings were mostly for ceremony, some laughs, and maybe a few bragging rights.

Lynn was now off the course and back in the throng of people who all wanted her ear. First to grab her attention was the tournament's operator, Max Schiff, a sort of kindly, aging little bird of a man who was remarkably easy to forget yet difficult to say no to. He'd been a key liaison over the past months between Lynn, Sachin, and the crew at O Triple C to get the event off the ground. Max took Lynn aside and recommended that now would be a good time to accommodate some media. There were two correspondents from competing local TV stations— affiliates from both ABC and CBS—who would love to get her for a few minutes, separately if possible, but would settle for joint coverage if that was all she had time for. Doing television work wasn't new to Lynn, though promoting her own tournament and charity was a different animal, one she was determined to take great care of. She'd actually love to just get ten minutes to herself, to decompress somewhere in a dark room in utter quiet, but duty called. She told Max to wrangle the two reporters, and she'd be happy to meet with them separately, allotting them all the time they'd need. She would just ask Max to remind them that the day was about shining a spotlight on breast cancer research, not the trials and tribulations of Lynn Sinclair-Moore. Max understood and toddled off. Lynn knew she could try to plant a seed with those wielding the mics, but come splash time, who really knew how things would go down. The media could be unpredictable like that, what with their hidden agendas and canned narratives that might or might not align with the facts on the ground. Oftentimes, they didn't, both truth and reality inconvenient. But they could be useful in their specific ways; one just needed to be wary, to the nth degree, of ulterior motives.

Lynn dashed over to the clubhouse to use the facilities and check on how she fared, hoping to look somewhat presentable, given she'd just played golf for the past four hours. She tidied herself up, adjusted her outfit and the Adidas visor she was paid great sums of money to wear as often as possible. The sun had given her skin a little kick. She makeshift brushed her teeth with warm water and her pointer finger. She thought she looked authentic, not glammed up, but literally someone who'd been on their feet all day, playing a sport to raise awareness and draw attention to the cause. It occurred to her that next year, she should have some of her own merchandise made up for the tournament, even hire someone to create a logo and some branding. Sachin would be good at something like that, or at least working with the creatives to bring that new element to fruition. She'd have to remember to speak to him about it later that night. Lynn looked in the mirror and smiled at herself, already pleased to be thinking about the tournament's second year in 1995, when maybe there could be more media, and who knew? Maybe even some television coverage of the actual tournament play.

Lynn had high hopes. The sky was truly the limit.

She headed back, found Max, and was ushered to the outskirts of the event, a quieter area but still with plenty of people gathering about in the background. The two production teams were there, and Lynn introduced herself to everyone, playing the role of good host. Logistics were quickly ironed out, and Lynn was amenable to just about everyone's needs. It would only take about a half hour to complete two interviews, both of which would ultimately go well. The questions were thoughtful, if not a bit predictable—which was welcomed—along the lines of what it was like to be back in Orchard Coils surrounded by family and friends. Was it true all four of her grandparents were in attendance? How did it feel to raise tens of thousands of dollars for such a great cause? What did it mean to her to give back in such a way? Lynn couldn't have been more pleased with the tenor both reporters brought to the interview, earnest and in sync with the spirit of the event. When they concluded their business, Lynn invited them all to stay for the pig roast, but she knew they'd have to get back to the station in order to cut the footage for broadcast that evening. The thought of the event getting TV time on two different networks made her slightly giddy, which she found amusing, considering she'd lived in the public eye for quite some time. But this was different. This wasn't about her or her looks or her golf acumen. This wasn't her trying to hawk some product or lifestyle. This was about something she'd helped create, something that was truly for the greater good. It was gratifying to Lynn to no end; it made her wish she hadn't waited so long to start giving back, to get off the sidelines and get something material done.

The television vans rolled out, and Lynn checked back in with Max to see if there was anything else she should be doing to further the event's success. If Max had told her she needed to serve hors d'oeuvres or tend bar, she would have without hesitation. But Max told her she'd done more than enough for now, that she should grab a cocktail or whatever her poison was and do a little mingling, cast some sunshine on her guests, have some fun in the process. There was still the write-up for the *Hartford Courant*, but the journalist would look to connect with Lynn in about an hour or so; he was still milling about, gathering background and exposition for his article. It all sounded great to Lynn, who drifted toward the stone patio for a glass of white wine and to hunt down some scallops from the appetizer tray and start working the room—even if they were all outside—happy to talk to anybody and everybody who'd made the effort to come out and support the day's event. She wanted them all to feel welcomed, appreciated for their generosity and willingness to contribute. And to remind them of the difference that could be made when people banded together against a universal threat, an affliction that needed to be eradicated in their lifetime.

The *Courant* writer was able to connect with Lynn about ninety minutes later while she'd been holding court over a table of diners, including the owner of a local electronics store who had volunteered a home stereo system if someone was able to get a hole in one on sixteen— which, to his mild relief, no one did. The table was amused by that, and Lynn told the store owner that she might head over to sixteen with her seven iron and not return until she sank an ace. The store owner put his hands up in mock surrender to Lynn's talents and begged for mercy. That got even more rounds of laughter from the table. The reporter tapped Lynn on the shoulder, introduced himself, and asked if now might be a good time to grab a half hour with her for the piece he'd been assigned. She cheerfully agreed. The two glasses of wine over the hour-plus had lifted her spirits even more, though she was hardly buzzed. Lynn was much like her father and brother in that respect, seldom taking the time to have a drink midday. But she did need to remind herself that it was a celebration by that point, and everyone appreciated a host who carried around a libation, even if it was more of a prop than anything. Besides, the company around her had been delightful all day, and she could scarcely believe she'd ever had any reservations about pulling off the tournament in her hometown—some wine was certainly called for.

All *had* been going well until Lynn sat down with Phillip Broadstreet, who started their little interview, turning on his pocket-size tape recorder device, with benign enough questions about the day, the cause, how she landed on it, what it was like being back in Orchard Coils— really not so dissimilar from what the TV news teams were asking. Almost to the point at which Lynn wondered if all these guys were working off the same script, identical talking points. Phillip, who looked two decades older than Lynn though hadn't turned fifty yet, had an uneven, coastal-like hairline and gin-blossomed nose—the skin of a man who didn't spend much time on its upkeep, probably someone who wanted to be on television at some point in his career but eventually came to realize that corporate executives would never allow it. There was a trace of honey in his voice, but he had broken shards of glass for eyes. His ears were slightly too big. There were yellow rinds around his shirt collar. Lynn tried to observe but not judge, to stay focused on the man's line of questioning, which eventually narrowed away from the charity and drifted to Sachin, her former golf coach whom she'd met at eighteen and gone on to marry. That was when the little hairs on the back of Lynn's neck stood up, a common reaction when Sachin's name was referenced in a certain context, by certain people, like the trigger of a defense mechanism—or Spidey-sense, if one preferred—to inform Lynn that an assault was forthcoming. Or, in this instance, an ambush. She wasn't wrong.

"What's your take on a coach, a man in a position of trust, who groomed you to the point where you've never been able to uncouple from him for almost fifteen years now?" asked Phillip Broadstreet flatly.

In hindsight, Lynn should have killed the interview right then and there—thanked Phillip for his time and excused her way back to the party, allowing this little man to write whatever preordained hit piece he'd already constructed in his mind. At the very least, contribute to it no further, not add fuel to its cruel and rehashed fire. It wasn't like Lynn hadn't heard it all before, those types of questions: that the beginnings of her and Sachin's relationship had been somewhat scandalous and under intense scrutiny during those early years, whether from her mother, who'd always had a sense for it and sniffed it out first, or the rest of her family. Or his family. The golfing community. Media. Advertisers. Even Tulane had stepped in at one point, the AD venturing from his gilded office to find out exactly what Sachin was on about, rumors swirling, wasting his precious time on a sport and gender he didn't give two hoots about, that brought in minimal revenue to the university. The point was that all this had been out there for a very, very long time. Asked and answered, a million times over. They were adults when they met. It was totally consensual. They'd been married now for over seven years—happily, she would add. What more was it going to take to show people it was the real thing? That the cloak of suspicion could be dropped for good?

For all those reasons and a few more, Lynn should have stormed off from Phil Broadstreet. *Grooming*. Was this guy a moron? Did he know the difference between twelve years old and twenty-two? Did he not believe that a sentient and sovereign woman could actually make her own decision and not be gaslit by pretty boys? For over a decade? She should have stormed off. But then again, maybe Lynn felt it wasn't her place to run away at her own charity event. Among her people, in her town. That this type of blind-side attack was not only unwarranted but nonsensical, given what she was trying to do for the community, for cancer survivors. And maybe, just maybe, Lynn figured to hell with this guy Phillip and the other cretins of his ilk with their stacked agendas. She wasn't afraid to go toe to toe with them. She was literally a world-class competitor with a steel-trap mind. There was nothing in her life she'd ever gained from backing down from a challenge, never mind a bully. So for better or worse, she stayed put. She engaged.

"I'd say, Phil, that I wouldn't be the champion I am today without all my husband has done for me," said Lynn proudly, staring into his mica-chip eyes. "Then and now."

"I go by Phillip. No one's arguing your success on the golf course," he said, checking his notes, his little tape recorder still spinning. "But the calls against Sachin's pursuit of you are hardly imaginary."

"And it's also been covered exhaustively in the press before, so if you were hoping for a scoop, Phillip, I'm afraid your colleagues beat you to the punch about seven years ago," said Lynn, pleased with herself, remaining cool. "I think the real story here is using golf to promote woman's health, some good in this world."

"Well, Lynn, I'd say the story can be more than one thing at one time," said Phillip, an air of resigned condescension he didn't bother to hide. "And maybe it's familiar territory to you, but it's news to me, so I'm going to ask all the same."

"Then let me save you some time. We fell in love, Sachin and I, simple as that. And we've been together ever since, so people really needn't bother themselves over it anymore."

"And what if you hadn't become wealthy? What if Sachin had never broken down and been forced to propose?"

Lynn could hear the faint din of the party in the distance, making her long for it. It would seem Phillip Broadstreet was legitimately out for blood, jugular-type questions and accusations, and her attempts to deflect were not slowing him down. She could hardly believe the temerity of his inquisition. She'd answered tough ones before, personal and intrusive and petty—but what this man was alluding to smacked of gutter journalism, tabloid material, nothing she'd expect from the *Courant*, headquartered only half an hour away.

"I don't trade in hypotheticals, Phillip, or you impugning my husband's motives," said Lynn, some of that previous coolness burning off. "I can assure you he wasn't forced into anything."

"Well, he was going to get the boot from Tulane, wasn't he?"

"He left voluntarily, of his own accord, another well-established fact."

Phillip checked his materials, the type of little book a cub reporter might use his first year on the job. It seemed to fit him. Lynn noticed his handwritten notes, atrocious penmanship, all but illegible.

"Perhaps a gentleman's agreement was made back then to spare all parties involved some bad press," said Phillip, rolling his pen between his fingers with the dexterity of a veteran drummer; he had musician fingers that didn't match his bloated wrists. "But I have it on some authority that his contract with the university was never going to be re-upped once your relationship came to light."

"I certainly hope you can back up that statement with a source if you choose to print it."

Phillip looked to the sky, playing coy as to whether he actually had a mole in the athletic department or elsewhere at Tulane to verify his claim. Or was he just fishing, trying to get an emotional rise out of Lynn, maybe even an inadvertent admission of guilt. He pressed on. To him, it was all the same; he could have been fastening pieces together on an assembly line for eight hours a day or deforesting a deep wood under heavy civilian protest—either way, a job was a job, and he'd get the work done.

"No one would hold Coach Moore's predatory behavior against you. He's a handsome man in a position of authority. Clearly you two had a connection. But your obfuscation that something at the very least creepy didn't happen when you were only a teenager feels like the opposite of female empowerment to me, which I know is something you profess to care about. Is that something you'd want for your own daughter twenty years from now?"

Lynn felt like a bucket of ice water had been tossed in her face, her emotions fanning— anger oscillating to confusion, then back to anger, only to remain stuck there.

"I've never had a daughter."

"Sorry, a hypothetical. I do traffic in them to prove a point."

Lynn reoriented herself, leaning on some of the media training she'd received over the years, along with her practical experience. It had been a while since she'd fielded so many cantankerous questions—most of her press had morphed over the years into positive interactions, more rooted in her golf and endorsement concerns, less so in her past with Sachin. It appeared to her that Phillip Broadstreet had a specific axe to grind against her, and she hoped to pivot away from it, gradually salvage the interview where she could, still hoping to score some points for the charity. That would require some course correction, perhaps some sweetness and grace.

"Thank you, Phillip, but again, I really can't comment on a hypothetical in that way. And I do think maybe we've exhausted the topic of my husband, if that's OK with you," said Lynn, trying to dial up the charm. "But I would truly love for your readers to know more about the day's event here in Orchard Coils and how they can fight cancer alongside us from the comfort of their own homes."

That seemed to connect with Phillip, who adjusted his posture and scribbled down a few more notes in his little book, a mess of scrawl on the page, the tiny gears of that recorder still grinding, the tape gently rolling and documenting the conversation for posterity. He seemed like he might be ready to move on to a different area of focus—away from Sachin. And Lynn was briefly hopeful that they could actually discuss in greater detail the real story of the day, get into some specifics of all the fantastic work that was accomplished at O Triple C during that weekend.

But again, Phillip disappointed her, in spectacular yet morose fashion.

"How much of your monetary success as a golfer do you attribute to being an attractive and physically fit woman?" asked Phillip, no signs of mirth or human empathy—just a man asking a simple question, no different from asking someone if they knew what time it was.

Lynn took a prolonged moment to regard his face—his sinewy jowls, the unfortunate bobble to his ventriloquist dummy's mouth—and how she'd like to break her right hand punching it in, how it might be worth forfeiting six months on the tour for the fleeting satisfaction of it.

But alas, she wouldn't.

She knew in that moment there was nothing left to say. She'd tried, but there was no rescuing the interview, no hopes of a decent write-up. It was a debacle she hadn't anticipated, nor had Max or Sachin. It boggled Lynn's mind, defied even her guarded expectations of the press. Why would they do this do a fellow Nutmegger? What purpose did it serve to tank a charity tournament; what was the angle there? She knew she wouldn't figure it out sitting before Phillip, his many vectors capturing all her reactions, attuned to her discomfort, hoovering the moments up. It was time for her to pull the chute and get out before things got uglier.

"I'm sorry, Phillip, but that's all the time I can spare today," said Lynn, getting up, composed, using the last ounce of her dignity to hide all the fluster she felt. "I need to get back to where I'm wanted. Pleasure to meet you."

She couldn't remember telling a more blatant lie to a journalist in her life. *Pleasure to meet you.* Hardly. She didn't bother to shake his hand. She walked away from the reporter, who actually called out after her. Lynn turned around with a sigh, and Phillip made a minor production of turning off the tape recorder, tossing his pen and closed notebook onto the table. Somehow, in those few gestures, the man looked different: vulnerable, defeated, the ice drained from his blood. It was the first time he'd looked vaguely human, a passive energy; he acknowledged his conduct and didn't blame Lynn for her reaction. He offered one final thought.

"My apologies for this," he said in a monotone, not offering any further elaboration. Lynn didn't know what to make of it, so she just walked back to the party, unsure of what exactly had just gone down.

* * *

By half past midnight, the card game was the absolute last thing going on in the Restaurant; all other stragglers who had kept an eye on it had finally left. A few had asked to join, but Grant rebuffed them nicely enough, speaking to the table's limited capacity and that they'd be calling it a night soon anyway. The former was somewhat true, but the latter was a falsehood as the game had continued on close to four hours. The waitress, Judy, was the only staff left, her newbie status at the club getting put to the test, although she already had a reputation as one who wanted to learn, do good work, and rake in some solid tip money. Those were all valued attributes in waitstaff; plus, her comely appearance and youth would serve her well with the night owls at the club. At one point, Grant had actually told Judy she could knock off for the night, that they could serve themselves, and he'd settle up with the GM in the morning. That Grant actually knew how to functionally close the Restaurant down for the night was a bit of insider knowledge, though he no longer exercised this much since his newfound sobriety. But it was foreign information to Judy, who just demurred, indicating she had nowhere else to be and was happy to hang around and help out, though now she was mostly loitering near the bar, seemingly out of earshot. But Judy had top-notch hearing and was picking up the occasional nugget from the table. It also helped that men drinking over cards always spoke louder than they realized, mistaking whispers for very audible speech, and normal conversation for bouts of half screaming. One could imagine what an actual heated dispute might sound like.

Judy busied herself with wiping down the countertop in between ferrying over light beers and half pours of tequila, picking up snippets of information from the eclectic table of patrons. She might have only been twenty-three, but she was smart enough to know you don't voluntarily leave a scene like that. You stay until each and every one of those men remember your name, until you're the last one out to kill the lights and set the alarm.

The actual card game, for the most part, had gone swimmingly. Despite the table being a mishmash of personalities, no one had stepped out of line or run roughshod on some agro streak. There'd been banter, but instead of it getting contentious, it more often veered into the jocular, self-deprecating. Grant had helped facilitate the good faith. Substituting card play for drinking over the past two years, he knew how to manage a ring game without anyone getting too bloodied, knew how to change a topic that looked perilous. He was also a good enough ambassador for the club, a diplomat with an even keel, though how much he should be trusted was up for debate.

Leo and Wes were probably down the most money, around two hundred each—really not so much after that many hours of play as they were career men with some disposable cash to burn. Sachin, despite his newness to the game, had managed to teeter around the break-even point, as had Grant, who'd actually hoped to win a little money that night and silently fumed over hours of weak hole cards, disappointing seventh streets that led him into dead ends, and second-best hands. Ronnie may have turned a small profit, but he was still struggling to find the correct balance of enjoyment, still self-conscious in Leo's presence and abstaining from drink when every fiber in his body wanted to have one with the fellows with no interest in getting drunk, even if it was just a light beer. But flashbacks to his narrowly averted DWI scare were top of mind, so water was all he'd allow himself. Cobb Webb was up a hundo and talking emphatically about how Texans had invented poker, tales of the Rangers creating the game to pass the time when out on assignments, weeks at a time away from their homes, patrolling homesteads and border settlements, forever engaged against the Comanche and other such natives who had mastered the horse, the ability to shoot arrows with lethal accuracy while riding. Until the six-shooter came along, then the tides started to turn. It was tough to tell how serious and factually accurate Cobb was—he was drunk and not hiding it, having a good time with the table, flirting with blowhard territory but somehow minding that line well enough that his antics were mostly well received. Wes had tried to tell him he was pretty sure cards were invented in France, but the Texan didn't want to hear any of that noise, begged Wes to not rain on his parade—which the table found funny enough, as many things were when you were drinking and gambling at one a.m.

The big winner so far had been Kirby Keener—the newspaper magnate and by far the wealthiest man at the table—even more than what Sachin and Lynn had. The man was a link in generational wealth, and it had grown exponentially under his watch. In the timeless tradition of the rich getting richer, Kirby kept upgrading his final card into boats and flushes, netting him close to four hundred in winnings. He'd also pulled a slick bluff against Ronnie, forcing him to fold two pair when he should have been raising into a pot he'd only half committed to. He lost heart and got flustered against the old baron, who had a look about him that an experienced player would recognize immediately: scared money don't win. Ronnie mucked, and Kirby showed the bluff, not unkindly, but quote-unquote, good for the game. Ronnie sulked inwardly over the laydown, sober and emasculated. He knew he'd be playing that one back in his mind for a long time, as all players do over certain lost hands.

Of course, those winnings meant little to Kirby. He made infinitely more money just sitting in a room alone, simply existing and appreciating in value, the empire he'd grown a money-making machine all but on autopilot with minimal input needed from him by that point. He served as more of a figurehead, though one who still very much set the tone, signed the checks. But the day-to-day stuff—he'd shed those responsibilities more than a decade before. All that said, a man like Keener didn't like to lose at anything, so if he sat at a table—any table, whether it was cards or a boardroom—he was playing to win. And he was adroit at doing so with a big smile on his lined face. He was accustomed to getting what he wanted.

Leo dealt a new hand that ultimately went to Kirby, hitting the wheel, raking in a small pot. It was hard not to notice a man running so well, the game coming to his front door.

"You're on a roll, Kirby," said Leo, now shuffling the backup cards. "Sure is nice when the deck hits you over the head."

"I'm just pleased you all haven't kicked me out of your little shindig here," said Kirby, flashing a wry smile at Grant.

"What did bring you here tonight, Mr. Keener?" asked Wes Baker. Stooge or not, he had enough awareness of who Kirby was and the deference that should be allotted—even if Kirby did seem like a pretty laid-back guy for being worth hundreds of millions of dollars.

"Oh, you know, Grant's been trying to get me to join for years now, reaching out through various channels, I thought it was time to finally pay a visit," said Kirby nonchalantly. "And given Lynn Sinclair-Moore's triumphant return to Orchard Coils, the timing seemed right."

"Kirby did issue a rather generous check to the cause today," said Grant.

A volley of appreciation was offered to Kirby, which he wordlessly accepted, bowing his head.

"Grant, you trying to convince our paper man to join us down here?" asked Cobb, not standing on formality, having some fun with it.

"Kirby knows he has an open invitation, and we'd be proud to have him as a member," said Grant in his most stately manner. "Though the truth as I learned it is that Kirby is a member of no club. He doesn't dabble in our dark arts."

"Is that right, Mr. Keener? You don't golf?" asked Sachin, who must have had a wooden leg, given he was showing little sign of being affected by all the tequila he'd put back.

"Can't say that I do. Tried for a few years, but a maddening game. Didn't have the coordination for it, the mind for it," said Kirby mildly. "I figured I'd better leave it to those far more patient than I."

"I'll second that. Game's a total squirrel fuck," said Ronnie, believing it.

"But it's still a beautiful game," said Leo, feeling obligated to defend it a bit. "The challenge is why we keep coming back, partly at least."

The table grumbled in agreement, though it was the kind of muted approval that might indicate less a love affair with the sport and more a tenacious habit that couldn't be kicked. Not everyone was as enamored with golf the way Leo was, a true acolyte to a game that was bound never to reciprocate in the way he deserved—or thought he deserved—as reflected in his scorecard.

"There's going to be some pretty big changes coming to the sport, I think, over the next few years," said Sachin, craving another hit of his THC dropper but not wanting to traipse out to his car. "The game's going to be getting quite a facelift."

"How do you mean?" asked Kirby, genuinely interested.

"Well, for lack of a better way of putting it, the game is overdue to come out of the country clubs and become more appealing to a broader swath of players. Both here and abroad."

"You talking about Tiger?" asked Cobb.

"Sure, if he can deliver on all the expectation that's been built around him, mirror the success he's had as an amateur," said Sachin. "He'll be a boon to the sport as it gets pushed into the twenty-first century."

"Not sure any man can live up to those expectations," said Cobb.

"Time will tell. I think we'll have some sense soon enough," said Sachin. "But on the woman's tour, the amount of international competition heading down the pike is extremely interesting. Way more diverse than it's ever been before."

"Is that going to be a good thing?" asked Ronnie.

"It should help with the tour's popularity. It doesn't get the respect it deserves," said Sachin. "But of course, a strong field of players will make it more difficult for Lynn out there."

"And how does she feel about stronger competition making its way into the LPGA?" asked Cobb.

Sachin took a moment to savor the table hanging on his words, his insider perspective—it was the kind of attention he'd hoped to get a little of that night, even if he did end up having to share some of that spotlight with Kirby Keener.

"She says bring it on," said Sachin, embellishing a little bit how Lynn truly felt about navigating through an even tougher, younger pool of global talent.

Sachin was handed a freshly shuffled deck and began dealing a new round, more comfortable with the cadence and order of the process than just a few hours ago. He was surprised to see how he'd enjoyed the card game and the comradery that accompanied it. He wondered if traveling around the world on his wife's hip—a blessing, no doubt—had maybe deprived him of these types of nights, of a certain male solidarity. When he thought about it, he didn't really have any close guy friends left—too many of his interactions were transactional, or he was charming associates into giving something he or Lynn would benefit from. He wouldn't trade what they'd built together for anything, but he wondered if there was room to introduce some new elements into his life. He didn't suspect Lynn would be overly bothered by the notion; in fact, she might encourage it. She was more than happy with the idea of Sachin hanging out with Grant and Leo tonight when he ran it by her toward the end of the event. She'd seemed almost relieved by the idea. She'd also seemed a bit off to Sachin, maybe worn down from all the day's exploits, stress being released after months of buildup. They'd have a thorough postmortem tomorrow to review what had gone well and what needed improvement for next year—Sachin knew Lynn would want to debrief while it was all fresh in their minds, gather feedback, formulate new ideas. He'd also want to hear how the write-up went with the *Courant*, read a copy, maybe get some tape on the TV interviews, see how those translated across the airwaves.

"No offense, Sachin, but if a number of these new players on tour look anything like Lynn, then we're going to see women's golf overtake the men in a hot minute," said Cobb, his Texas drawl reemerging a bit as the conversation got bawdier, more unguarded, and slicked with alcohol.

Sachin gave the man a knowing smile, an appreciative laugh to help set the tone on a borderline topic. It was common enough knowledge that Lynn was a smokeshow, and they profited from it, but it was a slippery slope nonetheless when her husband and brother were sitting at the table she was being mildly objectified at. A level of discretion would need adhering to, which wasn't easy, given the loose night they were having.

Fortunately enough, it was hardly unfamiliar terrain for Sachin to navigate.

"Well, you make light, but there's some truth to it. The women are under a lot more scrutiny than the men when it comes to appearance. Not only do they have to master the game, then beat other masters, but they're expected to look graceful, vibrant while doing so," he said, dealing more cards, wrangling loose chips into an orderly pot, all the while steering the dicey conversation. "Does anyone at this table give a shit about what the men look like while playing? Of course not. Many of them bear no resemblance to a professional athlete. All we care about is their distance from the tee and those impossible putts they sink."

More murmurs of agreement around the table while the men scrutinized their hole cards, hoping if they squeezed their eyes just right, those lowly fours will morph into aces—an alchemy of 20/50 vision that seldom works.

"It is a rather glaring double standard in the sport," offered Grant, folding his hand, sipping his club soda with its wilted piece of lemon still bobbing atop.

"Exactly. But the lousy thing is we want the prize money to increase, right? We want more eyeballs on the sport, both women's and men's," said Sachin. "So maybe it's naïve to think a woman's looks won't be a continuing aspect of the game, a selling point for growth. And not for nothing—it's not impossible to think that trend will bleed over into the men's game. Sure, the champions will be the champions, but I'll bet more of them may end up looking like print models if the sport ever wants to crack the top five in this country, maybe even find a way to surpass hockey or racing."

The room took a beat. Judy could be heard in the background, using a spray bottle on some surface she was pretending to clean for the third time.

"So what you're saying is you've given this a little bit of thought," joked Cobb, jettisoning his cards into the muck.

Laughter and merriment from the group. Times were good.

"I live and breathe it, but I'll get off my soapbox now," said Sachin as Wes threw in a green chip, pumping the pot. Ronnie folded while both Leo and Kirby called. Sachin double-checked his cards and announced his fold. He made sure the pot was good with three players left and dealt the fifth street, secretly pleased at how well he'd gotten the hang of it, a newfound respect for maestros who knew how to run a game.

"Well, Sachin, for what it's worth, I think your instincts are right," said Kirby. "I can't comment too much on the state of golf, but the underlying human conditions you're getting at seem spot-on to me."

"Thank you, Kirby," said Sachin, directing the action toward Wes, first to act, who was showing a pair of walking sticks—sevens to the uninitiated.

"Is that what you attribute your success to, Kirby, being a student of the animal kingdom?" said Leo, throwing a sidelong gambler's glance at the man, his words curt, not by accident. "Your understanding of the human condition is what helps move the morning paper?"

Kirby grinned. "I'm in a business where if I don't know what my readers want, if I don't give it to them, then I'll go belly up," he said calmly. "I'm not sure if that makes me an expert on humans, but I think it helps me know when something rings true."

"Rings true? That's a good one," continued Leo dismissively. Kirby didn't take the bait.

The table had gone uneasy, unsure why Leo had gotten chippy with Kirby for no reason, seemingly out of the blue. The hand carried on, Wes throwing in a ten-dollar bet, crunching the pot odds, a headful of math that told him a speculative bet was warranted, given he was one card away from a boat with two streets remaining. Kirby called the ten dollars, not bothering to check his hole cards again. Maybe he had them memorized to such certainty that checking them again would have been an affront to his nature. Or maybe he just didn't overly care about ten bucks. Leo, on the other hand—who, if people were being honest about it, was kind of a nit player who'd rather not gamble the pennies out of his loafers—continued to scrutinize the pot, then the players, then the pot, agonizing over the decision in a feedback loop that the others were tolerating as he'd been playing quickly enough all evening. The table was also aware that perhaps the light beers had finally caught up with him. Even Sachin's hackles were raised, concerned his brother-in-law was losing the thread, his normal symmetry starting to bend at the joints. Eventually, after much Hollywooding, Leo threw in the ten dollars, resigned, as though he'd just tossed his hard-earned money into a woodchipper. He turned back to Kirby as though the captain of industry had robbed him at gunpoint, despite it being Wes who technically led the action and popped the pot, not Keener, who just called and was along for the ride.

"You want to learn something about the human condition, you should try being a cop for ten years. That'll teach you something about people," said Leo grimly.

"Jeez, Officer Buzzkill, would you lay off the guy already?" said Cobb, trying to lighten the mood.

"I'm a sergeant now, Cobb."

"It's quite all right, Mr. Webb. Sergeant Sinclair certainly has a point about what he's learned of his fellow man walking that thin blue line, as they call it," said Kirby. "But that's not what's really on his mind, which I must admit, I'm not privy to either. So let me have it, Leo. Speak your peace.

Leo not unconvinced, at the moment, to say anything, so Kirby continued.

"Truly, maybe some of the others at the table are thinking the same thing, and I'm just the outsider here, totally in the dark. Though as a purveyor of information, I do loathe being ill informed, particularly if it's at my own expense."

Sachin didn't really know what was going on but quickly dealt sixth street to the three remaining players, doling out cards like hot potatoes, hoping the continuing action would settle down the rankled table. He motioned for Wes to act, but Wes wasn't going to do a damn thing in that moment, not before he found out if Leo really had something of interest on his mind, if he was about to dress down Kirby Keener for some unknown or long-forgotten slight.

"OK, good, I will," said Leo, looking relieved. "Why have your papers always looked to bash our club any and every chance they get?"

Whether that was the question Kirby was expecting or not, he provided no indication one way or the other, as though the man were now involved in two poker games, and his emotions were a garrison he'd defend to the death.

"I'm sure we've printed many complimentary things about—" said Kirby, only to be quickly interrupted by Leo.

"Hardy ever. And only when it's totally unavoidable, when there is no other angle to promote. The best we get is something neutral, and even then, there's some backhanded insult buried between the lines. And I want to know why that is."

"I'm not sitting beside my reporters telling them how to cover the myriad of stories we publish. That's what I pay the editors for."

"Oh, come on. Your family owns it, you're the boss, and the marching orders come down from the top," said Leo, keyed up. "The evidence is there for all to see that O Triple C has been repeatedly targeted by Keener publications."

Eyeballs were ping-ponging between Leo and Kirby, neither of them backing down per their respective styles.

"If you're telling me there's some deliberate pattern I should be aware of, I'll be very happy to have it looked into," said Kirby, still calm, almost amused. "I suppose, to use your word, some actual evidence would be of good use."

Leo looked about ready to pop a gasket. The cords in his neck had gone so taut you might have been able to strum them like a guitar.

"You want evidence? I'm your evidence, Kirby! I was born here, literally, on the fourth hole. The people here thought I was some miracle baby, whatever that was supposed to mean," said Leo incredulously. "It got written up in the *Courant* with all the emphasis on the staff not having the proper personnel or medical inventory to accommodate such a crisis. We're a fucking golf club, man, not a maternity ward, but your paper used my own birth announcement to cast another unprovoked stone at us. And that was almost forty years ago, and those stones haven't stopped flying."

Kirby's eyes glazed over a bit, clearly searching his memory banks for a story of a baby being born on the course that long ago. It came back to him, eventually; the old titan still had a strong mind. It was just filled with so much information that the more esoteric factoids took longer to retrieve.

"I do remember that story, vaguely. It was early in my career," said Kirby. "Does anyone else at this table have some examples of unfair treatment from one of my papers against your little slice of heaven here?"

There was silence at the table as they all looked at one another, curious to see if they were thinking the same thing, if anyone was willing to pile on to what Leo had already laid out. In the distance, Judy had been scrubbing down the same patch of crud on the bar for the past ten minutes, chemically loosening its hold on the varnish at a snail's pace, listening intently to what the table was arguing about and being fascinated by it to no end. *The things these old dudes care about.* It ended up being Cobb Webb who spoke first, clearing his throat of the alcohol film that had settled in, dialing up some needed sobriety as no one wanted to be the lone drunk punching up to knock some sense into Kirby Keener.

"I do seem to recall not so many years ago a story about golf courses and the excessive drain on water resources in the area," said Cobb, minding his elocution. "Pretty sure that was a Hartford piece, and our club absorbed most of the ire, even though there are a dozen courses in the county. And we're actually pretty efficient with our water usage. And there's also no water shortage whatsoever in Connecticut."

A piece of evidence.

"Then there was that New Haven paper always insinuating, and sometimes outright saying, that we're a glorified boys club," said Grant, surprising everyone by contributing to the insurrection against Kirby. "We've always prided ourselves on being a family-friendly institution. But many of those stories over the years have painted us like some frat house. You do own the *Register*, correct, Kirby?"

Kirby nodded in affirmation and continued to listen patiently, neither getting defensive nor refuting the examples. He sat still and paid attention to information he was curious about, had asked for.

"There was also that story when the Restaurant was accused of having rats, maybe some disgruntled ex-employee talking out of turn," said Ronnie, happy for the opportunity to back Leo up. "Only to turn out it was just hamsters smuggled in one of the members' kid's backpack. That story may have actually been retracted but not before a surprise inspection from the state health department took place, as I understand it."

More evidence.

"Hamsters," mused Kirby, as though he'd never heard the word before. "And how long ago was that article?"

"Just last year."

"I see."

All those stories were news to Sachin. He vaguely recalled Lynn mentioning something about the club not always getting the rosiest treatment from the local press, though admittedly, that wasn't something she actually ever paid attention to and would just be parroting secondhand information. It made him wonder even more how the day's media sessions had gone, how he wished he'd made a point to ask her more about them before they parted for the night. He'd also meant to ask her if she'd heard anything from the Gap people about the ad campaign, the big game changer they were waiting on.

"And I'm not even going to get into it tonight, Kirby, but how Peter Sullivan's death was covered at the time, my godfather, and the callous nature of it," said Leo, seeing red. "Trust me, I've read every word printed on it, and it sure as hell feels like someone has an axe to grind connecting his death to the overall culture of the club."

The table went dead quiet at the incantation of Sullivan, still a sore subject among many of the members, particularly Leo and the likes of Grant and Cobb. Even Kirby didn't need to search his mind to know why the name Peter Sullivan seemed familiar—he was well aware, though he hadn't necessarily known of the relationship between the dead man and the cop sitting beside him. Behind them, Judy had discreetly turned off the TV that no one had registered was playing, eliminating some white noise that wasn't serving any purpose—not so much because she was trying to signal closing time—no, she just wanted to hear them more clearly.

Apropos of nothing, having not spoken for a while and coupled with his own ignorance of the whole Peter Sullivan saga, Wes Baker decided to chime in, leveraging the topic he cherished the most.

"Let me tell you something, fellas, once this internet takes off, we'll be able to find and analyze all these different articles you're talking about right there on the computer," he said, trying to be helpful in his awkward way. "Eventually, they'll be written there. It'll all live online."

The fact that Wes had gone so many hours without bring up the internet was practically a cause for celebration. But no one was interested in his take on the future or the miracles of cataloguing that would have currently aided their debate if already in existence. Kirby may have been interested to hear more of Wes's take on it, given the nature of his print empire, but it was hardly the time or place. The man had asked for evidence and was just presented with a plethora of it: different sources, different papers, different angles, one owner. He felt mildly humbled, though didn't show it, still guarding his emotion.

"So what do you think, Mr. Keener?" said Leo, calmer, as though five minutes removed from a series of wind sprints. "You think this might be something worth looking into? And by that, I don't mean someone else. I mean actually *you*."

Kirby regarded Leo the way a young parent might when their kid makes a surprisingly valid point.

"I'm thinking both the PD and this club are lucky to have you, Leo," said Kirby, who never once broke his cool during the entire spat. "You have my word. I will look into this issue personally, see if there's some sub-rosa agenda going on that I'm not privy to. Truth be told, this is all very much news to me. I've never read an article about country clubs, or golf for that matter, in my life."

Kirby went so far as to extend his hand to Leo, an olive branch that Leo quickly accepted. He shook the man's hand. He might have been on edge only a few minutes ago, maybe even teetering, but he was all smiles now, coming down off his exaggerated high ground, burning some of that light beer out of his system. The table could feel the energy change, the pressure dissipating. It was for the best, truly; no one wanted to see a guy that wealthy get shown up or lose too much face. He could buy and sell O Triple C and turn it into a gravel pit without even noticing its impact on his bottom line, and that wasn't what anyone at the table was gunning for.

"Looking forward to hearing what you may discover," said Leo, channeling his inner diplomat now, even though he was quite sure Kirby knew more than he was letting on. He wasn't going to grill the guy any further past the promise he'd made to look into it.

"All right, gentleman, let's say we wrap up this last hand that's been stuck in suspended animation and get out of here before Judy calls the cops on us," said Grant, reminding everyone there was still a poker hand to resolve, a wink in Leo's direction.

The table agreed, and the cards were played out, softly, with Wes Baker filling up but not getting paid off. Checks abounded, a small pot finally concluded, and the session closed out for the night. Chips were exchanged for cash. Wins congratulated. Losses mildly lamented. The dregs of drinks finished. The bathroom hit one more time. Judy was left a most generous tip, pumped up with some of Kirby's winnings, money that was akin to him finding a nickel on the street.

The crew of them left together, down the wooden back stairs, out from the balcony-patio, still joking and chortling their way into the parking lot. Obligatory statements about getting home safe were proffered. Promises of future golf rounds were made. A few glances were issued to see what Kirby was driving—a modest Mercedes sedan, given the man's wealth. It had been a very long day and night, and no one was going to make a meal of their final goodbyes. Instead, all seven men got into their respective cars, ignited their engines and drove off to their loved ones who had been, in theory, missing them. Except Leo. All that waited for him was an empty apartment and a goldfish he'd already fed that morning.

He slept in his car—*What does it matter?* he thought. He believed in following rules as often as possible, and he didn't care if people hated him for no good reason.

* * *

An excerpt from the *Hartford Courant*, daily print edition, September 28, 1994, page 3, column 1, paragraph 1.

. . . having cut her teeth among the colorful characters at the Orchard Coils Country Club during her formative years may have been a portend, if not a contributing factor, to the love affair she developed with Coach Sachin Moore, a man ten years her senior who others have been said to be constructed of "loose moral fiber."

Surely, Lynn Sinclair-Moore's return to Orchard Coils will be heralded by many as triumphant, but this reporter can't help but observe the self-serving aspects of such charitable endeavors to "greenwash" indiscretions of the past. While the Moores are hardly the first to attempt such paths toward legitimacy, it shouldn't go unnoticed that a club known for rampant misogyny is now the venue for a fund-raising event geared toward women, as though sins from the past are so easily forgotten, if not absolved, through the cutting of corporate checks and a weekend of "best behavior."

Case in point, when one is so willing and eager to accept money from those . . .

Leo Sinclair took his first nervous step down the makeshift aisle, sixty feet away from the altar and bridal party—he was to be married that day in what was scheduled to be a short ceremony, hopefully no more than ten minutes. His betrothed, Janet, had already had an exorbitant wedding once in her life and was happy to admit that one was more than enough. That the excessiveness of her first wedding—and frankly, the wedding industry—served as a smoke screen for her relationship that really didn't have the footing to support a lifetime of oaths. The industry had become a concept corrupted by greed and co-opted by bad actors and false narratives—promises that the more you spend, the more special the day will be, the happier your life will be together. "Utter bullshit"—Janet's exact words to Leo on more than a few occasions. She was a straight shooter, one of the things he loved about her. A simple wedding would suit her just fine. She also didn't want a ring, hated wearing one, felt like it was always going to snag on clothing, like some vestigial appendage she had to be mindful of. The insurance on it. The dread of losing it. A costly symbol of union. She saw it as fleeting, unnecessary. An ancient chunk of carbon probably mined by child slaves. Horrifying. Again, bullshit.

Her finger would go unadorned, and she'd be no worse for wear.

All of which was music to Leo's ears, not because he didn't love Janet and want her to be happy. And not because he was a cheapskate—though no one would confuse him for being a big spender; he was a saver, an investor. But he had loftier ideas about what he'd want to spend that type of money on—something more practical and, in his view, better than hand ornamentation and a nine-hour vanity party. He was dead set on using his money to move Janet and her two young boys, Bo and Clay, into a nice big house with lots of property, something he couldn't fully afford but would make work all the same. Leo had held the notion, as he watched Bo and Clay grow up some over the past four years, that if he and Janet were going to take a run at it, a proper house for the four of them would be in order. That was the type of debt worth carrying, worth paying off.

Not jewelry and receptions—but a sturdy roof and three acres to mow.

So it had been decided that a small summer ceremony and party would accommodate their needs, and when Leo suggested using the country club as their venue, Janet thought it apt. The place was clearly special to Leo and his family—it was in town, convenient, and Leo was confident he'd get some price breaks on the big-ticket items. The two settled the issue quickly, requiring little of the debate or horse trading that often comes with planning a wedding. The plan also benefited from Leo being a well-liked member, maybe even a smidge feared around the club. His career had been going strong, his rank of sergeant untarnished for the past decade. He had long ago made the decision that he would not pull the chute after twenty years of service just to collect a pension and become an aimless man in his forties with nothing to do but moonbeam through a part-time security job or reinvent a second career midlife, probably in real estate. Leo didn't need a second career; he'd already found one he loved—so he wasn't going anywhere.

He was also on track to become the next chief of police in Orchard Coils, once the current one, Ray Wineski—who would be in attendance at the wedding—was ready to step down from his post. It was speculated that Ray had about one or two years left in him, but once he hit his early seventies and those Social Security payments got juicer, it would be time to call it quits and hang up his spurs. Chief Wineski had told Leo some years ago that if he stayed on the straight and narrow, he'd be the front-runner for the promotion. Leo had always considered the straight and narrow his default anyway, even if it wasn't the most exciting path a man could choose, so he wasn't too concerned with falling short of his boss's guidance. That said, he did adhere to the advice. He let Wineski know he unequivocally wanted the job, was the right man for the job, and would do whatever it took to ensure it was his once Ray was ready to retire, whenever that day might come.

The chief had grunted in approval, a good sign.

Leo's job as sergeant and career ambitions aside, most if not all the board and club administrators were excited to learn that the little prince of O Triple C—hardly a nickname anyone referenced anymore, but it still got mentioned from time to time—would be having his nuptials on their premises. The Restaurant was looking to bolster their events calendar, and a joyous ceremony was always a marquee event, as were college graduations and sweet sixteens. Wakes and funeral remembrances less so, but revenue was revenue. The current general manager had promised "a price," as he put it, and the staff was more than familiar with the groom-to-be, a mutual respect between those who served others, albeit in different ways. Even Cobb Webb, who'd managed to remain the head pro for close to thirty years now, promised to help out in any way he or his staff could, particularly around the exchanging of the vows bit, which was to be held outside his pro shop and patio, the fiefdom he'd lorded over for three decades.

Cobb had taken to poking fun at Leo's impending knot-tying, as had a lot of men at the club. No one was unkind about it, but Leo had been a bachelor all his life, though hardly monastic, particularly once he figured out how to leverage his badge and dark blues to his favor—nothing untoward, just leaning into the old axiom "A woman loves a man in uniform." For a long time, it seemed the man was unlikely to settle down. That sentiment had been shared by his father, Baxter, still with them, who would harken back to his own days in that drab green garb—rugged yet oddly regal attire that helped separate the men from the boys back then. Let alone when he wore his dress uniform, an effect that was not lost on his women at the time.

Baxter, during Leo's brief engagement days, would pontificate with his son about his own tomcat days, the hell he used to raise in Hartford before he met Ruth, also still with them, who changed his heart and opened a door to a world much grander than anything he'd ever encountered on a cramped dance floor or in a hotel room. It was fun to hear the old man reminiscence about his wilder days, though Leo wasn't interested in all the information and gory details. But he let his father digress, taking the long and vivid route with some of his exploits as many aging lotharios are prone to do. In truth, stories of the old days were preferable to Baxter. He was amazed to see the century turn over, further amazed he'd lived to see yet another sneak attack on the country, one of equal if not more devastation—though the historians would argue those ramifications long after Baxter was dead and gone. In his day, he'd rushed off to Europe; now they were rushing off to the Middle East—tens of thousands of men and women answering a new call, frothing with bloodlust, eager to topple regimes and propagate democracy and, well, whatever might or might not come after that. Baxter didn't know anymore. He'd laid his sword down decades ago and since grown old, and it was starting to look like a pattern hard to ignore, even to his bleary eyes, something Eisenhower had cautioned them over once his term petered out. It made him wish his own father, Roy Sinclair, was still alive, the self-taught historian, the armchair general—he'd for sure have a hot take on planes flying into buildings and no-bid contracts worth tens of millions of dollars. It made him miss the old man an awful lot, his mother, Esther, equally so. What he wouldn't have given for them to see Leo getting hitched. To see the life Lynn and Sachin had made for themselves, to meet their great-granddaughter, Olivia—noble thoughts, but nothing Baxter could make happen on this plane of existence.

In any event, apart from the gentle ribbing Leo had endured about finally losing his freedom and becoming a married man with an endless honey-do list and perpetual drop-off and pick-up schedules for two active kids, all those around him thought the stoic man was more than ready for his next chapter in life.

Leo took that second step down the aisle, easier than the first, then a third and fourth step and found them subsequently more comforting, less janky against his nerves. He found it funny, his apprehension, considering marriage was exactly what he wanted, had been for some time. He supposed that was just the nature of the beast. All life-changing decisions would be innately jittery. He followed his footsteps one after the other and was fascinated that it was actually happening, he was doing it; after all the talking and waffling and uncertainty over the years, the hesitation and doubt were fully behind him. There was nowhere else in the world he wanted to be. It was all he wanted now. He continued his measured pace, closing in on his groomsmen, the bridal party already in position, all waiting on him with smiles and good cheer. He saw his father and Sachin. He saw Janet's brother, Paul, watchful of his sister and nephews, though fully onboard for all Leo had in store for the remainder of their lives as a protector and provider. He saw his favorite classmate from his UConn days, Steven Hemmer. He saw his trusted friend from the station, Donald Ginelli—an older cop who had been as much a mentor to Leo as Chief Wineski had. He saw Ronnie Kemper, his buddy from the club, a friendship that had been rooted in an act of kindness, mercy—Leo's grace more than a decade before that turned into a very real and reciprocal bond between the two men, fellow town employees. And lastly, he saw his best friend, Oscar Ortiz, another brother in blue from the PD, a few years younger than Leo, just enough for Oscar to look up to Leo for guidance, stability—ironic, given Oscar stood at least a half foot taller than Leo on legs that moved like scissor blades, yoked with muscle from countless gym sessions where he'd gnash his teeth, quadding out on the squat rack, developing microfractures in his molars, much to his dentist's chagrin. Leo might have been the more tenured officer, but in his opinion, Oscar has ice sluices for blood vessels and lived a fearless, dedicated life in the service of others. He was the best young cop Leo had ever seen and was proud the man would stand beside him on such a seminal day, to see him off into a great unknown.

It was also possible, given his ridiculous shoulder-to-waist ratio, that Oscar had made a deal with the devil to reduce his body fat percentage to single digits, replace his organic muscle with loops of steel cable.

After a few more steps, he'd joined the scrum of men to one side of the altar, where the priest awaited to perform the condensed ceremony. Leo glanced over to Janet's bridal party, women he'd gotten to know over the past few years. Included among them was Lynn, who flashed her brother an enthusiastic, knowing smile. He looked into the crowd of people sitting to either side of the aisle, fewer than a hundred people in attendance, by design, all of them now waiting on the bride-to-be. Leo could feel his heart beating in a good way, his breathing measured and peaceful. It all felt right. He was ready. Then the music changed, pumped through the stand-up speakers—the traditional wedding march—and from behind the privacy screen, Janet emerged, looking radiant in full white regalia, flanked by her sons, Bo and Clay, their little suits nicely pressed and undoubtedly driving them crazy with itchy fibers and tight cuffs.

Janet's boys—giving their mother away.

She'd asked if Leo would mind if the kids participated in the ceremony somehow, maybe as ringbearers or something to that effect. Originally, Janet's brother, Paul, was going to walk her down the aisle, being the closest thing she'd ever had to a father figure. Sadly, Janet never had a relationship with her own dad—a deadbeat who literally went out for a pack of smokes one night never to return when she was only eighteen months old. Janet's mother, Dorothy, not surprisingly, had become fiercely devoted to and protective of her kids as they grew up without a father but had passed away prematurely with congestive heart failure, cutting her life short some ten years before.

With both their parents gone, Janet and Paul relied on each other that much more, as though attending to Dorothy's unfinished work of getting them comfortable in a world that didn't seem keen on offering either of them a break. So it had actually been Leo's idea to have her boys give her away and add Paul as one of his groomsmen. Janet loved the idea, as did Paul and the boys. It was settled. And after all those months of planning, the whole thing was coming together. All the parts were in place, operating as they were meant to. Leo's new family walking down the aisle toward him, witnessed by a merry audience of well-wishers and loved ones. Ensconced in perfect weather. Children behaving. Even the sound system was pulling it off without so much as a crackle of static, a glitch that had given them fits during the rehearsal. All in all, the stars had aligned, and standing at the altar, his destiny approaching, Leo couldn't help but think of the first time he'd laid eyes on Janet, the first time they'd spoken in the inconvenient presence of her former husband.

It had been over four years before, and Leo was at the Orchard Coils Memorial Hospital, off duty in street clothes but dragged into a skirmish that necessitated his attention. As he was leaving the hospital through the exit doors closest to the emergency department, he saw a man and woman arguing outside. Now Leo had seen countless people arguing over his twenty years of service and believed himself to have good radar for when it was just garden-variety bickering and when something might escalate into risky territory. What Leo saw with the two people that day fell into the latter category, particularly in such a public setting. It didn't bode well in his estimation. There was something to the guy's body language, his stance, the way his legs were spread out—too much energy built into the balls of his feet, the raise in his shoulders. And Leo didn't care for the look in the woman's eyes: too visceral, the sclera shining white with bloody murder. Both were gesticulating with their arms an abnormal amount, almost primitively.

So for the second time in the span of two hours, on what was supposed to be a day off from work—not that a good cop ever really got a day off—Leo proceeded to interject himself into a situation where he wasn't summoned, certain welfare might benefit from his intervention.

He approached the couple, cautious though resolute, as though he were the missing instrument in the conversation, the one who might resolve the harmony. He spoke casually, relatively unafraid of the situation but always amazed how his brain would remind him that even normal-looking everyday people loved to carry hidden weapons, nurse insidious fantasies.

"How are you folks doing today?" asked Leo, as though he wanted to sell them a timeshare in Key West.

The two combatants looked to the stranger addressing them, giving themselves a moment to catch their breath, their faces red and flushed with tempers spilling over. The woman seemed to quickly ferret out that the jig was up—the man, less so.

"What's it to you, guy?" said the man, pivoting all that ire from the woman onto Leo, comically so, the pathway of anger so easily channeled and redirected, like water. Leo preferred the negative emotion aimed at him. Better than to have it squared on a five-two woman in beat-up sneakers and a handbag hastily slung across her body.

Leo was more than accustomed to the slings and arrows of the public at large.

"Well, I'm actually the law around here," said Leo, pulling out his sergeant's badge and literally handing it over to the enraged man, the maneuver coupled with a turn of phrase Leo lifted from old cinema, from the TCM channel. Though not one for TV, he favored a western or noir when the mood struck and thought the line had a disarming quality about it when used in certain situations. Not that everybody back at the station house agreed with Leo on that particular tack. 'Why don't you just hand them your gun as well, Sinclair?'—he'd heard that one before from his detractors, when he and his colleagues would debate the means of crowd control, de-escalation techniques. Then, if more suspense was called for, Leo might finish with "So there isn't much that isn't my business in this town," which he did say to the hospital arguers before him. For a guy who didn't consider himself dramatic, Leo would acknowledge that his spiel dipped heavily into the realm of theatrics, though, he would argue, with good intent and positive effect.

That was enough to pipe the man down, literally still holding Leo's badge. As the sergeant watched, some reality set into his eyes, the tension ever so slowly draining out of his torso, his stance losing that prize fighter's pose, taking on a more contrite position as his weight shifted back to his heels as though anticipating a dressing-down from a town authority figure, even if the cop was dressed like he was heading to a farmer's market to buy fresh corn. The man moved to hand back the badge, but Leo just motioned for him to let the woman examine it, to ensure they were all on the same page as to who was in charge. She handled and regarded the badge as though it were an exotic fruit they were trying to promote at the IGA. Then she passed it back, thinking to herself that she'd thought it would be heavier, surprised at how tin-like it was, cheap even, an opinion she kept to herself.

"OK, so now that we've established why I'm here, why don't you all . . ."—he pointed to the woman—". . . explain to me what it is you're doing here, up to and including making a scene at this very sensitive and visible location?"

Leo could tell immediately that she wasn't going to be interested in that exercise, that she had more pressing matters at hand and believed she could have handled the situation without an interloper cop butting in. But it had already been an unlucky morning, so she wasn't too surprised that the good times kept piling up—"when it rains, it pours" kind of logic. She was in the jackpot now, knew it for sure, and there was no bolting from where she stood—she would spill; they all did—so she took a breath and summoned patience, the last scraps of which she hoped resided in some cranial logic center, to get this sergeant off her back, to keep matters from getting worse.

"My son had an injury—" she started, only to be quickly interrupted.

"Our son," said the man through an ever-tightening jaw.

Leo cop-stared the guy—he'd already learned much from the brief exchange: a hurt child, a shared child.

"You'll have your chance, sir," said Leo, pointing to the man, then motioning back to the woman. "Please continue."

"He was playing baseball, Little League, might have a broken wrist. We're not sure yet," said the woman, clearly upset just speaking the words. "My younger son and I were watching from the stands. He's sitting in the waiting room right now, watching TV."

"I follow. And I take it this gentleman is the boy's father?" asked Leo.

The woman nodded her head as though she were vaguely ashamed of the fact, her eyes cast down. Leo had already noted that neither of them wore wedding bands, so he was reasonably sure there was more going on than he could presuppose, but he was willing to ask about it anyway.

"To venture a guess: married at some point but perhaps no longer?"

"Divorced, somewhat recently," she said, lacking the enthusiasm that certain divorcees didn't bother to hide, particularly around their ex.

"OK, so now that I know what you're doing here, why don't you . . ."—he turned his attention to the man—". . . explain to me the general nature of the argument you're having, deliberately positioned far away from your other son, who is staring up at one of those corner-mounted TVs they have in there, maybe even watching cartoons or some animal program."

Unlike the woman, the man couldn't wait to unload on Leo and spill his point of view, all the injustices and fabrications that had been heaped upon him, if someone would just ask. And now this cop—who had just eerily and accurately described the situation with their youngest son—has asked him.

The man dove in, clearly not one to gauge the depths of the water beforehand.

"I'm only just getting here now, officer. I had to learn all about this from a text message one of the other fathers sent me from the field," said the man, his pupils rattling around his eyes as though they refused containment, such was his anger.

"I've been a little preoccupied dealing with—" attempted the woman, but now it was her turn for Leo to gently put a hand up to her, sans the cop-stare.

"Miss, please, allow him to speak," said Leo, returning to the man. "Continue."

"I mean, she has a cell phone. I know she doesn't like using it, but what's the point of having one if you're not going to use it during an emergency? If my boy's been hurt, I should be the first to know. I should be there." His anger ebbed slightly into concern, though most of what transpired was rooted in fear over someone else, a loved one. Not atypical, nothing Leo hadn't come across before—an injured child can make people act in very emotional and illogical ways, understandably so.

Leo had heard enough of the gist to wager these two had been divorced less than six months and were in that new territory of sharing custody, shifting schedules, swapping days, passing messages through the kids—all the ugly logistics of two parents forced to uncouple. Let alone the complicated feelings the two adults would share about each other: watching them slowly—or not so slowly—get on with their new lives, moving on to new adventures, new people, erasing certain elements of their past though forever tethered by two children. Leo had seen the varying shades of it over his career. And it was never not messy, even when it was somewhat good and amicable. And it could turn violent, quick as a viper strike—flashpoints reached in those who would have thought it impossible. Mostly men, but sometimes the woman. Attacks on each other. Sometimes the children. Once the animus had reached a certain level, all bets of civility were off the table per the institution of marriage, and it would then more resemble survival of the fittest, devolve into a Darwinian contest.

Leo directed his attention back to both citizens of his town, working to untie their domestic Gordian knot.

"OK, folks, here's what we're going to do. First and foremost, we're done yelling at each other in broad daylight, capisce? And really, it would be beneficial for you two to stop yelling at each other in most other situations. I can assure you your boys will sniff it out faster than bloodhounds," he said in full-on, serve-and-protect mode, though being a bit folksy about it, figuring these two didn't pose an immediate threat. "You've both had a pretty lousy and fast-moving morning. Now you have to decide if you want to make it worse or better. Sir, what's your name?"

The man said, "Billy."

"Billy, go on inside and see your boy, see what you can find out about the other one they're patching up," said Leo, Billy looking hesitant. "Go on now; they need you."

Billy went back into the hospital, leaving Leo alone with the woman.

"Miss, what's your name?"

The woman said, "Janet."

"Your ex-husband is playing a bit of catch-up here. Let him. It won't change anything, but it's going to make him feel he has a bit more control over the situation, which isn't a bad thing," said Leo. "Kids are always getting themselves hurt, right? It's practically their job."

Janet didn't say anything, just kind of stood there, maybe agreeing but not really knowing what to do with her body, with the wound-up energy coursing through her nervous system. For some reason, she wanted a cigarette, despite never having had a smoke in her life—anything to not feel the way she was currently feeling.

"Do you have any concern with your ex being around the kids in any way?" asked Leo.

Janet took a moment to regard the question; it was more loaded than Leo had intended, though less straightforward than Janet could do justice to.

"No, he's a good enough father," she said, trying to find the concise response to this cop, now mediating what had grown into a humiliating situation. "I mean, he loves them. He'd never hurt them; it's just . . ."

Janet trailed off, unsure or uninterested in finishing her thought. Leo persisted.

"Just what?"

"I just always worry he may say something to them about me, you know," said Janet. "That he gets frustrated and just dumps it on them, poisoning the well."

"Do you ever do that?" asked Leo.

"I try not to. Sometimes. I'm not always proud of myself."

"If there's one thing these family courts stress, after all's said and done and the legal stuff is over with, it's to not use the kids as sounding boards for the grievances of adults," said Leo calmly. "Don't speak ill of each other. He's still their father. You're still their mother. You'd be surprised how effective that piece of guidance can be with people getting on with their lives."

To that, Janet let out a little breath, venting some of the bad energy, hearing what the officer had to say, maybe for the first time really hearing him out and not just trying to get him to move along.

"And for what it's worth, I'm not a huge fan of cell phones either," said Leo, lightening the mood as the altercation was dissipating. "Just a new way for folks to find trouble, particularly while they're driving."

Janet laughed at that, a quick moment of levity in an otherwise shitty morning.

"OK, then, I can see my work here is done. I'm sure you're eager to check in on your son, and I do hope things work out for him," said Leo. Then he added, "And you."

"Thanks, officer. Thanks for being so decent about all this."

Leo reached into his pocket and pulled out what looked like a business card, which it basically was—dark blue with white font that he'd custom ordered for himself—and handed it over to Janet.

"This is my work number. Give me a call if you have any more run-ins with Billy or if you'd care to tell me how your son makes out with his wrist." He briskly nodded his head, mimed tipping his cap though he wasn't wearing one, and strode off, thinking himself an utter buffoon. He was convinced he'd never see or hear from her again. Then, to his surprise, she called him three days later to report that her son, Bo, had a cast on his wrist but the prognosis was good, and he'd be swinging a bat again in two months. Leo had been pleased to hear the good news. Then she asked him out for a drink by way of appreciation for the kindness he'd shown to them in front of the hospital, when she was hardly at her best. He eagerly accepted.

* * *

About seven months prior to his wedding day, in January 2003, Leo Sinclair had almost gotten his head blown off during a standard traffic stop, the sort of routine task he'd completed a million times before—sometimes even out of boredom—that would often result in a simple warning or, if egregious enough, a citation or even an arrest per an outstanding warrant.

It would be the closest brush with death Leo had experienced in his twenty-plus year career, culminating with him drawing his own weapon and actually firing off a single shot—the first time he'd ever discharged his weapon in the line of duty—at a lone vehicle speeding away.

The casing to that round would be recovered, though the bullet never found.

It had been a particularly cold night, the deep freeze of late January bearing its weight down on Connecticut and all of New England—back when the Northeast was prone to harsh winters, significant snowfall. The fluffy, ski-friendly powder of December had turned brittle and crusty from ice storms at the turn of the year; the sleet and freezing rain had hijacked the pastoral Christmas vistas and replaced them with barren landscapes—gray and treacherous and decayed in a way that was hard to compute but was top of mind the second you walked outside, particularly once the mercury had dipped to near freezing. True, it would all be melted away three months on, but those ninety days could feel like an eternity when you were constantly on the lookout for black ice, when you've barely seen the sun for two straight weeks.

Leo was nestled in his cruiser, minding a busy intersection that had a reputation for attracting people a little too liberal with obedience around stop signs and adhering to the concept of "no right on red." Oftentimes, a police presence got people thinking differently on just how easy it was to follow simple traffic laws. Every time, seeing those blue and red lights swirling was enough to show motorists the virtue in slowing down and allowing others to pass in an orderly fashion. Given the darkened conditions of January, the car's tinted windows, Leo would concede that his cruiser was actually doing most of the work, including keeping him warm as the engine idled. By eight p.m., the volume of cars had tapered off significantly, and Leo figured he only needed to spend about ten more minutes lording over the bisecting roads before he could move on and finish his shift, which was scheduled to wrap up at ten p.m. Those could be some long hours working in the deep-winter nights in Orchard Coils, where, honestly, there wasn't that much to do but sit and collect one's thoughts. And where Leo's thoughts had been pooling of late, particularly over the last few weeks, had been what his long-term future might or might not be with his on-again, off-again girlfriend, Janet.

Janet had been a fixture in his life for close to four years, though that fixture might be thought of as retractable, given they'd both initiated small breaks from each other at various times. They'd had periods of running very hot, only to reach a sudden cooldown. Their early years weren't pinned to exclusivity; both had their dalliances, though Leo would concede the more wandering eye was his. Janet was still a relatively young woman, but she was trying to raise two boys and manage an erratic ex-husband, so she was hardly painting the town red. And even if she did go out on dates with other men from time to time, none of it particularly bothered Leo, who carried an uncharacteristic hubris when it came to her affection for him, especially when they were running hot. He enjoyed her attention, some doting when they were on, though was cautious about making her feel she had another man-child to attend to—she'd already been down that road with her ex, Billy. The funny thing was that Leo didn't even necessarily think of himself as better than the other men she would date. He was sure some of these dudes were handsomer or richer or whatever, but wasn't going to get dragged into some dick-measuring contest over it. For some reason, he really believed that Janet would favor him the most, despite any of his shortcomings—which he held no illusions about; he possessed faults like everyone else.

So why did he feel such an entitlement to her, an ease to his position in her heart that bordered somewhere between virtue and arrogance? Was it her divorce, her standing as an all-but-single mom—? Even though Billy was still very much in the picture, he wasn't much of a disciplinarian with the kids since the split, which put a lot of the actual parenting squarely on Janet's shoulders. Did Leo hold some odd prejudice, watching her try to navigate those choppy waters? Was her endless love for Bo and Clay the hallmark of what a man should desire in a woman, or did it spotlight a certain type of attention that would never be fully shone down on him no matter what, despite the fact that he loved those boys as though they were his own? Would Janet's impending fortieth birthday, a milestone, play a role in the type of man she wanted to keep company with, the one she would want around the most? These questions both comforted and vexed Leo, as did his reluctance to muster the initiative and ask Janet to take the plunge with him, lay down some tent stakes, and create a confederacy between them.

His hesitancy was a conundrum, keeping him up at night. Lord knew everyone in his life had been subtly and not-so-subtly hinting and asking and outright prying as to how things were going on that front, despite, or perhaps because of the obvious lapses between the wayward lovebirds. His family made inquiries, though they were, surprisingly, not the loudest voices in the contingent, Those he heard more from were his contemporaries at the station, none more than Oscar Ortiz, who continually told Leo that he was waiting too long, that Janet was a catch, and any perceived baggage aside, she was going to slip away—the kind of frank advice one can only tolerate from their best friend. He also got an earful from the fellas at O Triple C, the ones who knew him well enough, knew he could handle a little back-door advice without being too on the nose about it. Surprisingly, or maybe not so, he heard it the absolute least from Janet herself, who, in fact, never brought up the topic of nuptials or, really, exclusivity. For more than three years, she'd been living alone with the boys in their small saltbox house, the only home they'd ever known. Billy had conceded it in the divorce, though he'd been allowed to stay there six months after the split until he could find a suitable apartment—a pretense Janet thought fabricated, just his last-ditch effort to save the marriage even after the ink had dried on the paperwork. Janet wasn't interested in reconciliation but had acquiesced because she wanted the house for the boys, some semblance of continuity. She would and did put up with Billy's squatting for five months before he moved into some bachelor's one-bedroom paradise a whopping four miles away.

So for those three-plus years, Janet and the boys had fostered their independence, wrangled custody logistics, and slowly built a new life, Maybe with all that going on, it wasn't so odd that Janet didn't have the time, energy, or inclination to hector Leo into proposals of marriage, an institution that had already not lived up to the bounty it was advertised as. And it wasn't like the word never came up or the boys never spoke an innocent question about it. Leo might get a little sheepish around the topic, and Janet would come to the rescue, coolly saying something to the effect that one marriage was enough, or there'd be time for that later down the road. Then the mood would pass, the boys would move on, and things would revert back to normal. She had a soft touch, graceful as a diplomat, cagey like a politician. Leo admired her disposition, something he'd had to work to develop over the years in pursuit of his career. Janet seemed to balance the wants and needs of others effortlessly, walking around with a full cup of water on her head, hardly making a fuss over it, as though it wasn't even there. She wasn't after him for a ring, and Leo struggled with whether he should be flattered, relieved or angered by that fact. He could keep kicking the can down the road, against advice from much counsel, but it certainly made him wonder. What did he truly want? What was he waiting for? What was he after?

One would think these would be easy enough questions. And if any of those answers didn't involve Janet and the boys, was it fair to keep them in limbo, even if it was unintentional, sans malice, even if they never protested his indecision? Then, even more the point, when the lights were out and Leo was in bed, either with someone or alone, he'd be forced to ask himself, staring at the darkened ceiling, before the dream could kick in, *what exactly is wrong with me?*

There were always more questions than answers—a certainty anyone could count on in life. The best Leo could do was treat them as thought exercises while he was staking out intersections during rush hour, but once the traffic abated and the thoughts grew too overwhelming, he'd know it was time to move on from both tasks.

He threw his car into gear and started to drive around some of the more commercial sections of town—the Stop & Shop, the Blockbuster Video, a few chain restaurants. There were some cars out, but not so many. The streetlights were changing colors to all-but-empty roads. It was Orchard Coils, after all, not NYC—hell, it wasn't even Waterbury. He checked in on the high school: a few lights on, a few parking spots filled. He checked in on some nearby woods, cul-de-sacs where teenagers were known to park en masse. Certain summer spots that were desolate in January. He drove by O Triple C, closed for the winter, though he still liked to keep a watchful eye on the place. The greens were covered with white tarps to protect them from ice, though a snow cover would actually provide a beneficial insulating effect. Neon-orange netting strategically put up around the maintenance road to dissuade snowmobilers from trying their luck on more tucked-away and gradient-prone holes. There were still two solid months before the course would open again; the Restaurant would probably need three before they turned the lights back on. Leo daydreamed of finally getting that first hole in one. Of finally cracking eighty strokes. He continued to drive around aimlessly, letting the denizens of his town know their police were out there, protecting and serving when neither were currently in demand. His radio had been collecting dust all night. He was bored, long enough on the job that he wasn't ashamed to admit it. It wasn't a mindset he cared to indulged, particularly at the taxpayer's expense, but sometimes, that's just how things shook out, when it was the truth of the matter.

He drifted over to some of the industrial parks, mostly day businesses, all but deserted at that time of night. That was when Leo noticed a sedan, nondescript as he rolled up on it, a Ford, with the right side bashed in some, the brake light and turn signal cracked and nonfunctioning. It didn't look like old damage to Leo, who'd developed an eye for such things, though he couldn't say how recent it was. He found himself with a choice to make. He could do nothing, drive around town for an hour, and call it a night. Or he could fire up the misery bar, have a quick chat with the driver to help pass the time, then head back to the station to clock out. The fact was that type of damage to the brakes and directional needed repair sooner than later. It was technically a hazard; the car wasn't roadworthy. So Leo opted for the latter, fired up his lights and sirens, and got right up on the Ford, clearly indicating to the motorist to pull over.

Which the individual smoothly did.

Leo parked his car a few lengths back, ran the license plate through the onboard, and awaited the results. The car and owner came back clean, registered two towns over in the same county, nothing to arouse suspicion aside from why they might be in the industrial park at nine p.m., though hardly a crime or even an oddity since it was still a free country, and folks could drive around as they pleased, getting lost or looking for shortcuts or whatever else tickled their fancy. It was the damage to the car that was the issue at hand. Leo gave it an extra minute, going through his little mental checklist for conducting a traffic stop, rote as it might seem; he found comfort in the ritual, strength in the training. He exited his vehicle and hitched up his belt, secured his pistol, the clasp now unfastened. He zipped his department-issued slicker up to his throat given the cold and windy conditions, minded the slippery road as the temperatures continued to drop, helping to turn the texture of the blacktop into a skating rink. He was ready and set. He took two more steps toward the sedan, and before he could even register what was happening, a head and then a body pushed out the driver's side window, then a flash and pop— as fast as anything you could imagine.

It all happened like a dream, a cliché Leo had heard before and had always dismissed as silliness, faulty recollection. But those few seconds of his life, infinitely small, would be so fast as to render them surreal and ephemeral—there and gone—as though they had never happened, a blip so fast as to escape documentation, the capture of time. But they did happen, were hardly imagined. It was a very real thing that occurred, that left evidence behind, that would have immediate, long-lasting, and hidden consequences in the life of Leo Sinclair.

The bullet was shot at a lethal enough range, though technically, it didn't graze Leo's left ear, never made any actual contact with him. It basically got as close to his head as possible without hitting him, then it sailed away into the night without ever being recovered, though it's casing would be. The force and feel of the passing round, however, were enough to spin Leo down, disorienting him, and ultimately causing the soles of his shoes to lose purchase with the slick ground. He fell. On the way to the ground, Leo's head clipped the metal guard on the front of his cruiser, a jarring blow that further crumpled him to the pavement. He wasn't knocked unconscious, and he still had the wherewithal to know he wasn't out of the woods against his attacker. He looked to the sedan woozily, expecting to see another muzzle flash meant to finish him off. He was sure of it. Maybe the driver would actually get out of the car and execute Leo at close range. The opposite occurred—the one functioning brake light came to life, and the car dropped into gear. For a split second, Leo thought the lunatic might slip the car into reverse and try to run him down. But the driver pushed forward, seemingly unconcerned with the fallen officer, heading out of the industrial park, not even bothering to speed, at a pace that wouldn't draw any additional attention.

Leo pulled his gun and fired a single, futile shot in the direction of the escaping car, an unsound attempt as he'd barely gotten himself onto one knee, his bell rung in a way he'd never experienced before. But the adrenaline in that moment, maybe some survival instinct, jackrabbited his system into a spike of bravado that wasn't going to allow him to not fire back, to not try and take this motherfucker's head off, as unlikely and nonsensical as that was. It was actually a small miracle Leo hadn't tried to unload an entire clip at the departing Ford, but his training restrained him enough after the first shot. A good thing—any more and it would have looked like Hollywood nonsense and possibly garnered a deeper investigation or, at the very least, created more uncomfortable questions. One shot could be easily explained.

Leo reholstered his gun, forgetting to fasten the clasp—something he never forgot to do—then took some deep, cold breaths that prickled his brain like an ice cream freeze. His hand went to the back of his skull where the impact with the bumper had taken place, and his fingers returned wet and sticky. He didn't need daylight to know it was blood, and not an insignificant amount of it. The radio he carried on his body had been damaged in the fall, cracked between his weight and the concrete. So he got up, unsteady on his feet, and returned to the driver's side seat of his car, where he called his station for backup, reported the shots fired and the make, model, and tag number of the Ford—data still logged in his onboard computer—and asked to issue an APB, armed and dangerous, proceed with extreme caution. The voice on the other end of the radio, a dispatcher Leo knew and liked, confirmed all he'd said and told him to sit tight, that the calvary was on the way. Leo clicked off the radio and did exactly as he was told—sat in his seat and waited—the endorphins sloughing off while the pain in his head and body were catching up, soon to take the lead in the race. Reality was setting in. He'd been shot at. The buzzing in his left ear was riding a frequency he couldn't decipher, that maybe only dogs could hear and understand at the same time. He checked his pistol again, unsure if he'd thrown the safety on. He had. But couldn't remember, amazed he couldn't remember something so vital. He holstered it again and now remembered to secure the clasp. He thought it would be a good thing to stay awake, to think a little. He'd had training on head injuries before. He'd dealt with Ronnie's crash all those years ago. He tried to recall what he'd planned to have for dinner once his shift ended. He couldn't remember. He couldn't remember his niece's name. He took a few more elongated breaths as though plagued by dehydration cramps, intent on staving off panic, which he knew could hijack his sobriety if he allowed it. He would not allow it. His vision was going blurry around the edges. Or maybe it had been for several minutes, and his brain was just acknowledging it. He didn't feel overly sleepy but knew for sure he didn't want to pass out; he wouldn't want to be found that way. So he replayed what had just happened to him, hoping to get his facts straight, that he hadn't done anything grievously wrong, that he'd followed the book. These thoughts slipped around his mind like eggs on Teflon. There and back, there and gone. It all seemed really bad to Leo, but there would be footage from the dashboard camera to help, to plug in what he might not be able to remember, to exonerate him if need be. Statements would be taken and retaken. He might be called before a board of his superiors. It was going to be a very real thing, and it made Leo wish he was back at that intersection, bored out of his skull, minding benign traffic, counting the minutes until he could head home by way of a Burger King drive-through.

Ah, BK, maybe that's what I was going to have for dinner.

He might have nodded off for a few moments after that revelation, only a minute or so of lost time, before he was roused by the blaring of sirens closing in—he figured them ninety seconds out, two minutes at the most. He thought about getting out of the car but realized his body wasn't going to comply just yet. At least he was seated in a somewhat dignified manner. He was grateful he hadn't pissed himself. He resolved to sit and wait, be still; he'd seen enough action for one night. *Let the rest come to you now.* It occurred to him that he might puke, but he pushed that notion aside. He thought of his dad, a warrior who'd seen countless nights of violence, way worse than this. A veteran who was shy about removing his shirt in front of others, lest they see what scar tissue looks like on an aging man once kissed by a grenade oversees. Leo didn't know. He figured he didn't really know much about anything anymore, probably never had. He wished his dad was there right now—him mom too.

He passed out briefly.

He awoke suddenly, with a start. Backup had arrived, a firetruck shortly thereafter. Leo's off-duty colleagues had been informed of the situation, everyone protective of their own during a time of crisis, of legitimate injury. The ranks would fold around him—it was a rare enough occurrence in Orchard Coils, for sure. The on-site cops kept checking on their compadre, making sure he was OK—not moving him yet, getting him to talk some, seeing if there was anything else he could share with them about the incident. Leo didn't have that much more to offer. The assailant had a ski mask on. And gloves. He'd moved pretty easily in and out that driver's side window, so Leo would guess he wasn't a big man. The person had never uttered a word. They asked about the shot fired at him. Leo could only hope his ski mask impaired his vision just enough to miss. The night, the wind and cold—who knew? It was too close to be a warning shot; the driver of the Ford had seemed resolved to put the cop down if need be. None of it seemed real; that's what Leo told his questioners more than a few times, as though he'd forgotten he'd already said it, repeating it: "It doesn't seem real." The gravity was more than setting in, and Leo had to excuse himself from their presence, pried himself out of that car seat amid their mild protests, found the side of the road, and threw up. The cops and firefighters formed a semicircle around the man, protective and at a distance, minding him with one eye, allowing him some privacy with the other eye trained elsewhere.

Leo finished up—mostly stomach acid, bile—wiped his mouth, and absently noticed the *T* on a neon storage sign from across the way had been blown out, lost its electric purple flare. *Kind of a shame*, thought Leo. *It's all fucked; everything's fucked.* His footsteps were less than steady, like so many of the drunks he'd encountered or pulled over during the past two decades. *Two decades*, he thought. Always the same line—"I'm fine, officer, I'm fine." Their favorite thing to say. The more they insisted on it, the more Leo knew it to be untrue. He put his fingers to the back of his head again—still soaked, now dripping onto his clothes—and looked at the blood on his fingers, flicking it to the road as to deny the logic of it.

The other officers had seen enough, coaxed him back into the cruiser, got him to lean up against the seat as they waited for the ambulance, which could now be heard, a couple minutes out. Leo was becoming fussy, obstinate like a child who didn't know better. The EMTs arrived, and the cops were asked to step aside to give them room to conduct their work. The examination began, right there in the industrial park, off to the side of the road—an area that had been quiet only half an hour ago before it lit up like a Mexican carnival. It took the two EMTs less than five minutes to assess that Leo was going to the hospital, tout de suite: they could staunch the bleeding, but he'd need to get some stitches in the back of his head. There were very real concerns about internal bleeding, a shock to the brain, the hematomas that accompany such trauma. He wasn't out of the woods yet. So they loaded him up on a gurney, per protocol, despite his fuzzy protests, and tucked him into the ambulance—one EMT driving, the other attending to their cargo. The ambulance journeyed its way to the hospital, eleven miles away, basically across town, escorted by a four-police-car convoy—all their sirens blasting, the kind of thing heard from great distances, just to let the denizens know some really bad shit had just gone down.

Spin the clock forward a few hours when some of the dust has settled but not much, Chief Wineski had been interrupted from his evening game of Scrabble with his wife, bickering over the validity of certain words and inevitably losing his challenge. The call had come in about Leo's plight, and the chief was out the door so fast his wife barely had time to remind him he was wearing sweatpants, to at least throw a quick pair of jeans on. Oscar Ortiz, also off duty, was given a call while home drinking an out-of-season pumpkin beer and sweating a Milwaukee' Bucks game he'd thrown a few sawbucks against with one of the more reputable and discreet bookmakers in Hartford county—the kind of hustler who knew how to pay and collect by Thursday and also forget every face he'd seen that week by Friday. Oscar was out the door faster than the chief—he'd already been wearing jeans—instantly forgetting about the stupid basketball game he'd been wrapped up in. The two men arrived at more or less the same time at the hospital, were directed to the ED's waiting room, relatively empty aside from the slew of cops and a few unlucky souls seeking emergency treatment on a Tuesday night, now having the misfortune of being surrounded by half the police department, all of them jumpy and extremely pissed off.

During that time, Leo had gotten his head sewn up and scanned by two different devices to the satisfaction of multiple techs and the senior doctor managing the department that night. No one was seeing anything troubling on the images—those ghoulish-looking black-and-white ones held up against the mounted wall lights, illuminating all the contours and imperfections of Leo's cranium. At least his head was still connected to his neck in all the right ways, and there weren't any fractures or bleeds to be found. They'd given Leo some mild painkillers to take the edge off. And while his thinking had straightened since he'd gotten his bell rung, the fog slowly clearing, his mind wasn't crystal yet. He told those attending to him as much; it seemed a worthy thing to be transparent about. He also told them, apropos of nothing, that he wasn't even born in a hospital like fancy people. Maybe he was making a joke of it. Or it was the concussion talking. But either way, the staff, despite the encouraging test results, insisted on holding the officer to observe his progress, preferring to keep him awake, somewhat vertical if possible.

Leo had been relatively compliant since arriving at the hospital, hadn't really asked for much, seemed content to be looked after by others. The attending thought this docility would pass, that the sergeant was still a bit addled, maybe even in mild shock, and could become agitated, even aggressive, without much warning or buildup. She'd seen it before. So they'd opted to get Leo into an armchair, made him somewhat comfortable, and brought in visitors two at a time. Leo consented, half-heartedly—in a certain sense, he didn't want to see anybody, didn't want to be there. He was ready to go home but knew well enough that wasn't happening anytime soon. There were plenty of police logistics that still needed to take place, and it was usually the sooner the better, given the unreliable nature of memory—its intrinsic fault in recounting the whole truth—especially when someone's nursing a head injury.

Chief Wineski and Oscar Ortiz were the first two to be admitted, and it didn't take long for the reunion to devolve into a display of machismo and haranguing, a lot of guy stuff said to deflect the core issue: that a man they both loved and respected almost got his ticket punched that night. It regressed into a roomful of jokes and ball busting and quips about the hotness of Lynn Sinclair-Moore. That Leo's lack of height got him to the ground much sooner, may have saved his life—imagine if he'd knocked his head from Oscar's verticality. That Leo had almost checked out a friendless virgin with no property or land to speak of—highbrow kind of stuff that men say to show they care. Not that it wasn't working—even Leo was laughing along with his boss and best friend. Again, maybe it was the concussion doing its thing, but Leo now felt like he was the center of a roast and was having a grand time with it. The nurse had to walk in to see what the commotion was, sizing up the room. Men. Cops. She left the room, both rolling her eyes and glad such fraternity existed. Then Chief Wineski got down to brass tacks with Leo regarding the incident, listening to his best sergeant tell the story—off the record for the first go-around—taking his mental notes, weighing if his boy would need a union rep. The chief told Leo that the whole county was out in force looking for the asshole who took a potshot at him, that they'd bring home some justice—whatever that technically meant. All of which sounded good to the seated man, fingering the thick bandaging on the back of his head, hoping that whoever that person was out there, they hadn't gone on to hurt someone else. The thought of it greatly disturbed Leo—that he couldn't prevent future violence, given his own failed encounter. He really didn't want to imagine it and promptly banished it from his muddy thoughts.

Oscar eventually jumped in to break up the chief's line of questioning, sensing Leo needed a breather, that maybe some dark thoughts were creeping around the periphery. He told Leo he'd read on the internet that it would be an early spring, a fabrication but a righteous one that he knew would please Leo to hear, which it did, prompting him to carry on about some golf clubs plied with lead tape that Oscar would barely recognize over a cricket bat or jai alai cesta. Oscar flashed the chief a look and was met with demure approval. Truly, if there was ever a scenario in which it made sense to let Leo Sinclair drone on about golf, it was in that hospital room that night, to keep him distracted, to keep him awake. The two men listened patiently as he tried to explain a facet of the club head called "bounce" and how degrees of it promoted distance and forgiveness. It went on like that for some time—the men noting Leo's cognition and motor skills, both hanging in there—until something occurred to Oscar, who interrupted Leo's monologuing over the proper way to rake the sand traps and asked if Janet had been told of what had transpired. Had anyone thought to give her a call yet? Leo hadn't a clue—it had been such a whirlwind that he hadn't made it that far, hadn't thought about it, given he was fine and would be released from the hospital some point, hopefully soon. No one had bothered with his emergency contacts—Leo was a cop, and many of his brothers and sisters had arrived to fill that occupancy. If Leo technically had an emergency contact, it was probably Lynn, written down for insurance reasons, not out of practicality, given her globe-trotting status.

Oscar asked Leo if he wanted him to call Janet, to let her know what had happened. Leo asked Oscar what time it was—close to midnight, which meant she'd be sound asleep, the boys too. He knew what his answer would be. And even if he would have loved to see her then—like that very moment, Bo and Clay too—he wasn't going to disturb them for his own selfish reasons. It was actually a decision that came easily enough to the chair-bound man, though he hoped it wouldn't come across colder than it was meant to. It was a pragmatic decision, though the line between the two could often be blurred and misrepresented. "No," he told Oscar, "Let them sleep; there's always tomorrow." Oscar furrowed his brow and couldn't help but wonder if Leo realized how close he came to not having a tomorrow, that banking on tomorrow in their profession—in any profession, really—was fool's logic. That tomorrow had never been and never would be promised to any human who had ever walked the planet. That said, he respected Leo's wishes and stowed his phone. Janet went uninformed and unsummoned that night. Then Oscar excused himself to allow a new officer to visit and to find a functioning TV to see if that Bucks game had pulled through for him.

* * *

They tied the knot, and all went off without a hitch: no cold feet, no objections from the small audience, no errant shots from seventeen hit in their direction, no lighting strikes from above in protest of their union. The ceremony was a tidy affair, ten minutes in total, as planned. Leo and Janet exchanged simple silver rings and kissed on command, and the priest introduced the world to Mr. and Mrs. Leo and Janet Sinclair. Cue the applause, on to the reception. It kicked off with a cocktail hour, still outside, where the weather remained temperate, before they'd eventually be moved inside to the Restaurant's banquet hall. Deviled eggs and bruschetta plucked from serving trays, lines forming at the open bar. People claimed little tables and chairs. Those in attendance who weren't members of O Triple C might mosey around the eighteenth hole, where they could see some players finishing off with chips and putts and take some digital snaps with the picturesque backdrop on full display.

Leo and Janet were squired away for about fifteen minutes by their own photographer, a few postnuptial pics in additional spots that had caught her eye. The happy couple were kind of photo'd out by that point but humored the professional, figuring she knew better than they did. She had the resume, knew how to work the clicky camera and interchange its preposterous lenses. Once they were able to sate the photog's creative ambitions, the bride and groom devised a plan of divide and conquer, splitting up to socialize among their throng of guests. A sound strategy. Janet reminded Leo to have fun out there, that it was his wedding day and he was only getting one of them. Leo told Janet he loved her and the way she thought and spoke and moved—he loved it all.

They parted ways and got to it.

Before Leo could start to enjoy himself with various friends and well-wishers, he sought out his parents, who were stationed at a small table—Ruth entertaining her granddaughter, Olivia, with some squishy toy, not unlike something a puppy would also be amused by. Baxter sat by, looking at ease, the way men do when they know their women have the young ones on lockdown. There was a glass of ice water before him, his face rosy from the day's sun, but he seemed to be hanging in there all the same. He wasn't as spry as he used to be and had lost a step or two in the recent years. Leo walked over to join them, and they almost got up out of their seats as though he were royalty, a visiting dignitary—though perhaps on your wedding day, you were—but he quickly motioned for them to stay put, giving his niece's arm a playful tug and pulling up a chair to sit beside them all. He breathed out a puff of contented air. The party was just beginning, yet he already felt exhausted, another happenstance of one's wedding day, he supposed. There had been warnings in advance, people reminding him it was a marathon, not a sprint, particularly if he wanted to be on the dance floor closing out the reception, which Leo did not. Dancing was hardly his thing, and he would happily pass on that tradition as much as he could.

"So how does it feel to be a married man?" asked Baxter, jostling his son's shoulder, his nearly eighty-year-old hands still full of strength and resolve, hardened by a lifetime of golf swings and the merciful absence of arthritis.

Leo took a beat for the words to sink in—he *was* officially a married man now, hadn't really had a second to reflect on it, He allowed the moment to pass.

"I'd say I feel about the exact same as an hour ago," said Leo. "Perhaps a little relieved it's over."

"That's a good sign."

"And you're happy, Leo?" asked Ruth, balancing Olivia on her knees.

"I am, Mom, very," said Leo. "And how is our Miss Olivia doing today? Where's her wayward mom and dad gone off to?"

"She's been very good, not too fussy at all," said Ruth. "Lynn and Sachin wanted to stretch their legs out. You know your sister, always scouting out ideas for her tournament in September."

"That does sound like her," said Leo. "And how are Grandma and Grandpa doing today?"

"Excited for their son," said Ruth.

"Your mother saw a bird she's particularly fond of near the first tee box," said Baxter, grinning.

"Is that right, Mom? Which was the highlight of your day so far?" asked Leo, teasing.

"Your marriage is the highlight. But I'd have to put a broad-winged hawk sighting a close second."

"Not a distant second?"

"It *is* a somewhat rare bird, Leo."

They were relaxed in each other's company—a joyous, weird, stressful, blessed day, but more than anything, a cause for celebration and being together. Weddings did have a way of bringing out the best in people, though also a way of surfacing old memories—something about looking toward the future could dredge up the past. People could get truthful with one another in a real hurry on such occasions. Maybe it was the notion of two people not bound by blood embarking on a great mystery together. Maybe it was the spirit of reconciliation in the air. Maybe it was the free booze. Probably some combination. The point being, it's not just the bride and groom going through the looking glass on such a day; everyone traverses it to an extent, feels it in their guts. A forum to play dress-up in their finery. Reconnecting with old friends and acquittances, making new ones. Even unburdening themselves to those who care to listen or just pretend to do so. Its result was a communal experience, cathartic; to think otherwise was folly, was to ignore that people were in search of something greater than themselves—weddings were often a reminder of that.

"So, what do you guys think? Some familiar faces here today, right?" asked Leo.

"Oh sure. Still a bit surprised you invited the Cornwalls," said Baxter.

"Club politics. Plus they'd find their way here anyway, so just easier to invite them."

"They were never so bad, more territorial than anything," said Ruth. "And Elizabeth has remained one of Lynn's staunchest allies when it comes to the charity event here."

"Another reason to keep them close," mused Baxter.

Leo enjoyed some of the palace intrigue talk, though before he could further weigh in, he noticed Mary Sullivan—of all people—on the periphery of the party, speaking with an older woman on crutches. He made a mental note to approach Mary once he could, not having noticed her during the short-lived ceremony.

"Are you two missing the club much, missing playing at all?" asked Leo, returning to his parents, shaking off the momentary distraction.

"We're still getting here from time to time, even play the occasional lazy round," said Baxter. "But make no mistake—even golf gets put aside once too many of those years pile up."

"As your father loves to say, don't get old, Leo," said Ruth, smiling at her husband, smiling at her granddaughter—generations apart, intertwined in her heart.

"I'll keep that in mind, but somehow, I doubt that the big eight-oh will keep Screws Sinclair from getting out there and knocking a few around," said Leo, clapping his dad on the back, much to his approval. "OK, then, let me make some rounds. You guys have fun. Don't hesitate to get me if you need anything at all. I'm still just your dumb cop kid, wife or no wife."

Ruth quickly leveled her son with a look that was meant to set the record straight among gods and men.

"You are the best of us, Leo. You and your sister," said Ruth, standing up to give her taciturn boy a long hug while still balancing Olivia in one arm, a real pro-mom move.

"Thanks, Mom," said Leo, feeling that javelin of emotion slice through his chest, a kill shot through the breast plate—simple words uttered by the right person, a mother, imbued with so much, with everything, He could hardly believe he was worthy to draw breath, to crawl the earth.

Leo had to turn his back and walk on from them, squelching down what would be many bubbles of emotion on that wedding day, lest they get the best of him, All that armor one builds up over a lifetime, battle tested and second nature as your skin, so easily defeated by the ones who know you best, whom you permit vulnerability around. He found the bar and ordered a much-needed beer—not even a light one—recognizing the kid tending as a Restaurant regular and offering him a hello, to which congratulations on the big day were immediately returned.

Leo proceeded to bop around, talking to a few members who'd been invited, even a few who weren't. He talked with some of Janet's friends from work, support staff for a prominent orthopedics group with over a dozen locations in the tristate area. They were less familiar with the layout of O Triple C, and Leo pointed out some of the finer aspects—how the course was bisected by the maintenance road, the whole I-6, X-12 language, where some of the newer coffee frond trees had been planted in anticipation of higher temperatures and a greater need for water conservation in the future. One of Janet's friends asked if it was true that Leo was actually born on the course. Leo confirmed it good naturedly—he'd long given up being annoyed or frustrated by the question that still found a way to be asked of him at least once every two months, more so when the season was in play. He even graciously pointed out the general direction of where on the fourth hole his delivery had happened, the path the ambulance took to reach him. Leo had even developed a little joke for when he was asked, for just such an occasion, telling people he'd been in a rush to get on the course since the day he was born. A bit corny, yes—but people liked the story and the happy ending, and he'd learned to embrace the dogged question's existence, not resent it.

He never brought up the fact that he was two months premature, and while that might not mean quite as much in 2003, it had been touch-and-go news in 1957, given the incubator technology, NICU development, and infant mortality statistics, No, Leo kept those charming details to himself, always.

He continued through the throng and sallied around: so many friendly, smiling faces to greet, to commiserate with. Leo had always been good with names, faces—had to be for his job—so he was skilled at approaching people, confident in calling them by their correct handle, jumping in with appreciation for their attendance, asking them how they and those close to them were doing. Holding court, being a good host—not necessarily his favorite thing, entertaining, but he was getting into the swing of it that day. His bottle of beer had been drained faster than he realized. The Restaurant's current GM bumped into him, purposeful and playful, a Greek fellow named Joe Mistikis. Despite the short and simple unabashedly American first name his immigrant parents had chosen for him, Joe was always called the Greek as many men of his ilk were called in small towns around this country. The Greek insisted that Leo do a special shot of liquor he'd brought from his private stock, and Leo had no qualms about placating the man. He took the liquid down, a briny twinge, not wholly unpleasant but still the kind of stuff that put hair on your chest, that maybe you only needed to try once in a lifetime. The Greek gave Leo a big hug, doled out some more shots to others around him, and returned to overseeing the staff, determined that everything in his power would be tip-top for Leo's wedding.

Hell of a guy, thought Leo, still tasting the seawater on his tongue.

Then someone asked Leo to pose for a picture using one of those digital cameras that were becoming more and more popular, pictures you didn't have to develop—they lived on the camera, maybe the computer somehow. Leo wasn't sure; he was still a Kodak guy. One of his cop buddies—a good egg, but the kind of dude who took illogical things personally, like rainy weather or a string of red traffic lights—cupped the back of his neck and congratulated him on having an outrageous year, saying he couldn't wait to see what Leo had in store for the holidays. The two spied Oscar Ortiz chatting up a bridesmaid, one of the few who was actually single, no doubt leveraging his best man status to achieve some hierarchy, anything that would put him in a favorable light, her good graces. That was another thing about weddings that people loved: the thought that they might be able to hook up, maybe even find the love of their lives. Those types of stories were important to certain people—did they meet at a wedding or a bar at closing time? Did they meet at a lavender festival, a garlic expo, or outside a hospital breaking up a quarrel over parenting decisions?

Leo caught Oscar's eye and gave him a sly look, wished him luck telepathically. Oscar saluted back with a raised cocktail, paying homage to the man of the hour.

Leo took a beat to track Janet, far across the way, talking to his boss, Chief Wineski— God, he could only imagine what that conversation must be like. For some reason, he was transported back to his youth; it had the feel of a parent-teacher conference where they'd discuss his flaws and foibles. Not that Leo really ever ran afoul of his teachers back in the day, but he was hardly a perfect child. He hoped Janet would keep it light with the chief. Then he hoped the chief would keep it light with Janet. Then he just hoped the two of them were exchanging pleasantries and would part sooner than later. Without asking, someone placed a light beer in his hands and walked off—it appeared no one was going to let him walk empty handed, and he'd have to remind himself to pace it in any hopes of staying upright the entire night.

Leo continued on, spotting Cobb Webb sipping a brandy, maybe a bourbon, holding court over a small group of members, pontificating about his own impending retirement, looking forward to some travel around the country with his newfound disposable time. The man had lasted a long time at O Triple C, longer than a lot of people thought the brash Texan could pull off, Leo included. But he'd made some adjustments over the years, course corrections when needed. Leo figured he was going to miss the guy, his wily ways, cagey personality. He also figured they'd be in good enough hands with their assistant pro, Michael Bouffard, a considerably younger man, who'd be taking the reins after apprenticing under Cobb for the past six years. It was going to be interesting to see what Michael had in store under his new regime, particularly as membership had seen a plateauing effect of late—the wait list not as hale as only a few years ago, and that's when there was a wait list—some dead-cat bounce phenomena had fostered a false belief that the industry was upticking when, in truth, the predictors were far more pessimistic. So young Michael Bouffard would have large shoes to fill and hands full, tapped to bring in new blood to a sport that could be dogged and barrier prone. He would be expected to lure in new prospects with more twenty-first-century thinking, leveraging certain technologies and concierge amenities that old Cobb just couldn't or wouldn't cotton to as his tenure wound down. Leo didn't envy the tasks laid before Michael. He'd help him where he could, but only time would tell if the kid could pull it off, if he could survive the way his predecessor had.

After about ninety minutes outside, the Greek personally announced that it was time to move the cocktail hour inside, that if everybody would grab their belongings, they'd now be seated in the banquet hall. The hundred or so people milled and thinned out, and Leo, despite having seen it many times before, couldn't believe how only a few staff members could facilitate a full wedding reception, even one as low key as his was meant to be. He really did share a great affinity for those in the service industry, made a mental note to ensure they all got a very big tip for taking care of him that day. For some reason, he thought of the old kitchen hand from his teenage years, Olaf Johnson—wondered what he was up to, if he was still smoking that pipe of his. Leo kind of wished Olaf was there and realized he was going to have a real sentimental type of day. He shook it off and spotted Janet again, with her boys and brother, Paul, ushering some guests inside. He saw his own parents heading in the same direction, along with Lynn, Sachin, and Olivia, who was just learning to walk. Then, to his surprise, he saw his mother speaking some words with Mary Sullivan, who appeared to be hanging back behind the dispersing crowd, soon to be alone, with just some of the staff picking up after the cocktail hour. Leo saw his chance and approached her, though not totally sure what to do, how she'd react. Mary noted Leo's slight hesitancy and took pity on his awkwardness, beamed him a smile, the boy she knew, now grown into a married man. She brought him in for a hug, still dear friends despite the forces that kept people apart, even when slightly estranged, even if they reflect some hard truths and unfond memoires.

Leo was relieved he could still hug his godmother, would have been secretly crushed if all had eroded to where that kindness couldn't take place. They released, and Mary gave Leo's shoulders a gentle patting down, straightened his tuxedo, and smoothed the fabric as though her hands were hot irons. She looked older than Leo remembered, having only seen her nine months before, though it was a very brief encounter, happenstance, hastily moved on from. They always had too much to say to one another, though never the words. Another function of a wedding day—polarities reverse, discourse made possible.

"Mrs. Sullivan, you came. I got your RSVP, but it said you wouldn't be able to attend," said Leo.

"I wasn't planning on it, Leo. In a sense, I'm still not," said Mary, sounding unsure, even more fragile than she had in the past. "I'm just so happy for you and Janet and what you two are going to build together."

"Thank you. I'd love for you to meet her. She'd be thrilled."

"Perhaps someday soon, but I can't go inside there. I can barely stand here," said Mary. "I haven't been inside since Peter passed. I'm sure you understand."

"Of course. I'm sorry you had to come here if it's too much . . ." Leo didn't know how to finish, if he should finish. Mary gently raised her hand.

"It's long overdue that I at least stepped foot back on these grounds, maybe just to prove a little something to myself," she said, showing some verve. "And there wasn't going to ever be a better reason than to see you on your wedding day."

Leo warmed to the sentiment, touched by the courage he knew Mary Sullivan had tapped into.

"How does it feel to be back?" he asked. Mary collected her thoughts, parsed her emotions into certain airtight compartments, bearing in mind she was speaking with the groom on his big day.

"Like something that needed doing, and maybe it hasn't been as upsetting as I'd built it up to be," she said calmly, her breathing choreographed. "It's been twenty years. All time does is move on, with or without you."

"Twenty years," said Leo. *Blink of an eye*, he thought.

"Peter would have been very proud of you today," said Mary. "He would have been overjoyed."

Leo remembered the man, remembered his boisterous nature, his life-of-the-party mentality. He would have been a huge presence on such a day, celebrating his godson, a reception that would not be forgotten if he had any say in the matter.

"I still miss him. Obviously, my loss isn't anything compared to what you and Chip have endured," said Leo. "But he would have been a great force in my life if he was still with us today."

"That's very kind of you to say, Leo."

"The fact that I've never been able to learn more about what happened that night, that I've never tracked down a credible lead or come any closer to the truth is the biggest failure of my career, of my life really," said Leo.

"I know you've never given up, and you keep that investigation close to your heart," said Mary. "That means more to me than I could ever tell you. But maybe there are just some things in this life we're not meant to know."

"Do you really believe that?" asked Leo, who'd been wrestling with similar thoughts. It had been eight months since someone tried to shoot him. They still hadn't a clue who it was, and the prospects weren't looking good they ever would.

"I have to; otherwise, how does one go on?"

Leo nodded his head, letting the advice resonate, wondering how applicable it was to his own situation, if it was a harbinger of how he'd have to continue on with his life—with this big, looming question hovering over him, forever unanswered.

"But none of this is what today's about. This is about your success and happiness and how we're all excited for your family," said Mary. "Including Chip, who sends his congratulations all the way from Japan."

"He's doing well?" asked Leo.

"Yes, thanks, his commission should be finished up in about a month, and he'll be home for a bit. Then, knowing him, off again soon to somewhere interesting," said Mary, always pleased to speak of her son and the success he'd had in architecture—though with a note of sadness as she knew he was prone to wanderlust, wouldn't stay in the States for than a few weeks at a time.

"Maybe I could bring Janet by when he's home, and the four of us can catch up in person?"

"I'd like that very much, Leo," said Mary, meaning it, though also forlorn. "Now enough hanging around with the likes of me. You've got a very big job to do. Get inside and attend to your guests. Make sure to enjoy this special day."

"Are you sure I can't convince you to come inside? I'll make sure you're seated with my parents."

"No, it's for thc bcst," said Mary.

She gave Leo one last hug, clearly holding back some emotion, and quickly took her leave of him, no need to tarry. It broke her heart she had so little to offer him—she couldn't even step inside the building where they'd celebrate his marriage to raise a glass of champagne and toast his new life. But she had shown up, even if it was just the outside property; despite her revulsion for the place, she'd willed herself to be present for Leo in some form, to show she cared, to show he was loved by the Sullivans—alive, dead, or abroad. She could leave now, her sense of duty fulfilled, departing the place she still felt held some culpability in her husband's mysterious death, even if she'd never been able to prove it or even define it. Nevertheless, it existed all the same—the way bones exist in your body even if you don't know all their names. .

The lack of evidence had never dissuaded her, and time had only hardened her position that O Triple C factored in somehow. That much, she would stake the husk of her life on.

Leo went inside, returned to his wedding party, and was ushered to his table in the front of the room, where he felt like a judge before a courtroom. It was a bit more exposure than he typically liked, but he knew to roll with it. Somehow, even more professional-grade photographs were taken; the photographer was tenacious if anything, She had blue hair and a stern resting face and seemed committed to dedicating her young life to the balance of light and dark, the medium of film, though Leo wondered if she had loftier artistic pursuits and then figured of course she did. He'd have to ask Janet how she came across her, as the photography had been Janet's department. It amused him that he was already excited to see the photos developed, despite the fact he was currently living through what would be in those captured moments. He hoped that didn't mean he wasn't being present, that he wasn't savoring his time, an accusation that had been foisting upon him from time to time. But he thought he was being present, mostly—even if some of the day had aspects that felt like a reality bend. He hadn't longed to be out on the golf course or the shooting range or back at HQ worrying over the niggling details lodged in his mind. Maybe the unexpected encounter with Mary Sullivan had thrown him a bit, but he thought himself in the moment and having a good time.

At the very least, he knew he was right where he wanted to be.

Leo was saved from the maze of his scattered thoughts with the chiming of cutlery on the water glasses, indicating he was to give his bride a kiss per the commands of his guests. They obliged, and Janet gave him a look to reinforce that all was well. They were good. Then the carts of seafood were rolled in, raw bar towers to all the tables, always a big hit at New England weddings, tapping into local and historic cultures but mostly tapping into people's affinity for fresh food that had already been shelled and cut octopus dipped in exotic mustards. These types of towers didn't stand a chance and would get picked clean as people washed down the ocean's bounty, paired with artisanal breads and very chilled white and rose wine. The DJ would fire up his act shortly, herding cats and lending some direction to how the evening was going to play out, how they were all going to celebrate the Sinclairs on their momentous day. Leo had instructed the guy, DJ Rodney, that a light touch would be preferable—less would be more, so to speak. DJ Rodney understood, knew how to accommodate such a request. Those mechanics wouldn't be a problem; a more reserved reception was the easiest to pull off and, when done well, the most tasteful.

Once everyone was seated and the seafood and drinks and music were in full swing, the party mostly progressed as typical wedding stuff for the next few hours. Folks eating too much, drinking too much. The kids out on the dance floor. Some old standards getting played. Some sly conversations taking place around the hall. Some members from the club side poked their heads in, Leo waving them in to have a drink at his open bar, where they'd congratulate him though questioning his decision to marry when he so clearly still needed time to get his handicap down to single digits—the ribbing never ending, not even on his actual wedding day.

Somewhere between the full dinner and dessert offerings, speeches were delivered. Janet's maid of honor orated a brief yet poignant testimony to the woman Janet was, the mother she was to Bo and Clay, and the wife she'd be to Leo. She prophesized a long and enduring marriage, and the whole room agreed with her. Then Oscar got up and belted out a whopper of a best man's speech, almost ten minutes that brought down the house. It was a rare opportunity for the man to express his real feelings for his buddy, but under the auspices of such a day, a little sentimentality was encouraged, Oscar let it all hang out—professing his love for Leo and Janet, delving into dodgy territory around their dangerous profession, the specter of 9/11, and even a subtle wink to the dangerous night Leo experience back in January. Oscar integrated the heady material quite well into the more thoughtful and saccharine fodder, a soliloquy that surprised more than a few people in attendance, including Leo, who hadn't known his mountain of a buddy had it in him. It really was a hell of a speech, aided by a little alcohol and Oscar's desire to impress any of the bridesmaids who might have taken a shine to him. But mostly, it was just a heartfelt rendition to the bride and groom, people who had his back as he had theirs. The room hoisted their flutes to the ceiling, toasting the sparkling couple. Oscar gave Janet a kiss and Leo a hug—a real one, not a bro hug, true brothers in arms. The three whispered a few words among themselves that wouldn't make it into the public record.

The night evolved, or devolved, depending on how you looked at it. The older and saner people, the families, begged off around eleven p.m., while the night owls took over, determined to keep the party going past midnight. The banquet hall was officially meant to wrap up at twelve a.m., but the Greek had other plans in mind. He and his staff had already committed to keeping the show going for as long as Leo and Janet wanted, which really wouldn't be that much longer, as the adrenaline of the day was winding down. Around one a.m., they were down to about twenty core guests. Much of the extended family had split; even Oscar had shimmied off into the night, not empty handed. The last of them were singing to nineties hip-hop songs, words and moves Leo and Janet didn't know well, but the younger folks seemed to know them all by heart. DJ Rodney knew the hits, knew the modern classics the later generation gravitated to. That carried on until Leo and Janet exchanged a few words, both ready to tap out, dead tired on their feet. Leo gave the DJ his blessing to shut it down. The happy couple took the mic one last time and thanked everybody for coming out—thanked DJ Rodney, Joe Mistikis, thanked all the staff and servers and bartenders for making it such a memorable night, perfect really. A final round of cheers was offered, and people slowly shuffled their way out of the building. The Greek brought DJ Rodney over to the member side of the building and treated him to any drink he fancied, customary for entertainers performing at the Restaurant, no matter who the current GM was. They left Leo and Janet alone in the now-cleared-out room, literally to themselves for the first time the entire day. The two pulled up chairs besides each other and took a load off. Janet removed her shoes with the relief of a marathon runner finishing up that last mile. Leo took her hands in his and kissed them like a blessing, sanctifying them. It was sublime to finally be alone with her, even if they were exhausted—it was clear to him she was happy. It was clear to her that he was happy.

"Tell me all the things you're thinking," he asked.

She'd do just that—she couldn't wait to share her life with him.

* * *

"OK, I want you to explain it again to me," said Janet, leaning forward and nearly out of her skin. "What does that mean—it was a bad traffic stop?"

Leo had had twenty-four hours to craft a response, to deliver the news about the previous night to Janet, but still felt there was no good way to do it. No matter how many different permutations of the message he practiced in his mind, they were all going to come out awkward or fumbled over. That said, his time was up, and he had to spill.

"A guy, presumably, had a punched-out taillight, so I pulled him over," said Leo calmy, sharing the couch with Janet. "I thought it would be humdrum, the way most of that stuff goes down."

"Aren't you always saying each traffic stop is its own thing?" said Janet. "Like a roulette spin, the past has nothing to do with the present. That's your line, right?"

Sometimes Leo hated how well Janet paid attention to people, especially him.

"Well, yeah, that's true, and it does mean you take precautions before each stop, hoping to ward off complacency," said Leo, pinned down by his own logic and diatribes. "But at the same time, when the ball lands on black hundreds of times in a row, it does get hard to imagine it won't land that way again."

"Except you're telling me it landed on white last night?"

"Well, red, but yeah, that's the gist of it," said Leo, clumsily. Janet motioned with her hands for him to continue.

"So before I could even approach the car, the driver pushed out the window and took a shot at me, then sped off like it was the end of the world or something," he said, well aware that his glossing-over skills left something to be desired and wouldn't suffice with Janet.

"I'm sorry, you said he took a shot at you," said Janet, her eyes bulging a bit, clearly not fooled by Leo's attempt at a slow roll. "You care to elaborate on that? Are you saying someone fired a gun at you last night?"

Leo stalled, bought himself ten seconds by pretending to clear a stray eyelash, a fake annoyance he fake skimmed off the surface of his cornea.

"Um, yes, that's what I'm saying but I don't want you upset by it."

"Don't worry about upsetting me right now. Let's just stick to the facts," said Janet, channeling the inner prosecutor who lives inside all mothers, wives. "Is that why you have that bandage on the back of your head? Is that from a bullet?"

"No, no, nothing like that. The bullet never touched me, just buzzed me," said Leo, still trying to downplay, though hearing how weak his own trump card was to his ears, none of it landing with Janet. "But it was enough for me to lose balance and hit my head on the cruiser. The road was icy."

Janet processed this information with computerlike stoicism. Of course she was relieved to know that Leo was OK, that he seemed lucid enough despite an overnight in the hospital for a head injury. The brief version Leo had delivered over the phone had been jarring, almost panic inducing—she'd insisted on seeing him that night. Her kids were with their father, Billy, for the next two nights, so the opportunity was there for her.

Leo knew better than to refuse her this one, even if he thought one night alone after the hospital convalescence was the better thing for him. But the truth was he did want to see her— had wanted to see her in the hospital—even if he wasn't feeling his best, like a wounded animal, more vulnerable than he liked to admit. So he gave her the green light, and she drove over to his place after work, impatient the whole day at the orthopedic practice, to find Leo reading some tome in his Bob's Discount Furniture recliner. His television was off, as always—Janet had never met a man so disinterested in TV and unafraid of missing out on those watercooler conversations about hit shows and pop culture—a zeitgeist that just didn't factor into his existence. The actual TV in his apartment, a Sony, basically sat there for aesthetics. Maybe it would be turned on to catch some sports, certainly some golf, maybe the Superbowl if he happened to be home that night. Otherwise, he could have just had a potted plant in that space, and it wouldn't have made much of a difference to him.

"What does that mean, buzzed your ear?" she asked, her inquisition in full swing, grinding her witness down. Leo considered the question, how to define the word.

"Got close but never touched."

"How close? Tell me when I'm there," said Janet, who extended her thumb and pointer finger out as far as possible from each other, then shrank the distance down to two inches, her makeshift units of measurement for Leo to gauge. He looked, almost squinted, as though he were trying really hard or the exercise confused him when, in reality, it was only bringing last night's incident into sharper perspective.

"I guess it was closer than that."

Janet halved the distance between her fingers to about an inch.

"Is this buzzed territory?" she asked.

"Maybe a smidge closer."

She halved the distance again, looking incredulous.

"Leo, any closer and it's in your ear."

"Yeah, no, you're right; that's about it," he said. Janet assessed the distance she'd measured then held it up for Leo to see.

"So this is the margin from you getting shot in the face last night?"

"Well, my ear getting shot."

"The ear is part of the face. And if the bullet had been two or three inches closer?"

"Yeah, well, then definitely in my face. But that didn't happen."

Janet took a beat, obviously screwing up her resolve to stay composed and keep her shit together in the face of Leo's contrived coolness. She was neither a computer nor a district attorney, so the fireworks inside her were just waiting to go ablaze, even in the face of Leo's approach, his hopes for a soft landing, which, rightly or wrongly, was infuriating her more. She started shaking her head back and forth, barely aware she was doing it.

"Leo, what in the ever-loving fuck are we talking about here?" she said, her hands getting in on the action with the exaggerated motion of a dog's leg kicking during a dream.

"I know, baby. It's fucked. I'm not trying to tell you any of it's good."

She moved over on the couch they'd been sharing, and he pulled her into his embrace, a long one that brought some life back into him, made him feel solid and real and less an illustration of some phantom power. Her warmth was comforting—not just her concern for him but the actual body heat she radiated, pressed into him, hearth-like and sublime.

"Are you OK?" she asked, as though some of it were truly sinking in, a reset of sorts, beyond the cross-examination, now into the territory of the longer version, hearing it and what could have been. "I mean it; are you really OK?"

"I'm really OK, I promise. I hit my head good, got some stitches, but I was monitored the whole night," said Leo, holding her hands. "The pain's not too bad. They gave me a script to fill if I need it."

"Let me see it," she said.

He handed Janet the piece of paper with the information on it from the end table. She read it over.

"This is strong stuff. I recognize it from people getting surgeries at our practice," she said. "Are you going to fill this?"

"I don't think so. Some Tylenols seem to be doing the trick—that and some rest."

Janet seemed relieved by that answer and placed the script back on the end table where a voluminous book dedicated to the antebellum conflicts on American soil lay bookmarked and dogeared.

"Light reading?" she asked.

"The print is just a smidge blurry, and I'm not absorbing every word, but yeah, I'd say if I can mostly read that, then I'm on the mend."

Janet finally allowed the faintest trace of smile to surface—softly, the kind in which more was revealed in the corners of her mouth, the curl of her lips.

"Look, the chief told me to take some time off, as much as I need, then get cleared and come back once I'm ready, no sooner."

"That's good of him," said Janet, still processing, still coming to terms with the events of the past twenty-four hours. "Do you want me to stay the night? Maybe you shouldn't be alone?"

"Need, no. Want, yes. But also, need, yes."

"I'll stay then," she said, then allowed the room to fall quiet for more than a few beats. "Did Wineski say anything about who did this to you? Did they catch the guy?"

"I got the license plate, but it's looking like a stolen car from some people currently vacationing in Orlando," said Leo. "Then this morning, the station got a call about a late-night mechanic shop robbed, owner bound and gagged, safe emptied, wasn't found until an employee showed up to clock in."

"That's terrible."

"They took the owner's statement, and he said the guy wore a ski mask, seemed like he knew what he was doing, like he'd been really planning it out," said Leo. "But then he heard a noise once the robber left, like a car hitting something. Looks like he might have clipped a dumpster he hadn't seen in the dark. There was apparently some debris around to suggest it."

"The broken taillight, the reason you pulled him over?"

"Seems that way."

"How far away is the mechanic's from where you first spotted the car?"

"Less than two miles."

"Jesus, Leo."

"Yeah, I know, like it was meant to be."

"So what are they doing now?"

"There's not much to go on given it's a stolen car, which he's probably already ditched somewhere," said Leo. "We'll see if there's any camera footage anywhere to use, shake as many trees in the county as we can, but if this guy's got half a brain, which it's looking like he might, he'll leave the state for a while and lay low."

"And if he can't leave the state for some reason?"

"Either way, the robbery now comes with an attempted murder charge, against a police officer no less," said Leo. "He'll be looking over his shoulder no matter what, maybe his whole life."

Janet took a breath, replaying Leo's words in her mind, "attempted murder." Her next question was a delicate one that she didn't totally know how to ask, but it needed asking all the same.

"Do you really think he was trying to kill you?"

A million-dollar question, one of a few Leo had been confronted with over the past twenty-four hours.

"I don't know. Maybe he panicked. Maybe he just thinks he's that good of a shot and missed on purpose," said Leo. "But by default, a bullet that close, I have to assume he was trying to put me down in some capacity. That's certainly how the law is going to see it."

Janet clamped her hands around his, tighter.

"I can't believe this happened in our town. And I know being a police officer is dangerous, but still, Orchard Coils . . ."

Jane trailed off, and Leo allowed it. All he could do was silently agree with her, even if he did know much more about the underbelly of their town than she did.

"And to think you were out there by yourself, then alone in that hospital," said Janet. "I wish someone would have called me."

"Well, I wasn't really alone. Most of the department was cycling in and out. And Oscar did ask if he should call you, but I just didn't want you or the boys to worry over something that was going to turn out fine."

Janet released his hands, slowly pulled them back to her own body.

"You actually told Oscar *not* to call us when he volunteered?"

"I mean, yeah, what would it have served? You'd have had to pack up the boys, get out of the house well past midnight just to see me sitting in a chair trying not to drool on myself, answering the occasional cognitive question."

"Yes, Leo, that's exactly what the three of us would have done," said Janet, a new quaver in her voice, tectonic and foreboding. "If there was even the remotest possibility you weren't going to be OK, we would have been there in a heartbeat. Even if you were totally going to be OK, maybe having some non-cops by your side would have been a good thing."

Leo could sense the choppy water he was in, felt some bloom of shame in his cheeks, conceding maybe he hadn't given this part of his explanation nearly enough thought.

"It was just a bad bump on the head, Janet, I promise you. I was going to survive the night, as I clearly have," said Leo reassuringly. "And you're here now. It hasn't even been twelve hours since I was discharged."

"You're not a neurologist just because you've had some police training on head injuries. You don't know how things could have gone last night," said Janet tersely. "And shouldn't your parents have also been called last night? If I'd have known, I could have picked them up too."

Leo felt that quick flash in his chest, a reptilian call to give in to anger. He stymied it, mostly, an adroit aspect of his truer nature.

"Come on, Janet, now you want my parents there too," said Leo, fatigued. "I'm not saying it wasn't scary because it was, but I need you to trust my judgment on these types of things. You being here right now means everything to me, but a room full of family for a one-nighter wasn't the move."

Janet could feel herself about to dig in, to let it all go at the same time. After four years, she knew this man very well: his strengths, his weakness, his blind spots, and the shit he'd barely be able to admit to himself looking in a mirror, mining his soul. It would be so easy for her to turn this into a fight, not entirely unjustified and one that would dip into other spots of bother in their relationship. Leo could be thickheaded and obtuse, proud when he felt vindicated, ambivalent when he thought others were watching too closely, when he'd forgo something to prove. She knew exactly where to go after him, the fracture that had never healed right, the trauma that left behind a soft spot—but she didn't. Janet dialed back her own anger, took a very deep and obvious breath so as to deny the moment its chance to define them as people, flawed people under immense pressure. Leo understood what he was seeing. And it wasn't like he was trying to bait or goad her into some grandiose argument—just the opposite, being too earnest for his own good.

In short, sometimes saying less, or the artistry of omission, was the better tack for all parties involved—a universal truth.

"All right, Leo, what's done is done, and there is no point harping on it, especially given the gravity of what you've been through," said Janet, softening. "I'm so sorry this terrible thing has happened to you. But I want to tell you something because maybe you don't fully understand your place in the dynamic here."

She paused to allow Leo a chance to say something, to interject a thought or objection, but he kept his trap shut, learning quicky and offering a hearty endorsement for Janet to continue, especially since he hadn't a clue what she'd say next, only hoped that it didn't end with her exiting the front door.

"You, for better or worse, are fully loved by me and Bo and Clay. You are not an outsider; you're not a surrogate or some stray we feed from time to time, even if you try to convince yourself you are," said Janet patiently. "You are a part of us, and there is nothing you could ask that we wouldn't take seriously. And I don't know if you even realize all this—maybe you don't—but God, we're the happiest when you're around."

Leo was not so much taken aback because he didn't have a notion of what Janet was saying, but it was still amazing to hear someone say that about him, to be brought into the fold, accepted as one of the tribe by the chieftain, no less. It was no small thing when a fierce woman, a protective mother, allowed you near her young, let alone trusted you with them implicitly. A woman who valued your input in raising them, molding them, punishing them. He still might not have been convinced that leaving them alone the night before was a bad call, but maybe he hadn't fully understood what he'd built with this woman over the past four years. That he wasn't just some piker along for the ride. That he needn't be dissuaded because they'd had some off-again moments, lost time. That he needn't look for something better when he already had something immeasurably special with Janet, right there at his fingertips if he would only man up and claim it. That he was already a part of something divine and needed to stop waiting for a sign or someone's approval. Or. Or. He could also nearly get his head blown off and maybe start actually seeing with the functioning senses he'd been blessed with—there was always that possibility, one reasonable way to approach it. Maybe that's what it would take for Leo Sinclair to understand what everyone else around him had known for some time.

Now he wasn't even sure if he could meet Janet's eyes. He averted them, only to see their black reflection in the television's bubble screen, mildly warped—which, as he thought about it, was a raffle prize he'd won some years ago with a lucky ticket, technology utterly wasted on him. He watched Janet's arms' outreach first through the TV, then in real life, and he inched back closer to her until wrapped in her arms again, leaning heavily into one another. They could feel the breath of life entering and exiting their frames in a less-than-hurried fashion, on their time.

He sighed, both defeated and triumphant. She whispered in his ear, a grand armistice achieved.

"You don't need to sort this all out tonight, Leo," said Janet, smoothing the day-old stubble on his cheek. Rare for him to not shave. "You'll find the right tempo."

Tempo, he thought—a golf lesson he believed in, that Janet knew he favored, but also a selfish tenet to live by, worth chiding himself over, as though his time was paramount.

They would talk more that night and into the following day, and Leo would eventually heal up and return to work in a week's time. He would see the boys; they would bake him a cake with the help of their mother. Things would start to feel normal again. Expect that Leo had more than made up his mind, after allowing a little time for reflection, mostly out of his pragmatic habits—he would propose to Janet on Valentine's Day, as cliche as that might be, on one knee in a local restaurant that served amazing eggplant. He'd ask for Paul's blessing in advance, in lieu of their wayward father, and he'd grant it enthusiastically. Corny and old fashioned—he'd long accepted that about himself. But that was exactly the kind of guy Janet wanted in her life. So she would say yes, with no hesitation—she'd even cry over the proposal, something she hadn't done her first go-around, and she knew the tears were well spent and for the right reasons.

* * *

A personal card and correspondence sent to Leo Sinclair from Kirby Keener, dated September 8, 2003.

Hello Leo,

It is with great enthusiasm that I write this note as word has gotten back to me of your recent nuptials. I offer my heartiest congratulations to you and your new bride, Janet, and sons, Bo and Clayford.

Though our paths have seldom crossed over the intervening years since our first encounter, I still fondly recall that evening and the education you provided me as to the lopsided coverage that was going on under my nose, among other biases that were later revealed. I trust you've more than observed the remedies put into place once I was able to ferret out that fifth column, a delicate task given the family nature of my business.

I seldom find myself both shocked and indebted, though such was the outcome of that fateful night of cards at your revered O Triple C.

Please accept a small wedding gift to you and Janet as your life together begins as one, a bottle of champagne that will be delivered to your doorstep monthly. It is my sincerest hope that you will have much to celebrate over the upcoming decades, and I've often found a little bubbly a time-tested and jovial accoutrement.

I'd hoped to deliver that first bottle personally, but alas, my health is not what it used to be, so I write this salutation from my sickbed, in hopes of not only my own recovery but also your continued success and happiness.

If I may offer one parting word of unsolicited advice as it relates to the trials and tribulations of marriage, a tenet that has served me well during my own union, it is never to stop dating your wife. This is where I'm hoping the champagne will come in useful from time to time.

Also know this is a gift that will continue on well past my remaining years of life, however many that may be.

All the best to you and yours,

Kirby L. Keener

2012

The last thing Leo wanted to see was his phone lighting up, an incoming call around ten p.m. on a Thursday, especially when it was Officer Fletcher on the other end, the kind of man who would never call unless it was urgent. There was zero chance this was going to be good news, so the real question was just how bad this incoming news would be. He peeled himself off the couch where he and Janet had been watching a DVD of a show she'd become obsessed with, finally convincing Leo to give it a chance despite his aversion to watching TV as a pastime. After a few episodes, Leo had begrudgingly admitted to enjoying the program—by the end of the season one box set, Mr. No TV was thoroughly hooked—who would have thought the New Mexico meth business could be so interesting? So Leo had made it a point for them to watch at least one episode a night together, two at the most—which they had just finished right before Leo's phone starting pinging with a new call. Janet was now off in the house somewhere, probably pestering Clay in some motherly fashion. Leo looked to that flashing touch screen, sighed, and took the call with as much cheer as he could muster, given the late hour, proceeding to say things into the device's little microphone such as "OK" and "I understand" in a calm voice, despite the waves of stomach acid that now roiled his innards. The news was not catastrophic, but most certainly not good. He thanked Fletcher for the call and told him he'd be on the scene in ten minutes, to keep everybody there, not to do anything further out of protocol.

He thanked Fletcher a second time and ended the call.

Leo went upstairs and quickly changed back into his work clothes, the ones he'd only been able to get out of a couple of hours ago. Janet was, in fact, on the second floor, hovering around Clay's doorframe, maybe helping him with his homework, though more likely just giving him the business, pumping him for information that her now fourteen-year-old, a newly minted high school freshman, was reluctant to give up, much to Janet's chagrin, though she'd experienced the same phenomenon once Bo had reached his teen years and moved on from middle school to the big building.

The funny thing about Bo was that once he'd hit seventeen years old, he'd decided to turn the spigot of information back on, sharing things with his mom and Leo, now boastful about his exploits as though there would be no reprisals, despite the fact that he did catch punishments when the offense was grievous enough, oddly to his surprise, but also devoid of anger and resentment. Janet liked to think it was because she'd raised a well-mannered and reasonable young man. Leo was less sure on that front but didn't want to remove his wife's rose-colored glasses as they pertained to her oldest. He instead pegged Bo as shrewder than he let on, not the dogmatic follower of etiquette his mother would like to believe but copping to things when it served his purpose somehow, even when a grounding could be leveraged to stay home and get out of certain things with his friends, maybe even to just have a quiet weekend to himself without it looking like his design. The kid had a closet homebody streak that Leo recognized in himself, not always easy to hide from your friends, who wanted you out every weekend to raise hell one way or another.

Sometimes you just needed a good excuse to stay in, to satisfy those home-drawn instincts that compel one toward familiarity, toward four walls and a roof that provide a simple comfort.

Bo also had a talent for getting what he wanted. The kid was cagey like that, not Mr. Manners as Janet would like to believe. Another theory of Leo's revolved around Bo being home to create an opportunity for his biological dad, Billy, to pay visits to his punished son or just to hang about a bit before he took Bo, Clay, or both of them for a few days per the long-standing custody arrangements, which had grown more fluid as the years piled up. Leo didn't consider Bo's finagling such a bad thing but found it interesting he'd lead the charge on such solidarity, trying to lend further peace to a situation that had actually been humming along smoothly enough for more than a few years—not that there hadn't been bumps along the way. Ten-plus years of work had gone into Janet and Billy working through their post-divorce issues, many settled, some tabled, and a few that would never, ever be resolved. But they had gotten to a place where they could be civil enough, almost happy, in each other's company, to in their common love for Bo and Clay. They'd found enough respect for one another even if they were no longer bound in the eyes of God or the ink of law. Billy had never remarried and seemed better off for it, quite content to carry on unencumbered and answer to only himself. Janet had found what she was looking for in Leo, raising the boys in a much more stable household.

As for Billy and Leo, they got along surprisingly well, much of that Leo's calculus toward how the situation would need to function long term. Billy's initial concerns were assuaged quickly enough when it became evident that Leo would be a sound stepfather—still a bitter pill for a man to swallow but a matter the courts weren't going to help him out on. They were stuck with each other; the saving grace was that no one rebelled against this fact with excessive force or childish tantrums. And now that the boys were older—Bo driving, Clay dreaming of his learner's permit—some of the early rigidity in their logistics, their attitudes toward one another, had softened considerably. Plus, Billy was savvy enough to know that running afoul of Orchard Coil's current chief of police wasn't going to get him anywhere. Even if Leo was an above-board cop, he was still a man with tremendous power in town, so Billy would rather engineer that to his advantage, which he had in small and useful ways, cagey—probably where Bo had picked up the attribute in the first place, either learned or inherited.

In any event, Leo was putting on his day-old clothes, finding his wallet, looking for some clean socks when Janet gravitated toward their bedroom, relenting off Clay and now curious to see what her husband was getting himself into. The house was very much her domain, despite her still working full time, and she liked to keep up with the pulse of it—such was her prerogative and a mechanism of control she enjoyed.

"Why are you getting into uniform?" she asked.

"Welp, just got a call, and it appears Bo and some friends snuck onto the course but weren't as stealthy as they thought they were," said Leo. "Patrol unit found them and are keeping them put for the moment. Fletcher gave me the heads-up, so I'm going to head over."

"He said they were going bowling," said Janet, shaking her head. So much for Mr. Manners tonight.

"No bowling alley on the seventh hole, last I checked."

"Seventh hole. Don't tell me."

"I'm guessing Devil's Altar. We'll see," said Leo, putting on his chief's cap. "Town folklore keeps getting built up higher and higher in front of our eyes."

"I'm sorry, Leo," said Janet, entering the walk-in closet and retrieving a belt Leo had neglected to put on.

"It was one thing when it was just the Halloween Trail and a ghost story for the kids," said Leo. "But after Sullivan, everything changed, and it's just taken on a life of its own."

"I know it's painful to see," said Janet. "But at least it's mostly just dumb teenagers doing dumb teenager stuff."

"Dumb teenagers that tonight apparently had alcohol, candles, and a dead animal and were reeking of pot."

"I'll kill the little shit," said Janet, not meaning it, but also kind of.

"I'm sure you will, but before that, let me go over there and find out exactly what our dumb teenager has gotten himself into," said Leo. "Then I'll bring him home, and you can tear him a new one if he deserves it."

"Hard to figure he won't deserve it."

"Probably, though one never knows."

Leo and Janet went back downstairs together, noticing Clay's door was now closed, which made things easier as he'd want to know why Leo would was dressed for work, why he was heading out so late. Clay was protective of his stepfather like that, actually worried about the dangers of the job—it could be sweet, when it wasn't neurotic. They were better off keeping Clay in the dark until they could learn more about what trouble his brother had gotten into that night. Like most younger brothers, Clay worshipped Bo and was highly malleable to his influence, oftentimes for good, but sometimes for the worse.

Janet saw Leo to the front door and gave him a kiss, and he left in their Chevy Impala. The golf course was only ten minutes away, which didn't give him much time to iron out his thoughts about what he'd be stepping into, based on the limited information Fletcher was able to provide over the phone. At the very least, it indicated some typical trespassing, though the paraphernalia mentioned was troubling—but really, it didn't sound like anything untoward was taking place, given the usual nonsense the PD was accustomed to seeing on the seventh hole from time to time, particularly after the sun had set, and the golfers were long gone. Those sightings tended to spike in the fall, deeper into the Halloween season by design, not coincidence. So much so that the course needed the cops to conduct routine check-ins on both October 30 and 31, after a spate of vandalism from more than a decade ago. None of this was major crime stuff, but it still cut close to home for Leo on a variety of fronts that were often hard to square in his mind. And now to have Bo in the mix—it just felt like a new vector of attack from the Quarry Witch legend, something he didn't want to believe in, but, at times, it sure felt like it believed in him.

A few years before, Leo had gone as far as to speak with some of the committee chairs at the club to recommend the retiring of the Halloween Trail, that it had become unseemly, given what had occurred in '78, that it was only helping perpetuate a bothersome campfire story, a sleepover tale the kids were taking too seriously. But Leo's request had fallen on deaf ears. Some of the committee members argued that the Halloween Trail was still a family favorite, others that history and tradition, even in eras when they might be uncomfortable or inconvenient, should still be adhered to. Some thought it was just the Orchard Coils police not wanting the extra hassle, as if their job patrolling a small town wasn't easy enough to begin with. But the unspoken reason, the one Leo believed held the most sway, was that the majority of those governing members thought it brought good and interesting attention to the course. To be latched to the town in a specific way, associated with certain lore, lent a brand recognition the club was willing to capitalize on—and, in truth, was eager to leverage more of. Leo wasn't so sure anyone was going to give the club a second look just because they had some loose affiliation with an old mining story or the tragic death of one of its members—these seemed like detriments to him. But then again, Leo was hardly a businessman and knew very little of marketing and free advertising, let alone this social media trend that had been gaining steam of late, something Leo hadn't the slightest knowledge of or interest in.

So the Halloween Trail carried on, and the kids still made their trek while their parents drank spooky punch in the Restaurant, further paying homage to the generational tradition and keeping their little indoctrination ritual alive on the seventh hole. Leo continued to dislike it as a member, a cop, a parent, and a godson—somewhat painfully, as he did have fond memories of it back when he walked it in the sixties. But now he knew of kids who had walked the trail only to return to the site as teenagers, even adults, to further indulge the fantasy, to pay respect to a deity that held court in a mine below—allegedly—her quarry still rich with untapped resources. He feared a magnetism growing toward the place, a Bloody Mary story that certain towns developed that attracted unwanted attention and brewed unwanted things. Leo had seen firsthand how it had taken on a life of its own and, despite being chief of police, he seemed to have less power to contain it. It would appear he hadn't even the authority to keep his own stepson away.

That was about all the thinking Leo got through before he arrived at the course and parked the car by the largest utility building, the Monastery, and hoofed it across the road despite the lack of light—a moonless night. He easily followed the cart path up to the seventh hole. This was territory he had wayfared a million times before; he could handle it in his sleep. He spied the figures in the distance, Fletcher standing tallest among the group that seemed to contain five kids, including Bo. Leo joined them wordlessly and sized up the motley crew, curious to see if he recognized any of them. There were two girls in the group Leo was unfamiliar with, but one of the boys looked vaguely familiar, though Leo couldn't place him. The remaining boy was very much a known factor to Leo—the son of the head groundskeeper of the club, Jocko Whalley the Third—the youngest hard-ass in a family line that prided themselves on being such. Also one of

Bo's best friends since they started attending the same high school, having already known each other a bit from earlier years around the club. A friendship Leo wasn't too enthusiastic about, not necessarily trusting Bo's laisse faire attitude to the wiles of a Whalley, though, in truth, Leo wasn't totally sure how far from the tree this youngest Jocko had fallen. For all he knew, it was Bo or any of the others acting as ringleader. He reminded the cop in him to keep an open mind, not to let his parent side jump to hasty conclusions.

He settled his gaze and process upon them.

"Chief," said Officer Fletcher, nodding his head, flashlight ablaze.

"Fletcher. What have we got?"

"Someone called in and saw our young friends here sneaking onto the course. Dispatch sent me to have a look-see," said Fletcher. "Didn't take long to find them. Recognized one of them in particular."

All eyes fell on Bo. Bo's eyes fell on the ground.

"Indeed," said Leo, shifting his attention to Bo. "Care to tell me what you all are doing out here?"

Fletcher shined the flashlight on Bo's face. The boy squinted from the glare but did so calmly. His overall demeanor suggested a coolness—genuine or fronting, it was tough to say.

"We're doing what everybody does up here," said Bo. "We're taking part in the ghost story. What else is there to do here?"

It appeared that Bo would take a more straightforward approach, perhaps involving some actual truth and maybe leveraging small-town boredom.

"And that would include drinking and the contact high I'm getting just being around you kids?" asked Leo, unamused, making an exaggerated sniffing noise to indicate he and Fletcher were no dummies.

"It's just a six-pack, Mr. Sinclair," said Jocko neutrally, which was basically his version of contrition.

Fletcher cast the flashlight onto the groundskeeper's kid as though it were a spotlight on a stage actor who had just flubbed a line.

"You want I should check their car, Chief? We got plenty of cause," suggested Fletcher.

"Naw, you did that already, found nothing, remember?" said Leo casually.

Fletcher was quick enough on the uptake to follow, nodding along in silent agreement with his boss—the car had been checked; the car was clean.

"You said something about finding a dead animal?" asked Leo.

"Yes sir, possum on the Devil's Alt—the fencing, that is," said Fletcher. "Had some lit candles around it which I blew out."

Leo shook his head, stared daggers at the kids.

"I hope I can go out on a ledge and presume you all didn't sacrifice a possum to this nonsense?" asked Leo.

"It was roadkill, sir," said the third, nameless boy. "We just moved it up here is all."

"Son, I don't know you, but if you handled that animal, you'd best be sure to disinfect the living hell out of your hands once you get home. That goes for all of you."

Fletcher proceeded to shine the flashlight on all their faces, some of them hanging low with embarrassment, others pointed up with a bit of defiance. After a while, Leo thought Fletcher was getting too cutesy or bored with the light show and shot him a look. Fletcher cast the beam down.

"You two young ladies, do you all go to school with these boys?" asked Leo, to which the girls slightly nodded.

"And they talked you into this little excursion tonight?" he asked, without receiving a reply. "Answer me, please."

A flash of mild anger from Leo or maybe just an exhibition of his authority and age, like a buck growing out a large rack, covered in velvet, not to be trifled with—he'd been here longer, staked his claim.

"It was our idea, Dad," said Bo. "No moon, autumn, it's what the Quarry Witch likes best from her visitors."

Leo got a little jolt of emotion when Bo called him "Dad," even under the present circumstances. He knew it was strategic; the boy tended to play that card when convenient, knowing Leo liked to be thought of that way, unable not to be moved by the notion. You couldn't have a child in your everyday life for close to fifteen years and not be susceptible to their affection, even when you know it's self-serving, caked in manipulation—as the adage truthfully stated, parents were the bone that children cut their teeth on. He'd seen his two boys butter up their mother a million times over. Or guilt Billy into allowing something inadvisable or downright reckless. They had refined a unique and effective touch with the many adults in their lives, including Leo. That said, Bo could call him "Dad" all he wanted, but start talking about the moon and candles and a fake witch, and all he was going to get was the evaporation of Leo's patience, an excuse for him to lace into the cabal of juveniles who did 't their asses from their elbows.

"You kids don't understand jack shit about what this place is," said Leo angrily, prompting even Fletcher to double-take, to stand more upright. "If you knew anything about the tragedy here, the real misery it's put people through, you wouldn't find any of this entertaining."

That piped the kids down. No one was meeting Leo's gaze now; even Fletcher seemed a bit nervous after that. Leo's distaste for all things Quarry Witch was well known at the station, but it was always another thing to see him wound up over it in public. He half surprised himself with the sudden revulsion he felt, the heartstrings that had been plucked only minutes ago now numb to the touch. He'd been on scenes like this many times before—as an officer and a sergeant, even as a golfer—but now he was the top cop in Orchard Coils, and there seemed to be no end to these petty crimes in sight, or at least it felt that way. If he had one gripe with his former boss, Chief Wineski, the man who had mentored him into the role, it was that he never took this shit as seriously as he should have, never saw it for the cancer Leo had identified it as. The truth was he was short of good solutions. But at the very least, there was one thing Leo could do—he could shut it down for one more night, close the book on it, and approach tomorrow as the new challenge it would be. Then the day after that. And so on, because this problem wasn't going anywhere—but neither was he.

"Where'd you kids park your car?" asked Leo.

"By the closed-off access road," said Jocko.

"That figures. Fletcher, I'd like you to escort these four back to their car, but you drive the young ladies home," said Leo, weighing his options. "Discreetly, no need for the show."

"Can do, Chief."

"Jocko, you're going to need to tell your dad about this," said Leo. "Because I assure you, the next time I see him at the club, he's going to hear my version of it. Maybe not the law enforcement version, but the man-to-man version at least. You following me?"

After some hesitation, Jocko the Third begrudgingly nodded his head in acceptance, already envisioning that conversation with his father.

"So we're not in trouble for this?" asked the third boy. Leo still didn't know his name and, frankly, didn't want to know.

"Listen, possum-boy, this is a quiet enough town, and we do our best to not arrest kids for being kids, even when they're being negligent and breaking about half a dozen laws before the weekend's even started," said Leo. "But bear in mind, Officer Fletcher and I got big mouths, long memoires, and never forget a face, so if we catch any of you on this course after hours, well, trouble is all you're going to get."

"Thank you, sir. You won't see us again," the nameless kid stammered out.

Leo grunted in approval, a maneuver he'd lifted from Wineski, who had the same habit when accepting concessions from those who didn't really rate with him anyway.

"Get rolling, Fletcher. Bo, you're with me," said Leo.

The quorum disbanded, making their way down the sloping hill, pinned in by fence and woods rife with scurrying animals and bleating insects, stalked by night owls and other birds of prey—bats eating late-season mosquitos and dispersing seed, pollinating as they traveled by sonar. The cart path was just as easy to navigate back toward the road, but the lack of moonlight did lend to an eeriness, a pall on an already weird night. They all got to the road, and Fletcher splintered off the group with his cargo in tow, heading for the cars that would ferry these wayward teenagers home. Leo hadn't been lying about their being off the hook since it had never been O Triple C's policy, or even town policy, to prosecute kids over what most saw as benign coming-of-age hijinks. At best, the goal was just to keep the recidivism down, which they mostly did. Leo had championed stricter policies but was routinely vetoed by the town hall and club committees—even lacking support from his own officers, who thought their boss had an unhealthy obsession with those who toyed with the lore.

So those soft policies contributed to new flocks of kids who found their way to the seventh hole, as the general word was no serious repercussions would follow, aside from a tongue lashing and maybe getting dropped off on your parents' doorstep. And that was only if you got caught. Hence, a sort of stalemate had developed, and Leo was in the unenviable spot of having to manage the situation year after year, with no will from the other parties involved to intercede. In his heart, Leo had started to believe that the only chance for real change would be something drastic happening, maybe even something tragic—but he didn't want that, would sooner just keep patrolling the area endlessly than something chaotic befalling the town again, which, in the dark recesses of his mind, he was convinced would happen despite his wishful thinking.

He was convinced someone else would have to die up there before they'd finally start listening to him, before any real change could occur.

Leo and Bo walked silently across the road toward the Impala. They both knew the real conversation hadn't started yet—that little group talk up on the hill had been the warm-up. They'd have it out, sort of, neither of them bombastic by nature or overly adversarial. But there would be some reckoning for what transpired that night, and it was minutes away. Both of them had the good manners and sense to save it for the privacy of the Chevy, the sanctity of their house. Somewhere in the distance, a confused hound bayed at the moon's absence, longing for something that couldn't be seen but was technically there, just hidden behind clouds or celestial orbits—but you try explaining that logic to a forlorn dog.

* * *

It took about ten days for Leo to cross paths with Jocko Whalley Jr. midmorning on a Saturday, when Leo had showed up to practice his flop shots at the range, his lag putting on the green—maybe squeeze in a few holes before he was missed too much at home or the station. He was technically off for the day, but since Leo never thought that an officer got a true day off, he certainly didn't think the chief of police would, given not a single day went by when his input wasn't needed on some decision or fire drill, oftentimes not even having much to do with policing, but with politics or budgetary wrangling. He was about seven years into the role and still felt at times the earth was unsteady under his feet, always learning about things he'd never had to consider when he was just a sergeant, things like mayoral races, ethnic power centers, overarching political battles, lawsuits against the department, revenue streams, besides being responsible for the dozen-plus men and women striving to be worthy stewards of the town, fallible human beings who made professional mistakes, often innocent ones—some who also lived messy personal lives that flared from time to time and might require a good talking-to or dressing down from a superior. It was a lot for one person to bear, let alone live up to and lead by example, even in a small town like Orchard Coils, while also married and raising two children—it made Leo wish he'd been more empathetic toward Wineski back when he had the chance, before the old codger retired and decided to live abroad with his wife—Jamaica, as it turned out.

Leo had thought of his old boss quite a bit during the past seven years, would reach out to him from time to time to solicit advice. Wineski, to his credit, always picked up the phone, always made time to talk with Leo for as long as it took. Then he'd retire back to his porch with a rum drink to feel the ocean breeze waft over his bald head. He and his wife still played those Scrabble games at night.

As for Jocko Whalley Jr., he was always one of the first to arrive at the club, six days a week, off on Mondays. He'd knock off around two p.m. once it looked like it would be smooth sailing for the rest of the day, that his crew had wrapped up the pressing tasks, and everyone understood what would be on the docket for the following morning. Jocko was very, *very* much into planning, into knowing what needed to be done well in advance of a target date—months, not weeks. Weeks, not days. Days, not last minute. His father, the head superintendent before him, had taught him that lesson with military-like verve. He had taught his son how to get his house in order, to keep it so, and to eschew surprises.

The Whalleys did not cotton to surprises.

Jocko Jr. would quiz his subordinates about what needed attending to three days out, when the next scheduled tournament was, when the kids' summer clinic would start up, what insects were known to swarm during various months, how invasive the turtles might be near some of the creek beds. Details, details, details. He tried to impress on his people that they were the grease in the well-oiled machine that was O Triple C—that all the extraneous parts in the world meant nothing, truly nothing, if friction went unchecked and prompted the whole thing to seize up.

And, much like Leo, he managed very human people, flawed souls who were even more prone to bouts of bad judgment, loss of clarity, sometimes just despicable luck. These were hard men, many coming from checkered pasts, background checks not all employers could overlook, searching for a new lease on life, some stability, and maybe even a little redemption. Jocko was talented at seeing the value in people that society had deemed problematic, unfit—he believed in second chances, even if they went against the grain of his rough exterior. The crews he assembled were tight by design. And while no man was going to get rich in their line of work, it could be the foundation for what a lot of these men were pursuing, certainly the possibility of springboarding into bigger and better things, particularly once you had Jocko's seal of approval. He was a ride-or-die boss, no bones about it, who'd promoted people before, gotten them better gigs elsewhere when the conditions were right—he also believed in keeping an industrial cooler inside the Monastery stocked with all the beer they'd ever need, on his dime, only to be enjoyed after shifts were over. Knocking back a cold one or two before heading home was totally permissible. There was no getting drunk on the property, no drinking while on the clock—to disobey either rule was a fireable offense that Jocko wouldn't hesitate to execute on.

All those in his employ understood and acted as though it were a holy commandment—heard the first time, believed the first time.

The orbits of these men didn't often collide despite their connection to O Triple C and having two teenage sons that were friends. Many times it would just be a quick wave or word of recognition between the two. But ten days after the incident, Jocko had spied Leo on the pitching green alone and made his way over. Leo saw Jocko heading his way, and while he wouldn't say he was afraid, it could raise one's hackles when a much larger man was moving in their direction with a purpose—particularly a man who had taken to inking sleeves of tattoos onto his arms in his forties. It was Leo's opinion that no one did such a thing unless they had a major beef with something or someone or maybe just the world at large. It was also the cop in Leo, a kind of mental reflex impossible to turn off—a piano-wire tension that kicked up from the smallest of catalysts—not easily controlled and not discussed enough either in the training academy or among the fraternity of peacekeepers. That said, the cops who could control it, wrangle it down with precision, reappropriate it to what may be common referred to as "the edge"—those were cops who were quite often able to go on to do amazing and heroic things.

Also, sometimes, horrible things.

Leo had stopped blooping shots with his sixty-degree wedge as Jocko was almost upon him. He didn't bag the club; he just held it inert by his waist, almost like an afterthought, as though he'd forgotten he was holding a blunt instrument in his dominant hand. He hadn't.

"Chief Sinclair, a word," said Jocko Jr., less a request than a statement of fact of something that would transpire, Leo tried to remember how Jocko typically addressed him— "Leo" or "Sinclair" or maybe sometimes "Chief," usually just one word, so "Chief Sinclair" was vaguely interesting and out of character for the superintendent.

"What can I do for you, Jocko?"

"I wanted to talk to you about what our boys got into last week."

"So Jocko told you the story?"

"You told him to, correct?"

"Sure, but I've told teenagers a million things over the past thirty years," said Leo, grinning, a splash of self-deprecation, which always went a long way in his book. "Hardly means they'll listen, despite the badge."

"Well, my boy heard you loud and clear. Plus you'd have mentioned it to me at some point," said Jocko, to which Leo agreed using a mild contortion of his facial muscles, sans words. "Anyway, I did want to thank you for keeping it low key, you know, mountains and molehills and all that."

Leo's grip on the club loosened—he hadn't realized he'd been squeezing it with more psi than necessary.

"Not a problem, Jocko. We don't put the kids through the wringer over the ghost story crap. And obviously, Bo was there, so I had my selfish reasons," he said. "If anything, it was Officer Fletcher who did right by us, calling me directly on my personal phone that night."

"Maybe you could pass along my gratitude to him?" asked Jocko, surprisingly contrite.

"I can do that."

Jocko allowed a beat to pass, took a moment to observe that the post for the ball washer on seventeen was askew and in need of fortification, made a mental note of it, and returned his attention to Leo.

"I'm to understand the kids got busted with a little beer? Had smoked some reefer?"

Did anyone call it reefer anymore? thought Leo rhetorically.

"Your boy really did confide the whole thing to you, didn't he?" said Leo, mildly impressed. "It's an interesting thing."

"How so?"

"It just sounds like Bo and Jocko are similar in that way, in that they don't mind telling their parents when they've gotten into something," said Leo. "Not sure what that's about, but it gives me some hope we're doing something right."

Jocko Jr. hesitated for a few moments, maybe unsure how he wanted to proceed, maybe distracted by a plume of spores drifting their way—absolutely the kind of man who might wonder exactly what they were, even if they were just off some patch of dandelions, and what impact they might have on his course.

"I'm not so convinced they tell us every little thing, Chief," said Jocko, back to a one-name basis, cracking a small smile, which was the best you'd ever get off the man. "But maybe they trust us just enough to be more forthcoming than other boys their age."

In the distance, a siren wailed—ambulance from what Leo could tell. Jocko shot the horizon a dirty look; he had an unchristian disposition toward noise pollution, particularly when he was trying to espouse a point.

"Trust is a beautiful thing in my experience," replied Leo.

"It's the invisible mortar that holds it all together."

The crux of Jocko's position, now concluded.

The two men piped down to enjoy the silence in their shared territory, their aligned thoughts on trust and what it meant to the world—a pleasant surprise when two grown adults, set in their ways, found others who prized similar beliefs, especially ones they held dear. Jocko took a moment to watch one of his men tending to some fallen leaves near the third hole. He didn't like how the blower was sounding and would have to have the bearings and battery looked over. Leo wondered if he had any text messages—his phone was on silent mode—but thought it would be rude to check it in Jocko's presence. He was still not a big cell phone guy, but Janet had finally made him get one of those Apples, third or fourth generation that came free with the plan, and he'd be lying if he said the thing didn't come in handy—a mini-computer—but would be damned if he became obsessed over it, a trend that was becoming more evident, not just among kids but adults as well. Too often, Leo would be out playing golf, trying to get away from the rigors and noise, only to see some other player out there staring at the screen, making a racket with all its beeps and boops—zombified—when they should have the thing pocketed and be focusing on their negative-angle striking, divot-size management.

As their respective distractions of seedlings and cell phones passed, Leo and Jocko returned to each other.

"So I don't want to keep you any longer than I already have, Chief, but I did want to let you know you'll never see Jocko trespassing on the course again," said Jocko Jr. "But I would ask, if I can borrow you for a few more minutes, there is something in Building One I'd like to show you."

"The Monastery?"

"If you like."

"I didn't think members were allowed in there," said Leo. "I wasn't even allowed in there when I worked here as a kid, back when your dad was in charge."

Jocko took a moment to pop a piece of gum out of a cellophane package, what looked like some type of nicotine replacement to Leo, as though the man had been struck by an urgent craving.

"There's truth to that, but considering what went down last week, I'd say you earned an exception," said Jocko. "Plus there's some stuff in there I want you to see. Might be worth a little of your mind space."

Mind space? Leo wasn't sure what Jocko was on about but figured he wasn't going to get a direct answer unless he saw for himself—which was fine by him since he'd always wanted to be invited inside the Monastery anyway, to breach the inner sanctum, where admittance was rare and furiously guarded. The other small offshoot buildings were pretty much fair game to anyone with a passing interest, but the Monastery was HQ, Whalley's rampart, and that bloodline had curated its traffic for nearly fifty years. And now Leo was being offered passage, a glimpse behind the curtain—for more than a few reasons, he wasn't going to refuse.

"I've got some time to spare," said Leo casually.

"Then follow me."

So he did, trailing the big man to Building One. Jocko Jr., despite his size and weight, his large bones and barrel frame, moved with a graceful stride. He had the build of someone you'd be tempted to call lumbering, particularly if you hadn't seen him in motion yet, if you were attuned to the fact that he worked with his hands, was on his feet all day long. But once the guy got going, there was a smoothness to how he descended on a destination—not quite predatory, but certainly catlike, spry, without much in the way of wasted motion or intent, mapped out in advance through some schema of the mind. Leo was about Jocko's age and wished his joints and muscles cooperated in such harmony—his own lifetime working on his feet and playing golf had hitched his gait just a bit, made it so the first half hour of every morning felt like a Mack truck had run him over. Don't get old—the advice he'd heard so often from the older men in his family, the older men at the club.

If they were closer friends, Leo might have been tempted to ask Jocko what his secret was—but they weren't, so he didn't.

They arrived at the Monastery, only a two-minute walk and Jocko entered through the unlocked doors as though he owned the place, which, in a very real sense, he did. Leo trailed behind and crossed the threshold into the formidable structure. The absolute first thing that struck him was how clean it was, how meticulously organized. He'd long had in his mind that the interior would be dirty, cluttered—like some junk drawer spilled out and reclassified as a maintenance hub—somewhat unfairly, given Jocko would never allow a building in his charge to function in a state of disrepair. In reality, it was the polar opposite. Some of the large mowers had been returned through the backside bays and were neatly aligned in the far corner, washed and rag dried, a Jocko policy. There were various types of seeder machines also stowed away, though those were mostly dormant that time of year. Accompanying the machinery was an assortment of weed whackers and niche cutting tools for intricate manicuring. In total, there were hundreds of thousands of dollars of equipment in that one building alone—maybe a million-plus—all key assets belonging to the club, where their upkeep and preservation were taken very seriously by the crew, none more than Jocko himself, who took pride in the longevity they got out of their gear.

Leo then noted a billiards table, albeit a small one, cloistered in a near corner, not far from the fabled cooler perpetually stocked with beer—rumors long heard by Leo now confirmed with his very eyes. There was also a giant yellow flag hanging on the back wall that read CONNECTICUT SHITKICKERS, which Leo understood to be the name of their fantasy football league. Jocko proceeded to lead him around the room a bit, not quite a formal tour but something to that effect. It wasn't like he was announcing things for Leo's attention, but rather giving him a chance to make his own observations. There was a workbench, clean and orderly, a home for every tool. Industrial-grade wet/dry vacs. Stacks of bagged landscaping supplies like mulch, pine bark, crushed rock, and such. Boxes of bulbs, random electrical components. Pest control materials. Algae control. Fungus control. Replacement parts for water pumps. Replacement parts for irrigation systems. Replacement parts for things Leo didn't have a clue about or even know how to identify. Basically, a lot of the things one would need to keep a large operation like a golf course running seamlessly, or as close to it as possible—which was important to the paying membership, who wanted to feel their dollars were going to the course's upkeep, that their monthly dues allowed for the functioning fountains and boulevard-like fairways and finely sanded bunkers. It fostered great pride and relief to most of the membership to see those dollars reinvested in the course they loved, as though it were a form of taxation, but they actually got a real say in how the money was used—representation—and they were pleased with the results.

Another thing incumbent on that type of work taking place: the transparency of it, that it not be hidden behind some veiled curtain. It needn't be a subprogram running behind the surface that couldn't be discussed, that no one could talk about, let alone see. Jocko's crew were out and about all day long, very much visible to O Triple C's patronage, though minding their regimented schedules that allowed for as little intrusion as possible as the golf was being played. The point of this was that the members liked the crew, liked seeing them attending to their craft, taking responsibility for those small details that helped make the place special. The golfers were more than happy to play around the guys cutting the lawns in the morning, even exchanging nods over a good shot, shrugs at a bad one—given enough time, all the crew knew who the hacks were, who they had to keep their head on a swivel when sharing a hole with. This all lent a sense of comradery, like they were in it together. Another Jocko policy. The members didn't want to be shielded from the effort it took to keep the club pristine—they wanted to know how the sausage was made. They even wanted to help where they could—small things like seeding divots in the fairway, plucking a weed, or just picking up stray debris.

The fact was O Triple C was never going to be the largest or most expensive or exclusive country club in Connecticut, not by a long shot—but that didn't mean it couldn't be gorgeous, that it couldn't host top-notch golf and be a hidden gem in the community. To that end, the authority of the Whalleys—first Jocko Sr., now Jocko Jr.—had grown steadily over fifty years, garnering their men wide amounts of latitude on how to get the job done. Junior was also given free rein on hiring his crew, training them up, an almost military-like endeavor he took personally with each new recruit, which was how he liked to think of them. Despite not being a military man himself, he had a deep admiration for those who carried the flag, guarded the fire. In turn, these men found discipline and, oddly enough, freedom in the discipline, then, with any luck, peace of heart and mind through that freedom—a convoluted journey perhaps, but not all roads are created equal, and anyone who tells you otherwise probably has some oceanside property to sell you in Kansas.

Such was the delicate nature, the relationships at O Triple C. Like a spider web, the smallest of vibrations could be felt everywhere over its surface.

After a few minutes of snooping around under Jocko's watchful eye and occasional quip, Leo found himself back to where he started—not exactly sure what it was Jocko wanted of him, wanted to show him. He'd seen the Monastery now, and, as interesting as the walled garden was, he was also ready to get back outside and maybe play the I-6 if nothing on his phone told him he couldn't. It also hadn't escaped Leo's attention that no workers had entered the building since they had; it should have been bustling at his time of day. Clearly word, had gotten out to stay away until they exited. Jocko, running whatever calculations through his mind, gave the chief a once-over, trying to gauge the man's disposition, his intake, and how he might react to certain information. Viewing the Monastery was more of a pretense, a precursor to the truth.

The fact was that Jocko had never really given Leo much thought one way or the other, kind of figured him as a little dude who, at the very least, didn't seem beholden to little-dude syndrome, which probably meant he had enough marbles rattling around his head and decent parents who brought him up right—the latter Jocko was positive of, having known both of Leo's parents. The brains and the roots were probably how Leo had been able to fashion a good life for himself, even rise through the ranks to become an influential man in town, though he made no show of advertising it. But now, Jocko needed a clearer measure of the man because if he was going to show him what he'd been intending to, it would behoove him to be right about Leo's character, his ability to be, for lack of a better term, cool. Many people had debated Leo's coolness in the past: some in favor, some against. Jocko couldn't decide if Leo being a cop—let alone a chief of police—was helping or hurting the cause. Ultimately, like a lot of tricky decisions requiring one to take a flyer, Jocko's inner voice told him to fuck it and not back out on what he'd planned to do—to reciprocate some of the trust he felt a Sinclair had levied on the Whalley family only ten days before.

"We have a lost and found of sorts," said Jocko, breaking the stillness that had fallen over the two. "Well, two of them, to be precise. The second one may be of particular interest to you."

"A lost and found? Don't they have one up at the clubhouse?"

"Sure, for stuff people are willing to admit they lost."

"Not sure I follow your meaning, Jocko," said Leo, kind of following but not wanting to assume.

"Maybe it's best if I just show you the first one," said Jocko, almost more to himself than Leo. "That might be a good primer for the second one."

Leo nodded noncommittally, really starting to realize his humdrum day off had taken an odd turn.

"Chief, what I need you to understand is that I'm taking you into my confidence here," said Jocko. "I'm not asking any promises of you, only that you remember how we got here in the first place."

"How about you show me what you want to show me, Jocko," said Leo calmly, his expression neutral like the mannequin face of a crash-test dummy.

Jocko and Leo walked over to a neatly arranged rack of metal drawers, basically columns of storage containers mounted into the wall across from the pool table. They all had large sliding doors with no discernable locks. They were unmarked—not so much as a piece of masking tape with scribbling on it. Jocko pulled open a waist-high drawer, seemingly at random. It opened smoothly, the wheels oiled along the rails, well maintained like everything else in the building, on the property. He stepped back and motioned for Leo to take a gander, which he did eagerly, though not without a modicum of caution.

"We find all kinds of stuff out there throughout the year, hold on to it on the off chance word gets back to us that someone wants it returned," he said. "Though as far as I know, a claim has never been made."

Leo looked through the drawer and inventoried the assortment of items, not so many as to be overwhelming but a decent amount of paraphernalia, most of which was noteworthy. The first thing Leo observed was a gun—two of them in fact: one a Glock, a model with real stopping power, the other a pearl-handled peashooter, might have been real, might have been a replica won from a penny arcade decades ago. There were also a variety of knives in the drawer, not utility or Swiss Army versions given out to groomsmen in wedding parties, but legit hunting knives, serious weaponry. Leo looked back at Jocko, who just nodded his head as if to say, "Yeah, all found on the course." Leo continued to examine the contents of the open drawer, saw a foot-long prosthetic penis tucked in the back. Some very yellowed Polaroids of some very naked people. He saw some type of puzzle box that had been sealed in wax. There was a silver molar large enough to have been taken from a primate's skull. A straight razor with a scrimshaw handle, an image of a whale being harpooned carved and inked into the hilt. Then there were the vials, lots of them, most with no labels, some with no lids. Leo picked one up and rattled the contents around, a maraca of uppers or downers, he presumed. He placed it back, looked at the other vials, then looked back at Jocko, more than concerned, almost frowning.

"I know what you're thinking, but we don't take any of that stuff," said Jocko. "A lot of it could be heart medication or weight loss crap for all we know. Most of it is loose pills that we add to the collection."

"Why?"

"To see how many we can fill," said Jocko. "It's not such glamorous work out here. We all need our little distractions and games."

Leo wasn't sure he was buying that, but then again, Jocko was under no mandate to show his collection anyway. He continued to sift through the stash some more, finding some water pipes, tins of European THC edibles. There were some small baggies with observable amounts of fine white powder, others with courser, darker powder. There was a rubber tourniquet with very obvious blood staining on it. An antique hand mirror with the surface scratched to hell. An ornate Zippo lighter.

"We throw the syringes out," said Jocko. "No one's comfortable storing them."

There was a photocopied manifesto, faded and weatherbeaten, written in the scrawl of an angry teenager, threatening violence against the world, page after page—it gave Leo the creeps just thumbing through it. There was a flash drive. There was cash, wads of twenties, a few hundos, gritty and grainy to the touch, almost like worn sandpaper. There were coins, heavy and foreign. Leo picked one up and examined it closely.

"Is this what I think it is?"

"A Krugerrand. Like they say, people love to conduct business out on the golf course."

Leo could only imagine the type of person who walked around with these coins, who could go so far as to lose one and not be compelled to report it, even if it was unlikely to be turned in. What types of dealings would that person be into? Or course, Leo understood how certain people valued their anonymity, might see the yellow metal as a safer mode of trade—not unlike the beaver pelt or tulip bulb before it, what a blockchain ledger would mean to people later—commodities for those who didn't trust fiat currencies, who didn't live exclusively on the grid.

"How can you be sure no one in your crew dips into this?" asked Leo, motioning to the wall of mounted drawers.

"Trust."

"Is that why you're showing me?" asked Leo. "You want to have a certain trust between us?"

"In part. But you've seen real evidence lockers, stuff that legitimately needs to be under lock and key, under surveillance. Our stuff has been built up over decades and decades. My dad started the collection, but I'm sure it doesn't even remotely come close to what your department confiscates over the course of a single year," said Jocko. "No, I'm showing you this so you'll believe what I have to show you next."

"It's not uninteresting so far, Jocko."

"Good. we call it the Museum," said Jocko, closing the drawer. "But maybe what you'll see next will be less interesting and more . . . enlightening."

* * *

"Does Mom know?" asked Bo, strapped into the passenger seat of the Impala, being driven around. Leo wasn't taking the straight path; he needed a longer, more indirect way home to allow for a tete-a-tete with Bo.

"She knows what I told her back at the house."

"Was she mad?"

"What do you think?"

Bo sank deeper into the leather upholstery.

"But maybe you and I can work together and try to contain this cluster of a night," said Leo. "And that starts by telling me whose bright idea it was to trespass on the seventh hole?"

Bo looked out the window as the long streetlamps tendrilled light into his eyes, obscured through the smudges on the glass as Leo had gone too long without getting the Impala washed and waxed. He realized he was still a little high, but that wouldn't stop him from bartering with this stepfather—he'd had a plan, after all.

"The truth can be murky," said Bo.

"Isn't it always? But try me anyway."

"Technically, me and Paul suggested going up there," said Leo. "But it was Lori and Jodi that had been talking for a while about wanting to see it with their own eyes. They'd been on about it since the school year began."

"Who's Paul?"

"The one that wasn't Jocko."

"Tell me you're not blaming this on the two girls?"

"I'm not."

"So you were trying to impress them?"

"Is that so hard to believe?"

Leo considered and conceded the point as an age-old axiom that has withstood the test of time—men would agree to do the stupidest things if they thought it would garner even a little attention from a girl they liked, who piqued their interest. He could remember his own exploits when he was Bo's age, Samantha Morris coming to mind, the way he chased her around for over a year, would have followed her to the world's end. He remembered his own father's stories, those post-war escapades. All the Oscar Ortiz tales, shared in the locker room at the PD, over a beer at the corner bar. Even his own pursuit of Janet, Bo's mother, and all the dopey things he did to leave an impression on her, like highlighting his job and membership at the club and marksmanship awards just to make this woman find him the least bit interesting.

So, yeah. Young men, old men, middle-aged men alike—all capable of doing stupid shit to curry favor with the fairer sex. Civilizations had been built on less and surely crumbled without the stress of men turning that crank for a woman's approval.

It appeared Bo wasn't so out of step with the times, had history on his side of the argument.

"OK, so which of them do you like?" asked Leo.

"Lori, the shorter one."

"And the taller one?"

"She has designs on Jocko."

"Leaving Paul the odd man out?"

"Story of his life."

"So the plan was to party up there and pretend to see some ghosts and hope it would convince these girls to start dating you," said Leo grimly. "Is that the gist of it?"

"In so many words," said Bo, sounding more defeated than he meant to, as though to hear the plan aloud reeked of folly, that their chances with Lori and Jodi were totally scuppered. "In my defense, it was the girls that brought the joint, and Jocko pinched the beer for us."

"So what did you bring?"

"The black candles."

"Jeez, Bo, that might be the worst of it."

"How so?" asked Bo, surprised to hear the candles were a greater offense than illicit drugs and underage drinking.

"Think, you know how," said Leo, a flush of anger. "And if you really don't know, you need to give a little more thought to what you know about me."

The tires of the Impala rumbled over a pothole.

"Come on, Leo. It doesn't mean anything, and it's not like any of us believe in the occult or whatever."

"The occult? For both our sakes, please don't use the word in front of your mother when we get home," said Leo. It did not go unnoticed that Bo had dropped the "Dad" routine.

"Fine. But you do believe me, right, that this was just about the girls?" said Bo. "We weren't trying to be disrespectful to anyone. It's just something you do when you live in Orchard Coils, like a rite of passage."

The kid has an answer for everything, thought Leo, mildly impressed, though none of it was the outcome he'd hoped for after decades of policing that area of O Triple C, seeing his failure reflected in the form of a child he loved.

"Sure, Bo, I believe you," said Leo. "I'm not sure your behavior and reasoning will fly with your mother, but I suppose I've been in your shoes before."

Whether Leo meant doing something to impress girls or gearing up to be in trouble with Janet, Bo was unsure—he suspected both. As much as he liked Leo, loved him really, he never found his stepdad to be the slickest of characters. His real dad was better at stuff like that, probably to a fault if he were to believe his mother on the topic.

The two drove around for a bit in silence, edging closer to home, still using a more roundabout selection of roads. Leo noticed all the political signs on people's front lawns, some for local races though many for the presidency, where a second Obama term seemed all but inevitable. Bo thought a little about Lori, how delicate her jawline was, something an artist would endeavor to sketch, never capturing its full grace. His current goal in life was to cradle her head in his hand by the holidays.

Then Bo snapped out of his reverie, a notion occurring to him that he'd suffered before, though now he thought it an opportune time to bring it up. He'd had some premeditation around it, the gumption newly in place to do so, as though he'd lured an inept prosecutor into opening a window, a space where he could ask what had long been on his mind without incurring certain wrath or diminishment. He took his shot.

"You never talk about him, you know," said Bo.

"Who?"

"Peter Sullivan. I'm not sure you've ever spoken his name to me or Clay."

"I've told your mother all there is to know. You boys were always too young to hear me go on about that stuff."

"Am I too young now?" asked Bo.

Leo paused and considered the question, distracting himself by minding the car's mirrors for passersby, of whom there were none. If he were to get on the topic of Sullivan, they'd definitely need more time on the road, a drive home by way of Massachusetts.

"No, I suppose you're not. But maybe I just thought you weren't interested."

"I've actually been very interested to know more," said Bo. "But it seemed like something you refused to talk about."

"It's not a parent's place to bother their kids with their problems," Leo said matter-of-factly, then took a beat. "But you're less a kid now, aren't you? That's what you're saying? OK, then, what do you want to know? Or maybe why don't you tell me what you think you know."

"I know it's unsolved, that it's a cold case like on TV," said Bo. "Also that there's only been three murders in Orchard Coils since then, all of them solved easily enough, which makes the Sullivan case that much more . . . problematic."

The kid had done some homework—that much was true.

Leo had been on the force for all three of those murders, and while he might not characterize them as being solved easily enough, he couldn't argue that they didn't stretch on even a fraction as long as the Sullivan case had. The first of the murders was in the late 1980s: a domestic dispute that turned violent when a husband put three bullets into his wife's chest after learning she'd been having an affair with a local orthodontist. The police caught him in the neighborhood of said orthodontist, skulking around, looking for revenge at being cuckolded, though luckily, the orthodontist was at another of his mistresses' house and not at home to be finished off by the jealous husband. The police arrested him in the area without further bloodshed, and he was swiftly convicted, despite his crime-of-passion defense, which fell on deaf ears with an unsympathetic jury. He was sentenced to thirty years, thought he would only serve seventeen, eventually succumbing to pancreatic cancer.

The second murder, which many thought should have been pleaded down to manslaughter, was only a few years later: a drunken fistfight between two hombres outside a roughneck bar on the outskirts of town known to cater to motorcycle gangs and rinky-dink drug runners—yes, even in Connecticut. It was the kind of place that had a little cardboard sign hanging in the storefront that read NO CLUB COLORS ALLOWED. The cops avoided it if they could. A woman was also involved—the one being argued over—though she was across town babysitting her sister's fussy twins at the time The long and short of it was that two dudes got in a fracas shooting stick inside the bar, words were exchanged over proprietary rights to this woman and the legitimacy of a scratched bank shot, they spilled out into the night, and one guy got cracked upside the head with a Lucasi brand and proceeded to fall and split his dome open on a curb. Cue the closing music, dim the lights, good night, and fare thee well.

They called the ambulance but just out of formality; the people who frequented that bar knew a dead body when they saw one, and no EMT was bringing that husk of meat back to life. The other guy left standing on his feet didn't flee, didn't really panic—just chain-smoked Kools until the police arrived, including Leo. The man was cuffed, transported, and booked into the local jail. He was ultimately convicted of a lesser murder charge, though murder all the same; served two dimes somewhere in upstate New York; and was eventually released on good behavior. As to his current whereabouts, the state of Connecticut couldn't say and didn't care— he'd honored his parole and then dropped off the radar, never to be heard from again.

The third and final murder since the Sullivan case had been about five years before, when a property line dispute between two neighbors boiled over, resulting in one of them being stabbed multiple times with a well-edged piece of gardening equipment, resulting in his bleeding out in the backyard. These two particular neighbors had had a bad history between them, seldom saw eye to eye on anything and weren't interested in a turn-the-other-cheek approach to each other's slights or alleged transgressions. They were two people who didn't require a perfect world, just a slightly better one that wouldn't have them as neighbors in the first place. But that wasn't how the world or home ownership worked. And after nine years of bickering and petty grievances, temperatures rising only to simmer for short periods of time, one of them met his unnatural demise over an argument about a tree branch obscuring certain vistas and a crumbling rock wall that had been mis-surveyed by the town years ago, creating confusion around a few hundred square feet of property. The aggressor in that particular instance, a married man with a middle school daughter, had to go back inside after the deed was done, covered in his victim's blood, utterly in shock from the crime he'd just perpetrated. His wife and daughter were home, saw him coated in red, and freaked out. The child was commanded up to her room, and, once she was secured, the wife pried the story from her shell-shocked husband, then called the police and proceeded to wash his hands clean in the kitchen sink.

She knew it was over before he could even snap out of his fugue state.

The authorities arrived and arrested the man without incident, bagging a pair of shears as the murder weapon. The deceased also left behind a wife and young daughter, who, on occasion, despite their fathers' differences, had found a way to play with the killer's daughter, amicably and devoid of parental bullshit.

That murder had been early on in Leo's tenure as chief of police, and he was apprised as the situation unfolded and the suspect brought in—a person still serving a life sentence with a chance of early release, despite a slightly checkered past, though nothing that would have portended a grisly murder. That was the first and only case with such drastic charges with Leo as the top cop, and he'd bird-dogged much of it, wanting to ensure everything was handled by the book, which under his watchful eye, it was. He allowed his officers to do their work, not looking to micromanage his people as though they were dolts, though did interject toward the end of the arrested man's interrogation, his statement with a lawyer present, pointedly asking, "Did you give in to anger; is that what you'd say you did?" Leo hadn't asked it to be cruel. He wasn't needling the man; he genuinely wanted to know, needed to know in his line of work, where, in a split second, a man could flush it all away over some wall rocks and a low-hanging branch. Two families now gutted. A town further traumatized. It was only natural for the chief of police to wonder what could possess a man to do such a thing. And it wasn't often you got to ask such a man that question to his face, in the flesh. But the neighbor/murderer didn't answer, clammed up despite the lawyer offering no objection to the question, despite his being forthcoming during the interview. Instead, he just started sobbing again. There had been plenty of that during the proceedings, signs of remorse that had probably earned him that parole chance with the judge who sentenced him, though the opportunity was still a decade-plus away. Perhaps he'd be a free man again, perhaps he wouldn't—that was the way these things worked. The blink of an eye, the beat of a heart—your whole life can be upended and marred until they lower you into the ground, scatter your ashes off a cliff—beholden to all the mistakes you'd never be forgiven for.

Those were the three murders that had taken place in Orchard Coils after the Peter Sullivan case—and Bo knew them well.

"I suppose this is all information that's easy enough to find online," said Leo. He'd worked hard over the years to get more comfortable with the computer, particularly the internet, which had all but become as important as a public utility.

"Among other things," said Bo.

"Meaning?"

Bo knew he was about to tread into shaky territory, went for it anyway.

"There's a lot of information out there on the Quarry Witch."

"How is that possible?" said Leo. "It's not even a real thing."

"The internet makes it real. Plus we know some of it's rooted in actual history—that mining tycoon that killed himself, the woman who was killed by his guard," said Bo. "Then all the other stuff gets piled on over the decades. It's more than enough for people to build their mythology, post their theories, create fan art, basically breathe life into the thing."

"You're telling me there are sites dedicated to this crap?"

"Sure, kind of. Mostly just social media platforms like Reddit or Wiki that I've seen it on."

Leo didn't know what those words meant—he'd have to evaluate what Bo was telling him, more techno-speak that, despite his efforts, he kept falling behind on, losing sight of the curve and unable to keep up with its rapid expansion. The generation coming up behind him was so adept with digital information, how to find it, how to separate signal from noise.

"Is there stuff about Peter Sullivan out there?" asked Leo.

"Some, but not so much," said Bo. "And what's out there seems really made up. That's another reason I've been curious about him."

"In what ways?"

"Well, you were his godson. It seemed like he really meant something to you, but you've never once told me a story about him—even, like, a happy memory."

Leo considered that, continued to drive in a drawn-out fashion, aware that Janet would start to worry over their delay, his tardiness. But there was little to be done about that. He wasn't about to cut short this dialogue with Bo, imbued with too much importance for both of them.

"He was a great friend to my parents. He and his wife were their best friends," he said. "And he was always watching out for me. Your aunt Lynn too. He was very protective of the people he loved, lessons he'd learned during the war."

"So he was a good guy?"

"I always thought so, but remember, I knew him only as a kid, a teenager before I went off to UConn," said Leo. "I never got to interact with him as a man, never got that perspective."

"And his wife was close to Grandma and Grandpa too," said Bo. "But she's passed on now, right?"

"Yes, Mary Sullivan, a few years back, around the time my father passed," said Leo. "We tried to stay connected with her, but it was . . . difficult."

Bo allowed the comment to stand on its own without further elaboration.

"And they had a son?"

"Chip. He came back to town for his mom's funeral. Then stayed around for a bit to settle the estate."

"Then he left for good?"

"He basically left for a good a long time ago. He didn't want anything to do with this town, only came back from time to time because his mom refused to leave."

"Why wouldn't she leave?"

"She didn't want to feel like she'd been run off," said Leo. "She was proud in her way, like all of us."

"What happened to Chip?"

"He lives in Japan," said Leo. "My mom and I still write him emails every so often. He's not so quick to reply, I'm not even sure he appreciates the outreach anymore, like it's a reminder both his parents are gone."

They fell into a silence—Bo getting a bit of what he wanted, a slightly better understanding of why his stepdad was so touchy about the Devil's Altar stuff. To Bo, initially, it really was just a silly game, make-believe with scant undergird. But hearing Leo speak of his godfather, a man he looked up to during his formative years, helped Bo understand that it wasn't just fan fiction scribbled on blogs, quips in the comments section—it was a terrible thing that actually happened on the soil he and his friends had been loitering on no more than an hour before. It was realer now, and he wished he'd been able to have this conversation with Leo years ago. And now that it was out in the open, Leo shared the same sentiment and would act on it, a valve of pressure released.

"Would you care to hear a small story about Peter?" asked Leo. "Something that's stuck with me over the years."

"Sure."

"So you know I worked at the club for all my summers during high school and into college, right?"

Bo nodded his head. He'd heard some of Leo's stories about hauling golf bags around for members before the carts took over, back when caddies would hump around the course carrying thirty pounds over their shoulders, developing giant calf muscles like the duckpins you'd see in New England bowling lanes.

"Well, we got stuck with a lot of grunt work, and one of the things they loved having me do when it wasn't too busy was hauling this plastic garbage can around the parking lot and picking up all the random crap that got left behind."

"Big parking lot to clean."

"Don't I know it. And they'd be happy keeping me out there for hours, picking up litter and broken tees and cigar butts and just about anything that shouldn't be there," said Leo. "That was my own little rite of passage there, seeing how much I could take without complaining, singing for my supper, you know."

"I thought you were supposed to be, like, this little prince of the club back then."

"Not everyone saw it that way, I can assure you."

Bo continued to nod along, not totally sure where Leo was going with this—if anything, it was starting to sound like another of his lectures on work ethic or something to that effect.

"Anyway, I'd drag that stupid garbage can around dozens of times, and for the most part, the only thing that happened was the lot got cleaner while I cooked out in the sun," said Leo. "Until one day, my mind goes numb from the tedium of it, maybe the heat, and I clip the front of a bumper, not even very hard, so I didn't think much of it, just carried on."

Leo glanced over at Bo to see if he was following him, which it appeared he was—not zoned out, not blankly looking out the window.

"Problem was the driver was still inside, and he either sees or hears whatever I did and proceeds to get out of the car and tear me a new one for the entire world to see."

"What, why? Did you actually do any damage to the car?"

"Not a scratch. It was an older car—a nice one, don't get me wrong, a Porsche as I recall—but they all had metal bumpers back then, if you can believe it. No way a plastic can is doing anything to that."

"So what was the guy's problem?"

"He was an asshole was his problem. Didn't have a great reputation around the club, lousy player, lousy tipper," said Leo, clearly reliving some of that rage. "Kind of guy that would light into a sixteen-year-old over nothing and think it was OK."

"What exactly did he say?"

"All kinds of stuff, mostly cursing. At one point, I distinctly remember him saying that the car was worth more than my life."

"Jeez."

"Yep, a real peach."

"So did you scream back at the guy?"

"Nope, I was kind of frozen, maybe a little embarrassed, like maybe I really had done something terribly wrong and didn't realize it," said Leo. "But then my uncle Pete showed up. He was coming out of the Restaurant and saw what was going on, saw me getting dressed down by this buffoon."

"Ah, so what did he do?"

"He went apeshit on the guy. Didn't bother to find out anything about what happened, didn't care; he just came to my defense, unconditionally," said Leo. "I mean, I could have keyed the guy's car, and it wasn't going to matter to Peter Sullivan. No one was going to act that way toward me if he was around. Let me tell you, it was something to see—those two adults going at it, me watching. Thirty years ago and I never forgot it."

"He had your back?"

"Sure did. And I don't think he ever told my parents about it. I know I never did," said Leo. "Like we both just knew it was something between us."

Bo gave that some thought, wondered who in his life would go to bat for him like that—certainly his parents, his uncle Paul, but he also figured Leo would too. Even if he wasn't blood, he was family and the kind of guy who shows up when needed.

"Thanks for telling me that story," said Bo earnestly.

"Yeah, sure."

"Can I ask you a favor, Leo?"

"I'm driving you home to be grounded by your mother, so not totally sure you're in the best position to be asking favors," said Leo wryly. "But go ahead . . . dead man walking."

"Hilarious. What I want to ask you is can we talk more about Peter and what he was like?" said Bo. "I'm not saying tonight. I just mean in general, so I can better understand the whole thing?"

Leo took another sidelong glance at Bo, speculating on his intent, unsure of his motives.

"This isn't so you can post stuff on the internet, is it?"

"No, I genuinely want to know more. It can stay between you and me."

Leo took a short beat. He wouldn't lie to himself—he loved the idea of discussing some of his fond memories of Peter Sullivan with his stepson, maybe even the unfond ones around the actual case.

"OK, then, I promise we'll talk more about it," said Leo. "But I need you to do me a favor in return."

"Sure, what is it?"

Leo gripped the steering wheel tightly, as though to brace himself.

"Don't call me 'Dad' unless you mean it. You follow?"

Bo felt the zing of that one in his gut, knew he'd been called out on something he thought he'd been getting away with.

"Yeah, I get it."

"Good."

They drove the rest of the way in silence, Leo finally settling on a direct route home. It wasn't such an unpleasant trip back, despite the fury that was waiting for Bo—maybe even Leo, to a lesser extent. They'd grown comfortable with the notion of returning home to face the punishment that awaited.

* * *

Jocko opened a second drawer from an adjacent rack and stepped back, allowing Leo a clean look. He recognized immediately what he was seeing, already more disturbing than the first drawer.

"Shit," said Leo.

"In a word," replied Jocko.

"For how long?"

"Since my dad's time," said Jocko. "People have been leaving stuff at Devil's Altar since before it was even called that. Though it's worsened after what happened there. And as you'll see, it's been accumulating over the decades."

In the opened drawer, Leo saw spell books, taxidermied black birds, silk scarves, glass baby bottles.

"Your dad started hoarding this stuff?" asked Leo.

"That may be your word for it. He thought of it as an inventory," said Jocko. "He had no affinity for this shit, but, yeah, it started out as dribs and drabs under his watch. Some of the early stuff got tossed away. But after a while, he got the feeling that some of it was worth stowing away, like a historical record of sorts."

"It's an actual evidence locker."

"If you like."

In the opened drawer, Leo also saw silver pentagrams, rosary beads, a bible, a wooden crucifix necklace, a small jar labeled HOLY WATER.

"What did your father make of all this?"

"He thought it was horseshit. Him and his crew used to laugh over it, no offense. Seeing what those weirdos were leaving up there, even after what happened to Sullivan," said Jocko, noting the pained expression on Leo's face. "Like I said, Chief, all departments have their little games, nothing to be taken personally."

Leo shook his head at the contents of the drawer, as though disavowing their assemblage—and in return, those inert objects mocked him from their resting place, hectoring Leo with their very existence.

"I've always known stuff was getting left up there. I've busted people trying to do it," said Leo. "But I didn't know the extent of it, an entire drawer's worth."

"Seven."

"Huh?"

"There are seven drawers' worth," said Jocko. "And counting."

Jocko proceeded to close the first of the Quarry Witch drawers—not to be confused with the lost and found drawers, as these weren't lost items; they were offerings—and opened the second drawer, motioning at all the adjacent drawers for Leo's sake, as though to indicate they were just as full as the first one they viewed.

In the second opened drawer, Leo saw candles, cornhusk dolls, bundles of incense, totems of wicker, dark ribbon knotted around tufts of what looked like human hair.

"I can remember when my dad showed me the first drawer. I was barely a teenager, back when there was only the need for the one drawer," said Jocko. "It creeped me out real good. I knew all about the ghost stories. The staff kids were allowed to walk the Halloween Trail, remember? I walked it. Same as my dad. And I've worked the trail too, just as he did."

Leo thought he detected some sentimentality in Jocko's voice, maybe some resentment, but he couldn't be sure, wasn't inclined to pursue it.

"And that was all before what happened in '78?" asked Leo.

"A few years before, yeah," said Jocko. "But like I said, after that, the trespassing got worse, and so did the tokens left behind. We knew the police were trying to run people off, contain it, but there was really only so much that could be done. You probably know better than me."

Leo nodded his head. He knew all too well the futility, further evidenced by seven large drawers of tribute for the Quarry Witch, all under his nose.

"I hate to say it, Chief, but I think these people consider it hallowed ground, like they literally revere it or something."

Jocko hated to say it, and Leo hated to hear it—both were true—but it more than jived with some of the stuff he'd learned over the past week. The day after he brought Bo home from getting busted by Fletcher at Devil's Altar, after his mother gave him holy hell and a two-week grounding, Leo had Bo show him some internet stuff he hadn't been aware of, which mostly amounted to social media sites and complex keyword searches. Bo showed him some online bulletin boards and message threads, crude aesthetics compared to what Leo was accustomed to seeing online but not uninteresting and not without a clear passion for the topic. These people were finding something in the lore to cling to. Or taking an ember and stoking it for more fire or, at the very least, more smoke to blow in their collective faces. These were early trolls playing off each other, sharing possible motivations of the witch, Peter Sullivan theories, why the quarry had been untouched for over a century—how that could even be possible?—alleged sightings of Agnes Schrader, the history of the land dating back even before Arnold Holm's time, why a golf course of all things had been built atop it, speculation that they tried orchards back in the day but nothing would flourish in the area for mysterious reasons, that the land was salted and lead ridden and courted death.

Leo read on and on and frankly didn't have a soft spot in his heart for people who wrote nonsense on the internet all day—they were losers playing make-believe, pretending to exist in a community of anonymous people arguing whether *she* showed herself more often in odd or even years, in solstice or equinox. Leo was particularly displeased when he read some of the theories that O Triple C was just a front to protect the Witch, to cull blood sacrifices in her name. That they indoctrinated children at the club, brainwashed them early and marched them in robes for yearly rituals. There were many of these threads, dating back years and years, some as early as the late nineties—and before Leo knew it, he'd been staring at the screen for hours with Bo or late into the night on his own, time having passed in a stream that defied logic, a rabbit hole, a wormhole. Leo was unaccustomed to the power of the web in that way.

He'd have to force himself to unplug, to attempt sleep despite a racing mind, firing neurons.

Though he'd be back, with Bo's help, finding more to read every night, scraping the internet to better understand what was being said of the Quarry Witch lore in the dark and not-so-dark corners of the virtual world, which was proving far more expansive than he'd imagined. He cradled a sliver of hope that he'd stumble on some nugget of truth, a clue, any idea that might lead him to crack the case that had gone untouched for so long now. It was too late to bring Mary Sullivan any peace in this world, but Leo still held out hope that one day he'd offer Chip Sullivan, all but hiding halfway across the globe, some modicum of relief, some explanation for and closure to his father's death. And if that meant Leo had to sift through the ramblings of mentally ill digital freaks, then he'd do so and hope to keep their taint from coloring his own outlook on humanity—which, for a straight-edged cop, would be a tall order and somewhat unlikely. He felt the judgments building inside him. He would not be charitable to any of their ilk: that was, if they ever left their dank basements.

His searching over the past ten days only further validated what Jocko had chosen to share with him that Saturday morning. Unlike the pixelated breadcrumbs, what he then saw in those drawers was real and tangible, another layer that infected his town, a plague both seen and unseen, offered then hidden. It disgusted the cop in him that it occurred on his watch, practically in his own backyard. He felt justified in his pursuits, his desire to quash it all. He idled his hands around the contents of the second drawer, felt the dark curios against his digits: fake jewels, small animal bones, woodwork with painted glyphs, tin punchouts of the moon, apothecary bottles, a broken music box. Some of the stuff he'd actually read about over the past ten days, a correlation forming, puzzle pieces fitting together in a way that could mean something or was just fodder for the delusional—unsettling either way.

"It really is mostly drawers of useless crap," said Jocko. "We're talking about shit that gets purchased at art or dollar stores, consignment."

"Yeah, well, not to sound ungrateful, Jocko, but in all these years, it never occurred to you guys to show this stuff to the police, even if it wasn't me?"

"Didn't think it was relevant. We were just cleaning up and getting a laugh out of it," said Jocko. "We figured you guys had a sense of it anyway. Besides, I'm showing you now."

"And why now, exactly? What's changed," asked Leo. "Because the boys are palling around, chasing girls, getting into some trouble together?"

Jocko gave that some thought, though when Jocko was contemplating something, it could resemble a bear deciding whether it was hungry enough to kill again. Leo continued to notice that no one had entered the Monastery since they had.

"I'm telling *you*, Leo, not the Orchard Coils Police Department. Make of it what you will," said Jocko. "As for why, maybe I think the whole Devil's Altar thing has gone too far."

"Now that it's struck so close to home, literally?"

"Something like that."

Leo took a beat. Jocko's reasoning tracked well enough, but who really knew his agenda, what he was thinking, and or else he may be holding back?

"Did your boy tell you they were trying to impress those girls?" asked Leo.

"He did," said Jocko, a faint smile over his hardened face.

"Yeah, I got that same story," said Leo. "Wasn't too hard to believe. Or maybe it's just what I wanted to believe."

"I follow," said Jocko. "Did you want to have a look in those other drawers?"

"I do, but maybe not right now," said Leo, thinking it over. "You mind if I come back some other day to take a more thorough look?"

"We can put that together."

And with that, their business was concluded. Jocko and Leo walked outside the Monastery, back into the light of day, to a bustling club filled with people who had no idea of the crazy collection, the Museum, that had been amassed inside a series of unlocked, nondescript cabinets. An hour ago, Leo had no idea about it. It brought to Leo's mind what Mary Sullivan had once told him ages ago, how there were secrets scattered all over the property, with gatekeepers protecting the serene surface of the club. Leo wondered if she was more right than even she knew.

The two men stood for a moment in an odd silence, not totally sure how to take their leave of one another or if maybe there was more to say. Leo noticed immediately how traffic back into Building One resumed once they'd exited, clearly indicating that the men had been kept away on purpose, on command. He thought it would be appropriate to thank Jocko, letting him get back to work, maybe shake the guy's hand, having just traveled through the looking glass together. But before Leo could act, Jocko spoke to something wholly unexpected.

"I was saddened to hear of your father's passing those years ago," said Jocko. "I always thought he was a class act around here. Your mother too."

Leo got a hitch in his throat, always did when someone brought up Baxter Sinclair, particularly when it was a compliment or fond remembrance, when someone referred to him as Screws, when someone was paying respect—doubly so when it came from an unlikely source. Leo couldn't recall Jocko Whalley Jr. offering any condolences back when Baxter had died, let alone showing up for the funeral or wake. But now, the big man, apropos of nothing, shared some kind words, not just for Baxter but for Ruth as well. Leo didn't know what to make of it but felt obliged to take it the right way, with wholesome intent, not belated skepticism.

"Thank you," said Leo, swallowing a bit of the loss he still felt every single day. "I've got to say I didn't know you had much interaction with them."

Something flitted over Jocko's face, what Leo first clocked as annoyance, but it passed before he could truly categorize it.

"I've been at this place my whole life, one way or another," said Jocko. "And when it comes to the people that stay here a long time, I always know the good ones from the bad ones. You want to guess who taught me that skill?"

"Who?"

"My dad, on these very grounds. He always thought it was important to know the measure of people you share space with."

"Sounds like a lesson worth learning," said Leo. "Apologies for not knowing this, but is he still with us?"

"He is. Getting up there, though. We got him in an assisted living community nearby," said Jocko. "Still sharp, though. How is your mom?"

"Same, moved into a nice condo with some home aide," said Leo. "Still see her a lot. She's healthy, still sharp, still independent."

The two men seemed to share a little solace in that—living parents, still able to enjoy life, family, and other earthly rewards, traversing eighty-plus years on a planet where civilization still required some grit and fortitude to make it through. Not all folks survived that kind of deal; in fact, plenty didn't, and plenty weren't even afforded the chance.

"You know, this might sound kind of stupid, but I sort of thought you and me were competing for the same thing back when we were kids," said Jocko.

"How do you mean?"

"You were sort of anointed, you know, given what happened out on four, lifetime membership and all, miracle story," said Jocko. "That kind of elevated your family here. Then your sister came along, grew up, came into her own. Just seemed like the Sinclairs were finding ways to walk on water."

"You thought that was taking something away from you somehow?"

"I don't know. Maybe I thought that a little when I was much younger. You were always a few years ahead of me, so it's not like we had so much contact," said Jocko. "But in a sense, I guess I thought me and my dad got shortchanged a little around here. Again, this was back when I was a teenager and still learning the family trade."

Leo roiled in a one-sided competition he'd no clue about, something that happened far more often than people ever realize. Resentments built when even certain parties were none the wiser.

"Sorry you felt that way, Jocko," said Leo, meaning it. "If it helps, no one around here's thought of me as much more than a cop for a very long time now."

"Naw, it hasn't mattered to me in decades. It was just an old whimsy I thought you might find interesting," said Jocko. "And yeah, lots of people are going to see the cop first, but you've still got some magic around here. People don't forget."

Leo hadn't thought much about what Jocko was alluding to for a long time. He supposed there was a time when his family was kind of special at O Triple C, particularly when his mom's parents were still alive, when Leo and Lynn returned for their summers from college. Even during their twenties, when Lynn had clawed her way onto the tour and Leo had lived up to the hometown promise, became a protector of the peace—those were golden days, but also thirty years in the past, and much had changed since then.

"My boys haven't shown much interest in picking up the game. Janet neither," said Leo. "And Lynn and her family have always been on the go. Not sure what magic will be left once I'm gone."

Jocko heard what Leo was saying, familiar and applicable to his own station in life.

"As much as I'd like for my son to take over from me here, keep that tradition going, I know it isn't going to happen," said Jocko. "He's going his own way, and I know I'd be a fool to stop it."

Leo started to smile to himself, chortled out a little mirth—fathers and sons, struggles as old as time itself.

"What's funny?" asked Jocko.

"Nothing, it's just that when men our age from this town confess something to me from the past, usually it's some story about them trying to ask out Lynn and getting rejected," said Leo. "I never know what I'm supposed to say to that."

"Well, I certainly did ask Lynn out back in the day and got shot down," said Jocko, grinning. "But I won't hold you responsible for that."

Leo nodded his head, then turned it as he heard his name being called over his shoulder, someone trying to flag him down.

"OK, Jocko, I'll let you get to it," said Leo, extending his hand. "Thank you for trusting me with all this this."

Jocko returned the handshake, and Leo thought it would be one of those overpowering ones with the grip meant to prove some type of manhood or finger strength. But Jocko's was normal, almost elegant, as though he had nothing to prove, as though he wanted the recipient comfortable in his company, in the folds of his bear paws.

"Thank you for minding our boys," said Jocko.

They parted, but Leo quickly turned back and offered Jocko one final thought.

"Hey, Jocko, let's not let so much time pass before we talk again," said Leo. "And I'm not just talking about those drawers. Maybe we got much more in common than we realized."

"I'd like that," said the big man, then he walked off, back to work.

Leo headed in the other direction, toward the member who was calling him over, wanting to see if Leo could fill in as a fourth to start a fresh round on the back nine, finish up with some lunch and drinks at the Restaurant, maybe a cigar. Leo checked his phone and saw nothing pressing from Janet or work—a rare opportunity to actually say yes to such an enticing offer. But he turned it down all the same. Then he fired off a text message to his mother, Ruth Sinclair, and told her he'd be swinging by for a visit to catch up, even though they didn't have much to catch up on—really just to relax in each other's company, muse over old times and inconsequential matters, mother and son.

She replied back quickly—said she couldn't wait. She'd brew some coffee, put some peanut butter cookies in the oven.

* * *

An excerpt from the eulogy of Baxter Sinclair by his daughter, Lynn Sinclair-Moore, April 23, 2010.

My father was many things, one of which was a peaceful, unassuming man you wouldn't suspect fought fiercely overseas, that he'd seen extensive combat and returned to our shores a decorated warrior, though plagued with his own brand of demons. He was a man who inevitably bested those demons through the act of family, falling in love with my mother, Ruth, a woman Baxter Sinclair would credit with changing his worldview, saving his life.

He was a man who would then go on to live for his children, Leo and I, an unrelenting dedication that we felt every day, even as adults. My father always was and should always be remembered as the salt of the earth. I say this without exaggeration or hyperbole. He was the literal salt of the earth, and if more men were cast in his mold, this would be a far more idealized version of the civilization we've aspired to.

To that end, we have all felt the collective loss of this great man, a tragic loss, and it is my sincerest hope that . . .

Leo waited in the warmth of the coffee shop, picking at a wedge of lemon pound cake and sipping a dark roast. He wasn't totally sure why he'd been summoned to that Starbucks on a cold January morning in Stamford, apart from the fact that the past had come a-knocking. Just after New Year's, he'd received an email to his work account from Samantha Morris—Sam, his high school girlfriend, whom he'd lost his virginity to in the gazebo on the O Triple C property back in 1974. She'd been the first love of his life and had summarily dumped him a few months before he departed for UConn, delivering him his first real taste of heartbreak.

That Sam.

She'd emailed him, hoping he didn't mind her reaching out, knowing he'd become the chief of police for Orchard Coils and using the town's online directory to look up his contact information. She wasn't even sure if she'd reach Leo directly or if her message would be triaged somehow, maybe never to be read by him. As it was, the address was very real, and Leo read the account daily, vigilantly checking it as he'd taken steps to get better with the Outlook software over the past decade. He would hardly call it his favorite part of the job, but at least he was far more comfortable with the notion of getting some work done online, though the account received less volume than one might have thought; in these smaller towns, the folks didn't clamor for their police too much. If it was something that could be emailed, they'd sooner try to solve the problem first on their own—sometimes advisable, sometimes not.

So Leo saw Sam's email firsthand and enjoyed the pleasantries of it, her recap of life in Stamford, a small Connecticut city where she'd spent her entire adult life. She made mention of a divorce, which she described as "long overdue," but offered no further elaboration. She also had two adult children who were her world, as she put it, and they were both doing well, one living in Boston, the other in NYC—distance for sure, but not light-years away. She wrote that she'd become adept at driving into both cities, something that had once worried her as she wasn't overly comfortable with long drives and tolls and parking. She also had little interest in using public transportation, despite living on the outskirts of a metropolis with a bustling transit system.

The point was, after she literally apologized in the note for rambling, that she was now an expert in getting into those two cities, knew all the best routes and travel times and even parking garages.

She went on to mention that she was a grandmother several times over—another reason it had been imperative to learn how to get into those cities on her own, a joy in her life that had been a boon against some darker days, which, again, she didn't elaborate on. She wrote that she was aware of Leo's marriage and hoped he'd fared better in that department than she had, which she imagined he would. She was also aware of his two stepsons, who would both be somewhere in their twenties now, and she wished them well, wherever they might be. It didn't take a genius, let alone a career cop, to realize that Sam had kept tabs on Leo or at least conducted a pretty recent Google search to see what the man had been up to, what information could be gleaned from the web. Leo wasn't on any social media, mostly because of his job, but also because he'd never join any of that shit anyway, and that was a hill he'd be OK dying on. But since he had held a very visible job for over a decade, there were enough easy searches out there to find some of his professional and personal milestones. Besides, Janet and the kids loved all those networking platforms, where inevitably information and pics would get leaked into the digital public record, the siphon of privacy as once we knew it.

It was more than obvious to Leo that Sam had done some homework. He recalled the last time they spoke, decades ago when he'd just joined the force and thought for sure he could crack the Peter Sullivan case all on his own, in his spare time, no less. He'd tracked Sam down to ask her some questions about Peter, particularly during the couple of years he'd been at UConn and Sam had stayed in town, had a better line of sight on his bon vivant godfather, still serving him drinks late into the night at the Restaurant. He remembered the conversation as cordial, if a bit strained—her being pregnant at the time and not volunteering as much as Leo had hoped, even benign observations that wouldn't have made much of a difference anyway. She was hardly rude, but she wasn't forthcoming or overly excited to reconnect with Leo, to rehash any of their past in the slightest. Leo wasn't looking to go down that path either or to perform a postmortem on their relationship, though her abrupt dissolving of their union had always stuck in his craw, made him feel he'd fallen short of her expectations. But truly, the sole reason for the outreach had been to try and learn if she had any insight into what might really have happened to Peter Sullivan, anything that might not have made it into the original case file from the late seventies. In the end, she'd had nothing new to offer, and they'd promised to stay in touch, though clearly, nothing of the sort came to fruition. They'd moved on with their lives apart, which seemed to suit them well enough—a not uncommon exit strategy in young love, for which one could only hope the good memories would outweigh the bad.

Until decades passed, inexplicably fast, and a random email popped up in your inbox—something that could have been relegated to a trash folder, what with the unreliable nature of anti-spam software—and all the old feelings came barreling back, a cavalry of nostalgia that didn't know how to take prisoners.

In any event, Leo emailed her back the next day—purposely waiting a day for reasons he couldn't fully explain—and expressed pleasure at hearing from her after so long, congratulating her on her children and grandchildren. He went on to tell her a bit more about Janet, Bo, and Clay and how they were all fine and healthy. He made mention of both Baxter's and Ruth's passing—Ruth not so long ago from pneumonia, making it into her eighties, still sharp, still an avid birder and protector of nature. Leo remembered his parents liking Sam, though wary of her being a year older, edgy in a way Leo wasn't. He wrote about his sister, Lynn, who had also gotten on with Sam back in the day, He summarized her marriage to Sachin; their beautiful daughter, Olivia; and their recent move to Florida, where they both continued to work in the golf industry. In typical guy fashion, apart from some small details about the town and club, Leo didn't have much more to offer up after that. It was about as long a personal correspondence as you were going to get out of the man, an entire screen's worth of his own typing. He signed off warmly and hoped to hear from her again, then hit the send button, and away it went into the electronic ether. He'd more or less put in out of his mind soon after, so he was surprised to see a response returned the same day. He wasn't sure a reply back was even necessary, given what he'd written; his note lacked follow-up or probing questions. He'd figured it was a brief stroll down memory lane for the two of them. But when he opened that next email and saw the screen fill with text, his stomach sank a bit, and his cop brain knew there was some issue at hand. No one wrote that much around catching up or trivial matters. He scrolled down without reading just to get a scope of how long the communication was—not a crazy length, but sizable for sure. Without even reading it, Leo summarized that Sam was either going through something or up against some wall and was reaching out for help—neither of those two options was Leo's preference, but he really didn't have a choice in the matter. Never would he just delete the email without reading it, so he would go through it carefully, find out what was going on.

He read her email twice, so disturbing was the content about an existence gone astray over the past decades, only to recently right herself and get back on her feet—it was a very different or perhaps a more complete recounting of her life than the shorter email she'd sent the day before. Leo had come to realize the first email was just a primer, a test balloon of sorts. The issues, in short—alcoholism, domestic abuse, emotional cruelty, all blights Leo had seen in spades across his career, even in his little bucolic town. Now Sam confessed to a lifetime of them. And Leo tried to square the revelation with the eighteen-year-old girl he once knew, once loved—it felt impossible, a misery-shaped block that shouldn't fit into the youthful shape of Sam, someone warm and funny and smart. He tried to recall any shades of it back during their days. Any signs he might have missed. Nothing came to mind, but if he was being honest with himself, he would acknowledge they hadn't even dated for a year, as kids, then only had sporadic contact with each other afterward, mostly at the club. He never really knew her as an adult, never gave much thought to where her track might lead. To reconcile the teenager with the adult without the benefit of the thirty years between would be foolhardy, bad police work. He thought it best to avoid that exercise as it would be rife with speculation and short on facts.

Her email concluded with a request, almost a plea the way it read—would he be willing to meet her in person? There were some things worth saying that should be said face to face, not written down. That surprised Leo a bit given how much Sam had already been willing to type out, extremely personal confessions, but he also thought he understood the sentiment: that leaving behind a paper trail on all things wasn't prudent, that there were some things better said in person. He wondered if her current troubles involved her ex-husband. Or was it some thorny legal issue? She'd left this decision to him, but there really wasn't much of a decision to make. Leo could have gone his whole life without hearing from Samantha Morris, and that would have been OK with him, no hard feelings. His life had been moving along just fine. But he *had* heard from her, twice in as many days, and now it sounded like she needed his help. And if there was anything that Leo Sinclair didn't shy away from, almost to a fault, almost to a point where it could be weaponized against him, it was helping out an old friend, especially someone like Sam, whose special standing had been seared in his mind.

He didn't wait an extra day like he had with the first email; that would have been callous, given all she'd revealed. He wrote back to let her know it wouldn't be a problem to meet up somewhere in Stamford. He was careful with his words, opting not to say he'd be happy to see her, to catch up—rather, that it wouldn't be an inconvenience, treating it as though it were a business appointment. He recommended something on a Monday or Wednesday morning, the earlier in the day the better—he'd be able to work out the logistics on his side to accommodate her as best as possible.

Send.

She replied back in less than an hour, choosing a morning two days out, a Starbucks on the periphery of the city. Leo was a bit surprised by the public location, for some reason thinking Sam was going to suggest they meet in her home for privacy's sake. But ultimately, the location didn't matter to him; it was her call to make. He checked his desk calendar to see if he had anything going on that morning or, more accurately, if whatever he was bound to have going on that morning could be pushed back a few hours. He didn't see any scheduling issues, so he responded to Sam that he'd be there at the appointed time and location. He gave her his cell phone number in case anything came up. He was tempted to tell her he was looking forward to seeing her again, though he opted against it as he'd been keeping his latter communications somewhat sterile. Then he asked himself if that was actually true. Was he looking forward to seeing her again in the flesh? He supposed so, though wished it were under better circumstances, less of the cloak-and-dagger routine. He restated the words in his mind—*It will be good to see her again*—as though trying to convince himself of it, trying to shelve the niggling sense of trepidation and unease imbued in their prospective encounter. The more he thought about it, the less well it sat, but there was nothing to be done. She'd asked for his help, so he would help.

That was how, a couple of days later, Leo found himself sitting in that Starbucks, early for their meeting given the unusually light traffic through Fairfield County, typically gridlocked during the rush hours on both the major highways. He ordered his coffee and pastry just to give himself something to do, a little sugar to calm nerves. He realized he was nervous, almost a bit flustered. That surprised him, given the career he'd chosen, the things he'd seen and experienced. But Leo wasn't one to deny the truth, which was, in that moment, one human being was anxious about seeing another human being after a prolonged separation. An oversimplification, but the molten core of the issue all the same. And perhaps the apprehension didn't make a lot of sense. They hadn't been on bad terms. Weren't enemies. She'd *wanted* to see him. But in a way, his leeriness did make sense: an opposing truth with just as much validity. There were plenty of reasons not to want to be in that Starbucks that morning, to be back in Orchard Coils, running the PD and hoping the cold of January helped keep his denizens in line.

That type of mental tug of war typically resulted in Leo reminding himself that he was a human, not a robot, which often comforted him, despite his admiration for robotics and engineering in general.

He crumbled that lemony cake into his throat, washed it down with acrid holiday blend, and wiped his mouth with one of those recycled-paper napkins the franchise was so keen on, fibrous and grainy and branded on all sides with their logo. He waited, not as patiently as he'd trained himself to be over the decades. He didn't like it when his patience waned. It projected weakness; it portended a fuse to be snipped short, quick to ignite. The coffee shop was emptier than he'd expected, still decorated for the season, even if winter was the worst season of all—not that it was winter's fault; it just did what it did, and apparently, Starbucks embraced that, celebrated the cold shroud. Leo was briefly reminded of his grandmother on his mother's side, who was prone to defend winter, thought it got a bad rap—an avid outdoorswoman who passed those traits onto Ruth, Leo's mother—all of them gone now, and Leo had to quickly flip that train switch in his mind to avoid going down those slippery rails. It was hardly the time or place.

Soon enough, a woman walked in, and he knew it was Sam, could still discern the young person hidden under the decades of life. If he hadn't been specifically waiting for her, he might not have known it, probably wouldn't have if he were being honest with himself. But it was her. He got up and waved his hand in her direction, hard to miss among the floor of empty tables. She smiled and walked over, and they greeted each other with a brief, cordial hug. Sam sat across from Leo on one of those hard, sleek wooden chairs the franchise was known for—pleasing to look at but not so much to sit on, particularly with an older body and a less-than-forgiving spine—a prime example of the small things one had to consider as they got up in age: seating options, late-stage ergonomics.

They settled in, and Leo asked if she'd like anything to eat, drink—as though they were in his house and not a public eatery in her city. His good manners were hard to turn off and didn't wane just because he was in a different county. He'd actually thought it a shame that being gentlemanly had somehow become out of fashion, now too often misinterpreted as condescending or patriarchal, even toxic. He'd always believed trying to perform those extra niceties was part of the fabric of a healthy society, that a lot of good could get done in those details, exploring those margins. Sam declined his offer, and Leo immediately wondered why she wouldn't have a coffee or tea. Not even a prepackaged scone. They'd barely spoken a word, and Leo was already inventing problems between the two—he needed to get out of his mind and get into the real and now.

"This is nice, seeing you again, Sam. I couldn't believe that after all these years, you even remembered me," said Leo, nervously, though not without enthusiasm. "An unexpected surprise to get that first email from you, a pleasant one."

Leo knew nothing he said was going to please him and had to resist the urge to find a rock to crawl under. He would press on and hope it got easier.

"You've never fully drifted from my mind, Leo," said Sam, which came out less provocative and more forlorn, like a statement of fact that would not allow retreat.

"I've certainly thought of you over the years," said Leo cautiously. "I was saddened to read of your troubles in that second email you sent. It seemed like maybe you had some hard roads."

"Yeah, the years haven't always been so kind to me, though some of that was my own doing," said Sam. "It's taken my fair share of time to face some of those truths down. But once I did, things started to get easier; things improved."

"That's good to hear."

To that, Sam said nothing, seemed lost in her own thoughts, though still somewhat present. She was having difficulty meeting Leo's eyes, nervously moving her hands around like an injured insect. Leo had seen similar behavior before, plenty of times, and it was seldom good. He needed to give Sam space, time to say what she'd come here to say. He needed to be patient, to quiet his own mind and not fill the void with inane chatter, his desire for people to be comfortable through the song of conversation. Eventually, she looked up from her braiding fingers, seemed to observe the coffee shop for the first time: the winter décor, maybe even its general emptiness. Their silence was somewhat awkward, but the thing was, once you were willing to concede to the quiet, it didn't need to be awkward. It was just the passing of time— natural and nothing to fear. Leo had worked over the years to hone this skill, employing it in hopes that Sam would follow his lead, which eventually she did, in a way that felt direct and even keeled.

"I'm an alcoholic, Leo," said Sam softly, almost defeated. "It still embarrasses me to no end to admit that, but it's the truth. I have a problem. I can't be around it. I can't have a single drop."

"OK, I understand. Please don't be embarrassed about it with me. I've seen plenty of it over my career and have seen people overcome it as well," said Leo calmly, warmly. "When was the last time you had a drink, if you don't mind me asking?"

"November 10, 2016. And it was half a can of beer—not even, probably four ounces. It was a stupid impulse, a mistake. I poured the rest of it down the drain, called my sponsor, and we went to a meeting that day," she said, clearly remembering the incident. "It could have been catastrophic, the wheels totally coming off, but I was lucky when it really counted."

"How long prior to that since you had a drink?"

"A little over two years."

"So in six years, you've had less than half a can of beer. I'd say that's pretty damn amazing," said Leo, always looking for that silver lining. "Clearly you're doing something right, and you should be proud of that."

"Do you really think so, Leo?"

"Of course I do. I don't imagine it's easy, but one day at a time, right? But I'd also imagine your life has improved dramatically over those six years."

"So much so," said Sam. "Most importantly with my sons. Neither of them fully gave up on me, even when I gave them plenty of reasons to. But now, I get to see them flourishing as adults, being parents themselves. It's been like a second chance at life."

"There you have it. Sounds like you're walking the line to me."

Sam took a beat, this time less defeated, more stout, likes someone who had traveled a long way to come out the other side, like someone who had learned to take a loss and find the gumption to carry on, to fight back.

"I wish it hadn't taken me into my fifties to figure this all out. When I think about how I let my boys down during all those years, when they were trying to grow up and also dealing with an unstable mother," said Sam, clearly heartbroken over it. "It's been their forgiveness that's saved me, that prompted me to actually do something about my life."

"And that's all that matters. The past is the past. Can't change it," said Leo. "What counts are the decisions you'll make today and tomorrow."

The bell over the front door chimed, a new customer entered, shaking off the cold, heading for the counter.

"Thank you, Leo. Still as kind as I remembered you."

Leo smiled and finished up the last bite of his pound cake, washed it down with his cooling coffee. He glanced back up at Sam, but she'd spaced out again, thousand-yard stare territory, as though wiped out by her admission to him. He thought he understood and continued to allot her time, which allowed him to regard her. She was still lovely, but it was apparent she wore those hard miles on her face, in her lines, looking older than she should for her age. Though in fairness, there were days when Leo caught himself in the mirror and could hardly recognize the old man staring back at him—which struck him as funny as he didn't feel old, didn't feel worn down or eroded by life. He hoped Sam felt that way or at least that the past few years had helped her rekindle some of that energy, some of that belief that while skin may lose ground to gravity, collagen and hair may slowly quit, it was the spirit that truly mattered, that actually accounted for one's age.

He could only imagine the trials she'd been through in her adult life, the desire to abstain from something and to be unable. The toll that it took on one's relationships, on one's outward appearance, their soul. She wore it well enough, but Leo could detect the weariness, see it in her still moments—Sam, looking out at the street traffic, waiting for someone, something. Leo figured she'd been doing better over the six years but that it was still a daily fight to salvage what remained of her life. He wondered about her physical health. About all the coils that slowly and not so slowly lose their spring over the years. Alcohol might be an effective lubricant of the tongue, but for the rest of the body, it was sand in the gears. And plaque for the mind. Though he did find Sam to be lucid, her emails read in a sober and detailed way—still, there was something not right about her as she sat. He wondered if there was a diplomatic way to ask, "How is your mind? How is your health?" It would come from a place of concern but also curiosity—nevertheless, a tough bridge to cross with someone who reached out from the blue, only to admit their failings and plagued days. He figured it would be OK to ask, gently and absolutely, in the spirit of making sure her footing was sound, even if he had to just blurt out his queries. He would tread lightly and was about to unspool his new line of questioning when she snapped out of her trance and engaged in her own discourse.

"Are you familiar with the twelve steps, Leo," she asked slowly. "The ones from the program?"

"In a general sense, kind of. Not that I could name them all."

"I'd say more than anything, committing myself to those teachings got me through the first year or two," said Sam. "It's actually kind of a weird doctrine to govern your life by, especially when you've already been alive for so long. Some people are better at following the sequence than others. For me, I had to bounce through those twelve principles a bit, getting good, falling short, circling back, trying again. It would feel like a cycle that had no end, that it would just be easier to give up and fall back on my old bad habits."

"But you didn't. And I would imagine a lot of people feel that way about the steps," said Leo.

"The best I can say for myself is that I stuck with it, got better at the progression as I struggled through it, didn't lose sight of the ones that came easier," said Sam. "It probably saved my life, but . . ."

Sam was about to drift back into her fugue. Leo wouldn't have it.

"But what, Sam?" he asked as he noticed she was now looking a little scared, trying to screw the courage up for something. She took a very deep and resigned breath.

"One of the steps—the hardest one in my opinion—is to make amends to people you've wronged in your life," she said, her voice ticking down to a wisp. "Even though the very next step says don't do it if you're just going to create more harm. But how do you know what harm you're going to create, if any? What if you've been carrying around something for so long that you hate, a secret, and you're ready to be free of it, might it cause harm? What if that person would want to know, even if it upsets them deeply?"

"I don't know, Sam," said Leo, a bit at a loss now. "Are you trying to say this has something to do with me? Is that why it was so important we meet in person?"

A reluctant nod from Sam, her eyes cast down again toward the breakfast-stained smear of the tabletop.

"If what you have to say will bring you peace, go ahead and say it. You don't need to worry about me," said Leo.

"You say that."

"I mean that."

The bell chimed from a new customer; a fresh puff of cold air rushed into the store.

"Harm in me," said Sam softly.

"Pardon?"

"Harmony. Sorry, just a mantra that helps."

Harm in me. Harmony.

Leo could feel the coffee churning in his stomach, the shop starting to feel too hot in his winter clothes, too crowed despite there being hardly any people inside. He was kind of ready to have Sam get on with it so he could bolt back to Orchard Coils. He was suddenly very, *very* ready to get on with his usual life.

"Sam, what do you have to make amends for with me?" asked Leo, prodding her until she relented, spilled, as they all eventually do.

"I was pregnant, Leo, by you," said Sam. "But I didn't see it through."

"What are you talking about?"

"When we were kids, obviously. I never told you. I never told anyone. Once I knew for sure, I had it taken care of before anyone could know," said Sam, trying to meet Leo's eyes, failing. "I thought it would be a secret I'd keep my whole life, but now you see I can't do it. And I felt you had to know even if it was decades ago. That's what I need to make peace with. And to make peace with you."

Leo sat back in his chair. And to think, his hope in that last minute had been that Sam would confess she actually knew something about the Peter Sullivan murder. How wrong he'd been—and there'd be no going back to his usual life anytime soon.

* * *

Leo Sinclair was practicing three-foot putts on the warm-up green, drinking from a bottle of Michelob Ultra—both odd, in that Leo often neglected practicing his short game and never liked to drink any alcohol before playing, favoring a light beer for after the round as a treat. Yet here he was, grumbling about lip outs while periodically running back into the pro shop to procure another beer that would occupy his hands when the club wasn't in them.

The putts weren't dropping. The empty bottles were lining up.

Leo had been spending a lot of time at the club, more so than he could remember over the past twenty years. Of course, he wasn't alone in that regard. A huge chunk of the membership, particularly those on the younger side, had been coming in droves to play copious amounts of golf, to use the range and practice facilities, even to exercise the two tennis courts that had finally been built three years ago after a decade of extensive delays, narrowly approved votes, and grousing over contractor fees. The current head pro, a man by the name of Lucas Brookings, who'd taken over from Michael Bouffard's short reign after Cobb Webb passed the baton to him, was scrambling with his assistants to get everybody who wanted to play out on the course, all hours of the day, seven days a week. The fact that it was a private club was their saving grace, with only a finite number of members eligible to play or bring visitors.

The word around the state was that the Connecticut public courses would remain open and were very much slammed with demand—tee times rapidly booked, daylight hours stretched to the minute—and a general shitshow atmosphere had not surprisingly developed on top of the current shitshow as certain people were clamoring to get out of their houses and actually *do* something outside. Bordering states that, in their own questionable wisdom, had shuttered their courses ended up driving their denizens onto the interstates, and Connecticut saw a mighty influx of people willing to pay fifty dollars to walk nine holes on some patch of dirt and creek that got grandfathered in as a municipal or executive course decades ago. There were plenty of those in the Nutmeg State, and many golfers had historically gone out of their way to avoid them, but given the demand for tee times in the spring/summer of 2020, even those worn-down munies were printing money, could hardly keep up with their phone ringing off the hook as they probably didn't even have online booking software, never needed it.

On top of that, all the pent-up demand wasn't just from existing golfers but also from people who had never played before or seldom got out there. Maybe they had an old set of wrenches collecting dust in the garage, hidden behind the ride-on mower out in the tool shed. Now these yahoos were coming out of the woodwork, tripping over themselves to mix it up with the everyday hacks and actual good players to share the same limited space, creating hodgepodge foursomes of disparate skill levels as the days of going out as a twosome, let alone solo, had been put on indefinite pause. That blending of talent created an awful lot of stories out on the links and, counterintuitively, a general sense of comradery that transcended these massive gulfs in handicaps. Given the extenuating circumstances of the time, charity was running high, and most folks were digging a lot deeper into love-thy-neighbor territory, particularly when they were outdoors and pleased enough to leave their masks back in the car. That said, did it mean you had to keep your head on a swivel because an errant shot from a newbie was more likely to be struck in your general direction? You bet it did. But it was better than the alternative—streaming more subpar material off Netflix's infinite scroll or putzing around the house looking for stuff that didn't really need repair or video chatting with old college friends while everyone pretended to be virologists, as though they'd ever heard the term *protein spike* before in their lives.

Some people were just willing to get comfortable in the shooting gallery and duck their heads instinctively every time "Fore!" was yelled, which was often and harrowing, but at least you were outdoors to hear the birds' singsong. Besides, there were currently more dangerous things occupying the air than squibbed golf balls—clearly. One just had to watch five minutes of cable news and their fear porn to be reminded of that.

So if you heard that ubiquitous warning screamed out on the course, you just protected your head and jewels, and if you happened to catch a stinger in some meaty or bony part of your body, you shook it off like you'd been there before and tried to act accordingly. Someone would probably offer you a beer in the parking lot for your troubles, commend you for taking the shot but keeping the pace of play in check. Ultimately, you'd have a little general anesthetic in your system, a good story, and a circular-shaped bruise to wear as a badge of honor—and not to belabor the point, but at least you were outdoors with like-minded people, rallying against the strange times and perhaps not succumbing to the doom and gloom trafficked through all walks of life.

Perhaps.

To be clear, it was the third week of June 2020, three months into the worldwide COVID-19 pandemic, and the golf sector was booming after the long, post–Great Recession slog of the 2010s—the industry getting a timely and much-needed shot in the arm after an exceedingly lean decade when the Tiger effect had waned, and disposable incomes had plummeted. Truly the most unlikely of catalysts that could have reversed the dwindling revenues of the game, the pandemic proved to be a godsend to the sport. In particular, Connecticut, bucking the guidance of adjacent states like New York and Massachusetts, opting to keep their courses open, and hoping the ever-changing science wasn't wrong about outdoors being the safer of spaces, even if neighboring governors weren't willing to wrap their minds around that inconvenient reality. Or, if one were being cynical, perhaps it just didn't play into their personal agenda or how the data jived with *their* narrative—take your pick. There were plenty of case studies in the Northeast to scrutinize around that particular emergency response. In any event, their constituents' loss was Connecticut's gain, and the out-of-staters were encouraged to brave the now-empty highways of 95 and 84 to play a few rounds in the Constitution State. Just be sure to book your tee time well in advance, and bring provisions because the restaurants and clubhouses were sure as hell closed.

As for Orchard Coils's own chief of police, the pandemic had hit him in a particularly odd way, an angle that people around him couldn't see and therefore didn't understand. Leo was still reeling from the news he'd learned from Samantha Morris in that Starbucks back in January but had opted to keep it to himself. It might have been logical to share his encounter with someone, maybe with Oscar Ortiz, certainly with Janet Sinclair, given they had a relatively honest and forthcoming marriage. It actually would have been more in his character to talk about it a little bit, even if he wasn't ready to go into too much length over it. But instead, he locked it away, told not a soul, pretended it wasn't anyone else's business. Not a word to Janet. Not to his adult kids. Not to Lynn or Sachin or Olivia or his brother-in-law Paul or Oscar or even Jocko Jr., whom Leo had become closer friends with over the past decade. Any of these people would have welcomed Leo's trust in them, understood his need to unburden himself, to solicit a different perspective. Served as a sounding board against his grievances and confusion. These were the people in his life, the trusted souls one cultivates through decades of filters and screenings, the people who would have walked on hot coals if it meant helping the man out. He needed only to ask, to open his mouth. But instead, he did nothing, clammed up, and allowed the revelation to fester in his mind in the unhealthiest of ways, souring his winter, projecting a vile mood out on those around him at home and work—also out of character for the man—which would be much of his trend for 2020.

His shortness with people was quickly noticed by those who knew him well, initially chalked up to his displeasure over the harsh winter, one that seemed likely to creep deep into April, if not early May. But as his disposition continued to worsen, people in his life started asking him if he was OK, saying he'd seemed off for more than a few weeks now. He dismissed their concerns, sometimes with grace, often with annoyance. More to the point, he continued to deny that anything was amiss, sometimes going so far as to say outlandish things like he'd never been better or make perplexing statements about functioning as a doormat his entire life—stuff along those lines. Those instances weren't helping Leo's case that he was, in fact, OK. They were boldface lies or cryptic nonsense, and the people around him knew something was up. For all the laudable and interesting things about Leo Sinclair, being overly complicated had never been one of them. He was a cop. A family man. A marksman. He loved hitting a small ball across yards of God's green earth. These were the things that made him tick. He didn't possess layer upon layer of un-mineable terrain—didn't have them, didn't want them. So when an amicable and relatively low-key person such as himself became withdrawn yet antagonist, as though channeling the angst of his inner teenager or struggling artist, people would eventually conclude it wasn't the abnormal levels of snowfall or workplace stress causing such a profound effect. They were going to figure something very real and difficult was going on in the man's life that he wasn't willing to speak to—and no one was going to get a guy like Leo to open up until he was ready. No amount of cajoling or picking around the edges would divine the truth from his reluctant mouth, particularly when he dug his heels into some prideful stand, which was precisely what he'd done, resulting in the guise of a bitter old man, cold and joyless—words no one would ever have associated with Leo prior to the winter of 2020.

A sort of nebulous consensus formed in lieu of an intervention that allowed Leo to wallow in whatever the hell it was he was dealing with, in hopes that he'd snap out of it on his own or eventually ask for someone's help—anyone's, really. It turned into this weird game of chicken that Leo was better positioned to win, though he knew that winning would be futile at best—if anything, winning might lead to a real deterioration in some of his most treasured relationships. The remainder of January and February passed with little change in his disposition, his mood slowly worsening as the mercury outside dipped. It was truly as bad a two-month stretch anyone could remember for the man. He himself was hardly under any delusions as to his behavior—he was struggling, and it was one of the rougher patches of his life, right up there with his parents passing, with almost getting gunned down in that industrial park some twenty years earlier. *Sam Morris did this to me*, he'd think incessantly. Indeed, the slog of those early months of 2020 had become a dark period in his existence, cutting him down to the marrow and reducing his zeal for even creature comforts, like food and sleep—he couldn't imagine how it could possibly get any worse or how he was going to get out of it.

Then March of 2020 was ushered in, and the world got properly fucked beyond anyone's wildest comprehension.

By that point, people had become less concerned with Leo's odd behavior as they now had more pressing matters at hand: panic at the grocery stores, lines at the gas station, masking, lockdowns, toilet paper shortages, daily presidential and gubernatorial briefings, homeschooling, working from home, Zoom, death tolls, two weeks to stop the spread, the loss of small and taste, legitimate and unfounded levels of fear, along with about a thousand other little things that every person on the planet had to consider, stuff they'd been able to take for granted their entire lives. People very suddenly found themselves in a personal nightmare they couldn't wake from, and given what little precedent existed for it in the modern age, there was hardly much guidance on how seven billion people were meant to react.

As for Leo, he was forced to curb most of his self-indulgent malaise and get down to the brass tacks of running the PD in a community of very scared and confused citizens. He took to the new challenge with great determination, and, like many of the men and women around him, he threw himself into the work wholeheartedly, burying that anguish he'd been roiled in, pivoting from his odd behavior to a workhorse obsession with keeping Orchard Coils a safe and lawful place, more so than ever under the specter of this encroaching illness. He rallied the people who worked under him, delivered newly impassioned speeches about what needed to be done, how it was time for them to step up, to provide stability and calm during these trying times. Leo had never been one for grandiose acts, but he laid it on thick with his squad, letting them know the high expectations set upon them, upon him. He told them point blank that if anyone didn't feel they could answer the call under the present circumstances, they could leave their badge and gun on his desk and call it a day. No one took him up on that option. No one backed down from Leo's gambit—if anything, they were encouraged to see their old leader back in rare form, full of piss and vinegar and determination, the glint of a hawk returned to his eyes.

Those first three months of the pandemic chewed through the man's hours as though the very construct itself threatened to fold under its own weight: dozens of calls to respond to, altercations to de-escalate, local checkpoints to enforce, maintaining a general calm that would comfort the populace while, at the same time, letting them know that bullshit would not be tolerated under the guise of COVID freakouts. It wasn't always pretty, and in fact, it sometimes teetered on martial law, but those early months did help set the tone. As terrible as the virus was, it was not the end of days, and it would not collapse the country or the little burg they held so dear. None of this was that different from other towns and cities around the globe, everyday heroes like cops, firefighters, nurses, docs, EMTs, community leaders, and even some remotely competent politicians banding together to brace the rule of law, preserving the fabric of their community and its place in society.

Leo worked tirelessly to be one of those cogs in the machine that was operating against this unexpected disaster, along with the mayor and other key figures, helping buttress the town's overall response as they crept into spring and its promise of warmer weather, which apparently the virus didn't cotton to, would cause the loss some of its transmissibility and perhaps potency. For a man now in his mid-sixties, Leo showed a tremendous amount of energy and vigilance in the face of what would have been viewed as a younger man's fight, particularly as it seemed older folks were in the greatest jeopardy of hospitalization and death. But Leo wasn't listening to that type of noise. He took to the workload as though he were half his age, and it didn't bothered him, which had the effect of erasing other people's recollection of his erratic behavior during the months prior to the outbreak, months that already felt like a lifetime ago—the slow-beating heart of a simpler winter people now longed for, wishing they could turn back time. But that wasn't how the construct worked; those clock hands would never cooperate under the wishes of mere mortals.

Of course, Leo had hardly forgotten those early months of 2020—he'd just further suppressed them under the intense burden of work, the subterfuge of a worldwide cataclysmic event. But his own cataclysmic event remained all the same: gestating, sculpted, and channeled into a certain type of output—useful, though probably not in a sustained way that could remain productive forever. It was bound to take other forms if buried too deep, if given too much time. A man's suffering could be cagey like that; it knew how to take on a host, to be patient with certain type of people, and to await its opportunity to manifest in the most insidious of ways. Horrible ways, bizarrely calculated. Beautiful lives had been ruined this way. And that suffering hadn't given up on Leo, not by a long shot—it was biding its time as the man tried to ignore it, lying in wait, still coming for him, hoping to strike him down.

After those first three months of COVID, and hard months they were, some normalization had set in, trickled down from global to local levels. Or maybe it was more grassroots from local to global—legitimately hard to discern. People developed a general understanding of what the virus meant to them and theirs. How it affected their risk-reward systems, something most people had never thought about deeply before. They realized the food and water wouldn't be turned off, and supplies would still flow, albeit at a choppy pace. Many would learn after those three months whether they still had a job or not. Whether their business would be shuttered. Whether their eviction would be placed into a moratorium—foreclosure too. Loans frozen. Schools taught virtually. Essential workers anointed. Religious gatherings fought over. Protests over government overreach, constitutionality questioned and requestioned. Once this new baseline was tentatively established and the initial fervor somewhat dissipated, most people got on with the concept of living their new everyday lives—even if they did look radically different from the way they functioned in the summer of 2019.

Policing became slightly less intrusive and started shifting back toward pre-pandemic levels, particularly in the smaller communities. In larger metropolitan areas, the police forces were contending with the fallout over George Floyd's death, a different type of viral material that had spawned civil unrest and prompted people to disregard COVID guidelines and take to the streets, sometimes rioting en masse, as a strong anti-police sentiment gripped the country right when it looked like it was getting its bearings from the airborne virus that had taken the lives of millions worldwide. Again, this was more isolated to larger urban centers, where they would have to weigh the pros and cons of progressivism and try to figure out exactly what they wanted of their police force: what the rules of engagement should be, the use of deadly force, the socio-economic makeup of their peacekeepers and how closely they should be a reflection of the community they were tasked to protect—not simple questions in areas where millions of people were packed into a dozen square miles, let alone when a global emergency was unfurling around them.

As for Orchard Coils, their PD didn't receive any backlash, and during those months, apart from the handful of anti-brutality protesters who liked to loiter on the green on weekends, the troubles from Minnesota's epicenter didn't disturb the applecart in Connecticut, including Leo's little fiefdom, very much. And after those three hard-fought months to establish calm, maintain order, and assure the community that life would continue, Leo found himself well positioned with all his subordinates, the vast bureaucracy, and even the public at large. He'd delivered on his mandates, and his approval rating was through the roof. Not that they had any actual hard data in Orchard Coils on the topic—the gauge would be the banter at wherever people could find a place to socialize, and the straw poll was in Leo's favor as his missteps from earlier in the year had all but been wiped out from public memory.

There was even chatter that Leo could be the next mayor—a job he had zero interest in or aspiration to.

The one person who wasn't quite ready to believe that Leo could walk on water was his wife, Janet—for truly, what wife in her right mind would concede that point? Janet had a front-row seat to how Leo had pushed himself over the past three months and did at times worry he was going too strong, doing too much. There were elements to his approach that she did find concerning, stuff she would try to bring up to him, that he would just shrug off as stress, unresolved tension from the day. Her job at the orthopedics practice had been mostly redesignated as a work-from-home position during the lockdown, though really, the practice was in a bit of hibernation until people felt comfortable enough to resume elective surgeries that would inevitably lead to weeks of physical therapy, necessitating more travel or perhaps someone outside your orbit entering your house.

All of the sudden, people had to worry about who they let into their homes—where they'd been, what they might be carrying.

Janet didn't have as much exposure to the outside world as Leo was dealing with, in both his prospects of infection and the unpredictable nature of the humans he interacted with. It wasn't something he lorded over her. He was thrilled she'd been able to maintain her job and could work from the safety of home, though a clear delineation of risk between the two had been drawn. Janet had never pretended that her job was more dangerous than Leo's and certainly didn't do so during the pandemic, so her point of emphasis was that her husband should do more to protect himself from the virus while he was slogging through those long days. Leo might get chippy over her concern—in his lesser moments, he'd accuse her of nagging, explaining to her he didn't have the luxury of social distancing when he had a town to protect, that he wore a mask as often as he could, disinfected his hands often, and bumped elbows with people in lieu of shaking hands. He had all the appropriate comebacks for her; they'd been drilled into his head as a steward of the state. But when Janet would press him, not so much on the machinations of his day but on whether he was fearful of the virus, of contracting it, he tended to pipe down, cast his eyes in avoidance of the topic. This was why it was good for Leo to have a wife, one who hadn't forgotten his unusual behavior in the early part of the year, one who easily took note of his cavalier approach to engaging with society, throwing too much caution to the wind, even if he liked to think he took certain prophylactic measures.

Janet could cut through those layers: his good soldier routine, his smoke and mirrors, his bullshit.

Leo might try to explain to her that he couldn't do his job and live in fear at the same time; they were incompatible, and no one's interest would be served by his bowing down to some microscopic threat that might only give him cold-like symptoms for a week. Janet thrashed that talking point summarily and reminded her better half that, yes, he was fit and healthy with strong lungs and a battle-tested immune system. He was also on the wrong side of sixty, and COVID could do a hell of a lot worse than put someone on bed rest for a few days—in short, he needed to accept that he was no longer thirty years old, and this thing posed a real danger to him. His not-me mentality was going to end him up on a ventilator in the makeshift pandemic section of Orchard Coils Memorial Hospital.

In short, the man was going to get himself killed—and it almost seemed like he was trying to.

Leo didn't necessarily refute all her accusations, some of which held more truth than he liked to admit, but he was going to ignore them all the same, to let them roll off his back and go about his job and life as he saw fit. He didn't think he was immune to the respiratory virus—he just didn't want to admit to Janet that he *wanted* to catch it. Or, to put it another way, he didn't give a flying fig if he did happen to catch it. He wasn't willing to cower. If his ticket got punched because of a germ, flooding his lungs, exacerbating some latent, preexisting condition, then so be it. The more he thought about it, what really was the point of being fearful anyway? The kids were grown and mostly safe from the illness. He'd survived being a career cop. He'd survived a bullet fired at his head. His parents were gone. He'd resigned himself to never breaking eighty on the golf course. And to punctuate his questionable line of thinking, his old flame from high school had let him know he was meant to be a father, a real father, unbeknownst to him, for a couple of months at least, until that was taken away from him, his agency disregarded, his counsel passed over.

So maybe that was the point of it all—everything got taken away in the end, either piece by piece or all at once. All roads led to the final destination.

If COVID had illuminated one thing for Leo, it was that we could all indulge our illusions of fortifying protection—banking money, eating fiber, looking twice before crossing the road—but the sole purpose of the universe is was remove everyone one by one, indiscriminately and without fail. Did this mean Leo technically wanted to die? Not really. But did he take that mask off every chance he got, despite the lines he'd recite to Janet? He sure did. Did he still shake hands with people? Yep. Had he given up washing his hands about a week into April? Absolutely. Did he give a damn about being in enclosed spaces, breathing in that communal, recycled air? He did not. He just couldn't care about this new indignation anymore, his tolerance tapped out. Samantha Morris had broken him back in January, splintered his mind and colored his outlook in a particularly unhealthy way at the very worst of times. And, laughably, as if the universe wasn't done taunting him, despite all the testing he'd gone through, basically every day as ordered by the town, given his job, the results were always the same—negative for COVID. He honestly couldn't believe that after three months of trying to contract the stupid thing, it was just another task he'd failed at. So many of his friends and family and colleagues had been infected. So many of them had gotten over it easily enough and then felt emboldened with their newly found natural immunity, something about antibody levels that Leo didn't fully understand. And it wasn't like Leo was walking around thinking himself biologically immune or that hospitalization or death wasn't possible, but by that point, he wanted to give it a go. He'd even settle for an asymptomatic infection, anything that would pop on those daily testings to let him know he was part of the tribe, that he had not been forsaken in ways unexplainable to him.

A more stable mind would not have been reduced to such folly, but Leo's headspace had succumbed to inferior lines of thinking, dangerous ones even. He wasn't the type of man equipped to battle such contrarian thoughts, to plumb those dark notes—no, he wouldn't be sharpened. Quite the opposite, he'd be crushed.

So when the dust partially settled midsummer, Leo found himself with some disposable time once again, which he squandered the bulk of at O Triple C. He became more social, not so much because he wanted to be around others—his day job saw to that—but because he wanted to test his body, its defense mechanisms, and the vectors around him that could spread the disease. The Restaurant's indoor dining had been closed, understandably, though much lamented by the membership, including the current GM who'd been looking to unveil a refurbished menu and modernized bar top of granite flecked with some kind of mineral shine. There were rumors that some outdoor setups would be implemented for July, the Restaurant chomping at the bit to get back to business in some capacity, especially given the heavy foot traffic on the course.

Leo found himself to be pretty popular at the club—not always the case, given his line of work—where people were eager to pick his brain about the town's response or just to congratulate him on a job well done. Some folks wondered if he had any secret information about the virus or its origin or the fast-tracking of a vaccine that the general public wasn't privy to. He assured them he didn't have an inside lane to any of that. He was still just a civil servant; he knew little more than they did. Most people didn't believe him on that one. Nevertheless, he was experiencing a minor flash of notoriety around the club—funny how a global disaster could change things, make strange bedfellows—though, to be sure, Leo was hardly of a disposition to leverage this popularity contest. In fact, he all but despised it and faked his way through the backslaps and offers of free cigars and Purell hand sanitizer.

The one thing he did try to impress upon people was that the virus probably wasn't going anywhere anytime soon. He listened to medical professionals, both local and online. He read up on it, particularly the history of fast-moving, breathable diseases. Educated himself on how hotspots and waves and post-holiday spikes worked. On treatments and regimens and hopefully some type of antidote. He learned what the difference was between pandemic and endemic, something he'd never imagined he'd need to research. None of it, in his estimation, pointed to something that they'd be able to turn the corner on in months; it looked like a longer game to him. This was also the opinion of many prominent figures who made their way onto cable TV, podcasts. But the thought of its lasting years was an unpopular outlook that people didn't want to understand, let alone accept. It was hard to fathom carrying on as they were for much longer, that society could fade a few seasons of this—but would they truly be asked to endure years of such precaution? Leo did what he could to prepare people for what might be a longer haul than they'd hoped for, but short of that, there wasn't much extra in the way of words to assist them. He'd be there for them in action, in spirit—he told them to not overreach for food and drink, to resist the impulse to decay into vice and, if they could, to get outside as much as possible, get some sun, exercise, play some golf, absorb some vitamin D as he'd heard good things about that particular hormone.

In short, protect yourself if you were so inclined because no one was going to do it for you.

* * *

"Sam, I don't. . . . What are you saying?" asked Leo, a little earthquake rattling in his voice box. "You're saying it was me?"

"Yes," she said, her simple answer.

"But how do you know. I mean, how do you know it was definitely me?"

"We were dating, Leo. Who else would it be?"

"Yeah, but I was maybe never sure I was the only guy in your life back then."

"Were you seeing anyone else during that time?" asked Sam calmly, to which Leo shook his head. "Neither was I. Why would you have assumed otherwise?"

"I don't know. You were older than me, seemed so mature. You were gorgeous, and we went to different schools," said Leo. "I never pressed you on it because I didn't want to screw things up."

"If I was holding anything back it was because my home life was such a mess. I would have been embarrassed or self-conscious about it, particularly given how close knit your family was," said Sam. "But it was just you during those months we dated, to be clear."

Leo was now aware his heart was jackhammering the confines of his rib cage in the most unhealthy of ways, as though it might flee his chest. He exhaled audibly, almost gagging, in an equally unhealthy way.

"Are you OK, Leo?" she asked.

He looked at her, saw his eyes, flame licked, like marred glass—it was everything she'd feared.

"Am I OK?" he said, his voiced raised. "No, I'm not OK. Are you seriously telling me you were pregnant with my kid and you . . ." Then Leo lowered his voice, continued on. "Aborted it?"

Sam's face flinched ever so slightly at the word, the implication, the accusation.

"I'm so sorry, Leo. I know this must be painful to hear," said Sam, trying to maintain some order, trying to remember she'd practiced this moment in her head hundreds of times, maybe thousands. "Perhaps I did seem older and more experienced back then, but I was barely eighteen, and plenty of that was just a façade. I mean, I was still a kid myself, and my parents were a wreck. The truth was I didn't know what I was doing half the time."

"But it didn't seem like that at all," said Leo, straining the words through his teeth.

"I was good at faking it, I suppose," said Sam. "When things aren't good at home, you get really adept at putting up appearances, especially when you're terrified people might learn the truth. But I promise you, I'm not telling you all this to hurt you. That is the last thing I want to happen."

The bell chimed, and a customer exited the coffee shop. Leo quickly observed that somehow, inexplicably, the lives of others were carrying on. The world hadn't froze on its axis.

"Then why are you telling me this?" asked Leo loudly, now drawing some glances from the sparse crowd, the barista microwaving a breakfast sandwich, the clerk at the register making change. "Is this part of your sobriety? How does *this* keep you from crawling back into a bottle?"

Sam let the slight pass. She wasn't in much of a position to argue with Leo's anger, his choice of words in the moment.

"Because it has weighed on me for forty years that maybe I should have told you back then, that you had a right to know," said Sam. "And I guess I'm even more scared of what it means to me in my remaining years. We're not young, Leo, not anymore. Surely you don't want to leave behind secrets and regrets and things left unsaid. We all want to be free and clear of those."

"So this is really about you trying to make peace with the future," said Leo. "This doesn't seem like anything for my benefit. If anything, it sounds like you're breaking one of your stupid AA steps to unburden yourself."

The cop in Leo knew how to find the vulnerable spot in the story, the soft patch in the interview, where he would then strike quickly, without sacrificing accuracy.

"I acknowledge that was a very real possibility," said Sam, controlling her breath. "But ultimately, while this process is designed to help me, it was also my belief that you'd want to know the truth."

"Your belief is self-serving horseshit."

"Be as angry as you want, Leo, but I truly would not have told you if I'd thought you'd grown into a man who didn't want to know how things really were," said Sam. "A person like my own father, who lived his life with his head buried in the sand."

"No one's burying their head, Sam. I've lived a long life perfectly fine without this information and would have been content to continue on that way."

"You say that now. And if it proves to be true, then I have made an utter fool of myself, and I wouldn't blame you for hating me the rest of our lives," she said, meaning it all, unequivocally.

Leo took a beat, considered what Sam was getting at—would he really rather not have been told? Obviously, he could have carried on with his existence sans the information. The absence would have had no material impact on how he'd live out his remaining days. But hadn't he always fancied himself as a man who wanted to know the truth, even when it was inconvenient, even when it was painful to hear? Had he not been now offered a glimpse into an alternative world, a different timeline? To look away would be contrary to the self-actualization he'd so prided himself on—an attribute that, in Leo's vainer moments, he had taken to a pedestal over, looking down on others.

He would have to keep pressing Sam, like so many interrogations, reluctant to believe they'd reached the bottom of it, more than likely, still just scratching the surface. And if it was going to hurt like hell to do so, for both parties involved, then so be it—he wasn't concerned with her feelings or her sobriety in that moment.

"Why didn't you just tell me back then?" asked Leo, collecting what wits he had left. "You didn't have to go through it alone. We could have made some decisions together."

"We had our whole futures ahead of us, Leo. You were smart and loved and had options. Can you really imagine being tied down as a father at seventeen?" asked Sam rhetorically, to which Leo didn't bother to respond. "I mean, honestly, do you even remember just how close you came to joining the military? How badly you wanted to serve like your dad?"

"I haven't forgotten," said Leo, recalling photos of Baxter Sinclair in his old uniform, his stories of Monte Cassino, the scarring on his back he was self-conscious of.

"You had a bright future, Leo, and you've made good on it. And me, I wasn't ready to be a mom at eighteen. And I know plenty about being one now. I was terrified of screwing it up back when I was twenty-five. And I did screw it up. And I'm still terrified. I've made mistakes that should have been irredeemable, but somehow, there was just enough grace in the world to spare me," said Sam, decades of strain in her voice. "But it was the right decision, what I did back then, for both of us."

Leo bristled at the suggestion. He would not be so easily swayed.

"A unilateral decision, Sam. No one really likes their life being defined by someone else, unbeknownst to them."

"I'm sorry, Leo, but if I'd told you, I think we can both imagine how it would have gone down."

"Really? Enlighten me on that one. You've clearly had time to think on it," said Leo, his hands gesturing in the air, his fingers spread in derision. "How would the seventeen-year-old version of myself react to his girlfriend getting pregnant?"

Sam sighed in frustration. How many years she'd imagined this conversation and the myriad of ways it could go. There were just some blows that couldn't be softened, no matter how much you wanted to; they were just always going to land like a lead pipe to the head—no way to outthink such raw emotion, outflank a quickly entrenched position.

"You would have wanted us to keep the baby," said Sam. "And I might not have been strong enough to refuse you."

"You were the one always calling the shots in our relationship."

"Not on something that big. You would have worn me down. Got your parents involved for sure. Guilted me. Maybe even evoked God or whatever," said Sam. "Anything, if you decided that the baby had to be kept. You'd have traded in all of your futures if you believed the right thing to do was the hard thing to do."

"The right thing to do is all but always the hard thing to do."

"I don't disagree. But in this case, those burdens needed to fall on my shoulders alone," said Sam. "It wasn't easy not telling you. In fact, it was horrible and lonely, and every day felt like a betrayal."

Leo piped down and sat quietly for a moment, wondering why he wasn't loved by the universe. Self-pity was not a trait the man wore often, but when he did, the scope could range galaxies.

"You can't say for certain I would have tried to make you keep the baby."

"Then tell me I'm wrong; now is your chance."

Leo said nothing, thinking it over, He didn't know what to say next, didn't know who was right regarding a decision made forty years ago without his knowledge or consent, a choice irrevocably denied. He didn't want Sam to be right, but maybe she was. Nothing about the conversation he was having in that coffee-chain restaurant was what he'd envisioned. He figured Sam needed his help with her ex, maybe a legal matter or one of her kids was in a jam—something for which he could flex his position in law enforcement and lend a hand, for old times' sake. And he was prepared to accommodate, happy to. But what she really brought him to Stamford for, what he hadn't seen coming, was an ambush, a long-set trap that had finally sprung, that he'd fallen prey to. It was not how his life was meant to go as he slowly neared the finish line—it was wrong and unfair, and his anger was stoked. The fumes rose.

"You robbed me of a chance to be a father, a real father," said Leo, boring a hole into the target of Sam's face, which had gone all but featureless in his flared mind, like all those faceless paper outlines he'd shot to bits over the years at the range.

"Leo, come on."

"No, that was my chance, and you took it away from me."

"You are a father, Leo, twice over, so don't do this to yourself because you're mad at me," said Sam, aware of the nerve that had been pinched. "You raised those boys, and they look up to you. You're their dad."

"No, they just call me Dad sometimes. They have a biological one, fucking Billy, always around, always reminding me of exactly what I'm not," said Leo, the words like bitter cherry pits to be spit out quickly. "I'm just a stand-in, the dormer you add to a house."

"I don't remotely believe that," said Sam evenly. "That's not what you are to anybody, let alone your family."

"How the fuck would you know what I am to anybody, Sam?" said Leo loudly. "Just because you googled me after half a lifetime doesn't mean you know shit about me or what I've been through."

"And you don't know the half of what my life's been like, not by a long shot," said Sam, not quite matching Leo's decibels but allowing her voice to raise for emphasis.

Again, the patrons of the coffee shop took notice of the older couple, clearly embroiled in some row, one that did not seem to be cooling down, the unsettled air about them only thickening, intensifying.

"If things didn't work out for you in certain ways, Leo, if you somehow feel shortchanged in life, that's not on me," said Sam. "A single abortion in the seventies you never knew about doesn't have much to do with your existence, and I think down deep, you know I'm right."

Holy murder entered Leo's eyes.

"You fucking cunt to lecture me," whispered Leo, as though he had a shot at controlling his rage, only to slam his fist down on the table with all his might, hoping to split the planet in half.

That was finally enough to bring the shift manager over from behind the counter to investigate what was going on between these two seniors on what should have been a humdrum morning. Usually it was much younger people causing such a disturbance who needed to be reminded to lower their voice, take a cell phone conversation outside, basically rein in their actions to accommodate the public space—not people old enough to swap photos of their grandchildren.

The manager approached the two with clear intent—purposeful and confident, skilled at dealing with the unruly masses or those just overly caffeinated.

"Sir, I'm going to have to ask you to lower your voice and mind your conduct," said the shift manager, whose name tag read Kayla. "Ma'am, are you OK? Do you need me to call for some assistance?"

"No dear, it's better if you just—"

But Leo didn't allow Sam to finish her thought—and Kayla, despite her best intentions, had inadvertently said the very wrong thing at the very wrong time. Sam knew it instantly, saw the proof in Leo's coal-stoked eyes, the brimstone leaking through his rictus of teeth.

"You're asking her is *she* needs assistance . . . Kayla," said Leo, reading the name tag slowly. "You should be asking me if I need assistance. She's the one trying to upend my fucking world."

"She's not the one yelling, sir. Or slamming her hands down or using foul language, for that matter," said Kayla, standing her ground. "So if you can't control yourself, the police are only a call away."

Leo didn't bother to hide his smirk.

"I'll do you one better, Kayla," said Leo, reaching into his coat pocket and slamming something down on the table—his badge. "I'm a chief of police in this state, the law around here. So my recommendation is returning to your counter and letting me get on with my business here. Do we have an understanding?"

A rhetorical question if Kayla had ever heard one. She didn't like it, but she also didn't need to butt heads with this officer, especially if he was a high-ranking one. The fact that he'd outed himself should force him to calm down some; at least, that was her hope. She glared at Leo suspiciously but ultimately moved along without further comment, hoping the worst was behind them, that this belligerent man would soon be on his way, and the well-composed woman would be freed from his company. Some of the customers in the coffee shop had taken it upon themselves to leave; probably some of the staff would like to have joined them. Leo's badge remained on the table as he and Sam looked back to one another, mired in a standoff, neither willing to admit a stalemate. She was waiting on a fresh salvo from Leo, no longer able to rule out that the man might cross some indelible line. His anger had been more than she'd anticipated, even along the spectrum her mind had faceted—he was redlining, and it was the exact reason she'd wanted to be cautious and have the conversation in a public place, for her own safety.

As for Leo, he was forced inward, going quiet, staring at his hands and what they could do in this world, what he should allow them to do. He'd played his badge stunt but was now hemmed in and needed to make some better real-time decisions. He took in some fast, shallow breaths—not out of panic, but the effect was almost like choking, fighting water out of his lungs—finding deeper, less labored respiration. He brought his heart rate down. Unballed his hands and threaded his fingers together. He regrouped. He eased out some words to Sam.

"What was it?" he asked, with a softer resignation.

"Sorry?"

"Boy or girl?"

"Oh. I'm not sure. I never made it long enough for that to be determined," said Sam. "I was only nine weeks along when I ended it."

"So I was a parent for those nine weeks."

"Don't."

"Could have been a son. Could have been a beautiful daughter. We'll never know."

"You have two sons."

"Not everyone sees it that way," said Leo, sneering at the thought. "Trust me, plenty of people over the years have been happy to point out that little nuance."

"Since when do you care what other people think?"

"Since always, Sam. I care very much about that sort of thing," said Leo. "That much about me hasn't changed much over the years. I'm not some free spirit, I'm not strong like that. I have a place in the world where I fit in, and it matters to me."

"Fine, fair enough. But small-minded people that would give you shit over how you built your family aren't worth a damn, Leo," said Sam, almost pleading with him. "Honestly, you're better than them, and you can't let their jealousies and ignorance define your place in the world."

Leo did his best to tamp down the roiling emotion, fearful of another outburst—instead, he scrunched his eyes tight, almost shaking, as if he could transform his body into a vessel that would draw the world inward, maybe even the universe. If it would not love him back, then he'd snuff it out of existence and take satisfaction in his revenge until he was nothing, until there was nothing.

"You're trying to calm me down. Placate me," he said.

"Jeez, Leo, you'd think one thing about me you'd pick up on is that I'm no longer in a position to lie about anything," said Sam. "I'm a drunk—yeah, a reformed one, but I'll always be one. I can't also be a liar. That's not how recovery works. So if I say you're right to ignore anyone who would so much as intimate that you're not a real father, then you can bet that's how I truly feel."

That was enough to give Leo some pause, reflection on Sam's word, while he tried to quiet the maelstrom roaring in his mind. It was working a little bit. He felt calmer, which was to say less homicidal—also trying to remember that more had been going on in the equation than just him, that Sam had outlined some hard stuff in her second email to him, details of a roughshod life in which her drinking had been both cause and coping mechanism. He knew there was more to the story.

"Your ex, is he still in the picture? Did he help you get sober?" he asked, attempting some type of pivot, a respite of sorts.

"My ex is a human piece of trash, Leo," said Sam stoically. "It took me and the boys a long time to rid ourselves of his toxicity."

"There was abuse there? Physical?"

"I'd rather not get into it now. He's just one of the many mistakes I don't care to relive," said Sam. "But I can assure you, Leo, from firsthand experience, there can be a world of difference from being a biological father and being a father that actually loves and raises his kids."

Leo nodded his head, took a sip of his now cold coffee. He removed his badge from the table, still lying there like a cursed relic from only ten minutes ago, pocketed it out of sight. He adjusted his body in the chair, the legs scraping against the ceramic tile. Kayla continued to clock him from her post behind the counter—Leo aware of and empathetic to her position, not holding it against her.

"So where do we go from here, Sam?" asked Leo, a trace of acceptance, though more likely defeat, sinking in.

"How do you mean?"

"I mean, you've finally been able to spill this big secret that I guess has been eating you up forever, trying to make amends, following those rules that help you," said Leo. "Does this mean you're that much closer to the cure?"

"There's no cure, and I'll never not struggle with it," said Sam. "But, yes, I think this will help me in the long run. I know it doesn't feel like it now, but you've done me an extreme kindness today just by hearing me out."

Leo scoffed at the notion.

"I've hardly been kind," he said.

"Haven't you? You didn't need to show up today. You didn't need to listen. You could have stormed off twenty minutes ago, and I'm not sure what would have been accomplished," said Sam. "So I'd say for someone you haven't seen in decades, in this small window, you've done more for me than you'll ever realize."

Now Leo was unsure if he could meet her gaze—somehow, despite being vicious to this woman, even if he had some provocation, she was thanking him for the scant help he'd offered—ironic, given he'd traveled to Stamford to do nothing but help her. Leo conceded to himself that it had been an extremely confusing morning, and he was no longer in a position to look at things objectively. He'd clearly need time.

"I'm not looking for your forgiveness today; that would be preposterous of me to ask. We'll part ways, and maybe I'll hear from you again, maybe I won't. I'll have to prepare myself either way," said Sam. "But in my selfish, greedy heart, because I don't want to lie to you, I do admit I hope there's a path forward for us, that you won't hate me for the rest of our lives."

Leo needed to leave, to get out of that coffee shop—that much he had more than realized, even if he had more questions, infinite questions. Even if he felt vaguely paralyzed sitting in that chair. He had to go before anything else could turn sideways, actions that couldn't be undone. So he got to his feet and threw on his coat, rushed but not erratic, only to struggle with one sleeve.

He would have time to think about all this on the drive back to Orchard Coils. During his day shift. During the long and cold winter months still ahead. His 2020 had gotten off to an unexpected and terrible start. He took one final look at Sam, his contemporary, a guidepost from the past. He could see how they'd grown old along separate tracks, how frozen in time his affection had been for her—the eighteen-year-old version he'd placed on a plinth, immortalized in marble. Now he was finally let in on the joke, tipped off to his folly. He now knew why she'd broken it off with him so unexpectedly all those decades ago. His obliviousness in full form, to bleed out in the light. It had all been thawed and altered now, perhaps to be frozen again in a new ice age, if his heart wasn't willing to see what Sam had clearly hoped for—forgiveness, growth. Leo was unsure if it was in him. But hope was a commodity not to be underestimated. The same could be said for resilience—both being better aspects of the human condition, worth fighting for, though not without their sharp edges, camouflaged thorns.

Leo offered his parting words.

"You'll hear from me," said Leo. "Maybe not soon, but we'll speak again."

Sam wordlessly smiled, and Leo left the coffee shop, the bell ringing above his head. Exit.

* * *

Seven months into the COVID-19 pandemic of 2020, and Leo Sinclair was still acting recklessly, as though he couldn't be bothered with the virus, the lack of vaccine, or the rising death toll. While the Northeast had found some relief during the summer months—more people outside, higher temperatures, direct sunlight, all things that supposedly stifled transmission—the uptick in case rates was worrisome for the fall, and serious questions were being posed as to how people should responsibly celebrate the upcoming holidays—and no one was liking the proposed answers. Seven months in and somehow it seemed like the experts knew less about it than before its onset. There were mountains of conflicting information about treatment protocols. Ventilators were being viewed as a death sentence—their use once heralded, now borderline lamented. The transmission rates were erratic at best, causing fits for those tasked with contact tracing. Even the origin of the virus couldn't be explained and was falling more and more into political camps, esoteric theories. There was a tremendous amount of hope being pinned on Big Pharma's ability to deliver on a cure, backstopped by the full support and resources of the federal government, an initiative known as Operation Warp Speed, though details were murky and generally withheld from the public at large. If an inoculation was coming soon, the release date was being held close to the vest.

As if all that weren't enough, a contentious presidential election would be taking place in a few weeks—this one particularly polarized under the shroud of COVID and mass mail-in balloting, and it was further dividing a populace already split into camps and exacerbating people's anxiety-soaked biases. The whole thing had a real powder-keg feel to it, and plenty of folks couldn't wait to just get the whole election cycle over with.

Combine that with the notion of canceling Christmas, and you get an autumn with just about everybody on edge.

As for Leo, despite his squirrely behavior of the previous months, the biggest consequence of October 2020 wasn't so much focused around viral loads or partisan bickering but finally breaking down and admitting to Janet what had been eating him up since the beginning of the year. It wasn't so much that she was able to pry it out of him, though she tried that tack at various times with no success. She'd even made the mistake of suggesting Leo should see a therapist—that only led to more of the cold shoulder, an iciness in the household Janet had never encountered before. Then she started to hope the thing might settle on its own, find a resolution without her interfering—though as the summer dragged on and Leo's absence from home grew more pronounced, that bit of serendipity seemed unlikely. These were bad times for Janet, a woman who had already escaped one doomed marriage and thought she'd found a far better suitor—had, in fact, as she and Leo had been happy for two decades together. But now something was amiss, and pushing him only made things worse, so she resigned herself to being patient, steadfast in her belief that problems had solutions, and she shouldn't involve Bo or Clay in their marital issue. She would let Leo work like a horse and play his golf and shoot his guns and ignore some of the realities that were literally floating in their faces. She would protect herself as much as possible, in more ways than one, but eventually, as the old saying went, something had to give.

When Leo was finally ready to sit Janet down and spill what had been on his mind for nearly a year, she truly had no idea what to expect. After twenty-plus years of marriage, it was hard to imagine what had unsettled her husband in such a profound way as she was pretty sure it wasn't the pandemic that had rattled his nerves. She also knew that most women would have jumped on the idea that some type of infidelity had occurred. Or that Leo had been tempted and strayed and was now bogged down in a type of remorse that was winnowing his will away—but Janet didn't think that was the case either. An affair seemed too pedantic for Leo, banal even. She never figured him for the cheating type, but if he did, she also figured him for the kind of guy who could hide it away, forever locking it up until the day he died. His would be the behavior of atonement, which was hardly the word to describe his demeanor in 2020. Besides, he was too pragmatic a man to let one slipup take him down, ruin all he'd built and diminish relationships dear to him.

No, not an affair and not COVID—it would be something more difficult to pin down, darker in nature, perhaps even loathsome.

She was right; it was loathsome—the point conceded. When Leo finally laid out all that Samantha Morris had dropped on him, Janet quickly understood why he'd been spiraling for so many months. She knew better than anyone what that kind of news would do to her husband, all the sore spots and exposed nerves it would inflame. She thought it cruel of this woman to interject herself back in Leo's life, to unburden herself at their expense. Even if this Sam was fearful of a future in which the secret would remain corrosive. Even if the tenets of her pseudo-religion all but mandated attempt after attempt after attempt toward some kind of transcendence, decades of strife toward a goal that could never be fully achieved.

To hear the story of an unborn child lost to a teenager's decision was sad, but Janet also thought it would have been a story better untold—as many of them are. Janet put that blame on Sam Morris and wasn't fully buying the hard-life excuse, the sob story. Janet's own dad had run out on them, her mom died young—neither she nor Paul had looked for solace in the bottom of a bottle and tried to encase the rest of the world outside the glass. Still, she did wonder, having never met the woman, what it would be like to be in her shoes. It was easy for Janet to sympathize with Leo, to comfort him as best she could—she'd taken a vow before God and family and friends to do just that. She believed he had every reason to be upset by the revelation; she just wished he'd confided in her sooner. Way sooner. She would have been able to help that much earlier. It was a lot for one person to bear though, of course, that had been Sam's point all along.

When Leo asked if she thought Sam was right to make the decision on her own, she had to get a little cagey with how she'd reply. Primarily, to make a judgment of that nature against a woman she didn't know, a young Leo she never knew, was inadvisable and mostly foolhardy. She agreed that it would be natural to feel frozen out by Sam's decision, that his ire had justification to it. But when Janet put it back on Leo, asked him in his heart of hearts if he wanted to be a father at seventeen, married to his very first, with his whole life in front of him, he balked. Janet asked him gently how much of this was wanting a voice in some long-ago important decision, and how much of it might must be a wounded ego? How much of it should be balanced against certain regrets, which all humans have if they had the stones to take a few shots in life—some to find their target, others to miss?

Leo wasn't quick to answer that line of questioning, and Janet was wise enough to not over-probe for now. It was easy to see that, at the core, a logistical problem existed, and it wouldn't be solved overnight. Let alone once Leo took the time to spell it out for her. She'd say one thing for the man, he'd held on to it for ten months, tight as a drum, but once he was finally ready to let it out, the floodgate didn't just open, it burst—nothing was left in reserve. They went back and forth on the whole biological versus stepdad issue, his rivalries with Billy, stressed joints Janet was well aware of. It harkened back to some of their old debates when they first got together, some real blowouts when they were still on the fence about making a go of it. Leo had been interested in fathering a child with Janet, but she'd felt those days were behind her, the Overton window passed. Bo and Clay were still so young, practically babies in Janet's eyes, even if that was hardly true. Billy was always hovering around, and when he wasn't asking for a favor from Leo, he was making some passive-aggressive quip to take Leo down a peg in the family hierarchy. It had been choppy waters for the two, difficult to navigate as Leo could only push so hard, and Janet could only relent so much. In the end, she stayed on birth control, and Leo took to being a stepdad like a duck to water. His love for the boys exploded once they were in the new house, and those old debates slowly fell by the wayside and, in time, were never brought up again, barely remembered with so much life going on under the one roof.

Until this Samantha Morris woman reappeared and twisted up her husband, trapped him in his skull box with neither a candle nor a key. Janet knew it was hardly a good place for a man like Leo, not keen on philosophical complications, and as they talked throughout the night, more of the puzzle shifted into place for Janet that would explain Leo's gruff behavior during the winter: his workaholic streak, his absence around the house, his indifference toward contracting the illness at his age, even his interest in actually acquiring the virus, which still, beyond comprehension, hadn't happened yet. Janet listened and realized his attempts to channel the bad news of the winter into a work effort that could benefit the town in their time of crisis—noble, though somewhat misguided.

It was more than obvious to her how little her husband had healed, and to point it out indelicately, if at all, would have been a colossal misstep on her part.

It also occurred to Janet—and this wasn't to excuse Leo and his blind spots and role in the sordid tale—that she wouldn't mind giving Samantha Morris a piece of her mind, though she knew this encounter was unlikely and inadvisable. Nevertheless, in her more selfish and petty moments, she envisioned it, and it didn't go well for Sam.

Once Leo had recounted the full story from that morning in Starbucks, twice actually, and Janet had some time to process it, connect Leo's behavior to the proceeding months, her first real question, as it related to what she saw as the issue at hand, catharsis, was whether Leo had reached back out to Sam since. Had he anything left to say to her? Was there any contemplation of a path toward acceptance, forgiveness? With nowhere left to hide and zero interest in lying further to Janet about the debacle, he confessed to her the progress he'd made or, more accurately, the lack thereof. He'd emailed Sam only once since then, sometime in late April, not a particularly long communication that centered exclusively on COVID, if she could believe that level of compartmentalization: how she needed to take the virus seriously and follow all the precautions out there to maximize her safety. He outlined the measures he thought most efficient, dismissed the ones that bordered on hysteria. He encouraged her to pass the information along to her children, though they wouldn't be in as much jeopardy as she would, nor would her grandchildren. Much of his note read as though it were penned by the surgeon general, antiseptic and to the point. Only toward the end did Leo make mention of the actual issue that had brought them together after a lengthy absence. He conveyed to Sam that he was still angry, still processing what he saw as a betrayal of his sovereignty. He wrote that he didn't care if he was being illogical or grandiose—that a lifetime of prudent behavior and service to others had earned him the right to trust his feelings on this, to relegate the logic centers of his mind to second fiddle. And his feelings remained white hot, a tempered needle in the eye. If that was inconvenient to her, then sorry—but also, not sorry. She had no one else to blame. These were the things he typed out, which he'd confess to Janet felt like an out-of-body experience, that he could hardly fathom now pertained to his life, codified with the click of a mouse: send. He'd signed off on the message to Sam indicating he needed more time, though he couldn't guess how much. They would all have to wait and see. He wished her luck against the virus and wrote only his first name by way of farewell.

That was half a year ago and he hadn't moved since. Technically, he couldn't say if Sam was dead or alive. She hadn't written back, either providing Leo his space or perhaps shuffling off her mortal coil, impossible to say.

Janet took in that information wordlessly, listening, allowing Leo to purge. She'd eventually get to her next real question: after six months' time, why was he not ready to reach back out to Samantha Morris? Leo had wondered that himself—even just to check in on her progress during the lockdown. He supposed the simple truth was his anger kept him static, that none of it had found a way to sit right in his mind. He'd never found the tranquility to set the information down, for it to not be a daily reminder when the invisible demons poked and prodded at inopportune times, during the briefest moments of vulnerability. That fact was, despite the most epic of distractions that COVID should have provided, the notion of a lost baby could not be jettisoned from his waking thoughts, let alone the manifestations that invaded his sleep. Try as he had—though he would admit to Janet his efforts were half-baked in those early months—his attempts in more recent months had failed, a splinter in his mind, lodged like the blade of Excalibur. He gave it more time, trying to solve the problem on his own—still not reaching out to Sam, still not confiding in Janet—only to get the same result, an overused definition of insanity but one that Leo was starting to regard as apt. What was he to do? And even if the answer was obvious—and Leo was a cop at heart who was trained to examine the obvious first and foremost—when one was mired in the dark and addled of thought, the obvious could often look like weakness, surrender, or impotence—to name a few.

Occam's razor could look like a coward's way out to some.

So nothing improved, and his capacity for forgiveness collapsed under the weight of his bruised id. He couldn't bring himself to write back if it meant giving up his anger, now almost cherished like a delicate token; taking that first step alone would mean its destruction. That was when he finally involved Janet. Upon his confessing his hatred of Samantha Morris, she could hardly believe her ears that her husband hated someone, a woman no less. The words were foreign, yet there he was, brimming with the most toxic of emotions, unleashed. Janet continued to listen carefully, knowing not to judge his position too soon—the fact that he'd finally trusted her was evidence enough. He'd found the end of his rope; the path of solitude had reached its terminus. She remained patient and crafted her advice mentally, knowing it would require tact, a soft landing—though, at the same time, she continued to see the problem as logistical, now an impasse to be bridged. Leo was immobile, and Janet eventually offered him a simple enough solution, gently—one that might appease the cop in him but also appeal to the man, a more sensitive man than he'd care to admit, who desperately needed to get unstuck.

Janet told Leo that all these months of not communicating with Sam *had* been his attempt to forgive her or, at least, to reconcile the bombshell leveled against him. Yes, he was angry, but he hadn't weaponized that anger against his tormentor. He hadn't written her hateful notes. Drunken screeds. What he'd been doing was waiting and waiting and waiting for something positive to dawn in his mind, anything that might have springboarded him back into some form of grace. The rub had been the stasis, the suspended animation he couldn't think his way out of.

And while that might have felt like an inability to forgive on Leo's part, Janet saw it differently, or hoped she did: that her husband was a wholesome man, deeply conflicted, who wanted to do the right thing but lacked the mindset to execute on it, rarely in his life unable to perform the hard task. Her advice to Leo was plain enough—write to Sam the following day, without the benefit of bearing good news or reconciliation or a modicum of forgiveness. No, write the woman and let her know that you're still angry, that you still feel betrayed, that you're still struggling to find an end in sight. She advised Leo that he need not resort to anything juvenile or obscenity laced; he need not bring her down or ridicule her steps toward sobriety. In fact, it would be best not to sugarcoat his feelings. He should communicate to Sam where his head was at, even if that made a resolution seem a million years out. Tell her, in a constructive way and, in that same proverbial breath, allow her to know, at the very least, he hadn't given up, without offering a timetable.

Leo hardly cared for the idea at first—it seemed too generous to him. Sam didn't deserve the information—he would be tipping his hand, so to speak, providing too clear a window into his mind.

Janet proceeded to remind Leo that this wasn't some game of poker, and if it were, he'd have to admit he was bleeding chips. It was Sam who had gotten what she wanted, unloaded the megaton on Leo to further her relationship with the twelve steps she believed would keep her on the straight and narrow, while Leo had gotten zilch for his troubles. But as Janet saw it, if Leo tried to maintain this radio silence for too long, eventually Sam would have to give up and just not care that Leo Sinclair wasn't able to get over it, wasn't even willing to discuss it further. And how would that help Leo in the long run? More than likely, it would lead to a far worse place, into the trappings of one who cuts off their nose to spite their face. Janet could all but see it; Leo lacked that clarity. So she told him to make contact again, ask about her family, COVID, how many days sober she was. Confirm she wasn't dead. Basically, anything—just get the ball rolling toward something that resembled progress, because honestly, as she put it to her husband, "Can you imagine going through another ten months of this?"

Leo said he didn't know—which amounted to a pride-shaped obstruction blocking the part of his brain where good decisions were usually crafted. In reality, he knew; it was just a challenge to get him there, her gambit.

Janet reminded him of an old saying his side of the family was partial to, and she as well: the only way out is through. She told him reaching out to Sam would be the second step of many he'd have to take to pull himself out of the abyss. Leo immediately wondered what the first step would be, and Janet, reading his mind, told him that finally confiding in her was step one. And at last, he cracked the faintest of smiles, after hours of talking—the laconic man might have never talked so much in his life.

Janet waited on him, watched him ponder, turning over her advice in his mind, balancing fear against absolution until he relented and agreed to give her plan a go. He would write Sam tomorrow and lay out some of those questions and maybe some of what he was still feeling and take it from there. Janet inched closer on the couch and pulled him into an embrace, gave him a kiss, told him she was proud. She now understood the year he'd had, why he was the best man she'd ever known, which wasn't to say he was a flawless man, just someone who couldn't shoulder the burden on their own, as much as they'd like to believe they can.

Women ask for help. Men seek redemption.

Leo let out a very deep breath, one that had been trapped in his lungs for nearly a year. He legitimately felt lighter, emboldened by this new plan, even if it did take an entire night to convince him of it. They quietly sat together for some time on their plush couch in their beautiful home, though in that moment, Leo couldn't shake the feeling that he was in some foxhole, and the very person by his side was the one who would have his back for all time. And that was a hell of a feeling for a man to come upon, to be blessed into—a feeling he would wish on others, for when it was true, life seemed that much more surmountable.

* * *

An excerpt from the eulogy of Ruth Sinclair by her son, Leo Sinclair, May 3, 2019.

. . . a woman who could oscillate from a quiet, intense energy to boisterous, heated debate, she was seldom afraid to voice a point of view, particularly during times when it was hardly fashionable for a woman to be outspoken.

Ruth Sinclair was unafraid in a fast and changing and often chaotic world and had a way of imbuing that courage in those around her. She was tough as nails but also kind and empathetic and a lover of nature, taking great care to appreciate the spectacles of beauty around her, around us, even in the most common of places. Whether they were the golden days of fall or rainy spring mornings, she found magic in them all. It was all magic to her, even at the end.

My mother was an enlightened soul, and I can speak confidently that on this somber day, while she'd allow for us to grieve, she would also demand of us, all of us, to remember our good times with her and not dwell on what has been lost but celebrate a blessed life marred with few regrets and no reservations. She would ask of us, in her polite yet firm way, that we carry on with full hearts and open minds to . . .

A funeral is seldom a happy occasion, neither boisterous nor uplifting, but the proceedings and wake held at O Triple C had devolved into an alcohol-fueled miasma, topped off with copious amounts of microdosing—particularly among the younger membership, who had fewer hang-ups about that sort of indulgence.

Schedule 1 still had a stranglehold on the harder stuff and was, despite some recent shedding, only growing in aggregate because of black lab proliferation around the world, synthesizing new compounds deadly enough to make five grams of cocaine seem like table sugar. What these unsavory chemists were up to in Brazil and Estonia and other places around the world was rejiggering molecules to escape certain patent laws and ultimately bolster the chemical hook toward transcendence, though flirting with dangerous level of narco-dependency. Somehow, there was money in this, a lot of money, even if it meant a certain percentage of their consumer's hearts would fail, brains would shut down—some would even be zombified. But the legalization a few years before of certain "softer" drugs had finally been deemed a worthy countermeasure to the poison being illegally on-shored. Substances like THC, MDMA, and certain psychedelics were decriminalized and sold openly through approved specialty stores, where Uncle Sam count get his cut, and the patronage need not skulk around in the shadows looking for their particular high of choice.

It wasn't such a terrible advancement, even if it did fly in the face of a long-standing war on drugs, and all but three states in the union had now fully adopted it. But it did lead to a constituency that all of the sudden wanted to know what a k-hole was. Was ergot something that could be experimented with? How safe was it to smoke dried toad venom? How dangerous was a morphine lollipop? And were those little mushrooms that grow on cow patties and horse dung really worthy of being called a designer drug?

The culture changes and so must the people with it lest they get left behind—a maxim that also applied to sports, institutions, even countries.

Not that any of these new mind-altering options were likely to make one's golf game that much better, though there were those who liked to believe it, even if only used as part of the nightly convalescing process. These would be the same ilk who swore by alcohol: that it stripped down certain inhibitions and allowed them to strike the ball cleaner, relax in the face of a sixty-foot putt. But in reality, as any professional golfer would tell you, alcohol while playing was just a painkiller for hacks. As would be the effects of these slick narcotics, which, hope as one might, just weren't designed to increase focus or concentration. But people did cherish their delusions, and since the game was hard enough on its own, to relieve them of their hash pen or nip of Jim Beam when it was perfectly legal was akin to the hectoring of some old schoolmarm. And who wanted to listen to such dogma when they were just trying to squeeze in a quick eighteen with a little something-something in their system?

The point being people weren't listening to the buzzkills any longer.

All that said, no one was playing golf at O Triple C on that auspicious funeral day. The club wasn't even technically open for the season yet. It was a Friday evening in mid-March, the day before the season would properly resume, when tee times would begin at sunup. That Friday night, the facilities and Restaurant were open only to members—no guests permitted—as a somber development had forced them together, like certain tight-knit pack animals mourning the loss of a revered alpha.

Of course, the members had seen this brand of despair coming for some time now. After the sport's COVID explosion had plateaued mid-decade, only to wane sharply, interest in the game had reached disturbingly low levels. Memberships lapsed; new entrants dropped. Revenue stalled while budgets became untenable. Thousands upon thousands of golf bags were relegated to the garage or tool shed. People spent time elsewhere, the familiar screeds resung: the game was too hard, too costly, too time-consuming, too stuffy—the usual suspects that had dogged the sport since ancient times. Not that they were necessarily false knocks; they'd always existed and needed to be taken with a grain of a salt, but now they were holding traction like never before. While the country's workforce was still slowly getting out of their pajamas and back into actual offices and places of business—the decade-long experiment with hybrid telecommuting no longer satisfying the bean counters with respects to their procurement-versus-productivity models—the paradigm morphed, and folks were back on the road, with far less time to sneak off and play a few holes.

That shift, coupled with the rising costs of food, fuel, education, day care, and health care, pinched disposal incomes in such significant ways as to rule out the indulgence of a costly pastime—particularly as the powers that be had also deemed in now legal to get stoned and stare at a firepit for a few hours for the cost of a ham sandwich, if not cheaper. Or get stoned and watch any number of the streaming services now available to them, their influx driving down prices to obscenely low levels—one of the few things that had realized a significant cheapening over the past few years. Or get stoned and just sit there quietly, consciously not spending any money on anything in that moment, which oftentimes felt like a win. There seemed to be no shortage of options that allowed one to numb their minds and stay home, stagnant and content, while the gears of reset slowly churned around them, out of sight and out of mind—again, just as the powers that be liked it—increasing tax revenue, docile citizens, and the delusions of grandeur of a high-functioning stoner populace.

So, yeah—for a number of reasons, golf was on a sharp decline in the year of our lord 2032.

The tipping point had been reached in a way the governing boards of the sport hadn't seen in over a hundred years—at best, they'd read about the highs and lows but had never personally experienced anything as bad as the post-pandemic dip, emphasized by the seemingly endless quarrels over the time and cost and difficulty with no bailout in sight. There were no identify politics to come to the rescue. The short-lived LIV experiment and ultimate consolidation under the PGA had its bump, though they mostly served to illustrate that globalization was tapping out, and even new markets were shrugging their shoulders at the game. There were no technological saviors on the horizon. No new respiratory virus forcing people outside, freeing up disposable time and stimulus checks. There wasn't even a tour superstar who could coalesce it all together, who served as either hero or heel to get people watching, performing feats that had never been seen on a course. For all these reasons and more, the sport was hemorrhaging money, sloughing off midrange players while not converting the casual ones into lifers. Furthermore, newbies were staying away as though it were a cult they'd been warned of several times over.

Golf was taking it from every angle—ironic, given that it was very much a sport of varying angles.

Clearly, something needed to be done to shake things up. Something drastic. The most drastic of which, in many people's opinion, was to go into effect on March 25, 2032, when the standard cup size on a green would change from the traditional measurement of four and a quarter inches across to an astounding circumference of one foot, an almost three times change from the long-held standard. This change had been suggested in the past to bring people into the game who were tired of racking up strokes once they were only a dozen or so feet away from the pin, after having already moved the ball hundreds of yards across the course. Naturally, the idea had been scoffed at for decades by the purists, believing it would utterly corrupt and diminish all the game had stood for—tradition, honor, determination. That said and with all due respect to the purists, the prevailing winds of change wait for no one—even if their gale takes years and decade—until the message came down from high above that a change would be enacted and, for sure, a drastic one. Dissenters be damned, there were greater things than purity at stake.

So O Triple C decided to have a funeral—gallows humor—and they threw a party the night before their official 2032 season kicked off with those one-foot cups. It was the Death of Golf procession, the third time in the club's history such a soiree was held. They would mourn the sport as they remembered it and celebrate its virtues by getting ripped in the company of the affected and bereaved.

Leo was there, obviously, and, despite not being a particularly sarcastic or cheeky fellow, had thrown his full support behind the mock party, believing the course change to be an utter disgrace and a massive overreaction to the ebb and flow of golf's popularity, which had shown resiliency in the past and ultimately withstood the test of time. He was a firm believer that it would come back on its own and that this gimmick, as he called it, would do nothing more than to attract the wrong type of player to the game. He thought a sport filled with posers was hardly a sport at all. The change was an abomination, he'd say—all day at the station or at home or alone in the shower rinsing shampoo out of his hair—an *abomination*, his new favorite word.

Janet was at the party too, being supportive of her husband and his buddies in their make-believe darkest hour. She'd heard plenty about this proposed change over the past decade and its impending implementation over the past year. She'd never remotely taken to the sport the way Leo had, finding the time commitment too grueling, the aches and pains the following morning unworthy of her physical bandwidth. She could technically play, owning a set of clubs and a full-fledged membership under Leo's banner, but with a handicap of over thirty—almost as many strokes as years of marriage to Leo—it was pretty clear the hook had never sunk in in a meaningful way. Nevertheless, she always enjoyed the Restaurant and some of the social aspects that went along with it. Leo had his notoriety around the place for a host of reasons—still the little prince, though that was mostly a wry joke now, given he'd be celebrating his seventy-fifth birthday in a few months. No one could have squeezed more out of a free lifetime membership than Leo Sinclair had. Given his stature at the club and around town, some of that pixie dust had rubbed off onto Janet, and she enjoyed the benefits, modest as they were. But still, who doesn't like to be treated with a little extra attention and courtesy?

Janet didn't really see the big deal in widening the holes to take some of the pressure off, move the game along. It wasn't like they were totally removing the concept of putting from the game entirely. There were still going to be bad misses and lip outs. There was still going to be grousing and prop bets and people impatiently milling about the green. The change was predicted to shave almost an hour off a full round of eighteen—a significant amount of time, given the sport was ridiculed for its snail's pace. Major League Baseball had enacted its own time-saving move a decade earlier, the pitch clock—also scorned by their purists and statistician wonks—though it had led to great success in shortening the game and was a contributing factor to baseball living to see another day, bolstering their resolve to make it into the twenty-second century.

The PGA now had similar ambitions.

In Janet's mind, that mock party was kind of an overreaction, thrown by people who had done well in life, who had the time and money to invest in such a demanding game. It wasn't quite unseemly, given that people were self-aware enough, in on the joke, but it did strike her as borderline silly. Of course, none of this was sentiment she would remotely share with Leo. If anything, Janet would be loyal on this one and stand by her man in the face of such an affront to the sport he cherished, even if she thought her husband's support for the Death of Golf Party III had been overly steadfast. He was hardly a frivolous man—quite the opposite—so if this was a notion he wanted to indulge with some fantasy, she figured it wasn't too much to placate him, to keep up appearances. Plus, Leo had had her back when she'd been sucked into something that time had proven to be banal or trite, and he typically wasn't one to call her out on it, launch the dreaded "I told you so" nuclear option.

So she would play along and mourn with the rest of them. Besides, at their age, why not enjoy a funeral-party where someone hadn't actually died—though she did think the requirement to wear only black a bit over the top.

As to the actual party.

The two of them were in a short line to get to the bar. Leo had been slow-rolling his light beers as usual; as crestfallen as he was, he still wasn't going to gravitate toward the harder stuff. Janet had been trying some new melon-infused cocktail out of Cuba that had been all the rage the past year, as a lot of Cuban-themed stuff had grown in popularity over the past five years as many of the old hostilities were buried and their new friendship with the American government proved genuine and eager to conduct business. For now. These things did have a way of going south, but the two nations had enjoyed a period of neighborly behavior—tourism and the lifting of embargoes and satellite-internet cooperation. There was even talks of building a Chunnel-like route from Havana to Miami, three times the length of the UK version, though many thought it pie-in-the-sky talk that sounded better in video clips from Florida officials than as feasible federal policy through any number of foreign or infrastructure agencies.

Still, an hour to Cuba and back—it was an idea to be jazzed about.

From somewhere at the front of the line, someone could be heard saying, "Yeah, he's doing good. He's taken to carrying around a buck knife wherever he goes, but still, he's good." There'd be a lot of that talk tonight: salty and unfiltered and irreverent, in keeping with the spirit of a funeral where no one had died, only a little piece of a woeful assemblage, a parcel of their collective soul.

In any event, Leo and Janet were waiting in that line to order when an intoxicated Ronnie Kemper, their longtime friend from the club—the man Leo had once spared from a DWI in their youth and had become legitimate buddies with over the decades—stumbled his way over to them. Ronnie, now pushing the big seven-o, hadn't lost much zest for life and tried to view the passing of time as an accelerant, much like the way an arsonist saw everything as fuel for his fire. He still loved a good party, a good argument. Ronnie had proven to be one of Leo's more emotional friends, a heart-on-the-sleeve sort of fellow—a characteristic that had always reminded Leo of his late godfather, Peter Sullivan, though Leo didn't like to dwell on the comparison. His thoughts on Sullivan were hard to abide anymore, and he'd mostly shut down that part of his mind years ago. Or at least, he'd tried to.

So Ronnie, retired and a pensioner now, found the Sinclairs waiting patiently in line and dropped his arms around them both like two soaked towels, heavy and spent of utility. His eyes were a glass factory, a failing one that would declare bankruptcy before the fiscal year's end. He hadn't bothered to shave for the proceedings, though he was fully adorned in the appropriate dark attire. His tie was knotted terribly, and Janet attempted to straighten it out, navigating under the weight of his limp arm on her shoulder, where it started to feel like they were the only things keeping the man propped up. When Ronnie spoke, it was like some abstraction trying to communicate from underwater—weakened and disoriented after some long escape from a determined predator. In short, the dude was a fucking mess.

"The hole in ones, Leo, haven't they given any consideration about the hole in ones," said Ronnie, half slurring, almost pleading.

"I know, buddy. Another sacrifice they're willing to make," said Leo, having had enough of being draped over and getting Ronnie steady on his feet, if a bit wobbly.

"The bastards could have at least left the par threes alone," said Ronnie.

"Preaching to the choir, Ronnie," said Leo. "And yet, it has happened all the same, with or without us."

"But how much more will they try to take? What are those aces going to look like now? A pitching wedge into a swimming pool?" said Ronnie, negotiating his balance, the bar line creeping forward. "It was one thing to horse around with the occasional big-cup tournament; those can be fun every few years. But to make this the new standard now—it's grotesque."

Leo was about to further agree with Ronnie, but the man continued on with his tunnel vision.

"I've never gotten a hole in one, and if memory serves, neither have you," said Ronnie, swaying slightly. "What's it going to mean to get one now? Might as well come with a carnival prize, a participation trophy."

"It won't be the same, that's for sure," said Leo, nodding in genuine lament. "It'll feel watered down at best."

"It'll be an era of asterisks is what it'll be, when they realize the mistake they've made and, in a few years, are forced to own up to their fuckup," said Ronnie, worked up and now fully swaying like a Vegas lounge singer. "They'll be forced to change back and hold someone accountable for a cluster of years with ridiculously low scoring."

"There'll be no reckoning, Ronnie. They'll give the time period some cynical name and move on, saying as little as possible, hoping history will erase their foolishness," said Leo.

The three arrived at the bar, Leo grabbing his beer, Janet her melon drink and a tall glass of ice water for Ronnie, despite his protests that he was fine and could fancy another bitter, though neither Leo nor Janet knew exactly what he was on about. Leo assured his friend that taking a round off to hydrate was the noble play, and Ronnie demurred. He'd always had a profound trust in Leo since the day he pulled him from that ditch by those old orchards left to seed. He'd drink his water if that's what the chief recommended. The three clinked their glasses and offered up a toast to the departed.

"To the death of golf," said Leo.

"The death of golf," repeated Janet and Ronnie, the former dispassionately, the latter as though the thumbscrews were being tightened.

"I'm going to do something about this," said Ronnie. "So help me God, I'm going to take action."

"What can be done?" asked Janet, truly wondering what had gotten into these men she'd respected for as long as she could remember—dedicated servants to the town of Orchard Coils—now enraged by a dash of modernization in their game.

"I'm going to start by ripping out that monstrosity on the fifteenth hole and filling it back in with any dirt or sod I can find," said Ronnie, looking quizzically at his glass of water, as though wondering how the hell it got there in the first place—*Right, right, hydration*. He continued, "Then I'm going to craft a proper cup as the ancients intended and restore fifteen to its former glory."

"OK, Ronnie, let's not do anything rash," said Leo, putting his hand on his friend's shoulder. "You know Jocko and his guys aren't responsible for this rule change. There's no need to wreck their work, especially when you know they'll just have to fix it. And I really don't think that would be good for anybody involved."

Leo threw down that gauntlet as gingerly as he could—translation: Jocko will take his revenge out of your ass, and there won't be anything I can do to stop it.

"Well, I've got to do something, Leo," said Ronnie, placing his half-finished water down on a table, storming off from the Sinclairs, hands in the air, calling over to another member, ready to commiserate over the sanctity of par threes all over again.

In the near distance, the following could be heard over the din of the crowd: "Have you ever seen a kangaroo flexing to attract a mate? It's unsettling."

"Is he going to be OK?" asked Janet.

"Sure, he just needs time. Acceptance is the hardest part," said Leo. "Besides, Jocko told me some of the more tech-savvy guys on his crew have installed cameras and aerial drones to cover the greens, so they'll be watching closely until tempers flare down."

"You're kidding me."

"Afraid not."

"Isn't that a bit excessive?" asked Janet. "Do the players even know that's being done?"

"It's almost irrelevant. Most people figure they're being recorded at all times in public anyway."

"The panopticon psyop?"

"That's the self-fulfilling prophecy we've chosen for ourselves."

To that, Janet and Leo took thoughtful pulls from their drinks—musing over the truth while surely the AI recorded them doing so, in whatever mode was available.

"Please bear in mind, my love, you did promise to take this party seriously," said Leo.

"I think I am. But you can't expect me to totally turn my brain off," said Janet, keeping her voice down. "I mean, look at this place. Every loon the club has to offer is in attendance. When was the last time you saw the Restaurant packed like this?"

She wasn't wrong—on either point. Indoors, the room was wall to wall with the eclectics, the faux-bereaved, all dressed in their dark finery. Some of the men wore sunglasses as though to hide the hurt. Some women wore veils for whatever reason a woman decides to wear a veil. The crowd would surely spill into the banquet hall on the other side of the building, if it hadn't already. Others would make their way outside to mingle—the March temperatures were already in the low seventies, a warming trend that hadn't abated and, despite your personal politics on climate change and energy policy, could no longer be refuted if you had even the most rudimentary understanding of the carbon element.

Over his shoulder, Leo heard someone say in a rich baritone, "Good luck looking directly into the eyes of an owl and not getting hypnotized into doing terrible things." It made him think of his mother and her affinity for all things birds, including the aforementioned owl.

In all the alcoves of the Restaurant, people were drinking and talking about how truly upset they were over the demise of their favorite sport while also whispering in covert tones about what additional substances they might have had coursing through their systems, along with the usual hushed gossip of money and affairs of the heart.

Inhibitions were down and would only slough off further as the party carried on.

Chemical enhancements aside, many of the members were spitting mad over what would commence tomorrow morning, the pins widened and open for business. Others were less outraged and more interested in a good party, especially one that hadn't happened in almost seventy years and only three times in Orchard Coils Country Club history. So, in a very real sense, per their little enclave, it was an auspicious occasion and not likely to be missed by many of the three hundred–plus members—a number that had toggled since the COVID scare a decade earlier, when membership had boomed to just over four hundred various contracts, to the point where capacity had been reached, and a formidable waiting list and initiation fees were enacted.

The current head pro, Lucas Brookings, had benefited greatly from the viral scare and ridden it successfully for many years, but he was now being looked at with greater scrutiny as to how he'd release the coattails of COVID and put his own stamp on the club's future—hopefully in a way his short-lived predecessor, Michael Bouffard, had never been able to figure out. That said, even if the sport had fallen on hard times since the spike circa 2025, you wouldn't know it by the sheer number of people rubbing elbows and swapping stories in the members-only dining room, a place that held a lot of memories for Janet and a lifetime's worth for Leo—mostly fond, though a few brutal—which was kind of the point. You took the good with the bad and carried on with your life.

"You know, I was actually in attendance for the last one of these get-togethers," said Leo, big grin on his face.

"Yes, you may have previously mentioned that," said Janet, grinning back, being a good sport. "You were, what, forty years old then?"

"Charming. I'd just turned thirteen, and it was a very big deal that I convinced my parents to let me tag along with them."

"What little boy doesn't beg to go to a funeral?" said Janet wryly, "Even if it's a fake one."

"Well, it did feel real to me. They wouldn't let Lynn come, too young. She stayed with my grandparents, I think."

"Speaking of, I don't know if you've told me what she thinks of all this course change business," said Janet. "Or Sachin, for that matter."

"I've told you; maybe it just didn't stick," said Leo, needling. "They're rightly mortified over it. The problem is they've seen the writing on the wall for some time now—the game in decline and all. They sort of agreed the PGA needed to do something."

"So they're OK with it?"

"They're OK with the league surviving. They also know the Saudis control the purse strings and don't have the fealty to the old ways of the game that maybe others do," said Leo. "So they're basically resigned to what's to come. Money talks."

Money talks. Janet left it at that, not wanting to push any buttons between Leo and Lynn, particularly as his sister was still in a public position as a brand ambassador and marketer of the league. The cup change had garnered a lot of publicity over the past few months that she'd surely had to contend with and, from what Leo intimated, get on board with lest she be left behind.

Leo and Janet drifted away from the bar area in search of a bit more breathing room, though the pickings were slim. They settled on a space near the far wall, under the plaques of past club champions dating back well over a hundred years. Leo has seen these plaques and their engraved names a million times before, but he couldn't remember the last time he took a moment to actually scrutinize them. He scanned them for his parent's names, which he knew he wouldn't find—neither of them quite had the chops to beat out so many in a crowded field, even if his dad could hit the ball a country mile, even if his mom could putt a fast or fuzzy green like no one's business. But Leo liked to look for their names all the same, through that era of the late 1950s into the '70s, when his folks were young and vibrant and still had much of their life in front of them, raising two kids in that post-war American dream when people unapologetically pursued things like a good job, house, two cars, family, friends, community, pastimes. Unlike today, when it had become fashionable to deride, even mock, that dream. Somewhere along the way, a core change occurred, and pretty much everyone in the Restaurant was confounded by it—even the younger members, many of whom felt unable to speak up in its favor, to attest that it was still out there, the myth being that it was always easily achieved when, in truth, it was never easy, but that seemed to deter fewer people back in the day.

Still looking at the plaques, Leo showed Janet a name etched in faux gold from the 1980s woman's club champions section—1984, Lynn Sinclair. He figured he'd shown it to her before, but not in a long time, and he always enjoy recounting the story, seeing his sister's name up there, anointed for all time. Lynn had been home for a weekend from Tulane back in '84 to play in the club tournament, something she'd never been overly interested in—oddly, given her competitive drive and acumen for the game. By Sunday, she'd made mincemeat of her competition, winning by almost ten strokes, then flying back to Louisiana that Monday morning, skipping some classes as she was prone to do. She had the aspiring athlete's attitude toward the relevancy of her studies—a notion reinforced by her coach at the time, Sachin Moore, who believed academics would only get in the way of Lynn's pursuit for the LPGA.

It was the only O Triple C championship Lynn had ever bothered to enter—and despite her many professional wins on tour, she would often cite that landslide victory in her hometown as one of her more influential, a crowning achievement she was fond of recalling.

As Leo continued to sidle along the wall, strolling down memory lane via the various trophies and certifications, he encountered a man who looked vaguely familiar to him. It took him a few moments to place him as Philip Cornwall, the youngest son of Grant and Elizabeth Cornwall, those old mainstays of the club, both of whom had passed away decades ago. Leo took it upon himself to reintroduce himself to Philip, whom he recalled as the more eccentric, if not snooty of the Cornwall brood. One might have even thought him the black sheep or, even worse, a malcontent—the kind of guy who rooted for the competitive figure skater to fall, for the ducklings to get mired in the oil spill, for the stage-one ovarian cancer to metastasize. They exchanged awkward pleasantries with little in the way of warmth as Leo observed that Philip did not look particularly fit of mind or body—not that it took keen deductive reasoning to suss this out. The man was haggard and bore the look of a few loose screws.

Philip was somewhat curt with Leo and actually confessed to crashing the party. He technically wasn't a member but figured the Cornwalls still had enough posthumous juice around here to keep him from getting tossed before he could do what he came here to do. Leo didn't like the sound of that and asked him what exactly that might be, his hackles raised as this slovenly man with his bad teeth and halitosis breath somehow still copped a pretentious attitude toward Leo, as though he were an actor consistently reminding you he'd been trained in the classical method. Leo was glad Janet had instinctively tucked herself away from this man, busied herself looking at the wall of memorabilia. Phillip said his parents would be spinning in their graves over the widening of the holes, and at least one Cornwall should be in attendance to properly commiserate. Leo looked blankly at the man, not fully believing him. He tilted his head and asked his personal opinion of the rule change.

Philip Cornwall, with his dead shark eyes, told Leo flatly, "I could give two fucks."

They parted wordlessly after that, Leo back to Janet, Philip to loiter around a different wall, one closer to the supply closet, where Leo suspected Philip would look for his eventual mark, to sell them either some dredged and drained swamplands in the Everglades or a hot new NFT, which was assured to make a comeback in this new decade.

As Leo returned to Janet, he heard a woman's voice rise above the local miasma, assured and resolute, without mercy: "Please, that guy's idea of living dangerously is mailing an envelope without a return address. "Leo had a momentary fear that the woman was referring to him. Perhaps she was.

"What was that all about?" asked Janet, eying Phillip across the room.

"A weird exchange with a guy I hope to never see again," said Leo. "But what else are these parties for?"

Over at the bar, a line of shots were being lit aflame—a spring break element seeping in, and it was barely eight p.m. The funhouse versions of those in attendance would be exposed in the next hour or so at such a rate, distorted yet true images plucked from the mirror, set into motion.

"So what do you want to do now?" asked Janet.

"Let's just stay in this corner and see what comes to us."

"As you like," said Janet, sipping her drinking. Leo watched.

"You know, you should let me take you to Cuba for real," said Leo, smiling. "I bet those cocktails taste even better down there."

"Don't you think we're a bit old to be traipsing down to Cuba?"

From across the room, some aristocrat yelled, "I've seen crows smarter than that motherfucker."

"As a matter of fact," said Leo, standing in the crowded hall of his contemporaries, under the plaques and pictures of those who had gone on ahead of him, those ghosts and bloodlines and legacies that still guided the way, "I do not."

* * *

In 1971, the second-ever Death of Golf procession took place at O Triple C, where Baxter and Ruth Sinclair found themselves on a Friday night in early April, the golfing season on the cusp of opening. They were sitting in the Restaurant, debating the health of the sport and recent events. The latest transgression that had triggered the second-ever party of this nature in club history was technologically based and had been building steam for almost two decades. Lending to the buildup most notably was the crafting of steel shafts into the clubs and the proliferation of the motorized golf cart. These were hardly minor offenses to the old guard, who valued the woodwork of hickory and the use of one's own legs to get them to and fro—properly surveying the course at a more gentlemanly pace, as bipeds were meant to do. But given the industrial boom of varying metals in both military and commercial applications, many were forced into an about-face, seduced by the promise of adding double-digit yardage to certain tee and fairway shots. As for the carts, well, too much walking could be hell on arthritic knees and brittle spines—plus the cup holders were useful for certain in-game amenities. They were also touted as a way to speed up the game, that consistent bugaboo that golf had always had to defend itself against. The real losers in the cart debate were the caddy shack kids, now being slowly replaced by machines that didn't need a bathroom break, could carry two bags without complaint, and never sulked over a lackluster tip—their generation's own little industrial revolution, like Whitney's cotton gin or Ford's automobile before them.

But kids today, as they were at the turn of the century, were resilient. They'd either hang on at the club somehow or get a different part-time job, perhaps grilling hamburger patties or guarding lives at the community pool.

These two notable changes passed through at a slow enough pace throughout the 1950s and '60s to garner little pushback, even if certain reservations were logged throughout the community, and a general sense of pumping the brakes was amplified to where it felt by the early '70s there'd been too much change to the game, that the players badly needed a static decade, a chance for everyone to catch their collective breath and not fret about what upheaval might be lurking around the corner. That supposed breath didn't last, and in the view of many, and way too quickly, yet another new substance was introduced into the bag, one with even loftier promises than the alloys of the prior two decades.

This introduction, at least in certain pockets of Connecticut, proved to be the straw that broke the camel's back—particularly when a random member of O Triple C showed up in March 1971, prior to the club actually opening the course, to use the range they'd made accessible ahead of opening day, with a new driver that looked, for lack of a better term, extraterrestrial. Inquiries were quickly made of this member, who shall remain nameless for his own protection, and the truth was revealed that an ominous and proverbial eagle had landed in their small enclave—it was a *graphite* club, brand new to the market, a very expensive Christmas gift from the man's wife and kids that had been sitting in his garage for three months, and he was now very eager to take it for a test drive.

Graphite—the newest affront to everything the game stood for: the simplicity, the purity, the notion fashioned hundreds of years ago of moving a ball around over some open land with whatever naturally occurring and somewhat inefficient instrument you had at your disposal, not using clubs made from materials that Oppenheimer would have been proud of and lauded.

Word quickly spread around the club, making its way to the Monastery, to the Restaurant, to the pro shop where the newish head pro, Cobb Webb, was expected to weigh in on yet another shaft type that was bound to proliferate and change the dynamic of the game, similar to the effects of steel over the past twenty years. Cobb, being new and still finding his feet among the Yankees at O Triple C, had neither the inclination nor the political capital to stick his neck out, so he shrewdly adopted the position of the club members, which from the jump had been an anti-graphite consortium. Cobb, if anything, was adroit at determining which way the wind was blowing and leaned in when it suited his own interests—even though, having taken a few hacks with a graphite club at the range, he knew it was here to stay, even if the members tried to eschew it.

From there, a three-week groundswell emerged that bubbled up all the way to the top, which, from the membership viewpoint, was the committee heads and club president. The actual owner or owners of O Triple C were a bona fide mystery, with scant official or public records leading one down a path of bland corporate names like Connecticut Golf, Inc or Nutmeg Sports, LLC—signatures that were almost indistinguishable, that could just barely be traced back to nondescript law firms based out of Hartford suburbs. Interestingly enough, it was mostly a moot point as it was understood that the owner, whoever it may be, was inclined to be extremely hands off and preferred the club to be managed in two directions—top to bottom, bottom to top—only to intervene in rare occasions and always through an assortment of proxies and intermediaries and emissaries who would sooner die than reveal their employer's true identity.

So long as the club didn't fall into a lower tier and managed to churn out a small profit, maybe break even during those leaner years, it was basically allowed to run itself—an arrangement that seemed to suit everyone just fine, though did create much fodder as to who the proprietors actually were. Some thought it was a side project of the then-owners of the New England Patriots, the Sullivan family—no relation to Peter Sullivan. Others thought it had to be tied to the Rhode Island mob. And others thought for sure it was the reclusive paper magnate Kirby Keener who secretly pulled the strings, though for what purpose, no one could say. There was much speculation out there, and it served as a favored topic of gossip among the members, though it often felt like a question never to be resolved.

In any event, the people who truly ran the club saw that swift and decisive action needed to be taken to tamp down the bloodlust riled up by this new space-age driver. So a determination was made that a funeral should take place, the second of its kind, resembling one that had occurred many, many decades before. In fact, perhaps they were long overdue for one, given the amount of change imbued into the game since the midcentury mark, since the Germans were beaten back to hell, and the Japanese acquiesced to the destructive will of Fat Man and Little Boy.

As a result, the Death of Golf Party II was voted on and approved, unanimously and with little dissent.

And much like the soiree their adult son would attend far into the future, Baxter, Ruth, and all the attendees were to dress in black, drink too much, and mingle until the wee hours of the morning, though with much less emphasis on drug consumption, as it was still very much illegal and embroiled in a culture clash, as was the specter of Vietnam hanging heavy in the air, seemingly omnipresent. The Death of Golf Party II would be an appropriate venue to lament the sport, but a certain level of unspoken decorum would surface—these were, after all, trying times, and the club was a community with many veterans in their ranks. And though they might hold different beliefs on the communist threat abroad, they all agreed that, in perspective, the threat of war was a smidge more important than what they'd assembled to fake mourn.

So in that crowded room, their voices would be considerably lower than what would occur sixty-one years later in 2032—more restrained, less bacchanal, despite just as much drinking—perhaps even more since that was a generation who knew how to hold their liquor and were reluctant to mix it even with seltzer, let alone melon-flavored chasers. There was also a different energy to the party of 1971: more somber, perhaps a bit more confused, bordering on businesslike, an office Christmas party run amok. It was technically the party to protest the speedy changes to the game, highlighted by the graphite shaft, but seeing as how the country had just gone through a turbulent decade, one that included several assassinations—most notably, the president only seven years prior—there was a rawness that still lingered for some, with high-profile blood still being spilled in a clash of the changing times. In the early 1970s, there were more than a few additional reasons to hold a ceremony, to mourn as it were—to collectively acknowledge that change happened fast, happened slow, could be difficult, was inevitable, and took place whether you were onboard or not. And, more to the point, it isn't afraid to be gory if it insists on birthing a new era.

As to the actual party.

The man sitting to Baxter Sinclair's left was a handsome devil, a club rake, dressed in a well-tailored charcoal suit and button-down white shirt, sporting onyx cufflinks and tortoiseshell glasses. The knot in his black tie was immaculate, as though engineered by NASA, mathematically sound and impervious to disruption. His thinning sandy-blond hair gave his head a kind of equestrian look that wasn't unpleasing from most angles, and he was cognizant of what angles to avoid. His noble nose only accentuated the point. Baxter knew the fellow as Haldermann but couldn't recall his first name—thought perhaps he didn't have one, as Haldermann was only ever referred to as Haldermann. He was seven years Baxter's senior, a nonsmoker who drank elegantly from a highball glass. One of his life's ambitions was to leave behind a stately corpse once his ticket was punched, hopefully of liver failure, quite sure the mortician would have to use copious amounts of powder to his by-then-yellowed skin and scant amounts of embalming fluid as he'd pickled himself diligently his entire adult life. Suffice it to say, Haldermann was a club favorite, and when he spoke, he sounded like an old Hollywood lothario, capable of asking a favor and making it feel as though he'd done the favor for you. At that moment, he struck up a conversation with Baxter, despite their having not associated much in the past, despite Baxter being mildly unnerved by the suave man.

"We've only just conquered the moon," said Haldermann casually. "Now it feels like we've plundered her materials to build sporting goods."

"I don't think we're quite there yet."

"I'm being droll, Sinclair. I'm aware the graphite isn't coming from moon rocks."

"But how many people in this room *do* think that?" asked Baxter, grinning.

"Too many. And more to follow once the night hits its crescendo," said Haldermann, returning Baxter's mischievous grin. "But truly, are you not the least bit concerned about the track we're on?"

"Perhaps for selfish reasons. My tee shot is my best advantage; the last thing I need is to lose ground because technology allowed weaker players to catch up," said Baxter. "That said, if this new stuff actually works, maybe I'll be able to roll one over three hundred yards."

"They'll never stop inventing, will they?" said Haldermann, more to himself, as though he'd forgotten he had a willing participant in the conversation. "Everything must be improved upon."

"Not if there's money to be made."

Haldermann seemed to agree with the sentiment.

"You've heard the rumors that graphite will be mined right down the hill," said Haldermann, half his mouth showing a row of well-proportioned teeth. "You've heard the Quarry Witch was hired as the foreman, stands to make a killing if all goes well."

"Bully for the witch. Maybe she'll finally be able to leave that shaft and buy some property along the shoreline."

While the men amused themselves, they could hear Ruth Sinclair on the other side of the table, getting boisterous over some conversation she was having with an adjacent table, her voice rising over the hum of the room in a way Baxter had become accustomed to, was no longer embarrassed by.

"I see your wife feels passionately about this graphite conundrum we find ourselves in," said Haldermann.

"Birds," replied Baxter, a bit to Haldermann's confusion. "I can assure you she's going on about the extinction levels of birds or sea slugs or some such thing. Maybe the use of petrochemicals that are ruining the planet. If anything, she finds the whole use-of-technology-in-golf argument to be a silly one, that these innovations are a way to democratize the game."

"How so?"

"Well, to paraphrase, the changes to the driver and woods will allow those not as strong or technically proficient to take more enjoyment while the carts will allow the less mobile to continue playing the game long after their legs have given up the ghost."

"She doesn't think there's a risk to watering down the sport?"

"She doesn't believe in solutions, Haldermann, just trade-offs," said Baxter conspiratorially. "She'll tell you that too."

From some table behind Baxter, in a measured and not-too-loud voice, some enthusiast proclaimed, "Hey, my man, you put the kinetic in Kineticut."

Haldermann took a reflective moment, as though weighing his desire to trust Baxter on one scale against the cool detachment he so prized on another, then proceeded in a way that suggested Baxter possessed the grander weight and was in store for some enlightenment apropos of nothing.

"Do you know what I like about a bowlegged woman, Sinclair?" said Haldermann, keeping his voice low. "There's something inherently sexy about them, a certain implication of talents, of predilections that, even if imagined, are still fun to muse over."

"Is that so?"

"Sure, you see one coming your way, the best of the deadly sins gleaming on the surface of their eyes, snapping chewing gum with a workman's purpose," said Haldermann, clearly visualizing in his mind's eye. "Pardon the digression, but I'm OK in this life admitting what I want."

Baxter tilted his head in a way that suggested they should carry on.

"My wife isn't bowlegged," said Baxter.

"I know. I was just sharing."

Baxter found himself on an odd footing with the older Brahmin, unsure of the etiquette or the type of dance being considered. He wasn't uninterested in what worldviews Haldermann held; if anything, he thought there was more to learn from him than many of his other cronies at the club. But how did one reciprocate what he'd just heard? He wasn't going to ask his thoughts on the Red Sox prospects for the year. Or trade notes on each other's handicaps. No, Baxter would need to offer up something a bit more interesting than that, somewhat personal, if he wanted that détente to continue, even if such frankness was a bit outside his wheelhouse.

"I like it when a woman older than me wears so little makeup you can barely tell she's wearing it," said Baxter, his voice low. "Let the cosmetics do what they can do within reason, and let's not move any mountains. Trying to set the clock back twenty years is unbecoming."

Haldermann smiled in approval and allowed his eyes to dart around the room, slowly enough not to disrespect the conversation he was enjoying with Baxter but quick enough to see what morsels might be out there. There'd been speculation, the occasional rumor, that Haldermann himself was more democratic in his selection process, taking men to bed if the mood or opportunity suited him, if and when certain stars aligned. These whispers may have hampered some of his upward mobility at the club, particularly with the old-old guard, though, vertical ascension notwithstanding, he didn't seem overly concerned with hierarchical status. The fact was he was fawned over by many, quick to spend a dollar on someone else before his own interests, not nitty when it came to gambling on the course or sullen when he lost, gracious to the crew that tended the grounds and served his food and cleaned his clubs—among many other little things that provided enough cover against untoward gossip, even if that rumor might have been true.

From two tables behind them, a man with a gruff voice, perhaps polyp laden, affirmed to anyone within earshot, "Socialists are just communists whose balls haven't dropped yet."

Haldermann returned his all-but-imperceptible lapse of attention back to Baxter as a thought had dawned on him that didn't involve his carnal nature.

"Correct me if I'm wrong, Sinclair, but your wife was an early user of the golf cart, right?" asked Haldermann. "If I've heard the story accurately, she was actually using the club's only cart when she went into labor?"

"True story."

"Not to poke at a sore subject. You can tell me to slag off if need be."

"It's fine. But, yeah, scary as hell. It all worked out though," said Baxter. "It's a well-traveled story, even made the local paper. I'm pleased to say we had our second child in an honest-to-goodness hospital."

"Cheers to a healthy family," said Haldermann, clinking his glass with Baxter's beer bottle. "Even if I've always said never trust a man with a family."

"Why is that?"

"Because it gives them a reason not to want to see the world burn."

Before Baxter could ask Haldermann to peel that onion back further, Peter Sullivan knocked into their table, his thighs hitting the rounded surface as he tried to traverse the crowded room and join his best pals, Baxter and Ruth, and his fellow barfly Haldermann. He was holding a tall, ladylike glass filled with something very pink, packed with crushed ice. Those seated at the table regarded his clumsy entrance, the dainty cocktail, then waited for how the man might explain himself.

"Don't judge until you've tried it," said Sullivan, reading their minds, taking a sip through the colorful straw. "My own damn fault. I told them at the bar, 'Dealers' choice.' Tasty,, though."

"I didn't say anything," said Baxter. Haldermann put his hands up in surrender.

Peter Sullivan put his drink down on the table, followed by his two hands, then leaned over and allowed a serious face to wash over what had, seconds ago, been a jovial demeanor. The man was getting down to business. He had their attention.

"Nuclear reactors," he said, without further elaboration, though with a palpable measure of satisfaction, maybe even gravitas.

"We're going to need more than that, Sullivan," said Haldermann.

"That's what graphite is used for, the core of nuclear power plants," said Sullivan, as though his point was an obvious one.

"Still more."

Sullivan slapped his hands on the table, baffled.

"You don't think it's crazy that our clubs are going to be made of the same shit used to tame the atom?" said Sullivan.

"Tame the atom?" said Baxter, somewhat exasperated. "Who have you been talking to? Please tell me they didn't let you into the town library."

"As a matter of fact, they did, and it was a fascinating experience," said Sullivan. "Did you know they still have librarians who will actually help you research the stuff you're interested in? That it's their actual job in life? In any event, I spent the better part of yesterday evening gathering as much dirt as I could on this so-called versatile substance."

The game was afoot, and neither Baxter nor Haldermann would have the heart to let Sullivan down—so eager was he, like a middling student who had actually completed their homework on time.

"And what were your conclusions?" asked Haldermann.

"Glad you asked," said Sullivan, taking another pull from that elegant straw. "For starters, it actually *is* a very versatile substance; that much is true. And it has dozens and dozens of real-world applications one wouldn't have imagined."

"Such as?" asked Baxter.

"From the lead in your pencil to the brakes in your car to the batteries in your portable radio, just to name a few," said Sullivan. "The more I researched, the more I realized I wouldn't even want to live in a world where graphite didn't exist."

Baxter and Haldermann traded quizzical looks.

"So, wait, you're not upset that the graphite is now going to be used to build clubs?"

Sullivan finished his lady drink with some undignified slurping through the straw.

"I'm of two minds, torn if you will. On one hand, weren't steel shafts enough?" he said, pantomiming with his hands as though they were the great scales of justice. "On the other hand, who are we to limit the use of such a miracle substance?"

Both men noted that graphite in Sullivan's estimation had been upgraded to miraculous from versatile before they could lodge a single protest.

"If you think it's such a miracle, why are you at a funeral where it's been labeled the murderer?"

"Since when do I skip a good party?" said Sullivan. The two men quickly conceded that point while Sullivan poked his finger past their shoulders in an accusatory direction. "And why, by the way, is Ruth ignoring me? Would she care to hear what else graphite can be used for? I have other examples."

"She's not ignoring you," said Baxter. "She's just passionate about the endangered warblers and seeking anyone that will hear her out."

From the back of the room, some inebriate proclaimed in a high-pitched trill, "There's something effeminate about men afraid of bees."

At which point, a thirteen-year-old Leo Sinclair snuck his way through the crowd to join his godfather's side, taking note of his mother carrying on at the far end of the table, his father pleased as punch to see him, and some random club member dressed like James Bond at a funeral. Haldermann regarded Leo's presence the way a cat might assess a cricket that had strayed into the house. He was not one who considered a bar appropriate for those of nonconsensual age.

"The not-so-little prince has deigned to join us," said Sullivan, cuffing Leo on the back of his neck. "How are you faring on this most somber of occasions? Or joyous. I still haven't decided."

Leo had become accustomed to his uncle Pete's eccentricities and barroom antics—he knew how to play along, ride it out.

"These people sure are taking this stuff seriously," said Leo.

"Indeed they are," said Baxter. "Leo, do you know Mr. Haldermann?"

Haldermann leaned out of his chair to shake Leo's hand in a kind of slow motion, as though a plane was nosediving from up high into Leo's palm. Haldermann was full of style and affectations that tried to bring the mundane to life.

"Pleasure, little prince," said Haldermann. "I was just picking your father's brain as to your origin story."

Leo didn't know what this balding weirdo was on about. The crowded room, the cacophony, the formal attire—it was hard for him to focus, and he wore his confusion openly on his face.

"He's talking about how you were born on the course," clarified Baxter.

"Oh. I wonder if there'll ever be an end to that story," said Leo moodily, some new gears he'd been developing since becoming a teenager.

"And what's so wrong with that story?" asked Baxter.

"It's embarrassing. Would you want people yammering on about how you were born?"

The three men granted that Leo had a valid point, which would only grow in strength the older he got. Still, he'd need to learn to be a gentleman about it.

"Be that as it may, I don't want you to be rude to people if it gets brought up, understood?" said Baxter, not unkindly, more like fatherly advice.

Leo turned his head to get the eye-roll out of his system, his own rebellious affectation recently learned though far from perfected, then turned back to his father, his eyes properly oriented in their sockets as though the slight had never taken place.

"I'm bored. There's no one here my age. Can we go home now?" asked Leo.

"You're the one who begged to come here when we told you there'd be nothing to do," said Baxter, annoyed. "Why don't you go outside and get into some trouble, something small and easy that you can work your way out of."

"Come now, I'll take the lad for a stroll. The air will do me some good," said Sullivan. "What do you say, Leo? Mary's outside, and she'll be wanting a piece of you too."

From the adjacent table, the following exchange took place in semi-hushed fashion:

"What's that called when you fuck on camera for money?"

"Porn."

"No, something more unseemly."

"Politics?"

"Yes, that's the one."

Ruth might have been involved in that conversation, and Baxter thought Leo going outside to get some fresh air was shaping up to be a most excellent idea indeed. His father told him to scram with the corporal, his uncle Pete.

Leo flashed them a peace sign, another new mannerism—the two bunny ears at full attention, rising above the bulwark of his hand—humorous enough to elicit a smile from these adults, these squares—even Haldermann was amused.

* * *

Leo and Janet continued to sift about the Death of Golf procession, chatting with those who still couldn't believe the new holes were in place and would be put into action the following day. That had been the prevailing sentiment of most—some in hushed tones, others singing it from mountaintops. There was, however, a small contingent of younger members at the club who not only agreed with the decision but vocally supported it. This contingent, which now mostly comprised the newest iteration of, yes, the stooges—that sect of contrarians O Triple C had never been able to shed—young and always reinventing themselves and now prophesizing to anyone who would listen how much more digital the world was going to become once the advancements of augmented reality got ironed out and achieved critical mass—hoopla the world had been hearing for close to twenty years. Their point was it would be nearly impossible to get people to go outside again once the singularity had been achieved—not that the older members had any clue what these new stooges were on about—nor did they want to know—and many longed for the days when they were just merry pranksters and not Cassandra-like soothsayers.

Their argument was that anything that made the sport easier, that actually encouraged people to go out and play, even if it felt like an assault on tradition, should be embraced—that it wasn't just golf at stake but the entire concept of being an active human being. There were some in the stooges ranks who believed the ship had already sailed on golf, and there was probably no saving it for future generations against the allure of virtual realities and quantum computing and that, at best, golf courses a hundred years from now would be granted designations like modern-day nature preserves or historical parks—best-case scenario. None of that was to say the stooges were necessarily right. They didn't possess a crystal ball, weren't clairvoyant despite their attempts at it—they now fancied themselves futurists, lesser prophets in a dying age. And if you were to get cornered by one into a conversation, which they were subtly doing at the Death of Golf Party III, and you weren't of the right mind to hear their tech-mech tales of what was to come, then you'd be advised to extricate yourself from their path—which Leo and Janet quickly decided on, beelining down the porch steps on the back side of the Restaurant, escaping those dark forecasts—including that a proper round would be reduced to fifteen holes by 2050, if not sooner.

Outside, there was the odd smattering of people, all in funeral garb, milling around for one reason or another. Some had found a quiet eave to be alone. Some were having a vape. Others were examining the putting green, newly reconfigured with one-foot practice cups—a weird sight that drew the ire of all those who passed by. Leo and Janet strolled a bit, enjoying the warm wind, talking about things of little consequence. It was shaping up to be a pleasant evening, even if it was themed on a funeral, even if maybe they—mostly Leo—had determined they were a bit too old for such a raucous party, even if one of such nature only occurred every seventy years. Leo started going on about Cuba some more, that perhaps they really should think harder on the idea of a vacation. Janet wasn't totally opposed to the idea, thought at the very least they were due a trip somewhere, not having left the East Coast since she could even remember. They started to drift back to the pro shop, holding hands, and that's where they saw Jocko

Whalley Jr.—the longtime head of the grounds and maintenance crew—loitering near the front door with what appeared to be a heavy duffel bag by his feet.

Close to seventy years old now, Jocko was still an imposing figure, not losing an inch of height to bone fractures, spinal compression, or the rigorous demands of his job—still burly, still barrel chested. He might not walk as fluidly as he once did—a noticeable hitch had taken up residence in his left leg—but he was still a man to reckon with, time not softening his attitude toward most people. If anything, the advancing years had made him more suspicious of his fellow man. Fortunately for Leo, the two had become real friends over the years, dating back to that shared incident with their kids trespassing on the seventh hole, horsing around with the Quarry Witch lore. From then on, the two men had made an effort to keep better tabs on one another, Leo even being invited to share the occasional beer in the Monastery, the highest of honors that the grounds crew could bestow on an outsider, let alone an officer of the law.

So when Jocko waved Leo and Janet over, it was received as a friendly invitation while others might feel they were about to be reprimanded over some infraction toward the course—like failure to drop fresh seed in a fairway divot or neglecting to repair a scuff on the green, both major no-nos in Jocko's code of conduct.

"Chief Sinclair, Mrs. Chief Sinclair," said Jocko, grinning. "Strange days are upon us."

"I'll say. I was telling Janet about some of the surveillance your boys have mounted."

"After seeing some of that party inside, the quote-unquote mourners, I'm starting to think we should have rigged up twice as many cameras," said Jocko. "And I bet we'll have to keep them running for longer than anticipated."

"It reminds me of the early 2000s when the Pro-V1 took the game by storm and replaced the balata ball," said Leo. "Rumor had it a Death of Golf vote was taken and narrowly defeated."

"I remember those balatas. We'd find them cut to hell from mis-hits, constantly shanked into the woods," said Jocko. "Probably in everyone's best interest that party never took place."

"Indeed. That ball was like hitting rock compared to those urethane covers Titleist came up with."

Leo could vividly remember those days—when most of the world was concerned with Y2K and the dot-com bubble bursting, golfers were wrapping their minds around this new ball technology set to change the sport forever. This was about four years before he'd met Janet, when she didn't know a single thing about golf or, frankly, want to know.

"Well, people sure are taking this change hard," said Janet neutrally. "What do you think of it, Jocko?"

"I don't play, so no real opinion on the gaming aspect of it," said Jocko. "Will be interesting to see the consequences and, more importantly, the unintended consequences, as it relates to the welfare of the actual grounds. Though truth be told, it won't be my concern for much longer."

"Does that mean what I think it means?" asked Leo.

"Yep, I've decided this will be my last season here, last season working anywhere. I'm going to retire once I hit the big seven-zero, which is right around when this place will go dark for the winter."

A drunken partygoer walked past the three of them, loudly blathering into one of those new Pulse phones that were all the rage, informing the unlucky recipient on the other end of the line, "You're not talented enough to go off script."

"Congratulations, Jocko. Are you excited for it?" asked Janet, distraction aside.

"I am, more so than I would have thought," said Jocko. "But I can collect my full benefits now, and surprisingly enough, the wife wants to see more of me around the house. Plus we have been grooming my replacement for a few years, so now's the time to pass the baton."

"This place isn't going to be the same without you," said Leo, a bit of gravel stuck in his voice.

"It'll carry on. I'll see to that. And I'll be around for another year or so in case they need to pick my brain on something or need me to swing by," said Jocko, clearly having given the issue much thought. "But after that, we'll be gone."

"Where to?" asked Janet.

"Unsure, but north, definitely north," said Jocko, not elaborating on the specific location, as though it were deeply personal or painfully obvious.

A silence fell over the three. The party in the Restaurant could be heard from where they stood, but they were preoccupied with Jocko's news, which was hardly a total shock—they'd spoken on the topic before—but still, when it had finally been decided, once the gears were set in motion, it became a different thing, realer and a stark reminder how all things moved on in some fashion or another.

"And what about you, Mrs. Chief Sinclair? When are you going to get him to hang up his spurs and spend more time on the homestead?" asked Jocko.

"It's coming. Whether he wants to face it or not, it's coming," said Janet, giving Leo a double pat on the back for emphasis. The best Leo could do was demur with a guilty head nod, a contrite act of someone who all but certainly had his issues with the inevitable.

"It comes for all of us, eventually," said Jocko. "Some just hold out longer than others."

Leo more than understood what the two were getting at. It had been widely speculated that the long-tenured chief of police would be stepping down soon—even some grumblings that, at seventy-five years old, he'd already overstayed his welcome and should have handed in his badge some time ago. Problem was that Leo hadn't much inclination to call it quits. He still liked the work, liked the people. He enjoyed the purpose it gave him to rise each morning and contribute to keeping his town safe. Of course, an awful lot had changed in his thirty years of being the chief: from the role of policing in America to the rise of privatized security in more middle-class enclaves to the expansive nature of surveillance technology—all told, it was a landscape that looked very different from when Leo had joined the force back in the 1980s.

That said and changes aside, he still relished working with younger officers and helping steer their path. He still took pride in the role and being a fixture in the community. And if he were being honest, he still enjoyed some of the prestige of being the top cop, even if it was big-fish-in-a-little-pond kind of notoriety. He'd been hesitant to give it up for all those reasons and more.

Jocko would empathize with him when they had their chats over it, and Janet knew better than anyone how Leo had been white-knuckling his hold on that wheel. But the writing was clearly on the wall, and those grumblings were going to turn into something more pointed and tangible in the corridors of the town hall if Leo didn't start planning to leave on his own terms. Either that or eventually be shown the door, despite broad approval from his subordinates. The former was the better and more ceremonious option for a man who cared about his legacy, how he exited a job he'd cherished for decades. And, for better or worse, Leo was that kind of man—he cared what others thought of him; he'd be embarrassed and wounded by a messy departure. He needed to go out with grace and dignity.

But it wasn't quite his time yet—it was Jocko's—and Leo was happy for his friend, though he did have a burning question for the man.

"So, Jocko, what's with this duffel bag?" he said, pleased to move the conversation along, toeing the bag with his foot. "You running away from home? Going to join the circus?"

"You joke. But believe it or not, I come bearing gifts tonight," said Jocko, taking a knee and zipping open the bag, rattling around until he found what he was looking for. "This, Leo Sinclair, is for you."

Jocko was back on his feet and handed over to Leo what looked like a metal cup, though oddly shaped, maybe not something you would drink from as there was no handle to speak of.

"Is this what I think it is?" asked Leo.

"It is. We've been moving these eighteen cups around the greens for more years than I can remember; now they're 'obsolete,'" said Jocko, using air quotes to contextualize the notion. "So I took it upon myself to appropriate these relics and distribute them among some of the more worthy members."

"Who'd have guessed you'd be so sentimental, Jocko?" teased Janet.

"I just couldn't imagine them getting thrown away, seemed like a waste."

"This is really terrific, Jocko, thank you," said Leo. "How are you figuring to give them away?"

"I know enough of the members. I know which holes might mean something to certain people for one reason or another," said Jocko. "Some might be a stretch. Others were a gimme, to borrow a term from your game."

"Which category did I fall into?" asked Leo.

"You were the easiest of them all, Chief," said Jocko. "And the first person that came to mind when I got the idea."

"Don't tell me," said Leo, his eyes widening through the wrinkles and puff. He turned the cup over to see a piece of masking tape with *4* written on it.

"Yes, sir, that's the cup from the fourth hole. Couldn't have gone to anyone else."

Leo handled the metal object in his fingers: the smooth exterior, the interior stained and chipped by time. It barely weighed anything, maybe a few ounces. It began to dawn on Leo what the gesture meant, the value of this object gifted to him by a reluctant benefactor, an unlikely friend.

"I don't even know what to say, Jocko," said Leo. "This might be one of the most thoughtful things anyone's ever given me."

"Well, little prince, I'm sure it's not the same cup from the 1950s when you graced the world with your presence," said Jocko. "But I do believe this one here belongs with your family."

Leo cleared some emotion out of his throat and shook Jocko's hand, thanking him again for thinking of him. Janet looked on, pleased as punch to see the two workhorses sharing a moment of mutual admiration, even a little vulnerability.

"It's my pleasure," said Jocko. "Now if you two will excuse me, I've got a few more of these to deliver. I also need to keep my eye out on the course, despite the surveillance—make sure some of the more unruly members don't get any bright ideas about christening these new greens in some unspeakable way."

Leo and Janet both reflexively thought of Ronnie Kemper without saying his name aloud, wondering where he'd gotten off to. They wished Jocko a pleasant evening, and the man walked off with his duffel bag slung over his shoulder, the remainder of the cups clanking around inside, like some golf course Santa Claus—though surly and content to relegate 99 percent of the world, if not more, to the naughty list.

The temperature had dropped a bit during their time outside, and the Sinclairs were without their coats. Most of the partygoers had retreated back inside, so the two of them were on their own—though, in reality, it was only uncomfortable when the wind kicked up, which was infrequent that night anyway. Leo offered his wife of thirty-two years an enigmatic look, not always the easiest thing to achieve after that long a marriage.

"What are you thinking there?" asked Janet.

"A random thing. How my dad used to call my mom cherry drop," said Leo. "I haven't thought about that name in years; now it just came to me."

"I remember."

"Isn't that funny? Not just when they were young, even, but as they got older. It didn't change."

Janet took Leo's hand, the available one that wasn't holding the obsolete cup from the fourth hole.

"There's plenty more time for you and me," she said.

"You promise?"

"I do."

He squeezed her hand to codify their pact, bind it through flesh on flesh.

"So what would you like to do now?" he asked.

"Hey, it's your funeral," said Janet. "I'm just along for the ride."

Leo gave this some thought, breathed in the cold air. It had been a far more nostalgic night than he'd anticipated—not in a bad way, but in a way that could churn up some old emotions, unearth memories that were almost forgotten. He was grateful he could actually remember quite a bit from the second Death of Golf procession all those decades ago. Thankful that his mind was still sharp, and a lifetime was safely stored in his bony head, the computer of his gray matter. *A true universe*, he thought—that's what every single being walking around was, a universe unto themselves. Leo found awe in that, perhaps some comfort. It made the value of life that much greater and the chaos he waded through a bit more tolerable—the punchline to the cosmic joke—"We've got no choice but to roll with it"—as if there were ever a choice to begin with.

Two yokels glided along, wordlessly nodding to Leo, then resumed their boasting of being in the Pipe Layers Union, Local Nine.

"You know what? I think I'm ready to call it a night," said Leo. "Let's you and I head home."

"You're sure? I don't mind staying longer."

"I believe I've mourned enough for one evening," said Leo. "Let's have a quiet one at the house."

"Lead the way, Chief Sinclair," said Janet, taking Leo's hand again as they went through the parking lot, husband and wife, trying to remember exactly where they parked in the full lot—just two content and weary souls, filled with the sudden prospect of returning home, as though after an arduous absence in a far-off land, even when they've only been a few miles away, even when it hadn't been that long.

* * *

Leo and Peter Sullivan walked the cart path along the first hole, jackets on, determined not to let the evening air get in the way of a good saunter. After running into Mary Sullivan outside the Restaurant and giving her an update on Leo's comings and goings, her husband spirited his godson away from the friendly inquisition. Not that Leo particularly minded. He loved his godmother and was happy to share with her all he'd been up to. Plus, he was just glad to be away from all the drunk adults and weird festivity, which was getting more uncomfortable, particularly seeing his parents socializing with such a motley crew under morbid and fraudulent pretenses.

Not that he hadn't seen debauchery at the club before, though as he got older, a certain amount of it was sinking in more—some in exciting ways, others more jarring, perplexing. And while a fake funeral had sounded kind of interesting beforehand, in reality, it struck Leo as kind of unseemly, even if there was supposed to be some tongue-in-cheek aspect to it. Ultimately, he was just glad to be out of the room, which was too hot and crammed with people, looking old and broiled and stitched into uncomfortable clothing, as was he in his little black suit that was probably one size too small for him now. It was better to be outside, in the cold air of nature, the waxing moon, in the company of his uncle Pete, who, despite being a gregarious man, was also good about allowing Leo to find his footing, not quick to force a conversation until the other was ready. Since the two were comfortable in each other's presence, it wasn't such a big deal to walk around in silence for a bit. Maybe it gave Peter a chance to actually zip it for a spell, always such a card around the adults, striving to entertain and be the life of the party—or the *lie* of the party, as some were keen to note on occasion, Sullivan's reputation as a fabulist preceding him around the club.

Leo would take the opposite tack in life from his godfather, endeavoring more to collect his thoughts, curate his speech in a way that promoted accuracy, that shielded him from embarrassment. From a young age, Leo had very little interest in being embarrassed around others. That said, he liked the fact that that he could speak freely with his uncle Pete—not quite blood, but family all the same. It allowed a back channel to the adult world that he couldn't access through his mom and dad, again sparing him certain embarrassments, allowing for more candid admissions.

Peter Sullivan was an ideal option for Leo's new batch of teenage-themed questions, his burgeoning curiosities, and, as Leo was learning, it was good to have options, good to have an advocate like Sullivan in your corner.

"Where's Chip tonight?" asked Leo, breaking their not-unpleasant silence, walking along the first hole's cart path.

"At home. Probably where you should have been, right?"

"Are those people all right in the head?" asked Leo.

"Who, the people at the party? sure they are," said Sullivan with a guffaw, giving his godson a gentle shove. "You know plenty of them in there. Lots of them are friends with your parents."

"I guess it all just seemed a lot weirder than I thought it would be."

"Look, Leo, one thing worth knowing is that adults are going to do some weird stuff too," said Sullivan. "You might think they grow out of it, and mostly they do, but you never totally give up on doing some silly, maybe even some reckless things on occasion. That's a part of being human."

"OK. But it doesn't seem like Mom and Dad ever do any reckless stuff."

"No, I'd put them more in the silly column, like your aunt Mary."

"But not you?"

Sullivan considered the boy's question.

"Your uncle Pete still has some recklessness left in him," said Sullivan. "And I suppose I will until I'm too old for it."

"Aren't you old now?"

That drew a bolt of laughter out of Sullivan.

"Everyone's old to a thirteen-year-old," said Sullivan. "Wait till you see how that changes as the years pile up. It's going to blow your mind how fast time moves, how you'll remember these younger versions of yourself."

Leo nodded his head along with his godfather, not totally sure he understood, but he figured maybe that was some of the point—he was too young to fully absorb it, but the advice might be worth storing for later use.

"But getting back to your original point, as it relates to this Death of Golf party, yes, it's all very silly," said Sullivan. "But what about you? Do you have any thoughts one way or the other about these new materials getting used to make clubs?"

Leo mulled the question over for a few moments—no one had really asked his opinion on it before—while minding his footing along the cart path, looking for cracks in the hard surface by the moonlight, his shiny, dress shoes squeezing his feet in a way that hadn't happened the last time he wore them six months ago, indicating a new pair might be in order. He'd have to ask his mom.

"Can I tell you what I really think about the graphite?" asked Leo.

"Please do."

"Who gives a shit what the clubs are made of?" said Leo, hoping his uncle wouldn't mind the cuss, maybe even view his opinion as more adult because of it. "You still have to hit the ball straight with whatever's in your hands, with good contact and tempo, which is all basically impossible to do."

More belly laughs from Sullivan. He never understood why people didn't think Leo a funny kid—sure, he was thoughtful and bookish and clearly not a dummy; those were qualities you could spot in the boy from a mile away. But the kid did have a certain dry sense of humor developing, even if he didn't aways know it. You just had to allow his sensibilities to register with you, like when he'd observe something absurd and recount it deadpan, almost comically mundane. Leo had an uncanny ability for that, and Sullivan thought it a hoot, that there was some natural timing in his godson that would only stand to get sharper with age.

"Don't tell yourself that the swing's impossible. That's a self-defeating prophecy you don't need rattling around in your head," said Sullivan. "Besides, look at Lynn. She seems to be getting the grasp of hitting the ball."

"Lynn's a freak. That's another thing that should be impossible—how good she already is," said Leo, kind of fired up. "She's like not even ten years old and doesn't even have a slice anymore."

"Life is full of impossibilities if that's how we choose to view things," said Sullivan cryptically, as he was prone to be sometimes, leaving Leo little recourse. If he was supposed to be happy that his kid sister was already better at the sport, *that* would be a demoralizing mindset he wasn't ready to adopt anytime soon, no matter what his godfather was getting at.

Leo and Peter rounded the first hole's green and walked around the promenade toward the second hole, making note of the pin and flag flapping in the breeze.

"And what else have you been up to these days?" asked Sullivan, feeling buoyant with some of that alcohol titrating through his system, a respite from the party allowing those good vibes to catch up with him. "How is school going? You're, what, a senior in college now?"

"I think you know I'm in eighth grade."

"Ah, that's right, my mistake. Must be the suit that makes you look older," said Sullivan. "So that means you'll be in the big building next year. How has eighth grade been treating you so far?"

"It's fine."

"Just fine? That's all I get? Come on, laddie, give your uncle Pete more credit than that."

"I mean, I'm doing well in my classes, so that's good," offered Leo. "My teachers are all nice, for the most part."

"OK, good, now we're getting somewhere. What about your extracurriculars?"

"I'm in an archery club I like."

"Also good. And everything's solid with all your little friends and what-nots?"

"Sure. I do see Chip in the building sometimes, but not a lot with him being in sixth grade, mostly down some hallways," said Leo. "But I always make sure to say hi to him whenever I see him."

"This I like to hear, Leo. It makes me feel better to know that you'll keep an eye out for the Chipster, the Chipmunk," said Sullivan, beaming. "Just don't tell him I used those names. He thinks he's too old for them now."

"I won't. And I do promise to look out for him when I can," said Leo proudly, pleased he could do something he knew his godfather appreciated.

And it truly did please Sullivan to no end—his son, Chip, whom he loved with all his heart and more, wasn't having the easiest go of it in junior high. He was a boy on the smaller size, a sensitive child, prone to bullies, a target to be picked on. He'd struggled to make friends, relying too much on the company of his mother, a happenstance Peter and Mary quarreled over often. Peter had tried to bring his son out of his shell, get him involved in athletics, the Boy Scouts, but Chip was uninterested, painfully shy, and more of an introvert. He had an artistic side, but his parents didn't really know what to do with that—at best, they just allowed him his doodles, offered him encouragement without much in the way of guidance. The Sullivans weren't bad parents, quite the opposite; they just didn't recognize their boy would gravitate toward things they'd never had an interest in. The fact that Peter knew Chip had an ally in the middle school building and would have one in a few years in the big building was a small solace that served as a beacon of light. If Chip could just keep holding on, he'd find his place, his people, and he'd come into his own—as all parents hope for their children, particularly the ones further back on that curve.

"And how goes it with the ladies?" asked Sullivan with a wry grin. "You got yourself a little girlfriend yet?"

"Not really."

"But kind of, maybe?" probed Sullivan.

Leo gave it some thought, trying to mind the cuff of his pants on some patchy gravel they'd passed over, knowing he'd hear it from his parents if he returned as though he'd been traipsing through the woods.

"There was this one girl that I thought liked me, but it wasn't the case."

"I find that hard to believe. What happened?"

"She likes someone else."

"Probably some jerk, right?" offered Sullivan.

Leo hesitated a bit, then blew out a plume of cold air. They were now traipsing on some wet grass, and Leo was caring less and less about dirtying his pants. He had other, more important things on his mind.

"That's the part that sucks. He's not a jerk. He's one of my good friends."

"Ouch, that's tough, kid," said Sullivan, lowering his voice, barely moving his lips. "This girl got a name?"

"Mindy."

"And does Mindy know how you feel about her? Does your friend?"

"No, I don't think so," said Leo. "It never really got anywhere. Then it became clear they were into each other."

"Unrequited love, it's a bitch," said Sullivan, looking at the moon as though it had the answers to Leo's woes. But for all of its romance and light, it was just another phony promise, only able to reflect the scraps the sun was willing to lend.

"What are you saying, Uncle Pete?"

"Unrequited is when you like someone from a distance," said Sullivan. "But they don't know, and it doesn't seem like they'll feel the same way about you."

"Seem?"

"You don't always know for sure how people feel, Leo, what's in their head, in their heart," said Sullivan. "That's not a bad lesson to get used to at your age."

Leo nodded as the two rounded the green on the second hole and walked down the fairway of the third—moving with some pace, Leo ruminating on his godfather's words.

"I'm not sure how distant we are, though, if I see her every day," said Leo. "Not sure I qualify for this unrequited thing."

"You're being too literal, Leo. Besides, it can also mean an emotional distance," said Sullivan. "You could be sharing the same house with the person, and they don't feel for you what you feel for them."

"If we're sharing the same house, then I'd think she already loves me no matter any distance."

"Let's just skip the distance bit for a minute," said Sullivan, mildly exasperated with the boy. "The point I'm trying to make is that you're not the first person to feel this way, and you won't be the last."

"Have you ever gone through it?"

"Almost daily."

Leo looked back on Sullivan, immediately confused.

"Forget it, bad joke. Did you tell your mom and dad about Mindy?"

"No."

"Why not?"

"I don't know. It's private, I guess," said Leo. "Besides, what can they do about it?"

"Your parents are great people. You might be surprised how much listening to their advice can help," said Sullivan. "That said, I also understand why you wouldn't want to advertise this all around town."

"No one knows, actually."

"Not even some of your best buds? No one's figured this out yet?"

Leo shook his head while Sullivan crinkled his nose against the cold air. He'd been treating his conversation with Leo lightly, a jaunt to stretch their legs, to take a break from the pandemonium inside the party. But now Sullivan realized he'd stumbled into new territory, stuff that should not be written off as childish affections, as puppy love. Leo was a full-fledged teenager now, and with that came a whole new set of rules and dynamics—coupled with a maelstrom of hormones. He was hardly a man but certainly less a little kid than only a year ago. And now, in his restrained and vaguely obtuse way, Leo was pouring his heart out—not to his parents, his sister, his friends, but to Peter Sullivan.

He didn't want to lose sight of that, needed to remind himself of its gravity and allow for it.

It made him think of Chip and how he'd want someone to help and guide him if he sought advice elsewhere than his parents. He tried to imagine Chip asking advice from Baxter or Ruth someday in the future. He hoped that he would. All kids need tutelage, and they need it from the right source, someone trusted, both experienced and discreet with their judgment. It very quickly dawned on him that he should be honored by the impromptu conversation, and maybe he could actually come up with something that would help Leo, a kid he'd literally walk over hot coals for.

"So let me ask you, Leo, why am I the only one to know about Mindy?"

It took Leo more than a few moments to form his response. During that silence, in the darkened woods around them, the animals scurried as predator and prey, roles often swapping as circumstances changed, while the birds that could see in the dark, posted high, bided their time, arrogant with their natural advantages, their embarrassment of riches.

"I don't know. I've been waiting to tell someone about her," said Leo. "I guess I just figured you'd keep this between us."

Sullivan absorbed the boy's confidence in him with a hearty measure of gratitude and restraint.

"I absolutely promise to tell no one if that's your preference, Leo," said Sullivan. "And if I may, I can offer you some actual advice if you're interested."

Leo nodded his head in the affirmative. He'd held on to this Mindy secret for a long time, and it was a relief to finally speak with someone about it, to feel less confused and isolated by its invisible binds.

"If this girl and your friend are going to take a run at it, then in my opinion, you're better off staying out of their way," said Sullivan carefully, minding his exact words. "I'm not saying it's going to feel great, but I think you have to let it play out and see what happens."

Leo considered the suggestion before responding.

"That means I'll have to watch them be boyfriend and girlfriend at school every day?"

"Yeah, probably, for a time at least. But here's the thing I remember from being your age—those little relationships don't always last so long," said Sullivan. "So if you give it some time, be patient like I know you can be, then you might get your shot down the road."

"OK, that makes some sense."

"But you got to take your shot, Leo, which I think may be the harder thing for you than the waiting," said Sullivan. "Once you got that window, you have to put yourself out there and live with the results: win, lose, or draw."

"But you want me to be patient first?"

"Yes, but only until it's time for you to show Mindy you got some cojones," said Sullivan, pumping his fist for emphasis. "Then you'll find out if she really likes you. And if she doesn't, you can stop torturing yourself over it and move on."

"What's cojones?"

"It's Mexican for courage," said Sullivan, then added, "Rejection can be a strong driver, but fear of rejection a debilitating one, so don't choose the latter."

Leo agreed wordlessly, and they continued down the cart path of the third hole, the lovestruck boy letting his godfather's words tumble around his head, permeating the folds of his brain. The advice didn't seem unreasonable to him, even if it forced him to the outside, having to wait to get in. If anything, it seemed more practical than Leo might have expected from his uncle Pete, who could have equally suggested a strategy that involved declarations of love in the cafeteria or grand gestures out in the schoolyard. He knew his godfather was a bit of a wild card, but he'd heard a lot of sound advice from the man that night, advice Leo suspected wouldn't be dissimilar to what he'd have gotten if he'd brought that conundrum to his father, solicited his counsel.

"And if they break up and I ask Mindy out and she says yes, what do I tell my friend?"

"You tell him to his face that you're going to hang out with Mindy for a bit," said Sullivan. "Say it as nice as you can without asking for his permission. Don't ever ask for some other man's permission to follow your heart unless it's the girl's father, and you want to marry her. And even then, if he says no, marry her anyway without his blessing."

"I don't think my friend will like that."

"And do you like sitting on the sidelines right now, watching them get together?"

"No."

"Then there you have it," said Sullivan. "Have you ever heard of the expression 'All's fair in love and war'?"

"Yes."

"Well, let me tell you from experience, Leo, war is fairer."

"I never understood what war had to do with love."

"Give it time."

Leo wasn't so sure about the love and war bit, but he chalked it up to something a guy like his godfather would understand, seeing as how he'd encountered both in his life, as had his father.

"Thanks for talking with me about this stuff," said Leo.

"Anytime, bud," said Sullivan, looking as though he'd like to share more of his knowledge with humanity. "Did you know that the heart doesn't get cancer, but that's also why it's not so good at self-repair?"

"No."

Sullivan took a deep breath. He was feeling a little mighty in the moment, borderline epic. Sometimes he forgot how much he had left to offer the world, and it was nice to be reminded, to pull rabbits out of hats, to still believe in magic.

"The heart doesn't heal," said Sullivan softly, as though the universe had asked him a delicate question. "At best, it scars over."

"Uncle Pete?"

"Pay no mind, Leo," said Sullivan. "Just remember, there's a time to wait and a time to act, and it's up to you to figure out the difference. You follow?"

"I do."

"Good man. And remember, it's great to talk to me about this stuff, and I'm here anytime for you. But it's OK to ask your parents too. I know it might seem weird, but they love you and would never steer you wrong."

"How sure are you about that?" asked Leo, grinning widely, an inside joke between the two.

"They are literally the two best adults I know, not including Mary. And they care about you and Lynn the absolute most," said Sullivan. "So I'm dead sure you can talk to them about anything."

Leo nodded in agreement, and the two of them stopped walking, only to find themselves next to the fourth hole tee box, the long fairway stretching ahead of them.

"Is it OK if we head back across the course?" said Leo. "I don't really feel like walking down four right now."

"Yeah, I get it. Who needs that reminder all of the time?" said Sullivan. "Let's go see what those stiffs are up to. Still grousing over the graphite I'm sure."

"I've heard rumors that it's actually a very versatile substance," said Leo.

"Well, let me tell you some things I learned about it in the library," said Sullivan, enthusiastically.

* * *

An excerpt from the *Hartford Courant*, weekly print edition, July 23, 2034, page 16, column 4, paragraph 1.

In financial news, upstart communications company Pulse Technologies closed the trading week at $8.92 per share on the NASDAQ, in what many analysts are calling a sluggish first week of their IPO, falling short of projections that had been speculated to wind up in the $18–$20 range.

When asked for comment, founder and CEO Klaus Porter emphatically stated that the integration of man and machine was not only a probability but an inevitability, and Pulse Technologies would be the tip of the spear of the change, successful IPO or not. The money, in the long run, will not interfere with the future he so adamantly believes in.

Mr. Porter went on to say, in the clipped and oddly cadenced pattern of speech many of us in the tech and financial sectors have grown used to, that Pulse would revolutionize the relationship between humans and information and the interfaces we may be willing to accept, along with those that some will most likely be fearful of and initially reject. He went on to say that failure to accept these eventualities will only serve to put the species behind the proverbial eight ball and cede authority to a higher . . .

<h1 style="text-align: center;">2042</h1>

Selected excerpts from the personal journal of Chief of Police Leo Sinclair, Orchard Coils Police Department (retired), dated May 2042, regarding case number H724-01: Open date of April 17, 1978, close date pending—Incident type: Death under Questionable Circumstances—Victim: Peter Sullivan of 1131 Howling Wind Road, Orchard Coils, CT 07215—Survived by wife, Mary Sullivan (now deceased); son, Chip Sullivan (now deceased).

It boggles my mind returning to this journal now, the moleskin purchased a lifetime ago, reading these old pages with faded ink, though it's still legible. There was a period in my life when I read and reread these pages all the time, the same way I'd return to the old Holm Quarry (never telling anyone) and just wait, hoping for some type of inspiration to hit me, clairvoyance to strike, anything that might help me figure out what happened to Peter Sullivan. (It never did.)

Now, in my advancing years, I find it odd to enter new words in this book that aren't just nostalgia, reflections on a crime I couldn't solve. (Truth is, it's been more than a few years since I've added anything of worth to these pages.) But now, there may actually be some new information about the case, something that had been withered and dead on the vine for so long. An individual came forward two weeks ago and has taken partial responsibility for Sullivan's murder (yes, murder), and if this person's account can be verified, to be followed up and corroborated, then the closure many of us have been seeking (though not all of us have lived long enough to see it) may finally be upon us, the mystery solved. (I'm going to write it all down where it belongs, at least what I've been told so far, what they'll allow me to know about an active investigation.)

Late last month, I was reading on the back porch, a book about the buildup to our involvement in Vietnam, a conflict I can hardly believe draws closer and closer to being one hundred years in the past. (Time is the apex predator that's never gone hungry, pardon the theatrics.) I like reading outside now more than I used to—the abundance of light makes it easier, the gleam off the white pages more welcoming to my old eyes for some reason. (I've refused to switch over to one of those tablet devices that have slowly been replacing proper books for decades now.) I also find the house too quiet midday, too empty. It has been three years since Janet's passing, and I still think I'm going to see her walk across the kitchen window, busying herself with some chore that never would have occurred to me needed attention. This has been happening less over the past year, though I'm not sure if this is progress per se or just time forcing something on me I don't necessarily want but need. (There's nothing about Janet or our life together that I want to move on from or forget, and if my brain tricks me into seeing her in the produce aisle at the market, then all the better.) Sometimes I am reminded of Bo and Clay growing up in this now-quiet house, all the noise and chaos their youth brought to bear. I was wise enough to mostly appreciate it back then, old enough too—not always, but better suited to it in my forties than twenties. But now the house is just an oversize wooden box that I was once so proud of, where I dodge the ever-present silence from space to space, though I suppose I'm not ready to part with it yet, as ridiculously large it is for just one person. (Sorry,

I'm scanning some of this and don't mean to get all maudlin, but the heart and mind drift, topics bleed together.)

Anyway, I was reading outside, and the Pulse pinged. I didn't recognize the number on the device—digits that were pegged to Arizona—so I just let the thing trill on, go to voice mail if need be, which was unlikely. (Scamming the senior population through any and all channels available has become such a boom industry, we've all become wary. Even if nonpartisan legislation is out there, it's mostly a paper tiger, no teeth, the telecom lobby putting the kibosh on anything restrictive. We seniors may vote in droves, but rest assured, whoever we put in office could care less if we get fleeced by confidence scams.) I was surprised that after a minute or so, my Pulse chimed with an alert to a new voicemail. I checked (not on a wearable, certainly not through a port), and sure enough, that Arizona number had left me something to listen to. It could have been a message of dead air or a wrong number, but right from the jump, the person on the other end indicated they were looking for the former chief of police for Orchard Coils, Connecticut, Leo Sinclair, yours truly. (I'd set my voicemail greeting to a stock electronic voice that didn't indicate my name, a tacit way of discouraging messages.)

The long and short of the communique was that a man who identified himself as Louis Minshew, the current chief of police in Flagstaff, might have some information regarding an unsolved death from back in the 1970s, and if I was the person who'd be interested in such a thing, I should please call him back. I could hardly believe what I'd just heard, actually having to listen to the message three times for it to sink in that I wasn't making it up, that it couldn't be some type of complex scam. (Which, while it could have been, I still have enough marbles rattling around to get to the bottom of it.) So I called Minshew back immediately and got him on the line directly as apparently, he'd given me his proper number, not some switchboard or intermediary (a small and favorable tell).

After a few pleasantries and the ubiquitous comments around my Hero of Hartford experience (enough years have passed where I wish people wouldn't bring that up, search engines would stop searching me), Minshew got down to brass tacks and told me they have in their possession a signed statement from a woman who claims to have been present the night Peter Sullivan was attacked and thrown to his death down a ravine, that it took place on some golf course late at night. I listened to Minshew recount the alleged murder of my godfather with an eerie degree of certainty, the likes of which I'd never been able to concoct, so muddled were the scant facts I'd had at my disposal, an examination over decades that led me nowhere (zero witnesses, Uncle Pete's increasingly weird behavior, his car never recovered, Mary's general distrust of the circumstances, etc.). There had always been so little to go on, as though the universe had taken him, but now, Flagstaff PD believed they'd turned up an actual eyewitness to the crime committed over sixty years ago (impossible to believe it's been that long). I tried not to express any disbelief until I heard Minshew out, though I suppose some of my silence betrayed a certain skepticism. He kept telling me that he knew it sounded unlikely, but I should hear him out, allow him to explain (as if I wasn't going to). The man sounded half my age, probably new to the top cop role the way I was half a lifetime ago, not that I'd hold it against him or even knew how true that was. (More a passing thought I had, like when I asked him to continue, this weird feeling like I was asking the younger version of myself to show me where I'd gone wrong, what I had overlooked, where I had messed up.) I'm sure I sounded eager. How could I not?

Minshew proceeded to ask me if the name Sophie Alba had any particular meaning to me. It took a bit of recall, but I remembered Sophie from the case file and my journal (documents I've read through a hundred-plus times). Sophie Alba was a part-time waitress at the Restaurant who also did a little bartending when things got busy. She'd only been employed there a few seasons, and even though shifts were varied, she was sort of like the twelfth man on a basketball team, somewhat unnecessary but a warm body, occasionally useful in a pinch. (There wasn't much overlap to our time there as those were my UConn days.) It was also my recollection (now confirmed) that she didn't even work at O Triple C in 1978, that she'd wrapped up her stint the season before with no issues or complaints, but when she was outreached the following spring to get her on the calendar, she never responded. Not much was made of this, given it was a very transient line of work for young people and the industry, always quitting or getting hired back or fired or moving on without another word. Ask any general manager in the service sector—they'll tell you turnover and staffing and scheduling are what keeps them up at night. (Also bear in mind all we had back then were landlines. Beepers were barely a thing, let alone mobile technologies.) Minshew did confirm she didn't work at the club in 1978 but hadn't left Orchard Coils. Instead, she was knocking around and had taken up with a slightly older man by the name of Horace Wizner (I'd never heard of him), who was a petty crook with a mean streak and high aspirations to criminality that wielded a certain nefarious charm he probably learned from watching noir movies as a kid. (Some of this, if not plenty, will be in Sophie's long confession through Minshew's mouth, transcribed by me in the moleskin for posterity.)

Minshew made a point of asking if the name meant anything to me, which I confessed it didn't. I tried to remember if any interaction with or hearsay regarding Sophie would have led me to believe she had someone in her life, but the truth was I could remember little of the mousy girl, a not-unattractive person who might have been mildly competent at her work but probably went out of her way not to make an impression on people, as though flying under the radar would suit her just fine. (I've encountered many people of this ilk in my line of work.) If she was involved with some older creep, I wouldn't have had cause to know it. It did make me wonder if my parents knew her better than me, given those were years they were at the Restaurant a fair amount. (I'm actually seeing Lynn soon. She's coming into town for a visit, and I can ask her, though we're bound to speak on the phone about it first.)

This also got me thinking that even if I didn't know Sophie well, Samantha Morris definitely would have known her, and they would have worked together for more than a couple of seasons. Sam was always the type to reach out to the quieter ones (as she did with me), particularly if they needed help acclimating or if she found them interesting once prodded from their shell. (She was always on the hunt for unmined gems—when she was younger, that is.)

Alas, all I can do is add Sam to a long list of people I'd like to ask about Sophie Alba but simply can't. Her passing, sudden yet not sudden, hits me hard at times. More than a few years after the pandemic, it still jars me in so many ways I can barely keep straight anymore. She and I had all those things to sort out: the amount of progress we'd made with still more to go, Janet encouraging me the whole way (rightly), eager for me to pluck that thorn from my side. Then, without much warning, Sam's time on the road ended, poof, leaving me on our road alone, which wasn't useful—the gains we'd made halted, my anger and resentment boxed—but at least more a part of me I could live with. That much I'd achieved with her. There's little for me to do about it apart from not allowing the regret to gnaw at my mind, maybe endeavor to do better in the future. (Some days I'm more successful than others, but at least I still care about the future, about being a better man.)

In any event, I was no closer to knowing who Sophie Alba was or why she would have been associated with this Horace Wizner guy. This much I told Minshew, and I could tell he was mildly disappointed. I couldn't ignore the pangs of ineptitude I felt that these persons of interest were tooling around Orchard Coils in 1978, apparently hiding in plain sight, and no one was the wiser about smoking them out. If Minshew sensed my unease, he chose not to harp on it and simply continued with his story, telling it in a patient way that suggested he was in no rush or wanted to offer me up a hearty serving of professional respect, perhaps both. (I couldn't have said how much work drew his attention in Flagstaff. It would seem too hot for the excessive movement crime requires.) (A joke.)

Minshew told me that Sophie's boyfriend was the man alleged to have thrown Peter Sullivan to his death, over the fencing on the green of the seventh hole. (He was clearly reading from his notes.) The way Minshew recounted the story, as told to him directly by Sophie in the flesh (she was now in her eighties), was that she'd gotten to know Sullivan a bit at the Restaurant over the years, particularly working the late nights. Sophie said she was never one of the more social girls that worked there, but Sullivan was always happy to give her the time of day, which felt welcomed as she often didn't fit in with certain crowds. Her opinion of him was that he was lonelier than let on, at least back then, even though he never had a bad word to say about his wife and son, even though he was well liked at the club, in spite of or aided by his barfly status. Sophie stated for Minshew that at some point her and Sullivan's little conversations drifted toward loftier ideas: ethics, theology, good and evil, right and wrong, even concepts like the existence of God and fallen angels and stuff like that. (These were weird topics to hear that my uncle Pete had taken an interest in. I'd never heard him discuss anything of the sort, but I also knew he wasn't above going down the occasional rabbit hole. He would have loved the internet age if he'd been around to see it.) Sullivan might have loved to pontificate late at night but seldom on matters deeper than finance or golf or carnal musings, though maybe he had a broader wheelhouse than I realized. To me, he was a mostly grounded adult who, despite some eccentricities, only really cared about his job and family and reining in the occasional duck hook that plagued his game. When he went to church, it was surely Mary's doing. So why would a guy like that, curiosity aside, get embroiled in other-worldly conversations with a barmaid half his age?

Minshew asked Sophie that very same question, and she replied that it was a field of study they were both interested in (news to me), though he'd come to observe these bigger questions after an unexpected hernia surgery. (A procedure I vaguely remember for him, but I couldn't recall if it was a big deal or not, maybe a one-nighter at Memorial that sidelined him for a few weeks.) She thought this surgery might have prompted him to start thinking about his own mortality, despite being a young man, despite having already been through war, and to start questioning the very nature of his existence in ways that didn't revolve around Christmas bonuses and newly imported bourbons at his package store, where the owner took special care in him. The repercussions of this surgery (apart from successfully repairing his abdominal wall) gave him convalescing time to contemplate the stuff Sophie was already interested in at a very young age. Since before she was a teenager, she claimed a philosophical curiosity had always been there, couldn't say where it came from, certainly not her parents, but it was there all the same, innate and undeniable. When Minshew pressed her on the topic, she had little else to offer. All she'd further volunteer was that those kinds of conversations never bored her. She also made the same comment about Sullivan—he never bored her. (This I could easily believe as my uncle was many things, but boring wasn't one of them.)

So, for at least two seasons at O Triple C, these two carried on this little intellectual relationship whenever their paths crossed, never outside the property and never to manifest into anything physical. (Old Sophie was adamant about that.) Minshew would tell me he pushed back awfully hard on that notion, finding it unlikely that despite all their time together, Sullivan's baseline for social inebriation, borderline hedonism, her being a young woman that also stirred his mind, that nothing of a sordid nature ever came up, not even so much as a passing flirtation that she'd have to shoot down, where she might have had to make it clear she only wanted something platonic. (Or maybe she didn't.) But her position was unchanging, Sullivan never laid a finger on her, and she'd never suggested he do otherwise, and in that vein, they got along swimmingly, even if they were an odd pair. Perhaps that lack of sexual tension and romantic feelings punctuated the companionship they found in one another, something more simplistic, less complicated. (Sorry, as much as I love Sullivan, I'm skeptical of this.) (The cop in me.)

The much larger problem had proven to be Sophie Alba finding a different kind of companionship with Horace Wizner (sexual), a sort of bad boy of ill repute that was adroit at plucking certain types of women out of a crowd, making them feel special, casting a spotlight, and warming them with the glow. Apparently, they'd met during the winter of '76 at some watering hole Sophie couldn't remember the name of, maybe in Glastonbury, while she was out celebrating something with friends on an equally forgettable occasion. The only thing remarkable about that December night (by her account) was being approached by this stranger, a somewhat unkempt, vaguely handsome short fella with hound-dog eyes and thick brows. He asked if she'd care to buy him a drink (toad!), with some devil-may-care confidence I guess.

Maybe it works sometimes, maybe it doesn't. But apparently, Sophie thought the approach odd and disarming in a seedy way that felt appropriate for the bar. (She told Minshew she wasn't much of a bar person, despite working at the Restaurant.) She peeled away from her friends, kind of a rarity for Sophie, and bought drinks for this stranger, who creaked open his wallet to return the favor by their third round. (She might not have been a bar person, but she was happy to practice her drinking at home, reading those heady tomes of dead pontificators.)

He introduced himself as Horace Wizner, and she thought immediately it was a phony name, like he was trying to pull her leg or pass something off. (Nope, it was his actual name, given to him by truly despicable people as I'm only just starting to research now.) After a couple of hours, Sophie's friends retrieved her to leave the bar, not willing to relegate their naïve friend in her current state (drunk-ish) to some random loner. (Horace had traveled to the bar alone, intentions unclear.) While Sophie protested mildly that she was fine to stay, much to their collective surprise, Horace agreed with Sophie's friends and thought it was in everyone's best interest if they took their leave, that the place was known to get a little rowdy after midnight. He also gave Sophie his telephone number in hopes she'd call him at some point. The move helped endear Horace to Sophie's friends and set the hook even deeper in Sophie herself. (Little did any of them know just how adept at and fascinated by the concept of the long con Horace was, cultivating assets, resources, and pawns in an attempt to use them later, disposable as they were, learning as he went that some of them would amount to nothing while others would ripen and bear fruit.) Sophie seemed to have no idea exactly what she was walking into (or did she?), and for all her intelligence and curiosity, she wasn't savvy enough to sniff out this grifter, charming as he may have been.

She called him the next day, nursing a mild hangover, eager to hear his voice, to make some type of plans with him on their own, away from the watchful eyes of her friends. When she finally got him on the line (multiple attempts were required), he'd said he'd love to but would be out of town on business for the next week. She was exceedingly disappointed, those visions of an immediate rendezvous dashed, his nature cool and aloof (as she'd recount), as though he'd expected her phone call, had been home and not picked just up to see how many times she'd try again, had this work trip lined up just to rain on her parade. He did ask for her telephone number and promised that as soon as he was back home, he'd love to take her out for dinner, maybe a show in Hartford, with the holidays fast approaching and some touring theater companies in town. Though unsure if she should ask, be so bold, she ended up inquiring as to what type of business trip it was. (He'd been mum about his work the night before.) Horace, for his part, didn't seem put out by the question and, in fact, was eager to explain that he was driving with an associate to Kansas City as chauffeur and protector. His companion was a jeweler that needed to transport some merchandise and didn't want to do it alone, so that was where Horace fit in. It all sounded rather exotic to Sophie, and she did wonder why the jeweler wouldn't just fly with the merchandise on him but didn't bother to ask. Horace promised he'd tell her all about his exploits once he'd returned. (A promise he did indeed keep, though whether he actually went on this caper to KC was anyone's guess.)

For the next year-plus, Horace kept Sophie on a long leash though a snug hook. He might disappear for weeks on end, leaving Sophie to her own devices: her banal job at the country club (his words), her incessant reading, community gardening, friends who apparently, after increasing contact with Horace, tried to caution Sophie about getting too infatuated with the guy, that these vanishing acts weren't normal and a portend of unhappiness down the road (advice she rejected, holding a grudge against the advisor). When Horace was around, they drove quite a bit in his beater muscle car that had a broken AC and barely functioning radio. From county to county, they tooled around Connecticut, looking at downtowns, posh watersides, bespoke neighborhoods. This seemed to be Horace's favorite thing to do, just seeing where other people lived, what they might be doing, how they went about their lives. He was fascinated by strangers. He loved the idea of them and what it would mean to befriend them, to hear what their voices were like and what they did for work, maybe gauge how wealthy they were. Apparently, he could be a real chatty guy when he wanted to be, but he was also quick to have the spell broken, the mystery resolved, and he'd be ready to part ways, move on to the next area, the next person (charming until he no longer wished to be). All the while, vacuuming up information with his eyes and ears, trying to learn, (Horace was evidently not a book person. Everything with him was experience and action.)

Sophie, sitting shotgun, would fill the car with chatter, much of it one sided as Horace preferred to drive without speaking, saving his words for when he was out of the car, when he was among those strangers. One of Sophie's favorite topics to bend Horace's ear with was her reading list, the books she was currently working on, particularly the philosophy texts that were taught in the colleges she wasn't able to enroll in. (Minshew didn't elaborate on this, so I'm unsure why college was a nonstarter for Sophie, though I'll endeavor to find out.) She seemed to have a real panache for the subject, as would later be revealed through her conversations with Sullivan. According to the statement to Minshew, Wizner not only tolerated her diatribes during the car rides but came to enjoy them. Always the con artist, he heightened his vulnerability with her by admitting his ignorance on these subjects she so adored. This admission emboldened her, and she continued to filter all she'd learned from these books into Horace's brain, to play the role of educator, to have a small amount of agency over him (by his design). This arrangement seemed to align with the man's sensibilities, literally with the way he viewed the world, how he liked to traverse its highways and coastal roads. He'd drive at a steady clip, fingers on the wheel, navigating new directions all the time, unconcerned with getting lost, listening to Sophie prattle on about concepts foreign to him. The windows would be rolled down to take in the new smells, competing with the occasional cigarette Horace would hack. (Sophie abstained—also, remember, no AC.) The whole world, even if it was just one state, zipped by their young eyes. It seemed enough to sate Horace during his down moments, when he wasn't working, as he called it. Sophie might have thought they were falling in love—she surely was—but him? Hard to say at this juncture. (Maybe he was, but honestly, what is a psychopath's love worth in the end? Absolutely nothing, I'd think.)

What Sophie hadn't known was gestating under Horace's calm-enough surface was a man looking to inflict real harm, to experiment with it in a way that would allow him to become a more formidable criminal, some force of nature out there on the streets. (She'd claimed she only came to understand this after what happened with Sullivan.) Horace had been in plenty of fistfights in his life, was tougher than he looked, and while he knew how to win a few, he also knew how to take a loss. It was those whippings that you grew from, that toughened your hide and proved you weren't a bowl of mush, that you were willing to mold your weakness into something less weak, time and time again, until what little weakness was left could hardly be seen with the naked eye. Horace had shown up repeatedly in Sophie's presence with fresh or fading bruises, split lips, cracked knuckles, sore ribs. He was unnaturally good with gauze and medical tape. Rubbing alcohol didn't sting after a while. He would patch his face up with one hand, nimble with a hand mirror, even a needle and thread. But, as she would describe to Minshew, Horace eventually allowed Sophie to conduct some of the repair work, though she'd learned not to ask him what had happened, that he'd just say it was work, and she needn't concern herself with his trivial injuries. Her time was better spent pondering her own life. (Sounded like another one of Horace's tactics, keeping her close without the appearance of it.)

So Sophie did stop asking, but she wasn't sure how she was supposed to not care. Horace was her boyfriend, after all, certainly in her mind, and a girlfriend should care when her boyfriend showed up on her doorstep from time to time beat to hell. By that point, it was somewhat obvious to Sophie that Horace must be involved in some kind of criminality, like maybe a stick-up artist, thief in a crew, maybe an enforcer. She openly admitted to Minshew that, at a certain point, she knew Horace was a crook, though probably not too violent of one, despite the occasional batterings, and he only stole from those that had it coming. What she would also admit to Minshew and, from the sound of it, pretty easily was that she didn't care if Horace stole for a living. She hadn't much in the way of rationalizations. (I doubt that.) She didn't need to perform mental gymnastics to stick it out with the guy, despite his line of work, as maybe a guy on the lower rung trying to climb some ladder. Horace never seemed to have any money, drove a ten-year-old POS, lived in a crappy apartment. and didn't seem to keep regular hours in the slightest. (By all accounts, he wasn't even that handsome, so why, Sophie, would you or anyone waste their time on this loser?) Minshew asked this question more than a few times during their lengthy time together, and the best Sophie could come up with was that she loved him, and it trumped all logic and reasoning, which hardly fully explains it, but also, if you'd ever been in love, kind of explained it enough.

As the two would go on to discuss in that interrogation room in Flagstaff, a topic Horace took a shine to during all those car rides with Sophie in the late seventies was the connection she had developed with this Peter Sullivan guy, some finance dolt with a family and two cars and a fenced-in house, who apparently liked to knock them back and commiserate on topics he knew plenty about or even little for that matter, guileless in that he'd admit to his ignorance on a subject he'd nevertheless carry on about (not inaccurate). Horace would ask about this man he'd never met, quick questions, brief prompts, which allowed Sophie to chat away about some of her work at the club, a subject Horace was infrequently interested in (apparently he thought of the club and its members as landlocked losers), but he did take note when something struck his fancy, filing it away in what Sophie would describe as a spooky-good memory. After a while, despite not being able to pick Sullivan out of a lineup, Horace grew to feel like he kind of knew the fella, or at least could appreciate what made the guy tick, and that he had the good sense to befriend Sophie, who Horace figured was head and shoulders better than anyone else working at the dopey Restaurant.

Sophie would tell Minshew over the course of her lengthy confession that Horace wasn't a jealous man and didn't begrudge her affinity with Sullivan or their late-night chats. (There would be more than one interview to extract as much detail from her as possible, a condition she didn't refuse for a variety of reasons, including her excellent recall for the details of those years. Plus, as Minshew would tell me, she seemed to have nothing else to do, was bored and old and under a great deal of stress.) Horace would have considered them like work friends, benign and useful in a way that helped pass the time, allowed an outlet to vent.

It was late in the fall of '77 when Sophie told Horace a new work story, one about the Halloween Trail that the club held every year for the kids, when the parents would attend a party at the club. (Sophie was to work that event for the first time in a couple of weeks.) This seemed to stir some curiosity in Horace as Sophie went on to describe some of the traditions and ghost stories and Quarry Witch lore that had clung to the golf course, particularly that time of year. He hadn't much sense of these tales, and Sophie, through her conversations with Sullivan, was now well versed on the ins and outs of the myth, including the spot on the seventh hole where one could peer over the fencing to see the long drop to the abandoned mines below, where the witch was said to be in residence. Horace told Sophie it seemed dangerous and reckless to have something like that on a golf course, which she'd agreed with. (What people don't realize, especially non-golfers, is that these New England and coastal-California courses, among others, get shoehorned into the terrain around them, particularly where land comes at a ridiculous premium, so some areas get created that aren't necessarily the safest, but typically, there's nothing that's so hard to avoid: treacherous, yes, but hardly a deterrent.)

All this spooky Halloween Trail business got Sophie talking more with Sullivan about their interest of good and evil, not so much the bible-thumping version but more naturalistic, the exploration of gray areas and what it truly took to be good in a world that was progressively getting weirder. (When hasn't the world gotten weirder?) Many times, Sophie would just let Sullivan talk on in his fanciful way, probably not unlike the way Horace let Sophie carry on during those long car rides. To Horace, it sounded like this Sullivan guy was going through some existential midlife crisis (perhaps), but Sophie would reiterate to her paramour that Sullivan was a very lucid man—a drinker and bloviator, yes, but not unintelligent and harmless enough in ways that people responded to.

Sophie would go on to tell Chief Minshew a very specific thing that Horace had asked of her, something she'd played off in the moment but had stuck with her, bothered her a bit. Horace had asked if she thought she could convince Sullivan to kill himself, to which she responded that of course she couldn't, and of course, she wouldn't want to. They were friends. Horace let it go, like a bad joke, but not before reminding her that they probably weren't friends, that she was the help at the bar he frequented, a lonely drunk that may or may not ever muster the courage to properly hit on her. (Sophie did not agree with this assessment but didn't press the issue.) She figured Horace's passing interest in the man would wane in time, as many things did with his scattershot attention. But what Sophie didn't realize was that she'd inadvertently planted the seed in Horace's mind, a mind that had become determined to kill someone just to see if he was capable of it, to see if he had the chops to get away with it. (I can't verify yet, but he had to have been influenced by all the cult stuff that grew in prominence in the sixties, bled into the seventies, and would frankly find some footing in the eighties, with all the devil-worshipping stuff.) A mind convinced he'd have to kill someone in order to reach a new stratosphere in the criminal ranks, to get past a moralistic, indoctrinated view of life and death, to create the ultimate reason he needed to be feared. (I'm speculating here, but from my experience and what Minshew told me, I don't suspect I'm not too far off.) Horace did not want to wait for some caper to go sideways to find out if he had the mettle to take a life. He wanted to get out in front of it, get the practice, get it over with. Ultimately, through those frequent car trips with Sophie, all her chatting about O Triple C (inadvertently choosing the victim, per her side of the story), Horace had formed a plan that centered around my godfather, my uncle Pete, that would serve his needs in more than a few ways, provided Sullivan died by his hands, and Sophie was forced to watch.

* * *

Lynn Sinclair-Moore finally arrived at her brother's house in Orchard Coils, many hours later than expected because of the inclement weather of the Southeast wreaking havoc on the carefully choreographed flight plans of hundreds of arrivals and departures—the tail end of hurricane season throwing a few parting jabs at the air travel industry, unpredictable weather still a wild card despite a hundred years of commercial aviation experience and planes now rigged with so much advanced computing they could actually take off and land themselves. That said, Lynn, an avid and frequent traveler her whole life, a patient person as part of her profession, was more than comfortable rolling with the punches of wind delays and missed connecting flights and vanished luggage and whatever else the fickle gods of travel—international or domestic—could throw at her.

Age had only made Lynn more patient; closing in on eighty years old, she was adept at not allowing stuff out of her control to zap her precious minutes, tax her already harried bandwidth. In many cases, these delays allowed her to channel her inner stoic, accepting that hiccups and wrinkles weren't just a possibility but a probability, and the true measure was how one reacted to them. It wasn't enough to just work through them; you mustn't hold a grudge. You had to do it coolly to truly succeed. So when Lynn was presented an opportunity to catch up on some pleasure reading, send some messages from her Pulse, eat at a halfway-decent spot as far as Terminal D restaurants went, she was up for it. She was a firm believer that there was plenty to do with newly opened time; it was just up to the individual to take advantage of those minutes gained, not lost. It was a specific mindset, a useful one, that Lynn had done well to cultivate in the second half of her life, and she wished she'd leveraged it more during her playing days. She wondered how more successful a career she might have had practicing the old disciplines, though she also conceded that if there was one thing that could break a stoic's soul, even Marcus Aurelius, it might be the baffling nature of golf.

There was a time in Lynn's life when she was a rather recognizable woman, when she couldn't *not* be spotted killing time at an airport or waiting in line at the car rental place. She was always able to attract attention from enthusiasts or, frankly, men in general. There were plenty of people jockeying for her attention during a brief and chance encounter—random moments when she was skilled at accommodating fans: autographs, pictures, a kind word, even gently rebuffing comical and not-so-comical advances and overtures from zealous admirers. She'd tactfully remind these would-be suitors that she was a happily married woman of so-and-so number of years, then play if off with a chuckle—good about not bruising egos, leaving these lotharios with a clubhouse tale they could exaggerate at their own discretion: "Did I ever tell you about the time I almost landed a date with Lynn Moore? She wanted to, but she was married, then she dipped into the airport Applebee's, and I never saw her again." Naturally, that attention had tapered off slowly over the decades. As Lynn moved away from being a professional golfer and spokesperson, as she receded from the limelight and moved into more behind-the-scenes roles for the LPGA, forging a second career in the advancing of woman's golf internationally, less of a public figure, which suited her just fine. After two decades competing in front of the camera's icy lens, Lynn was relieved to escape its capture and spend more time in closed-door meetings, on desk work and business lunches—basically anything that didn't have the properties of recording her while testing sound levels, lighting, and playbacks.

The fact that Lynn turned down numerous lucrative offers to be on-air talent for the league, highly coveted network deals her telegenic face and golf-riddled mind would have been perfect for, illustrated just how serious she was about leaving the camera behind, about helping the sport she loved in other, less visible, ways.

Time, as it does to everyone, had also chipped away at Lynn's appearance—though, in fairness, she had aged with remarkable grace and maintained much of her attractiveness over the years. Even into her sixties and beyond, it was evident to see what a great beauty she was, how she still possessed a handsomeness that many former athletes are able to sculpt after a lifetime of clean diets, sunscreen, exercise and, eschewing the lure of cosmetic implants, surgeries, repurposed diabetes medication, or whatever new shortcut some quack had invented to coopt the beauty standard into something Frankensteinesque. So long as you were willing to put in the hard work after your days of competition were over, while maybe using a dab of collagen-infused eye cream and not begrudging gravity as it did its thing, as gravity surely wouldn't hold it against you as you fought off its effects through exercise and ice plunges and sauna sessions. All this had been Lynn's approach, and it suited her well. Even if she wasn't the standout in a crowd the way she used to be, she more than carried herself with great dignity and confidence. And was grateful to walk about the world unimpeded, knowing full well who she was and who she loved and what she'd accomplished with her years not squandered.

Around eight p.m. on that Thursday night, Lynn deposited her two bags on Leo's doorstep and rang the front bell of the house she was very familiar with in Orchard Coils, where Leo had lived for close to forty years, most of them with Janet, where they raised Bo and Clay. A house not so far away from the one she grew up in, only a ten-minute drive. O Triple C was also close by. A trifecta of memories for Lynn, the swirl of them hitting her already, only back in town for five minutes—her mom and dad, grandparents, the years learning the game at the club. She knew it would be a lot over the next four days; it was impossible to avoid the swell of feelings that accompanied these trips back home. She'd been mentally preparing herself for what she knew would be an emotional visit with her brother, though hoping it would also be fun—unlike her last visit to Connecticut, for Janet's funeral, a painful gathering. Crushing to see Leo, Paul, her nephews torn up as they were—to feel torn to shreds herself over a passing that felt way too soon.

Leo answered the door and ushered in his little sister. Big hugs abounded as he took one of her bags into the downstairs hallway. Lynn followed, then deposited the second bag next to the first one. The two siblings regarded each other in the well-lit hallway, embraced a second time with more meaning, as though the first one in the doorway were perfunctory, and told each other just how good it was to be reunited. Lynn was somewhat surprised by her brother's outward nature. He'd always been on the more reserved side, what some would categorize as aloof, though probably not going so far as to label him cold. She figured that time and circumstances had slowly chipped away at him, the armor growing tinny and brandished—which needn't necessarily be a terrible thing. They agreed it had been too long since they'd seen one another—a trip Leo had taken down to Florida last year, a respite from the cold February Connecticut was mired in. The two did a fair amount of talking and screen time on their Pulses, using the video options when convenient, warding off the trap of becoming strangers in each other's lives. That said, Lynn was grateful to get a good look at her brother, to assess how he'd been holding up since the last time they saw each other in the Sunshine State.

After Janet's passing almost three years ago, Lynn had worried how a man of Leo's age might let himself deteriorate without that north star guiding the way. And even if Leo was cut from heavy and fire-retardant cloth, it didn't make him fully immune or unsusceptible to that specific brand of grief—a despair that can sneak up on you, even when you think you're maintaining, even when you think you've turned a corner, and quickly place you back in harm's way. Lynn would think of it as a maze, one you're meant to stumble around in, all dead ends and twisty turns, and while you're determined to escape, given enough time oscillating through hope, bumping into walls, you may start to forget you're even lost and grow resolved to your new reality. That was when things could go really bad, life and death bad, and that was what Lynn feared for Leo, looking into his face, truly an old man now but still with a shine and sharpness in his eyes that suggested he'd escaped the maze or never really fell into its clutch, or so she hoped. The fact was he seemed a bit jubilant, defiant in a way to prove he had much to live for—who was to say he didn't?—and she hoped her visit was a small part of that as she was there to hear about all the things Leo had been doing to carry the proverbial fire. And, in no small part, some of that would include a summation of the Peter Sullivan case being officially closed—that barb finally plucked away from their skin, six months after Sophie Alba had first come forward.

Once Leo could get Lynn settled into the kitchen, he reheated the pumpkin ravioli he'd prepared hours earlier, along with some baked Brussel sprouts and toasted garlic bread. It wasn't such a bad meal for a man who had never considered himself much of a cook, though he found himself with more time to indulge in such hobbies, which went hand in glove with enjoying wine and how it paired with different foods. He was hardly an expert, and his palate might never evolve much further, but at least he'd elevated his knowledge past red wine for beef and white wine for chicken and fish.

He poured himself and Lynn a glass of Malbec, fitting for autumn, and they sat together at the kitchen table with their meals before them as they had as children seventy years before, in a house not so far from where they currently were. They clinked their glasses. Lynn tried the pasta, then some more, and gave her brother a wry smile of approval, as if she hadn't known he had it in him.

"Not bad at all, Leo," said Lynn. "What kind of sauce did you cook this in?"

"Pesto cream with rosemary. Did I go overboard with the spice?"

"No, it's perfect," said Lynn. "Look at you. Who says you can't teach an old dog new tricks?"

"I'll take that as a compliment, the old part notwithstanding," said Leo, grinning. "Even if it's true."

"Well, it's true for both of us," said Lynn, trying some garlic bread, equally impressed that it was neither burned nor overly garlicky. "But at least we've managed some good health along the way. How have you been feeling these days?"

"Honestly, not bad, apart from the usual aches and pains. The eyes aren't nearly what they used to be," said Leo, sipping his wine, savoring it as he'd learned from the videos he'd watched. He still wasn't a heavy drinker, often capping himself after one drink. "But I still feel I'm able to do a lot of what I've enjoyed. How about you? How are you doing? How is Sachin?"

Lynn fortified herself with a quick gulp of the Malbec.

"He has his good days, but sadly, they are fewer and fewer. The home health aide, Carla, has been amazing, a real godsend, but there are some tough realizations I'm trying to brace myself for. It's just been way harder than I ever expected."

"Sorry to hear that. Are you talking about maybe a long-term facility?"

"Seems that way. The medication has helped him prolong him staying with us, but a sort of tolerance builds up, and then the condition seems to get worse. And eventually, even Carla and I working together won't be able to care for him properly in the house," said Lynn, clearly saddened. "I mean, he's ninety-two; it's just tough to imagine how much more quality of life we can give him. So much of it now just revolves around keeping him comfortable and calm, managing his confusion where we can."

"Impossible situation you're in. Does Sachin still know who you are? Does he recognize people?"

"Sometimes. But oftentimes not, and it's hard to get used to. It's upsetting every single time."

"It must be an incredible weight to carry every day. Are *you* doing OK with it?"

"I take it one day at a time, grinding it out like my career on tour," said Lynn, looking blankly at the caramelized sprout on her fork, neglecting to eat it. "I try not to think of the totality of it all. I think that would just consume me. So, yeah, I'm as OK as I can be, just working through it in increments. It's all I really know how to do, it's . . ."

Lynn didn't know quite how to finish her thought, rambling a smidge, but Leo had a sense of what she was getting at and took a stab at summing it up.

"It's fucked," said Leo, never prone to cursing, but when the occasion called for it . . .

"Well said," replied Lynn, a volley of wan smiles between the two.

"And how is Olivia handling it?"

"The best she can, equally devastated, of course," said Lynn, eating some more, idly moving food around her plate some. "She talks about uprooting her whole family and moving them all back to Florida to be closer to us."

"Is that something you want?"

"Selfishly, yes, which is why I've asked her not to do it," said Lynn. "There's not much she can do for her father at this point, and she's built this wonderful life out in Oregon that I know she adores, and I don't want to see her forced out of it. So I absolutely encourage her to visit as often as she can but to hold off on a cross-country move."

Leo regarded his sister, who had once been very much beloved in the public eye—and as popular as she was, her heights would have been tenfold if the world truly understood how good and decent a person she was—more than just a skilled athlete and charming spokesperson and ambassador for the game, she was a kind and loving soul.

"You're a good mother, Lynn. I can't tell you how much I think about you guys during these tough times."

"Thank you, Leo. We'll get through it one way or another," said Lynn. "I will say, seeing this disease up close and personal, I thank God every day that Mom and Dad never had to experience it."

"That's occurred to me too," said Leo, then allowing a beat, the kitchen becoming quiet as they retreated into their meals, the faint din of the late-season insects rallying outside against the encroaching winter they were powerless to prevent, with only a few moves left in their playbook: mate or molt or burrow or die.

"And how have you been holding up?" asked Lynn cautiously. "I've been curious if you've given any thought to selling this place and buying something easier to manage."

Leo cleared his throat as though the enunciation of his words needed sprucing up.

"I probably should. I hardly need all this space anymore," said Leo, somewhat unconvincingly. "But to be honest, I'm not inclined to do it just yet. This is where Janet and I lived, raised the boys. I know every creak in this house, every inch of the land, and I just don't think I want to give that up."

"Understandable. But it's not too much for you then?"

"Not so much. I still get around fine, and the landscaper and snow guys take care of a bunch of stuff I'm not up to anymore," said Leo. "And anything else I can't maintain here, I've got a list of people willing to help out, so I'm pretty much covered."

"I was actually referring to you being alone here, on your own."

"Oh, that part," said Leo, resorting to more wine, more shrugging of his shoulders in a way that suggested he'd heard this question a lot, and whatever came out of his mouth next would be, at best, a half-truth. "The good memoires far outnumber the bad, so it's not like I'm in some haunted house or something. I guess I'm reminded of stuff every day, but I really think that's for the best. In a way, it keeps me from getting lonely. But I'm still out and about plenty, so I also don't feel cooped up here either."

It was then time for Lynn to regard her brother, who, despite not being an overly complicated man—an opinion of himself he shared—could be a more enigmatic thinker than he sometimes got credit for and was good at hiding his true feelings, which would necessitate those around him to probe and plumb deeper if they thought there was more to discovered.

"Olivia and I do worry about you, Leo," said Lynn. "But if you say you're doing good here . . ."

"I am, thanks. Plus, I can still get the boys out here for a good number of visits. And I got you out here for a few days, so I guess I'm doing something right," said Leo, amusing himself. "Heck, I even got Olivia for that overnight last year when she was heading home from visiting you. It was awfully sweet of her to put up with all that extra travel and hassle to visit her old uncle."

"She still talks about that visit. You're her favorite uncle."

"I'm her only uncle."

"Potato, po*tah*to," said Lynn, smiling, digging back into Leo's cooking, somewhat mollified by his response. "So tell me everything the boys have been up to."

Leo lit up, a proud parent, always excited to field questions about the kids.

"The boys—it's funny how I still call them that, even though they're in their forties," he said. "No one tells you they'll aways be those little eight-year-olds in your heart."

"Oh, people tell you. It's just impossible to imagine until you've actually lived through those decades caring about something so much more than yourself."

"That's probably right. Well, in any case, they're both doing great. Clay is living his high life in the big apple, working in those digital currencies that I'm not going to pretend I understand. I like to call them imaginary just to get his goat, then he'll explain to me again why they're very much real."

"It does look like they're here to stay, though I won't pretend I fully get it either," said Lynn. "But do you think he knows what he's doing? Does he know how to be careful with it?"

"He says he does, and it's been his specialty since finishing grad school," said Leo. "He has a good enough head on his shoulders. I think he knows how to watch out for himself, even if he can be a bit of a risk taker in his field. I won't lie and say it isn't a bit frustrating that I can't help him with that type of stuff, but it's out of my hands."

"I'm sure, but you're right. It's his work now, and I'm sure he knows what he's doing," said Lynn. "Is he seeing anyone special to him?"

"I think they're *all* special to him," said Leo coyly. "That's the part that seems to trip him up."

"Look at you. Proud of your ladies' man, aren't you?"

"Hey, I can't help it he pulled the high card from the genetic deck," said Leo. "Besides, doesn't that remind you of somebody?"

"Yes, yes, except I never played the field quite the way Clay has," said Lynn. "Do you think he'll ever settle down with someone?"

"Maybe, but he honestly seems to be having all the fun he can handle and isn't in a rush to give it up."

Lynn puts her hands up in mock surrender, a go-with-God gesture.

"To each their own. But I can tell you from my experience, the attention can be great and all, but after a while, it's not all it's cracked up to be."

Leo regarded his sister with blatant skepticism.

"What part of it gets boring after a while?" said Leo, needling Lynn as though they were teens again. "The looks, the athleticism, the charisma, the . . .?"

"Yes, I get it, charmed life. . . . Though it still stings I never got that Gap campaign," said Lynn, grinning, squirming a bit in the hot seat. "But you were still the one people looked to when something had to get done. You were the trustworthy one, steady hands on the wheel and all that."

"You make me sound like an old sea captain."

"You know what I mean. You were the bedrock that never broke, the salt that never ran out on this town."

"Salt. Rocks. Now I'm really flattered," said Leo, half pouting. "You'll notice I'm not being compared to anything particularly exciting."

"Again, you know what I mean," said Lynn, openly teasing her brother, the two enjoying the banter. "And besides, there's nothing dull about a sea captain. You could do a lot worse than commanding your own ship."

"Maybe in the 1700s."

"Exactly my point. You're a timeless kind of guy."

"OK, I guess I'll pull the compliment out of that and take it," said Leo. "More grog?"

"Aye."

Leo poured Lynn a fresh glass and topped his off, the warmth of the velvety liquid settling down in him nicely—his joints relaxed, his bones at ease. He returned his gaze to his sister, who was eying him with a renewed scrutiny. Something had occurred to her that she'd speak her mind on, clarify, even if it would mildly embarrass Leo, even if he didn't necessarily want to hear it. He needed to hear it.

"In all seriousness, Leo, you are not an un-special person. You're one of the most honorable people I know," said Lynn—of the two siblings, the one to whom emotions came easier. "God knows what you had to do those years ago. And I know you don't want to talk about it, but still, you are a hero beyond any shadow of a doubt."

Leo averted his eyes, looked into his wine, then caught a reflection of his own eyes in the dark, shimmering surface, so he averted them again, but from his own mirrored scrutiny. Sometimes he thought the world his own personal labyrinth to escape, vain as that may be, but also, maybe the truth for any soul who crawled from the primordial ooze, who claimed the planet as home.

That said, how did one define *escape*?

"I'm more than happy to deny it," said Leo, a grimace on his face.

"Case in point. I don't want to dredge it up," said Lynn, bordering on a loss for words, as though she might lose the moment. "But what you did—"

Leo put his hand up, gently but with that cop authority that can shut people down.

"What I did was so beyond the pale of recklessness, Lynn, particularly for an old man," said Leo, embarrassed by himself. "Even if I did guess right and got the needed outcome, I took far too great a risk with the lives of others."

"He went for that Desert Eagle first," said Lynn. "You risked your own life too."

"There is that," said Leo. "I'm surprised you remember the make of the gun."

"How could I forget? I wish I could forget. And the thing is, Leo, you didn't guess. You had real information; you had forty years of training and experience; you had intuition," said Lynn. "You knew something was off that night, and you trusted your instincts, and when the time came, you acted. You did what had to be done. You call it a needed outcome, but people are alive because of you."

Leo heard his sister out—hardly the first time he'd been regaled with that sentiment, but it always cut a little deeper when he heard it from someone he respected, someone he loved. A significant milestone in his life, so utterly conflated with his own confusion, his revisionist history of what he should and should not have done that night some years ago and how truthful he'd been about it.

A dark note chimed in Leo's head—familiar and unsettling—one that had always been difficult to explain to others.

"You have to understand, Lynn. I lived a quiet life. I wanted one, despite this violent profession I took on," said Leo. "And I'd made it so long, but it still came for me in the end. I still can hardly believe it, but it came for me."

"What did?"

"All I'd hoped would never find me," said Leo. "I was a fool to think I'd escape it."

Lynn didn't know what to say, how to comfort her brother and the demons he now carried, stowed away in a heart and mind prone to opaqueness, bulwarked in a way few had breached—maybe Janet, who'd shuffled off and could no longer save the day, relegating Leo to his fortress again.

"Mom and Dad would have been so damn proud of you," said Lynn, choking up a bit, trying anything. "I hope you know that."

"Ah, jeez, don't go bringing them into *that* conversation," said Leo, not unkindly. "It's already hard enough, and you're going to make me cry into the ravioli or something."

"Knowing you, you're probably long overdue for a cry," said Lynn, holding his gaze. "I'll bet it's been years and years since you allowed yourself a good one."

Leo dropped his head in a bashful way, like a dog unsure of a small inbound punishment, though it would be Lynn who offered up the apology.

"I'm sorry, Leo. That was stupid of me to say. I should have known that without asking," she said, her mind flashing on Janet's memory, then and now. "But just hear this old lady out for a minute. What I'm trying to tell you is we're all proud of the work you've done—those of us still here, those of us that are gone. And don't forget the influence you had on Bo to join the force, to follow in his father's footsteps."

Relieved to see a way to move the topic off himself, Leo perked up and enthusiastically dove into the realm of Bo's career in law enforcement, a sergeant now in the New Haven Police Department, only a county away from where Leo used to serve.

"Now that's something I don't mind taking some credit for, probably more than I deserve," said Leo, eating again, his appetite envigored. "I tell you, though, he's got it way harder than I ever did in sleepy old Orchard Coils. Working in a city, even a small one—totally different animal. But it sounds like he's got a bead on it. At least that's the word that makes it back to me."

"You're keeping tabs on him?"

"People like to keep me well informed," said Leo, with a hint of mischievousness.

"Must be weird knowing so much of the profession, being proud of his rank, but also knowing all the different ways to worry about him."

Instinctually, all but unconsciously, Leo felt for the scar on the back of his head from when he was shot at and fell to the ground in the line of duty—a tangible reminder of the job's inherent danger and the fact that culprit had never been found.

"We all worry. Whether they become a cop or a financier or a botanist, it's just what we do."

"Still. New Haven's not what it used to be, with Yale and the other universities in decline," said Lynn. "As far as I understand it."

"It's true. The downtown has seen better days. But it sounds like it's slowly coming back. There are some interesting revitalization projects and legit tax shelters in the works, maybe more jobs in the health-care field coming in," said Leo. "But, look, you're not wrong, and I do worry about him working in that city, fighting the good fight to restore her glory. That said, there have been so many technological advancements made in policing, even just how the job has transformed with what we ask of them—it's radically different from when I was a sergeant. Honestly, it wouldn't surprise me, another decade from now, if we don't even ask them to carry a sidearm anymore."

"Wouldn't that be something?" said Lynn cryptically, as though it could be interpreted as either good or bad. She drained the remainder of her glass on that note.

"You want some more wine, Lynn? Maybe some water?"

"How about both?"

"Sure thing. You always could knock them back, better than I ever could."

"Just like Mom could always outdrink, Dad, remember?"

"Of course. She loved to remind him of it."

Lynn glanced down at her plate, totally cleared, even the sauced sopped up with bread. She could barely fathom it once being full. The day had been long, and time was getting a little bendy.

"I guess I was way hungrier than I realized," said Lynn. "Or maybe you're just becoming a better cook than I've given you credit for."

"Well, I hope you saved some room for dessert."

"You made dessert?"

"It's not so much what I made as what I remembered to buy," said Leo. "A couple of pints of chocolate peanut butter gelato."

"Still a favorite of mine. That sounds great, Leo," said Lynn. "Why don't I help you clean up, and we'll eat some ice cream in the living room, maybe open a second bottle of wine?"

"Works for me, but you traveled all day, so let me soak this stuff in the sink and deal with it tomorrow. You take a load off on the couch," said Leo, already busying himself with the cleanup. "As for a second bottle, not too sure how much steam I have left in me for that, to be honest."

Lynn leveled her brother a disapproving look, somewhat in jest but girded with a certain challenge, a call to action.

"Come on, Leo. I know you're not the biggest drinker in the world, but you're going to want a little more if we're going reminisce about some of our favorite subjects into the night."

"Really? How are you not exhausted?" asked Leo, who'd always been amazed by his sister's motor, her furnace metabolism that still hadn't slowed. "I'd be passed out if I'd had your day."

"Just the way I'm wired," said Lynn proudly. "So are you in?"

Leo mock-deliberated for the benefit of his sister, both of them knowing full well he'd acquiesce. She was the guest of honor, after all, and Leo could be dutiful to a fault.

"OK, I'll have some more, and we can get nostalgic over Baxter and Ruth Sinclair until we nod off in our chairs."

Lynn clapped her hands in glee, as though she were fifty years younger, as though she was about to step into a time machine—because in a way, she was, and she was primed for it, had been looking forward to it for many months now.

* * *

Selected excerpts from the personal journal of Chief of Police Leo Sinclair, Orchard Coils Police Department (retired), dated May 2042, regarding case number H724-01: Open date of April 17, 1978, close date pending—Incident type: Death under Questionable Circumstances—Victim: Peter Sullivan of 1131 Howling Wind Road, Orchard Coils, CT 07215—Survived by wife, Mary Sullivan (now deceased); son, Chip Sullivan (now deceased)

On the night of Peter Sullivan's murder, Sophie Alba and Horace Wizner had waited in the mostly empty parking lot as member's cars presumably trickled out into the encroaching darkness. Daylight savings would have just taken hold, granting everyone that additional hour of sunlight, allowing for a little extra golf in that early part of the season. April was never the most hospitable month to play, typically reserved for the diehards (like me), those with spring fever, or just those desperate to get out of the house for their own unique reasons. (Sullivan probably borrowed from all three categories.) He was still driving his Cutlass Supreme that Sophie recognized immediately, a kind of steely-blue she associated with the ocean despite not being a fan of the beach (her words). She would recount that she hadn't a clue why Horace had insisted they drive by O Triple C that evening, to park adjacent to Sullivan's car and await in relative silence. She remembered being nervous, or at least growing nervous, while Horace seemed at ease, lost in his own thoughts.

He hadn't mentioned Sullivan to Sophie in months, and with Sophie not returning to the club for the 1978 season (she claimed she found a better paying job in Hartford, though I'm unsure that's the full story), she'd figured his passing interest in the man had run its course. When she tried to ask him what they were doing there, he remained taciturn, noncommittal, apart from a low grumble. When she pressed further, he grew agitated and told her they were just there to meet the man. When she pressed him as to why, he told her to shut up. She was accustomed to his flashes of temper, so she quickly relented, not wanting to egg him on any further. She'd noticed that after her line of questioning, he'd become jittery, fidgeting with his hands the way a child might, when only five minutes ago he'd been serene. He didn't want to talk. And he wasn't interested in going for one of those car rides he loved. He just kept scanning the parking lot, anxious, then edgy. It was a combination Sophie didn't like; she preferred it when they were driving, in motion, as though safer from the world (or maybe the other way around). Staking out that parking lot of her old place of employment felt odd to her at the very least. When the occasional member would come out to their car to leave, she'd obscure her face, shrink her body down, not wanting to be seen, recognized, not wanting to have to explain her presence in a dark parking lot. (She'd practiced lame excuses in her head in case the situation called for one.)

The evening dragged on, and there was no sign of Sullivan for a long time. Sophie was hoping against hope that somehow Sullivan wouldn't come out. Or he'd come out with his wife and son. Or slumped over the shoulders of the Restaurant's GM, who'd give him a lift home or deposit him in a cab he'd called. Anything would have been preferable to whatever confrontation Horace had in mind with this man he claimed not to be envious of (a claim Sophie would go on to maintain). Sadly, it didn't come as the biggest surprise to Sophie once there were only two cars left in the lot—theirs and the Cutlass—and sure enough, Sullivan eventually ambled out with his loose gait down the rickety stairs from the back patio and made his way past the pro shop toward his car. (The Restaurant staff all parked their cars in a makeshift lot on the other side of the building, completely out of sight.) He was still wearing his golf clothes, clearly having played before grabbing some dinner and drinks at the bar, which would have been recently opened for the season. He was spinning his keys around his fingers like a man without a care in the world, cocky, impressed with his own dexterity, impressed with how some things in his life fell his way, even if other things didn't. (Apparently this was an image and a narrative that stuck with Sophie her whole life.)

Even though Sophie had described Sullivan's appearance to Horace many times beforehand, and the man was clearly heading for the last car in the lot, Horace still asked her to confirm it was him. She distinctly recalled not answering him at first, maybe her lips moving but no sound coming out. When he asked again, she just nodded, as though that were less a betrayal than saying his name, as if it wasn't all Horace needed to go on. He told her to get out of the car. Then he followed her, exiting and putting himself a half-step behind her, closing the short distance to the Cutlass. Sophie would tell Chief Minshew that a very real part of her thought Horace might draw down on Sullivan right there in the parking lot or at least threaten him in some way, though she would also say she'd never seen Horace with a gun before. But it would seem Horace didn't have a pistol on him that night, probably no weapon on him to speak of. He told Sophie to call out to Sullivan; they were all nearing, and he wanted the man to know it was her. (Sullivan would have clocked their presence by then though, given how dark it was, might not have been sure what to make of it.) So she called out something to the effect of his name, more than once, a greeting that surprised the man enough that the car keys he'd been spinning so adroitly on his fingers sailed off and landed on the concrete. He uttered a loud obscenity at the mishap. Once the flash of surprise had passed and he'd oriented himself to the fact that some unknown woman near his car was flagging him down, he took a closer look to realize it was Sophia Alba, formerly of the Restaurant. (Presumably, the little guard he might have thrown up would have instantly come down, figuring he was among friends, even if he didn't know the fellow by Sophie's side.)

At that point, as Sophie would recall to Minshew, she still didn't know what she was meant to say to Sullivan, how to explain their presence in the dark parking lot on an increasingly chilly spring night. In the short term, it appeared Sullivan bypassed certain questions of logic and reasoning (certainly feasible), picked up his keys, and dove straight into his niceties of fond salutations, even giving Sophie a friendly hug, exclaiming that it was so great to see her, that she was missed at the Restaurant by everyone (though it was unlikely anyone had registered her absence). He also took it upon himself to extend his hand to Horace, to make the man's greeting. (Sophie would describe Sullivan's behavior as a whirlwind, which certainly fit when he got excited about that kind of socialization, particularly if he had a bit of alcohol in him.)

Sullivan then launched into a round of questioning as to why she hadn't come back for the new season, was everything OK, was she still reading, that no one had heard what happened to her. He said he was surprised she never reached back out to the GM or even him to explain her disappearance or even just to visit and chat a bit. Sophie would remember that was when Horace chimed in, abruptly, though also friendly, to confirm they were visiting now, that was their intent. Sophie, somewhat brushing aside Horace's remark, told Sullivan she'd been very happy with her years at the club, but a better opportunity had presented itself near Bushnell Park, though she did feel bad about resigning from the club in such a rushed way, without getting to say goodbye to everybody, Peter in particular. (This seemed to placate my godfather, per Sophie.)

Horace then jumped back in and told Sullivan there was another reason they were there that night—in part, for Sophie to see some people—and sure enough, she remembered his car, and they decided to hang around. (It pains me to think Sullivan didn't sniff this out, why Horace and Sophie wouldn't have just gone inside the Restaurant, but I don't know that he would have been interested in questioning any of it.) Horace was the one to then bring up the Quarry Witch stuff, tales he'd heard as a kid that had been retold to him by Sophie over the past few months. He'd also heard there was an overlook of sorts where you could kind of see down into those storied mines. (Horace would apparently point out that Sophie had never been there, despite her years at the club, baiting Sullivan, it seems to me.) She couldn't quite remember if it was Horace that specifically asked to see it or if Sullivan had made the suggestion. It was such a churn of conversation that even in the moment, Sophie wasn't sure how it got put together. (I would tend to believe Horace made the actual suggestion. After hours, escorted by an actual member of the club, he was more likely to put that out there as a request than Sullivan to make the suggestion.)

However it shook loose, Sullivan told them he'd be happy to take them down for a look, that it wasn't such a far walk, that they could catch up as they journeyed, that he was already dressed for it, (Sophie said he was amicable about it, like it was a small adventure, without signs of concern or worry as to the odd request. She said he just didn't seem to have the antenna to pick up that something was amiss.) Instead, it sounded like my uncle Peter was more concerned about them, about how they were dressed, and literally asked if they wouldn't be too cold for such a walk. Horace told him that if little kids could manage it on that Halloween Trail, then they'd be OK to manage for an hour or so. (It sounded like Horace had landed on a good tenor with Sullivan, some of that selective charm being put to good use.) Horace also retrieved from his car a sweatshirt for Sophie (practical, but I bet also performative) and a silver flask for him and Sullivan to share, maybe some kind of brandy, certainly something Sullivan would have been game for as he played tour guide that night, a little nip to keep the cold at bay.

To hear Sophie tell it (which, of course, I haven't yet, at least not in the flesh; this is all coming to me directly from Minshew, who's been very generous with his time and granted me access to all the written and digitally recorded versions of Sophie's confession, which I've been pouring over), my uncle Pete was actually having a good time taking Sophie and Horace down the cart paths, around the Monastery, and over the utility road, asking Sophie about her new job, where exactly it was, and maybe he could take Mary and Chip there some night. (It pains me I'll never be able to ask Mary or Chip if they remember Sophie at all from those seasons in the mid-to-late seventies) He asked her about her reading: Had she been keeping up on it—her self-education, as he called it—had she gotten into any good discussions or theories that he should know about, pay attention to? It basically sounded like two friends falling back into an old pattern, though apparently her responses were a little brief, stilted, and she didn't offer up the same elaboration or enthusiasm she had in those late-night sessions in the Restaurant over the years.

Sophie would tell Minshew she was hoping Sullivan would pick up that something was off about the night. She remembered being cold despite the additional sweatshirt, which she called ratty and cheap, and that her shoes weren't the best for walking the sloping hills of a concrete cart path. She would say it felt like a soldier's march that she wanted no part in, but she didn't really know how to make it stop, didn't really know exactly what was going to happen. (So she says.) Horace kept the conversation going over the gaps and lulls that Sophie (theoretically) tried to create, asking his own questions of Sullivan, stuff about work and family and golf and money, maybe just to keep the patter going but also because Horace loved asking people he'd just met these types of questions, always looking for some insight, squirreling proof of human nature away in his mind for later use (my theory). Sullivan answered these questions with good cheer and posed his own back to Horace, getting-to-know-you kind of stuff from the sounds of it. Sophie would tell Minshew that Horace was responding with outright lies, stuff she recognized right away but that Sullivan was either too trusting or too polite or just didn't care to push back on.

It kind of sounded like the two fellows were having a decent enough time, sharing the flask, huffing the evergreen air, which would have been very crisp. Sullivan went on to ask questions of Horace about his relationship with Sophie, how they met, all those types of things, which Horace seemed to answer in a friendly enough fashion. In time, the conversation shifted to the Halloween Trail, and Sullivan explained how all the lanterns would get set up, the staff hiding in the woods making extra creepy noises, the parents getting blitzed up in the clubhouse (spooky punch!), the ghost stories, his own son, Chip, walking the trail less than a decade before.

Horace specifically asked Sullivan if he'd ever actually seen the Quarry Witch, half joking from the sounds of it. Apparently, my godfather said he had seen her once, then moved past the topic. (Not sure why he would have said that.)

The whole time all this back and forth was carrying on between Sullivan and Horace, Sophie would recount to Minshew that she was screwing up the courage to do something or at least to just stop, to walk right back to the parking lot. She didn't need anyone's permission, and if she'd just done that, with no explanation, then surely Horace and Sullivan would have had to follow her back, even if she was wordless. She could have just removed them all from whatever it was they were getting deeper into. (Honestly, she could have faked an injury, an illness, screamed in Horace's face that she wanted to go home, fucking anything to disrupt what she knew to be a bad situation.) She swore to Minshew that she wanted to, even if she truly didn't understand the depths of Horace's aim, what he was intending to do. She said he'd never laid a finger on her, that he was more of a wannabe, a punching bag that returned to their apartment beat up and cash heavy for the effort. It hardly seemed like he was out there killing people. She swore up and down that if she'd known how dark his true intentions were, she never would have led Sullivan out there, never in a million years. Or ever even brought up his name to Horace in the first place (a mistake she would cop to in hindsight). She and my uncle Pete were friends, and she didn't want to see him harmed in anyway, let alone killed. But as Sophie confessed all this to Minshew, much to her alleged shame, she still never said anything, never did anything to alter the outcome. Too much fear. Too much love. Too much denial, disbelief. She just allowed them all to carry on to that green on the seventh hole, a spot Sullivan had been hundreds of times, probably over a thousand, a place where he just wouldn't have had any fear, not even at night, certainly not with people he was having a ball with, and not with that liquid courage coursing through him.

Eventually, they arrived at the seventh hole, really not taking all that long to get there. Sullivan toured them around the perimeter of the pin, orienting them like guests, walking around the green as though assessing a difficult putt. (Sophie would liken him to a proud parent in a weird way.) He didn't draw out the showman act as it was getting colder, maybe had even been feeling it himself, and went about showing them the five-foot fencing with wooden slats that served as a barrier to the precipice below (not that anyone could miss it, even in the dark). The whole thing really was a geological oddity, the way the rock abutted the golf course, though really, it was the golf course that was built into the cradle of these ancient craters. Sullivan apparently told Sophie and Horace that the occasional approach shot was bound to plummet down the precipice or take some bad carrom out of play. (There was a designated drop zone for this, actually.) As far as deterrents went, the fencing was adequate, a stark enough warning for sure but also mildly decorative, certainly a conversation piece when bringing guests. (No golfer had ever died from falling off it—why would they?—and I've researched this extensively.) It was plain enough to see you needed to mind your footing in the area, stay off the fence—there was some small signage to the effect—but really, it was incumbent upon the players to not put themselves in harm's way by scaling a large fence and falling off a steep cliff (not unreasonable). This wasn't to say people didn't climb the low rungs and peek over, or try to. Countless people had (I had), but there was a difference between a safe lark like and taking it too far, which I suppose some people probably have, but to my knowledge, they've always reined it back before something catastrophic happened.

Sullivan proceeded to usher Sophie and Horace right up to the fence in question, cautioning them to secure their footing, to not lean up against the rail too much. (Sophie remembered him being none too concerned, delivering the warning in a rote way.) He went on to talk some more about the Quarry Witch lore, the cruelty of Arnold Holm, and the old ways of the mining industry, the whole time swapping swigs from the flask with Horace, holding court as he liked to. He went on about how being up the fence made him feel small, how looking down that cliff had a way of humbling men. He told them about the trinkets and tokens that were occasionally left up there by the looky-loos, often to be picked up by the members or discarded by the grounds crew. (This would have been back under the eldest Jocko Whalley's tenure, and I'm betting my uncle hadn't known the full extent of all that was left up there, the fact that it was being collected into the Museum, and certainly what his own role would be in the decades to follow, once the Devil's Altar stuff was crafted.)

Apparently, Horace asked Sullivan if he'd ever recovered one of these offerings that was supposedly left as tribute for the witch, if he'd dared keep something for himself. He said he'd once found some tin-pressed coins, worthless, but he kept them all the same, probably in his attic somewhere. (I can only imagine what happened to them once the estate was sold off.) Then Horace said something to the effect that maybe they should leave something up there, like a joke or something but also kind of serious, as Sophie would attest to. They were all loitering around the fence, occasionally climbing a rung and peering over, which does require some effort and doesn't really allow for much of a view. Horace started going on about it not being right to visit and neglect a tribute to all the legends. That was when Sophie finally spoke up a bit, not having said much in a while, finally suggesting maybe it was time for the three of them to leave, that they'd seen what they wanted to see. So she might finally have spoken the words, though who knew with how much conviction, but the men had been off in their own conversation, musing over why people gravitated toward this site. She tried again (per Minshew, questioning her veracity) but was met with a quick death stare from Horace while Sullivan wasn't looking, intimating that she should pipe down.

The way she described it to Minshew was that what happened next was very quick, so much so that she could still hardly believe it sixty years later. Horace proceeded to look down the ravine, just his head over the top of the fence, and started acting as though he could see something. Sullivan started to do the same, curious as to what might have caught the man's eye, despite the utter darkness that really made it impossible to discern anything down there. Horace then quickly hopped off the fence, took a few strides over to Sullivan. Sophie instinctively backed away (vocal cords frozen in horror, she'd say) and watched Horace grab at Sullivan's thighs and upend him over the fence he was looking over. Just like that. No preamble. No threats or speeches or pithy final words. No words at all, in fact. Just Horace executing on his plan, determined to kill a man for no reason, never that interested in making a production of it (though I guess he would start to fancy it as a tribute to the Quarry Witch, something he thought might also have value in ways I don't understand). The whole thing only took a few seconds, and Sophie would remember Sullivan's horrible screams as he plummeted down the ravine, far enough that they couldn't even hear the body land. She would say something to the effect that even his screams sounded lonely (fuck her). And that was that. He was gone forever. (How do I reconcile myself with this, if it's true?)

Sophie would tell Minshew, after her big confession, that she looked at Horace, whose breathing had become noticeably labored, and wondered if she was next to get tossed off the cliff, but all Horace did was dust himself down, remove a splinter from his hand, and take Sophie's hand, telling her it was time to go. She said he was relatively cool about it. So they left, not hanging around the crime scene, using the cart path and utility road to get back into the lot, empty but for the two cars. Horace produced Sullivan's keys (he'd lifted them from his windbreaker easily enough at some point back on the green, maybe even on the walk up) and started up the Cutlass. He gave Sophie his keys and told her to meet him back at the apartment, not to stop for anything, to get home, not to pick up the phone, and to wait for him. She would go on to tell Minshew that she felt catatonic, fearful of what Horace might do if she said anything, if she disobeyed even the smallest of commands. He asked her if she could get home safely, could she keep the car straight, not speed, not draw attention to herself. She recalled she must have nodded in the affirmative. Horace gave her a quick hug, told her it would be OK, it was almost over, she was doing great, stuff to that effect. He told her he was going to get rid of the car. (Which probably meant a chop shop or, more likely, he'd already scouted out some remote lake to drown the thing in, probably far away from Orchard Coils, stuff you could get away with easily enough back in the seventies, even walking or hitchhiking back to their apartment.)

The way it shook out, if Sophie's version is to be believed, at its core, all it took was the two guilty parties keeping their mouths shut and not ratting each other out. And from 1978 to 2042, all that time, it appeared that secret hadn't cracked. Even now, writing this all down, I can hardly believe after sixty years, the truth may be finally coming out, that I might actually live long enough to see some kind of resolution to this case. There's going to be more to follow for sure. This has only been breaking for the past month or so. To be honest, it's kind of a miracle, and I'm grateful for it, provided it's true. It seems true (or maybe I just want it to be true in a certain sense). I hope I'm ready for it, I've certainly waited long enough, almost as if I've been allowed to stay alive just to see it. I don't know. I'm going to lie down. I'm feeling lightheaded if I'm being honest . . .

* * *

Late that night, Leo and Lynn were well into the second bottle of wine, the ice cream devoured, the dishes stacked up in the sink as a chore set aside for the next day. They were in Leo's living room, relaxing on the big couch, loose from the food and alcohol, almost giddy with some of the belly laughs they'd shared. As Lynn had suggested, they'd been swapping stories and memories of their parents, gone now for so many decades but still very much alive in their minds, alive in the actions of their own children—the legacy the stood on blood and tradition, lines of tensile strength not easily broken.

Lynn harkened back to conversations she'd had with Ruth when she was at Tulane, shortly before graduation when she was head over heels for Sachin, but the age difference, his position as her coach, the fallout that could cause some scandal had all muddied the waters. She remembered all those talks with her mom, heated at times, about love and perception, about the nature of men and the power she was bound to have over them and how the right one could reverse that polarity on her. The whole time, Ruth never really told her daughter what to do: never laid down the law, a demand, an ultimatum, barely used her influence to steer Lynn one way or the other around the Sachin conundrum. Ruth wanted the world for Lynn, wanted her to find happiness, and thought her beautiful and talented daughter had the chops to do just that. But she didn't want to dictate what that happiness should be, to strip her of that agency, to pretend she existed in another's mind, even a child sprung from her own body. It was Lynn's life to live, to mess up—her wins to celebrate, her mistakes to learn from, her despair to climb out from.

In retrospect, Lynn would tell Leo that night, reminiscing, given how high the stakes were back then, it really was a supreme act of selflessness on Ruth's part to remain neutral, a sign of trust in her daughter to decide on the situation as the young adult she was. Sure, Ruth had expressed some misgivings about Sachin at the time. She and Baxter hardly knew him and were concerned for the obvious reasons. But Lynn had nothing but glowing things to say of the man during their courtship, as their relationship found steadier footing, particularly once she graduated. Ruth was smart and shrewd; she could see what he meant to Lynn, knew that the heart wanted what it wanted. Logic need not apply.

In time, and with a bit more effort convincing Baxter, Sachin was accepted into the family, and certainly once Lynn's career had taken off and Olivia was born, the truth expressed itself in a way that was undeniable—the two *were* meant for each other. Lynn told Leo that her world might not have come together is such a blessed way if not for the independence of their mother, a trait she now better recognized with the benefit of her own age, that she could barely see back when she was twenty-two, but now she hoped she possessed just of fraction of Ruth's spirit when it came to nurturing her own relationship with Olivia and the people she'd chosen to be in her life.

Leo could remember a time, only a couple of months after he'd been fired upon that cold January night in the industrial park, when Baxter had shown up unannounced at his apartment: no phone call, nothing in hand, no flimsy excuse to warrant a visit except a rush of compulsion to see his boy, to give him a hug a young child might demand of a parent, to never let go—somewhat out of character for Baxter, who wasn't a cold man but kept his emotions a bit closer to the vest. Imagine Leo's surprise when his father embraced him, and the man let out a few tears, coughing into his adult kid's shoulder, terrified at the realization of what a bullet two inches to the left would have meant—a ticket almost punched, a life snuffed out too soon. Of course, Leo had already covered much of that territory with his mother, someone who was far less likely to suppress her feelings, who flew into an outrage at what the world had tried to do to her son. But to see such an outburst from his dad, as though a delayed fuse had kicked in, was jarring, if not immensely heartfelt. He more than knew the old man loved him, but there was something in the encounter that made it more visceral, less a concept and more a tangible thing you'd die to protect, kill to preserve.

Baxter would clean out his eyes and his throat and shake Leo in a burly way by his shoulders, then hung around and drank light beers with the kid, sharing some of his wartime exploits in Italy—snippets he'd never mentioned before, that he now felt Leo had more than earned the right to hear, a fellow combatant now, a survivor and protector and a man who, despite almost getting his card pulled, was already eager to lace his boots back up and return to work as soon as he could.

Baxter told Leo how proud he was of that fact, but under no circumstances was he to ever get shot at in the line of duty ever again—not even so much as stub his toe serving the community. Leo took his father's sentimentality in stride, knew what the elder was getting at, and promised he'd never land in harm's way again—a promise both of them knew he couldn't make good on but a promise that felt holy in the moment, and, miraculously enough, Leo did mostly deliver on it over the course of a fifty-year career, ironically enough encountering one final brush with death not so long after his retirement, where the crown of hero had been rightly or wrongly placed atop his head.

They drank beers and traded war stories into the night, like brothers in arms. Seared into Leo's mind was this validation from the most noble and bravest man he'd ever known, who would fall asleep on Leo's couch that night, a phone call placed to Ruth to apprise her that all was well, all was right with the world, and she would see her son and husband in the morning.

When Baxter passed many years later, Leo would take possession of his father's Purple Heart—the recognition he'd received for peeling his skin and spilling his blood overseas during what some would call the last great war—and it would rest for decades on his bedside table, encased and polished and dusted without fail or disregard.

The tenor of that conversation went on between Leo and Lynn for two straight hours—Lynn shedding the occasional tear, Leo grinding his molars to paste when the emotion flared up. Then the two of them would laugh like teenagers over the more humorous tales, the silly stories and holiday debacles, of which there were many to reminisce about. Eventually, the conversation meandered from their parents to Peter Sullivan, as it was bound to, given all that Leo had learned of the case as it had progressed over the past five months. Of course, Leo had kept Lynn in the loop over that time, but this was the first real chance they'd had to speak to it in person, where it was bound to feel realer for Lynn, being in her brother's presence and seeing what his face looked like, how his features would further tell the story of something she'd thought would never find resolution. She'd been eager to discuss it, but she also knew to be choosey about the time and place.

"Is it too late for me to ask about the case? Should we wait until tomorrow?" she said, shifting her tone a bit. "I don't want to ruin the mood or anything."

"No, I figured you'd want to know. Wasn't sure if you were too tired to get into it."

"I'm wide awake. Let me have it. Are they going to prosecute this Sophie Alba for her role with what happened?"

"I'm not totally sure. They've kind of remanded her to the state, not that she's much of a flight risk, seeing as she's wheelchair bound and on dialysis," said Leo, his jaw set in a way it hadn't been previously throughout the night, as though it were preparing for a blow. "I guess she lives with her son, his wife, and their adult kid, her grandson."

"The one she's trying to keep out of the federal prison?"

"No, that's a different grandson."

"And how old did you say this woman was now?"

"Eighty-eight, soon to be eighty-nine."

"And this is what her life has become, at such an age?" said Lynn, with a mild disgust. "Does everyone truly believe she's never uttered a word of this story for all these years?"

"It's looking that way. And the folks in Arizona investigating her claims seem pretty convinced she's telling the truth, at least with what they're able to corroborate."

"Jeez, imagine carrying something like that around with you for so long, a lifetime, really."

Leo had more than pondered the notion but was equally curious about his sister's take on the situation, was in need of an alternate perspective, one he could trust, that he could place some real stock in.

"You feel sorry for her?" asked Leo.

"Not sure I'd put it that way," said Lynn, searching her own thoughts, feelings. "But I want to keep an open mind until I have all the available information."

"There actually hasn't been much new in the past few weeks," said Leo. "One of the reasons I think they might be close to a decision whether to indict or not."

"What charges do you think they'd go with, if they decided to proceed?"

"Could be anything. Conspiracy, obstruction, willing accomplice—plenty of things they could take their pick from."

"But getting convicted on even just one felony charge would probably be a death sentence for her, right?"

"In the sense that she'd die in prison, probably so, which may be exactly what she deserves," said Leo, testing the words out in the open air, gauging how much he believed them. "I do think they're struggling on this one, the optics in particular. The justice machine has leaned in to far more compassion over the recent decades, rightly or wrongly, particularly anytime narcotics plays a role, given the fallout from decriminalization in the past decade, the unintended consequences, and I think they're running up against that."

"And the considerations for showing her this mercy are somewhat obvious?"

"Yeah, her age and health are on the forefront. Plus, she did technically turn herself in, brought closure to a somewhat notorious cold case in the state."

"Though from the sounds of it, she didn't turn herself in for purely altruistic reasons. She has an addict grandkid who struck out enough times to finally face some serious jail time," said Lynn. "So, in some last-ditch effort, she barters this secret to keep him from facing decades in prison."

"You're not wrong, and that point certainly hasn't been lost on us," said Leo. "She's been asked point blank that if she didn't need this bargaining chip for her grandson, would she have ever confessed to what happened to Peter that night."

"And what did she say?"

"She said she was convinced she'd have taken the secret to her grave," said Leo. "That she'd never have write it down or speak to it, and that would have suited her just fine."

The room took a beat. Its occupants took some wine.

"What a piece of work," said Lynn, shaking her head. "Though not uninteresting she'd be so candid on the point."

"Lucid. Honest. A battle-ax," said Leo, agreeing. "Just a few of the terms the boys in Arizona have used to describe her."

"Doesn't seem like admitting you were willing to die with that secret would help your case."

"It probably doesn't, but I don't think that's what she cares about. What's important to her is that she has this chance to help her family out, to be useful in an important way. My guess would be, given her health, she hasn't felt useful in quite some time," said Leo. "Apparently, she only got a lawyer to make sure that DA doesn't screw over her grandson. It actually doesn't sound like she's even prepared much of a defense yet if it goes to trial."

"Could that be some type of ploy?"

"In theory, but so far, she's been honest about everything else," said Leo. "They tend to believe she truly doesn't care what happens to herself at this point, almost like once this mission is over, she'll have had enough."

Lynn took a moment to consider that, to contemplate this woman who, by all accounts, she should despise. Which she does; no amount of spin would change the core of the issue. But with that said, to hear that there was nothing left for her to care about in her own existence, apart from some broken family, that a prison death would suffice—well, on a human level, Lynn could see the sadness in that, even for a woman she had little empathy for, a woman who had contributed greatly to the pain and misery of the Sinclairs, let alone what she'd done to the Sullivans.

In truth, the thought of Sophie Alba out there in the world, infirm and wheeling around, chilled Lynn's blood—particularly how she'd lived decades with the power to illuminate this terrible secret without fear of retribution from the lunatic she used to run with, and yet she never stepped up and took responsibility, even anonymously. She eschewed all opportunities in a way Lynn considered unforgivable.

"What else has she said about Horace Wizner?" asked Lynn.

"What hasn't she said? He's her favorite topic," said Leo. "The man she both loved and feared. They have hours of her talking about him, just about that one night alone."

"What did she say about him?"

"That he became scary, particularly when the realization of what he'd done had sunk in, for the both of them," said Leo. "When it occurred to her that she was a witness, the lone witness, things obviously changed for the rest of her life."

"She actually said she was afraid Horace might try to kill her?"

"Not in so many words. Horace never threatened her directly, but he had his subtle and dark ways of reinforcing the notion they were in it together," said Leo. "That even if it was a line she hadn't wanted to cross, they were beyond it now, no going back."

"Yeah, but who's to say she didn't want to cross it?" said Lynn, following her train of thought. "Who's to say Sophie wasn't behind all this? Or that she knew exactly what would happen and wanted it for some reason she's not disclosing?"

Leo knew what his sister was getting at, knew she wasn't wrong in her skepticism—it was well placed and more than warranted, and that's where the case had its thorniest issues.

"I understand. But I've listened to all the recordings, multiple times, and I just don't get a sense that she had any real cause to harm Uncle Pete," said Leo. "I think she would have been happy working crappy jobs and reading books and driving around with that scumbag until she grew out of it or didn't, whichever came first."

"Hardy the way it worked out."

"The woman lived her whole life never getting in trouble with the law," said Leo. "Not so much as a parking ticket. That tells me something—a few things actually."

"And what exactly happened with Wizner?"

"He got what he wanted. After he killed Peter, it pumped him up. He started taking on bigger risks, bigger scores," said Leo. "He worked with heavier people and was willing to do heavier things."

"But it didn't last too long," said Lynn. "He died in the mid-eighties?"

"December twelfth, 1984. Shot twice in the head and left for anyone to see atop a snowbank in Woonsocket, Rhode Island," said Leo, sans emotion, facts now ingrained into his memory. "Not that anyone saw anything—just another unsolved case no one cared to solve."

"So no one has any clue what really happened?"

"Well, somebody does, or did. But criminal gangland activity was always assumed, a message of sorts; otherwise his body would never have been found," said Leo. "Honestly, speaking with some of the Rhode Island people that are still around, not so many given the years, but it sounded like not a whole hell of a lot of effort was put into finding Horace Wizner's murderer."

"So one unsolved case now clearly linked to another?"

"That's how it goes sometimes. When there's absolutely nothing left for law enforcement to do, no trees to shake, no rocks to turn over, all that's left is the slow passage of time," said Leo. "Not the most awe-inspiring method, but believe me when I tell you, it has its place."

"And he was, what, thirty-three when killed?"

"Yep, survived by his common-law wife, Sophie Alba, and their two young children, Susan, age five and Peter, age two."

"He really named his son Peter?"

"He sure did. Sophie told the Arizona boys he'd insisted on it, as if he liked the ring of it or something."

"Fucking nutcase."

"Indeed," agreed Leo. "And a not-so-subtle reminder, a daily one, about the man she loved, the man warning her to stay loyal to him, even after they scraped his body off the snowdrifts near a boarded-up Ocean State Job Lot."

"And it was Peter's son, Sophie's grandson, whose troubles prompted her to come forward?" asked Lynn, to which Leo nodded his head. "Jeez, it's like the ghost of Horace Wizner coming back for them."

"Not just them. Sounds like he'd hurt a lot of people after what he did to Uncle Pete, like he developed a real taste for it," said Leo. "Almost a surprise he made it to thirty-three, given the enemies he'd made."

"Thirty-three's too long if you ask me."

Leo agreed silently with his sister and took a beat, letting those facts of the case, what they'd learned in the past months, wash over them. Decades of uncertainty now being cleared up, in a speedy-enough, fashion given how long they'd waited, considering all the questions that lingered—all from a single source out of the blue, with her conflicted motivations and the unreliable nature of memory, let alone the prerogative of one speaking with almost ninety years of history on this planet. It would be enough to confound any man, let alone one so close to the victim.

"So what do you think, little sis?" asked Leo, rubbing at his eyes. "After hearing all this, do you think it's in the state's best interest to haul her back to Connecticut and put her on trial?"

Lynn massaged her knees as though she were planning a great escape, when really, they were just barking at the long day, even if she had been off her feet for hours—*Getting old isn't for the faint of heart*, she thought.

"I suppose it is more complicated than I realized," she said. "But ultimately, yeah, I think you have to, though maybe a plea deal is more likely than a trial, right?"

"And we do this for some type of justice for Peter Sullivan?"

"I don't know there's any justice left to gain in a story this old," said Lynn. "It's the rule of law that's worth standing up for—still one of the best things this country's been able to hold on to, mostly."

Leo considered his sister's position.

"It's not a bad take."

Lynn cocked an eyebrow, dipped her head.

"But one you don't agree with?"

"Partially. Yes, it's an old case, so many of the people are gone. Peter and Horace, obviously. But with Mary and Chip also gone, no grandchildren, one could argue there's no one left to appease," said Leo. "But the folks in Arizona are keen for me to weigh in, being Peter's godson, his closest earthly connection to the life he once had. They want to see if I'll endorse a prosecution against Sophie. Given all my background, that might ease some of those optics and doubts that have got them jammed up."

Lynn sat up ramrod straight for that disclosure, brow furrowed and worried.

"That hardly seems fair, Leo," she said, some outrage in her voice. "To put that burden on you because they're unsure what to do. Why don't you tell them to make up their own damn minds on it and leave you out of it?"

Leo paused for effect unintentionally.

"Unless," he said.

"Unless what?"

"Unless I do want to weigh in on Sophie Alba's future."

"Well, if that's true, Leo, and you want to factor in," said Lynn, a mixture of concern and incredulity in her voice, "what exactly would you recommend to them?"

And therein lay the million-dollar question, what the past five months had been leading to—forces on both sides of the debate, two states of the union, all jockeying to figure out what to do about this woman and her eleventh-hour confession—a treasure for some, a quagmire for others. There would be no kicking the can down the road on this one, no passing of the baton—Sophie already had too much visibility to sweep her under some rug, and Leo had been asked by the powers that be on both coasts to levy a verdict, multiple times in fact, and now he struggled to turn them away, despite believing they might not even heed his advice. But Leo couldn't ignore the responsibility he felt, that had been set upon him—a part of Sophie's fate had been placed in his judgment, and he'd be lying if he said there wasn't an impulse for revenge, as delayed and abstract as it might be. But there was also a call for something grander, perhaps a small stroke of the grace the world could always use, that was in short supply. But was it warranted? That was the trial Leo felt like the defendant of.

There were things Lynn needed to know about before he could fully answer her question. He needed her to understand his frailty as a man; he was hardly the rock she imagined him to be.

There was more to the story he needed his sister to know.

"Lynn, there was a woman once that wronged me in such a way I could barely see straight," said Leo, calmly, slowly shedding his reserve. "Or, at least, I believed for a very long time she'd wronged me and stolen something of great importance."

Lynn felt a gear change in the room, imperceptibly braced herself against the torrent that might come.

"Who?" she asked.

"Samantha Morris."

"Do I know her? The name sounds kind of familiar."

"My first girlfriend. You knew her a bit before you went off to Tulane."

Lynn took a pause, reaching into her memoires, quickly enough pulling up the name, the face, the time period—nothing she'd thought of in decades.

"That's right, I do remember her. I liked her. What did she take from you?"

"It's honestly too much to get into tonight, but I promise we'll talk about it tomorrow," said Leo. "But the point I want to make now is that I was slow to forgive her, the situation, my own bullshit, whatever you want to call it. And then she died unexpectedly, and it cut short any real chance we had at a reconciliation."

"I'm sorry, Leo. I didn't know any of this."

"No one did, only Janet. She was helping me through it," said Leo. "But now they're all gone, and you'll only be the second person I ever tell this story to, probably the last person that will ever hear it."

"I want to hear it, Leo, of course," said Lynn. "But how exactly does Samantha Morris relate to the police asking you what should be done with Sophie Alba?"

"In a word, forgiveness. It comes down to an exercise in faith, in clemency," said Leo. "And I don't know if it's in me, and I know I can't make up for past mistakes, but maybe I've learned enough to prevent a future one from happening."

"Like sending Sophie to die in prison."

He nodded.

"I just don't know what to do."

Lynn stretched her body out and shook off some of the wine fuzz that had been nipping at her consciousness. It had been an exceedingly long day for her and a particularly eventful night of conversation with her brother, one she would not forget anytime soon, if ever.

"Well, jeez, Leo, it's been a night," said Lynn, no longer able to suppress the yawns. "Hopefully, we'll also have some lighter things to tackle over the next few days."

"We will indeed. I'm looking forward to taking you to the club tomorrow. A lot of people still ask about you there," said Leo. "To this day, they still talk about those charity tournaments you ran all those years."

"I miss those. I always did enjoy coming back for them," said Lynn. "It also meant that the four of us were bound to be together again for the weekend."

"That it did. There's a few new things around town worth checking out, even around the county," said Leo. "A few new memories for us to create together—that is, if you're up for it?"

A wry smile from Leo, a knowing look returned by Lynn—still two kids, siblings, thick as thieves, and no amount of time was ever going to change that.

"I can't wait," she said.

* * *

A transcribed excerpt from PulseStream, an audio publication of the *Orchard Coils Courier*, released on April 7, 2043.

The town of Orchard Coils is pleased to announce the commemoration and celebration of the 150th anniversary of the Orchard Coils Quarry's closing, an inaugural event, to take place later in the year. First Selectman Cornwall has had this to offer thus far: "We are more than overdue to embrace the fanciful and thematic lore of our town, to partner with our varying institutions and invite others from around the state to share in some good old-fashioned spooky fun. I hope this will be the first step in furthering Orchard Coil's presence along the autumn trail of the Northeast while also educating those visitors on our town's rich history. . . . Preliminary plans are for a long weekend of festivities to be mapped out over the next six months."

The measure was all but unanimously passed by the town council by a vote of six in favor, one opposed. The lone dissenter was a former . . .

2050

Even if the years had been more than kind to Leo Sinclair, at ninety-three years old, he understood there were real physical limitations that his life would be pinned against, hemmed into. He didn't begrudge this for a multitude of reasons—the first being the soundness of his mind, still lucid and sharp and an absolute blessing that curtailed any complaints of other bodily deterioration. It was something he saw firsthand, as many do, when the mind of his brother-in-law Sachin Moore finally went—a brutally unfair condition to observe, even if that person was in the twilight of their existence.

Sachin would pass on not knowing who he was, who anyone was, even when he was surrounded by those who loved him.

Leo knew he'd gotten a good roll of the dice and wasn't about to waste his time or good fortune complaining about physical ailments beyond his control. There were still too many things he was grateful for at his advanced age: he could still drive, though no longer at night; he could still golf, though only nine holes and always with a cart. He'd been hitting the ball from the gold tees for two decades now and no longer felt glum about it, acknowledging he hadn't the strength to use his driver effectively—which was kind of the point of the golden tee box, to show some respect for the old-timers, to allow them a way to stay in the mix. Still. Leo would watch the younger players, men and women, spry and flexible, lacing shots from the tips, and it was impossible for him to see that ball zip away and not wonder where his life had gone, when the muscle had atrophied, and the joints become brittle, and simply standing upright without shooting pain qualified as a good morning. He never thought he'd have to reminisce about swinging the big dog with ease and fluidity, but there he was, and so it went.

He had moved along to concentrate on all the things he still could pull off, like practicing his chips and wedges and putts, still trying to drop that ball into that ghastly one-foot-circumference cup they'd refused to change back. Leo, like so many men and women on the wrong side of mounting years, had become a short-game assassin—his arena everything within a hundred yards of the pin—and he continued to practice because his body allowed it, because he was still enamored of the game, the puzzle of it.

As for whether that controversial rule change from two decades before had created an uplift in the sport, the consensus on that was, at best, a mixed bag. Some argued it was a resounding success, drawing in a new crop of enthusiasts to the game. Others pointed to the Saudis who had pumped competitive juice and unseemly money into the sport—a bribe toward legitimacy in the view of many—forcing the coalition of new and legacy leagues into a more unified global sport, not unlike how soccer had gone about dominating the landscape without necessarily being heralded in the United States. And still others pointed toward naturalism in the growing offshoot of young people willing to put down their Pulse products and actually do outdoors stuff, of both a challenging and a recreational nature. It was a movement unlikely to eclipse the expanding digital and AR options that propped up the zeitgeist, but there were enough contrarians in the fledgling generations willing to eschew some of these sedentary activities and bio-porting enhancements who actually found their way back to the golf courses, the demise of which had been falsely reported over and over again. Even if its heyday was behind it, the sport was alive and kicking and doing well enough—choose whatever reason you might prefer or choose some combination, which was usually the closest thing to the truth.

By that point, it didn't matter a whole heck of a lot to Leo if he'd been right or wrong about how golf would survive into the future. He was simply glad that it had, that the Orchard Coils Country Club was still viable, still a hub in the town he grew up in, which he loved. The old institution had not buckled, had not folded—old and young alike had found a place there. It still continued to squeak out a modest profit, those owners still content to remain hands off and hidden by a cloak of LLCs and C-suite officers. There was even a fellow at O Triple C by the name of Paul Spruce, one year Leo's senior, who'd joined a few years back, a transplant from Miami during his younger days—his eighties—who now took great pleasure in calling Leo "kid" when their paths crossed, as they occasionally did when Paul made his infrequent trips to the course. While most of their glory days were behind them now, there was still a comradery and commiseration to be shared at the club, at the Restaurant—where, Leo would selfishly admit, he felt like a minor celebrity for a variety of reasons that had transpired in his life. He was afforded an emeritus status and couldn't remember the last time he had to purchase his own drink—not that he could drink much alcohol anymore, absolutely one wine or light beer to sip on at the most, another facet of aging he'd been forced to accept.

He enjoyed that glimmer of reverence at the club and played into it more than his younger self ever would have—ironic that a golfer who never really improved past a bogey level should be afforded such status at a golf club. Stranger things had happened, he supposed, and it would be unwise to reject the affirmation, even if he wished it had more to do with being a scratch player or a former club champion, of which he was neither.

He was actually at the Restaurant for the "eagle heard around the world" shot—everyone's eyes glued to the TVs, his included.

Even given his acceptance of certain physical limitations, there was still one trek Leo wanted to pursue but would not be able to perform on his own. He wanted to visit the old quarry where his uncle Pete's body had been found so long ago. It had been decades since he'd gone down there, back to the excursions of his youth, when he was tasked with policing the area where he would contemplate the case in hopes of solving it on his own. Leo had once thought—as all cops think—that communing with the murder site might lead to some epiphany around what would be one of Connecticut's longer-standing and grisly cold cases.

Until it was solved, mostly, certainly on paper.

And all Leo's puttering around that mine in his twenties and thirties had done little toward a revelation or breakthrough—it was only Sophie Alba coming forward from across the country that had closed the books on the Sullivan case, in a rather convincing and resolute fashion, or so the powers that be declared.

Despite all that, Leo always felt he'd gained something from those years of sojourning down into the quarry, back when his knees were less hinky, and he was still decades away from the inner-ear degradation that would interfere with his balance up and down the large slopes, with a little persistent ringing, just to add some insult to injury. Back when he was down in the quarry, he felt closer to Peter Sullivan, would openly speak aloud to him as though he were still alive, as though he could ask advice of the man, listen to him guide Leo in certain directions that his parent's wouldn't have dreamed of or couldn't, given their closeness to their boy. It wasn't so much that Leo thought a line of communication had truly been opened—he was far too grounded to believe in mysticism; he barely believed in tangible things like acupuncture or cloud computing—but the process did provide some comfort, and after years of grasping at straws, trying to find any leads for the case, he'd been willing to try just about anything, including a plea to the dead.

But over time, Leo slowly gave up those visits after falling in love with Janet, marrying her, and becoming a father. Snooping around Holm's old property no longer struck him as a good use of his resources, even if justice for this godfather still burned like a lit cigarette stubbed out on his heart. Once he'd been promoted to chief, his days of chasing kids off Devil's Altar had ended, those duties relegated to subordinates, to the younger officers climbing up the ranks. Besides, it wouldn't have looked good for their new leader to be sniffing around that boneyard anymore, even if everyone understood why. People talked in a small town like Orchard Coils. There was always so little yet so much to jaw over—the smallest of gossip amplified beyond what its frequency should rightly hold.

But now, fifty years later, justice had actually been served as best as possible for the Sullivan family, and Leo felt a pull back toward those old, haunted lands. And while he'd tried to dismiss it over the past year, chalking it up to nostalgia or the musings of an old man, it would not be silent in his mind, would not abate. He was compelled to return. So much so that it was starting to feel like a remaining purpose of his long life, to visit that space one final time—even for a man heading into his mid-nineties, foolish as it may have been, it didn't seem implausible that something from the past might keep him moving forward, something unresolved. Though is there ever a resolution when something is stolen and not returned?

The idea allowed Leo to call upon his two boys, summoning them back to Orchard Coils—a move he wasn't prone to, but one he would need to employ to pull off this latest venture. The boys had set out on their own, as they should, to cities of their choosing, but they were good boys and would return if the old man lit the signal, would come careening home if he asked for help, which he was typically reluctant to do. But in this case, he would—he would ask his sons to return home and sherpa him into the decommissioned abyss to . . . what exactly, he couldn't say. Leo hadn't figured that last part out, just figured it was more his business than theirs. It would come to him when he needed it; that was his job. Theirs was to get the three of them down there safely—not so unreasonable—and Leo would figure out the rest once his feet left some new imprints in that mineral-rich dirt.

One thing Leo had to remind himself of was that Bo and Clay were no longer spring chickens themselves, even if they were young men in his own mind. Both boys had grown up strong, built solidly, into their forties. Bo was not so far off from his big five-oh. Not that Leo expected this to be a huge problem; the kids had taken care of themselves, both gym rats—Bo out of necessity, Clay out of vanity. They should be able to navigate their father down into the quarry carefully enough, perhaps not breaking any speed records, though speed was hardly the point. It occurred to Leo they could include Bo's oldest daughter, Allison—Leo's first grandkid—who had just hit her teen years. But then he thought better of it, figuring the nature of the trip wasn't really something he wanted Allison around for, despite the fact that he relished all the opportunities he got to see Bo's kids.

As he perceived it, there might be too much dark energy hiking down those closed roads, and he didn't need his granddaughter around that, around what conversations might ensue. He barely wanted to burden Bo and Clay with it, but he knew they were the right men for the job. Leo also knew that his two sons didn't talk to each other as often as they should—do they ever, in a father's opinion? They got along perfectly well, so it wasn't like some major falling out kept them at odds with one another. It was more a gulf of time, distance—brothers separated by hundreds of miles, leading busy lives, who had substituted the occasional digital message for actually seeing each other in the flesh or even just hearing the other's voice. They would see each other on certain holidays, or maybe when Clay dipped out of the city for a day and night via a train to New Haven, then travel to Bo's spread in the suburbs to spend time with his brother; sister-in-law, Charlene; and two nieces, Allison, and Claire. Sometimes Bo's family would take the trip into Manhattan to visit Clay in his high-rise condo overlooking the river, purchased a decade before at an exorbitant price as the city rebounded—still content as a bachelor, content with a whopping thousand square feet of living area in the right neighborhood and a doorman, pleased as punch to show Bo's family all the sights and sounds the big apple had to offer.

All that said, Leo was still of the opinion that the boys didn't communicate enough, were in danger of drifting apart, and, without Janet's guidance, the stickiness of her influence and masterful hectoring, they would continue to go their separate ways. Leo took it upon himself to fill that void, to nudge Bo and Clay closer together, when and where he could—not just the machinations of holidays and occasional visits but, in a less ephemeral sense, that they needed to be fixtures in each other's literal existence. He was more than convinced that was what Janet would want for them, maybe the only thing, so he championed that cause with all his vigor, took his opportunities where he could find them—case in point, bringing them back together to Orchard Coils for a mini adventure.

It had also occurred to Leo that it might have been easier to keep the boys united if their biological father, good old Billy, was more around to help, but he'd absconded down to central Florida, retired from a life of sporadic work, where he lived in a gated community for seniors with his Haitian girlfriend and twin toy poodles. The boys had a fine enough relationship with Billy but were only likely to see him once a year, maybe twice, as he was no longer able to travel long distances by plane. The family was rife with surviving men but not enough women willing and able to bind their patchwork together as a cohesive unit. That had been Janet's magic—a talent Charlene didn't possess yet—and Janet was sorely missed as the threads inevitably frayed, and everyone went their disparate ways—perhaps inevitable, even natural, but a more watchful presence, a true matriarch, would have managed the family in a more meaningful way than any assemblage of these men could. As a consequence, Leo tried his best, with mixed results and a weariness that betrayed his age, that escaped his core competencies.

With both Bo and Clay spending the weekend in their childhood home, the house Leo had maintained for decades, the house Leo specifically bought for himself and Janet to raise the boys, they'd geared up to head out on the warm-enough spring morning, parking their car as close as they could to the trail they'd have to set out on. Bo had maintained a physical presence through his position at the New Haven PD where, even as a sergeant, he'd still hoof around certain enclaves and barrios, trying to bolster a sense of community, even kinship with the denizens, with those who needed a police presence the most. He'd also gotten into some long-distance running over the past few years, his wind as strong as ever, even if his knees were losing some of their padding. Clay, apart from his gym obsession, had taken to rolling jujitsu for decades, slowly obtaining the rank of purple belt, determined to achieve a black belt by the time he turned fifty. Both, given their active status, were confident they'd be able to traverse down the quarry easily enough—both also having done so during their formative years, a sort of rite of passage for Orchard Coil teens, as was the Halloween Trail for club kids, which neither had participated in, per Leo's wishes.

Of course, they were hardly teenagers anymore. And escorting their elderly father would add a specific dynamic to the scheme, but given it was the old man's gambit in the first place, there wasn't much to do about it but take it slow and keep everybody on gravity's good side.

Which was mostly what they did.

Surprising to everyone, most of all himself, was how Leo handled the walk down the old road toward the quarry, which had actually been cleared of a lot of overgrowth and debris over the previous decade through acts of volunteerism, mostly emanating from the high school, though some of it self-serving as apparently bonfires were now common in the area on summer nights and senior ditch days. There'd also been calls from the town's historical society to clear the area out, echoed by the chamber of commerce and bureaucrats in the mayor's office. It would seem, without Leo really noticing, that more than a few people were interested in the accessibility of Holm's old stomping grounds, even if everyone did have their own reasons. So the trail made for a less cumbersome walk than he'd envisioned, even the fresh winterkill and widow-maker branches had been removed and discarded into the surrounding woods. With less to traverse around, the trip was more manageable, the arthritis in his knees only chirping from time to time. His boys were pleasantly surprised with their dad's sure-footedness, walking the mile-plus at a slow but steady clip, taking the occasional breather but determined all the same to arrive at the clearing in one piece. There were some areas where Leo needed to lean on Bo or Clay a bit—if the path got too narrow or rocky or choked with tree roots—but for the most part, he'd held his own and walked the path as he'd lived his life: by his wits, with few complaints.

The three men made their way down the pit with good cheer and in high spirits as, ultimately, the trek proved uneventful, apart from the occasional foot slip or bug slap. They shared a thermos of coffee, a generic brand that Leo preferred, brewed from a large tin purchased cheap at a bulk store. The warm liquid fought against the snap in the air.

It wasn't such a bad morning at all. They yammered and bantered—the three of them back together again, falling into old routines.

"How you feeling, Dad?" asked Clay. "You remembering if it's much farther from where we are?"

Leo never tired of hearing himself called Dad—even decades later, even if the boys were men in their own right.

"Yep, should be just around this last big bend," said Leo, suppressing his labored breathing as much as he could, though with less success than he might have hoped for.

"Why don't we take five then?" said Bo. "No need anyone getting hurt if we'll be there soon enough."

"You don't need to stop on my account," said Leo, though already slowing.

"It's more for Clay's sake. He looks gassed."

"This is a bit different than the spinning bike," said Clay, eyeing his brother. "Can't help noticing you huffing and puffing a bit there too."

"Let's just agree we could all use a breather," said Bo.

With that quick accord struck, no one wanting to lose face, they all slowed, taking personal inventory of their creaks and bodily pains, wiping the sweat from their brows, rubbing the trail dust out of their eyes, off their lips. Leo took in some water from a canteen he was traveling with, Bo freed a stray pebble from inside his boot, and Clay checked his Pulse for a signal that wasn't available.

"This might be the last place on earth with no frequency," said Clay, staring daggers at the inert tech cradled in his hand. "Weird to consider this level of disconnection."

"Consider not considering it," said Leo, who'd always had a complicated relationship with mobile technology, mixed feelings to say the least.

"I'm sure whoever this new woman of yours is, Clay, she'll be able to go a few hours without hearing from you," said Bo.

"Don't be so sure," said Clay, pocketing the device. "I can be very charismatic when I want to be."

"Not that we've ever observed," said Bo, now worrying over something in his hand.

"What's going on with your hand there?" asked Clay.

"Damn splinter from a few days ago still hurts. Got it right off the banister."

"The banister?"

"Use the thing every day, year after year, now I get this."

"Yeah, well, betrayal's a funny thing."

"You two pipe down for a minute there," said Leo sternly. "Clay, your brother was getting at something. You happen to have any long-term prospects out there, someone you might take the family route with?"

"If I find the right girl, I'm happy to throw my hat in the ring," said Clay.

"And how hard are you trying at it?" asked Bo.

Clay shrugged his shoulders, took note of the ominous birdsong coming from the deep woods—whispers and trills, like a hooded executioner's song for some soon-to-be departed.

"Allow my nonanswer to serve as my answer," said Clay.

"Figures."

"Besides, I like being the cool uncle. It suits me better," said Clay casually. "Maybe that's just my lot in life. Could be way worse."

"Cue the violins."

"Well, no one really asked you, tin star," replied Clay, the daggers he'd thrown at his Pulse now set on his brother, who, like all adult brothers, while probably not having fought in decades, were always curious how it would go.

"Enough, chuckleheads," said Leo, tamping his hands down in a cooling-off gesture he'd reserved for the boys when they were quarreling as children. "You can bicker with each other on your own time, but we're doing my thing today."

The two brothers clammed up, yielding the proverbial floor to Leo, who seemed keen on delivering some type of speech or insight—they could tell from his body language, the way his apple geared to bob in his throat.

"Now, Clay, you'd make a fine family man if you gave yourself half a chance," said Leo, adjusting his britches for comfort. "And Bo, not everyone at the end of the day needs what you got, understand?"

The brothers looked to each other, trying to suss out their father's logic, making sure they followed his gist.

"So you're saying it's time for me to settle down?" asked Clay.

"And that I should be less of an asshole?" said Bo.

"In so many words, yes, Bo, do just that," said Leo. "And Clay, no one's telling you to settle down or not, but stop acting like it's something to be fearful of when it's suited me and your brother just fine."

The boys nodded in a scolded way and muttered some charitable words of agreement.

"Good, 'cause I'm not always going to be around to guide you two out of your own way, follow me?"

"I'm not so sure, Pop. You've made it this far," said Clay. "Maybe if you'd quit eating all that bacon, you'd be able to make a real run at a hundo."

"Not giving up my pan bacon," said Leo, smiling, showing two rows of teeth that might not have been what they used to be but could still chew up a porterhouse on occasion, provided he was given enough time, and his guts were up to the challenge of digesting red meat.

"You'll outlive the lot of us, Leo Sinclair," said Bo, cuffing the old man on the back of this neck, gingerly, as if to feel the knobs of spine not so far below the papery skin. "And we'd have it no other way."

"All right, all right, I'm not going anywhere just yet. At least not today," said Leo, pacing a bit now, antsy to resume. "But you boys are hearing me, right? The thought of you two becoming distant like some far-away cousins that don't see eye to eye is not acceptable to me and certainly wouldn't be by your mother. So you two promise you won't get lazy about being good brothers to each other, if not for me, then for her."

Bo and Clay exchanged wary looks—funny sometimes how Leo could oscillate a conversation from banal to serious and then back again, but he was a master at it, something he must have honed interrogating people for decades.

"I don't know that we've been lazy about anything," said Bo, only to get the stone face from his dad. "But we hear you. We get it. Nothing's going to come between me and Clay."

Leo snorted mildly in approval, the way elders tended to, then turned his attention to the younger son, who needed less of a prompt than Bo did.

"I promise too. Bo and I will stay tight, like you and Aunt Lynn," said Clay.

"Good. Now that's how you settle an old mind," said Leo. "And it would please Janet to no end."

Sometimes Janet's memory could hit back in the right way, other times not. It wasn't always easy to tell how it would land, but in that instance, it was enough to get the men moving again, down that final turn of hardscrabble where some of the old mine cart tracks could still be tripped over. The three of them had slowed their pace for the final stretch, the ground slippery in patches with wet rock, slimy terrain. And even with all the enhanced cleanup efforts from the community, there were still gnarled trees and rogue vegetation to contend with, obscuring the lines of sight. The path had a way of narrowing, then opening up unexpectedly—repeating this pattern against a tableau that felt almost prehistoric, with few examples of man's influence, apart from some evidence of mining and the occasional stray piece of litter like a Snickers wrapper or an empty beer bottle.

Undeterred by their snail's pace, the three men eventually reached their destination—the very bottom of the path where the clearing was laid out, one that had been excavated over a hundred years before to serve as one of New England's preeminent mining hubs of granite, limestone, and any other material worth money on the open market. That was, until the events of 1893 shut down the operation forever—another mystery of sorts, how property so fertile had remained unmolested for all that time.

Leo had once done some snooping into it and hadn't liked what he'd stumbled upon, not unlike his research into the Quarry Witch during those early internet days with a young Bo as his tour guide. There wasn't anything productive to be found as to why the Holm mine was never touched again, and Leo jettisoned his interest in the spirit of letting sleeping dogs lie—or so he told people, but, in reality, it was only a half-truth. The remaining part he kept to himself for his own safety, for the safety of others.

Besides, with what he'd learned from Sophie Alba's confession, he'd also learned there was only so much brutal truth a man could take in one lifetime.

The three of them spread out a little and milled about the clearing, not that there was so much to see by that point. Anything of value had been removed from the site at its closing. And anything noteworthy or touristy had been plucked and pilfered over the decades since. The only stuff left was bolted into the ground, carved into the mountain, or tossed into the actual quarry, which would be too dangerous for any right-minded individual to explore—though rumor had it spelunkers had rappelled down at some point, unproven stories widely thought to be untrue. But still, one never knew—people were prone to commit foolish acts for their own reasons.

Slowly, as though drawn in by a homing device, the men converged on the boarded-up mine shaft, outfitted with fresh boards every few years, an esoteric line item in the budget of the town's parks department, tasked with ripping down the rotting and bloated boards only to replace them with newer and stronger ones. Leo, Bo, and Clay looked at those newer boards, contemplating what lay on the other side—the mountain's maw, the heights of which produced Peter Sullivan's death site, a location Leo had visited often in his youth, as a green patrolman, as a seasoned sergeant. What had once been a burning hot obsession was slowly fossilized by life and inaction until his vigils eventually ceased. Until he gave up on the place. He took a step backward, minding his movements as though his foot were about to trip a claymore, ensnare in a coyote trap. He looked long and hard at an unremarkable patch of wild grass, clumped with dirt and rocks and weeds, not remotely arable enough to grow so much as a scraggily onion. He'd scrutinized that stamp of land many, many times before, never knowing the full truth of what had really happened that night. Things tended to look different once you knew the whole story—one of the prevailing reasons Leo had been so keen to return before his days were up, to look upon the land with fresh and informed eyes.

"Is that it?" asked Clay, watching his father scrutinize the ground.

"Yes, that's where they finally discovered his body," said Leo, a bubble of phlegm worrying the back of his throat. "After three weeks of searching."

"Here all this time," said Bo.

"Thrown into the shadows," said Leo.

The three of them instinctively looked up, the glint of the fencing around the seventh green just visible from their position, provided the right amount of sun and that you knew what you were looking for. There was a lone hawk circling overhead, prowling for vermin, providing enough depth and context to truly crystalize just how far Peter Sullivan had been forced to fall before meeting his final reward.

They watched the hawk circle and cry. Some hunting grounds refused to be anything but, refused to give up their true nature.

* * *

Even though it really was too cold to be outside playing golf, Leo was outside all the same—playing golf—and it was making the new assistant pro, stuck with the closing Sunday shift, kind of nervous.

Heather Baker—her first year at the club when the season opened in March of 2050—watched Leo practice putting from her clubhouse window as she knew he was getting his body loose and warm to attempt a nine-hole round. This was Heather's first job in the industry, any industry for that matter, and she'd endeavored over the past ten months to get to know as many of the members as possible: who they were, what they did, when they liked to play, why they joined, what they wanted out of their membership, and, most importantly, how to keep them coming back. And after those first ten months on the job, corralling all the information she could like any new and eager go-getter, she could honestly say that Leo Sinclair was one of her favorite people she'd met during her freshman year at O Triple C. In her estimation, Leo was a charming and polite old gent who carried a quiet authority—a man who had given her the occasional pointer on how to approach her work and the varying fiefdoms at the club, such as the Monastery and the Restaurant, where she would learn that just because they were all part of the same system didn't mean they functioned in similar fashions or even had goals that aligned at all times.

At present, Heather spied Leo through the glass and worried over the safety of the ninety-plus-year-old man she'd grown fond of, out there in barely fifty-degree weather, overcast with the wind threatening to intensify, a hallmark of the unseasonably cold November they'd been having as the Thanksgiving week neared—so much so, the whispers of an early snow began circulating. It hadn't snowed in Connecticut in November for twenty years, but the mounting frost delays and atmospheric irregularities of late had the amateur meteorologists around the club tinkering with the odds, handicapping the probability of significant snowfall by the month's end. Several wagers had already been booked among the club's gambling contingent—which was to say, a broad swath of membership who now had a vested interest in what Mother Nature had up her sleeves for the next two weeks.

Weather and gambling aside, Heather Baker was not loving the prospect of Leo going out on the course, at least not solo: it was too late in the afternoon; the conditions were snotty; it got dark early and fast. Morbidly, though not unfoundedly, Heather was concerned about some medical emergency happening to the man while he was out there alone. The course would be sparsely populated and running on a skeleton crew so late in season, so it was hardly a stretch to think that if Leo were incapacitated somehow, there'd be no great way to know or react in time. And even if there were more cameras on the course than ever before, camouflaged into the tableau with remarkable discretion, feeding a bank of surveillance monitors cloistered in the back room of the pro shop, Heather couldn't be glued to them for the next two hours or account for every gap and blind spot that Leo might slip into. Plus, if he found out she was virtually babysitting him, she knew that wouldn't go over well either.

She found herself in a pickle.

Her timely solution came in the form of Jenny Mistikis, a seventeen-year-old player, daughter of long-tenured member Roland Mistikis, who'd enrolled in a family membership back when it was just him and his pregnant wife, Lucinda. Fast-forward seventeen years, and tragedy struck the Mistikis clan when Lucinda suffered an unexpected brain aneurysm and passed away suddenly, only a few days shy of what would have been her fiftieth birthday. Her death had occurred three months before, and Roland and Jenny still devastated, though their misery propelled them in different directions. Roland immersed himself in work. An engineer by trade, he specialized in the infrastructure of communication cables wherever humans might attempt to run them. Jenny, mired in her grief, threw herself into golf, a game she'd only ever had a passing interest in, typically preferring tennis, despite having full access to the eighteen holes, compliments of her parent's membership.

But over those three months, as Jenny returned to her senior year of high school, sleepwalking through her classes in a fog of apathy, she now counted the minutes until she could get back on the course—preferably alone—and walk the five-plus miles, lugging those clubs over her back, with just her thoughts to keep her company, a physical task that gave her something to focus on. It was better than having to think about her mom. It seemed to be the only thing that gave her solace, the only thing she vaguely looked forward to anymore. One could speculate—as Heather Baker did—that in the solitude of Jenny's play, her thoughts might drift to her late mother, to the mind-boggling unfairness of it all. And that her young mind was trying to suss it out, walking the course over and over again until some relief came to her, as part of a mechanism: coping or escape or otherwise. She was well within her rights to look for answers though too young to understand there would be none.

Heather Baker and all the staff were aware of the somber news that befell the Mistikis family—the three of them had been well liked and affable members of the club. For those three months, while noting Roland's prolonged absence, Heather had observed Jenny's obsession with heading off into the bowels of the course, seven days a week—weather permitting and sometimes not permitting. Each time, her heart broke for the wounded teen who was clearly in pain, a girl who really wasn't that much younger than Heather, who'd only turned twenty-four the previous month. It was easy enough for Heather Baker to remember what she had been like at seventeen and empathize with what it must be like to lose a beloved parent at such a tender age. Heather would fret over Jenny's well-being, not unlike her concern for Leo—an aspect of the job she'd been ill prepared for: actually caring about the people who would become fixtures in her weekly life, pleased to see them happy and elated but crestfallen when they struggled or seemed bereft of hope.

So when Jenny Mistikis came into the clubhouse to sign in for her round, Heather Baker noted that Leo appeared to be gearing up to head out too, and she got the idea to put them together, under the guise of young Jenny doing her a solid, as she would pitch it to the teenager: asking her to ride in the cart and play with the ninety-three-year-old, who really shouldn't be out there by his lonesome anyway. Jenny, not surprisingly, was hesitant at the request, still craving solitude, not really wanting to watch over some stranger, not really in the headspace to indulge charitable thoughts about helping out an elder, particularly one who might want to talk her ear off. Jenny hadn't a clue who Leo was or any of his notoriety around Orchard Coils—to her young eyes, he was just another stiff puttering around the course, always practicing his short game from the little she cared to observe of him. At best, she knew Leo by sight and figured him a harmless and frail hack who didn't know when enough was enough.

Heather Baker took it upon herself, sensing Jenny's reluctance, to let her know she should be honored to play a few holes with the man but didn't elaborate past that. She told Jenny that Leo would, at most, only play nine holes, at which point she'd be free to go off on her own and play till her heart's content, even using those LED balls paired with her Pulse to roam around the course after dark. Still, Jenny balked at the idea, but Heather was determined to play matchmaker and gave Jenny one final gaze, something she did judiciously while she was technically a cog in the service industry, a sort of guilt-me expression that could work on less battle-hardened kids, even if they happened to be grieving. The silence and stare eventually broke through, and Jenny relented. She would accompany the old timer, and Heather Baker pumped her fist in appreciation, not shy about celebrating the smallest of wins as those could be the most gratifying.

Their accord struck, Heather walked Jenny out and formally introduced her to Leo, asking Leo if it would be OK if they rode and played some holes together. Leo enthusiastically agreed, shaking the young lady's hand; she politely smiled back, though not quite matching the verve Leo had shown at the prospective pairing. Heather, satisfied with her success as social coordinator—another aspect of the job her PGA schooling hadn't trained her enough on—left them to it, hoping the canyon of generational divide wouldn't be too much to conquer, that some common ground would exist between that unlikely match—or, at the very least, the two would keep each other out of trouble, which had been Heather's primary concern from the jump. With any luck, maybe they'd find their way into some heady topics; the company of strangers had a way of opening folks up to that sort of free thinking, a communal bonding while trying to rein in a game designed to be all but impossible. Heather thought it could happen but hoped she wasn't getting too cute with putting Leo and Jenny together, realizing just how impromptu the idea had been, neither of them asking Heather to be paired off with a partner for the day to begin with. Too late now. Jenny had loaded her clubs into Leo's cart, and they sputtered off to the first hole, Heather left behind to hope the golf gods smiled down upon them—not so much with their long putts or shots around the diseased elms that should have been felled weeks ago, but to watch over these two lovely souls who had been in her orbit that first year, had been placed in her care, would traipse the property she'd been paid to oversee.

Heather Baker, impulsive and kind hearted, would watch the two when she could from that station of monitors tucked in the pro shop's back room. She'd hope for the best.

In the passenger seat of the cart, Jenny looked back one final time to see Heather tarrying under the doorframe, growing smaller in the receding distance though clearly gazing in their direction, a tractor beam of intent that had chosen to set them loose into the beyond. Jenny had grown fond of Heather over the past three months, looking up to her in a way—she understood it was her desire to impress her, to not let her down, that ultimately led to her acquiescing to ride shotgun with another player when what she really wanted was to be alone. And there was little to be done about it now. So she shifted her body and spoke her first real words to Leo, anxious to say what she'd been thinking for the past ten minutes, no matter who the audience might be, perhaps even in the spirit of breaking the ice.

"She can be really convincing when she wants to be," said Jenny.

A guffaw from Leo, no doubt as to who Jenny was referring to.

"This I have observed as well," said Leo.

Jenny nodded, and Leo parked the cart at the tee box of the first hole.

"Where do you like to play from, Jenny?" asked Leo. "I'm a gold man these days."

"The whites are fine, thanks."

Jenny hopped out of the cart and pulled her driver from the bag, teed up a ball, and gave the club a few waggles, a flight-path check, a clinching of the grip—then unloaded her full swing, heavily slicing the ball from right to left, creating just as much lateral movement as forward propulsion. It was a bad shot, kind of an embarrassing one right out of the gate, particularly while playing with a stranger on her home course, though she had little redress but to shake her head and cast her head downward, as though the laces in her shoes were the most interesting spectacle on the planet. She at least had the decorum to not curse or slam her club down, a move reserved for both young and old when hitting a cold shot askew, never to be lauded. It didn't escape Leo's attention how Jenny quietly returned her club to the bag and retook her seat in the cart, sans commentary or excuses for the mis-hit. She didn't ask for a breakfast ball. She didn't blame the atmospheric conditions. She did wonder if this Leo guy would be the type of player to immediately offer some unsolicited advice on her stroke, some quick fix to cure her slice—there were a lot of swing whisperers out there, all eager to improve others before their own house was in order—but that wasn't even in the ballpark of where Leo went.

"Always a treat to play with a lefty," he said earnestly. "Off we go."

Jenny felt a bit more at ease with Leo's response, watched the man guide the cart to his tee box, the golds—formerly known as the senior tees, but the age- and gender-related terms for tee box color had been retired a solid decade before. He got out and proceeded through his little ritual swings with the three wood, a process a bit drawn out for Jenny's taste, then he guided a clean shot down the center of the fairway, hardly a rip but carrying enough to find the short grass and gain an extra fifteen yards through forward roll alone. It was a crafty shot, struck by a player who knew his limitations, who wanted a specific lie for his approach shot. Leo looked on in appreciation, pleased with his target golf, then returned his club to the bag and got back behind the wheel.

"Any tee shot I can return from standing upright is a good one in my book," said Leo, poking fun at himself, Jenny neutrally nodding in return. "Let's see where you got to first; mine'll stay put."

They took the cart and headed left past a series of berms until they got to the tree line protecting the houses across the way, properties that had been plunked by errant shots hundreds of times, loaded with insurance policies and glass riders—an innate hazard of living near a club, having a hole-side view from your front porch but a hell of a vista during the golden hour. They found Jenny's ball, straight up in golf jail; it would require nothing short of a crisp punch-out to put her back in the mix, there being no better option as the branches would deter any shot with even a whiff of loft. Jenny grabbed her five iron and positioned her feet in front of the ball, a very deliberate setup for that type of shot, and swung down hard on the ball, jetting it forward with a satisfying crunch, a plume of dried pine needles kicked up in the air. The ball traveled low and far and actually accumulated a decent amount of yardage for a punchy punch, rolling to the other side of the fairway, giving her a clear enough view of the pin that should only require a slowly swung short club, probably a nine-iron given the pitch of the green.

"Nice out," offered Leo, still perched in the cart, no longer able to get in and out of the cart for every player's swing—a courtesy he believed in during his younger days, when his body was more cooperative. Now he was more invested in saving energy, an economy of motion to prevent small injuries.

"Thanks. I've had a lot of practice with those type of shots," said Jenny, a mix of pride and self-deprecation most golfers would be familiar with.

"Haven't we all."

They circled back twenty yards to Leo's shot, where he pulled a five-iron and took a stab, sending it low and straight, landing next to the hundred-yard marker, another safe and playable stroke that pleased the old ball striker right down to his bones. From their respective lies, Leo and Jenny proceeded with their pitch-like swings, both onto the green, eliciting smiles from both as the next club in their hands would be the putter, the penultimate goal of all holes.

They parked the cart near the tee box of the second hole; walked onto the green, putters in hand; and completed similar two-putts for a bogey apiece—not terrible for the first hole, certainly the type of start that can be built on, maybe even improved. Leo still couldn't get over the size of the cup, despite the fact he'd been playing over twenty years with them—they'd just never stop looking weird to him. He figured Jenny had never seen the old four-inch cups, that these one-foot monstrosities were all she'd ever known—*Sad*, he thought—but didn't bring it up to her, just put it out of his mind instead.

Overhead, a flock of Canadian geese were hightailing it somewhere, their honking sounding like ridicule cast down upon the terrestrial suckers below.

Leo could feel the wind picking up, blowing against the back of his neck, and it prompted his move toward the second hole, but then he hesitated, thinking there was some table setting left to do with this youngster. If they were to have a good time, their outing could be a better one— somebody just needed to be the mature adult about it. And since he was ninety-three years old and Jenny couldn't even legally vote yet, he figured the onus was on him, so he approached her as she was cleaning some stray grass off her putter head, and extended his left hand, a gesture within a gesture, accommodating the southpaw's dominant hand. She returned the shake with a surprisingly strong grip, which in golf, as in life, could mean a variety of things.

"Now that we've played a hole together and gotten that out of the way, why don't you and I actually meet each other?" said Leo, still shaking her hand. "I'm Leo Sinclair."

"Jenny Mistikis," she said, offering up more of a smile.

"Pleased to meet you, Jenny. Now I'm guessing that our friend Heather Baker may have put you up to playing with me today," said Leo, his smile regressing into a grin. "That maybe you had plans of roaming the course this afternoon without getting saddled with me. Does that sound about right?"

Jenny didn't want to lie, but she also didn't want to be rude to the man.

"Sure, maybe something to that effect."

"OK, then, I understand. But I would appreciate you tagging along with me for a few more holes if that's all right with you," said Leo. "I promise I'm not such terrible company once you get to know me a bit."

For reasons beyond her control, practically beyond her comprehension, Jenny could hear her mother's voice in the back of her mind, and she was not pleased with her daughter's aloof behavior toward the kindly older gentleman—that she was not being charitable with him. *Jennifer Marie Mistikis*, in her mom's foreboding tone—that's when Jenny knew she'd done something wrong, wasn't living up to expectations. It was a lousy feeling to experience and not how she'd want her mom to think of her, even if the whole exchange was just a function of her imagination, her grieving process. She knew she had to do better or at least try in a meaningful way.

"I'm sorry, Mr. Sinclair. I've just had some stuff on my mind," said Jenny. "I'd be happy to play with you today, as many holes as you'd like. I'm glad Heather suggested it."

"Excellent! But please, call me Leo," said Leo. "Mr. Sinclair is reserved for my father. He may play a few holes with us on the back nine."

Jenny looked to Leo with a sort of confusion that wasn't able to translate into a tactful question, let alone spoken language.

"Look at your face. I'm just kidding, Jenny. I told you I was good company," said Leo, truly amusing himself. "Now let's show this course what we've got today."

* * *

"What's it like being back down here, Pop?" asked Bo, not entirely sure what they were meant to do there; neither was Clay.

"It's strange. Even if I have been down here so many times before, it's like my return is making this place feel weird all over again."

"Plus we know what actually happened now," added Clay.

"I used to sit on an old wooden box right here," said Leo, pointing to the patch of ground near the boarded-up mine. "And just beat myself up about not making progress on the case. How I owed it to Mary and Chip and never got anywhere for them."

"You were always too hard on yourself about Peter," said Bo, an air of authority, both a cop and a son speaking. "It was the coldest of cases, something that happened when you were only a teenager, not much older than Allison. You didn't even join the force until years later, when they were already thoroughly stymied."

"Listen to Bo on this one, Dad," said Clay. "And don't forget, you saw this thing through to the end, never gave up hope, and look what happened. The thing got solved after all."

"And with any luck, Horace Wizner has been rotting in hell for decades now," said Bo.

Leo sighed and massaged his head, rustling his thinned-out hair, what little he had left to comb and, while doing so, wondered how much he should be listening to his boys and how much he should be ignoring their well-intentioned advice—filters and calculations that felt beyond him now.

"It bothers me to know that Mary and Chip never got that closure they deserved," said Leo. "Even if Wizner got what he deserved, I'd be lying if I said it doesn't bother me."

"You need to let that go, Dad."

"I know. I'm sorry," said Leo. "That's one reason we're here today. I'm trying to say goodbye to it."

Bo and Clay looked at their stepfather, the man who had actually raised them, with concern and reverence, watching him attempt to slip off this last shroud that had long weighed him down, cloaked his outlook with a dark and paranoid patina.

"You know, Pop, I don't know that Mary and Chip don't know that some kind of justice was found for them," said Bo, rolling up the sleeves of his flannel, the sun starting to poke around in the canyon. "Sure, maybe not on this plane of existence, but who's to say they aren't out there somewhere with this knowledge you'd like them to have. For all we know, the three of them are reunited somehow."

Leo was surprised to hear Bo speak that way, atypical of his sober-minded son—though he wanted to hear more, didn't want him to shy away.

"It's a comforting thought, son," said Leo, resuming some of his tight-circle pacing, like a pigeon, now fussing with the zipper on his nylon jacket, finally releasing it from its plastic hold. "Can't recall you ever putting much stock in that sort of thing."

"Yeah, Bo. I mean, are you talking about God or religion?" asked Clay. "Since when has that sort of thing crossed your mind?"

Bo heard what the men were asking him, looked around the desolate area they were currently occupying. One thing being a policeman had taught him was that hallowed ground came in all different shapes and sizes. That a city street corner might be just that to most but utterly sacred to others. A park bench was just a park bench, unless it was the one you lifted yourself off of, took one knee, and popped the question to your sweetheart. A damaged streetlamp on a highway where an accident took place became a makeshift memorial, peppered with flowers and teddy bears. A golf green. A quarry. A mineshaft. All these things were easy enough to visualize in a singular fashion but could hold very different meanings in the minds of others, how certain people hold them with sanctity in an esteemed way, despite their mundane nature. How these people might hear something the rest of us can't. See an additional layer of reality most of us can't observe.

Bo had never fancied himself an intellectual by any stretch of the imagination—didn't have the brains for numbers like Clay or the curiosity and reading acumen of Leo—but he had felt a touch of something growing in him of late, partly through his vocation, though much of it through raising his family. It was not something he'd been in a rush to discuss with others, apart from Charlene, but now it felt like something relevant, standing in that pit with his kin, his father's old demons pushing back, his brother's reticence about settling down. There was an aftermath to face, and he thought he might have gotten a bead on it, and it felt selfish to squirrel that away out of embarrassment or male pride, particularly when it could help the people he loved the most.

"I don't know if you need to label it God or spirituality or whatever. Maybe in the end it's just the labels that screw everything up, the shortcomings in our language," said Bo. "But I can't watch my kids grow, their own paths slowly branching out, and not think there could be something so much more divine out there for all of us. That maybe we just don't have the words or consciousness to even imagine it."

"Heaven?"

"That's a catchall term, appealing as it is," said Bo, speaking in a way that suggested he'd given this some clear thought. "I don't think there's a place where we all just walk about in bliss. I think it's some kind of threshold we're just not meant to understand."

More unexpected words from Bo, a man with such pragmatism he was prone to unplugging certain appliances at night out of safety concerns.

"Well, I hope you're right, Bo," said Leo. "I know we didn't raise you boys in the most religious of households, but I'd like to think we weren't heathens either. Maybe we tried to straddle that line so you'd figure your own way."

Leo and Bo looked over at Clay, who was toeing some dug-in stone out of the ground with his new overpriced hiking boot. He looked up to see the two sets of eyes feeling him out.

"What are you two staring at me for?" said Clay. "An afterlife sounds great to me. Sure, I enjoy an earthly delight or two, but I think I'll hold up OK to a real judgment. Besides, I see God or whatever you want to call it in all sorts of little things each day."

"Like what?" asked Bo, unable to fully mask his skepticism.

"I'm not listing off mini miracles for you, Bo," said Clay. "You'll just have to take my word that a higher power doesn't seem impossible to me either. That should be plenty good enough for both you two."

Whether his word was or wasn't good enough didn't get squabbled over any further as Bo and Leo allowed the issue to rest. Instead, Leo walked over to the old quarry, the actual remains of the pit, and stared down into it, wondering why it never seemed to stare back or, at least, he never imagined it did. Some people got that feeling—the call of the void, staring into the abyss—like some secret message being passed back and forth, but Leo never connected that line. At most, he'd felt humbled just standing along its perimeter, unworthy and small and ashamed in the face of his own inadequacies.

"Even when I stopped coming down here, I couldn't fully shake this place," said Leo to himself, to the boys, but also to the quarry that had never fully acknowledged him. "Every week, there felt like some new reminder, but in the end, what did I ever learn from it all?"

Bo and Clay weren't quite sure how to respond to that, watching their father struggle to reconcile it all into the past, to be clear of it for his future, however much time that would be.

"Did I ever tell you boys that Jocko Whalley, both senior and junior, kept drawers and drawers of the stuff people used to leave behind on the seventh green?" asked Leo.

"Sure, Pop, you told us," said Bo. "You remember when you had to come by and get me and Jocko that one night we were up there?"

"Yeah, I do remember," said Leo, looking at Bo as though he were sixteen again, somehow making Bo *feel* sixteen again under his gaze. "Clayton, you never did any of that Devil's Altar crap, did you?"

"No comment," said Clay, looking to avoid the hot seat.

"That's exactly what I'm saying," said Leo, an air of exasperation. "Even in my own household, there was no escaping it. When Jocko showed me those drawers, decades of relics from people that took the lore so lightly. But I was chief of police and I knew otherwise—that it wasn't a laughing matter, that it was a miserable and twisted-up—"

Leo stopped, tried to organize his thoughts in a way that would better express his sentiments, but he couldn't quite land on it—or maybe he just thought better of it in the spirit of putting the business behind him. Either way, he let it go, chalking it up to the futility of words, a weariness in never being able to convince the world of all its dangers, seen and unseen, sometimes hiding in plain sight—macabre delights that should be shunned in favor of a moral soundness.

Or, in short, just abide the signage: NO TRESPASSING.

"To hell with it," said Leo. "I don't want it anymore."

He tossed a stone down into the quarry as though to affirm his worldview, dissolve his one-sided pact with the site. He'd been loyal long enough, no more. Bo was now looking quizzically at his brother, who was also a bit baffled, only to turn back to his father.

"Just take it easy, Dad. No need to be so agitated by it any longer," he said.

Leo breathed out a gulp of air, as though it had lodged in his throat and finally had the daylight to crawl out. He thought he'd be OK about it, about the news he'd learned two months before, but being back in that place stirred up all kinds of old feelings, made him realize how raw and personal it still was to him. And as much as he wanted to imagine a catharsis in bonding with his sons and going on a little hike, he could now see that traversing down wouldn't be so simple—that maybe there was a little more he needed to lean on the boys over, not just in moving along a road but in getting something off his chest, something that was gnawing at him more than he figured it should.

"I wasn't going to mention it, seeing as how it happened back in February," said Leo, as though addressing a question that hadn't quite been articulated. "But I suppose it's weighing on me more than I would have thought, so maybe it's something you two should know about."

"What is it, Dad? What's bothering you?" asked Clay.

Leo took another breath, a pause to gather his thoughts, of which it dawned on him there'd been many between him and the boys that morning. He hoped progress was seeded in those lulls and silences, just as much as in their words.

"Sophie Alba passed away earlier this year," said Leo.

The boys said nothing, eyed their father, wordlessly encouraging him to continue.

"I don't know why it's so strange to me that she's gone now," said Leo. "Maybe that she lasted so long, given her condition. But I guess just about everyone involved with Peter Sullivan and me is . . ."

He trailed off, a dark thought worthy of abandonment.

"You weren't in touch with her or anything like that, were you?" asked Bo.

"No, nothing that direct. I only met her the one time back in '42 when the whole thing came to light, and I flew to Arizona," said Leo. "Apart from that, I didn't need to have an association with her. And she didn't need one with me."

"But you did end up believing her version of the story, right?" asked Bo. "You've told us that much before."

"It was plausible enough. But I suppose I also *wanted* to believe it, for more than a few reasons," said Leo. "And I felt that way even more after meeting her. It was strange, you know."

"How was it strange?"

"Just the way I met her—at her house, having a conversation. It wasn't so different from when Mary Sullivan used to have me over from time to time," said Leo. "Couldn't help noticing the parallels in it."

The boys exchanged full-blown worried looks over their father, not bothering to hide them.

"How did you find out she died?" asked Bo.

"One of the old boys from the Flagstaff PD sent me a note, thought I'd want to know," said Leo. "Been surprised it's stayed on my mind so much."

"Maybe you just need more time to process it," offered Clay.

"She would have been pretty old if she passed this year," said Bo. "And, as I recall, she'd been in a wheelchair for years. So maybe it was just her time."

"Sure. Still, though."

"Think of it this way, Dad. You're one of the guys that bought her those extra eight years, probably *the* guy that made it happen the most," said Bo, his hand on Leo's shoulder. "When you decided to vouch for her after you met in Arizona, you gave her that so she could continue on with her family, so she could be free for her remaining life."

"Bo's right. Without you recommending amnesty for telling her side of the story, she would have died in prison," said Clay. "Fact is you saved that woman in the end when you had plenty of cause to just let her suffer."

Leo could imagine the soft brackets of his body that held him together loosening all at once. His heart skipped beats. His throat constricted with emotion. To hear Bo and Clay lay it out for him like that, the admiration in their voices—well, it was enough to slowly undo him, as much as he would allow an undoing. He remembered the hand-wringing that went into his decision to forgive Sophie Alba. Even when he couldn't be totally sure of the truth. To put in a word for her. To stand before God and family and the law and maybe even the eyes of the departed and advocate clemency for this broken-down and flawed woman, who, by her own unwavering admission, only came forward to keep her own kin out of a federal penitentiary.

Leo had asked others to look into their hearts and see if the world had enough mercy left for Sophie, even if she was more culpable than she let on, even if the deal began to feel like a bad compromise, something perverse. Leo saw a futility in following through with the full charges against her—what some surely viewed as counterintuitive, as a lawman gone softhearted—but he recognized it as wrath masquerading as justice. The closest they could come to justice were her words, the revelations that had set the case free, that had further branded Horace Wizner a criminal and murderer of innocence. Leo could not find the value of locking this human being in a cage, despite an ardent belief that that was precisely where some people belonged, so he stumped for her release, and others followed his call, particularly the ones who held the mechanics of Sophie's future in their well-manicured hands.

She was set free, and perhaps her would-be jailors were relieved by it, not to have to follow through with the case, to have their scapegoat in Leo if things ever went sideways. And oddly enough, Leo found a peace in all that. Though what no one knew—aside from Lynn Sinclair, ninety years old and still puttering around in Florida—was that Leo couldn't help but think he was extending one final piece of compassion to another lost soul, Samantha Morris, the one he'd been too slow to reconcile with, the one his efforts and pride had fallen short with. Rightly or wrongly, Leo had intertwined the two and done what he thought best with the information available to him, as he had his entire life, to both great success and tremendous heartbreak.

Leo took a moment to compose himself, standing before his adult sons, still eager to be someone they could look up to, emulate. A man who never wanted anything more than to lead by example, to toe the line. Lessons he'd learned from his own parents, Baxter and Ruth Sinclair— the very thought of them enough to buoy his spirits, kick-start the old battery. There was still work to be done, always work to be done. The boys needed him; Lynn needed him. And it was a blessing to be in a position where things still mattered, purpose existed. A certain type of man might have pulled his sons into an embrace in that moment, and that would have been a fine moment indeed. But Leo, despite the emotion of the day, passed on the notion. It wasn't why he'd returned to the quarry, and if it became so, he'd prefer it not define his sensibilities past a well-worn track record. He would stay resolved in the face of that brief squall, adhere to his just-hold-on mentality. There would be other days, better days, to squeeze the life out of the boys— and those days wouldn't involve loitering at the bottom of some God-forsaken pit. So he tamped down those roiling feelings and spoke to his kids in a sober voice, even if some emotion was clearly leaking out, because honestly, there was only so much grit to muster in the face of all that life was willing to throw at you.

"Means an awful lot to hear you boys say that," said Leo, cheating his eyeline toward the sky, not their faces. "An awful lot you're here with me today."

Bo and Clay were relieved, their faces showing the ease to one another—they'd been in lockstep more than Leo realized, despite their differences, tighter than they'd been given credit for.

"What do you say, young man?" said Clay, draping an arm around Leo's shoulder. "You about ready to say goodbye to this place and all its bullshit?"

"Language," said Leo, grinning.

Then he nodded his head in a kind of self-affirming way, maybe trying to convince himself that such a thing was even possible.

"I suppose I am. Funny how I don't think I could have done it alone."

"That's what we're here for," said Bo. "Now let's put this dump behind us."

And with that, without much more in the way of fanfare or one last looks, the three of them gathered their bearings and headed out the way they came, turning their backs on the site that had held such sway over their lives, over O Triple C, over the entire town of Orchard Coils. A place that could never be truly forgotten but could at least be moved on from, even in the twilight of one's life. And that was very much where it belonged—in the past, not a second of their futures worth dwelling on it. Those seconds were far too valuable for misplaced curiosity, haunted terrain that, in the grand scheme of things, meant nothing and somehow offered even less in return.

* * *

The mood had indeed lightened after some of the initial awkwardness between Jenny and Leo lessened after the first hole. In particular, Jenny loosened up, realizing she wasn't out there to babysit some old kook but to actually spend some time with a man who knew the game well and had some interesting things to say about it. Leo, for all it was worth to him, was tickled to watch the younger golfer crush it off the tee with the reckless abandon only a developing player had— Jenny had bombed two gorgeous drives on the second and fourth holes, Leo letting out an appreciative whistle in both instances. Jenny, for her part, complimented Leo on his prowess around the green, his wedge and putter game lauded for their accuracy and control. These types of encouragements were common and good signs of people playing together for the first time getting on. There was also chitchat between the two as they played, a rhythm of patter to grease the wheels that allowed strangers to become fast friends out on the links, whether through those compliments or suggesting concepts to one another when appropriate or just commiserating over an unlucky bounce or a sailed downhill putt unable to find its angle of repose.

In some ways, it could be weird, like a courtship, a mating dance without the mating— people feeling each other out in a subdued fashion. Golfers had been meeting each other like this for centuries. And the ritual had been serving Leo and Jenny well. Despite the chasm of age, they had fallen into a smooth cadence of play and comradery ever since Leo reintroduced himself after the first hole, and she decided to give the old-timer a fair shake on that chilly November afternoon. She was glad she did. There was something charming about the guy, his easy nature, some corny jokes, though he didn't lack sharpness and projected an air of someone who knew how to get things done. Jenny noted a few of his mannerisms, his observational approach to their surroundings, his style of speech. She thought him someone her father would get along with, wondered if perhaps they knew each other. Maybe she'd ask him later that night at home if their paths crossed—if either of them was feeling the least bit talkative, given the conditions they were living under.

The two carted down the fourth hole looking for Leo's third shot, an iron he'd drifted and rolled into the rough, much to his chagrin. Jenny's ball was sitting high and pretty on the fairway, a dollop of white paint on a green canvas, just waiting to be express-mailed toward the pin with her second shot. They got out of the cart and trolled around some fescue, looking for the errant ball. With most of the leaves already down for the season, looking for a ball in the wind-swirled conditions could be an infuriating task, a kind of trade-off associated with playing in these more comfortable temperatures and gorgeous landscapes. Luckily enough, they found Leo's ball half-plugged and only partially covered by some brittle brown leaves. He cleared and cleaned the ball, unsticking it from the muddy lie, and placed in back down in the one-inch grass, fluffing its new position as much as he thought the rules would tolerate. He pulled his eight iron, the best club for where he was, knowing full well he had zero chance of reaching the green, and fired off a humdinger that died in the gusty and cooling air but still landed a tidy fifty yards from the green, well positioned for an easy wedge to get him on and a smooth putter stroke to take him home.

"That's a sweet shot out of this slog," said Jenny. "Kind of weird considering it hasn't rained all that much."

"Drainage on this side of four has always been spotty. Something to do with the water table and limestone that runs east to west as it's been explained to me," said Leo, loading his eight iron back into the bag. "They actually dig up and trim back some of the tree roots every few years. Supposed to help the perimeter get less swampy."

"You really know a lot about this course. How long have you been a member here?"

"My whole life, actually. My parents were members; so were my grandparents on my mom's side."

"Good stuff," said Jenny, getting in the cart's driver's seat, waiting for Leo to situate himself besides her. "Hey, have you ever heard that rumor that a baby was supposed to have been born out here somewhere?"

For a brief flash, Leo felt as though the universe revolved around him—and was more than happy when the feeling passed.

"I have," said Leo, grinning a bit.

"Do you think it's true?"

"I know it's true."

"How so?"

He could have let it go. In the past, he probably would have and not said anything. But his prerogative that day felt different—something about Jenny Mistikis—so he let it fly.

"I was that baby," said Leo, smiling now. "Born about fifty yards behind us on April ninth, 1957."

"Get out of here. That was really you?" said Jenny, truly amazed. "I kind of thought that was just an urban legend–type thing around here."

"Well, this place has plenty of those," said Leo. "But this particular one happens to be true."

"Wow, that's incredible. You were really born back there," said Jenny, looking over her shoulder, practically veering the cart back into the same soggy grass they'd driven away from, leaving behind some ellipsis tread marks. "What happened that day?"

"Premature labor, two months early. It was a dangerous situation for my mom and me," said Leo. "But there was an OB here, Dr. Corey Smith. Never forgot that name. He was able to get me out, and then an ambulance drove right up onto the course to take us all to the hospital."

"An ambulance drove out here?"

"Sure did. There were a bunch of people around trying to help. Some even took to their knees and started praying together like some makeshift congregation."

"Unbelievable, Mr. Sinclair—Leo," said Jenny. "You must think about that every time you play this hole."

"It's funny, but I really don't anymore. Hadn't actually thought about it much until you mentioned it," said Leo, looking over his shoulder just to make sure they weren't slowing down any golfers behind them, more out of long-standing habit than any real concern, given how empty the course was.

"Sorry if it's something you'd rather not talk about," said Jenny, noting Leo's distraction, hoping she hadn't ventured into choppy waters.

"No, not at all. It brings back some fond memories of my parents, what they must have been like when they were so young," said Leo casually. "I was always that type of kid—asking questions about what their lives were like before me and my sister were born. I think it was more common back then to talk about that kind of stuff with your parents. Maybe it's become sort of a lost art through the generations."

Leo dry-coughed a bit, and Jenny paused, taking in what the man was saying about his folks, how it might apply to her and the crisis she'd been living through for three months now.

"So you were really close to them, were you?" she asked.

"I was, very strong relationship between us all," said Leo, looking beyond the canopy of the cart toward the sky—hoping, feeling, believing in their presence. "You know, my father's nickname around here was Screws, and he could knock the stuffing out of the ball like you couldn't imagine."

Jenny had no clue what the word *screws* meant in relation to hitting a golf ball hard but figured she could look it up later.

"You think I can hit the ball as hard as your dad someday?" she asked.

"You bet. Of course, he wasn't a lefty, but I can see a similar wrist whip between you two, similar weight shift," said Leo. "If you keep it up, learn to rein in that swing path, you're going to be a real threat in the tee box."

"Thanks," said Jenny, turning over all that Leo had just laid out in her mind.

"My pleasure. Now let's see you stick this next shot onto the green," said Leo as they carried on toward Jenny's ball, fairway bound. Some clouds had started to roll in, the threat of rain wafting across the escalating breeze, that earthy, vaguely metallic smell.

They played the next two holes in relative silence—not an awkward variety, but more a concentration in the game. The thing about chatting when playing was that while it could be fun and social, it could also distract from the task at hand. When you were having a good hole, or the potential for one, people tended to clam up out of respect for those they were playing with. The same could be said when things were going sideways for a player, and no one wanted to say boo to them. It was sort of a strange phenomenon in golf—when it was appropriate to dive into conversation—and there was a certain artistry to it, an effect learned over time. Everyone understood that plenty of business got conducted during a round. It was also great for catching-up and getting-to-know-you kinds of days. But there was also something to be said for just shutting up and saving some of the talking for after the round, allowing the ebbs and flow of the game to proceed unobstructed to the white noise of the course.

That was the little dance Leo and Jenny were going through as their day progressed, as they moved through the fifth and sixth holes, both shooting well enough with no unforced errors. Jenny's mind had benefited from some respite, not thinking about her mom quite as much, which was the major point of being out on the course and challenging herself with something that required a lot of concentration, that demanded her full attention. Leo was just pleased his body felt limber, and his eyes could still see the ball as the sky slowly dimmed. He knew he was preposterously lucky to still be so strong of body and mind at such an advanced age, a true blessing he would not take for granted. He was still even able to go to his gun range from time to time, where all the PD would congregate, though he hadn't practiced firing in over a decade, had lost his taste for it after the Hero of Hartford county altercation had levied much scrutiny on him, more than he'd ever wanted. That said, and despite relatively good health for his age, he still had to go through the full regimen of medicines and creams and stretching every morning to keep him mobile, to ward off cramps and lower the probability of bone bruises or muscle spasms, which still plagued him despite prophylactic efforts. None of that was stuff he particularly relished, but he would go about it without complaint if it kept him active, helped busy his days, kept him in and out of that big, empty house he still ran—the house he was still clinging to.

A house that had in the garage a spare refrigerator, stocked with unopened bottles of champagne—Kirby Keener's wedding gift, still in effect long after his passing, long after Leo had enjoyed the last shared bottle with Janet. Now he gives them away when the opportunity arises, doesn't care to look at them.

By the time Leo and Jenny got to the tee box on seven, their respective moods had percolated to the point where a bit more conversation felt warranted, welcomed, given their recent success on the two previous holes. Jenny in particular could feel her guard coming down further around her affable new friend, wondering if he was perhaps a little lonely and talking with her throughout the day would be a boon. She didn't want to presume, but she thought it was a reasonable enough assessment from what she'd gleaned from the man. Given the nature of the seventh hole, there was always something worth mentioning about it. Of course, Jenny had no clue just how loaded a question about the seventh hole could be to Leo—no matter how innocuously and casually it was intended.

"I'm guessing you know all about that Devil's Altar stuff near the fencing," said Jenny, tossing grass in the air to gauge the wind. "Kind of crazy stuff when you think about it."

"*Crazy* is certainly a good word for it."

"Have you ever seen any of the junk people supposedly leave up here?" asked Jenny. "Like trinkets and tributes? I can't say I ever have."

Leo gave the question some consideration, not so much because he didn't know the answer—clearly, he did. He was just unsure exactly how much he should divulge to Jenny. He liked the kid and did want to share a bit with her, but there were precautions to take, pitfalls to be minded when opening up like that—also bearing in mind he was speaking to an impressionable mind, and one who wasn't kin, so it was hardly his place to speak out of turn, even if he was old enough to be her great-grandfather.

"Well, I guess I can tell you. I was the chief of police for this town for a long time," he said. "So I pretty much saw all the foolishness around the Quarry Witch stories and how they got pumped up over the years."

If Jenny was impressed or intimidated by Leo's former status as chief of police, she didn't let on, but she did continue her line of questioning with even more verve.

"So you must have walked the Halloween Trail when you were a kid, right?"

Leo nodded without comment.

"I did too, about seven years ago," said Jenny. "The club doesn't seem to shy away from all those old mine stories, the ghosts at the bottom of the cliff."

"Sometimes it's easier—or just more profitable—to let the history and the bullshit get mixed together, pardon my language," said Leo. "But I can tell you I was down there a few months ago, and there's nothing of interest to see."

"So was I. My high school helps keep the property clean now."

"I'd heard something to that effect," said Leo. "Why's the high school care about such a thing?"

"It's like an after-school program, for extra credit. It's like they want to keep those grounds clean or sacred or something," said Jenny, a little embarrassed. "It always seemed silly to me, but people seem to like those stories, and it makes it a bit easier to get down there, even though technically people shouldn't be going down there."

Leo pursed his mouth in a way to hide his disapproval, which only seemed to accentuate what he was actually thinking, which didn't escape Jenny's attention. They both hit their tee shots, long irons that both missed the green though not so far off they couldn't salvage a par, hole out an improbable birdie. They loaded back into the cart made their way up the steep path— Leo still thinking on what Jenny had said: *after-school program*. And she was right. People weren't technically supposed to go down there, but clearly they did, including him and his sons only a few months ago—a fact that wasn't lost on him for a variety of reasons, including being a cop who, for decades, saw people doing what they weren't supposed to be doing but did anyway, including himself.

Jenny then spoke up and freed him from his own thought loop.

"There really was a murder up here though, right, a long time ago?" she asked, not trying to press her luck or annoy Leo but genuinely curious and figuring he'd been around long enough to know fact from fiction. "I mean, you were a police officer; that's why I'm asking."

Leo clenched his jaw. He could hardly believe that with every generation behind him, no matter the century, not only did interest in the lore persist, but it also grew, helped along by natural curiosity, by all the local institutions that now celebrated it annually, which would seem to include OC High School. Leo had thought that at his age, he'd finally be done getting surprised by this reality, but he continually found himself out of step with its zeitgeist. Sometimes, in fact, he was utterly convinced that Orchard Coils aspired to be the next Salem, Massachusetts, or Sleepy Hollow or enchanted corner of New Orleans—towns that refused to let their legends die. They were too beloved, too profitable.

"Yes, there was a homicide here in April of 1978," said Leo.

Jenny did the quick math in her head—fifty-five years before she was born.

"And it was related to the quarry right, to all the old ghost stories?"

"It was, and it wasn't," said Leo. "The case was only solved eight years ago. There's actually a decent amount of reporting online. The *Courant* did a fair accounting of it; you'll get a pretty accurate sense of what happened."

The explanation didn't seem to satisfy Jenny's curiosity in the least—researching it through old links and reporting didn't seem nearly as fun or interesting as picking the former chief of police's brain, so she persisted, as teens often do.

"I heard it was a member," said Jenny, pressing, though in an earnest enough way. "You and your family have been at the club a long time, right? Any chance you knew the person?"

More pause and consideration from Leo, more calculus into how much he wanted to continue on this tangent, to indulge this kid's line of questioning, as innocent as it might be.

"I'll tell you, Jenny, but I suppose I'd rather not dwell on it much more, OK?" said Leo.

Jenny nodded in agreement.

"The man that was murdered was my godfather, my parents' dearest friend, and someone who personally meant the world to me."

"Oh my God, I'm so sorry. I didn't know any of that, I swear," said Jenny, truly mortified to have blundered into such a sensitive area.

They fell silent and finished the uphill drive to the green, where they attempted their respective chip shots—Leo lofting his into a clear parabola on the tightly cut surface, though he would still require two putts after an unfortunate lip out to complete a disappointing bogey. Jenny attempted an inadvisable bump-and-run shot out of a clump of grass and subsequently chunked her ball only a few inches forward into even worse bramble. Her frustration was evident though, to her credit, she kept her cool and used a nine iron to attempt a more apropos slash shot, this time to great effect, and managed to get the ball within fifteen feet of the hole. It could have been a good chance to save bogey, but she pushed the ball left and it missed the cup by an inch, forcing her to tap in for a double, cooling what had been four consecutive strong holes and marring her scorecard.

She hung her head and walked back toward the cart. Leo attributed her lapse in concentration to his admission that his family knew the man who had died here all those years ago and offered her a quick word of advice, encouragement.

"Head up. Don't let the course think it's gotten the better of you," said Leo. "You'll want to play those cards close to the vest."

To that, Jenny lifted her head, straightened her spine, felt what Leo was explaining was bone true, that it was advice worth heeding. They moved the cart up to the next tee box, a long par five that Leo had come to dread in his later years, the distance like a marathon to the man, a hole he was more than grateful to play from the golden tees. Jenny had the potential to do well on the hole. It played into some of her natural cuts of the ball, if she could keep her driver shot out of early trouble, of which there was plenty on both sides within the first hundred yards. They were going through their little pre-shot routines when Jenny asked an unexpected and tentative question.

"I know you said you didn't want to talk about it," said Jenny cautiously. "But can I just ask you one question about your godfather?"

Leo was silent for a bit, then softly nodded his consent.

"Were you really close to him? It sounds like maybe you were, that it was a great loss in your life when you were kind of young," asked Jenny. "Sorry if that's being too personal."

It was too personal, but Leo sensed something in the way Jenny asked, the nature of the question at hand. Call it instinct, intuition—call it being a cop for fifty years—but he felt there was more to Jenny's question, even just the temerity to ask it under the surface of simple curiosity. And in Leo's experience, there often was when a young person asked a question of a much older person because, honestly, most of the time a younger generation couldn't be bothered. So it was somewhat noteworthy when they probed, when they sought information from an elder, especially a stranger. For Leo's sake, he hoped he hadn't been misguided, opening up to the young golfer, that he was acting responsibly. Nevertheless, he would continue on with her, divulge, for reasons he wasn't totally sure of, but somehow, it still felt like the right thing to do.

"We were. I loved him like a second father, and he was incredibly close to my entire family," said Leo. "It was a terrible blow to us and, of course, to his own wife and child."

"That is so awful. I'm sorry you had to go through that," said Jenny. "And I'm sorry to have brought it up again. I won't bother you about it anymore."

"It's quite all right, Jenny," said Leo. "I appreciate the kind words."

Jenny nodded her head and gestured toward the tee box, ceding the honors to Leo as he'd scored better than she had the previous hole. Leo smiled, even bowed slightly, and proceeded to strike his tee shot, then Jenny hers—a wonderful low-bullet crack that split the fairway like the seam in a book. Jenny was all smiles, and the ugliness of the previous hole was quickly forgotten in the magic of moving on and recouping, the mind-erasing effect of a great shot. All golfers worth their salt learn to cultivate a short memory, the crux of the game in a certain sense and plenty applicable toward the pursuit of a fruitful life in general.

The final two holes on the front nine were played out smoothly enough. Leo and Jenny fell back into that quiet cadence—Leo being a bit winded and muscle-sore but determined to finish out at the turn while Jenny was focusing harder on her shots, brimming with energy and demons, a wily combination to tame, her mother's voice still pinging in her mind, reminding her of the world's unfairness, its random cruelty. She would admit that playing with Leo the past two hours had helped silence some dark thoughts, probably to an even greater extent than if she'd played alone. Yet they did persist all the same: sporadic, deflating, crushing. She'd tried to imagine herself as a knight on some great quest, alone and in pursuit of something divine, maybe ephemeral.

She would concede it was nice to have some company, at least for a day—two adventurers swapping tales, neither of them in pursuit of glory or gold.

They wrapped up the ninth hole, Jenny missing a long birdie putt and tapping in for a par while Leo double-bogeyed as the distance from his driver and long iron was depleted, along with an unlikely miss with his wedge. The exertion of the round had caught up to him, compounding his weariness in a way he couldn't have imagined even a few years before. In short, his tank was empty, and he knew it—knew he didn't have another hole left in him. *A pity*, he thought, as he was enjoying himself. He reckoned he'd never be able to play more than nine holes at any given time anymore, a depressing thought. But then he figured that number was bound to decrease again at some point, precipitously in all likelihood, so he should be grateful that he could still manage a full nine.

Leo motioned for Jenny to drop them off at the gazebo, the idyllic structure situated between the ninth and tenth hole, adjacent to the snack shack that had been closed for a few weeks, shuttered for the season, given the frosty mornings and waning daylight. Jenny parked, and Leo got out and took a seat in the gazebo. Jenny followed him, though not totally sure why, what Leo was on about, but she figured he knew what he was doing. Plus, she'd more than noticed his fatigue and remembered her mandate from Heather Baker only a couple of hours before. It was her job to keep an eye out for Leo Sinclair, a stranger at first but now someone she'd realized had an array of interesting stories, many of them taking place on the very grounds they'd just traversed.

So what would a few more minutes of companionship hurt anybody, particularly if the man needed a breather before heading back, particularly as she'd suddenly found herself reluctant to be alone? So they took their respective seats on the hard wood, slightly damp, and Leo let out a mighty sigh, glad to be out of the cart's confines and onto something more stationary and stable and airy. He closed his eyes briefly, then opened them, recalling that it wasn't outside his wheelhouse to nod off at inopportune times, in odd places—another unfortunate side effect of getting old and still trying to be active, a happenstance he quickly felt compelled to offer Jenny advice on.

"Don't ever get old," he said, grinning, rubbing his right shoulder with his left hand, kneading some of the stiffness that was already trying to settle in.

"I'll try not to," said Jenny, getting the joke though also not a big fan of it. Leo noticed her muted reaction.

"Do you mind sitting with me a few minutes?" he asked. "I know you've still got some daylight left to play a bit more of the back nine."

"Sure, I'm good to hang around for a few."

Leo nodded in appreciation and took in the view from the gazebo: bare trees, gray sky, some patches of burned-out grass that wouldn't come back until next year. The course had held up well during the season, but the onset of winter could be seen everywhere. There were squirrels foraging for acorns, birds looking to rob the ground of seed. Wild turkeys could be heard gobbling, loud and persistent, out of sight in the deep woods. The wind kicked up, a noticeable mist accompanying it, fine and clean and not unpleasant. By more than a few standards, it really wasn't the best day to be outside, but the two people occupying the gazebo didn't seem to mind—probably for different reasons, but they were kind of exactly where they wanted to be, even if the sky had already dropped one shoe, another one dangling.

Leo coughed a dry and scratchy cough and felt slightly embarrassed about it.

"I say don't get old, but I'm sure you're plenty ready to get on with being a young adult and all," he mulled. "So maybe don't take me too literally. Or just try to stop getting old once you hit thirty."

"I'll keep that in mind. Maybe science will have it figured out for me by then."

"Science has been promising that one since I was your age," said Leo. "I always figured it was best just to keep the body moving, the mind engaged. Those were the closest things we had to the fountain of youth."

"Seems to have worked well for you."

"I have no complaints. Now that anyone in their right mind should indulge my—well, you know. . . . Sorry, I'm rambling here," said Leo, piping down, going back to just enjoying the view. He started working his hands into his knees, massaging the sinewy meat around the knobby bone where the inflammation was prone to nest—a message from his body he wasn't interested in receiving. His patellae weren't afraid to lock up if he didn't warm them up or cool them down properly. From her pocket, Jenny's Pulse trilled repeatedly, some instrumental score they would have used in a fancy movie decades ago—clearly nostalgic, a throwback. She made no motion to address the persisting tone.

"Do you need to get that?" asked Leo, wondering where his own Pulse was, presumably in a weatherproof sack in the left sleeve of his golf bag, where he was happy to forget about it, happy to ignore the digital siren call that had enthralled the world past a point he could comprehend. It didn't escape his attention how Jenny had never once looked at the thing the entire time they were playing, for whatever her reasons were. Leo knew this to be an anomaly among younger players, especially the ones agreeing to the porting technologies, blasphemy in his view.

"It's fine, just my dad, finding some time to check up on me," said Jenny, a bit strained.

"Won't he be worried if you don't pick up?"

To that, Jenny just shrugged her shoulders, broke her eye contact with Leo in a way he'd seen a million times over his life—both as a parent to Bo and Clay and in his decades in law enforcement, dealing with citizens who were reluctant or refused to speak. Jenny had something to say, something to hide, and was deliberating with herself as to what she should do. Leo had sensed it earlier, was all but sure of it now, and allowed some room, some encouragement, for her to come clean.

"You know, Jenny, it's none of my business, having just met you and all, but I can't help but recall you telling me earlier that some things were on your mind, maybe why you were set to go off on your own today," he said, calm, measured. "Now I'm sensing that maybe you're avoiding your dad."

He stopped there, curious to see how Jenny might react to his baited nonquestion, a tactic he'd long employed when dealing with everyone from beloved family members to hardened criminals, oftentimes with success. Jenny seemed relatively unfazed.

"Was there a question in there somewhere, Leo?" she asked, not unkindly but making him work for it.

Leo clucked his tongue and nodded in agreement, slightly proud of the youngster for observing his ploy.

"Would you care to tell me what's troubling you?" asked Leo. "And if you don't want to, no hard feelings. I'll understand."

Now it was Jenny's turn to decide how much she wanted to impart to her inquisitor, a man she'd only met two hours before. She figured there were reasons to speak with him but also reasons not to. But the fact was she kind of admired the guy, the polite and old-fashioned manner of him. And it wasn't like she hadn't been asking all her own probing questions of the guy, who had seemed somewhat forthcoming in the face of her curiosity, her zeal to learn more of the Quarry Witch lore, his birth on the fourth hole. In a certain sense, Jenny could justify that she owed it to Leo to open up, a quid pro quo of sorts—literally a concept she'd just learned about in her Introduction to Law class at the high school. Or maybe she was just rationalizing what her gut was trying to tell her—*open up to the man, take him up on the offer.*

She would choose to trust her gut.

"This is probably a dumb question, Leo, but at your age, with all your experience, have you suffered loss in your life? And I know you've told me about your parents, your godfather, but have you had to deal with even more? Something even more horrible?"

Leo gave that some thought, not because he didn't know the answer but because only some of it warranted a response to a new acquaintance—plus, it was spot-on, he'd suffered plenty—it never seemed to end.

"My wife of many years passed away from cancer at too young an age," said Leo. "She was the love of my life and taken from us earlier than we ever could have expected."

"Us?"

"She had two children from a previous marriage. We raised them together."

"And you all got along?"

"Very much so. I love them. They're my sons, and the greatest joy of my life was being their father," said Leo, clearing some emotion from his gullet. "They're actually the ones that took me down to the quarry back in the spring."

"I see. I'm happy for that, Leo, truly. I bet you were a great husband and father."

"I certainly tried to be. But you asked about loss, and I'd certainly say I've been through my fair share," said Leo. "Is there a particular reason you wanted to know?"

A real question, direct and not hidden under the guise of cop tricks or getting-to-know-you golf rituals. Jenny could make her stand one way or the other right now. She decided quickly enough.

"Yes," she said, taking in a breath, uttering the words she'd been loath to say aloud for many months now, allowing them to accumulate cobwebs in the corners of her mouth, husks of dead words ensnared and never spoken. "My mom died a few months back, very suddenly."

Leo felt his stomach sink—too much tragedy for a teenager to endure. He instantly wanted to absorb her grief, his own parental instincts kicking in, but he also knew that was not how it worked. No one could free Jenny from it; the onus fell on her, and it would take the passing of slow minutes, thousands, maybe millions of them, all painful in their own right.

"I'm so very sorry to hear that," said Leo.

"Thanks, yeah, it's been really tough, as you'd imagine," said Jenny, upper lip stiff. "Things haven't been going so well the past three months."

"You do have people in your life to lean on, talk to? Friends? Your dad?" asked Leo.

"I do, which is good, I know," said Jenny. "Problem is that I don't much want to talk to anybody these days."

"That's understandable," said Leo, taking a beat. "Do you mind me asking—how did your mother pass?"

"Brain aneurysm."

"Tough way."

"Is it? That's not what people have always told me."

"What have they told you?"

"That it's mostly painless, quick, then over."

"And what have you learned about it on your own?" asked Leo slowly. "Because my guess is you've read everything you could find online as to what it really means to have an aneurysm."

The old man was right, and Jenny knew it immediately. She'd read what felt like volumes on the condition: papers, statistics, case studies, brain scans and imaging—anything to better understand what cut her mother's life short. She'd hoped it would make her feel better in the tiniest of ways, that maybe possessing such knowledge would offer some respite. It did not. If anything, it only served to underscore the treachery that had befallen Lucinda Mistikis, betrayed by her own body, a godless sky.

"Anything with the brain seems horrible to me," said Jenny. "I couldn't really tell what my mom might have gone through, but I don't see how it . . ."

Jenny trailed off. Leo collected his thoughts, spoke from hard experience, from his own sense of personal loss.

"People will want to comfort you, and they're right to do so," he said. "But as I'm sure you're noticing, there's only one person that's going to pull you out of this."

The wind ratcheted up a gear, only to lull just as fast. The golf course had become incredibly quiet, as though the two of them owned the land and all its machinations, acres to themselves where the woods creaked against the breeze, then fell stone silent, as though listening in on their conversation.

"You have a blunt way of talking, Leo," said Jenny. "More so than some of the others that have tried to help me."

"I don't mean to sound insensitive. It's just the cop in me. I've spent decades delivering bad news and sad truths to people I've just met," said Leo. "I was this . . . device that moved people along. Or tried to, at least."

"And now you'd like to help me move along?"

"I think you're doing that already; that's why you're out here," said Leo. "I guess I want you to know that even if you're the only one that can do the hard work, you don't necessarily have to do it alone."

Jenny considered the advice—the soft edges, the gritty surface.

"I'm out here on my own just about every day trying to do just that," she said.

"And you're angry?"

"Like nothing I can even believe."

"Then use it for good. Use it to get better."

"How? Why?"

"To come out the other side stronger, wiser. And sadly, to become far less innocent to the chaos of the world."

"Sadly?"

Leo paused a moment. He didn't want to get too into a philosopher's territory—he hardly considered himself that type of intellectual—but he knew he had some knowledge to impart to the child, some small nuggets that might just aid her in the tough journey she still had ahead.

"I read a lot, and protecting the purity of our young is a hallmark of many great societies, particularly in the West," said Leo. "And you, Jenny, have been forced to grow up way faster than you should have to."

"It's not fair—that's what you're telling me, right?"

"Correct, not in the least."

"But life isn't fair."

"Also correct."

Jenny absorbed the words. She knew there was something to them, given they were painful to hear.

"Can I tell you the one thing that's been kind of helping me, even if it's a bit silly?" said Jenny, to which Leo nodded. "I imagine my mom watching over me. I hear her in my head. And

I still want to make her proud, even if I'll never get to exchange another word with her again. Stupid, right?"

The two of them remained dry eyed, as though honoring some unspoken promise to each other. It would be their way; they were in it together.

"Not if it gives you comfort," said Leo. "But I think you're right, and I'm not sure if I ever had the pleasure of meeting your mother, but I'd guess she'd want you to be resilient and carry on, make her as proud as you can."

There were times when people would tell you what you wanted to hear, others what you needed to hear. The way Jenny figured it, Leo was threading some needle, adroitly and in a way that vaguely soothed her, his message resonating. He was, she had to admit to herself, an unlikely source.

"You said your wife passed away. What was her name?"

"Janet Justine Sinclair."

"And you still miss her?"

"Every single day."

"And that's probably what I have to look forward to for the rest of my life, always missing my mom?"

"Probably, yes," said Leo, leaning his lower back forward, a click of tiny bone only he could hear. "But that's not your life; that's just a part of it. A part you'll learn to manage."

"Is that what you do, manage it?"

"Yes."

Jenny took a moment to wick some moisture from around her eyes, maybe some budding emotion, probably just some of that fine mist—tough to say in the waning light, cooling swirl. She collected her thoughts, noticeably, and Leo allowed her the space to do so. The older man was unsure just how much of a balance he'd overstepped—if he had at all. One could never be totally sure when grieving people were involved, particularly a child. But Jenny remained calm, steadied her composure like an athlete adept at conserving energy, eschewing wasted motion. She looked solid and refocused her attention on Leo.

"Sorry, Leo, guess I wasn't planning on talking about any of this today," she said. "Let alone with a . . ." She paused, unsure, and Leo took it upon himself to fill in the blank, to save her the embarrassment.

"A stranger. A fogey. A cop. Take your pick, right?"

They smiled because they knew it to be true.

"No, you'd have come and played and kept it all inside your head," said Leo. "And while I'd certainly endorse the first part, not so much the second part."

In the distance, a volley of elaborate birdsong—maybe a mating ritual, maybe a cache of mealworms discovered—in any event, splendid to the ears.

"So you've played this game your whole life?" asked Jenny.

"Sure have."

"And I guess it goes without saying you really love it?"

"It need not go without saying since I love saying it."

"Can you tell me why?" asked Jenny. "Why does the game mean so much to you?"

Leo pondered, took note that there was only about an hour of sunlight left by the obscured sun's position. Instead of taking her leave, Jenny had opted to shoot the breeze with him in the gazebo—not quite the same gazebo he'd lost his virginity in with Sam Morris all those decades ago, a remodeled one on the same spot of ground, though he was hardly going to share that detail with young Jenny Mistikis. He realized he should feel colder, more tired than he did, but he didn't feel that way at all. He felt energized, a fact not lost on him, and when he instinctively motioned to rub the next crick out of his body, whether it be his neck or knee or wrist, he realized nothing was particularly barking at the moment. He felt healthy, at peace—a minor oddity, though welcomed.

"I suppose I owe you that much after all the questions I peppered you with about your mom."

"Little bit."

Some levity, some sheepish grins.

"Very well. What does golf mean to me?" said Leo to himself, tanking into his mind. "Probably anything worth saying or writing about the game has already been done by smarter people than me, so I won't waste your time pumping it up. You already well know how great the game is. I'll just tell you what it's done for me personally."

Jenny nodded in encouragement, anticipation.

"I've played my whole life, and I still kind of stink at it. You wouldn't think that would be possible, but it is. That said, I kept coming back for more. The challenge of it, the social nature, but also the option to strike out on your own, which I don't need to tell you about. Just to be outdoors for as long as you want to be, you against the course, you against yourself. It's like trying to push this really big boulder up a mountain while making little progress. Until eventually you actually do make some real progress. Then eventually, strangely, you don't care so much about your progress because you've come to cherish your time with the boulder."

"You've given this some thought, haven't you?"

"I have."

"And what's the boulder to you?"

"All the obstacles I'll ever face in life. Everything I'll have to accept and overcome."

"So you think golf is good practice for life?"

"In a parallel sense, I do, but that's just my opinion," said Leo, exhaling a faint puff of air. "You asked; I told you. Sorry if any of it sounds like I'm lecturing, but I truly do think it's a sport that makes better people."

Jenny chewed on his words for a bit. She wasn't totally sure if it tracked with all her impressions of the game or how it related to being a better person. From what she'd seen, there were a lot of people at O Triple C obsessed with the game, and they were total dicks. She wondered if Leo placed too much stock in the sport, its association with living a good life. But then again, she'd only been playing in earnest for a few months while he'd been at it an entire lifetime. Maybe she'd just have to trust his experience on the issue and find out what that mountain meant to her, just what her own relationship to the boulder would spell out.

It seemed a worthy pursuit, and she supposed there'd only be one way to find out.

"If it's OK with you, Leo, I'm going to take off on foot and squeeze out few more holes before dark," said Jenny, getting to her feet. "The cart is all yours."

"A fine decision, though I'm afraid I've wasted much of your daylight."

"Not a problem. I have a Pulse ball that'll work in the dark."

"Ah, yes, another long-promised advancement," said Leo. "Play after sunset, never lose a ball."

"I think they'll finally be using them on the tours next year, not that the pros need them so much," said Jenny. "But for all us hacks, they're not too bad."

"Won't that be something?" said Leo wistfully, wondering if a trackable Pulse ball might be just enough to trigger the fourth Death of Golf party. "Nothing stays the same."

Leo got to his feet and tried not to make a production of it in front of the young woman, even if some soreness had returned, what with the sun dipping and temperatures going down. The two walked over to the cart, where Jenny unloaded her golf bag and cleared her belongings. The two then stood before each other.

"It's been a real pleasure meeting you, Leo," said Jenny, extending her hand.

"The pleasure was mine," said Leo, shaking it.

"What will you do now?" she asked, her mandate fulfilled, now relieved of her charge.

"I'll take the cart back and head on home. I live close by," said Leo. "I've had a really great day today, thanks to you."

"After you return the cart, can you tell Heather I said, "Thank you" on your way out?" asked Jenny.

"Sure. For what?"

"She'll know."

To that, Leo just nodded—then they both took a moment to admire a crow wheeling above their head, cackling, having the time of its life taunting some other crow in the trees. Intelligent little buggers they were.

"I hope I get to see you again," said Jenny.

"Sure you will, and you know where to find me," said Leo. "I'm here anytime you want to play a few holes. Or even just to talk."

"Thank you, Leo," said Jenny, turning her back to part ways, only to turn back after hearing Leo call out to her.

"Jenny, would you do me one last favor before you head out?" he asked.

"Sure."

"Call your father. Let him know you'll be home for dinner soon, tell him you love him, OK?"

"I promise."

And with that, Leo loaded his bones into the cart and made his way back to the pro shop, sneaking a glance over his shoulder to see Jenny fidgeting with her Pulse, putting it to her ear, honoring her word to call Roland Mistikis.

The cart ride back to the pro shop was an easy one, particularly without having to mind other golfers and their errant shots. The place was deserted, and Leo crossed the road, gliding past the Monastery, whose crew would be getting ready to winterize the course over the next few weeks. It made Leo think of his old pal Jocko Whalley Jr. and what he wouldn't have given to have another one of their long conversations. Or Oscar Ortiz. Another one of his great friends who shuffled off the coil before Leo. He tried not to dwell on it for so many reasons but, in particular, because of the time he'd just spent with a young and promising soul like Jenny Mistikis.

Leo returned the cart to the bays where it would be cleaned and stored, the last of the kids working for the season giving him a nod as they proceeded to spray it down, inventory it for the night. Leo walked toward the pro shop to deliver Jenny's message to Heather, only to find her gone for the evening, the door locked up tight. Leo had seen that move before, a rite of passage for the junior assistant pros stuck on lousy shifts—dip out early when no one's looking, when no one will pay any mind. It was a fair play when shrewdly pulled off. One of the kids washing the cart asked if Leo needed help getting his golf bag into the car. Leo politely demurred. He lugged his clubs through the empty parking lot. Some chatter from the Restaurant balcony could be overheard, though not much—a few diners under the heat lamps, he supposed. He didn't make it in there as much as he used to, but he still liked to show his face from time to time, hold court for a little and share a story with anyone interested, inevitably running into someone who wanted to buy him a drink. There were plenty of people in Orchard Coils still eager to buy their former chief of police a light beer or glass of wine, though Leo often politely declined or simply enjoyed a small portion of the beverage.

Leo placed his clubs in the back of the Ford beater that he used for puttering around town, his days of driving long distances behind him. He slipped out of his golf shoes and slid on a pair of Sperry's, more comfortable and without the laces to bother with. He eased his frame into the driver's seat and turned the engine over, a satisfying grunt from the ten-year-old truck that was still ably doing what it was designed to do. He took a moment to look upon the course, the holes that could be seen from the parking lot, the way the all-but-departed sun knifed through the barren trees, shimmying around the skeletal limbs when the cloud coverage allowed for it. Leo thought it mundane and majestic at the same time—as were many important things in this existence. His radio played an oldie he favored. The heater was set too high. He sat back in the worn leather and contemplated Jenny, out there, moving her boulder, trying to carve that uphill path—scared and determined and in need of a little grace, just like all of us. He hoped more than anything his words would make some difference for her today, that she'd have the strength to come out the other side. He didn't know, but the optimist in him thought he'd done some good for the day, that she'd be OK. He might even have more advice to offer if she were ever to call on him again. He wouldn't mind that so much. In fact, the notion comforted him in a meaningful way. He liked to think of himself as unafraid of what lay ahead and would like Jenny, if not the entire world, to understand just how sublime a feeling that was. To be unafraid of what lay ahead. He caught his eyes in the rearview, smaller than they used to be or just more sunken in, and before shifting the Ford into gear to head on home, he announced to no one in particular or to any entity that might be listening a small declaration of his stalwart bravery.

"Not. Dead. Yet," said Leo Sinclair, a heavyweight in that moment of solitude, a prince who would honor his path to become a king.

He put the truck into drive, exited the parking lot, and traveled the four miles home, eager to change into more comfortable clothes, then pan fry a grilled cheese sandwich and maybe warm a small cup of tomato soup in the microwave. Oh, and a nice piece of slab bacon to boot!

* * *

An excerpt from the personal journal of Chief of Police Leo Sinclair, Orchard Coils Police Department (retired), dated March 20, 2053.

Though there may be little point to it, I'll document these thoughts as it seems this facet of my life finds new ways to crop up from time to time. Chief Minshew (of all people), still out there in Arizona, though retired now, reached out to let me know that Sophie Alba's grandson Levi, the one she'd traded in her big secret to keep out of a twenty-year federal sentence, died last month in a house blaze somewhere outside Yuma. It would appear he pulled an elderly couple to safety (it wasn't his house) and may have succumbed to smoke inhalation or burns a few hours later in a hospital. (Minshew has, for a second time, volunteered to send me all the information he has regarding a particular case, though this one should be far less enigmatic than the first.)

He quickly pointed out to me, before my brain could even remotely get there, that there might have been no rescue if Levi Alba (that side of the family having never taken the Wizner last name) had been incarcerated for decades, as opposed to the severely reduced sentence he'd completed without incident. It would seem that Levi did a good job cleaning himself up during his stint in prison, got right, found God, and put his life back on sturdy tracks. I suppose Levi wouldn't have even been fifty years old yet, and, if I'm being honest, I haven't thought much about him or even Sophie over the past few years, somewhat successfully putting the whole mess behind me. But now it's all coming back, and Minshew seems to be implying that this has led to something extraordinary, an act of valor and sacrifice. (I don't know.) I'll need to learn more about what happened, if what the former chief is telling me is true. Did Levi Alba really run into a burning building to save two strangers? The case files haven't arrived yet, but I suppose I owe it to . . . well, I actually don't know who I owe it to, but I'm going to look into it anyway. The truth is always more interesting than . . .

?

Gradations of Honesty
What Leo (really) Did

2040

The young man, on back roads he's not overly familiar with, in a county he's only ever had a sole reason to visit, has wrapped the front of his Toyota around a northern red oak. The catalyst for this accident—a mule deer—writhes and moans and has been incapacitated twenty feet from the Corolla's smashed-up grill. Many an accident of this nature has occurred along this stretch of dark, barely incorporated land. The young man does not know this and does not know if the deer will die. It sounds like it will, given its wails, the way they hollow out at the end. Hard to imagine anything could survive those guttural noises.

He hopes it will die. The young man is not one for the outdoors, not a lover of animals.

Still sitting in the car, he pinches the bridge of his nose with his fingers, allows for a moment of reflection to take hold.

The randomness of the deer, the absolute timing of the creature confounds the young man in a way that validates his opinions on existence. Though it is unbelievable, it should not have been unexpected. He feels vindicated in the most inconvenient of ways.

This conclusion allows him to bypass panic.

He inspects the steering wheel and confirms that the airbag did not deploy, which leaves some hope that the car will be drivable. He slides out of the driver's seat, grateful for the invention of seatbelts, that he is a man keen to wear one, that he always made his two kids wear one, even on short rides, despite their protests. He's out of the car and finds himself on sturdy legs, his stomach at ease. His bell has most certainly been rung, but it doesn't seem too bad. He wonders if the deer bore the brunt, absorbed the impact energy. It seems likely. That the deer spared the young man greater damage, that the Toyota may be salvageable.

The creature continues its woeful bleating.

The young man is fully aware he needs to get a move on.

He staggers over to the trunk, still clasped tight, the locking mechanism unaffected by the front-first crash. He tries to remember if he has a true spare available if, in fact, he needs to replace a blowout. In which case, he'll be forced to open up the trunk.

He'd rather not do that quite yet. He gets back in the car, the keys still dangling in the ignition, the battery functioning and some lights still on. He needs to see if the engine will turn over. He needs to see if he can uncouple his car from the great oak and assess the damage. He needs his mild concussion to stay mild. He needs to get away from this pitiful woodland creature and put miles between him and the county. He needs the forces of chaos to cut him a break just once. He needs all this to happen sooner than later.

There are a lot of things this young man needs.

But what he gets is the last thing he needs—an advancing set of headlamps, a car slowly coming his way from the same direction he'd been traveling.

This car comes to a standstill, parks, and idles, keeping its lights on, obscuring the vision of the young man. The lights are elevated, so it's probably some type of truck—it kind of has that rumbling sound to it, lots of millage, infrequent trips to the mechanic. The noise from the truck now competes with the deer, all of it slowly grinding the young man's frazzled nerves, the headlamps drilling into his brain. Maybe he has a migraine coming on. Accident residue against his addled mind. Stars behind his eyes. He takes a breath. He watches the driver's side door swing open and what he thinks is an older man getting out, a bit hunched and ambling his way toward the wreck, hands raised in a friendly gesture.

Empty hands—the young man is always assessing the hands of men, what they're holding, what they may be capable of.

The older man slowly approaches, waving his open hands in a neighborly way, leaving his truck running behind them.

The moon glows brightly above them—insects click, birds of prey screech only a stone's throw away, though unseen.

"Hit a deer," says the young man, jittery, getting right into it. "Came out of nowhere, then froze."

"Not uncommon out here. You OK? You hurt at all?" asks the older man.

"Shook up a bit, but I'm all right."

"Good. Let's have a look at your buck there," says the older man. "Sounds like it's in a bad way."

The young man agrees, silently nodding his head as they shuffle over to the deer. The older man has a bit of a limp or at least some hitch in his gait. He leads the way, the other man behind him. The young man goes about patting down his untucked collared shirt, like he's flattening it down or dusting it off. Feigning a finicky nature, maybe even a prissiness.

He feels the outline of the pistol tucked into the back of his jeans, affirms its presence, dug in, not visible.

The young man keeps his eyes on the older man at all times, without making a show of it. They arrive upon the wounded beast, and the older man goes through noticeable effort to take a knee and assess the animal. He actually uses some kind of mini flashlight clipped to a carabiner around his narrow waist. The young man is vaguely impressed with his economy of motion. The older man surveys the broken landscape of the deer, too weakened to cause much fuss against the humans. He does not bother with soothing words to the animal, does not speak to it. Doesn't even hush it when it rears up a kind of vocal rattle. He is clearly a man who has done this before, probably many times over.

He concludes his survey and gets back to his feet, rubbing at his chest to the point where the young man now feels compelled to ask if he's OK. The older man just waves him off, says what he has to say.

"We need to put him out of his misery," says the older man stoically. "I got something in my truck for that. You comfortable with us getting that done together? Shall we see it through?"

The young man contemplates what the older man is saying, maybe for a bit longer than is necessary, then just tells him something to the effect of "Go right ahead." He forces a bit of enthusiasm into his words, hoping to mask his hesitation.

The Desert Eagle digs into the small of his back.

The older man doesn't stand on ceremony or look to prolong the moment they're sharing. He heads back to his truck, slower now, the exertion building a cumulative effect, it seems. The young man has him pegged for late seventies maybe, a healthy-looking eighty. Tough to say in this light. He hopes they can dispatch this deer, then he'll send the older man packing, tell him he has Triple A or something, and he'll be just fine. He'll make the older man understand that his help was appreciated, but he's got it from here. Then he'll attend to his Toyota and get back on the road. Maybe it will only take another ten, fifteen minutes tops to get through this.

The older man kills his truck's ignition, blanks out the headlights, and a more pronounced darkness settles over the accident scene, apart from the earnest moon. The older man rummages around a bit in the flatbed until he pulls loose a weary Colt rifle—eventually making his way back toward the young man, releasing a labored puff of humid summer air.

There is a genuine nonchalance to how he holds the weapon, the ease of it.

Both men have noticed the deer moaning less.

The young man waits for the older man to ready himself, thinks he catches him taking a slightly extended look at the smashed-up Toyota but can't be sure. Even if he did, would that be so odd? Aren't people always drawn to rubbernecking accidents? The young man looks down at his badly scuffed loafers. Then looks at the older man's approaching sneakers. How little noise they make on the ground. They look comfortable if somewhat ratty.

The older man rejoins the young man and gestures the rifle forward, as though it warranted inspection, as though a ritual were taking place. The deer has all but piped down; does it know what's coming? Does the deer know the older man's scent, what his presence in the dead of night means? The older man makes it clear he's giving the young man the option of the gun to finish off the buck if he so desires. It is within his power to take possession of the rifle. But the young man just shrugs the invitation off, an affectation of dispassion. He takes a step back, signaling the deer is for the older man to dispose of.

The sooner, the better, thinks the young man.

The older man with his economy of time and motion, shuffles his feet a bit, pulls back the bolt and chambers the round. Takes aim at the deer's heart as it rustles painfully against its downed, broken limbs.

"Godspeed," says the older man, who then swings the rifle off the deer and aims it at the young man's chest, pulling the trigger and blasting a silver-dollar-size hole through his heart.

The older man does not even stay to see the body hit the dirt; he knows a kill shot when he's delivered one.

Instead, the older man is making for the Corolla with a newfound speed, agility. He goes straight for the trunk.

* * *

The old man drives aimlessly around the darkened back roads and lets his thoughts drift toward familiar pitfalls: namely, all he's lost in his life. He doesn't go about this exercise in a pitiful way. Quite the opposite. He is not a resentful man. To be resentful at his age would be not to understand the nature of existence, the high station he's achieved, living a long, happy life in America. He understands his luck and is grateful for it. Still. He has lost things. And perhaps it would be fair to say his place in the world has lost some brightness around the edges, has dulled over the decades. Components of his happiness have been winnowed away: wife, children, friends, vocation, health, passion. All of which can be tested with the passage of time, when the cards stop going your way.

Yes, the old man's thoughts tend to wander in his winter years.

He still loves driving these serpentine back roads, though; that much hasn't changed— same roads he grew up on, barely old enough to grow a mustache worth trimming.

He has lived in this county his whole life, plans to die here.

With one hand on the steering wheel, the other hand fiddles with the dials on his radio, his scanner.

There's an old newspaper on the passenger seat, couple of days past current, which makes it ancient in these times. The lead story on the front page is about a suicide in the adjacent county, a prominent local official mired in some kind of zoning malfeasance. *Damn fool*, thinks the old man. He considers suicide a coward's way out, an option that should only be reserved for the most dire of situations. Hardly worthy of a bureaucrat with his hand caught in the cookie jar. Some jail time might have done him good. He might have carried on, found a second lease on life.

Damn fool, he repeats.

The old man detects the judgment in his thinking, warns himself against such sly hubris. It is not his place.

Chalks it up to that wandering winter mind.

He skips his eyes off the newspaper and back on the road where they belong and, after a few minutes or so, happens upon the twin red glow of taillights in the tree line. He slows his pickup down to a stop and takes in the tableau of the accident, the sort of thing he's seen a million times before. A car has struck a deer, guaranteed. The exact type of accident he's assisted with a million times before. He can even hear the deer moaning through his open window—a male, he'd bet.

The old man leans forward in his seat and takes a long look at the crashed car: its make, its model, best he can figure under the washed-out beams of his own Chevy, the moonlight. He can't read the license plate from such a distance, plus it's a bit obscured by the angle. These old habits of his life that are impossible to kick. Or maybe he just doesn't want to. He spies the lone man standing near the driver's side door, trading eyelines with the pickup and the grounded deer. The old man knows it's badly injured; it has that sound the more his ears adjust to it. He leans over and opens the glove box, takes a peek, giving his stratagem some thought and thinks better of it. He shuts the box and goes empty handed. It occurs to him to silence his electronics, all of them.

There is a passage in the Bible he's partial to, prayer that carried him through his decades on the job. He recites it now in his mind, in his heart. He does this despite not being an overly religious man. He does this because he knows he doesn't have all the answers.

He reminds himself that life is not a series of coincidence, that it's hardly chaos, though it does a damn good job of disguising itself as such—at least that's his contention on how to soldier through.

He hops out of the idling truck, keeps his headlamps blaring, and makes his way toward the stranded man, throwing up his hands in greeting, offering up a disarming refrain.

As he draws closer, he sees the younger man is several decades his junior. They huddle and exchange bullet points on the accident, on the nature of these roads, the absence of streetlights, the need to examine the wounded animal.

They do so. And the older man can tell right off the bat that the buck is a goner, kind of knew it just by the tremor in its voice from a hundred feet away. Sad to see it, not that he'll let that emotion show. Such information shouldn't pass for free. Most of his assessment is perfunctory, kabuki theater. He is actually more interested in sizing up the younger man. The way his jeans look laundered with starch. The tassels on his loafers. The fact that he's unconsciously shifting his weight from one foot to the other. His behavior is pleasant enough; that much he won't deny. Plus the kid's just been through an ordeal, more than plenty that rattles folks. Though in truth, the younger man seems less rattled than most, more fidgety. The old man senses a struggle in the stranger: his desire to show patience, his hole cards begging him to fold. The old man has seen this before. On duty. He wonders where the younger man was off to. His Toyota is crunched up in the front, but that doesn't mean it's not drivable, could be mostly cosmetic damage. It's definitely a blue sedan, maybe only a few years old. Was probably a real nice ride up until a few minutes ago. Nicer than his Chevy. The kind of details that stick in your mind once you've been conditioned to do it, particularly when you refuse to give up the conditioning.

The same way you refuse to give up on these back roads, even if your eyes will one day get cloudy. You'll hold on to the wind whipping your face with a white-knuckled rage that seems disproportionate.

Perhaps it is—but he'll hold on to it all the same.

The old man gets up off his one knee with visible effort and a raspy grunt, massaging his chest over his heart, as though wounded from the inside out.

The younger man goes so far as to ask if he's OK.

The old man waves him off in a disinterested, noncommittal way, as though the gesture were to suggest "Are any of us OK?" Then words of logistical importance are exchanged. He proceeds to put his back to the younger man and moves slowly toward his truck. His pace is deliberate, and he hopes the jelly-quiver in his knees isn't too obvious. He hopes he has enough ice water left in his dried husk of a body to keep the moment peaceful, almost banal. He makes it a point not to look backward, not to see what the younger man may be doing, to steal hardly a glance at the Toyota.

A spell best unbroken, sanctified by the fireflies now coming out, signaling their life's intent. He reaches his truck, the flatbed, and pulls a canvas tarp aside to reveal guns, more than a few of varying gauges, some that require two hands to operate. A toolbox, the old man has come to think of it as. There is always the right tool for the right job though he must consider what that job is in this case. He allows his thoughts to spin. Tenets of hunting come to mind: ethical shots, reverence for the kill, the sharing of spoils. Spooking your target is another one. There is a gun or two he'd feel more comfortable using, but he opts for the bolt action. Old design. Less menacing. It looks the part, the kind of gun a man his age would wield, designed to put animals out of their misery.

The old man sneaks a glance back toward the younger one, still shifting his weight a bit pensively. He takes the opportunity to duck back into the cab, catches the banner plastered to the home screen of his Pulse, sitting upright and prominent in a cupholder contraption he bought off some late-night infomercial that targets insomniacs. He figured it might come in handy—such was his thinking on one of the many late nights when sleep wouldn't come.

The banner reads as it did about an hour ago, the alert.

Then he kills the headlamps and ignition, hides his keys under the seat, and keeps the door ajar.

He finds this new darkness preferable.

The old man rejoins the younger one, steady in his slow gait, a man of few concerns, nowhere else to be. He hazards a look at the Corolla and reads what can be discerned of the plate, given the variables. It is enough; it will have to do. His eyes don't linger. He is upon the younger man and offers him the rifle, gives the choice away. He will let the younger man hold the weapon. He will let him decide what's to happen next. It is the type of ten seconds that feels like ten years. He has known that sensation well over his career. Former career. The younger man defers coolly. He opts to let the old man to exercise his expertise in such matters, in dispatching of beasts not long for this world.

He wears the faintest of smiles, hiding the rictus of canines and incisors and blunt molars kept sharp and strong through modern dentistry, through the consumption of meat, through vanity.

The old man does not allow for much fanfare as the two adjust their steps, no strings of hesitation plucked. It really does happen fast. The old man takes his aim into the broadside of the deer and speaks the single word that will accompany the animal to whatever comes next.

"Godspeed."

Then he swings the barrel of his rifle and fires the one shot, straight and true, into the younger man's chest, dropping him dead, his face barely registering the vex.

The old man, spryer than he's let one, hustles toward the Toyota. It is the trunk he's interested in.

* * *

You don't know exactly where you are. What you do know is that she absconded to this weird rural county with bucolic street names and poor roadside lighting. You do know the road you're on is tree choked, that driving fast isn't a wise idea. You know that now, in hindsight. It's no wonder you plowed into a deer, even if you think it's the deer's fault, even if you're sure the county is overrun by them. You were distracted when it happened and probably speeding and may have heard some thuds in the back. You took your eyes off the road, only briefly—then cracked a deer, winding up front first in North America's strongest oak.

Your thoughts are a bit scuppered from the two impacts, and you're well aware now is not the time for impaired thinking.

You notice a few flecks of dried blood on your wrist and instinctively lick your hand to clean the mess away—not your blood.

You can hardly believe your crooked, chaotic luck and wonder if it will ever abate.

You have always hated animals, always.

You twist off your seatbelt and slink out of the car, grateful that the airbag didn't burst. This gives you hope. You know you should be moving; you need to get your ass in gear. You approach the deer gingerly, assessing your own stability, whether the accident has had any impact on your equilibrium, lucidity. They are bound to question your lucidity. But you feel all right; somehow, the chaos has left your faculties in check. The deer, on the other hand, is a mangled sight. Its death cries are grating against your already-singed nerves. It would appear the creature bore the brunt of the accident, serving some useful purpose. Clearly lessened the impact against the tree. Of course, if there were no deer, there would have been no collision to speak of. And you'd still be on your way.

These are things you can't change now. Among others.

You drift toward the trunk and listen for noises, inspect the lock's integrity. Still sound. You try to remember if you replaced the spare since your last blowout. You suspect not. You've been letting small things like that slide for months now, close to a year. And the small stuff doesn't stay small forever. It grows. Snowballs. Then bleeds into matters of consequence: work, family, relationships, optimism. It mutates in ways that can't be traced until its genesis is forgotten, its evolution unexplainable. That's how these things catalyze; that's how you find yourself without a spare tire when you may desperately need one.

That's when you find yourself unspooled and at a loss.

You know one thing for sure—you want this deer to die, you need it to. Even if you lack the luxury of time, you want to see it expire for the sake of your own sanity.

Your sanity.

You almost start laughing aloud, just thinking of the infinite branches of life that have brought you here. Then you see the headlights of an approaching truck, and your blood flash freezes.

This is the last thing you need.

You watch the truck come to a standstill, its engine still running, blaring its lights into your squinting eyes.

You feel a throb in your temple, ears ringing, a pulse in your neck, and it wouldn't surprise you if an aneurism were about to pop and pancake you to the ground.

Not much surprises you anymore.

You need to take a breath. You take a breath. This need not be the worst development that could happen. You just need to get into character, play the part—you're a distressed motorist; they happen every day. You hit a deer on your way out of the county. Then hit a tree. Only a few minutes ago. But you're uninjured.

These are true and incontrovertible facts.

You see what appears to be an older man shuffle out of the truck—at least you think he's old, certainly older than you are. You peer against the blinding headlights. Using your hands as a visor. Does this guy actually have his brights on? You take note of the Samaritan's gait, the swing of his arms, the bob of his head. It all seems innocent enough. But how can you be sure? Nothing surprises you. You'll never not be convinced that chaos doesn't court you at every turn. In varying forms, whispering in your ear.

A moot point now—the older man advances all the same, a solemn pace, a wrist flick in salutation.

You tell him you struck the deer, the resulting crash into the tree understood. You hope it sounds natural enough, unassuming.

You exchange a few more words, curated, given the current circumstances. You observe that he is, in fact, an old man, many decades your elder though he is not elderly. He is not necessarily feeble, but face-worn, bone-weary. It isn't that tough to spot in another. Like a projection in time. This older man could not outfight you. He could not outrun you. You have a clear upper hand against him, and this provides a modicum of needed comfort.

You agree to his inspection of the deer, the idea of it. He seems to have some kind of authority in this realm—not just his words, but his general atmosphere. He's probably a sportsman or was in his younger days. If he had kids, even grandkids, he'd take them fishing, camping.

You watch him take a knee before the deer, turn his back toward you. You wonder what it would be like to be so trusting around the unknown. To put your back to a stranger on dark, isolated land. At night. To stop and even help them out. To not think the worst of people all the time.

You figure it must be nice—but it's not your lot in life.

You smooth down your shirt and sneak a feel of the Desert Eagle tucked out of sight, the brief contact with your hand ever so reassuring. It makes you believe you can get out of this.

You are a believer. You *will* get out of this.

You watch the older man conduct what you think is an overly thorough examination of the pained animal, to the point where you wonder if he was ever a practicing veterinarian.

You hear him saying words to the effect of putting the deer out of its misery.

You hear him explain that he has the tools to get this done, asks if they should go about it and get it done.

You watch him as he awaits your response, your reaction.

You know you have to play it cool, despite not being remotely interested in having a new gun carried onto this scene, let alone by a stranger, by this interloper. But you have to stay in character, bear in mind what a normal person would do. A distressed motorist would want the older man's assistance, would be most appreciative of it. Would graciously accept it. To do otherwise would arouse suspicion, draw unwanted attention. It becomes kind of a nondecision—you have to let this guy go back to his truck.

So, as nonchalantly as you can, you tell him to have at it, in so many words.

You watch the older man move without haste, then reconsider his effort and move slowly, as though his body quickly reminded itself of certain limitations, a recalibration ensuing. You are aware that it's well within your wheelhouse to remove this stranger from the equation. If he poses a threat, if too many questions arise—or if the wrong question is asked—you will do what needs to be done. To move forward.

Like any cornered animal would.

But it hasn't come to that yet. Perhaps it won't, as this older man, this do-gooder, offers more in the way of potential than risk. You will kill the deer with him, get your Toyota unstuck from the oak, and drive away, no worse for the wear.

It's a plan rife with hope.

You feel surrounded by eyes—insects, birds, rodents—hidden in the adjacent woods, bearing witness.

You watch the silhouette of the older man run through his finicky process in his pickup's flatbed, cab. You wish he would get a move on. You're plenty anxious to get moving. You're grateful the deer has piped down a bit. The older man disables his vehicle, and a wash of darkness coats the scene. The moon is now their spotlight. You watch him amble steadily toward you, gun in tow, maybe taking a sideways glance at the Toyota, but you can't be sure. You may be imagining things, casting projections. Maybe you just really, really want to get this thing over with.

You bypass his offer to actually hold the gun, to kill the deer. You advise patience to yourself: act normal, be demure. Let this older man, this huntsman, dispatch his millionth deer. Let him think you've never held a gun in your entire life. That you are no adventurer. You stay in the character that's going to get you out of this jam. So you take a small step backward and allow the older man to adjust his footwork and pull the bolt back, taking aim at the dying animal, about to be relieved of its suffering. About to be relieved of everything.

You hear the older man say, "Godspeed."

You consider this mildly poetic, try to consider the value of this sentiment before you even realize the gun has been swung in your direction, and the trigger has already been pulled. All this in one fast and fluid motion with no hesitation by the older man. You find the swiftness, the economy of motion, uncanny.

Then you feel the hammer blow to the chest and are going down and hazily discern that you have been bested, and the older man is speeding toward the Corolla. You feel surprise—

actual surprise. As much as you're capable of feeling or registering anything in those last moments.

You hit the ground and are dead seconds after impact.

Your last earthly thought is that the deer has somehow outlived you.

You die.

* * *

You wonder if you've ever truly known anything. Learned anything. Have you ever taken something intangible and applied it toward better decision-making? Have you made someone's life better by just being present, by saying the right thing? Why do you feel like a glorified handyman? It's not like you aspired to be an academic, a professor. But after so many decades on the planet, you'd have thought you'd be more touched by some kind of intellectual enlightenment. That maybe you've acquiesced to unknown forces, holy plans. Based on faith. You've existed in this mechanical world. This binary of good and evil. And you wonder if it was a lazy path to walk, whether perhaps you've always been lazy and masked it through rote action.

Not that you begrudge any of it—if anything, you're grateful for your mind's elasticity, that the gears are still turning smoothly after all these decades.

You watch the trees fly by, the familiar bends in the road that shift your body in the grooves of the driver's seat, a truck you've owned for eleven years, six outright. A truck that you love, that you take pride in. You have the radio on, tuned softly to old rock songs, then mute it in favor of your police scanner. They let you keep it when you retired, not so long ago. No one would really miss it. Older model anyway. Still works though, same reliable frequencies. Plus you earned it. And it's getting plenty of use tonight, lots of chatter. Some bad stuff has gone down in the county, the kind of stuff the department doesn't see often, which isn't to say never. You listen to the crosstalk, and in a sense, you miss being in the fray, in the trenches with the officers who served under you. But in another sense, you don't want anything to do with what's transpired tonight; it's work for young people, eager to make a difference, who haven't been ground down by decades of shepherding human misery. You take a long look out your window to see the moon, shining full blast with an arrogance reserved for celestial bodies.

You glance at your Pulse; the banner across your home screen jives with the chatter over the scanner.

Bad stuff.

Your eye catches the headline of the newspaper in the passenger seat—more tragedy, the degradation and humiliation of others you don't know, you can't help. There were always too many people to help, too little time.

Nevertheless, you can't imagine punching your own ticket, especially over money crimes—that's no solution. That's not how you help yourself.

Your mind continues to wander on and off heady topics—no matter, you've nowhere to be, no one waiting on you. There's no sin in indulging in introspection, particularly if you think it's been lacking in the way you've governed your life.

Particularly when you're retired and have the time to do so.

Then you happen upon a familiar sight: the blazing demon eyes of taillights out on the road's thin shoulder, casting an eerie pall.

You immediately know what this is. Or so you think.

You slow your pickup down, park to the side of the road—you can already hear that a deer's been hit. It's hard to explain what that noise means to you at this point in life. It's the type of sentiment you wouldn't be in a rush to divulge. A lack of sensitivity you're not overly proud of yet feels well earned.

You look out your windshield and take note of the car ahead of you. It's not a hard connection to make. Or, at the very least, the way it pings on your radar, an involuntary reflex from conditioning that won't die. They train you to look for a certain car, so you look for a certain car. It's been out on the wire for close to an hour, incessantly and with good reason. You know instantly this is something you'll need to commit to. For better or worse. Your old oaths. You see the lone man. You see the car and know there's a license plate to examine; you just need to get a little closer, improve your angle. You need to do this under the correct guise. To confirm what this may be.

You swing open the glove box and study the pistol tucked in the back, cleaned and oiled and loaded, another souvenir they let you keep. Your buddies in the department knew you were a gun guy. So were they. No one was going to let you walk off into the sunset without it. You wonder what it would mean to take that weapon and tuck it into your pants? Is that wherewithal still in you? Is it the right play? You fancy yourself some kind of quick-draw artist this long in the tooth?

No. You shake off those foolish, youthful notions—you close the glove box, empty handed, and mute all the electronics in the truck.

The noise of the engine is now competing with the din of nature, an abomination to those that were here first.

You don't fully know what this is, not yet. It could be nothing, just the type of deer-and-tree headache you've encountered plenty of times before. But if you really believe it's nothing, then why has the skin on your arms broken out in gooseflesh on a muggy summer night?

You've honed these instincts for a reason. They've served you well; no reason to ignore them now.

You recite some comforting words from Luke 4:18; they float off your lips as you exit the cab, leaving the engine running, the lights blaring. You do this on purpose. All your movements, minute and sudden, will be scrutinized, underpinned with a purpose you hope will be unwarranted, moot. But you don't really believe that. Maybe you want it to be true. But you know you've been delivered here, in this position of providence. You can hardly believe where this path has led you, how these plans unfold.

You move toward this man who is so much your junior and throw an unassuming hand in the air. Then you discuss the brass tacks with him, all things wounded animal and smashed Toyota and insufficient street lighting.

You take it upon yourself to inspect the deer, but what you're really doing is surveying the younger man, his appearance, how he moves around your knee-bent frame. Is he jumpy? Is he nervous? You find him to be mostly calm. Mostly. Your training allows you to spot certain things. You are unsure how exactly this will bode for your survival.

You steal a few glances at the Toyota, and you'll be damned if that's not the car they've been looking for.

Damnation has staked a true and pressing claim on the scene.

So you have to ham it up a bit. Labor your breathing. Slow your motions. Rub at your chest to intimate the effect, double down on your appearance, your obvious age. Make the younger man wonder how you can still drive at night. How it isn't past your bedtime. Maybe all the theater won't be necessary. Maybe it will save your life. Maybe, the truth is, you are a bit winded from the past ten minutes, that it's not quite the act you let on.

The younger man asks if you're OK?

You shine him on, the way a curmudgeon might, exchange some concise words about the deer needing to be put down, how it should be done, who should do it. All of it mostly settled without debate.

You trudge back to your Chevrolet, and this is when you're positive you'll catch a bullet to the back of your head, turning those earthly lights out for good. Or maybe through the back, shredding your heart out your chest, the last thing you'll see before your reward. Before you see Janet again, your parents. Maybe. But you mustn't allow this anxiety to betray your body. The tightrope you're walking back to the pickup. If it's going to happen, then it will happen. It would have already been scripted to happen. But if it's preordained, inevitable, it won't be because you lost the steel in your legs, broke the character you were born to play.

It doesn't happen.

You are dead positive the younger man is staring daggers into your back, calculating, wondering if you'll look back. You don't—to do so would reveal your hole cards, of that you're sure. Your nerves hold true, and you reach the flatbed in one piece, pulling aside the old painter's tarp and start your own calculations. You know the younger man will fight back if given a reason, if he's spooked or figures himself boxed in. You know he will fight to the death. And you won't be able to overpower him. You can't outrun him. You probably can't out-snipe him either, though maybe you can level the playing field, darken the terrain. You're going to have to sell this from multiple angles. Which means using the lesser of your weapons, the one least fit for close combat.

You take the bolt-action and duck into the cab, read the Amber alerts plastered onto your phone's home screen, sitting in that plastic cupholder thing. You're proud to be one of these old guys who doesn't totally shy away from technology, that computer phones never really scared you. Mostly. If anything, you leaned into them. Kind of.

You hide your keys, then kill all the lights and electronics in the truck and amble back toward the younger man, holding your Colt with one hand, in a way that suggests your comfort with it but no immediate threat of using it.

You catch a better look at the license plate; despite the new darkness, the moon and improved angle free up a clearer view.

Yeah, you've seen enough.

You rejoin the younger man and offer up the weapon to him, an act of trust, an indication that all is exactly as it seems. You calculate it's the smooth play. A way to disarm the younger man's doubts if, in fact, he's harboring any. Which you have to figure he probably is, given what he's recently done. But you don't really know. You're mostly hoping for the best. Even if you're betting your life on it. Maybe even your soul.

The younger man concedes that you should kill the buck—playing his version of the same game right back at you.

You acknowledge to yourself that you've been patient, as patient a ten-minute span as you can ever remember, given the stakes. You know it's time to curb that forbearance, though whether that dismissal will be a blessing or a hellscape remains to be seen.

But seen it shall be.

You take a firm step backward and take aim at the deer. And you tell it the same thing you've told all God's creatures you've ushered off the mortal coil, whether they walked on four legs or two, whether it really happened or not.

"Godspeed."

Then you swing the Colt onto the younger man and blow a hole through his chest with an efficiency you weren't totally sure you still possessed, had hoped could be summoned on command.

It would appear you still possess it.

You quit the possum routine, mostly—you're still an old man and move with as much purpose as your frame allows. You make for the Toyota, try to open the trunk, only to find it won't budge, locked.

It occurs to you you'll need the keys. Are they still in the ignition? Yes.

You pay the fresh corpse no mind.

* * *

I'm fucked. I'm so very, very fucked!

I need to calm the fuck down. I need to get out of this fucking car.

I get out of the car and feel a bit woozy on my feet, but not so bad: kind of like a beer buzz or getting off the couch too quickly. It was a deer. Out of absolutely nowhere, a deer. There is always some element that's beyond my control. Always some new bullshit out to get me. There's a thumb on the scale. Myopic justice. If I could ever just get one day free and clear of my own personal chaos, then maybe things would have been different for me. Better somehow. Maybe none of it would've felt so uphill while everyone was coasting down, full of hugs and smiles. It's all been insurmountable. My life governed by the unknowable and the unforeseeable, and I'm expected to navigate it with a broken compass, blindfolded.

Case in point—a lone deer, this day of all days, this exact time.

The world hurling chaos at me, only to learn that I'm now willing to throw it back with a multiplier.

I shake my head a bit and start to assess the car's damage, edging closer to the pitiful, moaning creature. If it had just darted out of the woods five seconds later, we'd all be carrying on with our lives, no worse for the wear. But no. This stupid fucking deer and its mercurial nature and trance stare into oncoming headlights. It never ends.

And it looks like I hit the deepest-rooted tree in all the world, like it's hardly noticed the sedan cracked into it.

I drift toward the car's trunk, test the lock, which appears to be undamaged in the crash. Nothing about the Toyota's back end seems amiss. Should I open the trunk? Do I really want to know? Do I want to see *them* like that? It might be unavoidable if I have to change a tire. Do I even have a proper spare? Why the hell am I driving around without knowing that? Why have I gotten so lax with simple stuff a man half my age would be on top of? When did this decline start?

I take a breath.

Losing my head isn't going to get me anywhere. And I'm stuck in a real situation here, from way before I ever made contact with the deer. I need to get a move on. Nothing has changed that reality. In fact, it's just heightened the urgency. I need to get my tail in gear, and losing my cool and beating myself up for things beyond my control aren't going to help.

What's done is done.

I need not look in the trunk just yet.

I can feel my gun digging into the small of my back, and while it's a bit uncomfortable, there's also something supremely comforting in it.

So there's that.

First things first. I need to see if the engine will turn over. The keys are still dangling in the ignition.

But before I can step back toward the car, I see headlights advancing my way and instantly realize that it's fruitless for a man such as myself to concoct plans. Plans are for a different kind of enchanted human being. Reserved for those who are allowed some grace and margin in this world. It does not apply to me. I am more an insect that's being perpetually cornered by a house cat, batted and toyed with. The insect doesn't formulate plans; the insect just looks to survive one catastrophe to the next through sheer instinct.

The insect either buzzes the cat's nose with a spindly wing or stings or bites its paw—otherwise, it dies down a gullet, eaten alive.

I have every intention of surviving this latest catastrophe—by any and all means necessary.

To do so, I'll need to put on a friendly face, the veneer of a distressed traveler—and I'll need to be smooth about it.

I wait.

It looks like a guy is just sitting behind the steering wheel, but he's got his lights blazing and his engine grumbling, and I'm not exactly sure what he's on about. Maybe figuring out how best to help. Maybe dicking around on his phone. Maybe calling the police to report the accident. Impossible to say.

It's not impossible that the cops are already looking for me, though it seems unlikely. It only happened an hour or so ago.

How could they have found the body already? The bodies.

I register the gun nestled against my back again. This weapon has a history now, a legacy.

What the hell is this guy doing over there?

Then I see the door swing open and an older man lurch out, sturdy enough, though perhaps a bit compromised with age. He definitely looks like an older guy, but it's tough to see against the headlamps. Either way, he's heading my direction at a measured clip, giving me a wave like we're old buddies, like he's seen it all before. I take note of his hands. There is nothing in his hands. I'm always so fascinated by hands, particularly strangers', but I don't have time for that tonight.

He is upon me, and I need to say something that supports the visage.

"Hit a deer," I say, maybe a little too quickly. "Came out of nowhere, then froze."

The older man tells me this isn't uncommon, asks if I'm OK.

"Shook up a bit, but I'm all right," I say, slowing my speech down.

The older man seems satisfied and suggests we have a look-see at the deer. It seems like the reasonable thing to do, what a normal person would suggest and acquiesce to. I nod in agreement, and we drift over to the wounded animal. I watch the old man take a knee and run through his process, carefully inspecting the deer, using a mini flashlight looped around some key ring. He doesn't go so far as to touch the animal, but he's shifting around on his knees, assessing from multiple angles, running some kind of determination that's foreign to me, second nature to him.

All I can do is stand still, stay my nerves, wearing clothes ill suited to changing a tire or dealing with a mangled deer. And now I have to decide if I need to put this older man down. Does he pose a real threat? Did he call the cops while he dallied in his truck?

Does he somehow know what's in my trunk?

He hasn't mentioned the cops to me. I haven't noticed a Pulse on him. Maybe he's one of these old guys that doesn't even have a cell phone, hates technology and all that. I flatten out my shirt and can feel the contours of the gun, do my best to keep it hidden under the folds of clothing. I'd prefer not to kill him. And so far, there is no overwhelming evidence that warrants it. He's just some wayfarer, an old-timer, that stumbled upon me in a moment of distress. He doesn't know shit. He's looking to get me back on the road, so why not let him? I need to let this man help me, leverage his experience to get a move on that much quicker.

Here I am, still trying to craft plans when the universe will inevitably sabotage them. You'd have thought I'd know better—but I have to try.

The older man wraps up his examination and gets to his feet, rubbing the dirt and twigs and road pebbles off the knees of his pants. Then he starts rubbing at his chest in a pronounced, unhealthy way.

A normal person would ask him if he's OK. So I ask him if he's OK.

He brushes the query aside, which if fine by me. The last thing I need is this guy keeling over of a heart attack. He tells me we need to put the buck down—that he has a gun in his truck, and we can use it together if that's something I'm OK with.

My first instinct is to somehow refuse his proposition, if not forcefully, then tactfully. I do not need this man to have a gun in his hands. But as I let it play out in my mind, declining to put the deer out of its misery would only draw more suspicion. Allowing the older man to leave this scene with any kind of unfinished business, a sense of incompletion, would be a greater pitfall than having him execute the deer and see me on my way. There are no great options here. So it's about choosing what looks lucid, what helps keep this a two-man show. If the older man's intentions aren't true, he'll slip up first, make a mistake—then I'll deal with it.

In so many words, I tell him I don't have a problem with his proposal. I muster as much nonchalance as I can, even if it feels like all my neurons are firing at once, in scattered and conflicting arrays.

He doesn't hang around, just moseys his hitched gait back toward the pickup, leaving me to stand sentry over the dying beast. He's even older than I first assessed, might be pushing eighty, but still has his function, his utility. Makes me wonder how good his night vision is. He's going to have a gun in his hands soon. But so do I, difference being he doesn't know that. Difference being mine's a good three seconds away from being useful. I just need to stay cool, stay attuned. This is all going to be over soon enough. I'll be back on the road in no time, free and clear of this unfortunate setback.

Don't think about what's in the trunk. Don't think about what's in the trunk. Don't think about what's in the trunk.

It suddenly goes dark as the older man finally kills his headlights. I can see him rummaging around his flatbed, his cab, turning off the engine. He has his little processes; I suppose we all do in times of stress. My eyes adjust to the darkness, the moon now taking its rightful place. I watch the older man amble back toward me, rifle loosely held in one hand, almost an afterthought. I watch his clipped pace. His soft, soundless sneakers. His head tilts as he regards my smashed-up Corolla. A little too long a look for my liking, but I suppose it's natural. I'd be looking at it too.

I like the way this guy carries himself, I have to say.

It will be a real shame if I have to kill him.

Enough people have died for one day.

The gun digs into my back, slowly becoming a part of me.

The older man sidles up and offers me the bolt action, which I have to say confounds me. I hadn't considered he'd offer it to me. But I ultimately decline, shrug my shoulders, my character playing it cool all the way. I show no interest in handling a weapon, in taking a life.

I'm no threat, not even to an animal, let alone a fellow human being. I've given him no reason to believe otherwise.

Secretly, I can't wait to watch this stupid creature die.

The deer goes mute as we inch away from it. Soon I'll be on the road again. With what's left in the trunk.

The older man takes a final step backward to manipulate the gun, throws the bolt, and aims at the deer's still-beating heart.

"Godspeed," he says.

I think that's a fitting thing to say before the rifle is inexplicably swung in my direction, right at my still-beating heart. There is no pause. No words. No demands. No accusations. No explanation. No debate. No bartering. I don't even have a moment to put my hands up in protest, let alone initiate the three seconds to get my gun. There's just a single shot into my chest, and I go down with all my lofty and unhatched plans thoroughly dashed. I go down and melt into a pool of unseen chaos, slowly accumulating blood—returning to the chaos from whence I was born.

The last thing I see with my dimming vision is the older man racing toward the Toyota's trunk.

So he knew the whole time. And was willing to engage.

Then I see nothing.

* * *

I have grown old, and the hard truth is I just don't seem to have much left to offer this world. A career, a lifetime of public service, a desire to better society in my small way. But now it feels so uphill. There are fewer avenues for me to offer help. Less time and less energy for me to do so. Ironic, since in a way, I have more time: parents gone, wife passed, kids away and grown, friends dropping off too fast. A lot of empty hours in the day. Slow weekends. Restless nights.

There's only so much golf one man can play.

So, for lack of purpose, I drive. I drive an awful lot these days and listen to the radio and the old scanner to see what wickedness is still out there.

I've become prone to letting my mind wander, to evaluating my contributions to the world, my nuts-and-bolts value, my failings.

Things that have been taken away from me.

But I still really like driving, something I've been able to hold on to. My eyes are still good—proud I never needed glasses or surgeries. Good genes, I suppose. My mind is still sharp, truly, even if it's taken to slippery thoughts in my retirement, in creeping solitude. The losses I have suffered have not hardened my heart, made me angry. I am not a resentful man. I know plenty of people not allowed to get behind the wheel of a car anymore. I know lots of people now buried in the ground, ashes scattered on the winds. I know better than to drift into the seductive, bitter territory. I'm a better man for it, though, at the same time, I can acknowledge that reductions have taken place.

I float my hand a bit out the open window, like a surfer catching some big, blue Pacific wave. I'm driving down these curvy roads I know so well, a wind drafting off the pads of my fingers, over the contours of my knuckles.

It's a pleasant sensation, and I have enough marbles still rattling around to know how blessed I am, reductions or not—even if I seem to question my path more than I did only five years ago. My eyes glance at the newspaper in the passenger seat, and I'm saddened and confused and outraged by the spike in suicides, the varying addictions still plaguing the county. I don't read the newspaper the way I used to, despite the bloat of time to do so. I find it makes me judgmental. That is the last thing I want to be.

So I continue to drive along and think about getting some soft serve over at the DQ before they close for the night when I see some brake lights where they shouldn't be, on a stretch of road known for blowouts, skids, deer strikes. Sure enough, that's what it appears to be. I can spot it easily enough, can hear the deer bellowing from a distance. Sounds like a buck. I pull off to the side of the road, not much of a shoulder, keeping my engine on, lamps on. I take a moment to see what I'm actually seeing. The type of car that's been punched into the great oak. The same make and model they've been squawking about over the wire the past ninety minutes. The hint of a license plate I remember, conditioning engrained in me, but the odd vantage keeps me unsure.

I spot the man, hovering over the deer, apparently alone, kind of matching the physical description of the fellow they're so desperately looking for. And what he has absconded with.

What could possibly be the chances? Has something brought this to me? Am I even right? There are millions of Toyota Corollas out there. Popular sedan. Common color. What if it's just a coincidence? What if my intuition is perking up over nothing?

A certain level of irrelevance sets in as, of course, I'm going to pursue this—though I need to approach it with extra care.

This man—if he is, in fact, the man they're looking for—is extremely dangerous, a murderer.

I lean over and flip open the glove box and give some measure to pulling my handgun, trying to hide it on me. Or just letting it be known that I'm carrying, kind of out in the open, like maybe I'm going to use it on the deer. But this strikes me as somewhat presumptive, maybe reckless. I don't have the margin for recklessness. I don't know how this man will react to the sight of a handgun. Even the suggestion of one could set him off.

And there are other, more important lives at stake than mine.

So I close the glove box, begrudgingly and empty handed.

I decide to kill all the electronics—I don't need this younger man overhearing some news report, catching on that I have an operating police scanner.

I leave the lights on to dig into his eyes, impair his field of vision for whatever it's worth.

And I leave the car running, just in case I need to get the hell out of there, though that probably won't matter, given the distance between the two cars, the fact that I can't run as much anymore. If it comes down to me having to make a sprint for it, I'm probably a goner.

I'm not ready to be a goner. But I'm not going to do nothing.

I recite my Bible quote, the lines that have carried me when I thought I had nothing left. And I remind myself that I am on a path, even if I've questioned it at times, failed to see where it was taking me.

I walk out into the open, waving my hand as friendly as can be, watching to see if this younger man is going to make some move against me. To see if he's just waiting for a certain distance to close before he strikes. Or maybe he'll just let it play out a bit, see what my intentions are.

Or maybe he's just a dumb, run-of-the-mill stranded motorist grateful for some assistance.

As I pass by the car, I'm a bit too hesitant to get a proper look at the plate, my nerves kicking in, the stranger's eyes locked on me.

Then I'm upon the younger man, and he sure does fit the description of the guy they're looking for, now that I'm up close. Maybe I didn't want him to be, but I'd be lying if it wasn't a strong match. He tells me about the deer and the tree, and I ask if he's OK, and I eventually tell him we should have a look at the buck, even though I know it's already circling the drain. The deer knows it too. It may be the younger man is the only one who doesn't. The way he's dressed, his hesitance around the animal—I don't pin him for a sportsman. Or maybe he's just nervous. Maybe he's trying to decide if he needs to put a lead slug in me. The way he's wearing his shirt, fidgeting with his empty hands, it's hardly impossible he's got a piece tucked under his denim.

He may not know yet just how drivable his car's going to be. Maybe he'll jack me for my pickup. My gut tells me he's the guy—even if I don't want it to be true, even if I still want one clearer look at the plate. And I'd be lying if I said a part of me isn't feeling that old thrill coursing through my blood again, lighting up my bones—what had been dormant, now set loose. It's incumbent on me to keep it controlled.

I get up off my knee and rub at my chest for pure effect, let this younger man think I've got a bum ticker, that I'm sloughing off what limited energy I have left.

He actually goes so far as to ask if I'm OK. I'm unsure who the better actor is.

I wave him off like I haven't got time for his youthful commentary and tell him I've got the tools in my flatbed to put the beast out of commission, that it's the right thing to do. I say something to that effect and add some extra gravel to my voice to cement my expertise on such things. It seems to work as I don't get much in the way of resistance from the younger man. He seems to be at ease with the idea, maybe even a little pleased with the notion that it's about to become someone else's problem.

I walk away and put him in my blind spot, and this is when it gets particularly interesting for me since I can't be positive this man isn't going to draw down once I turn around. God help me, the hairs on my arms are standing straight up, and my heart is jackrabbiting away. Those ancient systems in my body trying to hijack my fight-or-flight impulses. Which I can't allow. So I slow my pace down even more, ever so noticeably, to further sell my story, to ward off a perverse fate. Slowly walking into my own blaring headlamps, like some kind of judgment test, a tunnel of blinding light.

My own divine path.

And maybe I've passed. I make it back to the truck in one piece, and I get along the side of the cab and strip away the canvas to look at my arsenal. I know what I want to put my hands on, what would cut the younger man in two even from this distance. But it wouldn't be the prudent choice, wouldn't align with the narrative I'm spinning. Wouldn't allow for one final look at the Corolla's plate. So I go for the Colt, which even a nonhunter would recognize as a gun worthy of putting down a lame deer.

I hoist it out of the flatbed, peering toward the younger man, who is noticeably shifting his weight from foot to foot, moving his head to the hooting of owls, the snapping of twigs.

I can feel in the pit of my stomach that our clock is winding down.

So I kill the lights on my truck, turn the engine off. Coat our scene in darkness, silence. I hide my car keys to deter him from stealing my car, whether he kills me or not. Take one last look at my cell phone propped up in that plastic holder contraption—best damn late-night $19.99 I ever spent. The Amber alert is still plastered to the home screen. Two missing children. Small enough to fit in a standard trunk. Abducted by their estranged father. It's usually someone you know. Their mother, the ex-wife, in critical condition with a gunshot wound at Memorial, fighting for her life, unlikely to survive. The new boyfriend executed.

It's been pouring across the wire for close to two hours now—fear mounting that this man will realize his plight, kill the children, then suicide himself.

I am not going to let that happen. I will do what I must.

In the new darkness, I walk back toward the younger man, who I believe to be the estranged husband and father—this man I can't overpower, can't outrun. I will need to bring something different against him.

And even though I'm scared too, I have to hazard one last look at the license plate, a real look, using a better tack as I pass it.

Conditioned to memorize how a license plate reads when you're told it's being hunted for.

I look.

Yeah, he's the guy, all right, zero doubts about it.

I rejoin the man, and before I allow the consequence of what I plan to do smother me, I gesture the rifle toward him, to see if he wants to lay his hands on the weapon, to put the deer down. To put me down. This is my final gambit to test the fates. To weigh chaos against destiny. There is a slight pause, but he just mildly dismisses my offer. And I am not interested in pressing my luck beyond pliable borders or giving him a chance to reconsider. I am not so foolhardy.

The best I can tell, I got him believing what I need him to believe.

So I take a step backward, putting an appropriate amount of distance between me and the deer—though really putting the distance I need between me and the younger man.

The deer has gone mostly mute by this point.

The man watches intently, shuffling his footwork about seven yards from me—still so close that if this goes sideways, if I fail, I won't get a second chance at redemption.

Get a move on, I think.

"Godspeed," I say.

Then I swing the barrel around, stiff like a pendulum, and level a shot into the young father's chest. If I can't outfight this man and I'm not in the arresting business anymore and these two kids are dead or dying in a locked trunk—well, maybe half-measures just aren't going to cut it. Maybe it's either him or me. And I ain't ready to go yet. So I'll just have to live with whatever comes next.

I know it's a kill shot, even if the man on his way to the dirt is trying to muster enough lucidity to worm himself out of the miscalculation, his latest mistake.

He cannot.

I haul ass over to the Toyota and try to open the trunk, but it's locked, and I need the keys. But I know exactly where they are, still hanging in the ignition cylinder—the younger man left the battery running, never removing them. So I grab them with some fumble and pop the trunk, which is weakly illuminated by a washed-out yellow light.

The whole time, there's a whole lot of praying I'm going through.

Praying for the obvious things.

I see two little bodies, bound and with duct tape over their mouths.

I fish for my pocket flashlight, shine it across their tear-streaked faces.

Up and down movement in their chests, wriggling with fear, pupil response to the light: alive, the two of them.

I scoop the kids out of the trunk, one at a time, and while doing so, I can hardly fathom the judgment and humility and righteousness and incredulity soon to barrel down on me like a runaway locomotive, newly abandoned by the only conductor she's ever known.

What have you done? What if you had been wrong?

The darting eyes of those little kids, their still beating hearts.

I'll accept whatever's coming to me.

* * *

Made in the USA
Las Vegas, NV
25 November 2024

12597680R00213